Heir of Embers and Eventides

M.W. THEODORE

Heir of Embers and Eventides
Written by M.W. Theodore

Cover design, Character Art, & Map by M.W. Theodore
First Edition

Published by Crest & Quill Publishing, LLC

To EKOLL—you are my heart, my purpose, and my greatest adventure.

To my friends—thank you for believing in me, for lifting me up when doubt crept in, and for reminding me that my words have worth. Your support made this possible.

And to my mother—thanks for the motivation. Turns out, I was smart enough to write a story after all.

Trigger Warnings:

This book contains content that may be unsuitable for some readers. It is recommended that individuals who are sensitive to certain themes exercise caution while reading as the content may be disturbing or upsetting. Reader discretion is advised.

Please be advised of the following:

Amputation, forced (off-page)
Blood/Gore
Bones: Broken/Exposed
Child, Death (off-page)
Child, Violence Against
Decapitation (off-page)
Genocide
PTSD
Racism
Religious Themes/Cults
Sexual Assault (off-page)
Sexually Explicit Scenes: MF/MM/MMF
Slavery
Torture
War

Table of Contents

I

II

III

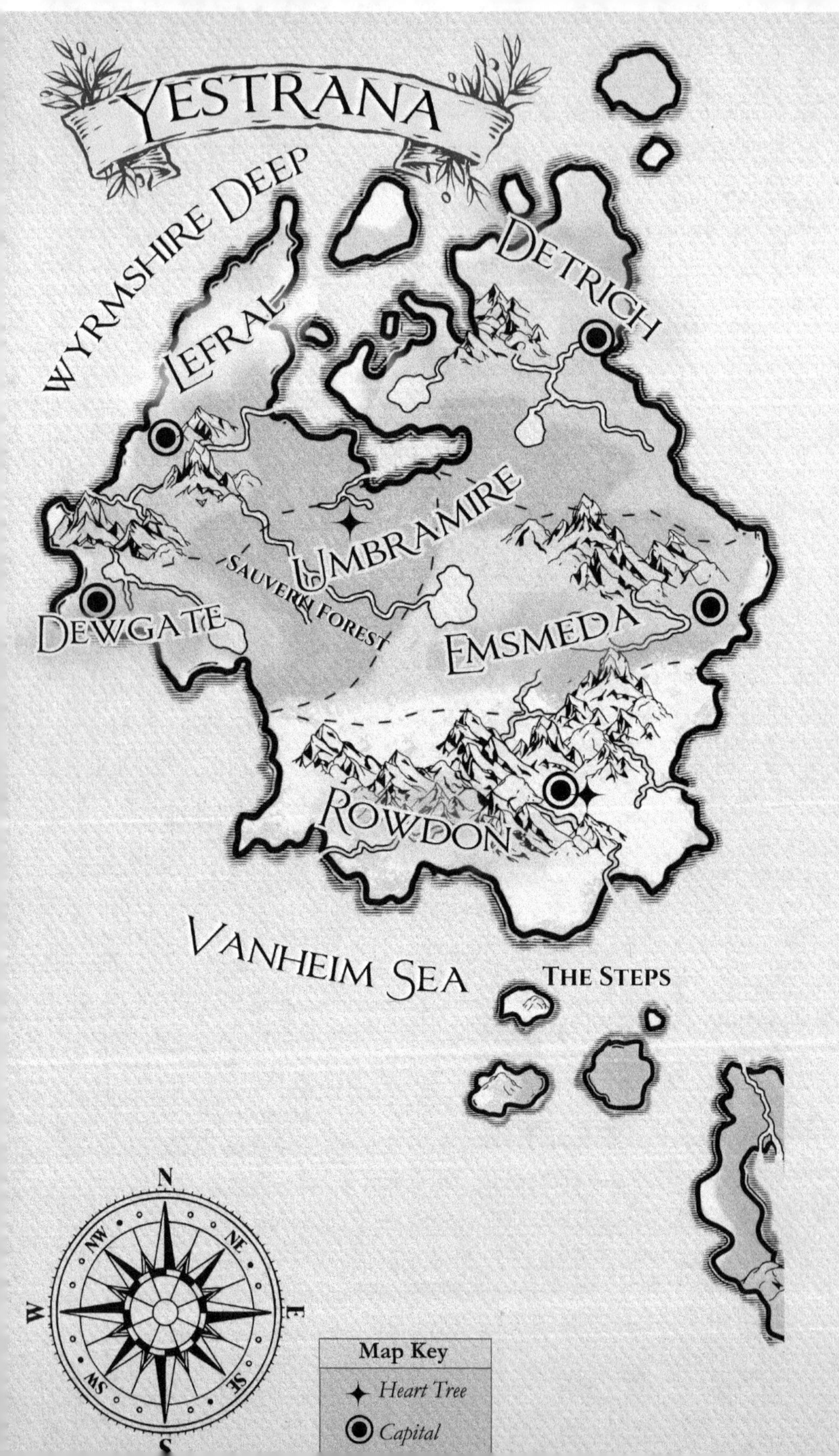

YESTRANA
WYRMSHIRE DEEP
DETRICH
LEFRAL
UMBRAMIRE
SAUVERA FOREST
EMSMEDA
DEWGATE
ROWDON
VANHEIM SEA
THE STEPS
N
NW
NE
W
E
SW
SE
S
Map Key
Heart Tree
Capital

OPRIEN
SCYREI
ASHAR
OSTRIA
SCHOLAR'S CITY
BURNING FIELDS
STRAFDEN SEA
VALORIA
CEANEA ISLE
HELGI TIDES
WAYWICH ABYSS

"When sun retreats from sight,
And darkness veils the land in shadowed might,
Children born under the eclipse's gaze,
Shall be marked by the gods in mysterious ways.

Gifted by celestial touch, they shall stand,
As conduits of power, by divine command.
Their minds like stars, their hearts aglow,
With ancient wisdom, that mortals shall know.

Borne of light that met the shade,
They'll wield the gifts that the gods have laid.
To heal the wounded, to call the storm,
Their destinies weaved before they were born.

Beware the envy of those who fear,
The might these children bring near.
For in their hands lies a force untold,
A power only they can hold."

I

Slumbering Roots

1

Between Two Worlds

"I was named after Faeturin, the god of the forest; I'm supposed to carry their legacy in my veins—but I can't shake the feeling that I'm not worthy of it. Not when the scent of smoke pulls me back to something I'd rather leave behind."

Faedi

Sual'viren, 2706

The Sauvern Forest, on the edge of the Umbramire, hummed with life, the air thick with the scent of earth and pine. As the creatures of the day settled into rest, those of the night came alive. The magic in the air grew more assertive as dusk fell, filling her senses and causing her skin to prickle.

It was a sensation unlike any other—the untamed energy of the woods filled the atmosphere and enveloped everything.

The forest was a wild, uncivilized paradise, stretching for miles in all directions. Balance reigned there, mostly untouched by human hands, and she loved it for that. The Guardians and Wardens of the Wood, along with the forest-folk, were the only ones who dared tread through it, careful not to disturb more than the ground beneath their feet. The creatures that called the forest home fiercely defended it.

It was primal and raw—something most people could never comprehend.

But she and her companion weren't most people. She and Lonan had been born there, raised among the Sauvern's pleasures and dangers. They had learned to live harmoniously in the wild. Where others found peril, they found peace.

They didn't just survive there—they thrived.

But the forest was restless.

Faedi crouched low, her fingers brushing the damp earth, checking under leaves for any disturbances. Then she pressed her palm flat against the ground, closing her eyes.

It was completely absent from what she was looking for.

Not a single fraction of it pulsed with the recent passage of heavy wheels, nervous horses, or the scent of iron and oil.

The parcel was pure.

If they haven't come through here, where did they go?

Lonan was nearby—she caught the faint melody of his song drifting between the trees—but she didn't call out to him. Not yet.

"Nothing?" Her falcon, Dusan, landed on the deer draped over her shoulders. She shook her head.

"Maybe they left the trails in the western parcels."

"Where they went missing won't matter when Dewgate is starving."

Dusan pecked at her hair. *"We can search after the migration."*

Someone has to.

Her gold eyes snapped open, narrowing as she rose to her feet. Her tail flicked once behind her in irritation.

With a low growl rumbling in her throat, Faedi quickened her pace—following after Lonan's voice.

Faedi's velveteen gray fur shimmered under the moonlight as it blended seamlessly with the shadows of the trees. Her wolf-like ears, tipped with silver and adorned with carved piercings, twitched at the sounds of the forest, the fur brushing against the air. In the dim light, her gold eyes reflected the moon's glow while they scanned the surrounding trees.

As they moved deeper off the beaten path, Lonan's song grew louder with a tune that was more cheerful than her mood.

However, his song hitched when he stumbled on the thick pine needles and fell, the deer he carried tumbling from his shoulders. Faedi stopped and watched, biting her lip to muffle her laughter as he scrambled to his feet. Moonlight filtered through the trees, highlighting his pale skin and violet eyes, his pointed ears sticking out from his messy black hair. The strands hid too much of who he was—the untamed beauty that matched the Sauvern's wildness.

A beauty she couldn't let herself look at for too long.

She hated that he wore a glamour in the woods. The Sauvern was beyond anyone's control or claimed land, but no Umbral left the Mire without one. There were too many in the world who feared and hated his kind.

Lonan stood a head taller than her, even with the weight of the deer slung back over his broad shoulders. His fur-lined cloak hung loosely over his hunting clothes, patched and worn from years of use. Even with the glamour, he looked every bit the Umbral he was, with shadows dancing around his feet as the magic of his disguise faltered slightly.

"I meant to do that," Lonan chuckled, his voice light.

Faedi rolled her eyes and leaned against a tree, inhaling the rich forest air. The falcon perched on the deer she carried ruffled its feathers.

"Of course you did."

The scent of smoke lingered—faint but undeniable. It pulled her back to memories she would rather forget—fire, blood, and the scars of twenty-two years past.

"There was a fire nearby."

"Was?" Lonan's eyes narrowed as he sniffed the air.

He would smell it too; his nose was just as sharp as hers. Were-folk were known for their keen senses.

"You're right." He cut his gaze to her before grinning. "What else does that nose of yours tell you? Does it smell dinner?"

His teasing pulled her back from the memories, and she shrugged with a smile. "It might—but I'm not sure if it smells clean dishes."

"I did them before we left." He laughed as he followed her deeper into the forest.

The weight of the deer they carried did little to slow them down. Faedi's muscles tensed under the load, but the strain was familiar—one she could accept. The pains in her body were always there, but she knew they would be worse after she slept.

In the morning, she would clutch her tea for stability until her herbs took effect.

"Who puts a fire out at nightfall?" Lonan mused, pulling her from her thoughts. "No other Guardians or Wardens were supposed to be on this parcel now, right?"

Guardians and Wardens of the forest were the stewards of the land, bound to the Sauvern—the lifeblood of the earth that flowed through roots, rivers, and all living things. Guardians, like Faedi, shared a deep connection to nature, able to commune with plants and animals as if they were kin. Wardens, like Lonan, were protectors, wielding their bond with the land to defend and uphold balance. Together, they ensured harmony, their souls tethered to the ancient forces that shaped the wild.

She shrugged. "Could be one of those supply caravans for Dewgate. Maybe they spilled water on a fire—you know city-folk are clumsy."

He scoffed. "Clumsy is putting it nicely, isn't it, Dusan?" He looked up at the falcon on her deer with a mischievous grin. "You were sturdy on your feet right out of the egg."

The falcon chirped in reply. *"Yes, but you're just as clumsy as the city-folk."*

Faedi snorted and shook her head when Lonan turned his attention to her. "He said you're clumsy too."

Faedi scratched the falcon's chin, translating Dusan's words for Lonan. She neglected to include Dusan's lighthearted insult, if only because of the tense relationship between the "civilized world" and those of the forest.

"Smart-ass oversized chicken." Lonan's laughter carried through the forest, blending with the night sounds.

It always had a way of unraveling her defenses, but she couldn't let it show. It was easier to roll her eyes at the banter than to admit how much his presence steadied her.

"He sure is loud for an Umbral," Dusan chirped in a rhythm that matched Lonan's laughter.

Faedi glanced between them and sighed. "You two are impossible."

As they walked, the thick trees thinned, and Faedi surveyed the fresh growth along the forest floor. It had come a long way since the fires that ravaged the land ten years prior. Healing was slow, aided by the forest's natural magic and the efforts of the Guardians.

The Umbral Watch had stationed them near Dewgate to restore the forest and guard the Umbramire's paths from trespassers. However, the proximity to the city meant they had to be careful—most city-folk weren't fond of Umbrals, and even fewer were comfortable around were-folk. Despite a more complicated truth, people often spread rumors of dark magic and ancient curses about Umbrals.

Fear and ignorance fueled the city's distrust, with whispers of Umbrals controlling the forests and even manipulating the minds of those who ventured too deep. And the Umbrals weren't the only people who faced fear and distrust.

Krelin, like Faedi, faced their own challenges.

Many in Dewgate were too wary of the forest-folk to understand their bond to the land, often mistaking them for dangerous were-creatures. While Krelin lived in harmony with the forest, some city-folk saw them as a threat, unsure if their fangs and claws were merely tools of nature or harbingers of a darker purpose.

Dewgate barred any Krelin who moved there from entering the city. Forced to stay on the outskirts, they worked the farms and tended to the livestock, their lives lived in the shadow of the stone barrier. This separation only deepened the distrust between the forest-folk and the city-folk, as the Krelin remained ever on the fringes of Dewgate, caught between two worlds and never fully accepted in either.

Tensions were simmering, with some factions pushing for tighter control over the borders of the forest, hoping to tap into its untamed resources. Faedi couldn't shake the feeling that, soon, the fragile peace between Dewgate and the forest would break.

The only thing that kept the residents of the Sauvern and Umbramire safe was the city's fear of the forest, but Faedi doubted that would last. As Dewgate continued to grow, so did its appetite for the forest's resources. The fear would soon turn into greed, and then there would be no stopping the push to claim what the land had to offer.

People faced their fears when they were desperate.

Through the evening mist, their home came into view—a small, weathered cottage nestled at the forest's edge. Ivy and moss covered its wooden walls, with vines of eventides laced among them, blending seamlessly into the surroundings. The air was quiet there, muffled by the mist, with only the occasional sound of owls and the nearby stream.

The tranquility was short-lived. As soon as they crossed onto the property, the silence broke with the sound of creatures rushing toward them.

"Here they come," Faedi said with a grin, descending the small hill toward the cottage.

"Brace yourself," Lonan laughed, running ahead to meet the oncoming herd. "Don't get your fur and scales in a knot. We brought food."

Faedi couldn't help but laugh as Lonan dropped his deer before a black adolescent drake and an indigo-horned, scaled feline creature—a diwha—who immediately pounced on the meal. They had raised both since finding them alone in the forest, lone survivors of poachers.

Lonan pulled a rope of rabbits from beneath his cloak and tossed them to the smaller creatures—a mix of foxes, lizards, spiders, and wolves—darting around his feet. For a moment, it seemed as if they would knock him down, but he held his ground.

After he fed them, he disappeared into the mist.

"I'll get some eggs," he called back.

"I'll pour the ale," Faedi replied, carrying her deer into the cottage.

Inside, their home glowed with warmth and light. The luminescent plants they had collected from the Umbramire cast a soft, shimmering glow over the room, their leaves like tiny stars. Shelves carved into the stone walls held pots of herbs and plants, drying in bundles. Furs and blankets lined the windows, keeping the cold at bay, and charred remnants of logs lay in the hearth.

She dropped the deer onto the large table near the fire with a heavy thud. Other creatures, too small or sick to be outside, scurried around her feet, eager for treats. Dusan fluttered off to the side and screeched at a mouse that had ventured too close to her boots, warning it to back away.

"*They act like they never eat,*" he quipped.

"So do you," Faedi said with a smile, pulling out a bundle of meat, innards, and berries. "You know I brought plenty."

She set their food into bowls, washed her hands, and headed to the bedroom to change. Crates of supplies sat stacked along the walls, and the bed remained untouched, covered in a thin layer of dust. She wasn't sure why they even kept a bed there anymore.

The one person she wanted to visit had been missing for twenty and two years.

As she changed out of her hunting clothes, she took a quick inventory of the crates. There was plenty for winter, more than they needed.

We can take the extras to the poorhouse.

She nodded to herself, tugging on fresh clothes before returning to the main room. Humming softly, she poured two mugs of ale before donning a leather apron and getting to work dressing the deer.

As Faedi worked, the steady rhythm of her hands allowed her mind to wander. She had grown accustomed to the quiet of the forest that the bustling city, with its narrow streets and suspicious eyes, held no appeal. However, the tension in the air outside the walls of Dewgate was always there—an undercurrent of warning and danger. The city's hunger for the forest's resources, driven by fear and greed, weighed on her.

She couldn't help but wonder how much longer the peace they had would last. She didn't know what would happen if Dewgate's hunger and hatred finally broke through the barriers of the forest. The Sauvern had its own magic, its own defenses, but Faedi knew it was not invincible. She'd seen its weaknesses firsthand before.

Her thoughts drifted to the rumors—whispers of religious and political action in Dewgate, of factions pushing for tighter control of the borderlands. If they were true, the treaties that promised peace would be broken. Like saplings, they were fragile, and with one gust to topple the scales of balance, what peace they had would be gone.

And where would that leave us?

Faedi paused for a moment, her hands resting on the table as she glanced at the glowing plants. The forest was her home, her sanctuary—and it had been for as long as she could remember. But it became more than that after she took her oath to the heart tree. It became her duty to protect. Not just from poachers or trespassers but those who sought to take it for their own gain.

She had grown up with the belief that the forest was sacred, that the Guardians and Wardens were its protectors, its voice. But as the city pressed even closer, she wondered if anyone could stop what would inevitably come.

"We've got eggs and six new chicks." Lonan's sudden announcement pulled her from her thoughts as he set a basket on the table. "Also milk—Daisy's calf is old enough for her to share again."

Faedi glanced at him as he rubbed his hands together, his glamour fading. Black shadows replaced his pale skin, shimmering like liquid night. His violet eye gleamed through the darkness, and, as always, her heart caught at the sight of his unhidden self—wild, untamed, and utterly him.

He finally felt like home again.

"This winter's going to be a rough one." He rubbed his arms for emphasis and shivered. "We're barely past the equinox, and the air's already biting."

"We've got an excess of supplies," she said as he moved to start a fire. "I think we should take whatever we don't need to the poorhouse and orphanage."

Lonan frowned. "None of the caravans made it to Dewgate, did they?"

She shook her head and continued working on the deer, setting aside pieces to be dried or smoked. "I don't think so. Ravyn's last raven said no one's been able to find them—and I didn't see any sign of them either."

He scoffed and stood to start cooking. "And no city-folk will find them because Lord Bastard kicked out Dewgate's only Hunt with his anti-were-folk laws."

Faedi snorted, trying to hold back a laugh. "Lord Bastard?"

"Blavier—Bastard, same thing," he said with a dismissive wave. "He'll run that city into the dirt… he's acting like an Orderling from Ashar with all his new rules and laws."

Faedi glanced out the window, the mist swirling just beyond the glass. The mention of Lord Blavier and The Order stirred a bitter taste in her mouth. Both were forces of destruction and ignorance.

The Order, known for their venomous hatred for anything they deemed unnatural, might have found a way to gain ground in Dewgate. Priests traveled the world to spread lies and stir up trouble. They preached balance and peace, but their version of balance was a world devoid of the very creatures who made it whole. If they had their way, the forest would fall under their control, and any creature not of "pure" blood would be hunted down.

Faedi shuddered at the thought. The followers of Ilos, his chosen devout, were relentless. Their hatred was a fire, and she feared that it might soon scorch everything that they knew.

They'd tried it before—and their next attempt might be successful.

When the moon was at its highest, Faedi relaxed on a pile of furs, mending clothes by the fire's glow. Lonan rested beside her, his long knives glinting in the flickering firelight as he sharpened them. Above them, Dusan perched in the rafters, his face tucked beneath his wing. Sleep would come, but neither was eager to end the quiet peace. The silence was easy, like a shared rhythm they had always known.

Every so often, Lonan would hum as he tested a blade against the furs, and Faedi would mimic the sound when she tested her stitches.

The fire crackled, sending flickering shadows across the rough-hewn walls, and the scent of burning pine resin mingled with the damp, earthen chill of the night. Faedi's fingers worked the needle through worn fabric, her movements practiced, but her mind drifted.

Of all the Guardians and Wardens who wandered the forest in search of the missing supplies, no one had seen anything. Not a single track, no overturned carts, no broken wheels, nothing. The forest swallowed sounds well, but even still, the utter lack of signs unsettled her.

Even if bandits took them, we'd find something.

"We could look for the caravans after we help the farmers," Lonan broke the silence. He must have known where her mind went. "If they haven't been ruined, we could deliver the supplies ourselves to Dewgate."

Faedi nodded, cutting her thread and folding the shirt in her lap. "I want to know why they're missing in the first place." She sighed and shook her head. "They've used those supply paths for decades and know not to leave the trails."

Lonan put his knives down and looked at the hearth. He was just as curious. One or two missing caravans might be a fluke, but nearly a dozen was something else. Soon, people would refuse to travel the paths the Umbral Watch protected and patrolled. And the poorest of Dewgate would suffer for it.

He knows it's something else—he knows it very well could be deliberate.

After the last siege attempt against Dewgate, the Umbramire had agreed to monitor and maintain the paths—an act of good faith that Blavier used but never repaid. Instead, he passed more laws to keep Umbrals out of the city, along with the forest-folk and were-folk.

If it weren't for Lonan's glamour, he wouldn't be able to go there with her—but every visit was a risk. The city guard heavily monitored glamours.

"We can ask the farmers if they've heard anything strange," Faedi said softly, pulling herself away from the knot of worry in her chest. "They always know what's going on, even if they're locked outside the wall."

Lonan lowered his head, his dark hair falling forward to shadow his face.

"Yeah," he muttered.

Faedi watching him for a moment, reading the weight in his posture—the way his shoulders curved inward, the way his hands stilled.

"Don't sound so excited." She teased gently, nudging his knee with hers. She let the contact linger, a small grounding touch, testing the edges of his mood.

When Lonan only grunted, she shifted closer, letting her shoulder press against his. Without thinking too hard, she tilted her head and pressed a light, quick kiss over his left brow—the place she knew he carried tension the most.

"Hey," She murmured against his skin, the word barely more than a breath. "If we're lucky, maybe we'll get some sweets out of it."

For a moment, nothing. Then, a flicker of life stirred in Lonan's violet eye, glancing at her from beneath lowered lashes.

"Honey and lemon cakes?" He asked, voice rough but hopeful.

Faedi smiled. "Maybe," she shrugged. "But we have to help with the migration first."

"I know, I know." He sighed, the tension easing from his frame as he put his knives away. Then he stretched out across the furs, arms tucked behind his head.

He glanced up at her, the faintest ghost of a smile tugging at his mouth.

"Think we'll have trouble with the city guard?" He asked, his voice steadier, as if he trusted her answer was that of a seer's.

"Maybe, maybe not." She said, standing to put the sewing away. "Ravyn said the newer guards are too soft to bother getting dirty."

"They're dirty—just not from honest work," he muttered, shaking out the blanket. He wasn't wrong.

There were more people in the poorhouse than the year before and even more than in the years before that. The temple of The Ancients was always full of people searching for a free meal, unlike when Faedi had visited as a child.

"They've gotten pretty lazy over the last ten years," Lonan said with a smile as she lay beside him. "When the next attack comes, they'll piss themselves before they can even draw their swords."

She stared at the ceiling while he pulled the patched quilt over them. "That just means more work for us," she sighed. "More Umbrals will be injured or killed defending that place while their Lord hates you for existing."

He chuckled, the sound warmer than the fire. "Just means he's not invited to our party."

"Speaking of which." She rolled onto her side to face him and grinned. "What do you want for your name day?"

He groaned, and her smile grew. It was the same game every year—who would ask the other first? They shared a day of birth and had been friends for more than half of their thirty-two years of life.

"I don't know; I've got everything I need here. A new whetstone, maybe?" he finally said after a pause. "What about you? And don't say more arrows. I make those for you anyway, and you ask for them every single year."

She feigned the most innocent look she could manage. "But the ones you make for my name day are prettier."

He turned to face her, unable to frown but not wanting to smile. "Is that seriously what you want?"

She hesitated before speaking, gripping the edges of the quilt as she searched for the right words. It wasn't that she thought he'd say no—Lonan rarely denied her anything—but asking was different that time. It wasn't just another name day. Not when the Sauvern hummed in an all too familiar way.

"I want to go camping in Emsmeda." She worked to keep her voice steady, though her heart pounded. "I want to see the lights on the Rowdon Mountains."

She'd heard that the southern plains of Emsmeda stretched out like a sea of silver grass, endless and open beneath the winter. In the colder months, the earth hardened and the wildflowers that once danced in summer breezes gave way to frost-laced brush and bare, whispering fields.

He remained silent for a time, studying her as if waiting for her to change her mind or still ask for the arrows. Eventually, he nodded and smiled. "We can do that." Without warning, he stood and went to the bookshelf to look through their maps. "Do you want to go before or after the solstice?"

She rolled to prop herself up on her elbows. "Your parents would kill us if we missed the solstice celebration."

He brought the maps back to their spot and lay down to examine them after she covered him with the quilt again. "We can go after; the stars will be brighter then." He nodded. "The nomads will be at the twins, too. We can ask them if there are better trails than we have."

She nodded and shifted closer to him. "You sound oddly excited about this."

"Of course I am," he grinned. "And don't worry, I'll still make your pretty arrows for you, too."

They examined the maps well into the night until the fire's light began to die. His excitement fueled her own, and she couldn't think of sleep for a while. Not when he wanted to plan the proper trails they should take.

However, her eyes grew heavy as the night stretched, and she pictured the lights. Everyone said they were beautiful, dancing brighter than the stars in winter's deep; but she didn't just want to see them—she wanted to see them with him.

They had never left the forest, and if she was going to see something beyond what she knew, she wanted to do it with him.

I can't wait for the solstice.

Though, as the fire burned low, casting its shadows long against the walls, a sudden gust of wind made the furs shift. Faedi glanced toward the door, half-expecting to see something there—something with a presence so commanding, so powerful, that all her hopes of seeing the lights vanished. But nothing was there.

Just the night's chill.

She nestled herself closer to Lonan, and yet, the unease lingered.

Somewhere beyond their quiet haven, something had happened. The caravans hadn't simply disappeared. The guards of Dewgate had grown softer. Blavier's laws were tightening. Something was coming—she just didn't know what.

2
Jam and Honey

Faedi

As the first light of morning filtered through the cottage windows, casting a soft glow across the room, one of Faedi's anshies screeched from the rafters. The sound startled her awake, and she blinked sleep from her eyes. She stretched, reaching across the furs for Lonan, but her hand met only emptiness.

Before she could pull away, a sharp nip stung her finger. Squinting, she spotted the culprit—a gray, bat-like fluff ball with a fanged beak. Dusan swooped down, flaring his wings at the creature, which squeaked pitifully before fluttering back to the rafters to sulk.

"Greedy thing," she muttered, sitting up. "I know you're not starving."

The scent of fried eggs and cooked venison drifted toward her, and her stomach growled in response. She turned her attention to the table where she had dressed the deer the night before. A covered pan and a cup of still-steaming tea sat on the aged wood. But Lonan was nowhere to be found.

Her back protested as she sat up, rolling her neck and shoulders despite her stomach's demand for food. Mornings were always bad, but frosty mornings were the worst. Her muscles and skin felt too tight, and the chill made the bones in her arm ache as if the slightest touch would break them.

Breathe.

She took a slow, deep breath. A soft floral scent filled her senses, easing the pain just enough to get off the floor and eat.

"He wrapped your herbs," Dusan informed her before he flew out through a cracked window in the greenhouse. She had forbidden hunting inside the house, but anything beyond the clearing was fair game.

When she removed the towel from the pan, she smiled at the sight of breakfast—eggs, sausage, toast, and a leaf-wrapped bundle of herbs. She could hardly believe she hadn't woken up while Lonan was cooking.

She quickly swallowed the bitter herbs and hot tea as the creatures inside the cottage begged for scraps. Once finished, she watered the greenhouse plants while sipping her tea.

As she moved the rows of greenery, she ran her fingers over the delicate petals of a nythbloom—a plant that only took root in lands where Sylvanism thrived. It pulsed with a faint glow under her touch, the magic in the soil still strong.

It will be ready to transplant soon.

"I'll keep you here until after the last frost," she promised softly before she turned to look out the window. Already, the corners of the windows had the faintest layer of ice. "It really will be a cold one."

Outside, the larger animals were calm—Lonan must have already fed them.

He was an early riser, an unusual habit for an Umbral.

At first, she had felt guilty about how much he did to ensure her comfort, but over time, she had come to respect his habits. He was always attentive, and she could only hope she did enough to repay him.

Sometimes, she wondered if he would tell her if she fell short in their friendship or if he would hold back because of their bond. Lonan had always been blunt, even as a child, but she couldn't help but worry that he stayed with her and helped only out of duty—or because of his assignment to their parcel of land.

She caught herself rubbing her right arm. He might have been blunt with everyone else, but he had always been kind to her. Maybe that meant he wouldn't tell her if she wasn't doing enough.

He would tell me—he tells me everything.

Shaking her head, she washed the dishes before heading to the bedroom to get ready. As she dragged a brush through her tangled black hair, she sighed. It was always such a hassle. It had been years since she had shaved the sides of her head after taking the marks of the Umbral Watch.

She traced the edges of her markings; the ink remained as bold as the day she etched it into her skin. Umbrals took different marks for various life stages, and she received hers when she was only ten and five. It was rare for an outsider, but not unheard of, and she wore them with honor, though haircuts weren't her priority living in the Sauvern.

Maybe Lonan will cut it for me—or should I wait until spring?

Once she finally managed to tame her hair, she tied it at the nape of her neck and changed out of her sleep clothes. The empty basket beside the door caught her eye, and she smiled. Lonan must have gotten up earlier than usual; laundry was typically her chore.

Whenever he did it, the clothes returned with more holes than they had gone out with.

She hummed as she pulled on a fresh pair of pants. A few more patches wouldn't take too long, and it would give her something to occupy herself with on quiet nights—more so if they ended up snowed in. However, she paused when her gaze drifted to the curtain-covered window. Lonan only did busy work when something was bothering him.

But what is wrong?

They helped the farmers every year after their last harvest, so that wasn't it. The missing caravans didn't threaten their survival, but that wouldn't have set him off either.

It could easily be Dewgate.

If caravans kept vanishing, it wouldn't just be traders losing coin—whole families would starve by midwinter. The last time supply routes failed, the city imposed heavier taxes, blaming the Mire for harboring 'bandits and monsters'. But she knew the truth: the city would rather let the poor and outsiders suffer than admit their own failings.

But Lonan wouldn't worry about that too much—not yet.

She frowned, mentally ruling out what wouldn't trouble him and arriving at the only possibility left.

Maybe he doesn't want to see the lights. Maybe it's too far from the Mire.

But he would have told her if he didn't want to go—he wouldn't have gotten the maps.

She sat on the edge of the bed and batted away dust when it plumed in the air. It had to be something else.

Lately, he had been staring at her without saying anything, more than before. Yet whenever she asked, he brushed it off. He'd claim to be lost in thought, but offered no details. At first, she had assumed it was Mire business, but as she pondered it, her mind wandered.

Maybe Myst and Rena teasing him about their bond had bothered him—or maybe Ravyn.

Her thoughts drifted back to the night of the spring equinox celebration. They had grown bored with the festivities and wandered into the forest. There had been wine, laughter, dancing, and… kissing.

Nothing had happened beyond that, though she had wanted to do more. Maybe it had upset him. Perhaps he regretted it. There could have been an Umbral in the Mire that he was interested in. He was well past the average age of marriage, yet he never spoke of it.

The memory came to her in pieces, like a dream she hadn't meant to remember. The lanterns floating through the trees. Laughter, wine, the crush of grass beneath their feet as they left the celebration behind. They'd said they only wanted some air, a break from the crowd. But it was more than that.

Faedi could still feel the pulse of the forest that night—lush, humming with new life. Ravyn had brought the wine, slung carelessly over his shoulder. Lonan had said nothing, but followed without question. She'd felt the heat of them both behind her, different kinds of gravity pulling at her ribs.

They stopped in a clearing dappled in moonlight. Ravyn sprawled across a moss-covered rock, one leg hooked lazily over the other, sipping from the bottle with a crooked grin. He looked nothing like the Elder she knew he was.

"Relax, Lonan…" he murmured, offering her the wine. "Let the glamour go."

Faedi took the wine from Ravyn's hand, her fingers brushing his. It sparked something in her chest—something reckless. She tilted the bottle back, letting the sharp-sweet taste of it burn down her throat, her eyes never leaving Lonan's.

His shoulders were tense, his shadows restless. But under the moonlight, with Ravyn watching, he let the glamour slip. Not all the way—but enough for her to see the shadows ripple around his edges and bleed into his flesh. Enough to remind her who—what—he really was.

Ravyn grinned, lazy and dangerous. "Better."

They passed the bottle back and forth, warmth blooming in her chest with every swallow. Laughter came easier, louder—slipping out of her as Lonan deadpanned a rare joke and Ravyn nearly choked from laughing too hard.

The night blurred at the edges. Ravyn's shoulder brushed hers when he leaned in for the wine, and she didn't move away. Lonan's leg pressed against hers, solid and warm, when he sat beside her. The glowbugs swirled above them in lazy arcs, like stars had fallen to dance just for them.

She didn't remember who touched whom first. Maybe it was her hand on Ravyn's chest, his breath catching. Maybe it was Lonan's fingers brushing her wrist, tracing up her arm. Maybe it didn't matter.

Ravyn kissed her first—wine-sweet and eager. His hand cradled the side of her face as though he already missed her. She leaned into it, lips parting, hungry for more. Then Lonan's mouth was at her neck, slow and reverent. Her breath caught, fingers fisting in his shirt as the three of them moved together, unsteady and desperate.

She kissed Lonan next, a clash of heat and shadow. Then he kissed Ravyn, and something in her chest twisted. She hadn't expected it—but the way Ravyn sighed into it, the way Lonan pressed closer, made her ache deeper.

They collapsed into the moss in a tangle of limbs and gasps. Hands roamed. Skin pressed to skin. The night pulsed with her want.

Lonan's hand skimmed beneath her shirt, and Ravyn's mouth dragged hotly down her jaw—and then he stilled. Drew back.

"Wait," Ravyn said, his voice hoarse. "We're drunk."

Faedi blinked, dazed, lips swollen, chest heaving. Lonan exhaled like someone had doused a flame.

Ravyn sat back on his heels, rubbing a hand over his face. "Not like this."

The silence that followed was soft but weighted. The forest no longer hummed—it held its breath.

Faedi pulled her shirt down, heart hammering. Lonan turned away, his glamour renewed around him. And Ravyn? Ravyn only looked at them both like he was already grieving what could've been.

They didn't speak on the way back.

And in the time that followed, none of them ever mentioned the spring equinox again.

She shook her head and glanced down at her arm, where black vines curled from her forearm to her shoulder. Dotted among them were blue flowers that faded to white at the edges—eventides, flowers capable of healing or killing. They had grown on her since Lonan had accidentally bonded himself to her fifteen years ago.

No one had ever seen anything like it or replicated it since. Not that she wanted anyone to. Beyond not wishing for anyone to suffer as she had as a child, it was a symbol of their bond—how he had healed her, how he had saved her life.

She quickly pulled on a long-sleeved shirt, covering the vines. While Lonan and the Umbrals knew about them, few others did, and she didn't need any extra attention. Not when they would soon be within arm's reach of the city guard. They would see her as a threat.

Just like that soldier during the war—accusing her of poisoning city folk. The way his eyes burned with righteous fury still made her skin crawl.

She pushed the memory aside and tugged on her boots, huffing in annoyance. Leave it to some fancy-armored idiot to claim she was trying to kill the very people she had been there to protect.

Bastard.

Faedi stepped outside into the crisp morning air, the scent of damp earth and dew-laced foliage wrapping around her like an old shawl. Lonan stood a short distance away, his back to her, dark hair catching silver in the light.

She watched him hang freshly washed clothes, but he turned as she approached.

"Ready?" He asked, eyes flicking briefly to the line of her collar. He never looked directly at the vines, but she sometimes caught the way his gaze hesitated like he could still see them.

"Yeah," she nodded, adjusting her cloak. "We'll make it before they start the move tomorrow—if we don't take it too easy."

That earned her a faint smile, the kind he gave when he didn't want to smile but couldn't help himself.

They started walking, boots soft against the path, the silence between them heavy but familiar. The kind that only settled between two people who had once saved each other's lives—again and again—and she didn't need to keep saying it out loud.

After a moment, she glanced sideways. "You'd tell me, wouldn't you? If you weren't happy?"

Lonan didn't answer right away. His hands were hidden in his cloak, shoulders hunched ever so slightly against the wind.

"Why wouldn't I be happy?" He asked at last. "I have everything I want."

She didn't reply.

Under the canopy of ancient oaks and towering pines, Lonan and Faedi walked in comfortable silence. The crisp air painted their breath white as sunlight filtered through the dense foliage, dappling the forest floor with patches of gold. The occasional rustle of leaves and the distant call of birds accompanied them, a soothing backdrop to the rhythmic crunch of their steps. Gradually, the nagging worries in Faedi's mind began to fade.

Dusan flew ahead of them, calling back occasionally to let her know where he was, but he did not warn of any danger.

As they walked, Faedi braided the sides of her hair and wove them into a larger braid that draped between her shoulders. She had not thought to do it before they left, and she knew she would regret it once they reached the farmlands. Nothing tempted her more to tear her hair out than livestock in a mood.

They were always grumpy about their forced migration, but there was only so much sympathy to be given. The herds had to be moved closer to Dewgate's wall, back to the farmers' homes, to be butchered, cooked, and preserved for winter.

She hoped they would not have to butcher all of them. They would need some for breeding to replenish what they killed.

They moved through the underbrush with practiced ease, scanning for tracks or other signs of wildlife. Their voices barely rose above whispers when they spotted anything of interest. Smaller creatures were everywhere, busy storing food for winter, and they even passed deer grazing in the distance. However, the deer remained unbothered by their presence, as if they had no fear of predators.

Blavier had gotten rid of The Hunt. Of course, they were not afraid.

Dewgate had been a city of warriors once, a bulwark against the tides of war when the gods clashed in the heavens—or so her mother told her. The scars of that time still lingered, etched into the ancient trees and wall. When the gods abandoned the realms, their followers were left to pick up the pieces.

Some, like the Umbramire and The Hunt, had fought in the shadows, assassinating warlords and severing enemy supply lines. But the victors of the war had rewritten history, and then, the descendants of the ancient warriors were little more than unwelcome remnants of a time best forgotten.

"We should hunt on the way back," Faedi suggested after they passed another deer.

"Spoil Penelope and Comet before we go searching for the caravans?" Lonan grinned down at her.

"Dry extra for them, too," she nodded. "Comet got cranky when we were down to only fish."

He chuckled. "I remember. I thought he was going to take your head off."

Faedi rolled her eyes before glancing up at him. "It wasn't that bad."

"You and I remember things differently, then." He winked at her, and warmth crept up her cheeks. His attention shifted to the trees. "Nests are higher this year."

She nodded and pointed to the branches. "It'll be cold and plenty of snow to match."

They fell silent again, the hours slipping by uninterrupted. By early morning the next day, the sound of bleating goats broke the forest's calm. Other animal calls filtered through afterward, and Faedi paused to sip from her water skin.

If they were lucky, the farmers would have extra horses. Otherwise, they would have to get creative.

Lonan glanced at her and smiled. "Ready?"

"You really want those cakes, don't you?" She narrowed her eyes at him before resuming their pace. He fell into step beside her with a chuckle.

"I do."

Faedi scented the air as they walked. The herd was large but not as large as the previous year. In a typical year, there might have been enough to butcher and breed, but not without the missing supplies.

She traded a glance with Lonan but broke from her worries when he smiled at her. "Maybe they'll give you some of that blackberry jam you like." He walked faster and waved for her to follow. "Come on."

"You think?" She asked, her steps quickening at the thought. "I can't figure out how to make it."

"I know," Lonan's laughter startled birds from the trees, and Faedi glared at him.

Of course, he found it funny. He had not been there for the disaster, just the aftermath—a kitchen painted in jam, her covered in the sticky concoction, and tiny creatures swarming to clean up the mess. She still did not know how she had managed to make jam explode.

His laugh had been the same then, after the look of shock and worry faded from his face. He had charged in after hearing the bang and her scream, knives at the ready, but he had not been prepared for that kind of sight.

The sound of that laugh lingered in her ears, bittersweet and distant, like birdsong before a storm. She exhaled slowly, letting the memory settle before the present reclaimed her attention.

A gust of wind stirred the branches overhead, and it came with the low murmur of voices and the clatter of hooves against stone. She crested the last rise, boots crunching on the fallen leaves over the forest floor.

The trees began to thin, and she spotted farmers on horseback beyond the herd of sheep, goats, and cows. Several carts sat scattered about, loaded with supplies and strapped to oxen. Horses were not wasted on pulling carts when it came to migration.

"There they are!" A young man, a Krelin, called, waving his hat and motioning toward them as they approached.

The Krelin had always been a part of the forest, their lives dictated by the cycle of land and the balance of seasons. Even then, their presence among the farmers was a testament to their adaptability. They had no stone halls or towering walls, only the trust that the earth would provide if they honored their ancient ways.

Faedi turned when something charged near them and smiled at the sight of an ashen-skinned elf racing toward them atop a chestnut horse. His white hair almost glowed in the open air, and his smile brought one of her own. He was a Guardian, Elder Ravyn—and one of their only friends in the city.

Ravyn's connection to the land ran deep—deeper than most Guardians she had met. His bond with his heart tree had been forged when he was barely more than a child, and even then, she could sense the hum of Sylvan magic around him. Like roots stretching beneath the earth. Few people in Dewgate understood the weight of that bond, how it shaped a Guardian's every action, every thought. Fewer still respected it.

He was feared and respected by many—not just because he was a Guardian, but because he was a Cinder Elf. An outsider from Valoria's burning fields, shaped by flame and war, a remnant of a bloodline too stubborn to die. People looked at him and saw danger. Faedi looked at him and saw something else entirely. Power, yes—but also grief, defiance, and a beauty like starlight dancing on the edge of a blade. He was a living echo of a history meant to be buried, and gods help her, she couldn't look away.

They had known him for ten years, since assisting Dewgate in their last war, and he was nothing short of breathtaking. All Elder Guardians and Wardens left those with much to learn in awe, but he was different. His knowledge and compassion were beyond anyone else's—yet he was always smiling and relaxed.

The honor and status of Elder never seemed to faze him, nor did the cross looks and fear he received for his race.

Maybe that's why I'm so drawn to him—he's how I wish I could be.

"You're early," he announced as he slowed his horse to a stop. "How is your brood?"

Faedi smiled, looking away as her cheeks warmed. "They're well. Daisy says hello."

He chuckled as he dismounted, then leaned in to press a kiss to her cheek. The moment lingered—light, familiar—and yet it sent heat flooding beneath her skin.

"Hello back," he murmured, his voice low and close.

Lonan clasped Ravyn's forearm and pulled him into a one-armed hug. "I thought we were late."

"They're packing up early," he replied and nodded. "Was the trip easy?"

Despite his age and profession, his face bore no signs of wear. His clothes, however, told a different story—rough, stained, and well-worn, betraying his well-respected status in Dewgate.

"It was quiet," Faedi told him. "More deer than normal, but that's to be expected. Still no news on the caravans?"

He shook his head. "Keep hoping they'll turn up or someone finds them."

The caravans were more than just shipments of goods. They were lifelines, manned by traders who had braved the roads for years, knowing every hidden path and ever danger that lurked beyond the safety of Dewgate's walls. Their sudden disappearance was no mere misfortune.

Faedi clenched her fists. If people's hatred for anything outside of their cozy bubble extended, their animosity could be extended to merchants who traveled through the Sauvern. The merchants who regularly traded with the Mire and with the Nomad Dwarves from the plains.

By default, they're outsiders—even if they have homes in the city.

Lonan patted the horse's snout while Ravyn gave Faedi the same hug as he had given Lonan. She tried to ignore the way her heart skipped a beat. "Faedi and I were thinking about looking for them after the migration."

He pulled away and looked between them. "Really?"

"We're going to try." Faedi shrugged before turning her attention to the herd. It was barely half of what the farmers had before—less than she had anticipated.

What happened?

"Blavier said he's not sending anyone to look—said supplies are coming by sea, but...I haven't seen any ships."

She glanced back at Ravyn, then at Lonan. It would not be safe to sail in a few weeks. If Blavier wanted supplies, they needed to arrive sooner rather than later. Winter along the coast was never kind.

"They could be late," Lonan offered with a shrug, though his frown deepened. "If it's this cold already, the fog could be bad near Ceanea."

"That's what I'm worried about," Ravyn sighed. "Blavier's been sending guards to take a cut of the farmers' stores."

Faedi narrowed her eyes, biting back a growl. "Can he do that?"

"He's the Lord. If the guards follow his orders, he can do whatever he wants."

Blavier was not the kind of ruler who led from the front. He ruled with a ledger in one hand and a knife in the other, always weighing what could be gained against what could be sacrificed. If he wasn't against starving the communities outside the wall, then he was capable of anything.

3

Livestock and Longing

"I've spent so many years hiding behind my walls, but now, everything is so much more compli-cated with them. Every moment with them makes me question if my feelings are a curse or the truest thing I've ever known."

Lonan

The farmers chatted with him and Ravyn while everyone finished packing their supplies. Though Faedi was preoccupied with the herd. Children ran about before being herded into carts by their parents, but something felt different from other livestock migrations. He just couldn't place it.

There were the usual jokes and jeers about how city-folk no longer came out to help or trade, some even aimed at Ravyn for his choice to live behind the wall, but it was all in good fun. The farmers were kind and grateful for their help.

"We've got horses for you," one of the farmers called, waving them over to a group of carts positioned like a makeshift fence. "Not the best pick, but it's what we've got left from the summer."

Lonan glanced at Faedi, then at the horses. "Were the summer storms bad this year?"

We hardly had any trouble with them.

The farmer hesitated before answering, rubbing his calloused hands like he could scrub the worry away. "It wasn't just the heat or storms," he finally said, voice low. "I've seen bad summers before, but this—this was different. They weren't just sick. It was like somethin' hollowed them out, left 'em too tired to live."

He exhaled sharply and shook his head. "And now the ones that survived won't even look at each other the way they should. They won't talk…" his eyes flickered to the herd as if he expected to find them watching back. "It ain't natu-

20

ral."

Faedi clicked her tongue, summoning the mounts, then looked at Ravyn. "What happened?"

"Peni and I couldn't figure it out. Some sort of plague," Ravyn said with a shake of his head. His eyes flickered toward Lonan briefly, and Lonan frowned. "We could heal some, but others were too far gone… but since then, the animals haven't wanted to breed."

He wouldn't have called it a plague unless it truly was.

Lonan exchanged a glance with Faedi and sighed when she bit her lip. She was thinking the same thing he was. An Elder would know what it was, but Ravyn's reluctance to name it outright was concerning. Either he didn't want to panic the farmers, or he didn't want to worry them… maybe both.

Faedi didn't seem to linger on Ravyn's words. Instead, she tilted her head when one horse approached. Once it was close enough, she reached out and stroked its forehead. "I can talk to them—see if we can figure out how to re-stock the herds."

The farmer stared at her, confused. "What do you mean?"

"I can talk to them. See if I can convince them to mate… make babies?" Faedi raised her eyebrows and made vague motions with her hands to demonstrate.

Lonan immediately choked on a breath, heat blooming across his cheeks. He glanced away as if the horizon might offer some reprieve, but the image of her hands—those delicate, calloused hands—moving so unhelpfully suggestive was burned into his mind.

Typical Liru.

She didn't mean to be bold. Or maybe she did. Either way, it was effortless. Honest. Purely her. No shame in it, just a desire to help, to understand, to fix what she could.

He risked another glance.

She was smiling, amused by something the farmer said, the sunlight catching in her hair and turning into glittering onyx. Her fingers still brushed the horse's muzzle with instinctive tenderness. There was no fear in her stance, no hesitation in her odd, brilliant offer. Only that stubborn heart of hers—so sure she could bridge the space between species, between people, between pain and healing.

She was impossible.

And perfect.

Lonan's chest tightened. He cleared his throat and tried not to look like he was drowning in her.

But Ancients, he *was*.

He focused on Ravyn, who also stared at Faedi, his own cheeks darkening. After the farmer said something Lonan missed, Ravyn turned to him. When Ravyn's gaze lingered, Lonan cleared his throat and looked back to Faedi.

She stepped closer to the horse, her expression softening as her palm pressed to its forehead. Her eyes fluttered closed.

Then she began to speak—not in common, not even in Umbral, but something older. Older than the written word—earthbound and lilting, the cadence less like words and more like song. Each syllable carried breath and intention, rising and falling like wind through trees. It wasn't a language learned so much as remembered in the bones.

The horse's ears twitched, and its muscles relaxed beneath her touch.

And he didn't understand a single word.

But Ravyn did.

Lonan looked between the two of them, heart hammering in his chest. That voice—that language—it didn't just speak to animals. It stirred something in him too. Something ancient. Something that whispered she wasn't just *of* the earth.

She *was* the earth.

And something, or *someone*, had hurt her—and the flock.

Lonan tried to shake off the creeping sense of unease, but it clung to him like damp wool. The plague—if that's what it was—wasn't just a problem for the farmers. It meant something bigger. Something wrong. But before he could chase the thought further, Faedi shifted beside him.

Her lips pursed in thought, her fingers brushing over the horse's mane in absent strokes. It was a simple gesture, but something about it struck him—how effortlessly she moved, how easily she connected to everything around her. No other Guardian had a bond like hers. And it wasn't fair how much space she took up in his mind…or how much of that space she shared with Ravyn.

Faedi wasn't the young girl he had met as a child anymore. She had grown into a striking woman, her laugh and graceful movements captivating him more than he wanted to admit.

He couldn't help but steal glances, but he couldn't tell her how often she crossed his mind, how much he wanted their bond to be greater than the one they already shared. How, after the night of celebration with Ravyn, he wanted her… and him.

Not just in passing. Not just with the low ache that stirred when she laughed or when Ravyn's gaze lingered too long. He wanted to be beside them both— wanted their warmth, their closeness, their hearts. And not for a night. For *always*.

It was stupid. Foolish. Dangerous.

He had no claim on either of them. Faedi never spoke of love. Ravyn never hinted at more. Multiple partners weren't unusual among Guardians, and the Umbral had no such limits either. But what he wanted wasn't just a quiet arrangement born of convenience or trust.

It was everything.

He wanted all of her smiles, all of Ravyn's steadiness, the soft moments, the private ones, the sacred ones. He wanted to be the center of something good. With all of the bad in the world, all the blood and the grief, everything Faedi and Ravyn had endured—did he even deserve that?

To ask for more, when he already had their loyalty, their friendship, their trust…it felt like asking the gods for a second miracle.

I'm one greedy bastard.

Before that night, he had thought he would only yearn for Faedi until he found the courage to tell her how he felt—but the Ancients must have wanted to test his resolve. He couldn't forget Ravyn's gentle touches, caresses, and kisses. They had blamed the lily wine and never spoke of it again.

But he wanted it again—and more.

He had confided in his sibling and a few other Umbrals, and they had warned him of what could happen. If he was lucky, they might feel the same, and everything would be fine. But if they didn't—if he ruined things between them—he couldn't bear the thought of becoming a stranger to them.

He didn't think he could live without Faedi—or Ravyn.

Ancients help me.

"Lonan, you ready?" Faedi's voice snapped him out of his thoughts. She was already astride a paint horse, her head tilted as she looked at him expectantly.

He nodded and quickly mounted the bay horse beside her while Ravyn mounted his own. He clenched the reins in his hands, forcing himself to focus on the leather pressing into his palm instead of the way his heart kicked against his ribs. It wasn't the first time he'd caught himself looking too long at Faedi—or at Ravyn—but it was getting harder to ignore.

Lonan had always been close to them, always known the warmth of their friendship, but it began to burn in a way he couldn't smother. He had never wanted to risk what they had, never wanted to be selfish, but Ancients help him, he wanted. And want had a dangerous way of unraveling everything.

He tried to ignore the twist in his gut and turned to the farmer. "Where do you need us?"

"Just keep 'em from wandering into the trees."

"We can do that." Lonan smiled at Faedi. "I'll watch for stragglers."

"Okay, see you in a bit." She flashed a grin and raced off, leaving him and Ravyn to follow with a chuckle.

The sun cast a golden hue over the fields as the farmers hurried their livestock away from the forest. Damp earth and trampled grass filled the air, mingling with the musk of the herd. The crisp bite of oncoming winter nipped at Lonan's cheeks, but sweat still clung to his back from the sun's heat.

Over the clamor of animal calls, shouts, whistles, and the occasional crack of whips, there was laughter—joy.

It was a well-practiced tradition, passed down through generations in Dewgate long before Lonan had been born. The farmers moved efficiently through the fields, dirt and mud covering them all, yet smiles remained on their faces. This was the last bit of work, the final rush of adrenaline, before winter inevitably shut everyone in.

Scanning the herd, Lonan searched for Faedi and Ravyn among the animals. They were farther ahead, moving among the more spirited creatures, gesturing and sometimes shouting at the reluctant ones. Where he and Faedi worked seamlessly in the forest, she and Ravyn had the same instinct when it came to handling animals.

He wondered if that was how people saw him and Faedi together in the Mire.

A smile tugged at his lips as he watched Faedi skillfully guide her horse with her legs, her hips moving in rhythm with the animal. She held her ground, even when a bull acted as though it might charge.

Her sharp canines gleamed in the sunlight as she shouted a warning at the bull, urging her horse forward. Lonan wasn't worried about her being thrown—Faedi had wrestled far larger and meaner beasts without a scratch.

Then there was Ravyn, weaving his horse through the chaos, leaping off to grab a downed calf. In the blink of an eye, he was back on his horse with the calf in front of him, urging his mount forward toward the bull Faedi had been arguing with.

They are amazing.

Faedi said something to the bull, pointing toward the rest of the herd as though chiding it like a stubborn child. The bull hesitated, then turned away from her, its fire lost, and scurried off with the others.

"She's a fiery one, isn't she?" A farmer rode up beside Lonan, an ewe draped over his saddle.

"That she is," Lonan replied with a grin. "You should see her handle wolves."

The farmer offered him a water skin. "She's the one who gave Elder Ravyn that direwolf, isn't she?"

"She gave him the pup," Lonan said, pride flickering in his chest. "And he gave her the falcon."

"It's good to see her happy," the farmer remarked quietly. "A lot of us were worried about her. She was the only one who chose to stay after the raids. You're taking care of her, right?"

Lonan hesitated. It wasn't just about looking after her, not in the way the farmer meant. She had stayed behind when everyone else fled after the raids. She had survived, even as her world crumbled around her. What could he truly offer her while the rest of the world continued to grow harsher? Could he keep her safe, or would the weight of the land crush her spirit?

It had taken her years to reach where she was now, but she still had nightmares. She still cried for her family when she thought he wasn't looking.

"She takes care of me," he admitted, steering his horse to block a confused ram. "The forest looks after her. Did you know the Lirulins?"

"I did. Her mother delivered my brother." The farmer nodded, resting an arm over the ewe. "But the rest of us Krelin are leaving—Lord Blavier's gone too far with his taxes, and we can't keep up. Anyone who doesn't give what he wants is jailed."

The farmer's words hung heavy in the air, and Lonan couldn't help but feel the weight of them settle in his chest. Lord Blavier had always been a man of strict order, but something about his recent actions felt desperate. He was afraid of something—Lonan just couldn't tell what.

"There's land, fields north of the Rowdon border. The Dwarves offer better trade, and there's no one there to give us trouble."

Lonan handed the water skin back. "You bought land?"

The farmer nodded, smiling faintly. "The king in Emsmeda practically gave it to us—said it was too close to the cold. The queen promised there wouldn't be taxes until we made the land useful."

Ancients, Lonan hoped they weren't trading one bastard for another.

"And Blavier's just going to let you take the livestock?" he asked, unsure if that would cause a problem for them.

"We're hoping to be gone before he notices, but the animals aren't his to claim. Last season, the Garvens tried to move their flock across the river…only one of them made it." The farmer removed his hat, wiping his brow. "We were going to ask tonight—see if there's a safe path through the forest."

He knew what helping them meant. It wasn't just about moving livestock—it was about defying Blavier openly. Putting himself, Faedi, and the Mire in the path of a man who was already looking for an excuse to crush them. However, if they did nothing, others would suffer from their inaction.

Lonan looked over the herd, back at the wagons behind them, then to Faedi and Ravyn in the chaos ahead. "There's one," he said with a nod. "It's wide enough for carts and livestock. Clearing the forest will take a few days, but you'll be safe. The wolves are farther north this time of year."

The farmer replaced his hat and looked at him with hope in his eyes. "Think we can get your help moving?"

Lonan hesitated.

They could help. Of course they could. But helping meant more than guiding the herd—it meant drawing attention. Blavier's attention. And Faedi would be right in the middle of it.

His gaze flicked to her. She was smiling, hands buried in the horse's mane, calm and unaware of the knot twisting in his gut.

He didn't want to drag her into danger. But he knew she wouldn't let them turn away. Not when people needed them.

"We can help," Lonan said at last. But as the words left his mouth, he felt the true weight of the decision settle over him. Instead of protecting Faedi, he could be putting her in danger.

"What'll we owe you?"

Lonan glanced toward Faedi again. "Blackberry jam."

"Jam?" The farmer stared at him, eyes wide. "Just jam?"

Lonan smiled and shrugged. "We don't need money. You'll need it to barter with the Nomads."

The farmer looked as though he wanted to argue, but Lonan urged his horse forward before he could. It didn't feel right to take their money, not when they were about to start new lives. They would need every bit of it—perhaps even to hire protection if Dewgate decided to retaliate over lost resources.

He didn't know what lengths Blavier might go to, but he could guess. The new laws he had passed spoke of desperation, fear—and hatred toward those who didn't fit neatly into his plans or worldview. It wasn't good for his relationship with the Umbramire, nor the forest-folk—or the residents in his city.

Once the farmers were gone, Faedi and Lonan would have to tread carefully. So would Ravyn.

He knew Faedi was suspicious as soon as they stopped for the evening. He watched her scan the horizon, her eyes squinting as she brushed down her horse. Their location wasn't a usual stop for the farmers during their migration. They were farther southeast, away from the farms.

"We're not going to Dewgate, are we?" She asked.

"Nope." He shook his head, pulling off his cloak. "Emsmeda."

Faedi turned to face him, her gold eyes darkening. "Why?"

"They're leaving." He frowned and shook his head. "Bastard's taxing them too much, and they got a good deal in Emsmeda off the Rowdon border. We might see them when we go watch the lights."

Her lips pressed together, and her eyes burned brighter. She nodded before turning back to her horse, but then she growled. Dusan shifted on her shoulder and flapped his wings. "They're leaving before the guards can take more of their supplies."

He knew she wasn't mad at the farmers for looking out for themselves. She was angry at Blavier and likely at Dewgate itself.

The city had been a sore subject for her since the raids twenty and two years ago. Dewgate had never sent help into the forest. Only the Guardians and Wardens of the forest, sworn to the heart trees, had helped search for survivors. Then, when the surviving forest-folk tried to resettle inside the city walls, they were met with resistance.

Most of them, especially the were-folk, had been forced to remain outside the wall as farmers—locked out by Lord Blavier's prejudice.

"Is that why Ravyn's still here?" It was customary for him to help with the migration, but it wasn't common for him to be armed. He had spotted the gleam of Ravyn's armor in his saddlebags before.

Faedi exhaled sharply, her shoulders tensing as she set the brush aside. "He mentioned being worried about guards coming when we got close to the city."

Was he going to fight the city guard?

He glanced over his shoulder, searching for Ravyn in the crowd of farmers near the communal fire. Ravyn stood out among the other races in the group. Cinder elves like him weren't common in Yestrana. Most remained in the east, in Valoria.

Ravyn stood taller than everyone else there, almost a head taller than Lonan, and his pleasant expression among the crowd sat on his face like a mask. Ravyn's eyes drifted to the west, behind them, toward Dewgate.

"I told them we'd help them reach the southern trail through the forest," he said, watching Faedi's fur-tipped ear twitch.

"They don't need us the whole way?" She looked up at him. "Everyone at home will be fine for a couple of weeks."

"I was thinking we could run interference. Trash the trail behind them, just in case Lord Bastard sends anyone after them." He explained, stretching his arms above his head as he circled the horse. "Ravyn won't stop them, the Guardians under him and the Wardens won't track them…but the guards? They might be sent after them."

"And they won't go where they don't think it's safe," she mused while braiding the horse's tail.

"Exactly."

She leaned to look at him on the horse's other side. "Ravyn said there are rumors about Blavier."

His eyebrows raised. "What kind?"

She disappeared from view, but he still heard her. "He has a gold-robed adviser."

Gold robes could mean only one thing—The Order was in Blavier's ear. *Fuck.*

He rounded the horse again and tapped the tip of her nose as he leaned down. "Want to see if we can hear more rumors?"

"You're just hoping they have cakes, aren't you?" She squinted at him, and he shrugged. "You're impossible."

He gasped, placing a hand on his chest to feign offense. "I'm just hungry."

She scoffed and grabbed his hand, leading him toward the group of farmers. "Hungry and impossible," she laughed. "Let's see what else they're saying about Lord Bastard."

He followed her, glancing down at their hands. Some areas on her palms were rough with callouses, but the rest were smooth—old scars from the raids—places where her velveteen fur didn't grow, revealing pale gray skin. He knew she hid more scars under her clothes, scattered across her arms, legs, and back.

He had committed each one to memory.

As they walked, he noticed the stiffness in her gait. Her legs and back were sore, but her hips swayed hypnotically with each step. Her tail flicked in rhythm, and he forced himself to look away before staring too long. Watching her for signs of pain was one thing, but watching her tail was another story.

Don't stare at her ass without permission.

"Are you two ready to eat?" One of the farmer's wives called from the fire. "Take a seat; I'll bring you some bowls."

"Thank you," Faedi responded sweetly, her voice slightly higher than usual.

He squeezed her hand. "Do you want to sit away from the fire?"

She shook her head and settled on the ground near the crowd's edge. "We won't hear rumors away from people."

"Alright." He smiled at her and draped his cloak over her shoulders. "I'll go get dinner."

He turned and headed to the woman at the fire, who held two wooden bowls in her hands. His breath hitched as he took in her features. Age had carved itself into her skin—fine lines webbed from the corners of her eyes, her cheeks sunken, and her lips pale and cracked from wind and time. But it was the burn scar on her neck that froze him in place. His shadows stirred, flickering with the force of memories he'd spent years trying to bury.

Twenty and two years had passed, but the scent of burning wood and blood still clung to his mind like a sickness. He remembered the screams echoing through the forest as raiders tore through the forest-folk's homes, their flames turning sacred groves to ash.

The Umbral Watch and The Hunt had arrived too late—too late to save the elders, too late to stop the cut of steel that ended so many lives. He could still hear them then, the children barely old enough to understand the horror around them, clutching at the lifeless bodies of their families, their tiny hands stained red.

I wasn't much older than them—Faedi wasn't either.

Guilt gnawed at him like a wound that never healed, and then, staring into the eyes of one of the few survivors of that massacre, he wondered if she, too, remembered how everyone failed her. He couldn't stop his mind from wandering, his eyes from going to Faedi as she stood anxiously beside the fire, if she blamed him.

Although worry tinged his face, he couldn't help but smile back. She was too old to start over again.

"Will you be coming with us?" She asked, her eyebrows raising and deepening the wrinkles on her forehead.

"Yes, *Vaelma.* We'll guide you to the trail and cover your tracks," he promised with another bow. "After the solstice, we'll bring supplies."

"You're too kind," she smiled, and her cheeks reddened. "We'll be fine once we're on better soil."

He nodded back toward the fields and led her to where Faedi waited. "Do you think the soil is the problem?"

"I do. The animals eat, but they keep getting skinnier. And they won't breed," she sat beside them, her voice growing solemn. "When I was a child, we moved with the season, but since the raids and the sickness, I think the soil's been drained—poisoned."

"And the Lord won't help? He has scholars, and the priestess is a Guardian," Faedi leaned forward to peer around him and focus on the old woman.

"Lady Callon had tried, as had the Elder Guardians." The older woman shook her head as she looked at the elf on the other side of the fire. "I know poor Elder Ravyn is at his wit's end. But those damned scholars never leave the wall."

"And yet he's still demanding more from you for the winter," Faedi scoffed, turning her attention to her bowl of stew.

"He hasn't always been this bad." Lonan asked, resting his hand on Faedi's shoulder. "Has something changed?"

The woman shook her head. "I don't know. He wouldn't even hold an audience with us after the livestock went ill. Lady Callon and Sir Sophir visited us, though—tried to help how they could." She sighed and turned her attention back to the group. "I fear he might be ill; no one sees him much anymore."

Lonan frowned. Sophir wasn't a name he recognized. "Who's Sir Sophir?"

"The High Knight," the woman replied. "He's new to the position."

It was difficult to replace High Knights. Most remained in their positions until death, and only a few throughout the decades had been removed for other reasons. But none in her lifetime had died or stepped down.

Faedi seemed to have the same thought. Her brows creased as she set her bowl down. "What happened to the last one?"

The elderly woman shook her head but didn't reply.

"He was murdered—they found him with his throat ripped out near the north gate."

Ravyn's smooth voice came from nearby, and the woman looked up as he approached. He sat in front of them, between Faedi and the fire. Only then did Faedi pick up her bowl again to eat.

Ravyn was one of the few people who could distract Faedi from her discomfort around fire, and he wondered if Faedi even recognized it. He never spoke about it when he diverted her attention—only steered the conversation in a different direction or directed her gaze elsewhere.

He wondered if he knew about Faedi's nightmares.

Faedi raised her eyebrows at him. "And the new High Knight?"

He shrugged and plucked a piece of grass from the ground. "Blavier wasn't happy when he took his oath on The Ancients."

"He's been working with Lady Callon—closely," the elderly woman added. "From what I hear, he's respected by most in the city. He was the only knight who left the wall during the raids."

Lonan turned his attention to her. "But he's in charge of the guards who take your supplies."

"He's never been with them," the elderly woman said with a shake of her head. "I don't know what goes on behind the city walls, but rumors of a rift exist. Lady Callon might be ousted, and Sir Sophir is already on thin ice with his oaths."

"He's a good man. A friend," Ravyn interjected. The woman glanced at him and caught his eyes lower. "He's been vocal about his distaste for how Blavier is running things."

Faedi huffed, swallowing a bite of food before speaking from behind her hand. "But he works for him and has to know Blavier's taking their supplies. Words and actions are two different things."

"I don't know what he does behind closed doors, but I do know that if Blavier gets rid of Callon, he'll get rid of Sophir, too." Ravyn shook his head. "He took his oath in the name of The Ancients—his oath was one the Umbrals took. He swore devotion to the city, to the land—not Blavier. Callon took the same one, along with the oath of the heart."

Lady Callon was powerful and a skilled Guardian. Lonan had seen her fight to defend Dewgate during the war. She was kind and soft-spoken, always helping the poor at the temple. If she were ousted, the city would suffer.

And if Ravyn was right about the High Knight, Dewgate would suffer without him, too.

"What did Lady Callon do that was so bad anyway?" Faedi's question pulled the woman away from the fire.

"Rumor is she attacked one of Blavier's other advisers," the elderly woman replied.

The woman watched Ravyn nod. "A member of The Order," he muttered with a wince as he watched Faedi. "He's got advisers from every path."

Faedi shuddered, and Lonan squeezed her shoulder. The Order was in Dewgate. Faedi had been adamant that they were behind the raids that had killed her family and so many other forest-folk twenty-two years ago. And few believed her.

"But, from what I've been told, the other advisers' voices are silenced." Ravyn's voice was quiet, but there was an edge to it—a weight that pressed against the air between them. "Blavier doesn't care about the city, not really. He cares about what it gives him—the power to control hundreds and shape his world how he wants. He's always searching for something, always reaching for more, and with his new Orderling adviser, he took his chance.

To him, Ilos' devout are just another weapon. He doesn't worship any god; he commands others. And those who follow him either believe his lies or fear what happens if they don't. He looks at people like you and Faedi, and he sees tools, not lives. You're useful when his world is under threat, otherwise, you're in his way. And the worst part?" He exhaled sharply, smoke and fog billowing in front of his face as his eyes darkened. "He thinks he's right. He thinks he's the savior of the abandoned city."

It isn't safe for Faedi to visit the Temple of The Ancients anymore.

"You should get some rest," the woman said, standing and offering Faedi her hand. "Everyone should."

Faedi took her hand, and the older woman gathered their bowls before bowing her head in thanks. Lonan mirrored the gesture and led Faedi away from the fire, his eyes drifting to the stars above. Why did they have to look so beautiful when his mind was dark?

If The Order had influenced Blavier to go against the treaty with the Mire, her kind might have to fight against the people they had protected for centuries. And she didn't know which side the Guardians and Wardens would choose.

At least the forest-folk won't be caught in the crossfire.

He glanced back at the group. If they were lucky, they'd be in Emsmeda with substantial shelter before the snow came—hopefully, far out of Blavier's reach.

Unless Blavier decided to retaliate, then they'd be defenseless.

Lonan watched Faedi's retreating form, the firelight casting flickering shadows across her back. If Blavier retaliated, it wouldn't be swift—it would be calculated, drawn out like a slow knife to the throat. He would use some of the Krelin as examples—hang their bodies for everyone to witness. He would call them thieves and traitors to the city, but he wouldn't stop there.

4

Thorns and Glowbugs

"I should be worried about the forest-folk, about what Blavier will do when he learns his farmers abandoned the city—but all I can think about is damned lily wine and solstices."

Faedi

As the last of the carts disappeared from view, Faedi crossed her arms over her chest and bit her lip. Three days of travel—chasing down rogue livestock, pushing carts through washed-out trails, and tending to odd injuries—had worn her out completely.

Ravyn returned to Dewgate as soon as they crossed into the forest, promising to delay anyone who might try to follow them, and he couldn't help but worry he might get himself mixed up in something dangerous.

Faedi also wasn't sure if the farmers would make it safely to their new home. She could only pray to The Ancients, hoping they would guide the group to a place with better soil and health.

"I'll follow them until they reach the outer parcel," Dusan had promised before taking off from her shoulder and flying after the group.

"We could chop down some of these pines to block the trail," Lonan suggested from behind her. "Where's Dusan going?"

Faedi turned back to face him. "Following them to make sure they make it out of the forest alright." She smiled and glanced him over. "Do you have an axe hidden somewhere I don't know about?"

"Ah," he rubbed his forehead and chuckled. "No, that I do not. My knives might take a while."

Faedi laughed, digging into the pouch on her belt. "Just vines and shrubs, then?"

"Eventides, too," he added while dragging debris onto the trail. "They won't go where they see poison."

Faedi nodded, walking along the path as she scattered seeds across the ground. "Good idea."

I guess we're lucky they're idiots.

Once the seeds were spread, she wove small designs with her fingers and began whispering to them. She had seen others command nature with harsh words, forcing it to bend to their will, but that always felt wrong.

The earth wasn't something to be dominated—it was to be respected—feared by those who meant it harm.

The seedlings trembled beneath her fingers like shy creatures waking from slumber. She poured her warmth into them, not just her magic but her intent—her care. The earth responded like an old friend recognizing a familiar voice. In its own way, it comforted her back, as if assuring her it would protect the farmers where she could not. Its pulse was slow and steady and wrapped around her magic like a heartbeat through the soil.

In that moment, Faedi didn't feel quite so helpless. She wasn't just hiding a path—she was sheltering hope. A smile tugged at Faedi's lips as little seedlings sprouted, one after another. It didn't take long for them to take root, and once they did, they blossomed.

She kept whispering, her words gentle and encouraging. The plants responded, covering the trail in a thick carpet of green. Vines wound around tree trunks, creating a natural curtain that draped the path. Bright flowers in crimson, silver, and azure bloomed, adding vibrant color to the lush greenery.

Eventually, the trail disappeared under the weight of the fresh growth, blending seamlessly with the rest of the forest.

Though the trail was hidden and the carts had vanished beyond the tree line, Faedi's mind could not rest. Every quiet second that followed was heavy, as if the trees themselves held their breath. The peace was temporary—she knew that. They still had to track the supply caravans, still had to find a way to help the city. And the longer they waited, the greater the risk that Blavier's soldiers, or worse, would catch wind of their path.

Stepping back, Faedi admired the transformation. The vines continued to thicken, and blue and white flowers opened between their thorns. Hours, or even days, of delay would face anyone lucky enough to try and get through. If they tried to burn it, they'd poison themselves with the smoke from the eventides.

"This should be good enough," Faedi said, placing her hands on her hips as she surveyed her work. "It'll spread more over the next few hours."

"I want to ask the Mire to send them supplies," Lonan said after tossing a branch into the recent growth. "Winter will be hard on them if they're building with what little they have. I don't know what resources are around where they're settling."

Faedi wasn't sure what they had to work with either. From what she'd learned, the southern plains had nothing. The harsh winds from the Rowdon mountains kept most things from taking root.

"We can ask while we're looking for the caravans?" she asked, glancing up at him. "The poor and orphans still need supplies, too. Just because Blavier's a greedy—" She sighed. "I want to help them, too."

"Were you about to call him something rude?" Lonan stepped closer, leaning in, his face inches from hers. He grinned, clearly enjoying himself. "What were you going to say?"

She tried not to let her breath catch as Lonan leaned in closer.

He always did that—closed the distance with a grin, his voice low and warm, like he didn't even realize the effect he had on her. Or maybe he did. She hated how easily he disarmed her with his laughter, how he could turn a weighty silence into something light.

Faedi rolled her eyes and tried to change the subject. "We need to go—we didn't bring enough arrows or rations to wander the forest looking for caravans."

"No, no. Tell me what you were going to say," he teased, holding onto her shoulders and following her as she tried to walk away. "I'm sure you've got some pretty colorful words you'd like to use."

"What I want to call him won't help anyone," she muttered, shaking her head.

"No, but you're adorable when your nose scrunches while cursing people. It's the best thing ever."

Faedi stopped and turned to look at him, crossing her arms over her chest. "Better than lemon and honey cakes?"

He paused, mimicking a scale with his hands as he silently mouthed things to himself. Faedi tilted her head to the side, watching him put on his little show. She couldn't help but smile. Even when she didn't want to—he always found a way to lighten her mood. But beneath his charm, she saw the ripple of his glamour— his shadow retreat—the weariness he tried to mask.

He carried as much as she did, more even, and never said so. It made her want to reach for him, not just in affection but in shared burden. The words stuck in her throat, so she let the silence linger between them instead. It was safer to let him continue his charade.

Eventually, he nodded, dropping his hands with a wide smile.

"If your nose gets scrunchy and your cheeks turn purple, it's better than cakes. But don't worry," he motioned for her to follow him. "I've got a surprise for you over here."

She trailed behind him, smiling as he picked up a pack and carefully offered it to her. She moved slowly to inspect the contents. When she unwrapped the cloth inside and saw jars, Faedi blinked in surprise. Blackberry jam—her favorite, a rare treat she hadn't tasted in seasons.

The gesture tugged at something deep in her chest. He had gotten it for her; even with everything else happening around them and with the farmers, he got it. She looked at Lonan, but the words she wanted to say were too big for the moment. Instead she closed the back carefully and whispered, "Thank you."

As they turned back toward the path, Faedi glanced once more at the wall of green they left behind. The forest would guard the trail for them. And with Lonan beside her, even the long path ahead didn't feel quite so daunting.

The forest was quiet—but not safe. Faedi kept her senses sharp, ears turned for the sound of pursuit that never came but always threatened.

They didn't have time to waste winding through careful trails. The sooner they made it home, the sooner they could get supplies and look for the caravans. If anyone had followed them, the brush of the forest would hide their tracks, but that comfort only went so far.

The last thing they needed was to lead someone back to the cottage. Only a few people in Dewgate knew where their home was. Elder Guardians and Wardens of the forest visited occasionally, and the forest-folk never came by. Any other communication came from ravens owned and trained by Ravyn.

As night settled over the forest and glow bugs flitted through the air like tiny stars, she couldn't help but worry. "Do you think they'll be alright?" she asked.

Lonan slowed to walk beside her and softly nudged her with his elbow. "They will be...Dewgate will be too."

She bit her lip and watched her steps through the brush. "What if we don't find the caravan—or what if the supplies are ruined?"

"Then we hope they ration what they have and accept help from the Mire," he replied, lowering his head. "All we can do is hope."

She glanced up at him, worry twisting in her gut. "Can the Mire help the forest-folk and Dewgate?"

"They'll try," he sighed.

The Umbramire might have been well-stocked and fortified, and plenty of people could use magic to help the community through the winter—but even magic had its limits. And if Dewgate turned away the supplies, it would be a waste. Blavier would burn them rather than send them away at the gates.

"Why is Blavier even such a— the Mire has had a long-standing history of helping Dewgate. It's not like there's a risk of betrayal," she kicked a stick. "There's a treaty to prevent that. It's not like we'll send wagons of supplies and try to blow up the wall like the port attack fifty and some odd years ago."

"Blavier's a human, and humans are fickle," Lonan shrugged, his frown deepening. "Next thing you know, he's going to ban more than Krelin from inside the walls just because anyone could be were-folk."

She growled, kicking a rock that time. She'd hidden her lycanthropy from almost everyone in the city, but it might not matter. "No more Temple trips for me."

Lonan laughed and swatted her tail. "You'll sneak in."

"They're monitoring glamours." She looked back at him. "It's safer just to stay away."

"Ravyn will find a way for you to talk to the gods," Lonan promised before he frowned and looked away. "As long as there isn't someone spying on his ravens."

She stopped in her tracks, turning to face him. It was just a thought, a possibility, but she caught the worry in his eyes. "You think he'd spy on Ravyn?"

"It wouldn't surprise me if he spies on everyone who leaves the walls… but Guardians and Wardens who regularly mingle with Umbrals?" He motioned around the forest. "He's got an Orderling adviser now. I wouldn't put anything past him."

Is Ravyn in danger there?

She dragged her hand down her face with a groan. Many Guardians and Wardens were of uncommon races, but only Ravyn was from one where The Order maintained control. The adviser could either look at him as a friend or a threat.

Faedi kicked another rock, harder that time. The words kept echoing in her head—*no more temple trips*. It wasn't just the risk of being discovered. It was the way it made her feel like her last connection to her mother was gone. The temple of the Ancients was the last place, the only place, that flames hadn't tarnished.

Ravyn might find a way. But it wouldn't be the same.

"We should still try to help," she began walking again. "It's the right thing to do."

Lonan fell into step beside her. "Agreed. Besides, if citizens see him turn away supplies when they're starving or at risk of it—maybe he'll be ousted."

She winced and shook her head. "I'm not sure that a civil war in winter would be the smartest idea for them."

"If it keeps The Order from ruining Dewgate like Valoria, it's probably the lesser of two evils."

They continued their trek in silence, their footsteps muffled by the thick layer of leaves and pine needles underfoot. The deeper they went into the forest, the denser the trees became, blocking out the sky until darkness surrounded them. The only light they had came from the glow bugs that danced in the surrounding air.

Her legs and back ached, and her steps grew slower with exhaustion. Occasionally, she glanced at the bugs. Lonan's hair reflected the faint light of the bugs drifting lazily near him, and she smiled when one landed on his head. Maybe it was as tired as she was.

They could make camp—but that'd waste time.

Lonan stopped as if sensing her thoughts and leaned against a tree to drink from his waterskin. Her eyes lingered on him longer than they should have. The soft flicker of a glow bug catching on the tip of his hair, the way the water traced his throat, the ease of his presence—it tugged at her chest the same way it always did.

He had always been there for her, a constant, quiet strength beside her.

But since the equinox, even years before—if she was honest with herself—she found herself wishing for more. For him to reach for her, not just in kindness or exhaustion, but in all the quiet moments between.

Faedi glanced away when her heart pounded in her chest—only looking back when he offered the skin to her. She accepted it with a smile, drinking as she leaned against the tree beside his.

"I love it when they're out," she murmured while watching the bugs fly around. "They're almost as beautiful as stars."

Lonan chuckled softly beside her. "Certainly in my top five favorite sights."

She glanced at him. "What are the other four?"

For a moment, less than a heartbeat, she caught him staring at her before he blinked and looked away. But there was something there; she knew there was.

It's that look again.

"Why do you always do that?" She straightened and huffed when he didn't look at her or respond. "Lonan?"

He glanced at her but didn't turn to face her. "Hmm?"

"Seriously?" She rolled her eyes and offered him his water skin back. "You've been looking at me like that for weeks now."

He took a step away from the tree and smiled.

"Maybe you're one of the other four," he winked at her before he started walking. "You should drink more. Only a little while to go, and there's still more work to do."

Ancients' blood, Tagi.

She shook her head before she took a deep breath and pushed herself away from the tree. She didn't move to walk beside him. Instead, she chose to stay several paces behind him. She didn't want him to think her purple cheeks were because she was mad at him.

They broke through the trees into the clearing around their cottage just as the first light of dawn began to filter through the canopy. Lonan and she exchanged a look, their hair and clothes damp with dew, before creatures rushed toward them with warm and hungry greetings.

Before entering, they handed them the small game they'd gathered from nearby traps.

She would have stayed outside to spend more time with them, but she was too exhausted. Her mud-caked boots might as well have been lead, and she abandoned them as soon as they were inside. Lonan's didn't stay on for much longer than hers. He didn't say a word and just closed the curtains before he collapsed onto the furs by the hearth.

He didn't bother lighting a fire, and she didn't ask. Their damp and muddy clothes were of no concern. They could be washed later.

She sank down beside him, their shoulders brushing beneath the blanket. His arm shifted under her neck without hesitation, pulling her close with the same ease as when he moved through shadows. She smiled as his glamour rippled away and his shadows enveloped them.

Her eyes were already closed when he tucked the quilt around them. The quiet of the early dawn outside surrounded them, the creatures rustling occasionally just beyond the walls.

"We'll figure out what to send when we wake up?" She whispered, her voice barely audible in the stillness.

He nodded. "After toast and jam."

She held onto his promise like a thread of warmth in the cold. *After toast and jam*, he'd said. Like it was the most natural thing in the world. Maybe it was. Maybe that was hope looked like—not a grand plan or sudden solution, but quiet mornings in a safe place.

The world outside might still fall apart, but for a few hours, they could pretend they had time to save it.

5

Shadows at Midnight

Faedi

Hrul'viras, 2696

A large man with a broadsword shouted over his shoulder as he moved to stand in front of Lonan and Faedi. "We can buy you time to gather the others. Go, now!"

Ravyn met Faedi's gaze and only stepped back when she nodded. "I'll be back with reinforcements."

Faedi watched him flee, her heart pounding as howls echoed in the distance. She turned to face the forest, but before she could process the situation, fire erupted from the shadows. Battle mages charged toward them.

The fire didn't sound right. It crackled too slow, like time itself was struggling to keep up. A scream echoed across the trees—a familiar voice? Her own?—but it was warped as it hit the smoke, curling into a whisper.

Nothing about the scene felt real, but the pain, when it came, was sharp enough to convince her otherwise.

A scream tore from Faedi's throat as she instinctively shrank back, firing her bow at one of them.

"Stay with me!" Lonan's voice cut through the chaos as he slashed his knives through the flames. *Stay with me, Liru!*

Faedi hooked her bow over her shoulder and outstretched her hands, summoning the roots under the dirt. Her palms burned as they responded. They shouldn't have, but they did. Beside her, the helmeted Dewgate soldier stood tall, unyielding, as he roared a battle cry and tore into the mages with his sword.

As the flames blazed around them, Lonan positioned himself before Faedi, deflecting arrows with his knives while she sent a blast of air through the fire, hoping to send the flames back at their attackers.

The mages were relentless, their spells crashing against Faedi's defenses with unmatched force. She gritted her teeth, her focus faltering in the heat. Still, she poured everything she had into holding the line while the soldier charged through the fray.

He practically cleaved them in two.

Together, they fought, refusing to yield an inch of ground to the assailants. As the fight raged on, Faedi's body ached, her muscles protesting each movement, but she pushed herself to continue. She didn't stop until the last mage fell and the flames were extinguished.

Faedi stood amidst the smoldering remains of the forest, looking at Lonan and the Dewgate soldier who remained. Each of them heaved with exertion, but they were alive. Unburned.

Then, a whistle pierced the silence between their breaths.

Lonan went down with a shocked shout, clutching his face, and a barrage of arrows rained down on them. Faedi stared up with wide eyes, her hands flying up on their own as a wall of thick vines and thorns rose to surround them. The projectiles clattered against the makeshift barrier, blood trickled down Faedi's face, and the arrows fell to the ground or were pinned in the vegetation.

But one arrow slipped through the barrier.

It moved in slow motion as Faedi calculated its trajectory. It wouldn't hit her or Lonan, but it would hit the soldier.

She could have let it hit him. He was armored; he would survive. Lonan was down, bleeding, and she needed to help him. But her feet were already moving. Not out of logic. Not even instinct. Something older. Something deeper.

Echoes of warnings from the forest rippled around her. The trees whipped violently in the smoke, their leaves casting twisted shadows around them.

Eryndar.

A chill shot down her spine, and she stepped into the path of the arrow without hesitation, as if her body made the choice long before her mind could argue. Her breath caught in her throat as pain ripped through her stomach, and the force of it nearly knocked her off balance. With a shout of shock and pain, Faedi took a step backward—into the grasp of the soldier—her hand instinctively pressing against the wound.

"Liru!"

The soldier's arms steadied her as she sagged against him, but her mind was already slipping. Lonan's voice reached her like it was underwater—panicked, distant. She wanted to go to him, to touch his face and tell him she was fine, even if she wasn't. But her mouth wouldn't work right.

Her howl had gone unanswered. Or maybe…maybe someone was coming. Ravyn promised he would return. She clung to that hope, barely conscious of the words on the soldier's breath, of the blood soaking the earth beneath her.

Her blood was warm as it seeped through her fingers, but the sensation felt almost foreign. She shouldn't have howled, but she did. She released the loudest one she could manage, praying to The Ancients that there was a Hunt nearby.

She wished Torix was there—even though she knew he wasn't.

Her vision blurred as shadows whipped around the wall of vines and thorns. Clashing swords and shouts echoed around her, but the sounds faded under her heart, pounding in her ears.

"They're here," the soldier's voice reached her as he lowered her to the ground as the strength in her legs gave out. "You did well, *Tia'min*."

Faedi groaned as she sat up on the furs, her back protesting as it screamed in pain. She shivered, blinking in confusion. Before she could fully process her surroundings, a bundle of herbs appeared in front of her face.

"What?" She asked, her voice heavy with sleep.

Lonan's face appeared, slowly waving the herbs in front of her. "You were dreaming of the war again."

Of course, he knew. He always did. Their bond let some dreams bleed through—sometimes they shared them entirely. He'd seen her nightmares more times than she liked to admit.

His frown deepened. "You overdid it with the migration."

She nodded slowly, her thoughts still catching up with him as she accepted the herbs. "Right."

Beneath her, the rough texture of the furs tickled her skin, a comforting contrast to the worn patchwork quilt that lay nearby. Lonan stood and lit a fire, then moved to fill the kettle. His movements were slow, sluggish. Even the shadows that usually swirled around him didn't move as restlessly as usual.

Faedi rubbed her forehead, forcing herself to stand. "Was it me dreaming about it, or you?"

"Probably both of us," Lonan shrugged, glancing at her. "Hard not to think about it when the city's gone to shit."

Faedi tried not to let the thought linger, but it was difficult. The next image to surface in her mind was Lonan without an eye, and his mother chiding them for their recklessness. She meant well, of course, but Ancients, she could fret more than any hen.

"I suppose ten years was long enough, wasn't it?" Faedi said, rummaging through the cupboards for bread and tea.

Lonan leaned against the table, sighing. "Probably." He grabbed a skillet and eggs. "Winter's the only thing keeping the city safe."

The warmth in their home soon spread as they worked on their late breakfast. Faedi didn't feel like humming while she worked—not with the war still so fresh in her mind. She had only served in one, only defended the city once, but the memory of the raids lingered.

It made her scars burn as if the wounds were still fresh.

She glanced at Lonan as she spooned tea leaves into a metal ball. "What if there's a civil war this winter?"

Lonan braced himself against the table, his frown deepening. "It would be... unfortunately interesting." He sighed. "If the Mire were forced to intervene, no one would like the result. Our oath is to the land, not the people...but Blavier and his loyalists would likely be the target."

"It'll serve him right," Faedi muttered, glaring at the tea until Lonan tapped the tip of her nose.

He chuckled. "There it is."

"What?" She raised an eyebrow at him, rolling her eyes when he scrunched his nose. "Oh, hush."

They ate, standing at the table, sipping their tea. Outside, the world continued on—the distant calls of birds, the rustling of leaves, and the soft steps of creatures moving about the cottage. But inside, time seemed to slow, wrapped in a soft silence until they were forced to do the dishes.

They couldn't delay the work that needed doing.

Before setting out to search for the caravans, they needed to separate their supplies to send to the poor of Dewgate. Even if they couldn't find the missing supplies, the people would at least have something to help them through the winter.

Crate by crate, barrel by barrel, they took stock of what they had, setting aside anything they could spare. By the end, they'd chosen to donate more than just their excess—they added the goods they'd set aside to trade with the nomadic Dwarves, too. The pile for Dewgate grew fast, enough to fill at least one cart, maybe two.

The process took hours, and when Lonan opened the greenhouse's back door, a symphony of crickets answered. The night was dark, and the creatures outside had already fallen asleep, but brisk air slipped into the house.

"They won't need firewood, right?" Lonan called to her as he reappeared with an armful of chopped wood. "We need more ourselves if we want it to dry before the snow."

"I don't know," Faedi huffed, closing a chest. "Hopefully, these crates of furs will be enough."

Lonan disappeared for a moment before returning with more wood. "Next year, we should skin everyone's food before we feed them… just in case."

"Good idea," Faedi said, sitting on a crate and resting her elbows on her knees. "Think The Watch will do the same if we ask?"

He shrugged before sitting beside her. "I don't see why not. We can start saving after we see the lights and check on the forest folk."

Faedi nodded silently, watching the flames dance in the hearth. The fire would go out soon if they didn't feed it, but she didn't move. The house was warm enough, and it would remain that way through the night.

They might need more tea if they decided not to sleep.

Faedi started to ask Lonan if he was thirsty or if they should sleep and return to a semi-normal schedule, but then the logs in the fire fell with a loud pop as one of their diwha kits yowled.

Faedi immediately snapped to attention and stood. "Someone's outside."

It wasn't someone they knew. Penelope would have chirped if it had been a Guardian, Warden, or Umbral. The other creatures would have made their usual greetings, but only growls and snarls came from outside.

Please go away.

"Fuck me, I wanted to go to bed," Lonan grumbled as he grabbed his knives. "Think we can just let Penelope and Comet handle them?"

"It might be someone from the caravans," Faedi said, shaking her head as she walked toward the door. Her hand trembled as she reached for the handle. "Put your glamour back on."

Ancients, let them be a supplier.

She opened the door and peered outside. Her eyes quickly adjusted to the dark, and just as they did, a surprised shout erupted as their young black dragon charged across the clearing. Then, the reflection of moonlight flashed off a blade.

That's not a supplier.

Wind rushed past Faedi as she readied herself. *"I'll get behind him,"* Lonan told her through their bond. *"Grab his feet."*

She did as instructed, flexing her fingers as she whispered a spell, a quiet plea for the earth to heed her.

Please grow.

The ground rippled, vines twisting and tangling around the soldier's legs. At first, he tore free of them, but Faedi repeated the chant, and the vines grew, wrapping around him until they reached his waist and arms. Just then, Lonan appeared behind him, his knives crossed at the man's throat.

The soldier stood tall, a head and a half over Lonan, with a hardened jawline and dark eyes that didn't waver. His armor was well-maintained, though his boots were worn from traveling. A scar marred his right cheek, a long, thin line that spoke of past battles.

The dim moonlight caught the gleam of his blade before it was lowered, and for a brief moment, Faedi wondered what kind of man would walk into the heart of a dangerous forest with no proper protection.

"Drop your sword if you don't want to become their next meal," Lonan warned.

"I yield," the soldier replied, dropping his sword. "I come in peace."

"Says the man who pulled a weapon on innocent creatures protecting their home," Faedi scoffed before snarling. "State your business."

"I was told you were going to search the forest for the missing caravans," the soldier explained, speaking calmly despite his predicament. "Elder Ravyn sent me."

The mention of Ravyn gave Faedi pause—an unease she couldn't fully place. She had trusted Ravyn for years, but the fact that he sent someone without forewarning felt wrong. He never moved without sending word first.

He didn't mention this while we were with the farmers.

"Elder Ravyn would have warned you about the diwha," Faedi narrowed her eyes at the soldier. "He knows what creatures live here."

"He said it was a kit. I thought it'd be smaller," he replied, his eyes never leaving the dragon and diwha that circled him. "But he did tell me...he hopes you bring the Valerian and night claw salve again for a gelding he's training."

Lonan's eyes flicked to Faedi's at the mention of the salve. Ravyn was the only person she made that for, and they called it something else entirely. Maybe Ravyn gave the soldier the ingredients for a reason.

"So I suppose we don't let Comet and Penelope eat him?" Lonan asked through their bond, his knives still hovering at the soldier's throat.

"He wouldn't send someone out here in the middle of the night," Faedi replied reluctantly. *"But Ravyn would be upset if we killed one of his friends. If this man is a friend. For now, we can let him talk."*

"No funny business," Lonan warned as he vanished and reappeared beside Faedi. "The Sauvern isn't safe at night. Especially without a mount."

"I sent mine back when I reached the edge of the forest," the soldier explained, slowly sheathing his sword. "She was too anxious."

Faedi eyed him. Ravyn wouldn't let someone he cared about wander the forest without something to keep them safe. "He didn't offer you one of his?"

The soldier shook his head silently. Faedi didn't believe him. *"Maybe we should let them eat him."*

"I want to see what information we can get off him first," Lonan said, squeezing Faedi's hand gently. *"I won't let him near you."*

He was right. Even if Faedi didn't want to invite a stranger into their home, it wasn't possible to leave him outside either. He was too much of a risk to their flock, just as they were a risk to him. If he was a friend of Ravyn, she couldn't let something happen to him—at least not without a good reason.

"Fine." Faedi sighed and waved for the soldier to follow them. "We'll talk inside."

"Keep the eventides hidden, just in case. He's wearing a glamour—I don't know what he's trying to hide."

Lonan's warning sent a chill down her spine, and anxiety twisted in her gut as the soldier's boots met their wooden floors.

Ancients, don't let it happen again.

Faedi's mind raced, her fingers tightening on Lonan's hand. She always had a plan—an escape route, a weapon within arm's reach, a swift, silent way to end a threat before it ever had the chance to escalate.

Her hair stood on the back of her neck as she regarded the soldier, his every movement calculated and observed, her instincts pulling her into the cold, calculating part of her mind that she'd learned to trust in chaos.

If he turned violent, she'd have the perfect angle to strike—her dagger would slip into his ribs, between the gap of his armor, for a quiet kill. But if that didn't work, she could summon the earth again. There was always a plan; because in their world, if she wasn't prepared, it was only a matter of time before someone like him would make a move. And when they did, she would be one step ahead.

I won't let it happen again.

6

The High Knight

"One wrong move…I fucking dare you."

Lonan

He leaned against the wall while the soldier, armored in Dewgate's crest, sat in a chair beside the fire and sipped the ale Faedi had given him. His eyes never left the soldier for a single heartbeat. He watched him silently examine the interior of their home while Faedi busied herself with the mending.

She was distracting herself, keeping near her bow and quiver.

Each crack from the fireplace made her flinch, and Lonan caught her eyes darting to him every time. If the soldier noticed, he didn't comment, but Lonan counted each one. Her golden eyes were dark, despite the light in the room, and her lips were pursed as she bit the inside of her cheek. It was the same reaction she always had whenever a stranger was in their home.

We should have sent him off.

Lonan waited for the mood to shift, for the soldier to reach for his weapon or whisper a spell that might signal danger. When the soldier's gaze shifted to meet his, Lonan realized that Faedi and he weren't the only ones tense in the room. The soldier might have thought they would kill him without warning—and he wouldn't have been wrong.

After what they'd witnessed, after seeing the destruction caused by those who pretended to be lost wanderers in the forest, they couldn't trust outsiders.

"You mentioned the caravans," Lonan said, pushing away from the wall and nudging Faedi. *"Drink some tea."*

"Yes," the soldier replied, nodding. "Elder Ravyn suggested I talk to you when I said I'd look for them."

Lonan watched as Faedi slipped into the back room, the greenhouse where she kept her sun-brewed tea. His mind raced. "So, he wants us to babysit you?" He turned back to the soldier, eyebrow raised. "You don't look like a Guardian or Warden."

The soldier's lips twitched, but he didn't immediately respond. Instead, his eyes went to Faedi as she bustled about in the greenhouse.

"Lord Blavier has them hunting for food," the soldier explained, his attention still on Faedi. "No one else wants to search the Sauvern for them, so I came. Ravyn said the two of you might help me."

The fire crackled in the hearth, its warmth spreading throughout the room, but it didn't reach the corners where shadows lingered. Faedi moved swiftly, gathering the tea and offering a cup to Lonan with steady hands. Her motions were fluid, but there was a sharpness in the way she gripped the cup—tension in her fingers.

I can't give it to him. Her voice entered his mind, and the small space suddenly felt smaller.

Lonan didn't need to ask why. He knew. He remembered the story—how her mother had offered food and drink to weary travelers. By nightfall, the strangers had killed her—her children—and only Faedi made it out alive. Everything burned. It had been the beginning of the raids, twenty and two years ago.

She's right, she can't.

Outside, the wind howled through the trees, the branches creaking as if in protest of the stranger's intrusion. It was a harsh, cold wind—one that might as well have come from the peaks of the Rowdon mountains. It was out of place for that time of year, and Lonan couldn't shake the sense that the Sauvern itself was watching, *waiting.*

He moved swiftly toward the soldier, offering him the cup with a silent thought of whether Faedi might have laced it with poison. He watched the soldier take a sip, studying his expression for any sign of hesitation or suspicion. But there was nothing in his eyes to suggest doubt.

When no immediate signs of distress followed, Lonan let out a quiet breath, his shoulders relaxing just a fraction as he turned to return to his place beside Faedi.

He reached out, touching her side, urging her to stand behind him. He didn't like the soldier's attention on her, didn't like the anxiety that rippled off her in waves, and he certainly didn't like him in their home. Lonan didn't believe him— Ravyn wouldn't have only sent him with words.

The man—something disguised as a human—turned to meet Lonan's gaze. Lonan wondered what he hid under the magic. The soldier was taller than him, far taller than an average human, and Lonan knew he could have ripped through Faedi's vines. He could have fought, but he didn't.

I don't like him, Lonan told Faedi, looking back at her. *He's not telling the whole truth.*

"I know."

As the tension spiked again, Faedi's hand brushed against Lonan's arm as she offered him her tea.

"So, what do we call you?" Lonan asked before sipping the brew. "The only name you've given us is Ravyn's."

The soldier shifted his focus between Faedi and Lonan, squinting as if assessing their trustworthiness. His composure was unnerving.

Like he has any room to judge us—he's in our home.

"Sophir Daygan," the soldier replied, and Lonan's brow furrowed. Daygan. It wasn't a common human name, but he didn't press him.

"As in the High Knight?" Faedi pressed closer against Lonan's back. His heart pounded in his ears. *"Do you think it's really him?"*

"I don't know, but I find it suspicious he's come here only days after Ravyn tells us they're friends."

"Yes, that is my title," Sophir nodded. "Ravyn didn't tell me your names, just where I could find you."

"That's a lie," Faedi warned. *"Ravyn would have told him something."*

Lonan glanced back at her while he debated. He'd given the soldier two names, and he likely expected two in return. Human or not, city-folk were entitled bastards.

It's better to keep the peace for now.

"Lonan Tagilson," Lonan introduced himself and motioned to Faedi. "And this is Faedi Lirulin."

The names hung in the air longer than they should have. Too sharp. Too real. His gut clenched as soon as they left his mouth.

He shouldn't have said them. He should have used their nicknames: Tagi and Liru.

Faedi's name was sacred, one only to be shared among friends—but he handed it over like a token. And his? His name carried a history that too many would know for the wrong reasons. Umbral. Warden. Watcher. A threat. A Warning.

If the supposed High Knight knew what his name meant—if word reached the wrong ears—they wouldn't just be recognized. They'd be hunted.

And worst of it all, he'd just tied her name to his.

Lonan's thoughts raced, but his expression remained cold. The flicker in his eyes when Faedi's name was given suggested that he knew more about her than what he was letting on. The mere thought made Lonan's blood run cold.

Sophir's gaze flickered back to Faedi, and Lonan couldn't help but feel a surge of protectiveness for her. If the man was lying, if he was manipulating them, it could mean everything they worked to protect was at risk. It meant *she* was at risk.

"He knows something about you—or your family."

"Good to meet you." Sophir bowed his head in greeting, and Lonan stood taller.

I don't like him.

Faedi and Lonan traded a wary glance. Sophir's calm demeanor seemed to carry an undercurrent of something more profound. It made the air heavy, and Lonan's skin itched. He wanted him gone.

"Well met," Lonan said, attempting to keep his tone as neutral as possible. "Back to the point—you need babysitters?"

Sophir set down his cup of ale but did not look away from them. "I need guides. People who know the forest as well as you do."

Faedi's tension rippled through the pressure of her body against Lonan's. She was scared—so was he. The forest was their home, their sanctuary, and the thought of leading a stranger through it made him uneasy. They would suffer the consequences if he did something to anger the forest.

"We're not tour guides," Faedi interjected, her voice steady despite her anxiety. Just as when she calmed angry creatures. "We're outside of Dewgate's claimed land—we don't have to answer to Blavier's High Knight."

There was another flicker in Sophir's eyes. He sighed and looked back to the fire. "This isn't about politics—it's about survival. Without those supplies, many would suffer, and the forest itself could be threatened if desperate men take what they need by force."

"Is that a threat?" Lonan narrowed his eyes at him. *"What do you think?"*

"It's a reality. I don't want to see blood spilled any more than you do," Sophir's attention returned to them, and Lonan bit back a growl. "But if those caravans and the supplies aren't located, the situation will escalate."

"And if he is the High Knight, he'll lead the charge."

A heavy silence fell between them, each crackle from the fireplace amplifying the tension, while Lonan's mind raced. He didn't trust Sophir, but the risk was hard to dismiss. If they didn't help him, they ran the risk of the city's High Knight dying or the city starving.

The fragile peace between Dewgate and the Mire would shatter, and when that happened, no one would be safe. The land would become a battleground, and the consequences would be far more dire than a mere skirmish.

The tension was not just between them and Sophir; it was between civilization and the wilderness of the land itself. He knew Faedi could feel it too. She could sense the slow, inevitable decay that would follow if they refused to help him. And yet, the fear that gripped her heart made her hesitate—just like him.

What price are we going to pay for helping him?

Lonan turned to Faedi. *"Outside?"*

She looked between Sophir and him, then nodded. "We need to discuss this—alone."

"Of course," Sophir nodded in agreement. "Should I step outside to give you some privacy?"

Lonan scoffed and took Faedi's hand to lead her outside. The tiny creatures in the house followed. "And risk you trying to cut down one of our friends out there? I think not."

The night offered no relief once they were outside.

Lonan's hair on the back of his neck stood as they walked several paces from the front door. Faedi's hand trembled softly in his, though he knew it wasn't from the chill—it was the anxiety that gripped both of them.

Faedi's gaze briefly met his before she turned to face the front window. Her expression darkened at the drawn curtains. Even without their beasts inside, there were still secrets they preferred to keep hidden.

"They're going to blame the Umbrals," Faedi murmured, her eyes still fixed on the covered window. "They'll ransack the Sauvern, and when they don't find what they want here, they'll turn their attention to the Mire."

And we'll have to kill them.

"That's if we don't find the caravans," Lonan sighed, running a hand through his hair. "But… if we find them, prove the Umbrals had nothing to do with it, they won't have a reason to cause trouble."

"No one's ever needed a reason before," Faedi countered, her voice tight. "And if Blavier's got an Orderling adviser—what if Mr. High Knight is one too? What if—"

Lonan gently hooked his finger under her chin, turning her face toward him. The worry and tension were all too clear in her eyes, and it tugged at him. She might not be an Umbral, but she was bonded to him, a Watcher who took their vows just as seriously as anyone from the Mire.

Faedi had seen the horrors that greed for land and power could bring. She'd witnessed firsthand the destruction wrought by those who feared the dark.

"We could leave," he whispered. "Take our pack and go somewhere else."

She frowned up at him but didn't pull away. "You'd miss your family."

"They aren't you," he replied, his voice low but steady. "They would understand. They'd appoint a new Watcher for this parcel, and we'd still visit for the solstices." He leaned down, resting his forehead against hers. The light in her eyes flickered back to life, and he smiled. "We can help the forest-folk settle. They'll need a grove for lumber. We can still help people, just without the risk of Orderlings."

She searched his eyes, and he swore his heart cracked when she frowned again. "They'll summon you back if there's war."

"I'll tell them not to," he promised, smiling once more. He stroked her chin with his thumb. "We're bonded, you and I, and I won't have you in a place that puts you in danger or causes you pain."

I'm not going to let anyone hurt you.

Faedi gave him a weak smile. "You have it all figured out, don't you?"

"Just the important parts," he grinned. "We look for the caravans, say we tried, and if anyone comes around again—we leave."

"Okay," she sighed with a reluctant nod. "But we stay cautious. We guide him, but on our terms. Stick to the caravan trails, far away from the Mire paths."

"Agreed." He smiled, stepping back, though he didn't want to. "We'll start at dawn, and I'll keep an eye on him tonight."

Faedi lowered her head with a sigh. "I'll see what we can do about mounts. Comet and Penelope aren't trained, and I'm not carrying him."

"I'm not carrying him either," he scoffed.

She stepped back, lifted her head to meet his gaze, and hesitated—only for a moment. Her lips parted, as though she might say something, but instead, she shook her head and turned, disappearing into the evening fog.

Don't follow her.

Lonan shook his head, then turned to face the house. He whistled, summoning the inside creatures to return. He hated himself with each step he took toward the house. Faedi was more than capable of handling herself in the forest—she'd done it countless times before—but he didn't like the idea of her going out there with a stranger in their home, whether or not he was a rumored friend of Ravyn.

People lied. They always hid their true colors.

Once inside, he spotted Sophir beside the hearth. The place looked as it should—nothing appeared out of place. If the soldier had moved, he'd returned to the same position they'd left him in. His cup was empty, too.

"We'll help you," Lonan announced, his voice firm. "But know this: you follow our lead. You don't get to boss us around. Whatever authority you have in the city doesn't matter in the forest."

Sophir inclined his head. "Understood. Thank you."

As Lonan settled back inside, the atmosphere remained thick with tension. He prepared rations, keeping one eye on Sophir at all times.

The soldier seemed lost in thought beside the fire but didn't speak. Maybe there was nothing else to say since they'd agreed to his terms, or maybe Sophir could feel the tension in the air too. Either way, Lonan didn't care. The silence was preferable to playing host to some pampered city-folk.

Of course, Sophir broke the silence when Lonan approached him with furs to cover himself as the fire began to die. "Where is Miss Lirulin?"

Lonan dropped the furs on him without ceremony and turned to resume his work. "Getting mounts." He couldn't help but let out a scoff. Faedi wouldn't enter the house again—she'd sleep in the barn just to avoid the Knight, and Lonan was tempted to join her. "There's a lot of ground to cover, and you'll need a fast escape if you piss anything off."

Sophir chuckled. Was he laughing at him? "You don't think highly of city-folk, do you?"

"No, I don't." Lonan glanced back at him with a derisive smirk. "Now, go to sleep."

Sophir kept his eyes on Lonan for a moment, squinting as if he had something to say. But he didn't. Instead, he turned back to the fire and settled under the furs.

Lonan stayed alert, waiting for the slightest wrong move that would give him an excuse to kick Sophir out and sic Comet and Penelope on him.

Don't give me a reason, Knight.

The night passed uneventfully, but the rest Lonan managed to get was fitful— filled with dreams of howling wolves, shadows, whispers, and golden flames.

When dawn broke, he awoke with a stiff neck and a deep hunger gnawing at his stomach. One he hoped a regular breakfast would satisfy.

Before the voices inside the home reached him, Faedi's anxiety washed over him like spring rain. His eyes shot open as he searched the interior, spotting a flash of gray from the greenhouse—behind the massive armored soldier. Sophir stood in the doorway, and Faedi felt trapped.

"Morning," Lonan announced as he stood quickly, brushing past Sophir to enter the greenhouse. "Need me to start breakfast?"

"I broke into some salted pork to eat on the trail," Faedi replied softly, her voice barely above a whisper.

Lonan stood between her and Sophir, his head tilting slightly to catch her gaze. *"Is he bothering you?"* She wasn't injured, but her anxiety was palpable. She could run at any time. "What needs to be watered before we leave?"

"No," she said, shaking her head. *"He was asking about my plants and standing too close to the Nythbloom. I don't want him to knock it over."* Her cheeks flushed slightly. She didn't want to cause a conflict, but her concern for her plants was clear.

"Can you get some skins of tea?" She smiled up at him and motioned to the pitcher of sun tea. "It'll be bad by the time we get back."

Ancients, don't be adorable this early in the morning.

"Of course," he smiled, but his expression faltered when he glanced at Sophir. *"Why does he stare so much?"*

"Because you have a pretty face."

Lonan pressed his lips together to hide his smile, but his cheeks warmed, and he hoped his glamour covered it. *"City-folk think Umbrals don't have real faces— but he probably likes yours. Maybe Ravyn's friends have good taste like him."*

He watched her cheeks turn violet while she bundled herbs, and she winked when she glanced his way. *"Ravyn's our friend."*

She was right—he was their friend, but that didn't change how he looked at her. *"A friend that blushes when he looks at you."*

Faedi cut her eyes at him. *"He blushes when he looks at you, too."* Then her eyes narrowed as she grinned. *"And you blush when you look at me."*

Did she notice that?

Of course, she would tell him something like that when they had an unwanted guest—one they couldn't get rid of without repercussions. Lonan didn't want to continue the silent conversation; he wanted to speak with her, but he knew she wouldn't talk frankly with him around.

She smiled at him sweetly, and he realized that's why she told him in his head. She was teasing him. "Tea, please."

Dammit, Faedi.

After filling the skins with tea, Lonan washed the pitchers and handed them and a towel to Sophir. He could work if he planned to stand there, make her uncomfortable, and prevent Lonan from talking to her.

To his surprise, Sophir didn't argue; he accepted the task without a word. His attention focused on the glass, rather than Faedi and Lonan, as he carefully dried it. Lonan noted how his hands moved as if he was afraid to break the pitcher, but he chose not to comment. Instead, he attached the skins to their packs and carried them outside, where three large direwolves waited.

He chuckled as he greeted the wolves. "Oh, this is going to be good." He scratched them behind their ears, making sure everyone got attention. "You're going to keep her safe, aren't you?"

The wolves growled and barked in response. Sophir wouldn't try anything with them if he knew what was good for him. The wolves were loyal, fierce, and protective of their pack. Faedi and Lonan were one of their own, their Hunt. If their backs turned to the High Knight, the wolves would see whatever they could not.

As he finished securing the packs, Faedi emerged from the cottage with Sophir behind her. Lonan watched Sophir's eyebrows rise at seeing the direwolves but didn't tease him. Yet.

He turned his attention to Faedi, who petted a large, slender, white wolf. "Ready to go?"

She nodded, giving the wolf an extra scratch before she climbed onto its back. *"Did he do anything last night?"*

"No. We'll see what happens when there are only wolves around." Lonan mounted his wolf, one a bit bulkier than Faedi's but just as white. "Ever ridden a direwolf, Knight?"

"I haven't had the pleasure, no," Sophir replied as he carefully approached the third wolf.

It was darker, closer to black than gray, but the sturdiest of all three. Faedi made sure whoever carried him would have the muscle to do so. The large predator watched Sophir closely but did not move away from him. Its ears turned slightly, its attention on Faedi as she whispered to it in beast-tongue. For wolves, it was a series of growls.

"He says he's bored and ready to run," Faedi told Sophir before she spoke with the wolf again. *"He also says he does not smell human."*

Lonan glanced at her, raising an eyebrow. *"How does he smell?"*

"He's hiding his scent—too powerful of a glamour to tell."

Great.

Lonan nodded for her to take the lead. She was the better tracker outside the Mire, and he wanted to keep his eyes on Sophir. If it meant he had to take up the rear for a while, he would do it to keep her safe.

7

A Fragile Accord

Lonan

The morning air was crisp and cool; the scent of pine and rich dirt filled the air as songbirds sang in the trees and the wolves dashed through the underbrush. Gradually, the forest grew denser, and the canopy above thickened, nearly smothering the morning sun completely. Once they reached that point, the wolves slowed, allowing Faedi to pass out their breakfast of eggs, bread, and berries.

Thank the gods, the food settled the hunger in Lonan's gut, and he sighed in relief. *"Did you hunt last night without me?"*

"I needed it for the wolves. I saved some," Faedi replied, nodding toward the pack on Lonan's wolf—the one that had been there when he prepared the mounts. She smiled at him, and he mouthed a silent thanks, relaxing slightly.

If the hunger returned, Faedi made sure he was cared for. However, her mood was far from relaxed. The further they got from home, the more anxious she seemed, scanning the trees worriedly. Dusan hadn't come back since they returned.

"Are you alright, Miss Faedi?" Sophir's question pulled Lonan's attention to him, and he narrowed his eyes. Had he noticed her anxiety, too?

Faedi stared at him with wide eyes. "Yes?" Lonan sighed and shook his head. Of course, she wouldn't know how to answer. "Everything's fine."

Lonan placed himself between her and Sophir. "Her falcon is still off hunting—she's just looking for him."

"Ah," Sophir nodded slowly, falling into silence.

As they walked, Lonan noticed that Sophir's serious mood didn't seem to change, but the crease between his brows disappeared as he studied their surroundings. He looked either shocked, impressed, or maybe even awestruck, but

Lonan didn't ask. He didn't trust the city-dweller to be truthful with them.

Sophir brushed a low-hanging branch and winced as thorns snagged his sleeve. Faedi moved her wolf closer to his, without pause, and untangled the fabric with practiced ease.

"Careful. Blackthorn bites back," she murmured with a smile.

"I'll remember that," he said, watching her with a spark in his eyes.

Lonan's gaze dropped to Faedi's hand, still brushing Sophir's arm before she moved away. It wasn't only him and wildlife she could calm with a touch. He clenched his jaw and looked away.

"Your bond with the wolves is impressive. They seem well-adjusted to people," Sophir finally broke the silence.

"They're part of our family," Lonan said, glancing at him while keeping his expression guarded. "They're only adjusted to you because Faedi asked them to be nice."

"And promised them treats," Faedi added with a grin.

Sophir looked down at the wolves. "What types of treats do you give direwolves? Meat?"

"I told them they could eat your toes if you misbehaved," Faedi replied sweetly, her bright eyes sparkling.

"I will be on my best behavior, then," Sophir responded, wide-eyed.

Lonan stifled a laugh at Sophir's reaction and scratched his wolf between the ears. He didn't know if that was what Faedi promised the wolves, but he didn't doubt her. She would give the wolves whatever they wanted if it kept everyone safe. With all the possibilities, Sophir's toes were the last things he needed to worry about.

Eventually, Sophir chuckled and watched Faedi on her wolf. "It's rare to see bonds like this—even with trained beasts."

Lonan watched Faedi narrow her eyes at Sophir and winced. Her reaction could go one of two ways, and he wasn't sure which route she would take for a reply.

"They're not beasts," she corrected him gently—though her golden eyes burned.

"No," he agreed after a beat, his voice softer. "They're something else entirely. Like you."

Lonan's jaw tensed. He didn't like the way Sophir looked at her—not disrespectful but curious. The kind of curiosity that often turned dangerous.

Hours passed, and Faedi's quick shortcut through the forest eventually led them to one of the caravan paths. She was the first off her direwolf, stretching her arms over her head before kneeling to examine old wagon tracks. Lonan was behind her in the blink of an eye, mimicking her motions.

"The last storm ruined these," he mused, sniffing the air. "Maybe two months old."

"You read the land well," Sophir remarked, crouching beside a broken shrub.

Lonan blinked. He expected criticism, not recognition. "Comes with surviving," he muttered. Still, something in Sophir's tone—quiet, even reverent—made him hesitate. Perhaps the Knight wasn't entirely blind to the world around him.

"We could follow it south to see where it left the trail?" Faedi looked up at him. "Two months or not… heavy supplies would break smaller trees and shrubs."

Sophir loomed silently behind them as Lonan nodded in agreement. The path went southwest and then rounded north toward Dewgate. It made sense to follow what trail they had.

"When was the most recent caravan supposed to come through here?" Lonan asked, glancing back at the Knight.

"A fortnight ago."

"Shit," Lonan sat back on the ground and looked up the path. "Then we either go south for this one or north to look for the newest one."

"North," Faedi sighed as she stood. "Someone lucky might have survived that long out here."

"How much hope do we have to find someone alive?" Sophir asked.

Lonan turned his attention to Faedi as she walked around the tracks and mused to herself. "They have a chance if they don't upset the Sauvern."

"You put a lot of trust in the wild," Sophir commented, eyeing the towering trees. "Even the most trained soldiers avoid relying on Sylvan magic or forest spirits. Too fickle—to dangerous."

"So are people." She replied flatly before she shrugged. "At least the forest doesn't lie about what it is."

Lonan watched Sophir's face carefully, noting the way his mouth pressed into a tight line. Maybe he hadn't expected a response with fangs. "We would have gotten word from the Mire if they had found anyone." He said, standing and dusting off his pants. "But someone careful or fearful enough could avoid Watchers."

"Do they tell you everything? You seem to have survived well enough outside of society."

Lonan turned to face the Knight and pursed his lips, debating a proper response. He knew they would have been told if the Umbrals had found anyone. They would have been treated kindly and shown a way out of the Mire, maybe even escorted to the cottage, but he didn't want to tell Sophir that. He didn't need to know how things worked in the Mire.

He couldn't resist asking, "What makes you think we're outside of Mire society?"

Sophir looked at them and shook his head. "It was my understanding that Umbrals don't live outside of the Mire." He was too flat to read—no hint of amusement or anything else. "People say Umbrals don't like to be away from the safety of their home."

Faedi faced Lonan and shook her head subtly. *"Don't."* Then she turned to face Sophir. "We survive because we were raised here. We know what plants are safe, how to hide from predators, how to defend ourselves… are merchants and suppliers trained to do those things?"

"Not to my knowledge, no," Sophir shook his head, studying them. "You were raised here?"

"Not on this exact path," Lonan said pointedly, quirking a brow at Faedi. "Think you can find out anything?"

"I can ask," Faedi smiled at him before wandering to the edge of the trail.

She hesitated, glancing over her shoulder at Lonan. Her eyes lingered on him, and he took in the expression on her face. It was as if she was memorizing him—or seeking silent reassurance. He gave a subtle nod, but his fingers clenched slightly at his side.

She would be safe alone. She always was, but it didn't change how her absence unsettled him.

Lonan watched her go and sighed, crossing his arms over his chest as her footsteps faded into silence. He didn't know how long she would be gone, but he knew she would ask whoever she could before she gave up. She was too stubborn to try only once. It could take a while.

Sophir eventually broke the silence, which had become too heavy. "Who is she asking?"

"The trees and animals," Lonan glanced at him. "Krelin can talk to them—some Guardians can, too."

"I see," the Knight mused while he began to walk the trail, examining it. "I wonder if the previous search parties tried that."

Lonan didn't respond and chose to watch him instead. Whoever had looked for the caravans would have thought to ask the forest creatures if they were smart. However, there was a chance that whoever they asked didn't know or didn't want to give the information freely. Wild plants and animals didn't care about the needs of city-folk.

"Was Faedi raised in the Mire with you?" Sophir asked, and Lonan squinted at his back, debating his answer.

There was a rumor he knew about: that Umbrals would kidnap children who wandered too deep into the forest or played too closely to it. One of many stories people told their children to scare them for whatever reason. He worried Sophir just might believe that rumor—and the others.

"No, she's one of the forest-folk. I met her when we were children," Lonan replied, returning his attention to the trees, listening for Faedi.

"I thought the forest dwellers relocated after the raids some time ago," Sophir's deep voice carried through the cleared trail despite his soft tone.

"You thought wrong," Lonan replied flatly.

He stared at the forest, watching the branches of the trees move as if in a storm despite the gentle breeze. He might not have known how to speak to the earth like Faedi, but he knew when the forest spoke. Just as he knew, the trees were talking to each other, to the animals and insects around them, and, he hoped, to Faedi.

Then everything went still.

A sharp, warbling whistle cut through the trees—a signal from Faedi. The wolves bounded off without hesitation, and Sophir's eyes tracked them before shifting toward the source of the sound. It was barely a glance, but Lonan saw it—the pause, the softness that didn't belong on a soldier's face.

He scowled, turning his gaze to the dirt again. Sophir didn't need to look after her like that. She wasn't *his* to watch.

They waited silently for nearly an hour before his examination of the trail ended. Either he was bored or impatient, but Lonan didn't care. He savored the silence, trying not to groan when Sophir finally turned his attention to him.

"She speaks to the forest like it's alive," he said, not quite a question. "It's like…she listens for answers."

Lonan's jaw tightened. "That's because she does. I take it you've never seen Ravyn do it either."

Sophir didn't respond, but the way his gaze lingered on the space between the trees made Lonan's hands curl tighter at his sides. He didn't like that look. He didn't like that Sophir noticed at all.

Are you looking for caravans or do you have plans for my bonded?

He took a step closer to the trail, pretending to study the tracks. Really, he was trying to keep a distance between Sophir and the space Faedi had vanished into. The Knight had that look again—too curious, too calm. He couldn't trust it.

"Your wolves look similar to Ravyn's," Sophir spoke slowly, carefully. "Are they related?"

Lonan debated answering, not wanting to carry a conversation but also not wanting Sophir to chase after Faedi. She didn't like an audience when she spoke to things that didn't make noise back. "They're from the same litter."

Sophir hummed with a nod, and Lonan thought the questions might end there, but he continued. "How long have you known the Elder?"

Ytna, kill me now.

"He's a Guardian—Faedi's a Guardian, and I'm a Warden. It's been a while." Lonan stared at him blankly, but Sophir's expression didn't change. Of course, he'd want an exact number. "I don't know…we took our oaths at the twins when we were children…at least twenty-some-odd years. We became friends ten or so years ago."

"So, before or after the war?"

Lonan turned away from him and focused on the trees. The timeline of their friendship with Ravyn didn't seem necessary to the task at hand, and Lonan didn't want to share personal information—not when he knew who Sophir would return home to. Friend of Ravyn or not, he was a dog of Blavier—even if he supposedly took his oath to The Ancients.

Dusan landed on a branch nearby, fluttering his wings. "Why does it matter?"

"In all the years I've known Ravyn, he hasn't mentioned you—but then, all of a sudden, he tells me you two are the only ones I can trust for help." Sophir's voice remained flat, and Lonan hated it. "And he asked me to protect you, too."

Protect us from what?

Lonan looked over his shoulder at him. Sophir wasn't any closer than before, but something was on his face. Lonan just couldn't place the emotion. "Ravyn knows we like our privacy," he told him pointedly. Bitterly. "The city failed forest-folk before, and the city isn't quiet about their dislike of my people. Of course, he wouldn't mention us."

Lonan thought Sophir might argue, might say something to excuse the city's behaviors—but he didn't. Instead, Sophir leaned against a tree with a solemn nod. "I remember the raids," his voice was soft. "And I've never agreed with banning the people who've joined the fight to defend the city whenever there's a threat."

"He's a good man—he's been vocal about his distaste for how Blavier is running things."

Ravyn's words ran through Lonan's mind, and though he wasn't ready to trust the High Knight, he couldn't deny the faith put in him. Perhaps, if he didn't piss Lonan off, he could give him the benefit of the doubt.

"Did Lady Callon really attack one of Blavier's advisers?"

Sophir made a sound, a snort, and Lonan narrowed his eyes at him. Was that a laugh? "He claimed it was an attack," Sophir nodded with tight lips. "And it might have been…if you count spilling hot tea on someone as an attack."

Lonan couldn't resist turning to face him fully, but he crossed his arms over his chest to save face. "Hot tea?"

Sophir nodded slowly, and his dark eyes brightened slightly. "The man in question made some distasteful remarks as Lady Callon passed by." His lips twitched, and he paused, trying not to laugh. "Being the woman of faith she is, she was disturbed, and when she turned to question him—he was drenched with hot tea."

It sounded like the time Faedi 'accidentally' pushed him into the stream when he teased her about loose patches on his pants.

"And what were you doing when this happened?" Lonan asked before he could stop himself. He wondered if Sophir had the same look then—trying not to smile or laugh at the scene.

Sophir shrugged and looked around Lonan at the trees. Lonan knew he was looking for Faedi, and he didn't like it. "I made sure she didn't burn herself, of course," Sophir replied matter-of-factly. "Thankfully, she was unscathed."

"You don't have to trust me," Sophir said, low and quiet, his voice carrying like a hush between the trees. "But I've watched enough men bark orders from stone walls while the forest burned. I won't be one of them."

Lonan didn't answer. He didn't *want* to find anything admirable in the man. But the words stuck, like burrs under his skin.

A sudden rustle snapped through the underbrush. Sophir's posture tensed as he reached for the blade at his belt. Lonan didn't draw his knives, but he scented the air silently. They didn't speak, didn't move. They just waited.

A deep bolted out from behind a thicket and disappeared.

"False alarm," Sophir muttered.

Lonan scoffed. "You sure?"

Sophir flicked a glance at him. "No."

Lonan almost smiled. *Almost.*

I won't like you just because he told a semi-amusing story.

8

Whispers of The Order

Faedi

The forest welcomed her as she stepped off the path, its shadows stretching long in the light. She crept, her fingers brushing against the rough bark of a pine as she passed, listening for the hushed voices of the trees and the rustling murmurs of the underbrush.

She wasn't sure if it was the best idea to leave Lonan alone with Sophir, but she hoped they wouldn't come to blows. Lonan would survive; he could flee in the blink of an eye, but Sophir couldn't flee into shadows. He could only flee into the trees or down the path—and Faedi wasn't sure he could survive in the forest alone.

If he's stupid enough to run off on his own, he deserves what the Sauvern gives.

Faedi dismissed the thoughts with a shake of her head and focused on her self-given task and what she did know. She knew that she couldn't hear the forest well when she was with them. Silence was needed to hear the subtler voices of the forest, and once she was done, she could return.

She knelt beside a patch of moss, placing her palm flat against the damp earth, and whispered, "Has anyone passed through here?"

The roots beneath the soil stirred, slow and thoughtful. They spoke of travelers long gone, wheels carving deep furrows into the ground, but their words were scattered, broken. The earth was reluctant to share.

It's afraid.

Her pulse quickened. Whatever had happened there had left a scar.

Pushing forward, she followed the unease threading along her skin. The scent of oak filled the air before she saw them—a grove standing tall and unmoving, their canopies thick with the weight of years.

She stepped into their circle and pressed her hand against the nearest trunk, feeling the hum of awareness beneath the bark. "You know something," she murmured. "Please, tell me what happened to the caravans."

"Hunters gave a disease to their prey."

Faedi stepped back from the grove of oaks as the black moss of their roots slowly peeled away, revealing the corpse of a human. The harsh stench of decay made her recoil, and she covered her nose. Her eyes watered, and her stomach turned.

The body was fresh, as if it had only recently perished hours before—but it reeked of rot left in the sun.

She pulled her scarf over her nose and slowly approached the deceased man. He wore no armor, only simple clothes. His mouth and eyes were wide open, gaping in silent horror—a black tarry substance leaked from them, as well as from his nose and ears. Faedi didn't dare to touch it.

"When did this one die?" She asked before looking up at the trees.

"Before the last moon slept. His hunters strung him up from our branches and begged their god for healing. They put the poison into him and said he would be purged of darkness."

She kneeled and rolled the body onto its stomach, hoping it would be bare— just as she hoped it wasn't the god she feared.

"We do not know their name. They called for golden flames."

A chill shot down her spine, and her blood went cold. There was only one god whose worshipers prayed for gold fire: Ilos, the new god of light.

The hunters' fire had charred the man's back. Holy flames. The bloodlessness he might have suffered was minimal because of the magic used. The fire had burned his clothes and flesh, exposing his blackened innards—the same black as the putrid filth pouring from his mouth.

Not even maggots dared to touch the wound.

One of three things killed him: the pain of the injury, the poison, or an infection. Either way, he would have wished for death long before it happened.

Ancients keep him.

She offered a silent prayer before standing and turning her gaze back to the trees. "Eventides should protect your roots and cleanse the poison. He will return to the soil," she told them as she fished for seeds from her pouch. "May I sow them?"

"You may."

Faedi gave the trees a sad smile before scattering a handful of seeds over the body and surrounding area. Then, just as she had done when she trapped Sophir's legs, she whispered her plea to the seeds and earth with her outstretched hand.

Soon, dark vines, adorned with blue and white flowers, covered the body, replacing the scent of decay with musky sweetness. Small silver glittering clouds of pollen danced around the petals, and then the forest went still.

"Thank you, little wolf."

Before backing away, Faedi smiled at the tree again and bowed. "I'll come back to check on you soon." Then she turned and raced back to where she had left Lonan and Sophir behind.

Ancients, let Lonan be in one piece when I get back.

It was a short walk back to them, and thankfully, there was no blood or sounds of pain waiting for her.

When she crossed the tree line, she whistled and the direwolves howled in reply. Sophir perked, but he did not approach her. Instead, he watched Lonan's back as he jogged to meet her. However, Dusan swooped down first and landed on her shoulder.

"Your friends made it to the last parcel." He told her while she scratched under his chin. *"There are more fires in the east."* That was the last thing she wanted to hear.

"What did the forest have to say?" Lonan asked as he leaned down to examine her. *"What's wrong?"*

"Nothing too useful, but we should look north." She smiled at him, unsure if Sophir could see her, and subtly shook her head. *"Someone attacked the caravan. There was a body in the trees—the grove said he was poisoned. Religious fanatics did it, and Dusan says there are more fires in the east."*

Lonan frowned, a faint growl coming from his chest, and glanced down the trail. "That's not good." He needed to tell The Watch but didn't want to leave. "North takes us closer to the Mire. Fuck."

Faedi hugged her arms across her chest and smiled. If the assailants were who she thought they were, the Umbrals would be a target if a Watcher pair was found alone. They needed to be warned. "I'll be fine," she promised. "Find the nearest one and make camp further north. We're going that way, anyway."

He grumbled something she couldn't catch before pulling her toward him by the back of her head. "Sing if you need me," he whispered, pressing his forehead against hers. "Be careful."

"You too." Faedi frowned up at him before she kissed his left brow. "Stay safe."

Then he was gone.

"I did not see any Watchers in the eastern parcels." Dusan chirped in her ear before ruffing his feathers as she turned to face Sophir. *"Why is he here?"*

"Long story," she muttered before she breathed to steady herself while her heart pounded in her ears. The Order of Ilos was in the forest, in Dewgate, and their safe-haven was no longer safe. They wouldn't stop their crusade to remove all darkness from the realm.

The only way to stop them was to kill them.

I'm not a helpless child anymore.

She composed herself and turned to face Sophir, who watched her intently. His expression was unreadable, but curiosity and suspicion rolled off him like the ocean's tide. It was unsettling.

Ancients, don't let him be an Orderling.

"We're leaving," she told him and mounted her wolf. "Lonan will meet us north of here and have a camp ready."

Sophir nodded and climbed onto his wolf. "Is everything alright?" Then he regarded Dusan. "Is this the falcon you were worried about?"

She nodded but looked away. She didn't know if he could see the lie in her eyes.

"Lonan's warning Watchers not to kill you," she told him before yipping to signal her wolf to speed down the trail. As soon as her wolf began running, Dusan flew ahead with a screech.

"I'll look for fire. Watch his hands."

The wolves ran until Faedi was sure they were clear of where the Orderlings had been. However, it did little to lessen her anxiety. Lonan was nowhere near; she was alone with Sophir, and only the gods knew where the Orderlings might be hiding.

Only the Gods know if Sophir is an Orderling.

"How do trees sound when you talk to them?" Sophir's question pulled her back to the forest.

She glanced at him before grabbing a tea skin to offer him. "Like anyone else, but they don't know the names for most material things." She took a skin for herself once he accepted his. "They call clothes bark and leaves—or furs."

He urged his wolf to walk beside hers. "What did they tell you?"

Her eyes went to the hilt of his sword and his hands. "The winter will be long, and the snow will be deep."

"I suppose that would be helpful for survival but not for the caravans." He sighed and drank his tea. "Anything else?"

She shrugged. "Just forest politics and gossip."

"What?" He stared at her, dumbfounded. "Trees have politics?"

She smiled and shook her head before correcting him. "No, they have all the gossip and news about politics." She couldn't blame him for not knowing. He wasn't Krelin, and he was a city-folk. "They know about the various packs changing territories and ravens leaving sparrows alone because the recent storms damaged their nests…also, a new colony of mice burrowed in the willow spring. They're quite pleasant, or so the toads say."

Sophir didn't look away from her, but the intensity of his gaze softened gradually until a strange sound rumbled from his chest. Was that a chuckle?

She squinted at him, studying his face, unsure if she should feel offended. "Is something funny?"

"I just…" He cleared his throat, but she heard another chuckle before it died. "Well, at least you're a fun *babysitter*," he muttered.

Her smile held, but her thoughts stuttered behind it.

She didn't know him—nor really. Not beyond his guarded eyes and the weapons he wore like a second skin. He was dangerous. Deadly. Like a panther. He could kill them if he wanted to. And if he hated her, hated what she was…

Don't let him see your fear.

She couldn't let him think she was like the stories they told behind the wall.

"I think you're teasing me," she frowned. "And you might be grown, but in the Sauvern's eyes, you are a baby."

That time, he didn't chuckle—and his smile fell as serious tone returned. "May I ask you something?"

She raised an eyebrow at him. "You may…but I may not answer."

She hoped her response would dissuade him from asking anything too personal, but she knew well enough how knights and guards were. They needed to know everything about everyone, all comings and goings, all in the name of safety.

Do they have to learn interrogation tactics before or after their vows?

"Why did you not relocate after the raids? Many of the forest-folk moved to the city." His voice was soft, careful, as if he anticipated she might react poorly.

If Lonan had been with them, she might have.

"I did move. I went deeper into the forest, closer to the Mire." She glanced at him briefly. "Life near the wall isn't for me. I prefer pleasant mice."

His eyes hardened as he studied her. Maybe he didn't like her answer. "Is there a reason you feel that way?"

She matched his gaze, her back stiffening. "Because animals don't lie about why they attack and kill you. You know it isn't for sport or hate. It's because they're hungry or protecting their home." She wanted to look away, but she held his eyes. "But people lie and will smile while you die."

I'm sure you'll smile when I die, too. All city-folk do.

Sophir didn't counter her. He didn't even open his mouth to speak. Instead, his gaze softened slightly before turning to the path ahead. She was glad when he had no response. It wasn't a subject she wanted to linger on.

She had more significant matters on her mind—like the Orderlings who would burn the Sauvern to the ground in the name of their god.

Hours passed as they traversed the winding forest paths. The cool breeze whispered through the trees, carrying the scent of pine and earth, while the scent of rot lingered only in her memory. Her wolf moved with a grace that belied her size, but her ears remained focused on her. The wolf seemed to feel her anxiety more keenly than she did.

Dusan must have felt it, too. He circled back shortly after they crossed into another parcel. *"No fires yet,"* he reported.

Sophir's wolf kept pace with hers, its eyes ever watchful of her for any sign. The High Knight appeared contemplative, his gaze scanning the surroundings while his near-constant frown deepened. He hadn't spoken again since she had mentioned death, but she knew he had more questions. They were etched in the deep creases of his brow.

I wonder if he kills people when he gets bored.

The thought came to her suddenly, and she shuddered. She had heard stories of how people would go to the city's dungeons to torture others for no reason. Was boredom the cause or something worse?

She kept her eyes on the forest and Sophir as they silently traveled. She examined every rustle of leaves for its source, observed his every deep breath for signs of him reaching for his sword, and prayed to be reunited with Lonan with each passing minute.

He reached out briefly—not to touch, but to brush his fingers against a low-hanging branch. Faedi blinked. That was…familiar. That was how Guardians passed trees without disturbing the rest. She didn't comment, but her grip on her wolf lessened.

Sophir cleared his throat, and she tensed instinctively. Her hand landed on the dagger at her belt. "May I ask more questions?"

Ytna, help me survive this without worrying myself into an early grave.

She sighed and nodded. "You may."

His eyes lowered, and a chill went down her spine when she realized where his gaze was. "I didn't realize Guardians encouraged dagger reflexes during polite conversation."

"Only when talking to Knights," she replied dryly.

Sophir gave her a look that might have been mock offense. She wasn't sure. City-folk didn't wrinkle their brows the same way.

"Earlier, you mentioned something," he began slowly, still cautious with his words. "What are Watchers?"

"Are the schools lacking in Dewgate?" Dusan quipped, and she bit her lips to keep herself from smiling.

She glanced at him and frowned. "The Umbral Watch." His eyebrows raised, signaling he wanted more. "The Watch is responsible for keeping the Mire borders safe and relaying messages between the Mire and the Guardians and Wardens of the Sauvern."

Sophir leaned forward and she eyed the hilt of his sword. He hadn't reached for it, opting instead for his water skin. "I thought there were still miles between us and the Mire."

"There are, but they also watch the forest and caravan trails. It's…" She trailed off, rubbing her shoulder as she thought. "The heart tree of this forest is the twin of the one in the Mire. We keep both of them safe."

He quirked a brow as he sipped from the skin. "We?"

"Guardians and Wardens work with The Watch." She held up her hands and threaded her fingers together for emphasis. "Every Watcher works with either a Guardian or Warden—like Lonan and me—we're bonded."

How does the High Knight not know that?

Sophir fell silent, strapping his water skin back to his belt while glancing around. "Ravyn isn't bonded to an Umbral...I fear I might know less of Umbral and forest customs than Lord Blavier."

That's entirely possible.

"Guardians aren't required to bond with Umbrals when they take their oaths," she explained as gently as she could. "Bonds are a choice, an honor, but you don't have to."

"I've heard of Umbral bondings in the past," he continued softly. "Though it was explained to me as more of a marriage."

She shook her head. "Not always… it's a partnership, a friendship, that can sometimes turn to romance—but the bond isn't made for love." She instinctively rubbed the side of her head. "Umbrals are known to take more than one romantic partner in life anyway."

He turned his head to face her. "They are?"

"Is that uncommon in the city?" She mirrored his motions. "Guardians and Wardens never seem surprised. Some of us take multiple partners as well."

*I don't know if Ravyn has, though. He didn't mention anyone when we—*not that he had to say anything.

He shrugged and looked away. "Uncommon, but not unheard of."

"You have more questions?" She asked, already knowing the answer. The crease in his brow was deeper.

"Why do the Umbrals continue to assist Dewgate whenever it is in danger?"

Funny, that wasn't the first thing you asked.

She faced forward and shrugged. She'd asked herself the same question countless times but had assumed he would know, being Dewgate's High Knight. "Centuries-old treaty," she began. "The Umbrals swore to protect the land and keep it free. It doesn't matter who rules Dewgate; their oath is to the land."

His gaze fixed on her again, but she didn't look at him. "But why?"

She motioned around them with an exasperated sigh. "To protect the heart trees and their forests." Maybe they didn't teach history in knight school. "After The Great War, people wanted to destroy everything… during it, even. I don't know why, but they tried. The only thing that stopped them was The Ancients, The Watch, Guardians, and Wardens."

"Why don't the Umbrals control Dewgate, then?"

She scoffed and shook her head. "It isn't theirs—the Mire is their home." What did they teach in knight school—was there even a school? "Why leave their home when there's no reason to? The Mire provides them with everything they need."

Sophir didn't respond, and when she glanced at him again, his eyes stared ahead. His brow crease deepened, if possible, and his jaw tightened. She wondered if she had offended him for a moment, but she couldn't think of anything she had said that might have been rude.

There isn't a creature alive that's harder to understand than people.

"What is it?" She asked, fearing the crease might dent his skull or he might crack his teeth.

He dismissed her with a shake of his head. "It's nothing, just adding things together."

What is there to add?

She frowned at him but didn't press further. She wasn't sure how history and traditions could be added. The Mire protected Dewgate, Wardens, and Guardians who resided in Dewgate, who were sometimes bonded with Umbral Watchers, and life was happy, for the most part.

She gripped her wolf's fur tighter. Caravans full of supplies to get the city through the upcoming winter were missing from trails that bordered the Mire. Despite everything the Umbrals did for Dewgate, no one wanted them around unless it was wartime. Blavier was going to blame the Mire for the missing supplies.

He's asking questions because he wants to know who would be a threat if Blavier declared war on the Mire.

Sophir paused when a raven cawed from overhead. He looked up, and something flashed across his face—loss, maybe.

Faedi didn't ask. She didn't need to, and Lonan would've said it.

He mourns something, too.

She didn't trust him. Not yet, but the silence between them had shifted. Just slightly. Enough to make her wonder what else he wasn't saying.

9

Fires in the Mire

Lonan

Veth'iral, 2689

Black mist and shadows swirled around Lonan as he reached the riverbed. It was his outing as an apprentice—he was almost a Watcher of the Wood. Soon, he would return to the Mire, bond with a Guardian or Warden, and serve the forest together, gaining a friend for life.

But his excitement was short-lived. Sitting by the water, he remembered why his apprenticeship had been prolonged. He could have returned months, even years, earlier, but he refused to go back. He couldn't return until he was sure that she was gone.

Acre by acre, he had searched the forest for any sign of her. It had taken five years—four longer than any apprentice of the Wood was allowed to be away from the Mire. The grove on the other side of the river was his last stop. Once he searched there, he would have covered the entire forest.

"I could go backward," he muttered before a faint cry caught his attention.

He stood and searched the trees as the sound echoed through them. It was haunting, yet familiar.

Following the sound, he moved away from the river and into a dense patch of underbrush. A massive oak lay on the ground, and the break in the canopy from its absence shimmered with silver pollen in the air. There, sprawled amidst a bed of fallen leaves and moss, lay a young, gray-skinned woman—a sight that shook him to his core.

It was Faedi Lirulin, his friend from childhood, the one he had sworn to bond with when they were little. He had searched the forest for her for years, and there she was, right in front of him. And she was deathly pale.

"Faedi," his voice cracked as he knelt beside her. "What happened? How did

70

you…what's wrong?"

Her response came out as a jumble of fragmented sentences, her words slipping in and out of coherence. She rolled in response to his touch, and the sight of her arm made him wince. Her right arm, swollen and discolored, bore the telltale signs of infection and poison—angry red and black streaks snaking their way from a deep wound that reached her bones.

"Save him," she murmured, her gaze unfocused as she cradled a tiny creature in her uninjured arm. Whatever it had been was long gone, but she didn't seem to notice.

It might have been a bird. She's covered in feathers.

His heart sank as he took in her condition. The infection was severe and threatened to claim her life if untreated. Yet, despite her delirium and distress, her concern was for the creature rather than herself—just like when they were little.

"Come on, I'm taking you home," he told her, lifting her into his arms and cradling her against him. Her skin burned like fire.

"No," she tried to wiggle away but collapsed against him. "He's there… hurts."

"We're going to the Mire," he explained as he ran. "Mam will help."

"Am I…dying?" She asked, her glassy eyes meeting his as his tears fell onto her face.

He shook his head quickly. "No. I won't let you."

A soft sob shook her, and he held her tighter despite his fear that he might hurt her. Her ramblings continued, and his heart broke with each one. The fever made her delirious, but some things made sense when he pieced them together.

Like the pitiful cries for her family and her mentor.

Does she even know they're dead?

He moved swiftly through the dense undergrowth of the forest, his steps silent over the needles and leaves. Among the scents of pine and damp earth, a faint hint of woodsmoke wafted by as he crossed a creek. Then came the distant bugle of an elk, and he couldn't help but smile as he ventured deeper before darkness wrapped around him.

The next place he stepped into was the deep shadows cast by a campfire. Meat roasted over the flames, and an Umbral and a Minotaur sat beside it.

"Rena, I thought you were north," he said as he approached and waved.

"Long story. There were parcel trades," the Umbral replied, standing and dusting off her pants. "Where's Liru?"

"It's another long story," he said before facing the Minotaur and bowing his head. "Good to see you, Enoch."

"And you," Enoch replied, bowing his large bovine head in return.

"Come sit," Rena motioned to the fire. "We have meat that isn't cooked yet."

"Thank you."

He moved closer to the fire and sat down, Rena settling between Enoch and him. The shadows lengthened behind him as he sat. They curled at his heels, twitching like restless dogs sensing danger.

It wasn't hard to sense the tension in the air. Their smiles didn't reach their eyes despite the warm greetings. Something had happened, and it wasn't good news.

"I think Ilos' zealots are in the forest," he told them, stretching his hands out to the fire. "Liru found a corpse, and the trees told her fanatics did it."

"They are his," Rena replied with a sigh. "They are why acres were traded. Younger Watchers were moved closer to the Mire… there was an attack from the east. They followed the Nomads in."

"What?" He turned to face her, his heart racing. "When?"

"There have been several over the past few months. We thought they were isolated… they all were coming from the north-east. Some wore Detrich armor, but…the King and Queen think something bigger is coming." She sighed, and Enoch offered him raw meat wrapped in a large leaf with a huff. "They knew where we would be on our rounds."

"Did they kill anyone?" He asked before biting into the chunk of meat. Deer.

"Two apprentices—their bonded are not fairing well either. One came down with a fever," she told him. "At least a dozen more were injured."

"Myst was injured in the attack. They've been pulled back to the Mire," Enoch said, and he froze.

The flavor of the meat in his mouth soured, and his stomach turned. Myst Tagild, his older sibling, had never taken an injury worse than a sprain and had never left their rounds. Even when they were still a Mireling, they pushed their limits and boundaries.

If they had returned to the Mire, their injuries had to be severe.

"What happened to them?" He asked, wiping his mouth with the back of his hand.

"The cultists caught them…tortured Myst," Enoch rumbled, lowering his head. "Their cub saved them."

"How did Espen kill them?" He shook his head in disbelief. The small bear cub was magical, but he doubted they were strong enough to fight fire-wielding cultists.

"We don't know; they grew and ripped the cultists apart. They wanted Myst, though," Rena added, leaning forward to brace her elbows on her knees. "They fought until they could flee. They…they were blinded by their fire when they tried to find Vishal."

His fingers curled into his palms.

Fire. Of all things.

Myst had always been invincible in his mind—sharp-tongued, clever, tireless. Even as a Mireling, they'd walked rounds others twice their age couldn't manage. He couldn't remember a single moment they'd shown weakness. The idea of them—tortured, blinded—made bile rise in his throat.

His body stiffened. They had been bonded for years; Myst must be a mess. "Where is Vishal? You said only two apprentices died but not bonded."

Enoch huffed. "Missing."

"We're hoping he escaped," Rena told him, but there was no hope in her eyes. "Myst has been in the temple since your mother healed them to the best of her abilities."

He watched the flames dance. "The blindness can't be cured, can it?"

"No," she sighed. "Much like Liru, but eventides can't fix eyes."

He dragged his hand over his chin and mouth, watching the fire. Myst was strong and could adapt to anything, but he didn't know if losing their bonded and their sight was something they could overcome, especially without The Watch as a distraction.

"When did this happen?" He turned to face Enoch and Rena.

"A few days ago." Her eyes didn't meet his, and his blood ran cold. Faedi had smelled fire before they went to help the farmers.

"Was Myst near the cottage? Liru smelled fire, but we thought it might be one of the caravans." He looked between them, frowning when they nodded. "Why were they this far south?"

"They didn't tell us," Rena said, shaking her head.

"What's your long story?" Enoch asked, offering him a skin.

"Dewgate's High Knight came to us and asked for help finding the caravans. Ravyn sent him." He told them before sipping from the skin. It was ale.

"At our last meeting, the Elders said Lord Blavier did not want to hunt for the supplies. Did he change his mind?" Enoch sat up straighter. "Or has this Knight said anything?"

"He's wearing a glamour and asks a lot of questions," he shook his head.

"Then he may not be the High Knight." Rena leaned against Enoch with a sigh. "But Ravyn wouldn't send just anyone to you."

"He could be lying about Ravyn sending him," the Minotaur said.

Faedi hadn't howled. That should have calmed him. But the woods were quiet, and the firelight left him feeling too exposed. Sophir had magic, questions, and a too-perfect smile. And Faedi was alone with him.

He couldn't let something happen to her. Not after the raids. Not after Myst. *She's been through enough.*

The fire crackled louder as he stood, the forest pressing in again—dense, dark, and listening.

"Can I take the uncooked meat? I don't want to waste time hunting," he asked them, bowing his head when Enoch offered him a bundle.

Before he could turn to leave, Rena stepped forward and pressed a small, glassy crystal into his palm. It pulsed faintly with embedded light.

"If it turns for the worst," she said softly, "use this. Your mother has us carrying them now—just in case."

Lonan curled his fingers around the crystal, nodding once in thanks. "Tell The Watch we have him under control for now. I want to see who he really is before violence breaks out. The last thing we need is for Blavier to have a reason to attack the Mire."

"Ancients keep you." Rena bowed her head before he disappeared into the shadows.

As twilight descended, he stopped at a clearing along the trail Faedi would take with Sophir. Dense fog blanketed the area, created by the steam rising from a nearby hot spring, and glowed eerily from the glow bugs flitting about. It felt wrong to make a fire and disturb the area, but he knew Sophir would need cooked food.

The flames that roared before him brought thoughts of Myst—and Faedi.

Lonan hadn't seen what they did to Myst. But he knew what the flames were capable of. Even after ten and seven years, the sight of Faedi in the forest riddled with infection was painfully fresh in his mind—the sight of her home, five years before that, and the scent of her family's burning flesh.

He stabbed pieces of meat with sticks and positioned them around the fire to cook. Once they were secure, he began kicking away dry grass and leaves from the flames while waiting for Faedi and Sophir. Should he howl for her? He quickly decided against it; the Knight might not react well.

What if he blindsided her, and she couldn't call him?

Pacing around the fire, he twirled his knives in his hands. Faedi was capable—more alert than he ever was—and fast. If Sophir tried to overpower her, she would run if she had to. The wolves would defend her, and Dusan would find him.

But what if he has magic beyond the glamour?

He shook his head and walked toward the trail. There were magics he could use to render her unconscious if he was talented enough in the arcane arts. Still, he seemed to prefer his sword. Either it was an act, or there was a good chance he didn't have magic.

Myst had been hunted, taken, hurt. Why not Faedi next?

He stared down the trail. There was no torchlight. Faedi wouldn't have used one anyway, but Sophir might have.

What if he's not a cultist and wants Faedi for other things?

He snarled at his thoughts and paced back to the fire. Sophir had done nothing but stare at her, watching her every move and asking questions since they met. Even if he wasn't a zealot, he could still take other nefarious actions that would hurt her.

However, if she was interested in his advances, then there wasn't much to do about it. He couldn't tell her not to; she was her own person, and his human glamour wasn't the worst thing to look at. Though, many used their good looks and charm to hide ill intent.

She'd cut off his cock if he tried anything.

He sat beside the fire with a huff, staring toward the trail. They didn't know anything about Sophir. They hadn't asked, and he wasn't sure he cared to. Anything he said might be a lie. If they fell for any tricks and the forest suffered because of them, he wouldn't be able to live with himself—not when a drop in his defenses might endanger Faedi.

He couldn't stand the idea of her being hurt again. But, if they befriended him and he liked them, maybe he wouldn't betray them.

"Ytna's tits," he groaned while dragging his hand down his face. "We can't trust him…but maybe we can get him to trust us. Knights are supposed to be honorable—if he likes us enough, maybe he'll second-guess killing us…unless Blavier commands it."

Knights and guards are just armored dogs.

10

Secrets in the Willow

"He's probably a worried mess. I hope the other parcels are alright…maybe it was just one small group of Orderlings."

Faedi

Night had long since fallen when Faedi spotted a campfire in the distance. Sophir quickly looked to her for guidance, his hand resting on the hilt of his sword, and she shuddered. She shook her head in response. The trees would have warned them of danger ahead, but they remained calm.

"It's Lonan," She promised him, urging her wolf to sprint forward. "He's at the spring."

"The one with your mice friends?" he asked as his wolf chased after hers.

"Yes," she replied, glancing back at him as a hand-cupped howl pierced the air.

It was Lonan, alright.

The direwolves howled in reply, and she smiled despite the leaves whipping against her face as they left the trail to follow the fire. As soon as she cleared the last tree, she leaped off her wolf, beaming as she spotted the Umbral running to meet her.

"Any trouble?" he asked, offering her a giant leaf filled with barely cooked meat. *"Did he say or do anything to you?"*

"Nothing, and the trees were quiet," she replied before quickly eating one of the chunks. *"He was civil. I taught him about tree gossip."*

"There's food for you beside the fire," Lonan said when he emerged through the trees. "The Watchers shouldn't be a problem so long as we don't get too far into Umbral territory."

"What if the caravan trails lead there?" Sophir asked as he approached the fire.

"Then it's an Umbral matter outside your control," Lonan replied sharply. Faedi gently squeezed his hand to calm him and kissed his left brow when he lowered his head. It seemed to help. "We will inform the Watchers if that's the case. They will take over the search."

"They will give you your supplies if they find anything," Faedi added, glancing over her shoulder at Sophir.

He didn't look convinced but didn't press the matter further. Instead, he sat down beside the fire and began to eat in silence. He seemed lost in thought, and for a moment, Faedi wondered what was on his mind, but she didn't ask.

"What else did the Watchers say?" She turned her attention back to Lonan. *"Did you tell them about The Order?"*

"Just talked about solstice preparations." He took her hands into his, squeezing them with a sad smile. *"They said a few got into the Mire but were killed before they could cause too many problems. They also apologized, thinking the incidents were isolated to the Mire and not wanting to worry us."*

"And?" She pressed, sensing he was hiding something. He wouldn't look her in the eye.

"They blinded Myst."

Her breath hitched. She felt it before she heard herself cry out.

"They what?" Her voice cracked louder than the trees could contain. Rage swelled in her throat like sap in spring heat.

Her knees nearly buckled, and Lonan's hands wrapped around her waist as if he knew she might go down. The firelight flickered behind her eyes like memories—Myst laughing, running through the trees and shadows, flashing their sharp grin.

"Is everything alright?" Sophir asked from beside the fire, and Faedi whipped around to face him.

"Yes." She snapped with a snarl before she blinked. "Lonan and I are taking a bath. We'll show you the spring when we're done," she announced as she grabbed Lonan's hand to lead him into the tress.

"I will watch him," Dusan chirped and flew to land on the tree nearest to Sophir.

However, Sophir's eyes hung onto their backs as they departed, but she didn't look back. He didn't call after them either or protest. Though, she doubted she gave him time to as she ran off into the willow trees to find the hidden hot spring. As she led Lonan, she hoped Sophir wouldn't follow them. Umbral matters were none of his concern, and she didn't want a strange man she didn't know to see her naked.

She might have been wild forest-folk, but she still had some modesty when it came to the depravity of city-folk.

Lonan remained silent until they were safely hidden among the trees, diligently following behind her. When the ground became muddy, she stopped and turned to face him. His violet eye glowed in the absence of light as he frowned down at her.

"What happened?" She asked, placing her hand gently on his chest.

"They did the same thing to their face that they did to your arm," he said, trailing his fingers over her right arm for emphasis. "My parents pulled them from The Watch and have them at home while they recover."

"I'm sure they're happy about that," she sighed. "Is Espen tormenting the house staff?"

"Myst is likely causing more problems than the cub," he chuckled before stepping back to remove his gear. "We should bathe so he's not suspicious."

"What if he followed us?" She whispered suddenly, glancing back toward the trees.

"He didn't," Lonan promised.

"He's a Knight. They're trained for silence. He could've hurt Dusan."

"We're trained too, and your sassy chicken is fine." His tone was light—but he looked over his shoulder too.

"Alright," she sighed, mimicking his motions with her weapons with shaky hands. "Did they know anything about our new High Knight friend?"

He looked up at her and shook his head as he kneeled after kicking off his boots. "They are worried he might be lying about his identity."

"He might be…he asked many questions he should already have answers to," she told him, leaning against a tree as he untied her boots. "He asked me why I didn't relocate after the raids."

Lonan stared up at her, pulling off her boots. Her heart pounded in response. "Did you tell him?"

Ancients, don't look at me like that.

"No. I said I preferred the company of animals." She grinned while she removed her belt and tugged off her shirt. However, unlike the other times they'd been naked around each other, her cheeks burned once her chest was bare.

For a moment, she swore she caught his eye shining brighter as his gaze lingered on her.

The Ancients are punishing me for teasing him about blushing—I know it.

"That you do," he said, dropping his pants after removing his shirt. She looked away so she wouldn't stare. Though, she wanted to. "Well, and Umbrals too, of course."

One Umbral specifically—don't go there, Faedi.

She shook her head and kicked off her pants before she followed him into the water. Almost instantly, every ache and pain in her body began to lessen as she sank into the spring's warm embrace.

Steam curled around their skin in lazy spirals, softening the edges of the world. The scent of moss and mint clung to it, heady and grounding. Somewhere above, an owl called softly into the night. A glowbug flitted across the surface of the spring, its wings humming softly before it vanished in the mist—then silence, as if the forest held its breath with them.

She leaned back to wet her hair and closed her eyes while Lonan settled beside her. It wasn't the first time she had bathed with him, and she doubted it would be the last. But it was the first time they had used a bath as a cover for discreet conversation. Then again, no one from Dewgate had ever asked them to lead them through the forest.

There was a first time for everything.

"How is your arm?" Lonan's voice broke into her thoughts, and she looked at him through heavy eyes.

"Not too bad," she shrugged, running her hand over the vines of eventides that covered her right arm. "How do we handle the night watch?"

Good job, stay on topic.

"Do you think he will try anything?" He moved closer, grabbing a fuzzy leaf from the edge of the spring. "I thought Knights were against backstabbing."

"Supposedly, they are, but—" she sighed when he began to wash her hair with the leaf, a minty scent filling the air.

Maybe sidetracking isn't bad. This feels too good.

"People lie," Lonan finished for her. "We'll sleep with the pack when it's his turn for a watch. He might be suspicious if we don't ask him to take one."

She glanced back at him with a frown. "What if he runs off trying to attack something? You saw how he was with Penelope and Comet."

"Then we try to make sure he doesn't die; if he does, it's his fault. We'll still look for the caravans and tell Ravyn when we deliver them." He shrugged, washing his hair once he finished with hers.

Is that a good plan?

"What about The Order?" She asked before dunking herself into the water to rinse her hair out. "I know we agreed to go to Emsmeda, but…they hurt Myst. We can't leave."

Lonan didn't respond. He didn't need to. The harsh expression in his eyes as they darkened told her everything she needed to know. He agreed with her. He knew just as well as she did that if the cultists were back in the forest, it wasn't just for a small group to kill merchants or attack a few Umbrals.

It would be like the raids that had displaced the forest-folk—or worse.

"We might have to choose, Liru. His mission or ours. We can't walk both paths forever."

She met his eyes and frowned. He was right and her heart sank with him as he went into the water to rinse himself.

"I know."

Once their bath was done, they dressed and made their way back to the camp. Faedi noticed Sophir still seated by the fire, though he hadn't fallen asleep as she had hoped. Instead, his attention was fixed on the flames. When he heard their approach, his dark eyes turned toward them.

"The spring is back that way," Faedi motioned behind her as she walked over to the wolves.

"Break the big fuzzy leaves for soap," Lonan added, collapsing beside her between the wolves.

"Alright," Sophir nodded and stood from the fire.

Faedi watched as he glanced between the flames and the direction of the spring before he turned and walked away. His decision not to take a torch surprised her, but she offered no suggestion. The path was short and safe; nothing would bother him while he bathed.

Faedi sat beside Lonan, leaning against her wolf with a sigh. Despite the job they had agreed to, she only wanted to go to the Mire. Myst was in capable hands and would be cared for, but Faedi craved seeing them with her own eyes. Myst would have done—had done—the same for her.

She clenched her fists in the wolf's fur, grounding herself. Myst had always been her friend, one of the few who could soothe the storms in her mind. It wasn't enough to hear they were alive. Faedi needed to see them—to know for certain they were alright. Or as much as they could be.

"Did he do anything?" Faedi turned her attention to Dusan, who preened himself in the branches.

"He ate, stared at me, then stared at the fire. He's boring."

Faedi rolled her eyes before stretching and petting the wolves idly. "Is Vishal alright?" She asked, realizing he hadn't been mentioned. "You didn't say what happened to him." She couldn't help but worry. *Ancients, don't let him be dead.*

"He's missing." Lonan propped his head in his hands as he lay back on the ground. "Rena and Enoch said they were attacked, and Myst was hurt trying to find him. They only got away because Espen killed the cultists."

"Espen?" Faedi looked down at him in confusion. "The little cub? How did he kill cultists?"

"I don't know," Lonan shrugged. "Do we still have tea? Enoch's ale tastes good, but it sits like sandpaper."

"We should." Faedi nodded and turned to the packs before she froze. "Do you think he'd drink the water?"

"What?"

Faedi handed Lonan a waterskin and looked back to the trees. "Sophir...do you think he'd try to drink the spring water?"

"Only an idiot would dri—Faedi, let him be stupid," Lonan called after her as she stood and ran back to the hot spring.

There was a chance Sophir was smart enough not to drink the water, but Faedi didn't trust it. He had survived long enough to reach their cottage on his own. She gave him that, but city-folk were notorious for their ignorance. They didn't know how to survive outside their precious city walls. Faedi couldn't trust that his intelligence differed from other city dwellers.

She found his armor, clothes, and sword set far enough from the spring to prevent damage and bit her lip. Then, a splash came from the spring, and she turned to face him. Sophir was waist-deep, cupping his hands full of steaming water and raising it toward his face.

Ytna's tits.

"Don't do that!" Faedi shouted a warning as she ran over to the spring and jumped in to pull his hands away from his face.

Sophir stepped back from her, raising his hands cautiously. "Do what?"

"Don't drink the water," Faedi huffed, swiping her hair away from her face. "You'll get sick."

He slowly looked between her and the water, then at his hands, before smiling. Then he chuckled, which turned into a full laugh. It continued until he leaned back against the edge of the spring to catch his breath.

Faedi crossed her arms over her chest with a huff. "I don't see what's so funny. You could have poisoned yourself."

"I was washing," he explained, splashing the water on his face. "See?"

Faedi stared at him while water dripped from his bearded chin. He smiled at her, his dark eyes brighter from the glow bugs flying around, and she sighed. Heat flooded her cheeks, and she shook her head when she realized she had worried for nothing.

So he's not as stupid as other city-folk.

"I see," she mumbled, backing away. "I'll leave you to it, then."

As she turned, he moved toward her and caught her wrist. Faedi glanced over her shoulder at him, her free hand resting on the dagger at her belt, and raised her eyebrows. He opened his mouth to speak but closed it again, his expression shifting to one of concern as the crease between his brows returned.

"What is it?" Faedi asked when he let her go and fidgeted with a silver chain around his neck.

It was tight against his throat, not enough to cut off air or blood, but as if a weight pulled at the back of it. Maybe it was another Dewgate crest he had flung behind him to wash. It made sense for someone of his status to have his crest in multiple locations, if not branded on him somewhere.

She lowered her eyes down his chest and abdomen at the thought, but quickly looked back to his face when she saw he hadn't worn anything for his bath. The heat in her cheeks spread to her ears, and she took another step back. The last thing she needed was for him to get the wrong idea.

"Is everything alright?" He asked softly.

"You're naked," she replied quickly, shaking her head. "Yes, everything is fine."

Sophir tilted his head with a quizzical expression on his face. "Do people in the forest wear their clothes when they bathe?"

"No, but..." Faedi sighed, making sure to look no lower than his shoulders. "We don't talk to city-folk while they're washing unless blood is involved—or they're about to drown."

He laughed, unbothered. "City-folk rules are a little different."

"Clearly."

"You and Lonan seemed worried earlier, more than normal." He stepped back from her, taking one of the fuzzy leaves to lather his arms. "Did the Watchers he met with have bad news?"

He must have been accustomed to bathing with a crowd. He didn't appear phased at all by her presence. However, Faedi wasn't sure if his behavior made her feel better or worse—not when she watched the suds cascade down his chest and slowly mix with the spring water.

His muscles have muscles.

"It's nothing to worry about," Faedi shook her head again. "Mire pre-winter business. He was also concerned you might wander off at night and get yourself killed."

"I may be determined to find the caravans, but I'm not stupid." He chuckled as he scrubbed his hair. "The two of you really don't think highly of the city, do you?"

"I think anyone who spends their life safe behind a giant wall shouldn't be trusted alone in the forest to survive." Faedi shrugged and crossed her arms again. "The city may have some problems, but...you don't have to worry about wild creatures and ancient magic that can kill you."

"Yet you live here," he countered, dipping under the water.

Faedi took the opportunity of him rinsing himself to get out of the spring, standing on the edge while she stared down at him. When he broke the water's surface, she tilted her head and watched him look for her before he found her above him. She smiled at him before motioning around them with her arms.

"The forest and Mire took care of me after the raids. Dewgate didn't," she frowned and looked away. "Unlike city-folk, I know how to survive here. I work with the land instead of against it."

"The farmers said that," he replied softly. "Before they left."

"As any Krelin would," Faedi shrugged dismissively. "Perhaps Blavier shouldn't have stolen from the people who fed him."

"You don't sound too surprised that they're gone." His gaze burned into her, and she flexed her fingers. "You sound relieved."

"They stayed longer than I would have. They waited until after the harvest, and most of their supplies were raided by city guards." Faedi narrowed her eyes at him. "Did you know everything they left wasn't enough to last half the winter? That the guards were going to take more? Blavier didn't give them a choice."

Sophir didn't reply—he only stared at her with wide eyes.

Don't look at me like that.

"Rinse your eyes with fresh water from your skin when you're done. The water can irritate them," Faedi told him before turning and returning to camp.

She couldn't tell if he was shocked by the news or because she knew more than he thought she did. All she knew was that she didn't care. Either he knew and played a part in the potential starvation of innocent people, or he was ignorant. Both possibilities were unfit for a Knight.

11

The Poisoned Path

"Maybe we should take him west…if we get close enough to Lefral, he might get scared and run home. Then we can deal with The Order without him around."

Character Name

The night at camp passed without incident after everyone ate and bathed, but sleep didn't come easily to Lonan. He remained on high alert, listening to every sound in the forest, while Faedi slept between the wolves, away from the fire, and Sophir remained near the flames. The High Knight didn't attempt to speak to him after Faedi drifted off. Instead, he took his watch in silence. Lonan had expected him to be more on edge, being away from the comfort of the cottage, but Sophir didn't react to anything. He only looked at the wolves with each noise, and Lonan had to admit, it was clever of him.

Morning came too quickly. The rustling of Sophir's pack jolted Lonan from his half-slumber. He glanced down at Faedi, her arm draped across his chest. Carefully, he maneuvered away from her, stretching his arms as he peered at the Knight. Despite being a city dweller, Sophir seemed at peace in the forest.

"We're going to continue following the path north," he announced softly, trying not to disturb Faedi. "There's a swamp in that direction where someone could easily lose wagons."

Sophir looked up from the fire, where he was roasting meat. "I've been wondering. Why would caravans leave the trail?"

Lonan shrugged, crouching beside the fire. "I guess they might have been scared by something in the forest." His attention shifted to Faedi's pack. She would need her herbs when she woke up. "The trails are monitored, but animals have their own minds."

"Perhaps," Sophir frowned. "I could see that for one or two caravans, but all of them? We haven't received supplies by road in months."

Lonan retrieved the herbs and winced when the wolves began to stir. "What about other people? Has there been an increase in priests and the like?"

"There are some who occasionally come, mostly by sea," Sophir leaned forward, resting his elbows on his knees. "Why do you ask?"

"There are some followers of certain paths that…well, they aren't exactly fond of certain races," Lonan shrugged. "Ones Blavier is making laws about…if resources are too low, they might be the first to be kicked out."

"You're referring to The Order," Sophir stated, his tone pointed. "Do you have a theory?"

Lonan watched Sophir through the flames, contemplating whether to reveal what worried both him and Faedi. He hadn't mentioned how he felt about The Order of Light; for all he knew, it might even have been Sophir's religion. It wouldn't have surprised him, given the Knight's suspicious nature and his question to Faedi about the raids.

"What if some of the more fanatical worshipers of Ilos are doing something to the caravans? Dewgate and the Umbrals have lived peacefully together, and we've assisted your city during numerous siege attempts. What if someone wants to see that relationship fail?" Lonan posed his questions carefully, watching for Sophir's reactions.

There were none. Sophir's face remained stoic, and he didn't even blink. He only straightened and bowed his head when the wolves moved. Faedi's hand appeared on Lonan's shoulder soon after, and he turned to look up at her, but her gaze was focused on Sophir.

She had heard everything.

"There have been some who think there's a chance someone wants to damage the relationship Dewgate has with your people," Sophir finally spoke. "There are many theories about potential culprits, though. Many would benefit from Dewgate losing Umbral support."

"What do you think?" Faedi asked, gently squeezing Lonan's shoulder after he offered her the herbs.

"We need evidence one way or another. I don't want to toss around accusations and get innocent people killed," the High Knight replied.

Lonan tilted his head. "What does Lord Blavier think?"

"If he has an opinion, he hasn't told me. However, he holds Lady Callon's opinion in high regard. She thinks it's likely an army or The Order," Sophir scratched his chin. "Whatever is happening to the caravans, it's not natural or a simple case of forest creatures scaring supplies away."

Lonan stood, turning his back to Sophir to focus on Faedi as she spoke into his mind. *Do we tell him about what the trees know?*

He shook his head. *You heard him; he wants proof.*

Okay, she frowned before turning and approaching the wolves. "I'll get them ready so we can continue the search."

Lonan nodded and turned to extinguish the flames but paused when he caught Sophir's gaze on Faedi as she walked away. He couldn't quite determine the expression in the Knight's dark eyes, but he didn't like it. His hair stood on end as he followed Sophir's gaze to Faedi's back, to her hips and tail as they swayed.

Frowning, Lonan returned to the fire and found Sophir's eyes on him instead. Without warning, he pulled his water skin from his belt and emptied it over the flames to extinguish them. Faedi would have put them out before they left, but Lonan didn't want to wait for her.

Not when he wanted Sophir's eyes off her.

The forest was unnervingly quiet, save for the thud of their direwolves' paws against the earth. Lonan's senses tingled with the stillness. The trees closed in around them, but he couldn't shake the sense that something was wrong. He scanned the shadows between the branches while Faedi took the lead, her form swaying with the motion of her wolf. His eyes narrowed at every slight movement, and he turned when Sophir moved.

His attention was on Faedi, seemingly watching her every move.

You better not be staring at her ass.

Lonan followed closely behind them, but the task at hand couldn't clear his clouded mind. He didn't like how Sophir's eyes lingered on Faedi, how he leaned in to speak to her and glanced back at him. Each minute that passed made his discomfort gnaw at him more intensely.

It was almost like he knew it ruffled Lonan's shadows.

He couldn't help it—his eyes kept drifting back to Sophir. The way the man's gaze lingered on Faedi, how his voice softened when he spoke to her, it stirred something in Lonan.

A knot twisted in his stomach.

The bond he shared with Faedi was deeper than anything Sophir could understand. The idea of him showing too much interest in her set him on edge. He had never felt jealous when Ravyn doted on her, when he kissed her, but watching Sophir glance at her gnawed at him.

He frowned at Faedi's back. *"What is he talking to you about?"*

"About the Krelin, how we live and things like that, and our relationship with the Umbrals," she replied, glancing back at him. *"He's also asking about rumors."*

Lonan narrowed his eyes. *"Which ones?"*

"About Umbrals being a creation of the gath-fauna and forest-folk being were-creatures," Faedi rolled her eyes before facing forward again. *"He hasn't asked if Umbrals steal faces yet, though."*

"The Order believes those rumors," he told her.

"I know."

Faedi wasn't one to show discomfort easily, but Lonan had known her long enough to notice the subtle shifts in her demeanor. There was a fleeing moment when her usual mask wavered, a tiny flick in her ears that spoke volumes. Something Sophir said rattled her, even if she tried to hide it. It didn't surprise him, but it unsettled him all the same.

His grip tightened on his wolf's fur as he silently urged them to catch up to Faedi, positioning himself between her and Sophir without warning. He smiled at her, determined to ensure that if Sophir wanted to ask questions about their kinds, it would be to both of them.

"Do you have water? I used mine on the fire," he asked her with a wink. *"He might be interested in you."*

"I knew I should have put that out myself," Faedi rolled her eyes before handing him her water skin. *"Interested how?"*

"As in, he might want to bed you. Maybe he's asking because he wants to know if he might catch lycanthropy from you." He sipped from the skin and watched as her cheeks darkened to a lovely shade of violet.

"Why would I want to sleep with someone who doesn't trust me or even know me?" Her nose scrunched as she shuddered and looked away. *"If I bed anyone on this trip, it will be you."*

Lonan choked on the water, leaning forward as he coughed and regained his breath. They had shared many things since childhood, but intimacy hadn't been one of them—if he didn't count that night with Ravyn and the wine. When they shared a bed, they slept—nothing more. Even when they bathed, it was simple and not romantic at all.

But I want it to be romantic—I want to hear her make the noises she made that night with Ravyn.

Just louder...Ancients, I want her to scream.

He offered back her water skin once he righted himself. *"Is that so? Are we moving forward with our bond then?"*

"Do you want to?" Faedi glanced at him with her eyebrows raised. *"I might not be suitable for an heir of the Mire."*

"Suitable? My parents love you, and so do—" he began to counter, but a glint in the trees caught his eye. "What's that?"

The wolves slid to a stop on the path, and Lonan readied his knives as he slid off his wolf beside Faedi. Their silent conversation would have to wait.

"There's an arrow in that branch," she announced, carefully approaching the treeline. "It isn't Umbral—too fancy."

It was the smell that hit him first—the heavy, acrid stench of something far worse than decay. His nostrils flared, his grip tightening on the knives at his side. There was a wrongness to the scent, a thick, cloying presence that made the air feel heavy. His gaze fell on the arrow embedded in the tree, its material slick and strange, catching the light in a way that made it seem almost alive.

"What material is that?" Lonan walked beside her and grabbed her hand when she reached out to touch it. "It smells foul."

He subtly shook his head when she began to protest and stepped back. She might have been immune to some poisons, but he didn't want to test their luck—not when they couldn't quickly get help.

He couldn't take Sophir to the Mire without risking their safety.

Whatever kind of material it was, it wasn't smooth. It had ridges, and the material glistened as if slick with oil. The bark had turned black and oozed discolored sap where the arrow had pierced the tree. It was undoubtedly some poison or magic.

Lonan's hair stood on his neck, a primal warning crawling down his spine. Something was wrong. The air was too still. He didn't like it—he hated the way the trees seemed to press in on them, the way the scent of decay grew stronger with every passing moment.

"I haven't seen anything like that used in the city," Sophir commented as he approached. "Do the trees here normally do that when they're cut?"

Lonan shook his head. "No. I'm almost certain there's some poison or magic in the arrow."

"The body I saw had the same thing pouring out of his mouth," Faedi told him before pointing at the ground. "There are tracks."

As he knelt beside the tracks, his eyes narrowed. The disturbance in the ground was too deliberate, too calculated. The footprints were from more than one pair of boots. Some of them scuffled, others dragging, uneven, and something about them felt wrong. Lonan's fingers brushed the dirt and leaves, noting something heavy in them, something ill.

It was an ambush.

"They went this way," Faedi pointed through the trees, and Lonan stared at the broken twigs on the smaller trees. "It smells worse that way, too."

"I don't like this," he mumbled as he followed her, leaving the path.

"Are there native poisons that do this?" Sophir asked from behind them as he drew his sword.

"No," Lonan shook his head. *"Ravyn mentioned something similar from Valoria, though."*

The Elder Guardian's grave tone came to mind. He had spoken of plagues in Valoria, something that burned the body from the inside out. The scars on his chest and back he'd shown them were evidence of the plague he suffered.

"He said that smelled of sulfur, not...decay." Faedi glanced over her shoulder before pausing, holding up her hand when there was rustling in the brush ahead of them.

Lonan watched her nock an arrow in her bow and crouch down. Her hair twitched—or rather, the fur-covered ears hidden under it did—and he rolled his shoulders as they waited. She was correct; the smell was worse in that direction, but whatever it was in front of them was alive.

Or moving, at least.

He sniffed the air, pulled his knives from his belt, and kneeled beside Faedi.

She was correct; as putrid as the scent was, it was nothing like sulfur. Raided graves smelled better than whatever wandered in the trees.

"The Watch needs to know about this. It could be a disease." he stared ahead and caught her ear twitch. She agreed.

"Two legs. It might be someone from the caravans," she replied. "Staggered steps; the left foot is dragging. They're injured."

"Are they a threat?" He asked just as a shadow moved behind the leaves.

"I doubt it," she told him, inching forward with her bow aimed ahead. "Go behind them?"

"Okay."

As he moved through the forest's shadows, he hadn't known what to expect, but the sight of the pale, haggard human they found was nothing close to what had crossed their minds. Faedi was right; the man *was* injured.

The human's arm barely hung on by a thread as he limped through the brush. He was unarmed, without armor, and his torn clothes wrapped around his limbs like makeshift bandages, all soaked through with blood as black as tar.

Lonan stood still, barely breathing, as the human shuffled past him again. A warning rose in his throat, sharp and instinctual. He didn't understand what he was looking at, not fully, but every fiber of him recoiled. His shadows wrapped around him like a shield, as he dared a step forward.

"Are you alright?" He eventually asked, as he turned past them again.

When he didn't respond or react, they stepped closer and tightened their grip on their knife. Unless the man was deaf and blind, something should have made him react. But instead, he seemed mindless.

The man's staggering steps echoed a nightmare Lonan rarely allowed himself to remember, but had been creeping in his thoughts since Faedi spoke to the grove.

Faedi, fevered and delirious, curled beneath dying plants, her skin slick with black blood. Even then, she had wept—not for herself, but for the animal she tried to heal, even as the poison infested the surrounding ground. He thought he might lose her again that day, and as he watched the husk of a man, he saw what she could have been.

He glanced at the brush, knowing Faedi was waiting for a signal. They wondered if Faedi might get sick again from exposure, but she had encountered a corpse like this before and had survived. Maybe her eventides protected her more than they thought.

"He's unarmed, but be careful," Lonan called out. "Something is wrong with him."

Faedi crossed through the brush first, her bow still aimed at the human, followed by Sophir. It was hard to tell what he thought of the situation, but he was the first to put away his weapon, keeping his distance from the injured man.

"There's no tourniquet. He should be dead by now," Faedi commented as she sidestepped to follow the human's movements.

"His eyes are glassed over, too," he agreed. "What else do you see?"

"Rope chafing around his wrists, his shirt and neck are burned, and the same black blood is coming out of his face...he—" Faedi stopped, her wide eyes meeting theirs. "His blood is killing the plants."

"Does that mean something?" Sophir asked from behind them, watching the human.

"This is not an illness caused by an infected wound," they said, watching Faedi's eyes glow as she turned her back to Sophir. "It's a curse."

"Is it the same as before?" Lonan put their knives away and studied the dead grass and saplings around the human's feet. *"Check Sophir's weapons for enchantments."*

She shook her head. "I don't know."

Her movements were subtle and calculated as she scratched the side of her head and glanced at Sophir. He followed her gaze to him, whose attention was still on the human. If he noticed her scrutiny, he didn't show it. Instead, his face held concern—but it was the kind born of theory, not of lived danger.

Either he didn't understand the scale of the threat...or he didn't care who got hurt in the pursuit of answers.

"Powerful glamour, but nothing else. Nothing on his weapons," Faedi told him before the glow in her eyes disappeared.

They moved to stand beside Faedi, ready for the living dead man to attack. "What do we do with him?"

"We can't let him wander around out here, killing everything his blood drips on," she replied. "We need to notify The Watch. There might be more people like him."

"I should take him to Dewgate. Lady Callon might help him or sort out the origin of the magic," Sophir interjected.

Lonan glanced at Faedi and sighed when she subtly shook her head. She didn't want to move the walking corpse, nor did he. It was too great a risk for the Sauvern, the Mire, and Dewgate.

However, he doubted the High Knight would take no for an answer.

Lonan stared at him. Did he genuinely lack common sense? "His blood is killing everything it touches, and you want to take him through the forest and into a city full of people?"

"It might not kill people," he suggested. "If he were covered appropriately, it would prevent too many plants from dying."

"It isn't just plants dying," Faedi scoffed, pointing at the ground. "Insects, there's a toad, and who knows how far into the dirt this goes. If you take him from this spot, you could spread this all over the forest. If this reaches root systems—"

"Do the Umbrals know what this is?" Sophir cut her off, and a growl rumbled in their chest. "Do they know how to treat it?"

"We do," Lonan told him with a growl of his own, standing in front of Faedi while she whispered a spell. Sophir's voice grated against his nerves, too calm for someone watching rot spread across the earth.

Does he not see the danger, or does he just not care?

He glanced over his shoulder, nodding once. *"Do it."*

"He's not going to be happy," Faedi warned. *"I'll grow eventides over the area afterward."*

"Don't worry about him. Just do what needs to be done."

Flames encircled the human and spread with a sickening hiss, curling hungrily around the man's feet. The scent of rot exploded in the air, thick and choking, and it lodged in Lonan's throat like ash. When the man screamed, the sound didn't rise—it collapsed inward, a wet shriek like lungs full of water.

Behind him, Faedi clutched at his shirt, and his shadows wrapped around her protectively. It was the best he could do to anchor her, to keep her grounded from the memories that he knew were clawing at her mind.

"What are you doing?" Sophir shouted over the roar of the flames.

"Protecting the forest." They glared at him. "Don't interfere."

Do not try to stop her—I will kill you if you try to touch her.

"Mages and alchemists should study him." The Knight did not stop his approach. "What if there is a cure?"

"You can't cure death," Faedi replied as vines shot around Sophir's feet to ensnare him. "I won't have you spreading a disease around my home or pack. We'll help you find your supplies, but anyone we find like this will be disposed of."

"Tell me what this curse is. We need to find a cure," Sophir pulled against the vines.

The flames grew higher, and their shadows rippled around them as they stepped forward. "It's a plague, and this is the only cure for it once someone reaches this point."

12

The Flame's Shadow

"It had to be done…I had to do it—but I still feel like I'm going to throw up."

Faedi

Sophir's silence was deafening. He hadn't spoken to them after the body had been reduced to ash or after Faedi had purified the soil with eventides. His eyes burned with fury, and each glare he cast their way made Faedi flinch. She instinctively moved closer to Lonan, seeking comfort in his presence.

"He's mad. What do we do?" She whispered, her voice tight with the tension in the air.

"Let him be mad. If we allow him to spread that plague into his precious city, he'll still be upset," Lonan replied, his tone steady.

Dusan's voice cut in, a touch of dark humor in it. *"You could kill him."*

Faedi shot him a glare.

"He isn't safe," Dusan added quickly.

Faedi turned back to the blooming eventides, their vibrant growth forming a barrier between them and Sophir. Perhaps he thought she might resort to violence at any moment, that she would lash out. He wasn't entirely wrong—if he had tried to take the animated corpse, she would have fought him. The forest came first, no matter what.

"We should follow his trail," she suggested quietly. "It might lead us to supplies…or survivors."

Sophir's voice sliced through the air, filled with accusation. "Do you plan to kill them too?"

"I didn't kill him," Faedi snarled, desperation creeping into her voice. "He

91

was already gone."

"How do you know?" Sophir shot back.

"I could see he was dead!" Faedi snapped, her frustration bubbling over. "He wasn't breathing—he had no heartbeat! Even Lady Callon would agree with what I did. Do you want to infect Dewgate?"

Lonan stepped in, his voice a calm warning in her mind. *We did not physically examine him, No doubt he doesn't trust the evaluation you did.*

Sophir's retort was biting. "Confident for someone who burns people who are still walking around."

His words struck deeper than Faedi wanted to admit. Even though she knew her decision had been justified, the sting of his accusation still lingered. She wasn't a murderer; she was just trying to help.

I did what I had to, I didn't have a choice.

"Faedi did what she swore to do by Mire oath," Lonan said, grounding her. "There are laws here."

"This is not the Mire," Sophir shot back, his eyes narrowing. "Your laws don't apply here, *shadow.*"

Faedi stared at him, wide-eyed. There was no way he didn't know the weight of his words. The ground rippled beneath them as she took a step forward, her anger rising.

You fucking bastard.

"Stay behind me," Lonan growled, his fingers tightening on his still-drawn knives. "Our laws are from oaths far older than the one you took to your precious city."

"He's too ignorant to know about them," Faedi seethed. "He doesn't know anything."

Sophir glared at them, his hand resting on the hilt of his sword. "I know the laws. I also know when a supposed Guardian, who is no Elder, steps too far from their path."

The surrounding trees whipped violently, and Faedi caught the scent of smoke. Looking up, she saw dark, curling clouds rising from the forest above.

"You don't know anything, you pompous—" Lonan started, but Faedi interrupted him.

"Stop it!" She shouted, grabbing his arm. "Look!" She pointed to the tree canopy above.

"No, he doesn't get to talk to you that way. He—" Faedi cupped his chin and forced him to look up. Lonan's eyes went to the sky, and his expression shifted as he saw the smoke rising. "*Oh.*"

"Dusan, go look," Faedi ordered, watching the black smoke billow. Her falcon didn't hesitate, taking off with a sharp screech into the trees.

The black smoke trailed thickly through the sky, unnatural and ominous. Birds fled in every direction, and Faedi's heart began to race. It might have been a lightning strike if it had rained, but there was no storm.

It's like the raids.

She whistled for the wolves, her words thick in her throat. "Call The Watch?"

"Call The Hunt," Lonan replied, his voice grim. He jumped on his wolf as it appeared at his side. "Do you think it's them?"

Faedi mounted her wolf, her instincts screaming for her to flee. But instead, she urged the wolf toward the smoke.

I'm not a child anymore.

"Why are you running?" Faedi called to the birds and creatures around them, desperate for answers. "Who made the fire?"

"We do not know them. They burn everything," a chorus of voices echoed back to her.

Chills ran down Faedi's spine, fear gnawing at her as she looked down at her wolf. Its hackles were raised, a growl rumbling beneath her legs, but all she could hear were the fleeing creatures' voices.

"Light touches where it should not. Light kills. Light destroys."

It's The Order—it has to be.

A feral whine rose from deep within her throat, and before she could stop herself, Faedi threw her head back and howled. The sound was raw, primal—more than she had ever allowed herself to make. It was the true voice of her kind. Lonan's howl joined hers, and their wolves ran in perfect harmony.

Faedi didn't look back to see if Sophir had followed. If he had any sense, he would have returned to his city.

As Faedi's wolf raced through the trees, she pressed herself low against its back, shielding her face as she listened intently for a reply from The Hunt.

There was nothing from the east, but she thought she might have heard an echo from the west, though she couldn't be certain. Before her thoughts could settle into worry, a reply came from the north—and it was close. They were near, hidden in the smoke, and they warned of a coming battle.

"It's The Order," Dusan's voice cut through the tension from further ahead. *"A dozen or more."*

The acrid scent of smoke and charred flesh reached her senses soon after, making the urge to flee grow stronger, but Faedi resisted. She wasn't the naïve, wide-eyed girl she once was. The cultists of light couldn't trick her again; they couldn't take everyone she loved. They wouldn't destroy everything she held dear.

I won't let them. I'll give them a good reason to hate the dark.

Then the sound of howls echoed from every direction through the trees. A smile crept onto her face, despite the fear that still gripped her heart. The other packs had heard them. They were coming, ready to hunt alongside them.

"The Watch is sending reinforcements," Lonan said beside her, his voice steady as he held an amulet against his chest, a token for emergencies. "We left the Knight behind."

"Good," Faedi replied, glancing over her shoulder. The wolf behind them was empty, and a wave of relief washed over her. Either Sophir hadn't had time to mount his wolf, or he had chosen not to join them. Either way, it was for the best.

"We'll track him later. He shouldn't be in the forest alone," Faedi said, her words more for herself than for Lonan.

"Maybe he'll go back to the city where he belongs."

Faedi nodded in agreement. The thought settled into her mind comfortably. Sophir could take the news of the plague back to Dewgate, and the city would have to find a way to survive the coming winter without the caravan supplies. It would be hard, but there were other ways to endure. The Umbrals would help, even if Sophir didn't trust them. Dewgate still had its seaside port.

No one would die if the rich in the city helped the poor. If they allowed greed to control them, they would face the consequences. A harsh winter was better than one burdened by both disease and famine.

"What if The Order is already in Dewgate, spreading the plague?" Lonan's question made Faedi bite her lip as she shook her head.

"I don't know. If they catch the signs early, they might be able to survive," she replied, her voice steady despite the dread creeping into her chest. She glanced at Lonan. "Gods willing, they will be alright. Ravyn is a good healer."

"Ancients and Ytna keep them," he said with a frown, his gaze fixed ahead. "We're close."

Faedi followed his line of sight and felt her stomach drop as the air around them thickened. The smoke was oppressive, but it was the shift in the forest's energy that made her skin prickle. The magic felt all wrong—abrasive, violent, instead of the comforting embrace it usually offered.

Then came the screams. The sounds of battle, the cries of the dying, and the clash of flames against the forest's shadows filled the air. The fire quickly overtook the darkness before them, reds, yellows, and oranges dancing wildly against the greens and blacks of the trees. Faedi's heart caught in her throat.

Run.

But she shook her head, dismissing the thought. They couldn't run—not if they wanted to protect their home. She owed it to the forest, for all the times it had protected her. She couldn't abandon it now, not when it needed help the most, even though terror clawed at her insides.

"Hurry," She urged her wolf, spurring it to run faster as she sat up and drew her bow.

"Faedi?" Lonan's voice was laced with urgency.

She glanced at him while nocking an arrow. "Yeah?"

"Stay beside me," he said, his violet eyes burning with fire, his black knives gleaming as he met her gaze. "Stay with me."

"Always." Faedi managed a small smile before their wolves leaped into the flames, and she bit back a scream.

I can fight them this time. They won't take anyone else from me.

Beyond the fire, chaos reigned.

The air was thick with the acrid scent of smoke and the metallic tang of blood. Red and gold-armored cultists wielded gilded weapons, commanding flames with deadly precision as they clashed with the Umbral Watchers and wolves around them.

Lonan was the first to dismount, stalking toward the fray with his black blades at the ready. He paused just long enough for Faedi to fall in step behind him before his speed increased. With each step, his pale skin darkened, shadows beginning to swirl around him as he twirled his knives, preparing to strike down anyone who came within range.

Faedi drew her bowstring to her ear, whispering an incantation. The arrowhead glistened with frost before she released it toward an Orderling of Ilos. It streaked through the air and embedded itself into the neck of a cultist. Before they could fall or remove the arrow, their skin turned to ice, and their scream was cut short.

She didn't feel proud watching the cultist freeze mid-scream—only a dull ache where her sympathy used to live. They burned villages. Poisoned trees. Slaughtered children. There was no reasoning with them. Still, it wasn't easy to look at corpses scattered like her brothers' broken toys across the burning forest floor and feel nothing.

Around them, the battle raged. Umbrals swirled and darted through the melee, their elusive forms hidden in the shadows cast by the flames. Wolves, direwolves, and humanoids with animal features leaped and snapped at the enemy without mercy. Their growls provided a constant undercurrent to the chaos, and other woodland creatures joined the fray.

Among them, Faedi caught sight of familiar figures: Rena and Enoch fought side by side; little Brin, no older than six and ten, ducking and weaving with daggers too large for her hands; and Quill, whose antlers glinted with frost as he rammed a cultist with enough force to shatter bone.

They weren't just Watchers—they were friends, kin by oath and choice. Seeing them bleed made her burn hotter than the surrounding flames with a need to end the threat.

A cultist charged her, but Lonan was quick to deflect the blow aimed at Faedi with a swift flick of his knife. In one smooth motion, he pivoted and drove his other blade into the cultist's gut. Faedi nodded her thanks, knocking another arrow and firing the same incantation into the ground between a cluster of cultists. Shards of ice shot out and pierced their bodies.

Just as she notched another arrow, her breath caught. A ripple moved through the trees behind them—not the fire or the wind, but something slower, watching. A cold prickle danced along her spine, not from the frost magic, but from something else entirely. She turned, scanning the tree line. But there was nothing.

Without warning, a wave of light surged toward them. Instinctively, Faedi raised her hands, surrounding them both with a barrier of wind. She dropped to her knees as the heat threatened to sear her skin. Lonan vanished from her side, and when she blinked, she saw his shadowy form looming behind the cultist who was still trying to burn her.

With a series of quick, lethal strikes, Lonan sliced through the cultist's exposed neck, armpits, and groin before they collapsed to the ground. Then, in the same breath, he was back in front of Faedi, helping her to her feet. His examination of her hands and arms was quick—over as soon as she wiggled her fingers to show him she was alright—and then his focus was back on the fight.

It wasn't long before the cultists became disorganized, overwhelmed by the forces against them. Bodies lay scattered across the forest floor as the flames began to die down with each cultist's demise. Several attempted to flee, to regroup, but Faedi wouldn't allow it. Each one fell to enchanted arrows embedded in their backs.

With the last cultist dead, Lonan stood from the corpse beneath him, pulling his knife from their mouth as his skin returned to its usual pale complexion. He looked up at Faedi, a smile spreading across his face—one she returned as she caught her breath. She closed the distance between them in just two steps, tilting her head back to meet his gaze.

A hush fell over the forest, broken only by the fading crackle of fire and the soft panting of their allies. Smoke clung to her hair. Her limbs trembled with leftover adrenaline. But in the middle of it all stood Lonan—steady, sure, and watching her like she was the only thing worth seeing.

She wiped the blood from his nose with her thumb. "You made that look easy." She smiled again. "No new cuts to worry your mother?"

"It was, and I'm fine," he shrugged, laughing when she rolled her eyes. "Your hands?"

"I think they're okay," she replied. "The heat scared me more than anything." She tried to look away, but Lonan cupped her cheek and leaned closer.

"*You* made that look easy," he said, his voice warm. "You were amazing."

Faedi opened her mouth to protest, to argue, but she couldn't—not when he leaned even closer, his mouth hovering so close to hers as he searched her eyes. He was waiting for something.

"You are amazing," he whispered, his lips barely brushing against hers.

Is he teasing me?

"Are you going to kiss me?" She blurted out without thinking.

Lonan chuckled, brushing his thumb over her bottom lip. "Can I?"

She couldn't find her voice with her heart pounding in her throat. Instead, she settled for her next best option—she tried to kiss him. Life in the forest didn't allow for romantic escapades, and she was sure that quick pecks on his cheek or those she gave animals didn't count as real experience.

Even that night with Ravyn hadn't given her enough confidence for that moment.

But Lonan didn't seem to mind. He cradled the back of her head and moved his lips against hers, soft and parted. Faedi mimicked the movement, holding her breath as his tongue slid against hers.

Their last kiss hadn't been anything like it—not with such care, not with his entire focus pouring into her like she was a secret worth keeping. It made her feel weightless and real all at once. And the way he held her, like he knew she might bolt, made her want to stay rooted in that moment forever.

The moment ended far sooner than she wanted it to and heat flooded her cheeks as his breath tickled her nose before he slowly pulled away.

She looked up at him, gently biting her lips together as her heart thundered in her chest. He beamed down at her, his smile brighter than a full moon, but then his gaze shifted behind her, and his smile vanished.

Faedi knew the change in his mood before he spoke.

"He followed us."

Echoes of the Past

Faedi

The remaining Umbrals of The Watch and the were-folk sat at the edge of the newly made clearing, tending to the wounded and burying their dead. Faedi leaned against a tree, her gaze fixed on the place where Lonan had last seen Sophir.

The High Knight hadn't approached them after the fight. He had only taken one of the Orderling's blades and vanished, not to be seen again. Faedi had sent the pack to search for him, but they had returned empty-handed.

Lonan tasked one of the younger Umbrals with tracking Sophir down, using one of their wolves to ensure he made it safely back to Dewgate. Faedi had sent Dusan along as well, to make sure Ravyn was warned about the plague. Lonan hadn't suggested they leave to find Sophir.

Instead, he sat beside her, offering a waterskin before he began to clean his knives.

She hadn't seen Lonan fight like that since the last siege attempt on Dewgate. There was something almost sacred in the way he moved—silent, swift, and devastating. His knives danced, never striking in the same place twice. The cultists hadn't stood a chance, not when moved like a shadow with purpose, as if each cut was a part of a vow written in blood.

"What do you think he's going to do with that sword?" He asked, breaking the silence.

Faedi eyed the pile of armor and weapons strewn nearby. "Not sure," she replied. "I don't trust what he might do. They turn black when the Orderlings aren't using them. He might argue it's an Umbral weapon."

The vibrant red and gold of the cultists' armor had vanished the moment they died. Now, there were no markings of Ilos, no golden flames, and their magic had dissipated. But those injured by the cultists' weapons bled black—a grim reminder of the battle.

The healers among The Watch worked swiftly, tending to the wounded. The dead were burned separately from the cultists. Words were sparse among the victorious. Even as the forest's magic began to settle, the tension in the air was palpable, thick enough to turn Faedi's stomach.

The young Lios'rin—too young for his twin blades—remained missing; she knew he was among the dead. He shouldn't have been there, but she'd seen him in the chaos. He wasn't even a Watcher, he was still in training. She knew the battle would take more than lives. It had taken promises, futures. And it would take more if The Order wasn't stopped.

She knew no one would sleep easily that night.

"If he blames the Umbrals, he's an idiot," Lonan nudged her, encouraging her to drink from the waterskin. "It'll be alright."

"He knows too much," Faedi murmured, taking a sip.

"At worst, we won't be allowed in the city anymore. Ravyn'll just have to meet us at the edge of the farmlands," he shrugged. "They can't make us leave the cottage; it isn't their land."

"They can try to make us leave," Faedi said, hugging her knees. "We should move closer to the Mire. Ravyn could get into trouble if word spreads that he was letting were-folk and an Umbral in the city."

"Good point," he sighed, wrapping his arm over her shoulders. "We'll still see him at the tree."

Faedi nodded. He was right.

They would still see Ravyn, and she wouldn't lose him.

Ravyn would meet them at the heart tree with the other Guardians and Wardens for regular meetings and celebrations. They could still see him there, and no one could complain. Forest matters belonged to the forest, and city rules could not reach them there.

However, if people found out Guardians and Wardens socialized with 'cursed races' in the woods, the gatherings at the heart tree might dwindle until only the forest-folk and Umbrals attended.

If Orderlings were allowed in Dewgate through the seaside ports, the Mire would be safer if no one traveled through the forest—even if it meant the city's people would suffer without supply transports. The cultists had already disrupted the winter stock caravans, and Faedi doubted they would stop there. They would continue to infect the forest, and perhaps the city, with their deadly plague.

But if no one traveled through the forest, people might be safe.

"You think too loudly," Lonan whispered. "Everything will be alright. We can rest in the Mire and visit Myst. Then, we can figure out a plan from there. We'll have to be on the defensive for a while...I don't think that was the last of the Orderlings."

"I think you're right," Faedi nodded. "We should talk to your parents about moving closer to the Mire. Myst's cub could use some friends, anyway."

"Penelope and Comet will like having kids to play with, too," he agreed, squeezing her shoulders.

"Myst will be able to visit more often. They'll like to get away from your mother," Faedi grinned. "We can get them into plenty of trouble while keeping everything up if we want to travel somewhere."

"I'm still going to take you to see the Rowdon lights," he promised with a smile. "And there are more springs closer to the Mire."

Faedi laughed, the tension in her chest easing a little. "I do like the idea of regular hot baths."

Night fell over the forest. Smaller campfires broke out, and food was cooked. The surviving fighters moved closer together to socialize and pay their respects to the dead. Ale was poured, and songs filled the air, but Lonan stayed beside Faedi, away from the fires.

She couldn't bring herself to sit close enough for warmth or food. Each crackle made her jump, and the scent of charred flesh lingered, twisting her stomach. She had seen and manipulated enough fire to last a lifetime.

Sleep was just as impossible as eating.

Lonan stayed up with her for as long as he could, but eventually, exhaustion overtook him. She knew he'd slept less than she had the night before. They would be safe around their allies as various Watchers patrolled through the evening, but that knowledge did little to settle her mind.

The flames stirred too many memories.

"I'm taking a walk," Faedi whispered as he slept, stretching her arms above her head. She slowly stepped around the sleeping Umbrals and away from those dozing under the trees and stars. She didn't plan to go far or leave the group's safety, but she needed to escape the fires and smoke.

She needed to breathe.

Crickets chirped in the brush as Faedi walked into the darkness, the soft sounds of mice and other rodents scurrying away from her boots. Most of the different prey creatures had long fled, driven off by the presence of the wolves, but some lingered—older ones or those with mis-healed injuries, resting among the trees. They were offerings—sacrifices.

She approached an old elk, its eyes wary. She scratched its nose when it huffed at her. The elk was here to be hunted, to feed the predators who defended the forest. It was one of the wood's traditions—a balance the heart tree provided.

Ravyn had once told her that animals behaved differently further from the tree, that in places where lush forests once thrived, nature lost its balance, leaving only feral or domesticated creatures. Those regions became barren, devoid of beauty. She hoped that wasn't the case in Rowdon.

Something shifted in the trees. It wasn't the rustle of prey or the whisper of a branch—it was quieter, measured. She paused, her senses flaring. A shadow moved against the darker black, and she caught the scent of wolf long before the voice came.

"You should be with the group," a deep voice growled from within the trees. "It's not safe alone with those cunts around."

"I'm not alone," she replied, searching the shadows and quietly sniffing the air. Wolf.

"Your pack is sleeping."

"I have allies awake in the woods." A smile crept onto her face when she caught his silhouette. "Were you here for the elk?"

"No. I came to answer the call, but the fight was already done." He stepped closer, and Faedi's eyes adjusted to his massive form. "I was delayed by another group of Ilos' worshipers to the east."

His skin was dark gray, his wild black hair framing a face she recognized immediately. His golden eyes bore down on her, one nearly closed, revealing a scar that wrapped around his cheek. She knew that face. He was a Warden, once a leader of The Hunt.

He had known her family well and was a frequent visitor to their home when she was a child. But she hadn't seen him since the day her family was murdered. She had tried to find him, desperate to bring him back home to help, but he had been impossible to track. Even after Lonan had found her years later, no Umbrals had been able to locate him, and Ravyn hadn't heard from him either.

It's you.

She had thought he died in the raids, but here he was—scarred but safe and sound.

She tilted her head, curiosity blooming in her chest. "Torix?"

"Yes?" His stare pierced into her, and she bit her lip. There was no recognition in his eyes.

Either he didn't remember her, or she had changed more than she thought over the past twenty and two years—even if she still felt like the terrified child she had been back then. But another possibility made her heart sink: he could remember her, recognize her, and be dismissive because he blamed her for what happened.

Faedi wrapped her arms around herself, the weight in her chest heavier than it had been in years, She didn't need Torix to remember her for the guilt to return. Just seeing him—alive, scarred, unchanged in the ways that mattered—was enough to twist the knife.

His presence should have brought relief, maybe even joy, but all she saw in his eyes was wariness. And she couldn't blame him. No matter how many years had passed, a part of her believed she didn't deserve forgiveness. Not after what she had brought to their doorstep.

Maybe he knows it was my fault.

"No one could find you after the raids," she said, hugging her arms. "Where were you?"

"I went hunting," he rumbled. He never was much of a talker.

Twenty and two years is a long hunt, even for you.

A flicker in his eyes caught her attention, something she didn't recognize, before he looked away, scratching his chin. She couldn't help but stare at him, taking in the changes. His appearance had always been rough, but his eyes had been brighter. His lips, which used to curl into hidden smiles, remained a frown.

It reminded her of the late nights when he spoke with her parents while her brothers and she were supposed to be asleep. He had always been serious around them, discussing bad news, but he never spoke of it when she was around. Instead, he had taken them on adventures.

He had taken her and Sylrie everywhere—she had survived everything because of him.

He had once carried her on his shoulders after her first kill and had given her a bow—just like the one she left beside Lonan. She'd commissioned it in the Mire as soon as she took her vows to the Watch.

I wanted you with me.

Ancients, she wanted to hug him like she did as a child. He had always made her feel safe, but she couldn't take how he looked at her. It was damning.

She frowned, taking a step back and glancing toward the campfires. The silence was too much. "Did you kill the other Orderlings?"

"I did." Torix turned his intense gaze back to her, and she instinctively took another step back. "Why are you here?"

"The same as you. We saw the smoke, and I called The Hunt." She could barely speak above a whisper under his scrutiny.

"You called it?" His eyes narrowed, and she felt her face burn. He stepped toward her when she nodded. "Your song isn't common in the forest—but you've called it before, haven't you?"

Was I not supposed to call it? Being a wolf was the one thing you didn't teach me.

Her shoulders slumped, and she looked away. Maybe it was better if he didn't know who she was. It was better to be an unknown Hunt.

"Only twice before," she admitted, hugging her arms tighter. "I didn't know if any hunts were around, but...thankfully, there were. I appreciate you coming."

I'm supposed to thank him, right?

"You should be careful about calling it again further from the Mire," he warned, his expression grave.

She nodded, her throat tightening as her questions faded. He was the one who had taught her how to call it, how to make her song carry through the trees and alert The Hunt of danger. It was the third time she'd done it, but the first time anyone had responded.

He hadn't come the first time—no one but Lonan had. He hadn't come the second time, either.

"I know—no one will hear me," she told him, the emotion tightening in her chest.

"That's not—"

"I should get back," she interrupted, finally finding her words. "Elder Peni and Ravyn will be happy to hear you're alive."

"I—of course," he said, reaching for her before pulling his hand back and lowering his head.

She turned and ran back to the camp, unable to endure his gaze any longer. Each second that passed only deepened her self-blame. It hurt more to know he had survived the raids; even if the dead could hold a grudge or blame her, she didn't have to look them in the eye.

The dead could only haunt her in her dreams, and she knew they would come to her as soon as she closed her eyes beside Lonan. If the flames and cultists hadn't ensured it already, Torix's eyes did. All she could do was hope that she didn't scream in her sleep or that Lonan would wake her before she could.

Why didn't you come when I called?

Even as she slipped back beside Lonan's sleeping form, her breath still carried the scent of ash, and her ears still rang with a silence louder than his answer.

14

In the Umbral Halls

Lonan

The convoy of Umbrals and were-folk moved through the forest, far from the trails the caravans would have used. Instead, they followed hidden paths leading to the Umbramire. Though they took the longer paths in case they were followed, adding a day to their journey. Their voices carried through the air like the morning songbirds, but the loudest sound was Faedi's silence as she rode her wolf beside Lonan.

She hadn't spoken since he had woken her, and her head hung low.

It wasn't the first time he'd seen her like this, but the waves of anxiety and sadness radiating from her were enough to sour his breakfast. He didn't want to draw attention to her in a crowd; embarrassment would only push her backward.

As they traveled in silence, he scanned the group for anything or anyone that might make her uncomfortable. No one carried a torch, and there was no smoke in the air, but a rugged man walked nearby, glancing at her occasionally. He was familiar, but Lonan couldn't quite place his identity.

Whoever he was, his attention made her uneasy. Lonan moved his wolf to position themselves between Faedi and the unnamed man. If he couldn't see her, maybe that would be enough to ease her discomfort. But it would be a long trip to the Mire if it didn't work. Unless...

"Do you want to race there?" He asked, glancing over his shoulder at her.

"What?" Faedi looked up at him, dark circles under her eyes, dazed. "What if there are more Orderlings?"

"The guards will take care of them." He shrugged and smiled. "The wolves are bored."

She shook her head before lowering it again. "I think we should stay with the group."

She never turns down a race—this is more than just cultist anxiety.

"Can you tell me what's on your mind?" He asked gently. "You're too scattered to read right now, and...I'm worried." He reached over to squeeze her knee gingerly.

"There was too much fire yesterday," she said, covering his hand with hers. "The past was too close."

"What else?" He pressed, trying to keep his tone as gentle as possible. "Is it that man who keeps staring at you?"

"He's staring at me?"

Faedi lifted her head and quickly scanned the group. Her anxiety flared as she searched for him, and Lonan sighed before slowing his wolf to reveal the man behind them. He followed her gaze and stared at the man, silently daring him to do anything that might make Faedi feel worse. But the man didn't react. Instead, he held their gazes for a breath and then looked away.

"Who is he? I think I've seen him before," Lonan said, keeping his eyes on the man.

No...I know I've seen him before.

"Torix. He was friends with my parents. He led the southern Hunt before the raids." She squeezed his hand, pulling his attention back to her. "I thought he was dead."

The name struck Lonan as he recalled when he found Faedi years after the fire. When she was a burned and bloody mess, crying his name. He only had vague memories of the man from their childhood, but he *had* been there at their home a few times.

"Shouldn't you be happy that he's alive?" Lonan asked, thinking it should have been a joyful reunion.

She turned her attention back to her wolf, scratching between its ears. "I was, but...I think he hates me or doesn't even remember me."

No one could forget you—or hate you.

"I'll eat anyone who hates you. Besides, you've grown up and need a bath." He nudged her with a smile. "Maybe he doesn't recognize you."

She shrugged, and he frowned, realizing what was wrong. It wasn't Torix who hated her. She hated herself. She was too afraid to bring up the past to him, terrified he might blame her for her family's murders—because she still blamed herself.

I can't eat her...Well, I—no.

"We can find out if he remembers you," he suggested, nudging her again.

"How?" She peeked up at him, curiosity flickering in her eyes.

"Simple. Your name isn't exactly common." He grinned at her before pulling his empty waterskin from his pack. "Faedi, do you have water? I ran out."

As he showed her his empty skin, he watched Torix for any reaction. At first, nothing happened, but then the man's steps slowed while he stared ahead. His eyes slowly shifted to Faedi and widened.

He most certainly remembered her.

"Here." Her reply pulled his attention away from Torix, and he winked at her as he accepted her waterskin. "Well?"

"Oh, he remembers you," he said after taking a sip and offering it back to her. "Thanks."

He caught Faedi glancing at Torix before she looked ahead and sighed. It wouldn't lessen her fears that he might blame her for what happened to her family, but he was determined to solve that, too.

He just needed to decide how.

It wasn't the best idea to dig up the past while they traveled, but he didn't want her to feel uncomfortable for the rest of the trip. It might be best for them to race ahead. If they did that, Faedi could feel however she needed to and freshen up before meeting with Torix—if he traveled to the Mire.

However, there was a chance he might leave. He had been missing for over two decades and was presumed dead. He could go again if he wanted, and Lonan wasn't sure if that would be better or worse for Faedi—not when the past continued to haunt her at every turn.

"We're only an hour's run away now," Lonan commented, glancing up at the canopy. It was well past midday. "I'll bet he doesn't hate you if he follows us."

Faedi grinned at him. "First one there gets the lily wine?"

Keep smiling for me.

"And the moss," he chuckled before smiling deviously. "Three, two—go!"

His wolf surged ahead of hers, darting around the others as he leaned over the direwolf. She was beside him before long, squinting at him as she tugged the fabric around her neck over her nose. In the blink of an eye, her eyes shone violet like his, and her blue skin paled to white as shadowy wisps danced around her. Once her Umbral glamour was active, she winked at him before urging her wolf to surge ahead of his.

Voices came from behind them, and he tilted his head back with laughter. They weren't the only ones who enjoyed a run.

"Are we racing?"

"Beat him, Liru!"

"Follow the Prince!"

He glanced over his shoulder and laughed as several others from The Watch summoned shadowed mounts to chase after them. But then, someone else caught his attention as he raced off. Torix's form shimmered and shifted, the massive wolf lunging into the trees behind them.

Lonan's chest eased just a fraction.

He was right. Torix didn't hate Faedi. And maybe—just maybe—that meant she could stop hating herself.

The forest's greens and browns swiftly shifted to blacks and vibrant, luminescent leaves that glowed in the shadows. Dark-cloaked archers perched high up in the trees, bowing their heads as he chased after Faedi. He spotted other guards mounted on ethereal felines and elks, hidden at the bases of trees, mimicking the archers above.

"Hunts are with us," he called out as his wolf ran past them. "Give them safe passage."

He didn't think they would attack anyone without an order, but the air felt too tense to trust common sense. Word of the cultists had already spread, and outsiders wouldn't be trusted easily. Even if he had not fought alongside them, he wouldn't have confidently spoken for them.

As he neared the black ironwood gates, he shook his head when Faedi raised her hand above her head, crossing the threshold first. He could have pushed his wolf harder, given her a better chase, but the way her bright eyes sparkled beneath her mask as she smiled back at him was better than any victory.

She needed the rush more than he did.

"You know they're going to stop us as soon as we get there," he said, finally catching up to her.

"I don't blame them for being worried," she replied with a shrug, slowing to a trot. "After what happened to Myst? I won't be surprised if they strip-search us for injuries."

"Don't give them any ideas," he groaned. "My mother hasn't seen me naked since I was a Mireling."

As they navigated the crowded cobblestone street leading to the center of the Mire and the Umbral Hall, he studied each passerby for any signs of illness or injury. When he saw none, he felt torn between relief and worry.

No injuries on the street could mean they were either dead or with healers. Myst couldn't have been the only Umbral injured by cultists; whoever was with them would have defended them. They were an heir just like him and would be protected like one. Anyone gravely injured would be in the Hall under his mother's care instead of the healing houses.

Ancients, let the Hall be empty.

"They've increased the guard patrols," Faedi commented as she dismounted her wolf upon reaching the massive ironwood steps leading up to the Hall. "Four at the door instead of two."

He nodded, his gaze drawn to the trees as he dismounted. "More archers, too."

"Overabundance of caution, or do they know something we don't?" Her brow creased, only relaxing when he took her hand.

"We'll find out," he said, giving her hand a gentle tug as he led her up the steps where his parents stood between the guards.

Lonan's mother, Vireya, stood poised and composed, but her presence held the weight of centuries. Her midnight-blue braids shimmered faintly under the torchlight, threaded with silver charms that chimed softly when she moved. Known across the Mire as both healer and high matron, her hands could mend bone and curse alike, and her gaze often saw deeper truths than words revealed.

Beside her, his father, Tagil, stood like a statue carved from shadowwood—tall, broad-shouldered, and silent. His dark armor bore no sigil, but the quiet authority in his stillness spoke louder than any title. While Vireya ruled with empathy sharpened by wisdom, Tagil was the sentinel of their people, a blade held in reserve. Together, they were a force, one that Lonan had spent his life both revering and quietly fearing.

He knew he couldn't live up to their legacy as their heir.

His stomach sank with each step he took when his mother's smile didn't reach her eyes as it usually did. He hoped she was just worried about their well-being, but he doubted it was as simple as that. His father's near-statuesque form told him it was something more.

Whatever it was, it was terrible news.

"The Gods bless us with your return," his mother said, wrapping her arms around him as soon as they reached the top step and kissing his cheek. She repeated the motion with Faedi before grabbing their hands. "Come inside."

"Mam, we're alright," he protested as she practically dragged them by their joined hands into the Hall.

"I'll believe you when you're not covered in blood and ashes," she told him before her voice fell to a whisper. "And when you're not in your glamours."

"Clear the Hall!" His father boomed from behind them, and everyone inside scattered like leaves in the wind.

"What do you see?" He glanced at Faedi as he followed his mother, rubbing between his brows with his free hand.

"Extra protective runes. Something powerful is near the roots," she said, glancing around the Hall idly and taking everything in. *"Some of these are strange. They aren't Gath'Faunan or Umbral."*

"You speak at least five languages," he said, dropping his hand and studying her eyes. She looked flustered—confused.

"Speak, not read...it looks similar to Gaelisk, but not quite. My mother had a book with runes like that on it."

He followed her gaze but didn't see what she saw. It was only dark wood, torches glowing with black flames, and the same décor as when he had left. He knew magic was hidden everywhere, even if he couldn't see it. Their protective spells had kept them safe for centuries, and he hoped they would continue to do so.

His mother didn't stop until they were led into the council room. Only then did she release their hands and turn to face them. She didn't wait for them to remove their glamours; instead, she waved her hands over them to dispel the magic herself. He knew she wouldn't take that chance even if they had nothing to hide. Not after he'd hidden his first dragon bite from her.

"Off with the cloaks and armor," she commanded.

"Mam—"

"You can keep your other clothes on, but take the rest off. Your belongings need to be enchanted before you leave again." She waved her hand dismissively as she sat, and his father moved to stand beside her chair.

"Alright," he relented with a sigh. *I swear she heard you.*

"At least you won't be completely naked."

He sat at the foot of his bed, rubbing his face as guilt washed over him. After his mother thoroughly examined both him and Faedi, she had sent them off to clean up before they were expected to gather. No one had asked about what they'd seen or fought against in the forest, and he couldn't mention it either.

He stared at his muddy boots, sighing.

And what about Torix?

He should have discussed it earlier and gotten it all out before they were sent away, but he had been greedy with his time. He wanted to breathe, to relax before the serious discussions began. He had wasted time planning to prolong that feeling as much as he could before facing the reality of their situation.

Ilos' cultists would continue their attacks on the forest; their attempts to cleanse the world of darkness wouldn't stop, and he would be forced to kill or be killed.

Let's live while we can.

He huffed and stood up, grabbing a change of clothes. His mother always demanded—in her gentle way—that he look civilized for meals, so he took the items with him as he turned to head for the bath. There was an enormous communal bath on the ground floor, but he wasn't in the mood for an audience.

Instead, he settled for the bath that separated his room from Faedi's. The room had once belonged to his sibling, Myst, but they had given it to Faedi when she arrived at the Mire.

He should have been thinking about strategy, about the growing danger in the forest, but instead, he found himself recalling the way Faedi looked when wind tangled her wild hair. How her laughter echoed like birdsong through the trees.

Is she still going to be able to laugh after this?

As he stepped inside the bath, steam filled the air. He heard movement in the tub before recognizing the gray skin in the water. Faedi was submerged entirely, and he doubted she knew he was there, so he turned on his heels respectfully and waited for her to come up for air.

He didn't need to stare at her.

He didn't need to; he already had her body memorized. Instead, he stared at the opened bottle of lily wine on the counter.

The scent of her lingered in the warm mist—crushed herbs, wildflowers, eventides, and something distinctly *her*. Even when she wasn't speaking, she occupied space so fully, like the room belonged to her.

For years, he had assumed his attraction was one-sided or merely a result of familiarity, even after that night with Ravyn, but then they kissed. There hadn't been enough time for him to process what had happened afterward—not with the cultists, his exhaustion, and Faedi's poor mood regarding Torix.

This is a horrible time to do anything.

"Sorry, I thought you were going to see Myst first," Faedi called out.

He froze as the water sloshed behind him, a soft trickle spilling onto the stone floor. Slowly, he glanced over his shoulder—just in time to watch her rise from the tub. Droplets glided over the velvet expanse of her skin, tracing the curves of her breasts and hips before pooling at her feet.

She wrapped a towel around herself, the damp fabric clinging to every dip and swell, leaving his mouth dry. His gaze lingered on the water beaded between her breasts, how the cloth pressed against them, barely containing her. He ached to taste those droplets, to chase each one with his tongue—until there was nothing left between them and she was moaning his name.

It was impossible to ignore how his cock hardened at the thought.

Stop it—say something.

"Y-you didn't finish your wine," he stammered, shifting awkwardly in the doorway. "You don't have to leave."

She smiled, and heat flooded his cheeks as her eyes took him in from head to foot. "You look like you have a lot on your mind."

Do I?

He glanced down at himself, worried she might have seen him strained against his pants, but she couldn't have. However, it didn't stop the tips of his ears from burning as if she had.

Thank the Gods he was holding his clothes in front of him.

"And I don't know if…um…" Faedi trailed off, biting her lips together as she ran her hand through her hair. "We kissed."

"We did," he confirmed, clearing his throat. "But we don't have to take it further than that or do it again."

I want to do it again.

She tilted her head to the side. "Do you want it to go further?"

Ancients, yes.

"I want many things, but I told you I wouldn't pressure you. We didn't know me helping you would bond us, and—"

"But it did, and besides, we already act like we're married," Faedi grinned at him.

"Maybe because I—" He froze, breath catching, the words rushing past his teeth before he could trap them. "—don't know how to act like I'm not in love with you."

Faedi blinked, her breath catching audibly in the quiet space between them. The smile slipped from her face, replaced by something softer—warmer—but layered with uncertainty. Her fingers twitched slightly at her side before she wrapped her arms around herself, her posture folding inward as if she needed to hold the words somewhere safe.

"Everyone I've loved—" her voice cracked, and she held herself tighter. "They always die. And you're…you're you."

She loves me, too.

His chest tightened. He wanted to step towards her but feared she might run. "You can't say it back."

She nodded once, then twice—her eyes on the ground—before she took a hesitant step closer. Her voice dropped to a whisper. "I'm scared. Not of you. Just of what will happen."

Lonan didn't move. He didn't dare. He just watched her, letting his shadows ripple around him, slowly circling her, silently begging her to come closer. "What happens is we complete our bond—I want you as more than my paired Guardian, my fellow Watcher, and best friend." He explained slowly, softly, unsure that his words could even be heard over his pounding heart. "I want *so* many things."

Faedi exhaled slowly, visibly collecting herself before a crooked smile tugged at the corner of her lips. "Is bedding me one of the things you want?"

He stared at her with wide eyes. Despite the subject, she spoke so casually and confidently as if discussing breakfast. Out of all their jokes and conversations, they had never really discussed their relationship. Their accidental bond existed, but it wasn't something they worried about. It was simply a matter they agreed to address if it ever became a problem, and his parents never pressured them about it either.

Despite his desires, he couldn't help but remember how their bond began. How her blood stained his hands, the way her fingers gripped his wrist—so suddenly astutely aware of what was happening despite her fever—not in fear, but in trust. That was the moment the bond took root, and maybe when he'd fallen for her too. He knew he couldn't lose her. He knew he couldn't live without her.

The bond, loving her, was not the problem. However, his desire to take her right then and there was.

"If we weren't supposed to meet with my parents—" he spoke slowly, his words catching in his throat when Faedi dropped her towel to the floor and his clothes tumbled from his hands.

"They're with the healers tending to The Watch," she said, approaching and tugging him closer by his belt. "Dinner is still a couple of hours away. I want to live while we can."

She was correct; there was time, and he wanted to savor every second he could.

15

Tides of Desire

Lonan

He should have known better—getting Faedi back into the bath was asking for trouble, the kind that left his heart pounding and his thoughts spinning out of control.

Once, he had found himself in the water with her; bathing while exploring her body had been impossible to manage. She was far too distracting, and even with her attempts to help him wash, he couldn't focus. Every time their eyes met, his heart raced, and his cheeks burned.

Everything felt different, even if it was the same as it had always been. And it was better than the night they had spent with Ravyn—so much better.

He realized he shouldn't have tried to kiss her while she scrubbed dirt from his hair, especially after soap slipped into his eye. But her laughter at his sudden, panicked flailing dulled the sting. She quickly grabbed his face, wiping his eyes gently with her thumbs.

"Are you alright?" She asked once he managed to open his eyes.

"Ow," he chuckled, holding his breath when she kissed his eyelids. "That's better."

She laughed, rolling her eyes. "You're worse than Comet at bath time."

Faedi was so close he could feel the heat radiating off her skin beneath the water, and each accidental brush of her knee against this thigh made his pulse jump. He couldn't tell if it was the scent of the lily wine or just her that made his head swim, but it was getting harder to resist her.

"You're making it hard to kiss you," he feigned a pout. "And the soap stung."

"Five minutes ago, you were worried about Espen smelling you."

"And five minutes ago, you weren't talking about sex," he countered, gently pushing her back against the wall of the tub. "But you did, and you're...beautiful."

Her gray cheeks flushed a deep purple as she stared at him with wide, bright eyes. She was nervous, just like he was, but she wasn't afraid. She trusted him, and that was the highest honor he could imagine.

That trust unraveled him more than any touch ever could—it was the kind of sacred, soul-deep gift he never believed he deserved but would protect with everything he had.

He caught her chin with his forefinger to keep her from looking away and smiled. "Absolutely beautiful."

Slowly, he trailed his hand down from her chin, past her neck, and into the water to caress her breast. He paused when she shivered, studying her face again. She bit her lips together as she stared down at his hand. It wasn't until he whispered her name that she looked at him and nodded for him to continue.

She met his gaze, her eyes searching his face for any doubt. When she nodded again, it wasn't shy—it was certain, her hand guiding his with a quiet kind of urgency.

"I'm okay," Faedi told him with a shy smile. "Do I...should I?"

"Do whatever feels right," he replied as he cupped her breast and rubbed his thumb over her nipple.

He wasn't sure if it was her sudden inhale or if she raised her chest upward on purpose, but he took it as a good sign and repeated the motion. She quickly wrapped a hand behind his neck, pulling him closer for a kiss. The scent of the eventides on her arm overtook him, nearly overpowering the lily wine that lingered on her tongue, but not entirely.

How many times have I imagined this?

Her breath was hot against his lips, warmer than the water that lapped around them. Her skin was like silk beneath his fingers, and when he rolled her nipple gently between his thumb and forefinger, her soft gasp echoed like thunder in his chest.

But then it was her turn to smile when she nipped his bottom lip.

His cheeks continued to burn as he explored her body with his fingertips. Above her left breast, just beside her collarbone, he found a scar—the third time he had ever truly feared for her life. She might have had it for a decade, but he remembered it as if it had happened hours ago. If it hadn't been for her lips on his neck, he wouldn't have been able to pull himself back from that memory.

Lonan's hand drifted lower, brushing across her ribs. There, just beneath the right side, his fingers traced the crescent of an old wound—thin and pale like a forgotten blade. She stiffened for half a breath but didn't stop him. Instead, she guided his hand back with her own, letting him feel the truth of it.

When he cupped her hip, his thumb brushed over a patch of bare, uneven skin—furless and warm—a burn. The fur there had never grown back, and it broke his heart anew to feel how deep the damage went. He recognized its shape—the width of a hand—cruelly familiar. He didn't say anything, just kissed the edge of it.

Then he reached the back of her thigh, and her leg shifted instinctively, but he still found the rougher patch of skin. It was uneven, like something had splattered and clung, burning through skin and fur alike. His touch softened there, and he let his lips follow—silently trying to make up for his absence in the past.

But the scars around her wrists rooted him in place.

She reached up to cradle his cheek, and as her hand passed by his eyes, he saw it again—that faint, circular brand. Raised and rigid like a bracelet forged in fire. He took her hand in both of his, lifting it to his mouth. She stilled. He kissed the inside of her wrist, slow and deliberate, and watched her eyes as her fingers trembled.

Around her ankle—when he reached it—was the same. Scar tissue tight and angry, especially on the inside where it dipped close to the bone. As he moved to trace it, her hand wrapped around his shaft, pulling him back to the present in a single, aching moment.

He twitched in her grasp, face burning.

"You're here." She whispered, her breath against his ear. "So am I."

He groaned, his eyes closing on their own. "Fuck."

"Fuck bad or fuck good?" She froze and stared at him with wide eyes.

"Good, very good." He nodded, leaning his forehead against hers. "We should have gone to bed."

"Why?" Her brow creased against his skin, and he chuckled.

"Because doing what I want may drown me." He admitted as he slipped his hand between her thighs.

He saw a brief flicker of confusion in her eyes as she parted her legs for him, an unspoken question lingering there—one he wanted to answer with his touch. His fingers found what he was searching for, though uncertainty coiled in his gut. Inexperienced as he might have been, he had listened when other Watchers spoke of their escapades. He'd tucked away their words with quiet fascination, wondering and hoping for the chance to put them to use.

And then there she was. Faedi. In front of him, guiding him, trusting him.

He had dreamed of that moment and imagined what it might be like to touch her, to learn her body the way he knew her laughter, strength, and fire. But nothing—not his self-explorations, not his fleeting fantasies—could compare to the reality of her.

Once he found the spot, after she guided his hand with hers, he quickly learned she was one of the women who enjoyed such a touch. Her breath caught, and her back arched so sharply it made his chest ache. The sheer force of her reaction sent a thrill through him, a heady rush of something almost primal.

Her fingers flexed around him, her eyes fluttering half-shut, dazed with sensation. He watched every shift of her expression, awed by how vividly she responded to his touch.

He instinctively thrust into her hand, shuddering against her. Her touch burned through him, branding him in ways he never expected. He knew his body well enough and had sought his release in the quiet of the night, but with her—

everything was different. Her fingers were hesitant yet eager, exploring him with the same curiosity he had for her. And every hesitant brush of her skin against his stole the breath from his lungs.

Faedi made everything better.

The bath had become a world of its own—steam curling like breath around their bodies, mingling with his shadows. The scent of soap and crushed petals was thick in the air. Water sloshed gently as they moved, their soft laughter and gasps threading between the droplets clinging to their skin.

Ancients, he loved it. Loved how she looked at him. Loved how she felt under his hands. He loved her.

She was his gravity, his tether, his undoing. And if that was the only night they'd ever have—if fate tore them apart the next day—he knew it would be the moment he'd dream of. Not just the way her body molded to his or how her voice trembled, but the way she saw him: not as an heir of the Mire, not as a weapon, but as a man she wanted.

Their bodies moved instinctively, surrendering to the rhythm they created. Soft moans, whispered praises, hands grasping and teasing. Learning. He wanted to know every inch of her better than he already did.

And beneath it all, an ache settled in his chest—a deep, unshakable longing that had been there long before that moment. Because Faedi wasn't just someone he wanted. She was someone he'd always craved, in ways he was only beginning to understand.

Before long, he couldn't restrain his desires any longer. He pulled her wrist, making her let go of him, and hoisted her up to sit on the edge of the tub. Her skin prickled from the absence of the hot water, and he briefly hoped she wouldn't be too uncomfortable before he took her knees to spread her legs. As he moved closer, he stared up at her.

"Do you want to keep going?" His voice was low, rough with need.

Faedi exhaled a shaky breath, her gaze dark and full of something that made his stomach tighten and burn. "Yes."

That single word sent a sharp pulse of heat through him. Yes. She wanted it—she wanted him.

He swallowed hard, barely able to breathe past the way she looked at him—like he was something precious, something worth holding onto. His grip on her thighs tightened as he leaned forward, pressing his forehead to her soft skin for a brief, stolen moment as if it might steady him. But nothing could. Not when she was so close, bare and open to him, trusting him.

His heart pounded, his throat dry as he trailed his fingers along the inside of her thigh, smiling when she trembled under his touch again. He wanted to savor every second, to worship her in ways words could never capture.

Lonan pressed a kiss to her inner thigh first—slow, testing, reverent—like each inch of her was sacred. He wrapped his hands around her to pull her closer, burying his face between her thighs. When he finally parted her with his tongue, it was with the kind of devotion reserved for prayer.

Not long after, he found that nub with his tongue, her fingers tangled in his hair, and she writhed against him with each flick and suck. Her moans and gasps grew louder—his name was a song on her lips, and he gave thanks for it with every flick of his tongue.

Thank the Ancients we're not in the communal bath.

Someone certainly would have overheard them if they had gone there, and he did not want to be interrupted. He'd feast on her until the end of time if he could. Her taste was divine.

Each sound she made was music to his ears, fueling him to continue. He was so lost in her, ensuring she was pleased and content, that he never thought to pleasure himself while providing for her. The idea didn't cross his mind until his groin ached as she tugged his hair tighter and cried out, her body trembling.

He pulled away and looked at her as she whimpered, sliding her hand between them. Her cheeks were flushed, her eyes wide, and her lips parted as she gasped softly for air. Then she smiled, and he melted. The gods could not have made anything more beautiful than her.

"Take me to bed?" She asked softly.

He didn't need any more encouragement than that. He stood to lift her in his arms, and she quickly wrapped her arms around his shoulders, kissing him as he stepped out of the tub. They appeared at his bed without a thought, and he gently laid her down on the soft furs.

He took a moment to marvel at the sight of her. The dull light in the room made her damp skin glisten while her hair clung to her shoulders and neck. The eventides on her right arm seemed brighter, their soft blue petals shimmering with silver specks, and their scent was also more potent. She was nothing short of intoxicating.

"Are you ready?" He asked as he kneeled on the bed between her spread legs. "We can wait—"

"I asked you to bed me," she cut him off with a smile.

"Alright," he nodded, lowering himself over her and positioning himself at her entrance.

Anticipation filled him as he returned his eyes to hers. That look alone could have undone him, and it might have if he had stayed there. However, a heavy-handed knock rapped at his door before he could even begin.

"Are you two done fucking yet?"

Lonan buried his face against Faedi's shoulder with a groan. "I swear to the Ancients, I'm going to kill them."

Ancients, kill me now.

Warm light from the low hearth bathed the room in gold, and the scent of damp soap still clung to the air. On the bed, a black furball happily rolled into Faedi's lap and batted at her still-damp hair like a cat with yarn.

Yes, distract her with your cute ways, Faunling.

Lonan grumpily fastened his belt around his hips. Faedi laughed softly, a blanket haphazardly wrapped around her, as she scratched the bear cub. Myst, his sibling, sauntered over and sat beside her. If it weren't for their recent injury, he would've thrown them out of the room for their disturbance.

Ytna blessed you, dear Myst…

"It's been too long since you've visited Faedi," Myst said, settling beside her like they owned the room. "You're keeping my little brother out of trouble, right?"

"She's the one causing it," Lonan muttered and winked when Faedi shot him a glare.

Faedi scoffed, "hardly."

Myst smirked. "Mm. That tracks for both of you—always following chaos around like a lost pup."

Lonan narrowed his eyes at Myst. "Says the one who convinced me to jump off the mill roof into the river."

"And yet I'm the one who broke my leg," Myst replied, pointing to themselves as if they were proud. "You stuck the landing. Always did have too much luck—a child of Aasis."

"Trouble always seems to find us," Faedi sighed, glancing at him before turning her full attention to Myst. "How are you healing?"

"I was lucky to be brought home before too much damage could be done. Poor Espen here used all of their magic protecting me, though." Myst petted the bear cub, who playfully gnawed on Faedi's hand, and Lonan's gaze softened.

They're probably tired of Mam hovering.

"Rena said the blindness is permanent?" He asked gently.

"Mam says it is," Myst nodded, touching the black silk bandages wrapped around their face. "Espen lends me their sight, though. We will be alright."

"Of course you will be." Faedi nudged them, and Myst returned the gesture with more gusto.

"Why didn't you tell me you two finalized the bond?" Myst leaned forward like they were about to interrogate a criminal. "You know there's supposed to be a ceremony—firelight, rootwine, offerings to the ancestors. I was *supposed* to cry."

"Plenty of people enjoy each other's company before the bond is sealed," Lonan cut them off, rolling his eyes when Myst huffed. "We'll light the damn marks later."

"You're no fun," Myst sighed dramatically.

"It was a spur-of-the-moment thing," Faedi's cheeks flushed, and her fingers brushed the edge of the blanket in her lap. Her smile was small, but it reached her eyes when she looked at Lonan. "It just felt right."

"Wait." Myst held up a hand dramatically, like they were trying to calm a chaotic vision. "Don't tell me you weren't rutting like forest beasts in heat this whole time. Because if not, that's a true waste of secluded time and soft furs."

Lonan dragged his hand down his face with a groan. "Ytna's tits. Please stop speaking."

"I've never gone into heat—that's natural-born weres. I wasn't like this as a child," Faedi said between a fit of laughter.

Myst never questioned their assumptions about his future with Faedi, but Lonan didn't think they believed they spent all their time in bed. In hindsight, it would have been a welcome way to pass the idle hours, but he didn't regret the time they took to accept each other as lovers.

However, his sibling's sudden interruption was something he would change if he could.

"Well then," Myst stood and gathered Espen into their arms. "I suppose I should let you get dressed before dinner...I would pack, though, if I were you."

"Why?" Faedi sat up straighter on the bed, her smile gone. "We planned to stay and help."

"I overheard them talking—they think there's someone who can help, someone outside of the Mire. Papa said they might help if you go," Myst explained. "I tried to get more, but they started talking about refugees."

Lonan snapped his attention to his sibling. "Refugees from where?"

"They didn't say. Just that they were oath-bound to take them."

His jaw clenched, and he turned to look at Faedi. The only people they had an oath to were Dewgate. If they had called in on the oath, the situation was worse than he thought. The Mire didn't offer sanctuary lightly, and Dewgate had never asked for it before.

Faedi reached for his hand, squeezing it tightly. He didn't need to say the name—she already knew who came to his mind.

Ancients, let Ravyn be alright.

The next several hours passed in a blur, and before long, dinner was over.

Lonan hadn't heard a single word anyone said. All he knew was that Faedi had taken charge of retelling everything that had happened since Sophir had enlisted their help to find the caravans.

His mind drifted back to the last time he had seen the High Knight. He dug his fingers into his knees, recalling how the knight had stayed at the tree line, watching the survivors of the fight. There had been too great a distance between them for him to read the expression on his face, but he sensed something—maybe anger, given his reaction to Faedi's treatment of the animated corpse.

Maybe he realized there were too many Umbrals around to interrogate them again.

"We need the Dusk Elves' assistance."

Lonan blinked, focusing on his father as his words broke his thoughts. At first, he thought he might have misheard, but Faedi's wide-eyed expression told him he had heard right. They wanted help from the elves in the mountains—the same elves who had damned the Umbrals for years.

He was a child when the Dusk Elves withdrew. One day, their scouts and traders simply stopped crossing the borders. No messages. No reasons. Just silence, like the mountains had swallowed them whole. Rumors grew teeth— whispers of purists and bloodlines, of ancient laws twisted into something cruel. Lonan didn't need stories to know how they looked at Umbrals.

Like they were ghosts. Like they were mistakes.

"Why would they help?" He asked after a long sip of his wine. "The Dusk Elves hate us."

"Warden Torix told us King Haldin could be swayed," his mother answered softly.

"Torix?" Faedi squinted and shook her head. "What does he have to do with the Dusk Elves? They don't let anyone near their territory."

Lonan nodded in agreement with her. The King of the mountain killed any- one who trespassed on his land. They had ceased all trade with other countries, and most Dusk Elves who lived elsewhere had returned to the mountain. He hadn't seen more than a handful in at least fifteen years, maybe more.

"Torix is a Dusk Elf," Tagil said.

"No…he's a natural-born were-folk—and a Krelin," Faedi said, staring at him blankly. "The man has a tail."

"So do you," his mother countered.

"Because I'm Krelin—"

"Faedi, dear," his mother spoke softly, reaching across the table to take her hand. "You should talk to Torix in private. This subject is too much to come from an outside party."

Holding his breath, Lonan looked between them, the two most important women in his life. There was a hint of sadness in his mother's eyes, while con- fusion and anxiety rippled over Faedi. If there was one thing she hated, it was secrets. She often said they were as dangerous as lies, only kept when necessary.

"A secret is a knife, and I only trust myself and you with a blade."

He recalled her saying that when they had gone to Dewgate together to assist with the war. It was the same night she had been hit with an arrow while defending a Dewgate soldier. The third time he thought she might die.

He nudged her gently. "Do you want me with you?"

Faedi didn't flinch when he asked, but her shoulders pulled in just slightly. She didn't like not knowing things. Secrets were too close to chains in her eyes— gentle at first, but tightening with time.

Her tail twitched once, betraying the stillness in her face.

The calm she wore wasn't real. Lonan had seen it before, the same look she'd had in Dewgate when they told them the Mire's casualty reports had been doctored. She hadn't raised her voice then, either—just turned and walked out.

Three days later, the commander who lied to her had resigned without a word.

"I'll be alright," she shook her head and stood up from the table. "Where is he?"

"The library," his father answered, his voice softer than usual.

Faedi turned and gave him a small smile, but it didn't reach her eyes. Her anxiety washed over him, and even as her scent gradually vanished from the room with her departure, the dread in his gut remained. He started to go after her, but Myst's sudden hand on his shoulder stopped him.

"Someone tell me what's wrong," he growled. "Now."

He stared at his parents and his sibling, digging his fingers into the table. The wood splintered under the pressure as his nails sharpened to claws.

Myst's hand curled over his, not firm, just enough pressure to say "I'm here." It was the same way they had steadied him after his first shadowshift. His world had gone half-mad that night—his body not quite his own, his mind a storm. It had been Myst who pulled him back from the edge, sitting with him for hours in the charred remains of Faedi's home. Silent. Present. Steady.

That same calm flowed into him then, chasing the claws back into his hands.

As he calmed, his father refilled his cup. "Have some more wine, son."

He downed the wine, the tartness grounding him. Faedi was walking into something built on omission. If Torix was truly a Dusk Elf…what else had he been hiding from Faedi?

16
Beneath the Surface

Sophir

He had tried not to focus on the wars of the past during peacetime. He didn't want to remember the bloodshed or the sounds of death, but he couldn't shake the memory of a scream—one of raw terror—from years prior.

It was the same scream he'd heard when Lonan and Faedi ran to fight the cultists.

Dewgate's evening temple bell rang, snapping him from his thoughts as he walked through the forest side gate. The scent of fresh bread filled the air while shopkeepers pulled tables out in front of their storefronts, stacking them with various goods. Traders from other regions filtered through the gates, having been inspected by the guards, and were greeted warmly by the other merchants.

It was peaceful—the longest peace Dewgate had seen in a century. For ten years, the port city had remained untouched by those who coveted its resources or plotted strategic maneuvers against their enemies. His duties as High Knight had been simple until the hunt for the caravans began. Then everything changed, and he knew it wasn't for the better.

The time of peace was over—he knew it as soon as he saw the plagued man—the man who was meant to travel to Dewgate.

It had only been two days since they parted ways in the woods, but it felt like a lifetime. The screaming hadn't stopped echoing in his ears, and the stick of scorched flesh still clung to his cloak.

Was he attacked and plagued in the forest, or was he ill before he crossed the border?

He shifted the sword under his cloak and marched toward the Lord's manor through the cobblestone streets. If anyone in Dewgate might know how to manage a plague like the one he had witnessed, it was Lady Callon. She always had some sort of trick up her sleeve regarding bad news.

However, as he moved deeper into the city, the heaviness grew.

He searched the crowd and buildings for whatever might be the cause. Disheveled people scattered the alleyways, their faces covered by scarves. Each of their eyes was dark—almost hollow. However, before he could approach the nearest one, a flicker of gold caught his eye above the temple, and he froze when he saw a golden flame fixed to the tower—the flame of Ilos.

The flame glinted like a beacon of judgment, unmoving and unnatural in its brightness. It didn't belong there. It devoured the sky above the temple, and with it came the weight of centuries of dogma and war. His stomach churned.

That flame wasn't hope—it was a warning.

Sophir's eyes darted across the street, his pulse quickening. His thoughts churned as he turned his back on the unsettling sight and walked toward the nearest alley. A hand gripped his arm and pulled him into shadow.

"You're supposed to be in the Mire," a thick masculine drawl growled as he whipped around, ready to attack the hooded figure.

However, he stopped when the man lowered his hood to reveal his face. He had ashen gray skin, red eyes, pointed ears, and thick-lined tattoos on his neck. It was Ravyn, the Cinder Elf Guardian, who had sent him to Faedi and Lonan.

"I came back when we found one of the travelers sick with a plague," he hissed, raising his cloak's hood to mirror Ravyn's movement.

"They were supposed to take you to the Mire," the elf said through clenched teeth. "Lady Callon said a messenger would meet you and take you there."

"There was no messenger—just a plagued traveler. They ran off after Faedi burned him alive, and I took one of the cultist's weapons to bring it here—"

"Faedi burned someone?" Ravyn cut him off. His eyes widened, and he frowned when Sophir nodded. "Well, shit."

"That's more surprising than anything else I've said?" Sophir rolled his eyes. "Why wasn't I told about a plan for me to go to the Mire—where Lonan and Faedi were adamant I not go?"

"Not here." Ravyn shook his head and motioned for Sophir to follow him. "There are eyes and ears everywhere."

Sophir followed behind the elf through dark alleys, carefully watching the corners of buildings. As they walked, his mind drifted back to the defaced temple. There was no set religion as people from everywhere migrated to Dewgate, but the only temple was dedicated to the Ancients, and the cultists had tarnished it.

"There are some followers of certain paths that—what if someone wants to see that relationship fail?"

Lonan's words echoed in his mind. He thought back to how he and Faedi behaved, their secrecy and silent conversations in soul speech. He knew it was rude of him to listen to their discussions, but he needed information. He needed to see if they knew anything about the caravans, and they didn't seem to trust him.

The moment they realized he wore a glamour, they became just as suspicious of him as he was of them.

Their silent conversations hinted that they had something to hide. As he pictured the large gold flame on the temple, he realized why they were concerned. Lonan had asked about priests in Dewgate; they spoke of religious fanatics and danger.

Lonan always kept himself between Faedi and the campfire. She even hid behind him when she burned the plagued man, and she spoke of liars who smiled while they killed. Faedi said she relocated closer to the Mire after the raids—she believed The Order was responsible for them.

Other Guardians in Dewgate had thought the same, but there was never any proof.

Then, he recalled the expressions in her and Lonan's eyes when he protested her treatment of the plagued traveler. They thought he was an Orderling.

He'd judged them too quickly—let his suspicions speak louder than their fear. Maybe he thought himself better for staying calm, but calm had become complacency. And in that moment, he understood: he had heard, but he did not listen. Not to their words. Not to their warnings. And certainly not their pain.

I'm an idiot.

He pressed a hand to his temple, the dull throb behind his eyes pulsing in time with his heartbeat. It had started after he returned to Dewgate—small lapses at first. Names. Routes through the city. Faces of soldiers he'd served beside. Then the holes grew wider. Entire conversations lost. Memories that felt *edited*, as if someone had rearranged them while he slept.

He remembered the war clearly enough—the screaming, the smoke, the dying. But the years since settling in Dewgate were blurred around the edges, like a painting left out in the rain. Sometimes he caught glimpses of what was missing—flashes of symbols carved in light, voices whispering a language he knew but shouldn't.

It left him uneasy, always second-guessing what was real. Even Ravyn, the one person he trusted without question, couldn't quiet that gnawing doubt. Every time the elf was near, that same low hum stirred in the back of his skull—a sound that felt like magic recognizing itself.

He'd buried the truth of his blood long ago, sworn to hide the parts of himself that glowed when touched by power. But lately, the veil between what he was and what he pretended to be felt thin. Too thin.

Sophir remained silent, lost in his thoughts as Ravyn led him into his home and shut the door behind them. During the short walk, he replayed his interactions with Faedi and Lonan—including their silent conversations.

Their fear and concerns had been justifiable, and he knew he had done nothing to raise their confidence in him. Had he stopped and listened, Faedi wouldn't have anchored him to the ground while she burned the corpse.

Stupid.

He dragged a hand down his face and grumbled but paused when Ravyn grabbed his shoulder and turned him to face him. The stern expression on Ravyn's face didn't reveal what to expect, and Sophir almost held his breath, waiting to see what he would do. If Ravyn wanted to strike him, he wouldn't stop him—he deserved that much, at least.

His grip wasn't harsh—but there was steel in it. He wasn't just angry. He was scared. For Faedi. For Lonan. Sophir's thoughts drifted to something he had heard between Lonan and Faedi while Ravyn looked him up and down.

"A friend that blushes when he looks at you."

"He blushes when he looks at you, too."

"Did you touch the corpse? The ground it poisoned?" Ravyn's question snapped Sophir's attention back to him, and he silently shook his head. His eyes narrowed, as though he didn't believe him. "Take your clothes off. I need to be sure you're not infected."

Sophir's brow creased as he shook his head again. "I'm not infected."

"Prove it." Ravyn took a step in his direction, daring him. "Not like I haven't seen you naked before."

Sophir's mind briefly flashed back to the time Ravyn had seen him without his clothes, without his defenses. It had been a different time—just when his life became complicated. Just after Blavier sank his claws into him.

Blavier's voice still echoed in the back of his mind, a cruel command dressed as duty. He hadn't forgotten the night he was ordered to the chamber where Lady Callon waited, pale-faced and trembling, forced into performance for a tyrant's amusement.

They had both known what was coming when Blavier joined them. The weight of that night had carved itself into his bones, and it was Ravyn who found him afterward—shaking, stripped of everything but shame. Ravyn had touched him like he was still whole. That night between them had never been about desire—it had been about anchoring a drowning man.

He remembered the brief, uncomfortable silence after, the way Ravyn's eyes had traced his skin, as if trying to figure out a puzzle. Then there was the pity, as if he could see the corruption Blavier left behind in his wake.

Since then, Ravyn and Lady Callon were the only two people in the city he trusted. Perhaps that was why he couldn't find a way to trust Faedi and Lonan—even if he should have.

Sophir sighed and began to remove his armor, then his clothes, while trying to ignore Ravyn's eyes on him. He was right; Ravyn had seen him before, but it had been under entirely different circumstances, and he didn't like the idea of being examined. He'd had enough of that from Lonan and Faedi.

Ravyn didn't waste any time examining him, his eyes glowing like Faedi's had while he checked every inch of Sophir for signs of the plague curse. He wondered if it was something only Guardians could do, but he didn't ask.

Sophir tried not to flinch at his touch—clinical though it was—but the warmth of his fingers stirred a familiar flutter in his chest. Ravyn's presence had always unsettled him, not out of fear but because of the things he made him feel when the world was quiet.

Ravyn hummed to himself as he stood, a soft sound that made Sophir raise his eyebrows. "Well?"

"You better not be hiding something under that glamour of yours." Ravyn's voice was sharp as he warned him before stepping closer. "Are you?"

Sophir frowned. "You know I'm not."

Ravyn's eyes narrowed again, and he took a moment to examine Sophir's face. "I want you to leave in the morning," he said, his voice softening as he tilted his head to the side. "Go to the Mire—we're sending people there."

Sophir didn't like the tone of his voice. It was too close to a goodbye.

"You always look for answers in other people's choices," Ravyn said quietly. "But this time, Sophir, you need to make your own. The Mire will need you—Faedi and Lonan might need you. And if you stay here…I'm not sure I'll be able to protect you from what's coming."

His words sank into him, more than any physical blow. His words were too final, too sure. If he stayed, what would it mean for him? For Ravyn? A bitter pang hit his chest. Ravyn knew something he didn't.

His shoulders stiffened. "What about you?"

"I have my path," Ravyn answered, taking another step. His chest brushed against Sophir's when he inhaled. "I'll be around when you get back." His voice was soft, but Sophir heard the tremor in it—a rare crack in his otherwise unshakable calm.

The scent of iron and fire filled Sophir's senses as he studied Ravyn's face. He smelled more like a smith than the stableman he was. There was a forge on the property, but Sophir had never seen him use it.

Slowly, he tilted his head to the side and examined the soot stains on Ravyn's neck. "What are you up to, Ravyn?"

"Preparing for *his* flames." Ravyn's gaze darkened and glanced down at Sophir's still-bare body. "I have gear for you. You shouldn't wear Dewgate armor when you leave."

Sophir watched Ravyn's cheeks flush and chuckled. "Do you plan on giving it to me before I catch a cold?"

"You won't catch a cold," Ravyn promised before his lips crashed into Sophir's.

Sophir's breath caught as the kiss grounded him. In that moment, it was just the two of them—everything else blurred into the background. Everything could wait, just for a while, before they moved forward into the flames.

We need to unwind.

"The cultists took over the day after you left."

Sophir watched as Ravyn poured ale into a mug and sat across from him. The fire in the hearth beside them crackled, and he was dressed again in the new studded armor Ravyn had provided him. He couldn't help but wonder how Faedi always flinched whenever the campfire popped. Lonan always soul-spoke to her in those moments—calming phrases or simple questions.

"And no one resisted?" Sophir finally forced himself to ask as Ravyn slid a plate of food toward him.

"Their priests came with winter supplies—people don't resist when they don't see a threat," Ravyn sighed. "Lady Callon knew it was coming. She's been sending their usual targets to the Mire for the last few weeks. Wardens and Guardians delayed their returns from patrols. I warned them to stay away when she said it was time."

"And you sent me to them without telling me because?" Sophir tore off a piece of bread and took a bite.

He leaned back in his seat, holding his mug to his chest. "We both know if you'd known what was coming, you would have fought. Then Dewgate would be nothing but ashes with plagued corpses."

He didn't argue. Because he would have fought. And he would have lost more than the city.

Sophir rubbed his forehead with a sigh. "So you knew about the plague?"

"They've changed it since they used it in Valoria, but yes. Some of us— Guardians and Wardens—saw the plague during the raids. We thought they were survivors, just ill with infection, but..." Ravyn trailed off and took a sip of his ale. "Then the fevers came—their eyes turned black and they started weeping black blood."

"There was no cure," Sophir finished for him with a sigh. "Faedi said burning them was the only option."

"She isn't wrong. Once they reach that point, scorching their remains and everything they touched is the only way to prevent it from spreading."

It seemed like Ravyn knew far more than Sophir did—more than the High Knight of the city. "And no one told me because?"

"Lord Blavier appointed you as High Knight—oath to The Ancients or not. Lady Callon worried you might not uphold them," Ravyn explained slowly, almost apologetically.

"It seems I'm a good suspect. You, Lady Callon, Lonan, and Faedi..." Sophir turned his attention to the food. It might be his last meal if the cultists decided to purge the city. "I thought Lord Blavier listened to Lady Callon. He's always taken her opinion seriously at council meetings."

"He did, until a priest gave him visions of darkness taking over the city.

They told him the Mire would see Dewgate starve and freeze."

"I don't know of many seers who can show people their visions," Sophir mused, looking out the window. "Even Lady Callon can't do that."

"But there are people who can show you the fears you have brought to life."

Sophir leaned forward, bracing his forearms on the table as he processed everything. Even if he hated it, their concerns and actions were valid. He had been outspoken about some of Lord Blavier's policies but had never acted beyond his words.

"If he doesn't listen to her…is she safe?" He asked, gesturing vaguely toward Ravyn. "And you? Why didn't you evacuate with the refugees or leave to regroup with the other Guardians?"

"She's being held prisoner." Ravyn shook his head, his gaze darkening. "I stayed just in case you came back. The Orderlings won't bother me; I've been purified."

Sophir froze. He didn't ask what that meant—mostly because he wasn't sure he wanted to know. He'd heard enough horror stories about Valoria to know that whatever happened wasn't kind.

"They've replaced the city watch and soldiers," Ravyn added grimly. "Took their oaths, wore their colors. Most citizens here haven't noticed, but they will— once the gates close for good."

They ate in silence for a while until Ravyn eventually asked how the trip had gone. His concern was more focused on Faedi and Lonan's well-being than on what they had found. It was almost as though he already knew about the plague. His eyes widened when Sophir mentioned the Myst individual he had heard Lonan tell Faedi about. The sudden shift in their mood that night made sense when Ravyn explained that Myst was Lonan's sibling and was supposed to be their messenger.

"Lonan said they were blinded," Sophir finished his ale. "Faedi dragged him off after that."

He watched Ravyn's eyes widen before his brow creased. It seemed Ravyn knew Myst as well as he knew Lonan and Faedi, and Sophir couldn't help but wonder what his relationship with them was. He had never spoken about anyone from the forest before, yet here he was with connections Sophir knew nothing about.

"What is your relationship with them?" Sophir asked carefully, swirling his empty cup. "They're both fond of you."

Ravyn shook his head and poured more ale for him. "We're friends."

There was more than that, Sophir knew he was holding back. He leaned forward and rose his eyebrows, silently asking for more.

Ravyn chuckled, some light returning to his eyes. "I've known them well since the war but met them in passing before then." Then, his smile grew as he leaned forward—one elbow braced on the table. "Why? Are you jealous?"

Sophir scoffed and rolled his eyes. "Why would I be jealous of you having other friends?"

Ravyn chuckled and leaned forward to brace his forearms on the table. "Are you worried that I might have passed on lycanthropy to you?" His smile grew when Sophir wrinkled his nose. "They're just good friends."

"We're good friends," Sophir countered with a smirk.

Ravyn didn't smile right away. His fingers tightened around the mug, just slightly. Sophir saw it—a flicker in his eye and crease between his brows. There was something he wasn't telling him, but he didn't push him for an answer.

"They—" Ravyn started but was cut off when someone pounded on his door. "Well, fuck. Pull your cloak up."

He left the table and approached the door, pausing to grab an axe and holding it behind his back. His grip was tight—tighter than Sophir had ever seen—knuckles went white, and his jaw ticked once before he schooled his features.

Sophir turned and faced the table as soon as he saw torchlight. He held his breath when Ravyn asked why they were there, so he could better hear their response.

"One of the maids overheard Lord Blavier. He permitted them to cleanse keepers of dark wildlife—they killed the farmers who left. Your Krelin friend has creatures at their cottage, right?"

"When did they leave?" There was a scuffle on the floorboards before the door shut. "Tell me."

Sophir stared at his empty mug, still in his hand, tracking the time he had spent with them. It had taken nearly an entire day for him to reach the cottage on foot after he left Dewgate, and he arrived at midnight. They were on the forest trails for two days before they separated. He assumed they would have rested after fighting the cultists in the forest. However, he didn't know if they went with The Watch to the Mire or returned home after.

"They rode out before the evening bell."

Sophir glanced out the window beside the hearth and stared at the sky. They had a four-hour head start, and he had no idea what mounts they were on. He knew Lonan and Faedi had wolves that could cover great distances if allowed to run free. If they returned home after the fight, they would already be there if they left at first light. They would be asleep when the cultists inevitably set their home on fire.

She'll lose everything again.

The mug shattered in his hand.

17
Roots of the Tide

"She knew something, but wouldn't tell me. How is she an outside party? She's been in my life longer than Torix ever was…I don't know if I can look at him."

Faedi

The air in the hall was cold, scented faintly with parchment and the lingering smoke of blown-out lanterns. Each step scraped against the ancient floor like a knife dragged through stone.

In her experience, footsteps were always louder when they marched toward bad news.

She should have known the people lost in the woods were up to no good when the leaves crunched too loudly under her bare feet—they had never made that sound before. Just hours earlier, when she raced away from the inferno behind her, those same leaves had been silent. Her boots during the war had only scuffed against rocks when soldiers attacked them by surprise. And the floorboards in the greenhouse had creaked the day they left with Sophir.

She paused at the library door, her hand hovering over the knob as she stared at the dark wood grains. Torix's scent lingered just behind it. He was there; he hadn't left, and she was supposed to talk to him.

Torix remembers me, but he isn't happy to see me. Why would he be, though?

Her heart sank as she closed her eyes and opened the door with her head lowered. If he had any information that might help the Mire, she would hate herself if she walked away. A moment's discomfort would be worth it if she could help Lonan's people.

A chair scraped the floor, and papers fluttered nearby, but she didn't look up. Instead, she shut the door behind her and leaned against the wood for stability.

Waiting. If Torix was anything like she remembered, he wouldn't speak unless he genuinely wanted to.

She watched shadows dance on the floor from the lantern's light until a larger one swallowed them as Torix approached. The tops of his boots were barely in her sight until she looked away.

"You look like her," his sudden gruff voice made her flinch.

She glanced up at him before quickly turning her attention to the rows of shelves. "Who?"

"Your mother," Torix elaborated, his tone softening. "I thought you were her in the forest for a moment."

She noticed the herbology book wasn't where it was supposed to be; someone had shoved it next to religious texts. She huffed and walked over to retrieve the book and put it back where it belonged. Torix remained where he stood, his eyes boring into her back.

"Tagil said those Eventides grow on you."

"They do," she confirmed with a nod.

"Did you know they were wiped out of the Mire?" He raised his eyebrows at her when she glanced over her shoulder. "Endi brought them here with her when a fever came. I didn't think they could be re-cultivated, but she proved me wrong."

She glanced down at her arm, remembering the vines that grew over their house and how every breeze filled her room with their scent. They didn't smell as pleasant when they burned.

"They mask your scent well now," he told her. "I thought you were a ghost sent to haunt me."

She studied his expressions carefully; he was too hard to read. "Why didn't you say something?"

His hand rubbed the back of his neck, slow and tired—like the motion was muscle memory from years of worn-out apologies. "At first, I thought I was going insane. Then came the guilt when you said my name." His arm dropped. "I tried to find you—and the bastards that got away—for years. How could I hope to find you, only to tell you that I didn't slaughter everyone responsible?"

"You shouldn't feel guilty." She leaned against the bookshelf, her gaze dropping to the floor. "I'm the one who took them there."

The words fell like stones into a bottomless well. No matter how many times she replayed that night, she always ended up there—at the moment she opened her arms to strangers and let evil into her home.

She hadn't told anyone besides Lonan—not another soul in seven and ten years.

"What?" He straightened, steps quiet as he moved closer.

"They were lost—or they said they were. They weren't wearing armor, didn't have any weapons… one of them was bleeding and…" She quickly wiped away the tears that stung her eyes. "And I took them home. I thought—"

She didn't hear him move over the sobs that rose like a tide—couldn't see through her tear-blurred vision. She only felt it—his arms, solid and careful, wrapping around her. He cradled her head to his chest like he used to, as if she hadn't grown. As if she could still be saved by being held.

Torix didn't speak. He didn't growl. He simply was—present and steady as the world crumbled around her again.

When her knees buckled, he moved with her, lowering them both to the cold floor. He tucked her hair behind her ears, hands rough but gently, and rubbed her back as her sobs softened.

"It wasn't your fault," he whispered. "You did what you've always done. You tried to help them, and they took advantage of your good heart—of your mother's heart."

She whimpered as the tears threatened to begin again. "But I took them there."

The pain twisted deeper, testing her resolve. She'd learned how to grieve in silence—holding herself together while the world crumbled. But there, in Torix's arms, some small part of her dared to believe she could fall apart and still be caught.

"If you hadn't, they would have killed you, and the raids still would have happened." He wiped under her eyes. "You would not have escaped and called The Hunt, and more people would have died."

She shook her head. "The Hunt didn't come."

"We did. All of us did," he frowned. "But we were too far. The raids were too well planned; they knew the forest-folk were comfortable and unguarded. They were too fast and organized. There was no evidence I could take to King Haldin to preserve his relationship with the Mire."

Why would the Dusk Elf king care about raids in the Sauvern?

They hadn't occurred in Rowdon; his people weren't in danger. Unless Torix thought they might have their eyes set on the mountain next. Ilos' light was always targeted at creatures of the dark.

"Why would you take them there?" She forced herself to ask after a shaky breath.

He hesitated, his gaze heavy with a weight Faedi couldn't name.

"Because your mother was a Dusk Elf," his eyes met hers, and she froze. "Endi was Haldin's daughter."

Her breath hitched.

Torix didn't flinch. His arms stayed loose at his sides, but a tightness clung to his shoulders, like he expected her to bolt—or strike.

She stared at him. Her mother had always looked like a Krelin. So did she. Short and soft gray fur, dark nose, dark eyes. The only difference was she had a tail and her mother didn't.

"Then how do I look like a Krelin? Unless you're going to tell me that I'm adopted—"

"You're not," he said firmly. "She used a glamour. She chose the Krelin face because it meant safety. Because no one would look at a soft-furred family, known for their peaceful ways in the woods, and think they came from Haldin's blood."

He looked older. Not in years, but in wear—like the forest had carved him into something unyielding, and guilt had etched its story in the lines beneath his eyes. "I held you first." He added, his voice tight. "Endi was shaking. She thought she'd lose you and Syl. But when you cried, she wept like the Ancients had blessed her."

Her eyes narrowed. "Then why didn't anyone say anything?"

"To protect everyone," He said, eyes flicking to the closed door as if he half-expected someone to eavesdrop. "If enemies of the Tide found out who you were…it would have been worse than the fire."

"The Tide?" She echoed, clutching her arm.

"Eventides." He gestured to her vines. "They're the symbol of your house and their oaths to the Ancients."

The vines itched as if they, too, could feel the tension building. When she flexed her fingers, the stems curled gently as though reacting to her unease. She stared at them, she'd always seen them as an oddity or accidental result of her bond with Lonan, and inched her head to the side.

They're only there because I had seeds in my pocket.

Faedi let her arms fall, staring into the flickering shadows between the shelves. "And there are more enemies than just cultists?"

"Far more." He stepped away, slowly pacing, like the truth unsettled even him. "Ilos' zealots are manipulators. Their roots spread wide. You'll find sympathizers in places you'd never expect."

She shivered and hugged herself. Her mother's reasons for hiding made more sense. But Haldin's hatred of the Mire still didn't.

"If I go up the mountain…" Her voice wavered. "Will Haldin help the Mire?"

Torix stopped pacing. "He'll do what he can. But his oaths bind him to the mountain. He can't leave it undefended."

"The mountain is at risk from Orderlings too?" She turned to study his face.

"Anywhere that houses creatures of darkness is a target…but I was warned the Mire might be a distraction. For now," his jaw clenched. "They don't want to repeat their mistakes in Valoria."

She flinched. She didn't need the details—not when she knew what the plague could do. The Order craved destruction in the name of purification.

Faedi paced the length of her bedroom with a glass of wine in hand before stepping onto the balcony. Her mother, the kind and wild-haired woman who danced barefoot in the forest, had been a princess of the Dusk Elves. She had left the mountains to honor the alliance between her father and the Umbrals, to help protect their home, and to aid her people in returning to theirs.

The treaty between the Umbramire and Dewgate had not been between the Umbrals and the free city. Lonan's ancestors had sworn an oath to her ancestors—to protect the Dusk Elves' ancestral home until they could leave the mountains and return. Someone had stolen Dewgate from the Dusk Elves centuries ago, erasing the true ownership from history.

But why?

Torix didn't have the answers. He claimed even her mother hadn't known why history had erased the Dusk Elves from Dewgate. Her grandfather, whose daughter's murder had caused him to break his alliance with the Umbrals, had been involved. The daughter, whom Lonan's parents had known as a Krelin, had been a Dusk Elf.

Torix had told her that they hid their identities, along with the identities of her father, brother, and herself, when they had made their home in the forest. He had been her mother's sworn protector, a wolf of the crown, and her departure from the mountain had been with King Haldin's blessing. But when soldiers from Ashar had attempted to lay siege to the mountain, starting a decade-long war, her mother had been told to remain safe in the forest.

Then Asharian zealots had tracked them down in the forest. The war had come to them.

Afterward, King Haldin had closed the Rowdon borders, moved his people into the mountains, and killed anyone who dared step on the snow. He had damned the Umbrals for failing to keep their oath to protect his heirs.

But they hadn't known who she was until Torix had told them—they had never made an oath.

"Faedi? Can I come in?" Lonan's voice broke through her thoughts, and she turned to look at the door.

"It's unlocked," she called back.

The bedroom door opened slowly, and Lonan stepped inside, shutting the door behind him. They stared at each other for several breaths before he swiftly moved in front of her, pressing his forehead against hers as he wrapped his arms around her.

"They told me what Torix said," his whisper tickled her face. "Are you alright?"

"If he meets me…maybe King Haldin will help against the cultists." She didn't look at him when she said it—didn't want to see her doubt in his eyes reflected back at her. "He might help his heir."

He frowned and pulled away, shaking his head. She knew he hated when she avoided his questions, but she didn't know how to answer him. She didn't know if she was alright. Her mind had fractured beneath the weight of everything Torix revealed, the edges of each thoughts dulled by shock.

"There might be another way to fight the cultists. We don't have to go to Rowdon. Maybe Lady Callon knows something to help," Lonan suggested, though doubt laced his voice. "The Dusk Elves could kill us before we even reach the King."

She sighed, fastening a button he'd missed on his shirt. "Torix said he would travel ahead and leave a safe path."

He tilted his head to meet her gaze. "Do you want to go?"

"We can see the lights," she managed to give him a small smile. "And we're good at being sneaky."

Lonan fell silent, studying her face. His violet eyes moved over her, and she could feel his worry ripple off him like a river's current. But they both knew it was the only option that might provide a solution for the cultists. They had to go to the mountains.

A messenger couldn't share her existence, not even by Torix. She would have to be seen to be believed.

"They said your mother had a glamour on you," he told her. "One to make you pass off as a Krelin. Mam said it must be powerful if she can't remove it."

"Torix said the glamour was woven into my blood. That maybe Haldin can break it." She touched her forehead as if the magic still pulsed there, coiled beneath her skin like a secret waiting to wake.

"So…" He took her hands and led her to sit on the bed before refilling her wine. "We follow Torix's trail through the mountains, see King Haldin, and… hopefully he helps."

"I want to stop at the cottage and send what supplies we have to Dewgate for the winter. We didn't find the caravans, so what furs and food we had should go to the poor there. Ravyn can make sure they're taken care of," she told him, hoping the detour wouldn't take too long.

"I was thinking of going back there anyway. That picture you have of your family is hidden in the chest beside the bed. We should take that," he squeezed her knee gently.

She bit her lip and stared at the floor. "Torix didn't blame me…but what if Haldin does?"

"Then we leave," Lonan said, his voice firm but playful. "Kill some cultists. Have our ceremony so Myst can cry. And your grandfather? Definitely not on the guest list."

He nudged her shoulder like he hadn't just mapped out a war followed by a wedding.

She laughed softly and shook her head. He really did have all the essential parts figured out. Survive, save the day, and have their bonding ceremony. It sounded simple when put that way, even if she knew the first task would be the most difficult.

Cultists. Mountains. Her grandfather.

It wasn't just survival—it was walking into the jaws of every nightmare she'd inherited. Only then they could celebrate and get married.

Wait…he still wants to complete the bond?

She stared at him, her jaw slack as she tried to piece the question together.

She'd never known Lonan to be prejudiced against Dusk Elves, but he was an Umbral prince, and she was supposedly a princess of people who hated his. "You—"

"We should leave tonight," he blurted. "If more cultists are coming, the cottage won't be safe for long."

"Torix said he would take the river path before going south. I can catch his trail from there," she set down her wine glass with a nod.

"Alright then," Lonan stood and offered her his hand. "Let's go get our supplies. We'll take Umbral mounts and let the wolves rest."

She stared up at him momentarily, then sighed as she smiled. His support meant more to her than she could express. She knew he had a drive to protect his home, just as she did, but he also supported her. He was willing to avoid an actual chance at help if it meant she would be comfortable, and she didn't think she could ever repay him for that.

18

Under the Ancients' Eyes

"Everything is fine. We were going to go to Emsmeda anyway to see the lights. Maybe they'll be brighter on the mountain, and Faedi will enjoy them more. She needs a good reason to smile."

Lonan

It didn't take long to pack their supplies; they were accustomed to traveling light. However, he was sure to include warm clothes and sturdy new boots. He wasn't certain if their other gear would be enchanted in time, but he would get supplies from the armory anyway.

No one would stop him.

He held Faedi's hand as they walked through the black flame-lit hallways, a pack slung over his shoulder. They needed preserved food, he told himself. If they were going to send all their supplies from the cottage to Dewgate, they had to make sure they had enough to eat. He wasn't sure how the hunting was in the Rowdon mountains, and he knew there wouldn't be much when they reached the peaks.

"What do we know about Dusk Elves and were-folk? I know Torix is one, but…" He trailed off, frowning. It was dangerous enough for him to go as an Umbral—they might try to kill him on sight.

"I don't know," Faedi shook her head and squeezed his hand. "If Torix thinks my being an heir could persuade them, maybe it won't matter? I didn't think to ask him about that… we could try to find him before we go?"

"That might be a good idea. Admittedly, I don't know much about them," he said, giving her an apologetic shrug.

"I know my mother told me stories, but I don't know how much good they'll do. Everything she said felt more like… history. Maybe fantasies? I don't know," she sighed, lowering her head.

Her nightmares are going to come back.

It had been a while since she had woken up screaming—reliving the death of her family—but Lonan didn't think she would be lucky enough to avoid the dreams for much longer. Not with so many reminders coming into her life one after another.

"You'll have to tell me these stories on the way." He nudged her lightly.

He smiled when she did—until movement in the doorway ahead made him stiffen. His mother waited at the turn toward the armory, arms full, eyes bright with mischief and something more.

Of course, she knew.

He grinned sheepishly at her and bowed his head as they approached. He hoped she wouldn't make a fuss, but he wouldn't blame her for being worried. Serving in The Watch and living alone with Faedi was nothing like facing cultists who killed anything that got in their way.

"Trying to sneak away without saying goodbye?" She asked with a smile that eased some of his worries.

"We were going to say goodbye," he told her, letting go of Faedi's hand to lean over and kiss his mother's cheek. "Faedi has a picture of her family at the cottage we can show the King, and we wanted to send our stores to Dewgate before we follow Torix."

She offered him the large bundle in her arms and stepped back, looking between them. Her expression shifted—something fleeting and sharp, like sorrow dressed in pride—but it disappeared the moment he noticed. Lonan blinked, unsure if he imagined it, but the weight in his chest told him he hadn't.

"Mam," he shifted the bundle of gear in his arms. "What's wrong?"

"Even if it's for a good cause, I don't like sending my son into danger. Torix will get you an audience with King Haldin, but that won't protect you from cultists or whatever else the gods want to test you with. I want to see you, both of you, back here healthy and whole," she said. "Mothers worry, Wisp."

"I'll keep us off the common trails," Faedi promised. "Even if the Dusk Elves don't help, we'll be back soon and devise another plan."

"I never wanted to see any of my children in war," she sighed, holding Faedi's shoulders. "I want all of you safe."

"I won't let them hurt you the way they hurt me," Faedi's voice trembled.

Lonan watched his mother wrap her arms around Faedi and lowered his head again. He hated that she blamed herself and hated that his mother worried, but he knew he couldn't stop either of them from feeling their emotions. Even if he shared his mother's sentiments, he wished the world were better for them— that no one had to suffer.

"Maybe you could…start planning the ceremony?" He offered gently. "Something to focus on, after all this with The Order?" He didn't say *in case we don't come back,* but the thought stuck in his throat all the same.

"That would certainly boost my morale," his mother said, narrowing her eyes as she whispered, "I will hope to see it come to pass."

Before he could question her wording, Faedi nudged him with her elbow and raised her eyebrows.

She grinned at him, her cheeks darkening. *"If she's worried, we could do it before we leave."*

"Do you want to?" He inched his head to the side. *"I don't want you to feel pressured or—"*

"Am I making you feel pressured?" She quickly countered with a mischievous grin.

Dammit, Liru.

He chuckled and shook his head. Just when he thought he understood all her edges, Faedi tilted the world again.

"If you have time to plan something quickly," he turned his attention back to his mother. "We could have a ceremony before we leave. Nothing too large to take away from preparations or our defenses, just us—and Torix."

The lines of anxiety on his mother's face instantly vanished as she clapped her hands together and smiled. He shook his head when she quickly hugged both of them and kissed their cheeks, immediately rattling off the things that would be needed. She summoned one of the armory staff to take their items and put them in the stables before motioning for them to start down the hall.

"We'll need to get to work, then. I'll have someone fetch Torix, and then we can—Faedi, dear, do you want someone to paint you instead? I don't know if your grandfather will—"

"If the Dusk Elf King doesn't want to help the Mire because I took traditional Umbral markings when I bonded myself to the Umbral Prince, his head is up his ass and is no family of mine." He glanced at Faedi, his eyes widening. "Paint washes away. My bond is not temporary; my markings shouldn't be either."

"Spoken like a true Umbral," Lonan said, pride blooming in his chest like firelight.

"Indeed." His mother echoed, her smile soft with approval.

Lonan paced the length of the main hall, staring at the backs of his hands. His still skin itched from the magic his mother had used to create the bonding tattoos—small dots that would eventually form into full markings once his bond with Faedi was complete.

If she didn't change her mind.

He shouldn't have worried; he knew she wouldn't second-guess her decision, but his stomach twisted as he walked from one end of the hall to the other. He turned on his heels to walk the same path again.

"Oh, my Wisp," his mother sighed from her place against the wall. "Your father did this before we were bonded."

"He did?" He stopped and looked over his shoulder at her. "How do you know?"

"I watched him from that doorway." She pointed to a door beside the staircase.

He chuckled. "You wanted him to sweat to death?"

"I wasn't sure if he wanted to be bonded. Our match was arranged," she said, approaching to take his hands. "We were lucky; love came easy. You and Faedi are different, though. The love is already there. You've grown together, both in and out of the bond. You protect and understand each other in ways even fully bonded matches can't. This ceremony is just a show for something you two achieved years ago."

"She's been through so much already," he sighed, shaking his head. "I don't want this to hurt her. If the cultists—"

"Gods forbid something happens to either of you," she interrupted, her gaze softening. She knew where his mind wandered without him saying it. "If the worst happens and either of you is left alone, you'll carry centuries of regret for not doing this. If that happens, you'll have this to comfort yourselves instead of an aching regret that you didn't do it when you could."

"Is that why you said you wanted to see this? Because you don't want regrets?" He whispered, his voice barely above a breath.

"I don't want anyone to regret missing this day. When it comes to battle, hopes do not keep us alive."

He pulled his hands away from hers and wrapped his arms around her. Mothers worry, she always said, and he hoped it was just anxiety. She had an uncanny sense of knowing things, and he worried she might have chosen to hide something from him. But he knew she would deny it if he asked.

Fate couldn't be changed, she told him.

"You will be happy together," she said as she squeezed him. "All of you will be."

He smiled as he pulled away and kissed her cheek. Just then, footsteps echoed in the hall, and he looked at the main entrance as his father and Myst entered, both wearing bright smiles. Espen waddled behind them, and he laughed when the cub bounded at him, demanding to be petted.

I wish her family was here.

Shaking off the sting of that thought, he scratched between the cub's ears. At least Faedi had Torix with her. She wasn't completely alone; even if her family didn't come, his accepted her. He hoped that was good enough for her.

"She is on her way with Torix," Tagil told him.

"She is?" His attention snapped away from the cub. "Is she… I mean—"

"She's fine," Myst patted his shoulder. "Don't worry. Espen let me peek, and Torix is even smiling in a strange…unsettling way. It might've been gas."

"It was a smile, I assure you," his mother sighed, rolling her eyes.

Following her instructions, he moved to stand in the center of the room as more footsteps reached the hall. There was no fanfare, no one from The Watch, or even guards in the area to witness it, and he knew Faedi would be relieved without a large group. He didn't want a fuss, either.

His heart stopped, just for a moment, when Torix stood in the doorway, offering out his arm. Then, the world moved in slow motion as Faedi stepped into view. Like him, she was dressed for travel, but the way her golden eyes shone under her fur-lined hood made him hold his breath.

Her cloak dipped low, exposing her chest, just as his untied shirt did, and her sleeves were rolled up above her elbows, revealing her hands and arms. She smiled shyly at him as she approached, lowering her head before Torix whispered something. He saw a flicker of something on her face before she returned her gaze to his.

His hands trembled as Torix placed hers into his, and heat rushed to his cheeks when he realized her hands were also shaking.

"Ready?" He managed, smiling when she quickly nodded, her lips bitten together.

"Tonight, before the eyes of the Ancients and our cherished kin, we gather to witness the union of these two souls. As you speak, know the Gods will mark your words with their eternal blessing," his father's voice echoed through the room, drowning out the sound of his pounding heart. "Speak now and let your hearts and souls be bound."

The room was quiet, save for the remaining echo of his father's voice, which seemed to reverberate off the walls, growing louder despite the absence of words. He watched the gentle smoke of incense wrap around Faedi, wrapping around her head almost like a halo, and it wasn't until she blinked up at him with her wide eyes that he realized he was supposed to start the vows.

"I, Lonan Tagilson," he paused and breathed, chuckling at himself. "Pledge my unwavering love and devotion to you, Faedi Lirulin…"

His voice wavered at the start, a breath caught somewhere between love and fear. His hands shook as he held hers, but the trembling wasn't just from nervousness—it was from the weight of what he was about to promise her. His eyes never left Faedi, trying to lock the moment into his memory, trying to hold on to the reality that she was there, with him, in that moment.

All while trying to ignore the low growl from Torix.

"From this day forward, I vow to stand by your side through joy and sorrow, prosperity and hardship. I promise to be your shield, confidant, and partner—to grow with you as we wander together through life's paths."

As he spoke, he watched Faedi's eyes travel down to his chest, light dancing in her eyes. When he finished his vows, her gaze returned to his, and she smiled.

"I, Faedi Lirulin, pledge my eternal trust and companionship to you, Lonan Tagilson." He glanced down as she spoke her vows, watching her chest and hands glow as patterns formed on her exposed skin. "From this day forward, I vow to stand beside you, support and uplift you, and share your dreams. I promise to be your shield, confidant, and partner—to grow with you as we wander together through life's paths."

In unison, they smiled and breathed before reciting their final vows.

"Together, we are stronger. Together, we are whole. Our spirits are bound; our hearts are one. Under the eyes of the Ancients and our most precious kin, we seal this bond tonight forevermore."

As they spoke the last words, the lit markings on their bodies shimmered before dulling, leaving behind tattoos on their arms, chests, and necks. He reached forward and traced his index finger over the line that trailed onto her chin, smiling. She was his, and he was hers.

Finally.

The silence stretched between them for a heartbeat, a moment where time itself seemed to hold its breath. His chest tightened, and for the first time since they'd met, he allowed himself to feel the weight of their connection, their bond.

Faedi's smile was brighter than the candles in the room, and for that moment, everything else faded away.

II
Scattered Embers

19

His Golden Flames

"Get everything to Dewgate, get to Rowdon, and talk to the king. We can do that, right? Torix said it will work…maybe Haldin is more reasonable than Blavier."

Faedi

Darkness swirled around Faedi as she and Lonan appeared in front of the stream bordering their cottage, two Mire draft horses behind them. She hadn't expected his mother to weave such magic to get them there, but she was grateful for the assistance. It would give them extra time to find Torix's trail when he headed south. However, despite the journey ahead, her mind was focused on something else entirely.

All of their creatures were gone.

She rushed toward the barn and coop, but nothing ran out to greet them or demand food. Both stood empty. While Lonan quickly secured the horses, she scoured the property in search of them. There was no blood or damage to the buildings, but even the freshly hatched chicks were missing.

"Peni left a note in the barn," Lonan said, jogging over to her and handing her a piece of parchment.

The forest is no longer safe. Your brood is at the tree. May the heart keep you — Peni.

She pocketed the note, trying to quell her rising panic. "Maybe Sophir warned them about the cultists?"

When she looked at him, his glamour was on once again. To anyone else, he looked like a pale elf—not of Dawn, Dusk, Cinder, or Shadow—his shadow-forged presence cloaked beneath a hunter's charm. But she still saw him.

Some of her panic turned to a simmered rage.

One day, you won't have to do that anymore.

"Or someone else found them out here, too." He led her toward the cottage. "They know Peni; they should behave for him."

"Was the old cart still behind the barn?" She sighed in relief when he nodded. "At least we can send the horses with supplies."

Lonan opened the door for her and led her inside with a smile. The interior was dark, untouched since they had last left, and relief washed over her when she realized Peni had taken the creatures inside as well. They wouldn't have to worry about them when they left.

If the cultists came, there would be nothing for them to find—except her plants.

They worked quickly, dragging out all their furs and preserved food. It wouldn't be enough to feed everyone, but it would do no one any good if it stayed there. They had supplies for travel and could hunt for anything else they needed.

After loading the cart, they returned to gather what they needed. With their packs in front of the unlit hearth, Faedi huffed, placing her hands on her hips as she glanced out the window. They only had a few hours before they needed to leave.

What was to come sat heavy in her chest—possible war, loss, the unknown. How many more quiet moments would they have before everything changed? She didn't know, but she wanted that one—wanted him—while she still had it. But before she could speak, Lonan took her by the shoulders and turned her to face him.

He slid his hands down her arms; one laced his fingers with hers, and the other settled on her waist as he began to hum, leading her in a dance. She smiled, laughing softly, and followed his lead. As skilled as he was with a blade, he was no dance master, but that didn't matter to her. Not when she danced just as poorly and stepped on his toes more than once.

"What are you doing?" She asked when they tangled their feet together.

"There's typically a feast and dancing after a ceremony." He explained, attempting to spin her before pulling her against him. The scent of leather and the Mire clung to him. "Before the bedding."

"We had dinner." She bit her lip, grinning. "And we're horrible dancers."

"We are," he agreed with a laugh.

"Bedding, however, you are…" She trailed off, warmth creeping up her neck. The firelight played along the strong lines of his face, making the gold in his irises flicker. "Talented with your tongue."

"Am I?" His grin sent butterflies through her, anticipation winding tight in her belly. She nodded sheepishly.

"It's late, but I'd rather have you than simply sleep."

"Then take me," she challenged him with a grin, unfastening her cloak and letting it slip from her shoulders like a fallen shadow.

His eye glowed in the dim light, pupils swallowing the amber. He watched her for a breath—two—his nostrils flaring as he took her in. The air between them thickened, heady with the musk of sweat, pine, and the faint metallic tang of old steel.

He took his time undressing her, his calloused fingers rough against her soft skin. Each brush of them sent a shiver up her spine, raising gooseflesh in their wake. His lips followed, pressing reverent kisses over the marks of their bond, his breath hot against her. She mimicked his motions, peeling layers from him like unveiling something sacred.

He guided her to the furs spread out on the floor and knelt before her. Her breath hitched as she followed him down, her back sinking into the furs beneath her.

His body covered hers, solid and burning with heat. The weight of him pressed her into the wood, grounding her in the moment. His breath ghosted over her face, warm and laced with the lingering spice of wine. She trembled as she felt him—hard, insistent, pressing against her thigh.

In that moment, she ached for him more than she ever had before. And she loved it.

A deep growl rumbled in his chest, the sound vibrating through her. His grip was firm as he spread her thighs wider, his fingers pressing into her flesh like he was claiming every inch of her. His left eye burned brighter as he leaned down, his breath hot and damp against her skin.

The first brush of his lips against her inner thigh sent a jolt through her, heat pooling low in her belly. Her hands clenched the furs, resisting the urge to pull him closer, to urge him on. His stubble rasped against her skin as he nuzzled her, inhaling deeply before pressing a kiss to the sensitive flesh.

Another growl, deeper this time, just before his mouth found her. His tongue flicked against her clit, slow at first, teasing, tasting. Her back arched on instinct, a breathless gasp escaping her lips. He hummed in response, the sound sending another wave of pleasure through her.

His fingers joined the dance, sliding into her with practiced ease, curling to find that place that made her come undone. Her toes curled into the furs, her thighs quivering around his shoulders. Her breaths came fast, uneven, sharp gasps swallowed by the fire-lit dark.

She hadn't realized it could feel better than it had in the bath.

She was close, and the sounds leaving her were raw, unfamiliar, but she didn't care. She wanted more—she wanted all of him. But she couldn't form words, not when every inch of her burned with need.

His mouth never faltered, his fingers never ceased their steady rhythm. And then she shattered, a cry ripping from her throat as pleasure surged through her in waves.

Even as her body trembled, he didn't stop. He licked her clean, slow and thorough, as though savoring the taste of her. Her legs twitched with aftershocks as he finally pulled away, his lips glistening, his expression smug and satisfied.

He crawled up her body, his skin hot against hers, his length dragging between her thighs, leaving trails of heat in its wake. He kissed her, and she tasted herself on his lips—salty, sweet, intoxicating.

But before she could savor it, a loud bray shattered the moment. One of the horses kicked at the stable walls, the sound jarring in the quiet.

Lonan groaned, dropping his forehead against hers. "Ytna, please," he muttered, his voice husky with frustration.

"It could just be an anshy," she told him while they waited to see if the horses would calm down.

An offended squawk came from outside. *"I am no common anshy!"*

"Of course, he would come back now." Lonan shook his head, sitting back. "Can he stay outside?"

"I have news from Dewgate."

"I suppose not. The Ancients blessed our bond, but nothing else, it seems," Faedi scoffed, glancing at the window where Dusan sat perched with his back to them. He strutted along the windowsill with all the grace of a noble delivering a royal decree—even though he was tracking in straw and looked as though he'd just fought off a squirrel.

I should have just sent word to Ravyn to take our supplies. We might have had peace in the Mire.

"There are miles between here and the mountains." Lonan stole a kiss, and her heart pounded in her ears. "I will have you. Soon."

Dusan hadn't lied when he said he had news from the city.

The forest-folk had been attacked as soon as they exited the forest. Some had managed to escape, but many had been killed, and the same fate had befallen their livestock. Their attackers hadn't even taken the corpses of the animals with them when they were done.

The attack hadn't been about resources.

Then came the worst news. Orderlings were coming into the forest to purge dark creatures from the Sauvern, and they would find them sooner rather than later. Their cottage was on the parcel closest to the city; there was no way to miss it.

After Faedi told Lonan everything Dusan had said, he lowered his head and cursed. "What do we do?"

She shook her head, carefully standing from the pallet of furs. "I don't know."

Lonan frowned and stood behind her, draping her cloak over her shoulders. "Do we leave early or stay and fight them?"

"Elder Peni already took the animals; we should leave. There's nothing here to defend." She looked over her shoulder at him with a frown.

We should have gone with them.

"I'll get the packs and furs." He nodded, tapping her nose gently with his index finger. "Do you want to hitch the horses?"

She nodded silently and quickly put on her boots before grabbing her bow and walking outside to wake their mounts. Halfway between the cottage and the treeline, she paused and examined the property. Everything was silent, and a dense fog had settled over the ground, thick enough to hide the forest's edge and beyond.

But it wasn't thick enough to hide the trees as they began to whip violently. Shadows flickered in the fog, too fast and unnatural to belong to any native creatures. Then, voices chanted somewhere, just out of sight—low, steady, unnatural.

That's Asharian.

"Hunters are here." The trees warned through the wind as her blood went cold.

"Faedi—run!" Lonan's voice boomed in her mind—just before a bright light shot at her through the fog.

She barely had time to dive to the side before it whirled past her. Even without it hitting her, the heat singed her hair. She rolled to her feet and nocked an arrow to her bow as her heart pounded in her ears. The fog was dense, but she swore she saw a shadowy figure before she blinked.

Before she could find a target and release her arrow, another flash of light came from beside her, and she was too slow to get out of the way. All she could do was turn and hope her quiver of arrows took most of the blast. It didn't offer any protection, and the force of the impact knocked her off her feet, tearing through her with searing pain.

Just like when she had been a child.

The dirt muffled the scream that erupted from her mouth as she clawed at the ground, trying to crawl away. Footsteps approached from behind, and someone stepped on her back to keep her in place, pulling her head back by her hair. Then Lonan's blood-curdling scream echoed through her haze of pain, and she stared ahead as the fog turned red.

It glowed like a dying sun, shifting in gold as the fire raged. Wood cracked and collapsed in the distance, and her lungs burned with every inhale. There was no denying it, The Order had come for them.

"Let the darkness here be purged while you are purified, child," a raspy voice spoke from above her. "Beg Ilos for forgiveness and mercy. Your life may begin anew."

"Lonan," she gasped, sinking her fingers into the dirt as the fog danced in hues of red and yellow. Fire. "Ancients save him."

"The dead gods will not save either of you." He slid his boot down her back and knelt on it, wrapping his hand around her face and squeezing her cheeks. "Beg."

Two new voices shouted in the distance—one fierce like a cracking whip, the other low and filled with wrath. The screams echoed oddly in the fog, warped by the heat and smoke until they sounded like spirits wailing through the trees.

The metal on his gloves sliced into her skin, but she didn't care. Not when the new voices in the fog shouted for her and Lonan. It was Ravyn.

And Sophir.

Save Lonan. Please save him.

"Kill them if they interfere," the man on top of her commanded people she couldn't see, covering her mouth.

Please grow. Please grow.

She glanced at the ground as best she could, watching the dirt. There was nothing—no ripple or crack in the earth, just pain, fear, and the chorus of screams coming from within her home.

The cultist above her continued to taunt her, demanding obedience, but his voice felt miles away. Instead, all she could hear was her heart and her labored gasps against his glove. All the while, she continued to mumble her pleas for the forest and Ancient Gods to help her.

As she lay on the ground, the pressure on her back grew, and the cultist's grip tightened on her face. His demands became more insistent while his glove cut deeper into her cheeks.

She felt it before she saw it—life pushing back against death. A pulse in the dirt. A tremble in her bones. Then, the scent of eventides overpowered the smoke, and she closed her eyes in relief.

Her arm began to ripple and move like the earth, and then vines shot out from her shirt and the ground to engulf the man on top of her. He shouted in surprise, flailing around and falling backward, but they were faster than him.

She pushed herself onto her hands and knees, her body still weak, and watched the vines tighten around his neck. Others restrained him on the ground as she crawled over to him, grabbing his face the way he had done to her. A growl rumbled in her chest as she leaned down, her nails turning to claws that sliced through his skin like parchment.

"Beg," she snarled. "Not your god—beg *me* for mercy."

"What are you?" He gasped, his eyes wide, his fear overpowering the scent of the eventides.

"I am the forest, and you aren't welcome here." She leaned closer to him as the vines traveled into his gaping mouth. "Neither is your god."

She released his face when he began to choke, his eyes rolling back as the vines grew and tightened around him until she could no longer make out his form. It wasn't until more shouts and screams echoed from the cottage that she turned away from the cultist and shakily got to her feet.

"Faedi!" Ravyn emerged from the fog and grabbed her shoulders—moving her behind him as arrows shot at them.

A wall of rocks and dirt created a barrier between them and the projectiles; he winced as he examined her face. His eyes burned brighter than the surrounding flames when she recoiled from his touch. Despite his gentleness, it hurt too much.

He released an unnatural snarl as he turned and extended his hand—causing the sand and rocks to fly out into the fog. Shouts and screams echoed less than a heartbeat later, and she stumbled back from him.

Lonan was still in the house.

The fire continued to blaze wildly in the fog, and she stumbled through the pain radiating from her back and down her limbs. Her fear was more potent than the pain, and it differed from what she usually felt when she looked into flames. She didn't want to run from it like she had as a child.

She wanted to run into it, and she did without hesitation.

The flames inside her home bit at her skin and clothes as she stumbled into the cottage, smoke filling her lungs. Cultists lay dead among broken furniture, and others fought against Sophir, who stood in front of a bloodied Lonan in the corner. He lay motionless against the wall. Blood trickled down his temple, mixing with soot.

Ancients. Sudek, don't take him from me.

She knew no one would last long in the fire and smoke, not when breathing was almost too difficult. Then she remembered something she had done a decade prior during the last siege attempt on Dewgate. It wasn't something she had tried to replicate again, but it was worth a shot.

"I've done it before," she murmured to herself. "I can do it again."

She limped forward and stretched out her hands, weaving intricate patterns with her fingers as the flames began to draw toward her. Gradually, the flames inside the cottage began to encircle her, the closest ones wrapping around her hands and fingers. Her flesh burned, and she screamed, but she didn't stop. Not until there were only flames around her and no one else.

"Get him out!" She shouted at Sophir. Arms wrapped around her, breath washed over her cheek, but she didn't look back.

Her attention returned to Lonan before she directed the flames at the hearth with every ounce of strength she had left.

20

The Scarred Smuggler

"Fuck, he has a good left hook."

Scarred

The air in the tavern was thick with the scent of sweat, blood, smoke, stale ale, and a hint of the sea. Wooden beams groaned overhead, supporting a ceiling blackened with the soot of countless candles and torches. The light flickered, casting shadows that danced across the faces of the crowd gathered around a makeshift fighting ring in the center of the room.

The ring was nothing more than a cleared space on the dirt floor, marked off with a crude rope between posts. Around it, a motley collection of onlookers cheered and jeered, their faces flushed with excitement and drink. Coins exchanged hands rapidly, and shouts of victory or groans of disappointment echoed over the faint music in the tavern.

In the center of the ring, Scarred straightened, his bare chest heaving with exertion. Numerous necklaces rattled and chimed with each breath. Sweat and blood glistened on his tanned skin as it rolled over his muscles and dripped onto the grime-stained wooden floor. He sniffed, pushing his long, umber hair back out of his face.

The cheers grew louder as the deep scars marking his cheeks and brow were revealed. He snatched a rag from the nearest wench before kneeling beside his defeated opponent, who lay groaning at his feet, clutching his ribs. Rolling his eyes, he tossed the rag onto the man's chest.

"Better luck next time?" He said, standing as a wiry human grabbed his wrist, attempting to raise his arm in triumph. They barely managed to lift it to the height of his shoulder.

"Ladies and gents! The winner, tonight's undefeated champion—Scarred!" The crowd erupted into a mix of cheers and boos, some throwing their mugs into the air in celebration while others muttered curses as they watched their lost bets disappear into the hands of winners.

Scarred followed their gazes and the announcer's gesture that pointed to the long scar running from his collarbone to his opposite hip. With a grunt, he pulled his arm away from the announcer and stepped over his fallen opponent to retrieve a mug of ale. As he drank, his bored gaze scanned the room. Beyond the crowd, he spotted a woman seated in the corner, her red eyes matching his own, hidden beneath choppy brown hair.

She smirked, raised her mug, and rolled a gold coin over her knuckles before it vanished. He moved through the crowd, watching her as the patrons parted. When he was only a few steps away, she leaned back in her seat and waved for service.

"You're early, Rage." He announced, taking the chair beside her and pressing his back against the wall.

"You took your time with that one." She nodded to the woman who approached. "Whatever's fresh—rare. Enough to feed this ox."

"I was bored." He shrugged, waiting for their privacy. "Are the ashes safe?"

"They landed where they should—however, flames are growing in the west."

He grumbled, finishing his ale and setting the mug on the table. He glanced at her hand as she tapped on the table. She wore a silver ring on her middle finger and a black snake on her pointer, but the black one on her thumb was new.

"The next shipment?" He asked as she pulled out a skin and poured a honey-colored liquid into his cup.

"The hard work is done," Rage said, the skin vanishing as soon as his cup was full. "They'll be waiting at the ashen tree—take them to their pond."

"And the flames?" He took his cup, raising it to his nose to sniff. Mead.

"Growing," she leaned forward, resting her forearms on the table. "They want this solstice to be a bright one."

"The eyes there say the second is coming?" His eyebrows rose, and he frowned when she nodded. "Fuck."

"It's about to get interesting, my friend," she sighed.

Interesting is one way of putting it. There's going to be war—real war.

They sat silently long after their food arrived, eating while another fight began. Scarred watched them move; the larger one was sloppy and slow. Whatever talent or strength he had was dulled by drink. He knew the smaller one would win—he had enough speed to outlast the blundering rage of the other.

"There's extra pay if you make a stop tonight." Rage set a gold coin on the table.

"Where?" He asked, taking it and slipping it into his pocket.

"The priest in the corner?" She subtly nodded in the direction she wanted him to look. "His silver piece."

He followed her eyes and studied the man in the corner. He wore a deep red robe trimmed with gold and a golden flame pendant. A frail-looking man with silver hair sat beside him, their heads lowered, shoulders tight, skin pale.

"Where do you want it?" He sipped the mead and licked his lips. She always had the good stuff.

"Just uncage it. Then, after you're done with the fish…go to the ones sleeping when it's time." She looked at him with a mischievous twinkle before standing. "You'll know when to go."

"You're a pain in my ass, you know that?" He leaned back in his seat.

"And you need to put on clothes. I hear it's cold where you're going." He rolled his eyes as she laughed and bowed. "May the Ancients keep you, Scarred."

"Yeah, fuck you too," he cracked a smile as she vanished into the crowd, leaving behind a shirt, cloak, and a bag full of coins.

After tugging on the shirt and tucking the bag away, he finished his meal while watching the priest. The man's cup was refilled by the frail one four times by the time he was done, and his cheeks grew redder with each one. His voice raised in volume as he professed his many blessings and good fortune—all thanks to Ilos.

Time for work.

Scarred stood, draping the cloak over his arm, and sucked his teeth as he approached the man's table. If the priest had anyone with him, they were too drunk and lost in the crowd or outside. Or he was just plain dumb and cocky. He assumed the latter by the numerous jeweled rings on his fingers.

Spell weaver—leader—highly adored in Ashar.

As soon as the priest's eyes landed on him, Scarred turned, leaning on the edge of the bar's counter to order another ale. The priest didn't look away, and he bellowed over the crowd before the keep could make it over.

"Mighty fine victory, Scarred! Join me!"

There we go.

Scarred straightened and turned, accepting the chair opposite the priest. "Hope I earned the flame some coin?"

"You did," the priest chuckled merrily and snapped his fingers.

The silver-haired man immediately refilled his cup and poured a second for Scarred. He studied him; injuries unmarked his thin wrists, but his pale skin had a ghastly pallor. A Dawn Elf—sick, or at least underfed.

Scarred nodded silently as the man offered him the cup with a bow of his head before turning his eyes back to the priest. Human, fat from gluttony and greed, and beyond the drink that flushed his skin, he was healthy. Well cared for, spoiled by the riches people in Oprien gave to their temple for miracles and protection.

Liar—backstabber—murderer.

"Will you be fighting again tonight?" The priest asked, raising his glass. "I'll bet on you."

"Not tonight, no," Scarred said, shaking his head and raised his cup. "I leave for Ostria tonight."

"To better coin, whores, and wine—" the priest exclaimed before drinking again.

Scarred merely smirked, his mind already on the job ahead.

He glanced at the fight and nodded. He could take the man; the fool was already sluggish and worn thin. The nimble one still had plenty of energy to outlast him.

"I wager he'll be done before I even walk to the ring," he commented idly. "The lanky one would go down in one hit."

"I didn't take you for a betting man." The priest's eyes bore into him, and Scarred smirked as he turned his gaze back to him.

"Care to take me up on it?" The priest raised an eyebrow.

"What's your wager?" The priest slurred, leaning forward.

Scarred pulled the coin pouch from his side, holding it in his palm with a jiggle. When the priest's brows lifted, he flipped it over and poured its contents onto the wooden table. Gold coins, silver, and jewels spilled out in a small cascade. Before the priest could reach for a single one, Scarred swiped it all back into the bag.

"That's a fine fortune—one a humble man such as myself can't match in one night." He wiped spittle from his chin before nodding to the man beside him. "If I win… you can give me him. My men will be bored on the way to Ostria and need someone to warm their beds."

The Dawn Elf man cowered in his seat, his jaw tightening with a shudder. Scarred watched as the priest turned his gaze to the fight in the ring. Anxiety rippled off both of them. The silver-haired man slowly began to put his bag away, but the priest slammed his cup down and offered his hand.

"If the oaf doesn't go down before you reach him, you lose—then only one hit from you on the boy."

Scarred grinned and clasped his hand. "You have yourself a wager."

It was a nasty game to play. He hated the way the priest's eyes gleamed at the thought of trading flesh and coin. But sometimes, to free a bird, you had to let a bastard believe he'd sold it.

He shoved his hands into his pockets and casually strolled toward the ring. With each step, he whistled a simple tune, though it was quickly drowned out by the crowd's cheers. As he neared, the tune grew louder—just as the smaller fighter charged his opponent.

Scarred stepped over the ring's rope just as the large man collapsed. The lanky announcer from before approached the victor but hesitated when Scarred continued his advance. Whistling, he rolled his shoulders, watching as the smaller fighter raised their fists to guard their face.

They barely reached his chest in height. Their smoky green eyes widened as he closed the distance. Slowly, they tilted their head, a braid decorated with bronze and shells slipping into their face. Then they smirked.

"Place your bets!" The announcer cried just before the fighter lunged, launching a flurry of punches.

Scarred didn't move, taking the hits to his abdomen and chest with little more than a grunt. His hands remained tucked in his pockets as he waited for his opponent to step back. When they did, he began his tune again, nodding as if to urge them on.

Come on.

The fighter stepped back, panting, eyes locked onto his face. They took a moment to size him up, to plan an attack. Scarred remained calm. Bored, even.

He waited, hands still casually tucked away. The fighter huffed before launching into another series of rapid punches to his stomach and sides. Scarred barely flinched. He glanced toward the priest with a smirk.

Then, in a single fluid motion, he withdrew one hand from his pocket and flicked his wrist. The slap was almost casual—a mere afterthought—but the force behind it sent the smaller fighter sprawling.

For a moment, the crowd fell silent, shocked by the suddenness of the strike. The fighter lay on the ground, dazed, eyes wide as they stared at the ceiling. Scarred placed his hand back in his pocket and stopped his tune.

"Well, that settles it!" The announcer finally shouted, breaking the stunned silence. "Looks like Scarred's still got it!"

Scarred turned on his heels and stepped back over the rope with effortless grace, not bothering to look back. He couldn't—not when the silver-haired man lifted his head to meet his gaze, his expression nothing short of fear.

"I'll take my winnings now," Scarred said, shifting his attention to the priest, who sat frozen in his chair.

"H-wh-how—" the priest sputtered.

"Away from him. Let's go. The man of the flame gave his oath; you're mine now." Scarred curled his middle and pointer fingers, gesturing for the silver-haired man to stand.

He watched as the man glanced toward the priest, who still sat dumbfounded, before he hurried to stand before him, head lowered. Scarred studied the priest for a moment, ensuring he wouldn't start a scene, before nodding in satisfaction. The silver-haired man grabbed his cup, offering a subtle nod of defeat.

It didn't bring as much satisfaction as Scarred had hoped.

"May his flame light your way," he murmured before stepping out of the tavern, the silver-haired man following close behind.

May Sudek use it to burn your fucking corpse.

21
Between Embers and Dreams

"It's okay…Faedi got away…she's fast. They didn't kill her…but I think they killed me."

Lonan

His eyes fluttered open. He expected to see fire or smoke, but the world around him felt different. It was familiar, yet strange. He lay on a bed of soft moss, surrounded by towering trees whose leaves shimmered with a silvery light. The air was cool, infused with a subtle sweetness reminiscent of Faedi's eventides.

As his senses adjusted, memories flooded back—frantic shouts, the crackling of flames, the desperate fight in the burning cottage. He remembered the cultists in their gold-lined robes, their faces contorted with hatred as they unleashed chaos upon his home. He hadn't seen Faedi in the chaos, only heard her pained cries echoing in his mind.

Pushing himself up with a deep breath, he took in his surroundings. The canopy above glimmered with silver and green from glow bugs, while shadows danced among the ferns and wildflowers, creating an otherworldly mosaic of light and dark.

He was in the Umbramire.

He wasn't injured.

Is this a dream or the afterlife?

Rising to his feet, he began to wander the forest. The scent of eventides grew stronger when he turned left, urging him to follow. There was a chance she was here, and he needed to know what had happened to her—if she had died because he couldn't reach her.

The scent led him along a babbling brook alive with shimmering fish, past thick willow trees swaying in the breeze. The silvery mist thickened with each step. The forest opened into a grove, and in a small clearing of deep green grass, he spotted her. She was on her knees, head tipped back, staring at the sky, facing away from him.

"Faedi," He called, rushing over to kneel in front of her. "Are you all right? What happened?"

"You're alive?" She flung her arms over his shoulders, nearly tackling him to the ground. "You weren't moving. I couldn't see you breathing."

Her body trembled against his, and he realized she had been crying. That turned into sobs when he held her. His heart pounded as he processed her words. She must have gone into the house after he fell, but he didn't know if the cultists inside had attacked her.

He pulled away once she calmed herself. "What happened, Faedi?"

"Cultists were… I killed the one on me. I left Ravyn fighting the others and went into the house." She wiped her eyes and released a shaky breath. "When I went inside, Sophir was there. He ran in before me. You were on the floor; there were still some inside, and Sophir was fighting them. He wouldn't let them get to you. Everything was on fire, so I sent it all out of the chimney. I think I passed out."

Lonan stared at her, checking for injuries. "So we're not dead?"

"I don't think so," she said, shaking her head. "I think it's a dream? We've gone into each other's before."

His hand reached her cheek, thumb rubbing gently. "What about Sophir?"

"I told him to get you out."

He caught a tear slipping from her eye and frowned. The news of Ravyn and Sophir's assistance surprised him, and he wasn't sure how to take it. If the High Knight had come to help them, to save them, he would owe him a debt. But he didn't know his motives.

There were plenty of ways to thank Ravyn.

They still needed to travel to the mountains. They needed to find a way to stop the cultists, and he doubted Sophir would want anything to do with it—especially after his reaction to Faedi burning that walking corpse. But maybe his mind had changed after fighting the cultists to defend him.

Perhaps they could trust him.

"So… if we're not dead and they helped us," Lonan said, sitting back and holding her hands. "What do we do?"

She shrugged, biting her lip. "Wait to wake up?"

"What's on your mind?" He tilted his head before pulling her into his lap. "Talk to me."

"He wasn't wearing Dewgate armor," Faedi said, resting her chin on his shoulder while he rubbed her back. "There was a silver pendant on his chest. He kept trying to grab it, but the cultists were too fast."

Lonan breathed in the scent of her hair. "Were you close enough to see what was on it?"

"A fang… and I think it was Rakgrah? I recognized one from one of Torix's books." She nodded against his shoulder, confirming her assumption. "I think it's his glamour."

"And we already know it's powerful," he mused, tracing circles on her back. "Do you think he's an Itmis?"

"It would explain his unnaturally large size," she said with a shrug.

"Why take up in Dewgate as a Knight, though?" It didn't make sense. Itmis rarely left their mountains in the sky, and those who did were wanderers.

"Maybe family business? My mother said one of their mountains was between Dewgate and Rowdon."

He stared at the trees, continuing to hold Faedi against him. If Sophir were an Itmis, the glamour would make sense. Some, mainly on the Eastern continent, hunted dragon-kin for sport or enslaved them. But hunters traveled to follow their prey. Even the Mire wasn't completely safe from them.

"I suppose… since he helped us," Lonan sighed and shook his head. "We should give him the benefit of the doubt."

"Agreed," she said, nodding against his shoulder before he turned to kiss her cheek.

"Now," he murmured, nuzzling into her hair and neck. "How else do we pass the time?"

"You have an idea?" Her voice lightened as she laughed.

"We almost died…we might die," he whispered, pressing a kiss to her neck. "I want—I need you."

She tilted her head, giving him better access as she clung to his clothes with a whimper. If he could only have her within a dream, he would take what he could get. They had almost died, and he would be damned if he didn't make up for every lost moment before someone ended them.

"Better hurry then—I don't know when we'll wake up," she whispered, smiling at him.

"As you wish."

23

A Fractured Bond

"Ancients, everything hurts."

Lonan

He groaned as he opened his eyes, trying to shield his face from the morning light. His limbs felt heavy, protesting each movement. He must have been badly burned; everything hurt.

Lonan shot up, scanning his surroundings. He heard the river first, then took in the trees, and finally, the furs beneath and over him. His heart raced when he looked down and saw Faedi. Her eyes were closed, but the furs covering her rose and fell with each breath.

"You're awake."

He turned toward the voice, his hands instinctively searching for his knives, but they were missing. He froze when he saw Sophir. The Knight wasn't in Dewgate armor; instead, he wore rough studded armor, and a silver pendant caught Lonan's eye. He was unarmed, and Dusan looked far too comfortable perched beside him.

"You're here," Lonan replied, wincing as his throat protested the effort. "When—"

Pain pounded through his skull as he recalled the attack. The cultists must have already been in the house—but he and Faedi hadn't seen or heard them. He barely had a chance to get his knives ready.

After that, all he could see was fire. Then someone had knocked a cultist off him. Then…nothing. Until he dreamed of Faedi—he had thought that might have been the afterlife.

The cultists had already gotten into the house—but he hadn't seen or heard them.

After that, all he could see was fire. He had fought anyone he could and screamed for Faedi to run, but then someone had knocked a cultist off him. Then there had been nothing. Until he dreamed of Faedi—he had thought that might have been the afterlife.

"Ravyn received word cultists were coming for the cottage," Sophir explained as he offered him a skin of water. "I hoped you weren't there."

"We came to send supplies for the winter," Lonan said after drinking, feeling some relief as the pain in his throat lessened.

He leaned over Faedi to examine her. Her jaw was tight, sweat covered her brow and neck, already staining her shirt. The clothes she wore weren't the ones from when they had been attacked, and neither were his. He paused as he leaned closer; there was no scent of eventides.

No…no, no, no.

With as much care as he could manage, he rolled up her sleeve, hissing as he revealed the deep scarring on her arm. Hardly any vines remained, and every last bloom was gone. Her skin was discolored and stretched tight, sitting on top of her bones in a way that made his stomach turn. It wasn't the scar that made him ill—it was knowing how much pain she would be in when she woke.

Without the eventide vines to support her, her arm was practically useless; the pain would be so severe she wouldn't be able to speak.

"What's wrong?" Sophir asked as Lonan stumbled to get out of the cart. "You should rest."

"Faedi needs medicine," Lonan snapped, sidestepping him when he tried to stop him. "Don't. I—she's going to be in pain when she wakes up."

He expected Sophir to argue or try to force him back into the cart, but he didn't. Instead, he looked between Lonan and the cart, pulled a dagger from his belt, and offered it to him.

After a sigh, he turned his eyes back to Lonan. "Tell me what we're looking for, and I'll help," he said, motioning to the forest. "We shouldn't stay in one place for long; I don't know how many more Orderlings are out here."

"Do you know herbs and native plants?" Lonan squinted at him, sighing when Sophir shook his head. "Get the river moss; it's fluffy and black on the trees. Don't bring anything green. I'll get the other herbs."

Lonan watched Sophir head off, searching for the moss, before turning in the opposite direction. Sophir was right; they didn't need to linger, but he couldn't risk Faedi's pain. Not if it was bad enough to make her scream. If anyone were nearby, they would hear her.

The warning in his mind pushed him to rush through the discomfort in his limbs. He wished they had some of her eventides; they would help her pain more than the other supplies he gathered. If they were lucky, they would find more while they waited for the vines in her arm to regrow.

Once confident he had everything he needed, he returned to the cart and approached Sophir. He held out the moss for Lonan to inspect, and Lonan leaned over his hands to sniff the bundle. Despite his lack of herbal knowledge, Sophir had done well—nothing smelled terrible.

As Lonan straightened, his gaze lingered on the pendant Sophir wore: ancient markings, a tooth, and pure silver. Despite the soot and grime on his clothing, the necklace was pristine. To Lonan's knowledge, Dewgate didn't have any dragon artifacts.

"It's my glamour," Sophir announced. "Dewgate is not friendly to certain races—I didn't know how they would behave around someone cursed."

"You wouldn't be High Knight," Lonan told him as he climbed into the cart to mix herbs. Faedi was better at making medicine.

"Lady Callon was rather adamant I keep it on," Sophir said, handing him the moss when Lonan reached for it. "Is there a direction we should head in?"

"Rowdon. We're going to the Dusk Elves."

Faedi's arm lay covered in a poultice of herbs as Lonan sat in the cart while Sophir drove the horses southeast. To his surprise, Sophir agreed that they should stay in the forest for as long as possible before crossing the open plains north of Rowdon's border. He hadn't asked why they were traveling there; he simply nodded and directed the horses along the trail.

"Why did you come back?" Lonan eventually asked when Faedi seemed to relax.

"I was worried you might have gone home after your fight in the forest," Sophir replied.

"We're not city-folk," Lonan looked up at him. "We're not your people to protect."

"Would you have preferred I leave you to die?" Sophir countered, his eyes still focused on the path ahead.

"That's what city-folk do to shadows, isn't it?" Lonan scoffed, rolling his eyes before turning his attention back to Faedi. "Anything past the trees doesn't matter to you unless we have something you want—like your damned caravans."

An awkward silence settled between them. Occasionally, Lonan noticed Sophir glancing back at them, but he didn't let his gaze linger. It was the same kind of snooping glances he had given before, making his skin prickle.

"I was afraid," Sophir finally sighed. "When I heard they were in the forest to purge it—I worried it would be like the raids. I've buried enough people."

"We aren't yours to bury," Lonan snapped, turning to look at him. But the expression on Sophir's face gave him pause. "What?"

"I swore an oath to Ravyn when he told me how to find you…I promised I would bring no harm to you—that I would defend you if you were in danger," he said, gripping the reins tighter. "I might not have trusted you when Faedi burned that corpse, but I didn't mean you any ill will. I wanted to follow you—to fight with you, but—"

"But what? You believe what the cultists do, and us darklings made you question your faith?" Lonan cut him off, unable to hide his disdain.

"I hope The Ancients snuff out Ilos!" Sophir turned to face him with a growl. "Mumir's flame was stronger than anything that bastard god creates."

"Then why didn't you honor your oath before? You watched us leave and only came when the fight was done. Then you ran away, only to return when our home was in flames. Why?" Lonan stood on the cart, bracing himself on the rail to put himself between Sophir and Faedi. "How do we know you weren't with them, waiting to play the victor?"

Sophir was fast, but so was Lonan. He dropped the reins and grabbed him by the collar. The dagger Lonan pressed to his throat didn't deter him. Sophir pulled him closer until their noses almost touched, his hot breath washing over his face as he growled again.

Lonan should have hated him—the arrogance in his voice, the way he loomed over him like he had every right to act like they owed him something for helping them. His hand fisted in Lonan's collar, his grip unyielding, his breath hot against his skin. Fury burned in his chest, but beneath it, something else coiled—something he despised as much as he craved.

Sophir was close—too close—and Lonan hated that his body reacted before his mind could stop it. He was drawn to the heat of him, the sharp edge of his anger like a blade he wanted to press against his skin just to feel the cut.

"I swore to Ravyn on the Ancients and to the Oath-Keeper," Sophir said, his voice lowering to a rumble. "I didn't go with you because I couldn't bring myself to look you in the eyes. Not after I insulted you, and Faedi looked at me like she does at fire…"

Lonan tightened his grip on the knife, matching his tone with a snarl when he mentioned Faedi. He was right; she was afraid of him, and he hurt her when he insinuated she was a murderer.

"I followed to ensure you were safe and then took the blade to Dewgate," Sophir continued, releasing Lonan's collar. "When I learned you might be in danger again, Ravyn and I went to your home as quickly as possible. When we arrived—they were already there. The house was on fire, and I thought both of you were inside."

Even though he released him, Sophir didn't move. He remained nose-to-nose with him, waiting for his reaction. Slowly, Lonan put his blade away and glanced to the side when he realized the horses had stopped walking. Then, the silence between them was broken by a whimper.

"Lonan…" He watched Sophir's eyebrows raise and his eyes widen as he turned to crouch beside Faedi.

"I'm here," he whispered, brushing her hair out of her face. It was damp again. "I have herbs."

Faedi's face contorted in discomfort, and Lonan quickly helped her sit up as she gasped for air. He offered her a bundle of moss and lock, then water after she chewed the bitter mix and gagged. If he had found any honey, he would have taken it for her, but she had to do without.

"Just breathe," he said, rubbing her back as she cradled her arm against her chest. "We're going to make camp soon."

She looked up at him, tears glistening in her eyes. "What?"

"Sophir came and took us from the cottage," he explained slowly, offering her another bundle to chew. "I couldn't find any eventides. I hadn't smelled any."

"That wasn't a dream?" Faedi opened her mouth, allowing him to feed her the leaf-wrapped bundle before she looked back at Sophir. "Did he say any-thing?"

"Just that he was with Ravyn when he heard cultists were coming. We would've died without them," he said, kissing the top of her head as she rested it against his shoulder. "And we had a heart-to-heart."

"After the cultists…did you have a dream?"

Lonan stared at the trees and nodded gently. It wasn't one he had experi-enced before, but it wasn't unwelcome. However, Sophir's unexpected appear-ance lingered in his mind.

"I did. Maybe the gods pitied us for nearly dying," he teased her.

"I suppose now is the time to say I can hear your soul speech," Sophir's sud-den announcement made Lonan tense, heat flooding his face.

He tipped his head back to look at Sophir as he urged the horses onward. "You what?"

"I'm an Astral Itmis. We can hear soul speech like it is spoken word."

Lonan glanced down at Faedi as she gripped her arm tighter and laughed. He had heard everything they said to each other but hadn't told them. He thought he should have been angry, but it was challenging to feel that way after what he had said.

That may have been why they had both welcomed him in the dream. They knew he came for them and helped them. He thought he had a faint recollec-tion of Sophir holding them in the river, but he had dismissed it as a dream. He should have felt cold, but it had felt like a warm embrace.

"Did you heal us?" He asked softly. "After the cultists? I should be burnt to a crisp."

"Ravyn and I did," Sophir confirmed simply, offering no further informa-tion.

"Are Itmis always as secretive as you?" Faedi chimed in from beside him.

"I don't know. I believe mine is a force of habit," he chuckled before clear-ing his throat. "I apologize. Please, ask me anything you like. We have fought together and are now, I assume, on some kind of mission to save the Mire. I will tell you whatever you want to know. I hope to learn more about you two as well."

"You might learn something," Lonan told him as Faedi nodded, eating an-other bundle. "Why did you pick Dewgate, and why become High Knight?"

"My sister. She said she saw me there in the armor. She said that was where I needed to be," he explained, and Lonan frowned. There was something in his voice, a hint of sadness. "Did you help in the war ten years ago?"

"We did," Lonan nodded. "We were with The Watch and helped heal wounded soldiers."

"With eventides?" Sophir shifted in his seat, and Lonan looked back at him to nod. "Were you caught?"

Faedi spoke once she finished her herbs. "Someone thought I was poisoning them and chased us into the forest—"

"You were glamoured as an Umbral–that makes more sense," Sophir said softly as he nodded to himself.

Faedi winced as the wagon bumped over a large rock. "How would you know that?"

"I was the soldier with Ravyn who chased after you."

Lonan fell silent, encouraging Faedi to take another sip of water. That night was burned into his memory—Faedi lunging in front of a soldier when a barrage of arrows came at them, making a shield of vines. Some arrows broke through, and she was hit. They both were the scar on her chest, a reminder of the danger they faced.

"Were you in Dewgate during the raids?" Lonan asked softly, kissing Faedi's head when she tensed.

"I was. It was before I was appointed High Knight," he said solemnly. "I helped the Wardens and Guardians bury the dead."

"The Lirulin's home?" Faedi whispered, feeling warm against him as he brushed his fingertips over her forehead.

"Yes, their home was the first I went to. It was the first time I heard The Hunt summoned."

"You have a fever," Lonan told Faedi, pouring water on an old cloth to wipe her face. "We need to make camp."

"Alright."

Sophir didn't waste any time directing the horses to the first substantial place he could find. What took only minutes seemed to drag by as Faedi's body continued to heat up. Even after Lonan threw the furs off her, she still burned.

Lonan thanked Sophir when he brought more water and cloth to help ease Faedi's fever. Even though he hadn't completely processed everything Sophir had said before, he was grateful for the help. They were too far from the Mire for any genuine assistance, and any nearby Watcher couldn't provide what they needed. All he could do was hope that it wasn't the same fever Faedi had suffered from before.

"Ytna…" Faedi whimpered, shying away from them. "The gods hate me."

"What do the gods have to do with a fever?" Sophir asked, offering her a skin of water.

Lonan frowned as Faedi tried to scramble back from them. He quickly grabbed her good wrist, and she stared up at him with wide eyes, looking between him and Sophir as she panted for breath. Then, the sweetest scent flooded his senses.

Ancients.

"She's going into heat," he told Sophir before tugging Faedi against him with a low growl, wrapping his arms around her waist. "But only natural-born weres—"

"Could we worry about the possible implications later?" Faedi shook her head, hiding her face against his chest. "I—I don't—I can't—"

"Should I take a long walk?" Sophir asked, his tone significantly softer than it had been before.

"Yes," Lonan snapped over his shoulder at him, gasping when Faedi nipped at his exposed neck. "Please."

25

Fevered Temptations

"I should have a better sense of self-control. I can work through this. We should be on our way to Rowdon, not rolling around on the ground—Ancients, help me."

Faedi

Her body thrummed with a longing so intense it burned like a fever. The ache deep inside her, the hunger, was unlike anything she'd ever felt before. It wasn't just heat; it was something primal, a force clawing its way to the surface— wild and ancient. Her muscles trembled under the weight of it all.

She told herself that it was only Lonan she needed, that his touch alone would satisfy the burning inside her. But when she turned her head and met Sophir's gaze, a quiet but insistent hunger stirred within her for him, too. The instinct was undeniable, wild, and overwhelming.

Reason faded away, drowned by the pull of desire. There was no room for thought, only the rush of flesh and the intoxicating scents of their presence.

Lonan's eyes held her with an intensity that made her pulse race. He tore her shirt open with a single motion. The night air should have cooled her heated skin, but it only intensified the fire. She shivered, not from the cold, but from the growing need that consumed her.

Lonan's lips pressed against her neck, his teeth brushing against her pulse in a teasing bite, and a soft gasp escaped her. "Gods, Faedi," he murmured, his voice heavy with desire. "You're stunning."

A low, whine slipped from her throat, her fingers digging into his back as she lost herself in the sensation. She felt the weight of Sophir's presence beside her, his closeness sending an almost electric charge through her.

He knelt beside her, his gaze dark and intense, eyes flickering with something untamed. His breath was warm against her skin, and his voice rumbled low. "Ancients," he whispered. "Your scent—"

Lonan's voice cut through the tension, low and warning—though he continued to trail his lips down her body. "You're supposed to be walking."

No—I want him to stay.

But Sophir barely noticed, too enraptured by the pull between them. "I've never smelled anything like this," he said, his words a growl. "It's intoxicating."

The words stirred something in her—something that needed to be claimed, cherished. She wasn't sure who it was meant for, but it didn't matter. There was only the heat, the hunger, the connection that laced between them.

When Sophir took his pendant off, her breath caught in her throat.

Yes—without the glamour.

Sophir's glamour shimmered away, revealing his true form—his sharp features, his long, curved horns, and the fierce beauty that made her pulse quicken. He leaned in, brushing his lips against her ear before his teeth grazed her skin, the touch sharp but tender.

A strangled sound slipped from her lips as Lonan's mouth found its place at her core, his touch both gentle and firm, pulling her deeper into the haze of want. Her fingers tangled in his hair, her body trembling as Sophir's scent wrapped around her, ancient and enticing.

Sophir's lips traced down her neck, his hands pressing just shy of breaking skin on her breast as he marked her with his touch. His every movement was a delicate balance between tenderness and intensity, a contrast to the way Lonan's touch ignited the raw, unrelenting ache within her.

"More," she breathed, pulling Lonan closer, urging him to deepen the connection.

Lonan froze only for a heartbeat, then growled, the sound vibrating against her before his fingers dug into her thighs. He pushed her legs open roughly, moving closer to her while he kissed up her stomach—teeth dragging over her skin.

Sophir's chest heaved, his breath ragged, pupils blown wide as he stared at her like prey and salvation all at once. "More?" He rasped, voice breaking on the word. "What—do you need?"

She trembled as his hand trailed over her skin. "Everything."

"Ancients," the moonlight flashed on his fangs, and she locked her thighs around Lonan's waist. Sophir's hand quivered against her skin before his restraint snapped. He crushed his mouth against hers, kissing her with a brutal hunger.

Her body arched between them, caught in their pull of hunger that matched her own. Her nails raked down Lonan's shoulders, her breath rapid as she begged with broken gasps. "Please—don't stop—don't you dare stop—"

Lonan's answering growl was pure darkness, primal and possessive, while he hooked his arms under her and lifted her up. Her chest pressed against his while he thrust into her mercilessly. Sophir moved, his breath coming in snarls and groans against her ear while he pressed behind her.

Every part of her body was pulled in two directions—claimed by one, desired by the other, both of them feeding the fever that consumed her. And still—it wasn't enough.

More. More. Give me more.

Sophir said something—too heavy with a growl for her to understand; an ancient sound that shook her marrow. His skin burned against her, his heat rolling off him like a furnace. When he pushed inside, fire seared through her. Scorching and perfect, claiming the part of her Lonan hadn't.

Lonan's thrusts grew rougher, deeper, as he rutted into her. Shadows licked over his skin, wrapping around her—dragging her down. Harder. Faster. His shaft swelled at the base slowly, and each thrust stretched her. Burned her. Until, with a guttural snarl, he locked inside her.

The relief was savage, perfect—her body clamped down, instinct meeting instinct in feral surrender.

Her scream tore free, wild and raw, as her body clenched down on both of them, dragging them with her. Lonan's snarl was sharp and possessive as his knit pulsed inside her, locking him in place—the pressure holding Sophir in place, and his fire surged into her with searing heat.

Ancients' blood.

As the waves of pleasure slowly faded, Sophir's hand tightened in her hair. A soft smile curved her lips when he whispered, his voice thick with desire, "Gods, you're beautiful when you come."

It was perfect—almost complete—but there was something, just out of reach, that she couldn't quite identify.

Something has to be wrong with me.

As the urgency of her need began to subside, her body swiftly reminded her of past injuries.

She sat beside Lonan against a tree, watching the starry-scaled Itmis gather furs and food. Lonan fed her another bundle of herbs, and she bit into a piece of dry meat to mask the taste. She offered both of them a silent smile of thanks.

Once her mind returned to clarity, she felt too awkward to speak.

Whoever coined the phrase *pillow talk* likely never experienced heat or shared intimacy with two beautiful, powerful men.

"How is your arm?" Sophir asked softly.

"It hurts a bit more than usual," she admitted, hissing as she tested the arm in the sling. "A lot more."

"It always hurts?" Sophir leaned back, and she flinched slightly under his gaze. "What happened?"

"The raids? When…" She bit her inner cheek, struggling to put her thoughts into words. "One of my brothers got me out of the house while it burned. I ran to find help, but two of them chased me. They burned me on my arm, and… I didn't know any healing magic. It had already healed when Lonan found me, but the eventides helped ease the pain."

"So that's why you're covered in burn scars." Sophir sighed, nodding in understanding. "How long were you in the forest? An injury like that would have taken months to heal."

"Five years," she replied, tilting her head when he stared at her in disbelief. "What?"

"You survived alone, with your arm like that, for five years?"

"Only the gods know how long I had the fever when Lonan found me." She glanced at him, and Lonan grinned at her with pride.

"You were the first person ever accepted into The Watch who wasn't an Umbral."

"I'm sure your expertise in the forest is an asset to them," Sophir smiled, then his expression turned more serious. "Will the eventides grow again?"

"Eventually," she nodded. "There was an accident during a solstice a few years ago, and it took a while for them to regrow on my forearm. I don't know how long it will take for…almost all of it."

Lonan gently draped a fur over her shoulders. "Hopefully, there will be something to support it better before we reach Rowdon."

"Why the Dusk Elves?" Sophir asked. "Don't they hate Umbrals?"

She glanced at Lonan after Sophir's question, wondering how he would react. He had told them the truth, and they had shared a rather intimate time together. When he nodded, she turned her attention back to Sophir, sighing.

"I'm King Haldin's granddaughter and bonded to the Prince of the Mire," she said, waiting for him to laugh. She wouldn't have blamed him if he did. "If they want an heir, they have to learn to accept Umbrals."

"You're both…" Sophir trailed off, rubbing his chin. "That suddenly makes more sense."

She leaned forward, despite the sharp pain in her arm. "What?"

"My sister, Cera, she said something before I left. Something about stars merging with twins' shadows again." He shook his head. "Sometimes, she was more poetic with her prophecies than I could follow."

"Well… I'm fairly certain both of you made me see stars. Maybe she saw my heat," she teased, grinning when both men laughed and their cheeks flushed. "Oh, Ancients, don't act like maidens. I should be the one blushing—until to-night, I was a maiden."

"What?" Sophir stared at her, then glanced at Lonan. "You're joking."

Lonan shrugged with a chuckle. "We both were."

"Blessed, Ytna," Sophir stole her water skin and took a sip.

"And her tits," Lonan chuckled, laughter growing. "She finally stopped send-ing people to interrupt us—now I suppose she's sending them to join us."

She laughed and shook her head. If the gods had sent anyone else to join them, she would have been unsure of what to do with herself. Having both of them with her was unexpected and exhilarating, enough that the thought made her clench her thighs and shift on the ground.

As incredible and mind-blowing as it had been, she doubted they would want to do it again. Lonan, she was certain, would still want her, but she wasn't sure about Sophir. Maybe, in the dream, he'd reacted just because she would be in heat soon.

"Are you uncomfortable?" Lonan asked softly.

"No," she smiled at him, her face quickly flushing. "Just thinking."

He grinned mischievously. "Are you fantasizing about us?"

Sophir crossed his legs, bracing his elbows on his knees. She knew he was still naked beneath the fur in his lap. "What's on your mind?"

They all were.

"Not much now," she admitted, her eyes widening before she shook her head and looked away. "I was just… well, Lonan and I are… but you…"

"You're wondering what my intentions are with both of you?" Sophir nodded with a chuckle. "I'll admit, when I was sent to you for guidance, I wasn't looking for partners. I thought myself incapable of making such bonds. But I won't deny my attraction to you—both of you."

"You are?" Lonan sounded as surprised as she felt.

"Yes." Sophir nodded, his eyes lowered. Bashful.

"Your human glamour doesn't do you justice," Lonan commented, and she chuckled in agreement.

"It wasn't my intention to be attractive," Sophir mused, his voice low and rumbling, sending a shiver down her.

Do that again.

Heat spread over her face when his eyes met hers, and he smiled—then rumbled again.

"Is that a common noise for you?" Faedi squinted at him. She didn't know if she could handle hearing that daily without her core aching.

"When I'm not hiding myself," he told her with a grin before his eyes darkened, and her heart pounded.

She bit her lip as he tucked her hair behind her ear, looking away as her cheeks warmed. Lonan's fingertips traced over her thigh, idly before gently gripping it. Her breath caught in her throat, and she glanced between them with a soft whimper.

Sophir raised his eyebrows. "How long do heats last?"

"Up to a week," Lonan answered. "We might need to be creative with the arm."

"I don't know if it'll take a week for me," she shook her head. "This hasn't happened before. If it lasts a week, it'll be extremely inconvenient. It'll slow us down."

"Well," Sophir shifted beside her, sliding his hand over her neck. "We still have to camp at night, giving us time to learn from each other. If you feel urges during the day, I can direct the cart while Lonan helps you."

"It's a good idea," Lonan agreed, his hand moving further up her thigh.

She huffed. "You're both incredibly nonchalant about this."

"We'll still get to the mountain," Sophir promised, his breath washing over her ear. "There's nothing wrong with the trip being pleasurable."

Ancients.

25
Faltering Boundaries

"I should have walked away. This will not help their feelings towards me—I took advantage. How do I even apologize for this? How can I apologize when I want more?"

Sophir

It was impossible to keep track of the times he and Lonan had shared quiet moments with Faedi through the night. Her bursts of need were unpredictable, leaving her often apologetic, uncertain, and casting nervous glances between them. He knew she had been asleep during his earlier conversation with Lonan, but he couldn't help but wonder if she sensed something between them—something unsaid, but felt in the air.

Lonan tried his best to keep the mood light, as Sophir did, but Faedi was astute. She was always alert, watching everything around her. He had no doubt that it was that vigilance that had kept her alive for so long in the forest. That, and perhaps a bit of luck.

Sophir glanced at her as she slept curled under a blanket of furs. Only her head was visible from his spot leaning against the tree. To his surprise, Lonan had stepped away after Faedi had fallen asleep to gather water and look for herbs.

Despite the fatigue weighing on him, sleep didn't come easily. It wasn't just the events of the day that kept him awake, but the lingering scent in the air—intoxicating, yet so powerful it almost overwhelmed him.

His reaction to her heat left him unsettled. He had every intention of giving them privacy, of stepping away, but the scent clung to him. It was impossible to ignore. It took everything in him not to follow the pull that urged him toward her. Watching Lonan with Faedi had been fulfilling in a way he hadn't anticipated, and yet there was a part of him that yearned for something more.

What have I become?

In his past, he had always maintained control, never once losing himself in the heat of the moment. Yet there he was, questioning his restraint.

It's like Blavier's aphrodisiacs…but without as much guilt.

With a sigh, he wiped his hand over his face and turned toward the trees, hearing the soft rush of the stream in the distance. Lonan had been gone for some time now, and a nagging sense of worry began to gnaw at him. Lonan hadn't fully recovered from the earlier strain, and Faedi's arm was a reminder of how taxing their journey had been.

He stepped carefully through the trees until the sound of running water grew louder, and soon after, he heard a groan.

"Lonan?" Sophir called softly.

"Go watch over Faedi," came the sharp response, but Sophir could hear the frustration in his tone.

Sophir frowned but didn't argue. It wasn't hard to find him—Umbrals had an affinity for darkness, and even in the dim light, Sophir's senses led him straight to Lonan. As he approached, the scent grew stronger, not diminishing as he had expected, but intensifying. It was different from Faedi's, rich and deep, like an exotic blend of spices.

Confused, Sophir drew closer, his heart beginning to race. He found Lonan seated by the stream, his head leaned back against a rock, eyes shut in apparent distress.

"Are you alright?" Sophir knelt beside him.

Lonan's violet eyes flashed open, filled with irritation. "I told you to go back to Faedi."

Sophir hesitated, his gaze softening. "Is it only natural-born were-folk who experience this?"

Lonan nodded, a frustrated groan escaping him. "It won't stop."

Sophir frowned, his curiosity piqued. "Your scent—it's like hers, but different."

Lonan's breath hitched, and he struggled to compose himself. "I...developed some traits when I bonded with Faedi. She wasn't a were-folk when we were children, but now...it's confusing."

Sophir's gaze softened, and he spoke gently. "Could it be your ability to take different forms that's causing this?" He chose his words carefully, sensing how delicate the matter was.

"I don't know," Lonan murmured, a pained look crossing his face.

Sophir hesitated for a moment before speaking again, his voice softer than before. "Do you want help?"

Lonan's eyes searched his face for a long moment before he finally nodded, his expression filled with a mix of vulnerability and longing. "Yes," he whispered.

Sophir's heart pounded in his chest, a rush of emotions flooding him. He could feel the warmth between them, stronger now than before, and it was almost too much to bear. His voice trembled with a mix of desire and tenderness. "Then let me help you."

Sophir struggled to maintain control, each passing second pushing at the edges of his patience. When Lonan slowly pulled his hand away, the air seemed to grow thicker with the scent that had already begun to overwhelm him. Sophir's gaze flickered downward, his breath catching as the subtle hint of moisture on Lonan's hand sent a rush of heat through him.

He reached out to take Lonan's hand, his fingers brushing gently against his skin. Without thinking, he brought it to his lips, tasting him in a tender, almost reverent gesture. The taste was darker than he expected—smoke and earth and something sharp that lingered on his tongue. It left him lightheaded, craving more.

Lonan's gaze met his, wide-eyed and filled with a mix of surprise and something more vulnerable. He fumbled to shove his pants down, his hands clumsy with need. Sophir caught the movement and steadied him, helping with sure fingers. They had enough to contend with, and clothing would be the least of their worries.

Sophir's heart raced as he surveyed him, uncertain of how to best help Lonan through this storm. He knew so little of Umbrals and their needs, but he could tell that whatever was happening between them wasn't just physical—it was something deeper, something more profound.

Lonan's breath hitched as Sophir urged him to stand, but when their eyes met, it became clear. There was no hesitation left. The pull between them was undeniable, and Sophir could feel the connection sparking in every fiber of his being. His actions were driven by something far greater than instinct, and he gave himself to it completely, even as his mind raced with the urgency of the moment.

Lonan's voice faltered as Sophir leaned in, pressing a soft kiss to the edge of his jaw, feeling the shudder run through him. Their breaths tangled in the quiet night air, and Sophir allowed the intensity of the moment to unfold naturally.

"Do what you need," Sophir whispered, his voice rough.

Lonan's hands found his horns again, pulling him closer with an urgency that left no room for doubt. Sophir met him halfway, giving him what he sought, his mind clouded only with the pleasure of their shared connection.

Every movement, every touch, was a testament to the bond between them, a bond that neither of them could deny, no matter the complexity of the moment. Sophir's heart beat in time with Lonan's, each pulse a promise.

And when they finally gave in to the overwhelming tide between them, Sophir's final words were soft but filled with all the intensity he felt. "Mine."

Sophir could feel Lonan's body trembling beneath him, the heat of the moment swirling between them as they shared a connection deeper than anything he had ever known. Lonan's breath came in uneven gasps, his fingers clawing at the ground as though grounding himself, but he never once asked for Sophir to stop. Instead, he pressed back against him, his body urging Sophir on.

"Lonan," Sophir's voice was thick with need as he moved. Lonan's back arched under him, a low gasp escaping his lips. Sophir could barely contain the overwhelming sensation, his heart pounding in his chest. "You're..." he wasn't sure how to put into words the depth of what he felt.

"More," Lonan whispered, his voice soft and pleading, his hands digging into the dirt as though desperate for more of Sophir's touch.

With each shift of his body, Sophir felt Lonan melt into him. He gripped his hips, urging him to relax, to let go. "Let go, Lonan," he murmured, his voice rough with desire. "Stop thinking."

Lonan responded with a soft moan, his body pressing back against Sophir, craving the connection that seemed to pulse between them. The rhythm of their bodies became fluid, a perfect harmony of need and response. Sophir lost himself in it, in the way Lonan moved with him, as though they were two parts of the same whole.

"Do you want me to stop?" Sophir asked, his voice soft with concern as he pulled back slightly, giving Lonan a chance to decide if he needed a moment. "Lonan?"

Lonan glanced over his shoulder, his eyes dark with desire, before he swayed his hips slightly in response. "Did I say stop?" He asked, his voice teasing, low and sultry.

Sophir smirked. "No," he replied, his heart racing as a wave of primal desire washed over him. "You didn't."

And with that, Sophir surged forward again, losing himself in the movement, in the feeling of Lonan beneath him. The sounds of Lonan's breath, his soft gasps, only fueled the fire inside him. They were moving together now, as though nothing else existed but the two of them, wrapped in this shared moment.

"Ancients, it feels good," Lonan gasped, his fingers pressing into the earth as he met Sophir's movements with his own. He pushed back, his body hungry for more, each thrust matching the rhythm of Sophir's. "Please...don't stop."

"Make me," Sophir growled, his voice thick with a challenge. "Show me how much you want this."

Lonan turned his head, their eyes locking for a moment. His breath hitched, and Sophir felt a thrill run through him. "Take me harder," Lonan whispered, his voice low and full of longing. "Harder. I need you."

Sophir responded to the challenge, his body moving faster, deeper, as though he couldn't resist the pull any longer. The world around them seemed to fade as he became lost in the heat, in the feeling of Lonan's body against his, their connection stronger than ever.

"Yes!" Lonan cried out, his back arching, and he arched into Sophir as though he was trying to draw him even closer. "Show me what you can do."

Sophir's grip tightened on his waist as he moved faster, the words coming out of his mouth a low growl. "You like this, don't you?" he rasped. "You want to feel me—want to be filled completely?"

"I want everything," Lonan cried, his voice full of desperate need. "Don't hold back."

Sophir's heart raced at those words, and he moved with even more urgency. Each thrust seemed to pull them both further into the depths of what they shared. The intensity of it overwhelmed him, and yet, it felt as though this was where they were always meant to be.

Lonan's hands gripped his shoulders, urging him on, his voice trembling with need. "Give it to me," he whispered. "Please."

Sophir's pace quickened, his focus entirely on Lonan and the way his body responded. They were both lost now, caught in the intensity of the moment. The sounds of their breaths, their words, everything around them seemed to become a part of the melody of their connection.

"Don't stop," Lonan whispered urgently, his voice strained with need. "Please."

Sophir gave him everything—every ounce of strength, every bit of desire. "Come, Lonan," he demanded, his voice rough, as he moved to the rhythm of their shared pleasure.

And then, with a cry, Lonan shattered beneath him, his body trembling, his breath coming in gasps as he came undone. The sight of Lonan breaking beneath him dragged Sophir over the edge, his body giving in with a shudder.

As the world around them settled, Sophir pulled back gently, both of them catching their breath. He watched as Lonan slowly regained his composure, his back marked by the lingering traces of their connection.

"I need to check on Faedi," Lonan said softly, his voice still filled with emotion.

Sophir nodded, watching him disappear into the shadows. He remained standing there for a moment, his thoughts swirling. This night had not solved everything, but it had shifted something between them. It was a beginning, and perhaps that was all he could hope for.

He moved to the stream, washing away the remnants of the moment, but the truth lingered. When he returned to their camp, he leaned against a tree, lost in thought.

Nothing between them was simple anymore. But as the night held its silence, Sophir knew one thing for certain: none of them could pretend the night hadn't changed everything.

But, for a time, he could wait to see how they would react.

26
Shared Bonds

Sophir

He walked beside the horses while Lonan sat on the wooden bench, directing them to follow Faedi. His eyes scanned the horizon, constantly alert for any sign of enemies. There was a silent understanding between them: they would watch for cultists while Faedi hunted for a trail.

As they traveled together over nearly a week, their time was divided between near-mindless rounds of heat beddings and moments of comfortable silence or learning about one another. Those long stretches of quiet no longer felt uncomfortable, as they had when they first met. Instead of suspicion and fear, familiarity began to extend between them. It was refreshing, even if Sophir suspected it was mainly due to the heat.

The mood soured when he learned about the forest-folk farmers who were slaughtered. Ravyn hadn't mentioned them when they were together, and Faedi hadn't said anything until the second day of her heat, when Lonan gave her a jar of jam. The happiness in her eyes vanished almost as quickly as it appeared, replaced with tears.

Then they told him what happened.

Sophir knew Blavier would be furious at their disappearance, that there would be repercussions come spring when no one would be left to sow the fields, but he hadn't expected anyone to hunt them down and murder them. Given Blavier's habits, he thought the worst he might do was imprison them—though that would have been unjust, considering they broke no laws in their departure. But they were murdered instead.

No one mentioned the forest-folk again, and Faedi didn't eat the jam. Sophir thought Lonan would discard it, but instead, he hid it on the back of the cart under a pile of furs. He didn't offer an explanation when his eyes met Sophir's.

He didn't need to.

It was something Faedi loved; Sophir saw it in her eyes before the sadness took over. He had witnessed her happiness and excitement over such a simple thing and knew that joy had been stolen from her, taken by hatred and greed.

After hours of silence, Faedi gradually began to name the plants they passed, explaining their uses. At first, Sophir thought she might be uncomfortable with the silence, but then he noticed the way Lonan would frown and look away whenever she mentioned the adverse reactions to certain herbs.

She was teaching them, preparing them for the worst in case they were separated—or worse.

Sophir didn't want to dwell on those possibilities, but he didn't interrupt her. He diligently worked to remember everything she said. If teaching and preparing them made her feel better, he would have been wrong to deny her that peace of mind, even if it filled him with dread.

As she searched for Torix's tracks, Sophir observed how she gathered herbs as the scenery shifted around them. Her falcon also frequently flew off for hours, only to return with herbs in his talons for her. Sophir didn't think to ask her what they were or what they were for unless she offered the information freely. He didn't want to make anyone uncomfortable with his questions.

He told himself he was only watching her because he had nothing better to do, that it was simple curiosity, nothing more—but the longer he watched her, the more he became aware of the quiet grace in the way she moved.

In a way, she was like Ravyn; the practiced care she used when she plucked each herb, how she seemed to sway slightly with the wind. The world answered her, and him, in ways it never would for Sophir—bending to her touch, yielding to her voice. And he envied it.

Her falcon returned, dropping something small into her waiting palm before perching on her shoulder. She murmured to him, running a gentle finger over his sleek feathers, and Sophir clenched his fists. What would it be like to have that softness turned toward him? To have her hands linger, not out of duty or necessity, but because she wanted to?

He tried to shake the thought away, but it lingered, curling in his chest like a fire too stubborn to die.

He kept his distance, unwilling to let his thoughts betray him, but it became harder with every step. Every time she turned her head, the sunlight caught in her dark hair, turning it into something almost ethereal, something that made him ache in ways he refused to name. She was focused, lost in her task, while he warred with himself, pretending he didn't want what he couldn't have.

His heart had no right to that longing. No right to wish for her gaze to linger on him the way it did on the forest around them. And yet, as she knelt to inspect the ground, her brow furrowed in concentration, he couldn't stop the thought that stole through his mind—he wanted to be something she reached for.

The dense forest began to thin, the towering trees growing sparser while the underbrush became less tangled. Sunlight, which had struggled to penetrate the thick canopy, now streamed through the gaps, casting dappled patterns on the ground. Even the air felt lighter, and as Sophir relaxed from the oppressive magic of the forest, he noticed that both Lonan and Faedi appeared more tense.

It made sense when he considered it. The Mire and Sauvern provided safety, and each step they took moved them further from that protection. The plains and mountains were unknown territory, full of danger.

"If any cultists are this far east, they'll be easier to spot," Sophir commented, noting how the horses' hooves echoed less in the open space.

Faedi looked over her shoulder at him. "The nomad dwarves might handle them."

"Do they normally venture this far south?" He raised an eyebrow. "I heard they preferred farther northeast in Emsmeda."

"They trade with us closer to winter," Lonan said from the cart. "Some of them stay with us through the season—family members of The Hunt."

Sophir nodded, recalling what he had heard about the nomad dwarves worshiping the gods of the hunt. It made sense for them to stay close to the most extensive grouping of were-folk on the Western continent. But he couldn't shake his worry about the dwarves. The cultists were ruthless, and if they learned of the dwarves' friendship with the Mire—

"Found it!" Faedi exclaimed suddenly, bouncing on her toes as she pointed at a tree. "It's his mark, and… he left us supplies!"

Sophir rushed over as she tried to pick up a large pack hidden in a log, hoisting it onto his shoulder after she snagged a black bow from the side of it. Her wide smile surprised him, her near squeal of delight like a child receiving a name-day gift, but he didn't comment.

His attention turned to Lonan, whose wide-eyed expression revealed his shock.

What's wrong?

"This is his bow," Faedi mused, examining the intricate carvings in the wood. "He said… this is his."

"Torix's?" Sophir asked, carrying the pack to the cart.

"Yes," she confirmed with a half-mesmerized nod. "It's a family heirloom. It has a sister—they were made from the twin hearts centuries ago. The bow and an axe."

"Torix didn't have an axe," Lonan stated, his tone firm. "He had a sword."

"He had an axe when I was little. I remember him showing it to me and Sylrie. I couldn't even pick it up, but Syl…"

Sophir watched as the joy faded from her eyes when she mentioned her brother's name, her shoulders dropping in defeat. Anger washed over him as he observed her trace the intricate carvings on the bow. It threatened to erupt when he saw her quickly wipe her eyes.

"We move south from here," she announced, rushing to lead them away from the tree.

I'll kill them all and their bastard god for doing this to her.

His fury continued to simmer as Faedi hurried ahead of them. Her quickened pace and forced composure were betrayed by the tears she refused to let fall. Painful memories overshadowed the joy she had moments before.

He turned his attention to Lonan, studying his expression. Concern was etched on his features; his head lowered as he stared after Faedi. The sorrow in his eyes was evident, and Sophir wondered if he should push for more information.

"What is her relationship with Warden Torix?" he asked softly.

"He helped raise her—he was friends with her parents," Lonan sighed as he rubbed the back of his neck. "He… was like a second father to her. He presented her at our bonding ceremony."

"And Syl?" Sophir pressed gently.

"Her twin brother. He's the one who got her out of the house," Lonan said, clicking his tongue to urge the horses to follow after her.

"Torix… he couldn't find her or Syl's corpses when he buried her mother and…" His voice trailed off as he thought back to the names of the other two. "Genris and Gelen."

He looked over at him, shocked. "What?"

"He was under the assumption that there was nothing left of them. He buried two eventides instead," Sophir said, nodding as he recalled the memory. "I helped him bury them."

Lonan's gaze lingered on Faedi, his jaw clenched. He appeared deep in thought, and Sophir hesitated to question him further. Eventually, he shook his head and turned to face Sophir again.

"You should tell her," he urged. "Just… not right now."

Sophir tilted his head, intrigued. "Would her knowing help anything?"

"I don't know, but she hates secrets and lies," Lonan shrugged, settling more comfortably on the cart. "It makes me wonder, though… she got away, which explains the absence of her corpse, but Sylrie… what if he made it out too? If he went a different way than she did—"

Sophir watched Faedi walk further away, though she remained in sight. "Was he as educated about the forest as she was?"

"He was," Lonan confirmed.

"Then perhaps we should hope for him," Sophir nodded, as if he had already decided. "We'll hope for both of them."

Faedi's herb lessons stopped after they turned south, and the air grew colder with each step. It wasn't long before they had to raid the supplies in the cart for more layers, but they pressed on. There was too much ground to cover between them and the mountains, and their peaks were still too small on the horizon.

Dusan's gifts of herbs also ceased, but he continued flying off for other things: small game and fowl or anything else they could eat. During that time, Sophir learned that Faedi didn't like rabbits. Or rather, they assumed she didn't. On the few occasions Dusan brought them back, she'd frown and eat very little—though Lonan tried to coax her to eat more for strength.

They'd stopped using soul speech around him, and neither used it to speak to him.

As they traveled, Sophir worried that whatever aid they might obtain would arrive too late. The cultists would likely attack the Mire soon unless they had reinforcements already on the way. No one knew the exact number of Umbrals or creatures available to protect them, and if what Lonan and Faedi said was true, they had Dwarves and The Hunt to contend with, along with the Guardians and Wardens Ravyn had sent away from the city.

The number of cultists Sophir had seen within Dewgate—even if they had the entire city's population—wouldn't last long against all that.

"How far ahead do you think Torix is?" Sophir asked when the silence grew too heavy.

Faedi looked back at him. "How long were we unconscious?"

"Two days," he replied, hoping that wasn't too long and that Torix hadn't taken them too far off course. But they couldn't change time.

"He'll be at least three or four days ahead of us then," Faedi said, pointing at another mark on a tree. "He said he would leave the Mire after we left, and his path would have been straighter south than ours. This one is at least a couple of days old."

"Was he at the Mire with you?" Sophir asked, though they hadn't seen the Warden in years; his face was hard to forget.

"He heard Faedi call The Hunt when we went after the cultists and came," Lonan explained, rubbing his hands together to keep warm. "He told us about her being the heir of the Dusk Elves and said he would prepare King Haldin for us."

"Prepare?" Sophir quirked a brow, not entirely understanding the phrase.

"King Haldin hates the Umbrals because he blames them for my mother dying," Faedi explained while she walked, examining the pale plants they passed. "Torix said he would try to make him agreeable to meet with us. He made it sound like he thinks I'm dead or that I don't exist…it's hard to keep track of all the lies and stories."

"Although he still might not be happy," Lonan added. "She might be an heir by blood, but she and I completed our bond in the Mire."

"When you say completed," Sophir looked between them, "is that what caused your…heat?"

"We got married," Lonan beamed, and the traveler smiled. "She stands to take the throne with me."

"It might have been the ceremony. Natural-born were-folk have heats or mating seasons. I didn't sing my first song until after Lonan found me and healed me. My parents—I don't know if they were or not. Our disguises are Krelin."

"I didn't sing until then either—we assumed she might have come in contact with something in the forest, and that's how I developed some were-folk traits," Lonan added.

Sophir turned their attention back to Faedi and frowned. If she didn't know her mother was an heir to the Dusk Elves, there were likely many other things she didn't know about her family. However, he didn't press the issue; he didn't want to upset her, especially after seeing her face fall simply at mentioning her brother's name.

"Is that why you two have similar tattoos?" Sophir asked instead, thinking it seemed a safe topic. He hadn't seen the tattoos before, although he hadn't seen them naked until after the ceremony.

"Every Umbral bonded to their partner takes the marks when they have their ceremony," Lonan explained, glancing down at his hands. "My parents advised us to wait until we were older and decided to take the bond since… well, I accidentally started the process when we were younger."

"I wouldn't be alive if you didn't," Faedi called over her shoulder, her voice light.

"You bond by healing?" Sophir paused, sitting back on the cart's bench. "Is that a common occurrence?"

"The betrothal bond is sealed when the parties make a blood oath and heal each other, yes?" Lonan stared at him, and then his jaw went slack. "*Oh, Gods.*"

"You healed us after the cultists." Faedi stopped walking and turned around. "Were you hurt? Did you heal yourself?"

"I was more focused on the both of you," Sophir admitted, scratching the back of his neck and shrugging helplessly.

"I don't intend to force either of you to complete some kind of bond with me," he added quickly. "I admire and respect you both, and I wouldn't take back what I did either… but I also don't want to force you to—does the bond make you have feelings for someone?"

"No. My mother said she and my father fell in love after marriage." Lonan rested his elbows on his knees. "The bond does not remove free will."

Sophir should have been relieved. The bond didn't force feelings, didn't strip away their choice. It meant that whatever was building in his chest, twisting tighter every time Lonan and Faedi spoke, every time their gazes flicked to them, wasn't some trick of magic. It was real.

And that terrified him.

He watched Lonan, the way his hands curled loosely between his knees, the way shadows cast over his face. He was trying to be careful, measured, as if the weight of his words might break something fragile between them.

Did they know how the sound of their voices settled under their skin, how their presence filled spaces he hadn't realized were empty? Sophir wanted to reach for them, the way Faedi reached for plants and wildlife, to test if the pull they felt was tangible. But he didn't.

Because he knew himself, knew the hunger that stirred in them when he let his guard slip. He kept their wants buried beneath duty and reason. Releasing his hold on his more primal desires was one thing, when it was in service to their time of need, but he wouldn't—couldn't—let go otherwise. Not when he knew that if he let himself go, if he gave in to his desires, he wouldn't be able to stop.

Because I'm ruined.

"You've forced nothing." Faedi's voice pulled Sophir from his thoughts, and his heart stopped when she smiled at him. "Whatever you feel about us, if you feel anything, is you."

Her words hit harder than expected, settling deep in his chest and leaving him feeling raw. Exposed. She said it like it was simple, like it was something he should have already known, but he wasn't sure what to do with it.

She hadn't said what they felt for him; her statement was too open-ended to make assumptions or have hopes. However, if the bond wasn't shaping their feelings for him, what he felt pressing against his ribs was real; there was no excuse—his heart was pulling him toward her. Toward them.

And Ancients, he was already too far gone.

"I—that is good to know," Sophir returned her smile before looking up at the sky. "We should find somewhere to camp."

He swallowed hard while he searched the sky for something to ground him. The vast openness hadn't ever failed him before; it was steady, unchanging, and a constant presence no matter where they stood. But then, it was different—too open, too full of things he wasn't ready to face.

Ravyn would have known what to say to put his mind at ease. He always did. He would have laughed, made a simple joke—or maybe he would have changed the subject with a simplicity Sophir could never replicate.

He exhaled sharply and forced themselves to look away, to push back the ache that suddenly formed in his chest. He saw Ravyn, only for a moment, and the pain in his eyes when he commanded Sophir to leave. He'd never looked at him like that before, and he couldn't help but wonder.

Did he…did Ravyn create a bond, too?

27
A Walk in the Past

"The stars shine so much brighter outside of the Sauvern and Mire. I wonder if they look the same in Rowdon and Valoria. I should ask Ravyn when we get back."

Faedi

She lay on the ground with her hand behind her head, studying the dots in the sky as they twinkled overhead. She connected imaginary lines to create constellations while Sophir and Lonan chatted about Umbral traditions and customs. A smile tugged at her lips as she glanced at the Astral Itmis, seeing him wide-eyed, completely enthralled by everything Lonan had to say—like a child listening to a story.

He didn't ask questions until Lonan paused, either too engrossed in his words or too polite, but each question led to another explanation from Lonan. The trend continued for hours, eventually shifting to the bonding ceremony. Lonan compared what they had to a traditional one, and Faedi couldn't help but laugh when he recounted their failed dance attempt in the cottage.

Sophir's eyes sparkled with excitement as he expressed a desire to see a traditional Umbral dance, eager to compare it to what he knew as an Itmis.

"Faedi and I are horrible dancers," Lonan chuckled.

"That just means you need a better teacher," Sophir said, standing in one fluid motion and holding a hand out to her. His eyes were still bright, eager, and Ancients help her, it was impossible to resist that kind of enthusiasm.

"I don't think you understand how bad we are," Faedi warned, but he only grinned. Before she could talk herself out of it, she let him pull her to her feet.

Lonan groaned behind her. "You're going to regret this, Sophir."

"We'll see," Sophir said with a teasing chuckle, already moving them into position. His hands were warm as he adjusted her stance, one on her waist, the other guiding hers to his shoulder. "Just follow my lead."

The moment he stepped forward, she stepped back—straight onto his foot.

She winced and started to apologize, but Sophir only laughed and tightened his grip so she wouldn't stumble. "All right, maybe you weren't exaggerating."

Lonan smiled up at them, still seated, and looked far too amused. "Told you."

"Oh no, you're not getting out of this." With a sudden shift, Sophir pulled Lonan up and into their little circle. "If we're dancing, we're all dancing."

Lonan sighed dramatically, but his smirk gave him away. "Fine, but when Faedi breaks your toes—don't say I didn't warn you."

Faedi rolled her eyes. "You're just as likely to break digits." She would have said more, but her words vanished when Sophir spun her—gracefully that time, no foot-crushing involved.

His confidence made it easier to move, to find the rhythm in his steps, and she couldn't help but smile. When Lonan joined, clumsy at first but adapting quickly, the three of them moved together in a way that she wasn't sure was any sort of traditional dance—but it was theirs.

And for a while, under the quiet glow of the stars, the weight of everything didn't seem quite as heavy. Even when the dance took a turn.

Sophir shifted to guide them into another step, and Lonan hesitated enough to throw them off. Her foot caught his, Sophir moved quickly to correct it, and in the chaos of tangled limbs and misguided steps, they all went down in a heap.

Faedi landed on top of Lonan, who let out a very undignified oof as Sophir crashed beside them, barely catching himself before his elbow jabbed into Faedi's ribs. For a heartbeat, there was silence, then Sophir started to laugh—a deep, full-bodied laughter that was utterly contagious.

Lonan groaned beneath her, his breath caught while he tried to laugh. "This," he started, his voice strained, "is exactly why we don't dance."

Faedi tried to glare at him, but she was already laughing too hard. "I think we did pretty well."

Sophir, still grinning, sat back on his knees. "You lasted longer than I expected." He reached out and tucked a loose strand of hair behind her ear, and Ancients help her, the warmth of it sent a shiver down her spine. "But maybe next time, we'll try something slower."

Lonan huffed a laugh, shaking his head. "Next time, huh?" He looked between them hand grinned. "Then you're going to see that Myst is the better dancer. They always show me up at solstices."

"I was sorry to hear they were blinded," Sophir bowed his head. "Ravyn said they were supposed to be a messenger to get all of us to the Mire, but the attack stopped them."

"A messenger?" Faedi sat up, raising her eyebrows as she accepted the food from Lonan. "They didn't mention it."

"Ravyn said it was a plan with Lady Callon. I assume it was about the refugees being sent to the Mire, but he didn't give me much information. Either Lady Callon didn't tell him, or he still didn't trust me entirely," he explained.

"The refugees are from Dewgate?" Lonan asked as he settled between them. "What else did Ravyn tell you?"

"Just that Wardens and Guardians are not returning to the city and that Lady Callon sent people of less…cultist-favorable heritage to the Mire," Sophir shook his head. "He also mentioned that she was taken prisoner."

"They arrested her?" Faedi asked, picking at the dried meat.

He nodded and tossed the stick he used to clean from under his nails. "Sadly."

"She is devout to the Ancients," Faedi confirmed, tilting her head. "The Orderlings could have done worse."

"I'm surprised they didn't burn her when they defaced the temple with Ilos' flame."

Faedi clenched her jaw at the news of the temple, a chill shooting down her spine. It made sense for the cultists to desecrate a place that didn't belong to their god, but hearing it still made her heart ache.

She remembered her first visit there with her mother, how the imposing building had felt intimidating upon approach, but became home the moment she stepped inside. The priestess had smelled of sweet smoke, and the woman in the back had fed her stew while sewing a hole in her pants. They healed illnesses and fed the poor there.

Of course, they would taint a place of healing.

"Does Ravyn intend to stay there?" Faedi asked, pulling herself away from the memory.

"I believe so, or nearby. He said that he had his path and that the cultists should leave him alone. He's already been—"

"Cleansed in Valoria," Faedi cut him off. "They started their practices in the east. His family came here after the purges."

"He said for years that Ilos' devotees did the raids, but we could never find proof. I thought he might have been wrong when we went so long without any other attack." Sophir frowned, avoiding his food. "Even the soldiers in the last war, their fire was different—manipulated from torches rather than conjured out of nothing. Yet, they infiltrated the city and influenced the Lord."

"It isn't surprising," Lonan commented with a shrug. "He was the one who outlawed were-folk from the city. Ilos' followers could have been there for decades, just waiting for the right time to attack."

"But why now?" Sophir shook his head, and Faedi frowned.

That was the question no one seemed to have an answer to. If they had been there longer than they assumed, there would have been plenty of opportunities to move. They could have taken Dewgate in the last war, after the raids, or even before—but they waited.

"Did they say anything to either of you or near you?" Sophir asked, trying to break the silence.

"Other than commanding me to die? No," Lonan shook his head, and Faedi shifted as their gazes turned to her.

"He told me to repent and be purified," Faedi admitted, her voice barely above a whisper.

"What about the ones from the raids?" Sophir's voice was soft but made Faedi jump as if he had shouted.

"They were unarmed. I thought they were lost. One of them had been attacked by something; he was bleeding and needed healing. I…" She trailed off, looking away as she forced herself to remember instead of shoving the memory away. "I took them home. I knew my mother could help them. At first, they were kind and thanked us for helping them. They ate dinner with us, but one of them said something—I don't know what language it was. My mother's skin… it changed. Papa told us to hide, and then there was fire."

She hugged her knees to her chest, taking a breath before continuing. "Wait, before the fire… one of them said 'it's her' when Papa told us to hide. He grabbed a stone from the hearth. I couldn't hear what he said; Sylrie and I were too far away. We took Genris and Gelen to the back door; we were going to hide in the forest, but there were people outside. They called us shadow-kin and… said to kill the Krelin mutts before they…"

"It's alright," Lonan spoke from behind her, wrapping his arms around her. She hadn't noticed he and Sophir had moved closer. "Breathe."

"You don't have to continue," Sophir whispered, offering her water.

"They burned Genris and Gelen in front of us," she choked back a sob, wiping her face with her hand. "Sylrie picked me up and carried me into the cellar. There was a window we used to sneak out of the house to watch the glowbugs. One of them followed us. Sylrie… he dropped me when they burned him and took a wood axe. He told me to run while he tried to keep the cultist away, but the fire… I couldn't see the window; it burned my hands, and… Sylrie pushed me out. He told me to find Torix. Then they chased me—they said to catch me, but… they burned me."

"That's when we got there; we saw people using flames outside," Lonan nodded, wiping her tears before encouraging her to drink more. "Myst and I came with The Watch when we saw the smoke. We killed the two, but we couldn't find Faedi."

"Was the fire they used on your other brothers different?" Sophir's tone remained gentle, cautious.

She shook her head. "I don't remember."

"I have an idea if you are willing to try," he said, his eyes catching hers. She bit her lip. "I can see your memories, be in them, and witness things you could not. Your memory would allow me to experience the moment as a whole."

"Would I see it too?" She didn't know if she could bear to witness it again.

"You would," he frowned, sighing. "You would see yourself and everyone else. See the moment for what it was. It can be confusing for some, for their memories to occasionally differ from what they remember. I only suggest it because there might be something—anything—that can tell us why the cultists chose now to act."

"Is that an astral dragon thing?" Lonan asked softly.

"It is," he nodded. "A gift from Shivr, the god of history, to my ancestor, Mumir."

Faedi looked at the sky while she considered his idea. She knew it would be wrong to deny his request if it meant information that could help the Mire or aid them when they met her grandfather. However, she didn't want to relive it. She didn't want to see them die all over again, powerless to stop it.

She wanted to forget.

"What about Lonan?" she asked, still gazing at the stars.

"He will guard us while we are in the trance," Sophir replied. "What will feel like hours to us will only be minutes for Lonan."

"How much will we see?" She squinted; some constellations were dimmer than they should have been.

"It depends," his voice dropped to a whisper. "I will remove us if it becomes too much."

She turned away from the stars and looked at him. "Do it."

"As you wish."

Sophir beckoned for her to join him beside the cart, and she steadied herself before she approached. He spread his legs and patted the ground between them as he removed his pendant. After his glamour vanished, she stood between his legs and looked back at Lonan. He was already on his feet, eyes on her—waiting and watching.

"Sit with your back to my chest," Sophir instructed gently. "It will be more comfortable."

"Alright," she nodded, biting her lip as she did what he said. "Now what?"

"Just close your eyes and breathe. Think about the moment you found them in the forest."

He pressed his hand gently against her forehead and leaned her back against him. She took a last look at Lonan, trying to smile, but it wouldn't come. Instead, she sighed and closed her eyes as Sophir began to rumble softly behind her. He whispered something, the words too quiet for her to piece together, and soon her body felt weightless, as if she were on the cusp of sleep.

"Shake me three times if there is danger," Sophir's instruction to Lonan faded into the distance as if she were submerged underwater.

"Open your eyes," Sophir whispered in her ear.

"I'm scared," she admitted, shaking her head. "I don't think I can."

"I thought you said the eventides grew on you after the raids."

"They did," she replied, opening her eyes and looking back at him. "They grew when Lonan—"

Sophir smiled and gently turned her chin, pointing at… her. Her dark brown hair was a tangled mess, stuck to her cheeks and ears, with leaves and twigs poking out of the waves. Her clothes were smeared with mud, her pants torn at the knees, and her feet were bare against the leaves.

A single eventide was tucked behind her ear.

She sat crouched by a stump, cradling a mouse as she spoke to it about the best places to find seeds where the squirrels and birds wouldn't bother it. She was completely unaware of their presence, even though they were only a few steps away. Nothing pulled her attention from her conversation with the mouse.

"Mama had us wear them whenever we went into the forest," she told him. "She said it would keep predators away and that Torix could find us if we got lost. It was the first thing she taught me to grow—I kept a pouch of their seeds in my pocket."

"You were adorable," he mused with a chuckle.

"I was a terror," she corrected him. "Sylrie said I would get eaten because I always ran off. My little brothers were terrified to be away from Mama and Papa."

His bright eyes twinkled with delight. "Well…you had valuable information to provide the mice."

Her laughter faded when leaves rustled nearby, and she watched her child self leap to her feet and hide behind the stump. Sophir wrapped his arm over her shoulder and squeezed gently, but her attention was drawn to the trees. They didn't whip around violently as they had when the cottage was attacked. The trees didn't know there was danger.

They would have warned her if they had.

"The trees are quiet," she whispered. "The forest had never seen them before."

"This was twenty and two years ago?" Sophir asked softly, and she nodded. "So if they came through the forest before, they did so without causing damage."

"They would have warned me if they knew they were dangerous," she told him, watching the humans approach.

Just as she remembered, they were unarmed and without armor. One had his arms draped over the shoulders of the two beside him while blood pooled around the rough bandaging around his waist. She snarled, wishing she had left them for dead as she watched her child self slowly peek from behind the stump.

She smelled the blood.

"That's them," she told him, and the memory paused. "What—"

"I want to see where the others were," Sophir announced as he walked away from her and into the trees. "You said there were more outside of your home; they would have followed from nearby. They might have said something."

"You can stop time in the memories?" She chased after him.

"I can." He confirmed with a nod before he pointed to the left. "There."

She followed his finger and squinted into the trees. A glint of gold caught her eye. She approached cautiously as if they might move or attack at any moment, but they were motionless. There were twelve of them, their armor hidden under brown cloaks. Even further behind them were two more, with a horse-drawn cart—a cage.

"I am going to start the memory again," he warned her before the disguised cultists began to move.

"We can't kill them, can we?" She stepped back beside him.

"No," he frowned and shook his head. "We'll move through them and anything else here if we try to touch them."

"Damn," she huffed, glaring at the group.

"Did they find one of them?" One of the cultists whispered before they were hushed.

"It's a child," another told them. "Don't scare it away."

"A child?" Spoke one near the cage. "No one said anything about children."

"We go where Ilos leads."

She squinted at the one in front, who spoke of Ilos, then looked at the one who seemed disturbed about children. They were younger. Hidden under their silver hair and scruffy facial hair was a deep scar from the left side of his forehead to his chin. The eye, partially closed by the scar, was white, while the other burned red like hot coals.

He was not human—he smelled like…a predator.

A silver chain around his neck rattled, and he bared his teeth as if in pain before he stepped back and shook his head. The other person beside the cage glanced at him, her eyes red like his, and whispered something in a language she did not know. The scarred man nodded, and then they turned their eyes forward—to where she was with the other three.

She pointed at the two with the cage. "They are slaves."

"Do you recognize them?" he asked, examining the man and woman through the cultists. "They are chained to the cart."

"No, I've never seen them before." She shook her head. "What else?"

"Binding runes." He leaned closer to them and studied the man's face. "Barely visible. I don't recognize the markings."

She bit her lip as the group began to move slowly, and she followed along with them. Sadly, they did not speak about their plans. They remained silent while they followed their allies, led by her child self. However, as they walked, her skin began crawling like someone was watching.

The group stopped again before she could find the source, and she looked through the trees. Her childhood home was just on the other side, past a clearing. Smoke plumed from the chimney, the stone and wooden sides were covered in eventides, farm animals skittered about the property, and her two little brothers played outside with wooden swords.

They were alive—but they wouldn't be for long.

28

Prophecies and Truths

Sophir

*H*e wondered if it had been wrong to suggest that Faedi relive her worst
memory, especially with more detail than she likely wanted, but it was too late to
turn back now. Unless she asked him to stop, they would remain in this moment
while they searched for answers. He couldn't ignore the way her eyes widened,
filling with tears as she watched her twin brothers, Genris and Gelen, playing in
the distance.

Soon, they would be burned before her eyes.

"You should not be here."

Sophir looked away from Faedi, his senses tingling at the unfamiliar voice,
but nothing seemed out of place. It was just the cultists, their chained slaves,
Faedi, himself, and her family on the other side of the trees. Then, his gaze met
the red-eyed woman's. Her eyes turned white as she stared at him.

He spun quickly, glancing over his shoulder to see what had caught her
attention. Perhaps something in the trees had drawn her focus, but there was
nothing there—just branches swaying gently in the breeze.

"He knows you are here."

Sophir focused on the woman again and opened his mouth to speak, but she
shook her head quickly. The motion was barely perceptible, but it was enough.
She could see him. She could see Faedi.

"Who is 'he'?" He asked, squinting at her, then glancing at the chained man
who appeared unaware of their presence. *"Him?"*

"Ilos," she replied, standing motionless. *"And his allies. They know you are here. Whatever you are looking for—find it fast."*

Sophir tilted his head, feeling a twinge of concern. *"How do they know we're here?"*

"Ilos has been in her mind before. He knows when it is tampered with."

"How?" His brows furrowed. *"She is devout to the Ancients—"*

"One of his worshipers gave him access when she was a child." She cut him off, her frown deepening.

Sophir stepped back, glancing at Faedi, who was still unaware. *"Do they know where our bodies are?"*

"No, not yet. And don't tell me where you are. They might find out. They torture them in Ashar for the information we share. I don't want them to hurt them more," she warned quickly. *"They are going to destroy the Mire. They will kill the Umbrals—they want to tip the balance in their favor. They will kill anyone who does not bend to them."*

"Them?" He asked, trying to grasp the weight of her words.

"Captured eclipse-born who have a connection to divine magics. Like Faedi and like her."

"Her?" Sophir glanced around the group, searching for another woman, but there was none.

"Ragna, this poor soul I'm speaking through. I don't have much time. They want to destroy the Mire and twin hearts. Ilos will not stand for the Dusk Elves to return to Dewgate; he will wipe out the western continent before he lets that happen. Do not let his men get your friend. She is eclipse-born—they will enslave her and sacrifice her to Ilos with the others when the time comes."

"How do you know this?" Sophir narrowed his eyes before looking back at Faedi. How could this woman know when Faedi was born?

"Ragna told me his plans."

"When will they sacrifice them? How many do they already have?" Sophir's mind raced as he tried to piece together the gravity of the situation. If what she said was true, the chained woman was fighting against Ilos in whatever way she could.

"I don't know, but they will sacrifice them when the moons and sun align with the earth."

Sophir furrowed his brow. He might have been an Astral Itmis, but he had no idea when that alignment would happen. The second moon didn't appear nightly like the first one, and he hadn't seen a glimpse of it in years. However, with the cultists' sudden shift in tactics, he assumed that the alignment would happen soon.

"How do we stop them?" He asked, turning his gaze back to the chained pair, his frown deepening. Were they eclipse-born?

"Find the crowns."

"What crowns?" He bit back a groan. He doubted she meant literal crowns. She spoke too much like his sister—like a seer.

"Find me, and I can tell you. Look for me in the stone, with frozen hearts and leaves. Please, get here before they do."

Before Sophir could ask any more questions, the white tint faded from the woman's eyes, and the cultists began to move again. He turned to find Faedi still standing beside the same tree. Her tears hadn't spilled yet, but she remained motionless as the cultists passed her. Whoever had spoken to him had given him crucial information, but he wasn't sure if there was more to learn.

"Faedi?" He placed his hands gently on her shoulders. "We can go."

"No," she shook her head quickly. "I need to see."

"Are you sure?" He asked, his frown deepening at the tremor in her voice.

"I need to know Torix buried the right bodies. I don't want any of these bastards beside my family."

Sophir sighed, watching her as she followed the cultists. It was a valid concern, and he would help her remove anyone who wasn't welcome near her family's graves, but he worried it might be too much for her. It could even be too much for him—to witness innocent children murdered in the name of a twisted god. But he wouldn't leave until she was ready.

Even as his heart pounded in his chest, he followed her.

From what Faedi had told him, the scene would shift quickly. He would witness everything for himself, and he hoped she wouldn't hate him for making her relive it. Even if she claimed to want to stay and ensure her family was properly cared for after death, he knew the pain might change her mind.

There was no time to admire the home's beauty or consider what he had been told—not when he knew the danger lurking inside. He could have stopped the memory and given himself time to appreciate the surroundings. He wondered if he should have. There were markings along the doorframe, hidden under vines of eventides, but Faedi was already inside by the time he thought to ask her about them.

Sophir paused outside the door. The screams hadn't begun yet, and Faedi had said there was time before the attack. Maybe there was time for him to learn more before the chaos erupted.

He sidestepped around the house, taking in the details. The materials were all from the area—no stone or wood sourced from outside the forest. A bundle of hay in the back had been painted as a target and held two differently sized arrows. One was made for an adult, but the other was child-sized. He remembered Faedi's excitement over the bow earlier and frowned.

The arrows were likely hers.

He continued while the scent of eventides masked everything else. Laughter slipped through a crack in one of the windows, and he peered inside. A boy, a bit taller than Faedi's child self, chased a little boy with a sewn toy—a dragon. The boy's squeals of delight brought a sad smile to his face.

"Mumir will fly you through the skies!" The older boy, Sylrie, called as he chased the other boy.

They knew the old stories.

Sophir shook his head with a chuckle, finishing his quick examination. Faedi was inside, and he worried how she might react if he stopped it, so he moved as swiftly as he could. There was nothing outside to indicate a target, no traces of magic, but something felt off. He just couldn't place it.

Maybe Faedi knew something—perhaps her mother had used a spell to shield them from prying eyes. It made sense for a princess in hiding. However, it seemed unlikely that the Umbrals wouldn't have noticed unless she had used a glamour before reaching the forest.

The home's interior had been calm as Sophir walked through the wall after Faedi. Her family had been gathered in the common area, and a Krelin woman had bustled about, feeding the cultists. Nearby, Faedi and her siblings had played while a male Krelin sat by the fire, patching their clothes. But that calm had been short-lived.

One of the cultists cast a spell quickly when Faedi's mother offered him a bowl of stew. Sophir watched in horror as her glamour had rippled away, revealing heavily tattooed dark blue skin. Her dark eyes had ignited like fire, and her teeth had sharpened as she turned to shout a warning. Then, the events Faedi had described began to unfold before Sophir's eyes.

Her child self and her twin had ushered the younger two away while her mother had launched herself at the three cultists in the room. Faedi's father had hurried to the hearth, speaking into an object he grabbed from the mantle. Sophir quickly realized it wasn't a stone but a crystal meant to amplify soul speech over great distances.

"Send them in. Kill the young ones; the eldest are eclipse-born."

"Papa?" Faedi's small, confused voice had made Sophir's blood boil.

She looked up at him, her eyes wide with disbelief. Faedi hadn't followed her younger self; she still heard everything with Sophir. Her father had been one of them, and he had just ordered her brothers to be killed. The revelation had hit hard. The woman who had spoken through Ragna had been right. The cultists wanted to capture Faedi and her twin.

"Gods," Sophir had breathed, turning Faedi away from the scene just before her mother had been engulfed in flames.

"He—" Faedi had stared up at her, her tears finally spilling over. "He knew."

Sophir wrapped his arms around her as she flinched at the screams of her little brothers piercing the air. He tried pulling them both from the memory, but Faedi ran away. Sophir chased after her, determined to get her out before she witnessed any more, but Faedi was been too fast; she knew she was going.

She ran for the cellar.

"Faedi, run!" Sophir heard her brother shout over the roar of the flames as he hoisted her child self from the floor and shoved her toward the window. "Go—go get Torix."

Sophir winced as she watched the boy scream, his arms burning, but she hadn't been able to look away. Faedi stood nearby, her tears silently falling as she glared at the cultist with an unmatched fury in her eyes. Sylrie turned with a feral snarl and stumbled as flames shot at his chest, but he managed to pounce on the cultist, tearing into him with his teeth and claws.

"Kill him!" Faedi had shouted at her brother, urging him on, while a faint howl had echoed from outside. "Take him to Sudek."

Sophir braced herself, waiting for Sylrie to fall, for him to succumb to his injuries, but he hadn't. He kept fighting, and once the cultist had lay dead, he went to the window and climbed out. Faedi left first, and Sophir followed closely, just a few steps behind. Sylrie stumbled and limped through the forest. The boy had only looked back once, blood and soot caked on his face, before turning to run into the trees.

"I didn't go that way," Faedi told him. "I went north...he's going south."

"He got out," Sophir said, touching her shoulder. "He didn't die."

"Can we follow him?" Faedi looked up at him, hope glimmering in her eyes. "Can we see if he makes it to safety?"

"No, it's your memory." Sophir shook his head. "Once he's too far from where you are, we'll move backward."

Faedi frowned, returning to where her brother had disappeared into the trees. She took two steps after him before lowering her head with a sigh. At that moment, Sophir wished nothing more for her to follow, for his abilities to be more remarkable than he was, but he couldn't. The only solace he had was that they'd learned something valuable.

He could only hope that her brother's survival would help soothe the sting of her father's betrayal.

But then, a flash from the north had sent a shiver down him, followed by a shriek of terror. It was Faedi. Sophir grabbed her hand and dashed toward the light. Despite Faedi's presence beside him, Sophir couldn't shake the terror twisting in his gut.

Faedi was scared, injured, and alone.

Sophir skidded to a stop when he spotted two cultists standing over Faedi, who was scrambling backward on the ground. Four others closed in, two carrying strands of silver chains. The other two were the ones who had been chained to the cage earlier.

They were coming to take her.

"Please grow, please grow," her child self cried as she threw a handful of seeds at the cultists. Nothing had happened, and they laughed at her.

"She's a child," Ragna had snarled. "What danger is she to your bastard god?"

"Leave her be," the scarred man shouted at them.

I like you two.

"You're here to track, not give commentary," an Orderling said, and the pair hit their knees as the cultists tugged their chains. The silver glowed gold.

"I don't remember this," Faedi shook her head. "Lonan came with The Watch, but I never saw them."

"I don't see The Watch," Sophir replied, stepping closer. Tiny leaves dotted the ground where her child self had backed away. "You said there were two when he arrived?"

"Yes."

"Then it isn't time yet." Sophir turned his attention back to the chained pair.

They exchanged glances; the man nodded, and the woman stood. The man wrapped the chains around his wrists and pulled on them with a snarl. The woman lunged forward, wrapping her chains around one of the cultist's necks. As she tightened them, she screamed when the metal shone brightly, but she hadn't stopped.

The man moved next, despite his neck smoking from the chains, and sunk his claws into another cultist's face. The glow from the chains illuminated his face eerily, and Sophir hadn't been able to help but smile when he thrust his other hand, wrapped in burning chains, into the cultist's mouth.

The red-eyed man snarled at Faedi. "Run, child!"

"Go to the Mire; Ilos can't reach you there," Ragna added quickly.

Sophir's brows shot up. They intended to kill the cultists, but there was a chance they might fail. The chains were burning them, their strength waned, and despite their efforts, their bodies trembled with pain and exertion. Yet, even in their pain, they were trying to protect Faedi.

"What's happening?" Faedi's voice pulled Sophir from the scene, and she faced the child on the ground again.

Her eyes hadn't been golden; they were pitch black. Shadows crept up from the ground where flowers had grown and stretched toward the chains. As they moved, they traveled up the cultists above her, holding them in place. Her child self mouthed something, but no sound reached Sophir's ears.

Sophir rushed over, kneeling to listen, narrowing his eyes in concentration. It hadn't been the common tongue, not any form of elvish, Umbral, or Faunan. It was been older—it was been the language of the Ancients.

"Leave. Them. Alone."

Sophir's eyes widened as the shadows swallowed the light, and the chains broke. The pair of slaves stood stunned, their eyes wide only for a moment before they turned their attention to the child. Ragna was the first to bow, and her companion followed suit as the shadows enveloped the cultists who lay dead on the ground.

"Run."

"We will see you again, Faetorin," Ragna promised before following the command with the red eyed man on her heels.

"How did I do that?" Faedi asked, shaking her head in disbelief. "I can't do that."

Sophir hadn't had time to answer before black, misty figures had surged through the trees. The two remaining cultists were quickly dispatched, unable to fight or flee. Sophir tilted his head as two shorter Umbrals emerged from the shadows, both with bright violet eyes and armed with black blades, but their focus hadn't been on the cultists.

"Faedi!" One shouted as they sprinted toward the blaze, a small ball of fluff trailing behind them. "Sylrie! There are people inside!"

"She's not in there." The other shook his head, and when he turned, Sophir recognized him as Lonan. "She isn't here."

Sophir looked down to where the child Faedi had been only moments ago, but she was gone. The shadows had vanished, and aside from a small spot of blood, there was no sign anyone had been there. It was as if she had evaporated into thin air.

Without warning, the memory had frozen and rippled. The shadows cast by the fire grew, and Sophir wrapped his arms around Faedi. If she remembered what happened next, they would have gone with her. The scene would have changed if she had traveled too far, but the memory was gone.

"Time to go."

29

Whispers of Stars

"This is going to start her nightmares again. I should have stopped her—nothing good can come from this. She's strong but doesn't need more scars to test her strength."

Lonan

He thought it wouldn't take long, but his patience wore thin as minutes stretched into hours. He paced around the cart, scanning the surrounding areas for any signs of fire. Each time he rounded the cart, he caught glimpses of Sophir and Faedi, and if he didn't know better, he would have assumed them to be asleep. They looked so peaceful, but he knew the memory they were in was anything but.

He hoped the effort was worth it. If what had happened to the Lirulins happened to his family, he wouldn't want to relive that nightmare.

Rubbing his shoulder where Sophir bit him, he walked, glancing up at the stars. Something was unsettling about the night sky; he had never seen some of those stars before. He recalled his stargazing nights with Faedi, where they'd lie together, tracing constellations and making new ones.

"Tree or flower?" He mused to himself, reaching out to trace lines between the stars with his finger.

Suddenly, he heard Faedi's voice, filled with fury. "That fucking bastard!" She stood from the ground, her teeth bared, and his heart raced.

He rushed over to her. "Who?"

"My *father*," she spat.

"What about him?" Anger burned in her eyes so brightly that he thought she might be capable of killing someone with just a glare.

"Her father communicated with the cultists," Sophir's voice was low and dangerous. "He told them to kill her little brothers and that she and her brother were eclipse-born."

Lonan felt his heart sink. "Oh, Faedi," he breathed, placing his hand gently on her shoulder. He could feel her trembling under his touch. "I'm…so sorry."

Sorry didn't even cover it.

"I thought everyone died. What if he made it out?" She took slow, deep breaths, shaking. "I'll kill him."

"We'll make it hurt," he promised, wrapping his arms around her as she fell into him.

Her hot tears soaked through his shirt quickly, and she didn't make a sound as she cried. Her good hand gripped his shirt tightly, the fabric tearing, and he turned his attention to Sophir, who stood nearby, his gaze downcast and solemn.

"What do eclipse births have to do with cultists?" Lonan asked him. "Another one of their prophecies?"

"There was a woman who spoke to me in the memory," Sophir explained, still avoiding his gaze. "She knew we were there. She said they plan to sacrifice the eclipse-born to Ilos and that he aims to destroy the Mire. I've never had someone speak to me in a memory before. It could be the truth or a trap. However, she seemed attached to two people the cultists had with them in the memory. They were chained to a cage—Ragna and a man."

"What else did she say?" Lonan rubbed Faedi's back gently.

"She said she could not tell me where she was. Said to find her in stone, with frozen hearts and leaves before they do." Sophir shook his head. "She said Ragna shows her things, and she knows Ilos' plans."

"If she escaped, how does she know his plans?" Faedi asked, wiping her face quickly. "They got away."

"They could have been captured again—or she knew from before," Sophir shrugged. "She stopped talking to me before I could get much more information. She said he knew we were there, though. I don't know how, but…she sounded concerned."

Lonan was almost afraid to ask. "What else did you find out?"

"Sylrie got out of the house," Faedi whispered.

"What?" He gasped, looking down at her. "He survived?"

"The fire, yes…but he was hurt. The same fire they used on my arm, they used it on him. They might have caught him, or he could have died in the forest," she looked away. "We couldn't follow him."

Lonan turned his attention to Sophir, who nodded with a frown. He assumed they couldn't follow him because of limitations on Sophir's abilities, and it wasn't a simple choice to remain where they were. He trusted that if Sophir had been able to follow Sylrie, even to appease Faedi's curiosity, he would have done so.

"Faedi also spoke in the Ancients' tongue," Sophir added. "She used magic to break Ragna and her companion's chains before she vanished. She did not run when you arrived. She disappeared."

"Where did you go?" Lonan looked down at Faedi and sighed when she shook her head. "That's alright. We have more information than we did before."

"The woman told me they want to sacrifice eclipse-born when the earth aligns with the sun and moons," Sophir told them.

"The cultist who grabbed me…" Faedi whispered, backing away as if she were reliving the moment. "He told me to repent. He was on me; he could have killed me…but he didn't. Was he trying to capture me?"

"It is possible," Sophir nodded. "If he scared you into doing whatever he said, he could have taken you. If not, he likely would have continued until you lost consciousness and taken you then."

Lonan clicked his tongue and shook his head. How their original plan to find missing supplies for the city had spiraled into this wild religious escapade made his head spin. Less than a fortnight prior, he had been focused on how to surprise Faedi for her name day on the winter solstice, planning to take her to the heart tree and—

He shook the thought from his head. They had completed the bond; it didn't matter. He wished the circumstances were different and that he could give her everything she deserved, but he couldn't—not with the threat of a bastard god and his zealots looming over them.

"It's a four-day trip to the first peak," he announced. "We should rest. I'll take the first watch."

It was better just to let Faedi sleep as much as she could.

Hours passed into the night before Lonan knelt beside Sophir and gently shook his shoulder. The Itmis had donned his glamour again, protesting Lonan's decision to take the first watch, but in the end, he'd lost the argument. Lonan needed the time to think; sleep eluded him, especially after Sophir's revelations echoed in his mind.

Faedi wasn't the only one born during the eclipse that night. Lonan had been born the same night, during the nearly two-day eclipse. The world had gone completely dark when night fell, and all light was swallowed in the vast shadow. In the deepest darkness, when even the Mire's light had faded, he had entered the world.

At least, that's what his mother had told him. He had no memory of it.

"Sophir," Lonan murmured again, shaking his shoulder until his eyes fluttered open. "Your turn."

Sophir blinked up at him, still groggy. "How long was I asleep?"

"A few hours," Lonan replied, glancing over his shoulder at the horizon. "We should leave before daybreak, though."

Sophir was on his feet in an instant. "Did you see anything?"

"No," Lonan said, still kneeling on the ground. "But if that woman was right, and Ilos knew you were here… what if there's magic to lead him here?"

"It's possible," Sophir agreed with a brief nod, his gaze serious.

"I also wanted to talk to you," Lonan admitted, his voice soft. His gaze flickered toward Faedi, asleep nearby. "About matters less severe, but perhaps equally complicated."

Sophir raised an eyebrow. "Let's walk then," he said, offering a hand to help Lonan rise. "I assume this has to do with the bond?"

"It does," Lonan nodded, taking his hand as they moved a little further from Faedi, giving her space.

The silence between them felt heavier than it should, but Lonan was reluctant to break it. His hands were clasped behind his back, and he resisted the urge to glance at Sophir. Without Faedi by their side, Sophir seemed even more imposing, and Lonan couldn't deny how the Itmis' presence stirred something in him, something he hadn't expected.

The bond had always been there, but the growing connection between them felt like it might be more than just a shared mission. Sophir, too, seemed to be changing before his eyes, maturing in ways Lonan hadn't anticipated.

They walked further, the night air cool against their skin. Sophir glanced at him, a teasing smile playing at his lips. "What is it?"

Lonan hesitated. "We haven't really spoken about what happened with the heat."

Sophir tilted his head, his expression thoughtful but not uncomfortable. "Was there something you wanted to discuss?"

"I wanted to make sure you were alright," Lonan said quietly. "The bond might not negate free will, but…I'm not sure what it does when emotions, like the heat, come into play. You…reacted to it."

Sophir was quiet for a moment, then he turned to face Lonan fully. "How do you feel?" He asked, his voice gentle but with an edge of curiosity.

Lonan was taken aback, but he met Sophir's gaze, feeling the weight of the question. "About?"

"About me," Sophir said, motioning toward Faedi in the distance. "It's clear you love her. Your auras dance together like sunlight on water. But what about me?"

Lonan paused, considering the words carefully. "At first, I thought you were a pompous ass," he admitted with a small, wry smile. "But…beyond that, you're honorable. Not something I encounter often."

Sophir's brow lifted, a glint of amusement in his eyes. "Is that why you kissed me?"

"I kissed you because I wanted to," Lonan replied, rolling his eyes but feeling a warmth spread through him at the memory. "It wasn't just the heat, Sophir. It's not every day someone defends an Umbral in an inferno."

Sophir's eyes softened, and his voice dropped to a low murmur. "I thought I had lost you that night," he said quietly. "I couldn't tell if you were breathing. I thought they had killed you."

Lonan felt a flicker of emotion in his chest at Sophir's words, and he reached for Sophir's arm, squeezing it lightly. "I'm here, Sophir. And... thank you. For coming back. For healing us."

Sophir met his gaze with a quiet sincerity that made Lonan's heart beat faster. "I shouldn't have doubted you. You and Faedi showed me kindness when I didn't deserve it. And all I did was repay that with suspicion."

"You came back," Lonan whispered. "You defended us. And... we've been growing fond of you, too."

Sophir smiled at that, stepping closer. "Fond how?"

"I think I mentioned your glamour was appealing for a human," Lonan teased softly, a smile tugging at his lips.

Sophir leaned closer, his breath warm against Lonan's skin. "And now?" he asked, his voice low and enticing.

Lonan's heart fluttered in his chest, but he held his ground. "This is about what you want," he said, the words heavier now. "I'm trying to make sure you're comfortable with all of this."

Sophir chuckled softly, his eyes twinkling with mischief. "What I want?" He mused, his fingers gently brushing Lonan's jawline. "I want to hear you say my name... when I make you lose control."

Lonan felt his breath catch at the thought, but he stepped back slightly, trying to regain some composure. "You're sure about this?" He asked, his voice shaky but determined.

Sophir's expression softened, and he reached for Lonan's hand, gently pulling him closer. "I'm here, Lonan. And I'm more than willing if you're comfortable, too."

30

Passion and Promises

"This is turning into my relationship with Ravyn. I don't know if that's a good or bad thing. Helping them through their heats was one thing—but this…I want this."

Sophir

Lonan was like a flame, flickering, reaching, and always pulling him in further. He pushed him, teased him, made him wait, until Lonan lay there in the soft grass, breathless and pleading. Each time Sophir pulled away, Lonan's silent challenge urged him back, hungry for more.

Lonan never told him to stop. Instead, he welcomed each touch, every sensation that Sophir gave him, as if he couldn't get enough.

Even as Sophir traced his fingers across Lonan's skin and pressed him gently into the earth, Lonan's gaze never wavered. There was fire in those eyes, a fierce desire that made every moment together feel even more intense. The quiet sounds of his breath, the soft moans, the way he whispered for more—it all added to the heady connection between them, making the air itself feel thicker with tension and longing.

Sophir could have stayed in that moment forever, but he couldn't help but tease, to make the experience last even longer. "Are you ready?" He asked, his voice low, coaxing. He couldn't resist the smile that tugged at his lips when Lonan nodded, speechless, his chest rising and falling quickly in anticipation.

"No more smart comments?" Sophir asked, his amusement clear.

Lonan's eyes gleamed, and his voice was thick with need. "Less talking— more touching."

A chuckle escaped Sophir's lips. "I should have seen that coming."

He moved closer, aligning himself with Lonan, determined to be gentle at first, to savor the moment. But the bond they shared—the pull of the Umbral—was too strong to resist. As soon as their skin met, Lonan pushed himself up onto all fours, urging Sophir forward with a subtle yet insistent movement. The sound that escaped his lips caught Sophir off guard, and he quickly reached to cover his mouth, not to hide the moment from Faedi, but to keep her from waking. Faedi needed rest after the night's events, and there was plenty of time ahead for them to share moments like this.

Lonan's rhythm was intoxicating. Sophir let him set the pace, his eyes following every movement, every ripple of shadow across Lonan's skin. But the position wasn't enough. He wanted to see Lonan's face, to see the pleasure and emotion in his eyes. So, with a soft tug, he guided them both into a new position, lying back in the grass.

Lonan's response was immediate, eager. He moved to straddle Sophir, and Sophir watched, transfixed, as his body glided against him, limbs moving with the grace of a shadow, his face softening with every sound, every breath. The way his expression changed with each shift of his body, the way he moaned, how he looked at him with shock and wonder—it was like watching a work of art come to life.

"Say my name," Sophir murmured, his voice thick with longing, as he moved with him, urging him closer, harder.

Lonan's breath caught. "Demanding bastard," he whispered, his voice laced with a smile, though he was anything but unaffected.

Sophir chuckled softly, his gaze darkening. "Lonan," he warned, the word a promise. He pulled him closer, his body moving in rhythm with his, his need growing stronger. "Should I stop again?"

Lonan shook his head, breathless, and leaned forward, bracing himself on Sophir's chest as he moved faster. "Don't stop. Please," he urged, his words a plea.

"Almost daybreak," Sophir warned, though his voice was rough with the growing intensity. He could feel the way Lonan's body trembled with every movement, could see the way his eyes were starting to flutter, as if he were losing himself to the moment.

A soft rustle in the grass caught Sophir's attention, pulling him out of their intimate world for just a second. It was Faedi, standing quietly by the edge of the camp, her golden eyes reflecting the soft light of the dawn. She smiled, a gentle expression on her face, as Lonan cried out his name in release, and Sophir followed, his own breath stolen away.

"He'll be napping in the cart," Faedi murmured, her voice a soft echo in the quiet morning air, as she turned to walk toward the cart.

Sophir chuckled, breathless, though his gaze never left Lonan. As he caught his breath, he noticed Lonan hadn't even noticed Faedi's presence, still lost in the aftermath of the moment, still trembling beneath him. Before he could say anything, Sophir gently guided him down to the soft earth, pressing a lingering kiss to his lips.

"Time to go," he whispered, his voice tender, yet firm.

As Faedi had predicted, Lonan was fast asleep in the cart by the time we left the camp. She didn't comment on his exhaustion, simply covering him with furs before leading the horses south. Sophir considered whether he should say anything to her about being alone with Lonan or the memories of their time together, but he didn't know how to approach either subject. He didn't think she was upset with them—especially after she smiled at them—but he couldn't be sure.

"Is my back that interesting?" She asked over her shoulder, breaking the silence.

"It is more beautiful than barkless trees and grass," Sophir replied, grinning when her cheeks flushed. "I was debating how to talk to you."

"You talk to me rather frequently," Faedi replied, turning to walk backward with a playful smile. "What's different about today?"

His smile faded slightly. "You saw a lot last night."

"Sylrie might be alive," she countered quickly. "And I plan to ask Torix if he buried my father beside my mother."

Sophir didn't respond. He knew that wasn't what she meant, but he wondered if she was changing the subject because she was uncomfortable. Still, the look in her eyes made him think she knew how uneasy he felt.

"And what about this morning?" Sophir asked carefully.

She stopped and let the horses catch up. "What about it?"

"I just wanted to make sure there weren't any… ill feelings?" He wasn't sure if that was the right way to phrase it.

"Would you be mad if Lonan and I had sex without you?" Faedi asked, gently stroking one of the horse's snouts as she met his gaze.

"No." He shook his head quickly.

"Then why would I be upset? I told you, it's common for Umbrals to have multiple partners," Faedi shrugged and turned to walk again. "If you both enjoyed yourself, and it sounded like you did, I'm glad."

"And if I said I wanted time alone with you as well?" Sophir asked, a slight warmth creeping into his voice.

Faedi looked at him again, and a playful smile tugged at her lips. "Then I would be glad that my attraction is not one-sided," she winked, her laugh light and carefree as she walked ahead.

Sophir watched her lead the way, a smile forming on his lips. Despite the unease he had, her response wasn't surprising—not really. Since he met her, she had taken everything as it came, even through her pain and sadness. Sophir couldn't help but admire her strength and resilience. It was easy to see why Lonan loved her as deeply as he did. And in time, Sophir could see himself sharing those same feelings.

They continued our journey mostly in silence while Lonan slept, pausing only when the horses grew tired. The landscape shifted as they moved south, and he noticed Faedi murmuring softly, casting spells to encourage the flowers to re-grow. After the second time, Sophir realized she was trying to nurture the plants in the same way she had in the past.

A slight frown tugged at his expression when he noticed she no longer re-turned to the cart for herbs as often. Sophir leaned back and checked the pouch where Lonan kept her bundles of herbs. They were almost gone.

She's trying to make it last.

Sophir scanned the area around them, hoping to spot a flower or mushroom he could point out to her, but there was nothing. Even Torix's trail had become sparse, with little to guide them. The mountains loomed ahead, growing larger with every step, and he assumed the trail would pick back up once we reached the snow.

"Come sit with me," Sophir called to her as a frigid gust of wind cut through the air, and he saw her clutch her arm with a curse.

"I can't track a trail from there," she replied, shaking her head.

"You can track him when there's something to find. You're cold," he said, patting the seat beside him. "The trail will stay even if you sit down."

Faedi relented with a sigh, and he stopped the horses, dismounting before she could reach him. He offered his hand to help her, and after a brief moment of hesitation, she accepted. She sat down with a huff, and he climbed on beside her, urging the horses forward without saying anything further.

Sophir wondered why she hesitated but didn't ask. He knew she didn't dis-trust him; it was probably pride. She didn't want to appear weak, or perhaps she didn't want anyone to worry about her. He glanced at her, wondering how often she hid her true feelings for the sake of others.

The wind howled again, sending a sharp gust through the valley. Faedi tensed beside him, and without thinking, he reached up to pull the fur lining of her cloak higher, wrapping it more snugly around her shoulders.

She blinked, clearly surprised, but he only shrugged. His fingers lingered for a moment before he pulled away. "You're shivering," he said simply.

"I'm fine," she mumbled, but the faint flush on her cheeks told him other-wise.

"Sure you are," Sophir smirked, leaning back slightly.

She huffed but didn't shake off the cloak or argue further. Instead, she turned her gaze forward, watching the path ahead as the horses trudged on. After a few moments, a hesitant weight pressed against his side—just for a mo-ment, the briefest lean before she straightened again. He didn't comment on it, but he smiled to himself.

"Does this bond… influence feelings?" Sophir asked, his voice careful. "Lonan said it doesn't take away our free will, but…if I were angry or scared, would either of you feel it?"

"Lonan's emotions have never influenced my own," Faedi replied, her voice steady. "I know how he feels sometimes, but that's probably from how long we've been together. Why do you ask?"

"Maybe," Sophir said, scratching his chin. "What about injuries?"

"We feel those," she said, propping her feet up on the cart and leaning back with a sigh. "But not old aches and pains."

"Your arm hurts?" He asked, pulling off his cloak and draping it over her.

"Always," Faedi whispered. "It's more uncomfortable without the flowers. Like the other burns."

He studied her face, noticing the way her brows pinched together, the slight clench in her jaw. She had been in pain before, like that night when she and Lonan bathed in the spring. She had never said a word, not even in soul speech.

Sophir thought back to the memory he had walked through with her—the one where her brother pushed her through the window, and the fire had burned her hands. The scars on her arms and legs, the evidence of torment.

"Have you ever told anyone?" He asked before he realized what he had said. Sophir softened his tone. "Or did you block the memory?"

She cracked her eyes open and looked at him. "Told someone what?"

"That you were tortured."

Faedi didn't respond immediately. Her eyes closed again, and she released a shaky breath. She hadn't blocked the memory—she remembered it as well as the day her family had died.

"You don't have to tell me about it," he added gently.

"I didn't see who did it," she whispered. "The shadows swallowed me, and I ran. Then…it was bright."

Sophir tightened his grip on the reins, staring ahead. It had happened when she was a child, and after everything else she had endured, this was yet another cruel burden she had carried.

"It happened in my dreams before the fire," she continued, her voice soft. "There was a man's voice—Sylrie said he dreamed the same thing. He could hear me scream. Our mother carved on the house after that, and it stopped…but it happened again after the fire."

"The protective runes on the door," he said, nodding. "The fire destroyed them."

"He never told me his name," Faedi whispered. "But it hurt. I heard someone else, too. He was kind. He told me to run before it made it dark again." She sighed, her voice distant. "I was in a different part of the forest after that, near Detrech, and tried to find Torix."

"You haven't heard him since?" Sophir asked, turning to her again. She shook her head.

That was strange. If the man had once tormented her in dreams, why had it stopped? Perhaps, as she had suggested, it was only the shadows that had reached her. He hadn't seen her use that magic in some time, and neither had she mentioned it.

"The woman who spoke to me in the memory said that Ilos has a connection to your mind," Sophir admitted softly. "I wonder… if perhaps that light was him."

Faedi shivered beside him, and he tightened his cloak around her again. He grabbed a spare fur and gently draped it over her shoulders. She didn't protest but stared up at the sky, her jaw set tight. After a moment, she sighed and rubbed her brow.

"Even if it wasn't him," she murmured, "why hasn't it happened again?"

"Maybe whoever helped you did something to keep him out of your mind," Sophir suggested. "Or maybe his attention is elsewhere."

She huffed, curling under the cloak. "Why do we only get more questions when we get answers?"

He chuckled softly. "I believe that's life's greatest mystery."

Sophir raised his arm, inviting her to come closer, and after a moment of hesitation, she scooted beside him, resting her head against his chest. She tensed when he draped his arm over her shoulder, but he quickly adjusted, placing it between her arm and waist.

"I can't wait until this is normal again," she murmured.

"I'm sure the flowers will regrow soon," he reassured her, squeezing her knee. "But can you promise me something?"

"What?" Faedi looked up, raising an eyebrow.

"Tell me," he frowned gently, "if it ever hurts too much."

"Okay," she whispered, a soft smile on her lips.

31
Among the Ashen

Lonan

For four days, they traveled, their eyes fixed on the mountains, and not a
soul crossed their path—not a dwarf, not an animal. Nothing. If not for the
occasional scribbled marks Torix had left behind on rocks, Lonan might have
thought they were lost—that all life had been wiped from the planet without
their knowing. It could have happened while Sophir had taken Faedi into her
memory, while Lonan had guarded their bodies, and no one would have been the
wiser.

Yet the sun continued to rise, followed by one of the moons, and Lonan
found himself searching the sky for the second moon—the one that hadn't been
seen in years. He knew that if it broke the horizon, his anxiety would spike. That
moon heralded the countdown for a mass sacrifice of presumed innocent people
to the bastard god of light.

The Ancients would be furious.

"Do you think we should stop and check on the farmers?" Lonan asked
suddenly, noting wagon tracks in the dirt. "See if any of them made it?"

Sophir looked up at him as he walked beside the cart. "You know where they
went?"

"They have land on the border of Rowdon," Faedi called over her shoulder
as she paused to stretch. "I think we should. We can give them the supplies cart
before we go up the mountains."

"What about the Mire?" Sophir asked, glancing between them.

"They said they would send a warning if there was an immediate threat," Lonan replied, pulling a crystal from his shirt to show him. "So far, they've only dealt with a few small groups. Scouts, most likely. They're testing defenses and figuring out where the city is. It could take them months to find it."

"If they wanted a timely response and resolution, they would have sent us here instead of the cottage. I think we should have time," Faedi agreed, turning to face them. "We should know their location anyway. If Haldin agrees to help us, I want to ensure they're also protected. They were always friendly to my family—the king might be sympathetic."

"Do you think Torix would have stopped with them?" Sophir turned to Faedi. "Would we lose his trail?"

"His marks match this wagon path," she confirmed before continuing.

"You probably shouldn't wear your glamour, though," Lonan told Sophir. "They didn't speak ill of you, but…they might worry you were sent to find them."

"They'd be less fearful of an Itmis?" He asked, raising his eyebrows.

"One way to find out," Lonan chuckled, snapping the reins and clicking his tongue to urge the horses forward.

They traveled silently along the wagon trail that wound through the rolling plains, marking the border between Emsmeda and Rowdon. The midday sun beat down on them mercilessly, casting long shadows of their horses on the grass. Still, they remained alert, scanning for any signs of the cultists' trademark fire.

As they reached an old crossroads marked by a waystone, Faedi stopped to search the area. Sophir sipped from his waterskin and walked wide around the stone. Lonan halted the horses and climbed down to examine the marker. The southward marker had been carved out, but he knew it was meant to point to Rowdon.

"There's smoke," Sophir announced, his gaze on the sky rather than the ground.

"I hope that's from campfires and not the alternative," Faedi whispered as she moved to stand beside him.

"If their focus is on the Mire, I don't see why they would bother the farmers," Lonan said, shaking his head, but his confidence faltered at the stern expression on Sophir's face. "What is it?"

"I don't trust it," Sophir replied, shaking his head as he returned to the cart. "The raids targeted the forest-folk, and many of them became farmers. Are Krelin dark to them?"

"Might be—feral features and traits could mean they aren't… light enough?" Faedi hugged her slung arm to her chest and looked for Dusan. "Can you go check?"

Lonan watched the falcon fly off with a screech and frowned. There wasn't any cover for him if there were Orderlings, and he wasn't sure if they would find him suspicious.

Sophir rumbled low before looking between Lonan and Faedi. "Should we continue?"

"We should reach whatever is there by nightfall. Maybe they have some supplies we can trade for," Lonan said, climbing up beside Faedi and taking the reins while Sophir settled into the back.

He urged the horses forward, following the faint tracks through the grass, but he couldn't shake the unease creeping into his chest. As he glanced at the mountains again, dark clouds surrounded the peaks, cloaking them in a haze. He hoped the storm would weaken by the time they traveled up them. The cold wouldn't be kind to Faedi's arm and would only make their journey more perilous.

They did not pick up their pace until Dusan returned and informed Faedi it was safe. As promised, they reached the outskirts of the farmers' encampment just as the sun vanished over the horizon behind them.

Approaching the perimeter, a wary group welcomed them, their cautious eyes peering from behind makeshift barriers of carts and tents. Lonan exchanged glances with Faedi and Sophir as they climbed out of the cart, tension crackling in the air. The farmers visibly relaxed when Sophir and Lonan left their weapons behind.

"Who goes there?" A weathered man stepped forward, squinting into the fading light. His thick beard hinted at a life spent outdoors, and his accent was distinctly not Emsmedan.

"Watchers from the Mire," Lonan raised his hands to show they meant no harm. "Where are the farmers from Dewgate?"

The man's hand went to a knife on his belt, but he did not remove it. Instead, his eyes narrowed as he studied them. "They're here," he replied, stepping closer. "Bit far from the Mire, aren't you?"

"They're friends of ours," Faedi said, her voice steady. "They knew to expect us."

"Aye, they said they knew the Umbrals…thought they were lying," he laughed, his skepticism giving way to amusement. "And a Krelin and Itmis too. Sounds like a bad tavern joke."

Lonan chuckled silently, shaking his head as he glanced at Sophir. The man wasn't entirely wrong. Their small group looked out of place in the peaceful setting.

"We wanted to make sure they made it here all right and hopefully trade for supplies before we move on," Faedi explained, absentmindedly petting one of the horses.

"We've got hot food and places to rest your horses." The man's wary expression softened when he looked at Faedi. Then his eyebrows shot up in concern. "Ancients, you're injured. Come with me; I'll have my wife look after you."

She shook her head quickly to dismiss his concern. "That's not—"

"Thank you for your kindness," Sophir interjected, and Lonan couldn't help but grin as Faedi glared at him while they followed the man.

Sophir hadn't even hesitated. The moment Faedi tried to brush off her pain, he stepped in, cutting off her protest with that quiet authority of his. Lonan watched the way Sophir's shoulders squared, how he stepped closer to her side, almost as if he was making sure she didn't slip away from the offered care.

It wasn't possessiveness—it was something gentler, something steadier. He didn't want her to bear her pain alone.

Warmth settled in Lonan's chest. Had Sophir always looked after her that way? How long had he known about her pain? Lonan thought over their interactions since they'd met while he watched him.

He recalled Sophir standing close to the Nythbloom in the greenhouse, lingering near even while drying dishes. Did Sophir know the plant was deadly? Had he been trying to protect Faedi?

He had noticed her anxiety so easily while they traveled. She had given no indication, had not said a word about worry, yet Sophir had known something was wrong. And he had come back for them.

It wasn't just duty that motivated him; he had proven that already. It wasn't just the bond, either. It was him—his concern was genuine and unwavering. And Ancients help him, Lonan respected him. Maybe more than he should.

"He's right. You need more herbs," Lonan added, trying to stifle his laughter as Faedi's glare shifted to him.

"I'm going to put pebbles in your boots," she threatened, her cheeks darkening.

"You need other herbs, too," he said, tilting his head in mock seriousness. "Unless we want to tempt fate? You were in heat."

He let his grin linger, but his thoughts had already drifted elsewhere, tracing emotions he wasn't sure he should put to words. It was more than respect, something deeper, but he wasn't sure he was ready to name it. Yet as they followed the man toward shelter and warmth, he knew one thing for certain.

He wasn't the only one who wanted to keep Faedi safe. And maybe—just maybe—that longing wasn't his alone to carry.

Faedi's expression darkened further just as Sophir cleared his throat, steering the conversation forward. As they passed through the barriers of carts and tents, Lonan noted how the makeshift defenses suggested they had faced trouble from outsiders before. They huddled their children close, their warm smiles betraying the wariness in their eyes.

The weathered man led them to a large communal fire where a pot of stew bubbled, the rich aroma wrapping around them like a comforting embrace. As they gathered, the man waved a woman over from a tent before returning his attention to them.

"I'm Jaref. Elected mayor of our little community here," he introduced himself as the woman who appeared to be near his age joined him. "This is my wife, Odessa."

"Lonan," he replied, offering a firm handshake. "These are my bonded, Faedi and Sophir."

The words left his mouth before he could think twice, smooth and certain, as if they had always been true. *My bonded.* Faedi and Sophir. The moment stretched thin as realization struck, and a slow, dawning weight settled in his chest.

He had claimed Sophir—not just in passing, not just for convenience—openly and without hesitation.

Sophir inhaled sharply, and Lonan glanced at him with raised eyebrows. He hadn't expected to see the wide-eyed expression Sophir regarded him with, nor the brief mistiness in his eyes before he looked away.

He noticed.

Ancients, Lonan didn't regret it. If anything, the thought of taking it back felt wrong, like trying to undo something that had already been woven into place. They were his—and he was theirs.

"Well met," Jaref said, smiling as he nodded at each of them. "The Dewgate folk speak highly of you. Suppose there are kinder people here."

Lonan watched as Faedi inched further from the flames while Odessa approached to examine her arm.

"Where are you from?" Faedi asked.

"Work camps in the east," Jaref replied, glancing over his shoulder to call for someone to fetch the Dewgate farmers.

"All of you are?" Sophir raised his eyebrows, and Lonan exchanged a look with him. Ravyn had never mentioned work camps, but neither of them had ever thought to ask.

"The whole camp was bought," Jaref confirmed with a nod. "We thought we were going somewhere else to work for another fancy lord. We were dropped off in Detrich and brought here. The King said we could have homes if we made them."

"Bought?" Lonan traded a glance with Faedi, then looked between Sophir and Jaref. "Like property?"

"They were slaves," Sophir's deep voice rumbled from beside him. "The work camps in the burning fields are full of slaves clearing the plagued land. The only way out is to be bought or to die."

"Did the King buy you?" Faedi asked, pulling away from Odessa.

"No," Odessa shook her head. "We thought they were pirates… a bunch of rough people bought us. They saw us off when we arrived and promised us a safe trip. One of them, Scarred, said we would be safe in Emsmeda near the border."

"Farmers from Dewgate showed up a few days ago and told us a lady told them the same thing," Jaref added, nodding in agreement. "Scarred was a big fellow. I didn't think Dusk Elves could be as large as him—but no one's seen one of them in years. Must be good food on the mountain."

Lonan glanced at Faedi and Sophir. "I thought Haldin called everyone back to the mountain?"

"He did," Faedi nodded subtly. "How many of you are there? We have supplies we can trade to help."

"Not quite fifty with the Dewgate folk," Jaref replied, shaking his head. "Some of our younger ones stayed in the city; others joined Scarred's crew. Many did not survive the journey, but they died free and were buried in good soil."

Lonan lowered his head respectfully at the mention of death, closing his eyes momentarily. Jaref seemed at peace with their deaths, but Lonan was not. No one, least of all children, should have been enslaved in work camps.

"Where are the farmers?" Sophir asked after the pause for the dead passed.

Odessa cleared her throat, her anxiety clear on her face. "In one of the tents for healing. Those that survived weren't well off." She lowered her head. "Some died shortly after they arrived."

Faedi stiffened. "Which tent?"

Lonan knew she wouldn't be persuaded to eat until she had checked on them.

Jaref pointed to a larger tent next to a smaller fire. "They're in there. Most are resting."

"I'll check in on the farmers, and we have some supplies and toys we can give to the children," Faedi announced before she darted back to their cart without explanation.

"I'll help," Sophir said before following her, and Lonan smiled, shaking his head. He had almost forgotten the toys she had carved for Dewgate's orphanage, stored on the cart before the cottage burned.

"You travel with toys?" Jaref asked, confusion etched across his features.

"Not typically, but it has been a strange few days. We were going to send them to the orphanage in Dewgate," Lonan explained, standing when Odessa began serving bowls of stew. "Let me, please."

Not long after the food was served and eaten, Faedi returned from the tent with Sophir, carrying bundles of hand-carved wooden toys. Lonan smiled as a crowd of excited children quickly surrounded them when Sophir announced what they had, watching Faedi happily pass them out. However, he noted that one child remained at a distance.

"Is that one well?" Lonan asked Jaref, nodding toward the small cloaked child several paces away.

"Shy one, she is," Jaref frowned. "Lost her parents to a fever days before Scarred bought us. Many of us have tried to take her in, but she always goes off alone by morning."

"A fever?" Lonan straightened, offering the spoon back to Odessa.

"Aye," the man nodded. "Folk here call it the ash plague. You know it?"

"I do," Lonan replied. "Excuse me."

He approached Faedi and Sophir, carefully stepping around the children who ran about happily and took one of the toys. Silently, he nodded toward the lone child. Faedi followed his gaze, her eyes widening as she offered him more toys.

Sophir, however, stared at the child with raised eyebrows. His surprise quickly turned to sorrow and anger as the girl attempted to hide behind a cart, peeking out timidly around the wood.

"She's an Embral Itmis," he stated.

"She is?" Lonan looked between him and the child. "How can you tell?"

"Because her soul is crying—she's afraid of herself."

"Ancients bless her," Lonan murmured.

He watched as Faedi carried her armful of toys toward the girl, but her steps were slow, and she didn't walk around the cart. Instead, she sat on the ground and placed the wooden toys before her. The girl's head disappeared behind the cart, her exposed legs stepping away from Faedi, but she didn't flee.

Dusan fluttered to the cart the child hid behind and inched his head to the side. Lonan couldn't tell what he was saying to Faedi, but he watched her tail flick behind her in silent acknowledgment. Maybe he was observing the child for her or checking for injuries.

Lonan held his breath, watching Faedi lift her good hand, holding it out before her. With a flick of her wrist, wishing flowers sprouted, and the girl stepped closer. Faedi blew the flowers, sending their seeds in a small flurry into the air.

"All the other toys have friends now," Faedi said softly. "These are still alone."

She took another step forward, and the girl's hood became visible again.

"I like this one best," Faedi picked up a miniature replica of their Diwha. "Have you ever seen one of these before? Everyone thinks they're scary because of their big claws and teeth, but they're very nice."

Slowly, the little girl approached and sat across from Faedi, hugging her knees to her chest while staring at the toys but not reaching for them. Instead, she whispered something Lonan couldn't hear over the laughter of the other children nearby.

He fell in love with her all over again.

32
Unspoken Truths

Faedi

"Is he mean and scary?"

Faedi leaned closer when the girl whispered, studying her wide amber eyes. She glanced at Sophir momentarily before turning her attention back to the child. Gold scales dotted the girl's cheeks, and Faedi could make out the lumps on her cloak where her horns were beginning to grow.

"Him? No," Faedi shook her head. "Well… I'm sure mean people think he's scary. Are you mean?"

"No," the girl quickly shook her head.

"Then he's not mean or scary at all," Faedi assured her, slowly offering the toy she had carved. "What's your name?"

"Emmaline," the girl answered softly as she accepted the carved creature. "What's yours?"

"Faedi." She smiled and sat back, watching as Emmaline examined the toy. "That's Sophir and Lonan over there."

"They said you're friends with the farmers. You helped them come here," Emmaline said, looking up at her. "Are you like Scarred? I thought he was scary, but he was nice. He let me steer the ship and taught me how to tie knots."

"That sounds fun. I've never steered a ship before. You must be really strong," Faedi said, noticing how the girl's body language became less tense, her eyes brightening.

Emmaline giggled, turning the toy in her hands. "No, I'm too small. Scarred helped a lot." Her gaze grew distant, her voice hushed with awe. "We saw sirens—they were really nice, too. They swam around the ship and sang us songs."

Faedi noticed more golden scales on the girl's knuckles, catching the light from the nearby campfire. Her nails, claw-like like Sophir's, gleamed gold instead of black. Despite where she had come from, she appeared unharmed.

She's probably had time to heal.

"I've never met one before. I heard their songs were beautiful, though," she said with a smile, wanting to keep the child's spirits up.

"Are you going to stay and help them build houses? Everyone says it's going to be too cold soon."

Faedi's smile faltered. She glanced back at Lonan and Sophir before shaking her head. "No. We're going to Rowdon."

Emmaline's eyes widened as she stared at Faedi, then turned her gaze south. There must have been rumors about the Dusk Elves in the east—mystery at the very least. It wasn't every day an entire race hid themselves away for decades on end.

"How are you going to get up the mountain?" She whispered.

"Very carefully," Faedi said, knowing that much was true.

"But everyone says the Dusk Elves kill people who go there."

"There might be some bad people there, but I'm sure there are good ones too," Faedi said, crossing her legs where she sat. "It's scary, though—not knowing who is good or bad."

"Like some of the nice people at the camps? And Scarred? He dressed up like them." Emmaline looked back at her. "He didn't like wearing their clothes—he said their god was bad."

"Their god?" Faedi worked to keep her tone level. "Do you know which one?"

"Ilos. All of the guards there wore a gold flame... they made it out of our scales. Everyone had to give offerings to him. They got mad if we didn't," Emmaline shifted uncomfortably as she explained. "Scarred and his friends hurt some of them. They dressed up like us and got on the ship."

"He sounds like a good person," Faedi told her.

"It's okay if nice people do bad things? That doesn't make them bad?" Emmaline looked back at her, brow furrowing.

"He was protecting all of you, wasn't he?" Faedi tilted her head, trying to guide the girl's thoughts.

"But what if you hurt someone on accident?" Emmaline lowered her head with a sniffle.

"It's only bad if you hurt people on purpose and want to be mean. But it isn't bad if you're protecting the people you love." Faedi leaned forward, bracing her elbows on her knees. "And accidents don't make you bad. Everyone makes them."

Emmaline remained silent, clutching the carved toy closer to herself. Faedi didn't press her to speak or move the conversation along. The girl had been through enough, and she didn't want to make her uncomfortable.

Had their plans not involved a dangerous trip up the mountains, Faedi would have stayed with the farmers to help however she could. Or even gone back to the Mire. Emmaline and the others needed somewhere safe. The elderly freed slaves likely wouldn't survive the winter without shelter, and the children were at risk as well.

"Does he help other people who aren't his friends?" Emmaline asked at last.

"He does," Faedi said, leaning closer to whisper, "Do you need help?"

"Yes."

"Alright then. Come on," Faedi said, standing and offering her hand. "He'll help."

She smiled as Emmaline took her hand, leading her toward Sophir and Lonan. Both men smiled as they approached, and Faedi gave the girl's hand a reassuring squeeze before squatting down beside her.

"This is Sophir and Lonan," she told her gently, then turned to her bonded. "This is Emmaline, and she wants help."

"Well met, *mal'ki*," Sophir said, kneeling and offering the girl his hand.

"Good to meet you," Lonan said, smiling down at her before shifting his gaze back to Faedi. "Sophir says she likes you."

"She's adorable," Faedi said, smiling up at him. "What kind of help did you need?"

"I don't know how to use my magic—I burned someone," Emmaline admitted, her voice small and trembling. "Well… two someones. They stabbed Scarred, and I burned both of them—but Scarred wasn't mad. He said I was brave."

Faedi studied the girl, a swell of admiration rising in her chest.

I just met you, and I know you're braver than me.

Faedi laid her head on Lonan's shoulder while watching Sophir with Emmaline several paces away. He sat with her in his lap, both their eyes closed as they connected. Faedi wasn't entirely sure how it worked, but Sophir had explained that he could help Emmaline learn about her magic through his own.

Faedi assumed it was similar to the time Sophir had spent with her in her memories, but she didn't want to bring up that sour subject—not after learning that her father had been a murderer and a liar.

After returning to their cart and eating, they had stepped away at Emmaline's request. Faedi trusted Sophir to keep her safe, but she still felt anxious. She knew Lonan was too; even Dusan had shown interest, but he had roosted for the night while Lonan and Faedi kept watch over the two tranced Itmis.

Lonan draped a blanket over Faedi's lap with a sigh. "How many farmers survived?"

"Very few," she muttered, her jaw tight. "Too few." Her fingers curled into the blanket as anger churned in her stomach, thick and bitter. The joy she had found in the smiles of the children was gone. "I did what I could to help them, to ease their pain and speed their healing, but it wasn't enough. It's never enough."

The words came out harsher than she had intended, her frustration bleeding into every syllable.

Lonan hummed softly before reaching out to gently flick the tip of her nose. Faedi blinked, caught off guard, as he grinned at her. "There it is again," he teased, his voice warm despite the weight of their conversation.

She narrowed her eyes at him, but the sharp edge of her anger dulled just a little. "You're impossible," she grumbled. But when he chuckled, she couldn't help the reluctant smile that tugged at her lips. "Utterly impossible."

"Maybe," he admitted, nudging his shoulder against hers. "But at least I got you to stop looking like you were about to kill something."

She huffed and rolled her eyes. "Blavier would be a good start… they wouldn't have been hurt if they hadn't left, and they only left because he—"

"I know," he cut her off with a sigh. "But maybe they'll be safe here." He nudged her again before pulling out his knives to sharpen them.

Silence settled between them as Faedi watched Sophir and Emmaline, but she couldn't escape the memories of what she had seen in the healing tents. Charred injuries, all too close to the scars on her own arm, and dazed expressions of horror. None of them seemed to recognize her or much of anything around them.

Suncrest leaves.

One of the Valorians in the tent had said it was the herb they used to sedate them and prevent pain. It was a native plant to their land, something they used while toiling away in the burning fields—a plant Faedi knew nothing about. If she had been in a better state, she would have asked for more details or a seed, but she didn't care to at the time. Not with her heart so heavy.

"What do you think he's doing, exactly?" Lonan mused while sharpening his knives.

"I don't know," Faedi shook her head. "They seem alright, though."

"I don't think he'd do anything that might hurt her," Lonan sighed, resting his head against hers while continuing his work. "Maybe she'll let someone care for her when she's less afraid."

Faedi frowned, her gaze turning to the stars. "If we weren't going up the mountain, I'd take her with us if she wanted to come. Sophir could help her more than anyone here."

"I was thinking that too," Lonan agreed. "It's too open here. We don't know where all the cultists are traveling from, and they don't have suitable structures yet. I would have taken the farmers to the Mire for winter or longer if I'd known about those Ilos bastards."

Faedi sighed as Lonan spoke. He was right. If the cultists came upon the small encampment, they'd have no way to protect themselves. And Faedi doubted the cultists would be kind to the freed slaves of Valoria. After everything they had done to them, to her family, Faedi wouldn't be surprised if the cultists killed them all.

Moving them to the Mire would take at least two weeks, and some of the farmers could die traveling through the forest. It would also delay their trip to the mountain. They would have to start over again, and Faedi didn't know if they could spare that time, even if she doubted their success with speaking to King Haldin.

If his daughter, her mother, was disguised and hiding her identity from everyone, his hatred for the Umbrals would be unwarranted. She couldn't place her faith in someone who might damn an entire region for something they didn't know about. Even if Torix thought he could help, Faedi didn't share that belief.

"You're worrying," Lonan nudged her gently. "What's on your mind?"

"Haldin," Faedi sighed and rubbed her face. "Torix was so confident he would help and that the Mire was a primary target—but I don't trust it. For all we know, he'll kill us as soon as we step foot on the mountain, and then no one is any better off than before."

"You don't think he'd be happy finding out he has a granddaughter?" Lonan set his wet stone aside and wrapped his arm around her waist.

"We were there for years, and then the fire… if our child was gone for years and then we found out they were murdered…" Faedi pulled away to face him. "What would you do?"

Lonan's eyes darkened, and he looked away from her, clenching his jaw. Faedi watched him process his thoughts, giving him time to think. She didn't know exactly what he would do, but she knew he wouldn't stay hidden away on a mountain or blame an entire region of people.

"I'd hunt everyone involved down and make them pray for death long before I gave it to them," he told her, staring ahead at Emmaline and Sophir. "I'd be happy, though… if I found out we had a grandchild."

Faedi looked up at the stars, feeling the weight of uncertainty. "And if that grandchild played a part in your child's death?"

"I'd recognize they were children and that adults took advantage of them— lied to and used them. I'd know they hurt my blood in more ways than one." Lonan straddled her legs, resting his forehead against hers to capture her gaze. "I wouldn't blame a child for the evil of men."

Faedi searched his eyes, biting her lip. He hadn't lied, and she hoped Haldin would be the same. But she knew there was a chance he would be like her, blaming her for what happened, just as she blamed herself.

"It wasn't your fault," he whispered. "I'll tell you every day until you believe me if I have to."

"You don't have—"

"Yes, I do," Lonan interrupted, kissing the tip of her nose. "I want to see you happy one day when you talk about your family—when you tell about how you and Sylrie climbed on top of the house and scared your mother when you convinced the tree to bend down so you could climb it and put a bird back. To hear about how Sylrie scared away a badger that frightened the boys… I want to hear you laugh when you talk about all your adventures with them."

He wiped her cheeks with his thumbs as her eyes grew blurry. Her lip quivered, but she couldn't help but laugh when Lonan started recounting their mischief—trying to teach chickens to race and stealing wolves to ride. He hadn't been there for all those things, but Faedi realized she must have told him when they were children.

"How do you remember all of this?" She laughed when he trailed off. "Some of that was almost thirty years ago."

"Because I remember everything I learn about you," he pulled back and smiled at her.

"Really?" Faedi raised an eyebrow, skeptical yet hopeful.

"The color of fog on the trees is your favorite; you love blackberries but hate raspberries; your favorite season is the first frost—even if that isn't a real season," he laughed when she rolled her eyes. "You also hate rabbit."

"It never tastes right," Faedi shrugged. "Those are easy. What else?"

"I know you love me, even if you're too scared to say it. I know you won't tell me because you're afraid someone will take me away if you do."

"To be fair… you were almost killed by cultists right after we got married." Faedi hugged her arms to herself.

"I was, but I didn't die. No one is taking me away from you." He leaned down again, tracing her bottom lip with his thumb. "They can try, but I will always be with you. In this life and the next."

"You better be," she told him before tugging him by his collar for a kiss.

33
Hollow Waters

Scarred

The salty breeze filled Scarred's lungs as he stood at the ship's helm, his jaw tightening as he watched the wind fill the sails. As the sun set on the horizon, painting the sky with hues of orange and red, his eyes wandered over the endless expanse of the ocean. The faint cries of seagulls faded as they left the shoreline far behind.

"No shore!" One of the deckhands shouted from the crow's nest, waving their hand overhead.

"Out of the eye!" Scarred shouted back, nodding as he glanced around the deck. The crew cheered, and he added, "Stretch your legs! You earned it."

The hands removed their masks and cloaks as he looked around, and glamours fell away. The once-gruff human crew revealed themselves as a wild mix of races from the east and west—skin, fur, feathers, and scales of various colors covered the deck. Scarred sighed in relief as he removed one of his many necklaces.

Shoving the necklace into his pocket, he glanced over his shoulder when he heard a chuckle. Behind him stood his first mate, a man with chestnut hair pulled back, some in braids adorned with shells and brass rings. His pearly white smile grew as he faced Scarred, crossing his arms over his chest.

The bruise on his cheek had faded, but his lower lip was still scabbed over.

"Who do you want on the helm while we're below?" Danik, first mate asked, raising his eyebrows.

"Put Osred on it—he's got the most practice this far south," Scarred replied, starting down the steps as his mate followed behind him. "If they handle things well, you should take the wheel when we're done with them. I don't want them jumping overboard before we're near the Isle."

"Red—to the wheel!" He shouted before hurrying to match Scarred's stride. "I don't know how long they've been in there. Most of them might not handle legs well."

"We'll string nets in the hold if we need to. Extra beds for them to rest until they're ready," Scarred sighed, rubbing his temples.

He walked past several stacked crates once they reached the dimly lit corridor below. He stopped in front of a seemingly ordinary panel and pressed his palm against a hidden latch. There was a soft click, and the panel swung inward, revealing a dark passage.

Stepping inside, the door shut behind them with a *thud*, plunging the space into darkness. A match struck, and his Danik lit a lantern. As the light flooded the space, Scarred counted the cloth-covered rectangular boxes lining the walls and center of the room. However, movement caught his eye, and he tilted his head with a scowl when he saw a frail silver-haired man several feet away, clutching a knife.

"Stay back!" The man shouted, holding out the knife with a shaky hand.

"Danik?" Scarred turned slowly to look at his first mate. "What is he doing on my ship?"

"I believe the term is called a stowaway, my friend," Danik said, his lips twitching as he tried not to smile.

"I know—fuck." Scarred lowered his head with a sigh before lifting his eyes to the man. "That coin would have given you a perfect life anywhere…why are you here?"

"Why do you have innocent Helgi in cages?" The man asked defiantly, blinking up at Scarred. "Wait… what?"

"When I won you," Scarred began to walk toward him, grabbing the knife's blade when the man tried to jab at him. "I handed you a bag full of coins and gems. Enough to buy you passage anywhere and live out your days more comfortably than most can afford. I left you on the docks, beside one of the finest ships to travel across the sea—so why are you here?"

The man stared up at Scarred as he ripped the knife out of his hand and tossed it against the wall. Only a fool would give up the chance for freedom—unless he was still loyal to his former master. Scarred glanced him over before grabbing his wrist and twisting him to hold his back against Scarred's front.

"Check him for a crystal," Scarred told Danik as the man tried to wiggle away.

"You were working together—you conned the priest," the man stammered, recoiling from Danik as he began to pat him down.

"Oh, poor priest," Danik rolled his eyes. "Ilos has given him another slave to pour his drinks."

"I was helping people," the man protested, tugging against Scarred's grip.

"He doesn't have anything—not even the coin," Danik said.

Scarred let him go with a grumble and glanced around the room. Nothing appeared disturbed, but that didn't mean the man hadn't hidden a crystal somewhere. He could have tossed it into one of the covered crates if he had heard them approach.

"I don't think we're letting them out slowly," Scarred warned Danik. "Bind him, put him in the corner. There could be a crystal somewhere in here or on the ship."

"I don't have a crystal!" The man protested, grunting as Danik wrestled with him to tie him up.

"I'm not risking the Helgi or my crew's safety on your word," Scarred said, ripping the fabric off the nearest container to examine the large box.

It was fashioned from metal and wood, but the one he uncovered had a plank pulled away, and water sloshed out from the top as the ship rocked. Carefully, he began to peel away the wooden slats, revealing glass beneath, with several holes in the top for air. A soft hum came from inside, and Scarred shook his head as his head began to grow light.

"Danik…" he mumbled, feeling the unease settle in. "They're awake."

"*Fuck.*"

Scarred stood beside Danik, watching the hesitant faces that looked up at him with wide, uncertain eyes. He kept his shoulders low and his hands visible as the group exchanged a series of hums, varying in tone and volume. Some looked worried at the silver-haired man in the corner, but most stared at either Danik or him.

It wasn't until a small boy, likely no older than six, peered around a woman's legs that Scarred's jaw clenched tightly. His damp curls clung to his cheeks, and a pair of bright, ice-blue eyes stared at Scarred with wonder rather than fear. Slowly, Scarred took a knee and smiled at the child. Some of the other Helgi stepped back, a few hissing with their sharp teeth bared, but the boy took a step forward and tugged at the woman's hand.

The boy hummed something as he pointed in Scarred's direction and then to his hair. Scarred glanced to his right, where a braid rested against his cheek, adorned with the same bronze rings and shells as Danik's. It had been there so long that he often forgot it was there until Danik demanded he redo it every so often.

"I'm a friend," Scarred said softly before whistling a low tune of three notes.

"Friend," the boy repeated with a smile, slowly approaching. "My name… Iatai."

"Scarred," Scarred said, tapping the center of his chest with a smile. He glanced up at Danik, who hummed at the child.

"He likes your tattoos," Danik told Scarred with a chuckle. "What is it with kids and tattoos?"

Scarred shrugged and rolled up his shirt sleeves to show off more of the black markings on his skin. Most of them were disrupted by scars that littered his arms, but Iatai didn't seem to mind. Instead, he traced over each of the lines and hummed happily—until he reached Scarred's bloody palm.

Iatai hissed, looking up at Scarred wide-eyed and humming at a higher pitch. Scarred narrowed his eyes and glanced at Danik, who made a similar tune but didn't seem to recognize it as anything but an unhappy one.

"He wants to know if you were hurt helping them," Danik translated, humming again at the child before returning his attention to Scarred. "Go ahead and talk to them; I'll translate. Everyone is calm enough to understand."

"I won't claim to know what you've endured on the Ashen Isle," Scarred began, staring slowly at the group and observing Danik for cues. "But your time there is over. We are sailing to your home where you will be free. I only ask that you don't try to leave the ship early and only come above deck at night. We are still in waters patrolled by Valoria and Ilos' followers—if they catch you in the water or see you on board, they will attack. I can't promise safety until we are in the Helgi Tides."

Scarred waited for Danik to complete the translation, returning his attention to Iatai, who listened closely and nodded slowly. With each word, the spark of hope in his eyes grew more prominent. When the translation was complete, he looked back at who Scarred assumed was his mother, humming a response that Scarred recognized as happiness.

Gradually, more hums came from the group, and Scarred relaxed when Danik sighed in relief. However, a woman in the corner, watching with wide black eyes, pulled Scarred's attention. They shared a short conversation before Danik looked down at him and smiled.

"They agree to the terms but want these tanks gone."

"We can do that," Scarred nodded, standing. "Tell them we'll house them in the cargo hold; they'll only need to return here if anyone boards us. Have the crew break these down for supplies. I'll take them up deck; the stars should be shining now."

Danik nodded and translated while Scarred turned to the silver-haired man in the corner. For a moment, Scarred wondered if he should leave him there but decided against it. As long as he was watched closely, he wouldn't be able to cause much trouble.

"Come on," Scarred said, hoisting him up by the ropes that bound him. "When was the last time you ate?"

The man scrambled to keep up. "What?"

"Food," Scarred glanced down at him. "You've been on this ship for days; no one has seen you, and no supplies have been reported missing. When did you last eat?"

"I don't know. There's no light down here."

"Ytna, help me," Scarred groaned, turning for the mess instead of the deck before calling out to Danik. "Take them up. Tell anyone who wants food before air to follow me."

Scarred half-dragged the silver-haired man beside him, keeping a firm grip on the ropes that bound his wrists. The mess hall wasn't far, but the path was tight, winding through the ship's lower decks, where the air grew colder and damp with the scent of saltwater. The man stumbled, clearly weakened, and a pang of pity hit Scarred's gut.

"I can walk, you know," the man muttered, his voice barely above a whisper.

"Then walk faster," Scarred tightened his grip. "The sooner you eat, the sooner you get fresh air."

They continued down the corridor until they reached the mess hall—a cramped space with a few wooden tables bolted to the floor. A handful of shiphands were inside, finishing a late meal. Their chatter ceased when they saw Scarred and the man, exchanging wary glances before quickly returning to their meals.

Scarred led the man to an empty table in the corner and pushed him onto the bench.

"Stay here," Scarred ordered, then moved to the small galley, where a pot of stew simmered over a low flame.

He grabbed a bowl and ladled a generous portion into it, along with a chunk of stale bread. Glancing at the wall where cups and a barrel of water waited, Scarred sighed before filling one and carrying it back to the table.

"Eat," Scarred said simply after depositing the bowl and cup on the table.

The man hesitated, then picked up a spoon and began to eat ravenously. Scarred watched him for a moment, noting the sharpness of his cheekbones and the hollow look in his eyes. He knew that look well; it belonged to someone who had suffered for far too long.

"I don't know what you're planning." Scarred narrowed his eyes, leaning closer and lowering his voice. "But if you intend to bring harm to anyone on my ship, I'll send you to meet the god your priest loves so dearly."

"I thought you were slavers," the man looked up, his spoon paused mid-air. "I was going to free everyone and—"

"And what? Take over my ship with an emaciated Dawn Elf and a couple dozen tanked Helgi?" Scarred raised an eyebrow. "Would a slaver give a fortune like that to a slave they won?"

"Maybe if he felt bad for damaged goods, or the money was stolen, and he didn't want to be caught with it," the man shrugged, returning to his meal.

"I was paid to free you," Scarred leaned back in his seat. "My job was to get you away from the priest—I did that. Then I went to my next job, picking up the Helgi and taking them home."

"So you get paid to free people?" Suspicion was evident on the man's face.

"Not everyone in Valoria is friendly to the flame—some of us see past their lies." Scarred leaned forward again, glaring at him. "Some of us know what they do to the dark in Ashar."

The man set his spoon in the bowl and stared at the table. He didn't speak, but Scarred could see him considering his words. He let him take his time and sat back to watch some Helgi take seats and eat, sharing soft hums among themselves.

Excitement—uncertainty—hope.

Scarred scratched the corner of his nose before sighing and shaking his head. It would still be days before they were out of patrolled waters. They could have sailed directly west to cut time off, but that would have increased the risk of being discovered.

Instead, they would skirt the southern seas and risk shared waters with pirates and sea monsters. A death to either of them would be kinder than what would happen if followers of the flame caught them. Most would be enslaved, the crew would be killed, but some would face an even worse fate.

They would be taken to Ashar—to the source of Ilos' light.

34

A Lone Hunt

Faedi

The morning was quiet; a gentle hush had settled over the land as Faedi sat with Lonan and Sophir, surrounded by the group of freed slaves and farmers. The cold bit through their layers of woolen clothing, and she couldn't help but worry as she watched them shiver beside the fire.

Winter had barely begun to show its teeth, but it was already harsh enough to make her bite her lip in concern.

She busied herself mixing tea to help fortify them against the cold while Lonan and Sophir unloaded their cart of supplies. The hearty breakfast, a mix of leftover stew from the previous night, was served first to the children. A sense of satisfaction settled over her as she watched them eat; it was a small comfort amid the uncertainty.

Lonan and Sophir sat beside her, sharing the meal quietly while she continued her work on the tea. It was a small gesture, but every bit helped. She glanced around, noting how animated the group was, happily chatting and laughing despite the biting cold. They seemed unbothered by the risks they faced, their laughter breaking the crisp morning air. To them, winter was their only danger.

Delicate snow flurries drifted lazily from the sky, landing softly on the ground. They shimmered in the pale morning light, melting into glistening drops. She watched as the children chased after the snowflakes while Dusan flew between them, their innocence warming her heart despite the chill.

"We should warn them," she suggested, setting aside a jar and starting on another.

"We should," Sophir agreed, his eyes following the children with a hint of pride. "But not yet."

She spotted Emmaline among them, her hood down as she ran free with the others. Whatever Sophir had done with her had given her newfound confidence, and Faedi couldn't help but smile.

"Does it snow in Valoria?" Lonan asked softly.

Sophir shook his head. "Only ashes fall there."

Her heart ached at the thought, and she leaned back to watch the children play, torn between wanting to protect them and knowing they needed to wait a bit longer before warning them.

"They need protection," she insisted, returning to her work.

"I can ask the eastern Watch," Lonan suggested. "I'm sure they can spare a few to help them."

"You think your parents will send help when they should be strengthening their defenses?" Sophir raised an eyebrow, skepticism evident in his tone.

"If the Mire falls because we were helping to defend others, it will have fallen for a good reason," Lonan replied, grinning at Faedi when she squeezed his hand. "I'm not leaving them unprotected."

"A few Watchers and their bonded won't be missed," she agreed with a nod. "Besides, they can double as a patrol to see if anyone comes through here."

"How many fighters does the Mire have?" Sophir's brow creased in thought. "Beyond your assistance ten years ago, I don't know much about your forces or defenses."

"Everyone is taught to hunt and fight as soon as they are old enough," Lonan explained. "Even if their talents call them elsewhere, no one goes without basic training to defend themselves and their family."

Faedi nodded, remembering the first time she had met Lonan. He had just been a young Mireling, barely able to hold a physical form outside the Mire, yet he had already known how to trap and hunt. Myst had always been by his side. Those memories were bittersweet, reminding her of simpler times.

"Call the Watch, see who's nearby… We should talk to Jaref," she said as she finished the last jar of tea. "Tell them to bring supplies if they can. They'll need more than this if it's snowing already."

Lonan nodded and reached for his hidden crystal to call them. Faedi turned her attention to Sophir, who stood to find Jaref and Odessa. She hoped they would accept any help they could offer, especially for the children's sake. If the cultists turned their eyes toward them, the snow would be the least of their concerns.

"Ilos' zealots are talented manipulators."

The voice of Torix echoed in her mind, a chilling reminder of the lurking dangers.

She bit her lip. They might not attack the way they had at the cottage, but she feared they would try to win the group over with kindness and false promises. If they didn't get what they wanted through deception, they could become violent.

Faedi reminded herself that they needed to know if any of the people here were eclipse-born. More importantly, they had to warn them to forget that Faedi and the others had been there. If the cultists discovered they had helped, they might use any means necessary to extract information from them.

As she rubbed her cheek, she recalled the metal glove of the cultist that had cut into her face. The warmth of the fire flickering nearby did little to ease the chill in her heart.

Faedi watched as Jaref sat beside Odessa, her hand gripping his lap tightly while he absorbed everything they had told him. Sophir had warned them that the cultists might come under the guise of offering aid, just as they had in Dewgate, or they could face an outright attack. Faedi had cautioned them about the approaching winter and the frost that would soon harden the ground, while Lonan reassured them that Watchers and their bonded would arrive within a few days to offer support.

"All right," Jaref said, his voice steady despite the weight of the situation. "How do you suggest we best prepare?"

"If the carts are torn down, you can use the wood to build some kind of shelter. I'll see what I can do about getting more supplies," Faedi suggested. "Anyone who can wield a scythe should start harvesting whatever they can from the plains. You'll need it for warmth."

"Sophir and I can help with that as well," Lonan promised, determination clear on his face.

Faedi noticed Odessa glancing between them, concern flickering in her eyes. "I thought you needed to leave soon," she said.

"We do, but I don't want to leave without offering what we can," Lonan replied. "We shouldn't linger too long, though." His gaze shifted to Faedi, silently asking if she agreed.

After a brief pause, Faedi spoke. "Was anyone here born during an eclipse?" The question had been pressing on her mind, and she needed to know.

"None from Valoria," Jaref said, shaking his head. "They took the babes born on each eclipse as soon as they took their first breath."

A low growl rose in Faedi's throat, but she bit it back, clenching her jaw. It shouldn't have surprised her that the cultists were willing to steal newborns—not after what they had done to her little brothers—but hearing it still sent a fresh wave of rage through her. With each revelation, her hatred for them only deepened.

"If any of the farmers were eclipse-born, I doubt they would have been allowed to leave," Sophir said, his voice low and thoughtful. "Or someone would have tracked them down by now. Blavier seems to have fully sided with Ilos' zealots."

"That could be a good thing," Lonan added, a trace of hope in his tone. "If no one here was born during an eclipse, they might not turn violent when they arrive.”

Faedi nodded, but unease still gnawed at her. There was a chance Lonan was right, but she couldn't shake the worry about how they would treat the freed slaves from Valoria. If the cultists tried to take them back and were met with resistance, it could still lead to bloodshed.

“Do you have proof that you were freed according to Valorian law?” she asked, keeping her voice gentle.

“Aye, Scarred made sure we all had the right documents,” Jaref said, patting his chest, the faint crinkle of parchment audible even over the wind.

“Then maybe they'll be safe,” she murmured, glancing between Lonan and Sophir. “Would that be enough to pacify them?”

“Ravyn said they didn't threaten him because he had already been cleansed,” Sophir noted. “I didn't ask what that entailed, but he's also from Valoria.”

Faedi sighed and pushed herself to her feet. “We should focus on your shelter,” she said firmly. “It will protect you from the cold and any outside threats.”

Despite the unease twisting in her gut, she forced a small smile. But as her eyes lifted toward the sky, dark, heavy clouds loomed on the horizon. The ground was still warm, but if the snow began and didn't let up, it wouldn't take long for the earth to freeze solid.

If they didn't act quickly, time would run out.

And when she and the others returned, she feared they might find nothing but frozen corpses.

As the afternoon dragged on and night crept closer, Faedi sank beside a small grove of pines with a heavy sigh. The weight of the day pressed down on her as she watched their branches sway gently in the breeze. They weren't large trees, nor were there many of them, but she hoped there would be enough to harvest to build a structure capable of sheltering everyone.

A longhouse would keep them warm, trapping their body heat efficiently. More trees would grow in time, and after resting, she could spur additional growth, ensuring a steady supply of materials throughout the winter and into the following year for kindling and construction. They might not have a forest's worth of resources, but it was a start.

The promised Guardians would be able to offer further assistance once she left. The seeds had been sown, and new saplings already dotted the ground—all they needed was magic and encouragement to grow quickly, just as the livestock would need encouragement to breed in order to sustain the settlement's food supply.

If Haldin is kind, I can also ask him to help them.

A gust of wind whipped around her, making her joints ache. She hugged her arms to herself, shivering against the cold. It was only going to get worse. The journey up the mountain would be miserable, and she began to wonder if it was even possible. The elements could kill them before they reached the Dusk Elves.

"Tea?" Sophir's voice called from behind her, and she turned to look up at him.

"You're pale," he observed, kneeling beside her.

"My fur is as gray as ever," she replied, accepting the steaming cup from his hand.

"Your lips never match your fur, though," he countered, removing his cloak and draping it over her shoulders. "Odessa has a team of women working on new clothes for the trek up the mountain."

"They should save their supplies for themselves," she frowned.

"I didn't have the heart to deny her. She seemed too happy to help," he admitted with a sigh, settling beside her.

"How did things go with Emmaline?" Faedi asked, taking a sip of the tea. "I saw her playing with the other children."

"She needs practice but is growing more confident in her abilities." He nodded and wrapped an arm around her, sharing his warmth. "She wants to come with us."

"The trip isn't safe," Faedi warned. Sophir's warmth eased the ache in her limbs, but the danger ahead remained unchanged. "Lonan and I are eclipse-born… the cultists might hurt her if they find us."

"I know."

She looked up at him, frowning as she realized he *wanted* Emmaline to come but didn't want to put her in danger. His expression mirrored Lonan's from the night before. They all wanted her with them, yet none of them knew what to do.

"If Haldin is… agreeable," she said slowly, choosing her words with care, "maybe we can bring everyone to the mountain. The Dusk Elves have lived there undisturbed for so long; maybe it would be safer for them rather than staying here in the open."

"It's possible—if everyone consents to it," he said, looking down at her. "You would ask that of him?"

"If I'm his heir, then why not?" She exhaled sharply. "He may be content to isolate himself from the world in a decades-long temper tantrum, but these people need help. I can't gamble on the Mire being safe just because of Torix's assumption." She shook her head. "The mountain has been safe for the Dusk Elves for a long time—it would be safe for them, too."

"You might ruffle some scales if one of your first acts as heir is bringing newcomers to the mountain," Sophir chuckled, nudging her to drink more tea.

"Let them be ruffled. He's a *temporary* king of Rowdon. His throne is in Dewgate, and it's not just meant to rule over Dusk Elves." She squinted up at him as he laughed again. "What?"

"That stubbornness of yours must be a royal trait."

Faedi rolled her eyes and let out a small laugh, shaking her head. Her mother had taught her many lessons that had once seemed strange—proper etiquette, courtly manners, customs that had little relevance to a life in the forest. Perhaps she had never intended to keep them there. Maybe she had been preparing Faedi to reintegrate into a noble house once they returned to the mountain. Or maybe they were simply habits her mother had never been able to let go of.

"I—" Faedi started to speak but abruptly stopped, straining to listen.

Sophir frowned, studying her face. "What?"

She shook her head, but the sound came again—louder this time. A howl. Then another.

"The Nomads never mentioned wolves here," she said, scanning the area quickly. "Get everyone together."

"What's wrong?" Sophir asked, already following her as she strode back toward the communal fire.

"There hasn't been any prey since we left the forest. If they're hunting, a mass of people here is an easy target—especially with domesticated livestock. They'll come here," she explained hurriedly.

With each step she took, the howls grew louder.

Then came the scream.

35
Into the Ice Plains

Faedi

The forest-folk and freed slaves organized quickly, forming a protective circle around the campfire. Anyone too young, old, or sick to fight was moved to the center, away from the edges where the wolves might attack. Tension hung heavy in the air as the howls grew closer and more frenzied, mingling with the sounds of hurried movement and anxious murmurs. Some grasped makeshift weapons—bows, spears, anything they could find to defend themselves. The children huddled between the adults, clinging to them with wide, terrified eyes.

Faedi stared out into the fields as she prepared. The howls were more spaced apart than before and remained just far enough away to avoid sight. The scream she had heard likely belonged to someone who had strayed too far from the safety of the camp. The pack should have swarmed whoever had cried out; they should have howled to signal a meal.

But they hadn't.

"Something doesn't feel right," she murmured, glancing at Lonan and Sophir.

The three of them stood in a triangle formation around the others, ready to spring in any direction if something charged. A moment of silence passed between them before they nodded in agreement. Her gut was rarely wrong, or perhaps they were just as wary as she was.

"This is rather organized," Lonan said, scanning the area. "I think there are more of them than the howls suggest."

"How can you tell?" Sophir asked, his eyes darting across the field.

"It sounded like they were signaling earlier, but the number doesn't match the howls. I don't think these are normal wolves. I think it's a hunt." Lonan looked at Faedi. "Call ours?"

They should have been close enough to hear. They would have followed after the fire.

Faedi bit her lip, gripping her dagger tightly. She wished her arm were functional enough to draw a bow, but she knew she couldn't wield one effectively. Her magic and blade would have to suffice, but if Lonan was right and a pack of werewolves surrounded them, a dagger would do little.

"It won't hurt to try—they've already smelled us." She drew in a deep breath and tilted her head back, releasing a long, clear howl. Lonan's voice joined hers shortly after, their calls echoing into the night. She prayed they would hear.

The tension in the air thickened as they watched and waited. Faedi's mind raced through potential scenarios. If a group of werewolves lurked in the darkness, they shouldn't have approached where one was already present—unless they intended to kill.

Dusan swooped down, landing on her good shoulder. "They're were-folk with a pack of direwolves. It's a Hunt."

The howls grew louder and more erratic. Faedi's eyes scanned the darkened fields, searching for any sign of movement. Suddenly, a commotion erupted on the far side of the camp.

A figure staggered into view, clearly wounded and panting heavily. One of the freed slaves—a man who had been gathering grass—collapsed near the edge of the protective circle. His clothes were torn, blood dripping from multiple wounds.

"They're coming!" He gasped. "At least a dozen of them…wolf men."

Faedi's heart sank. The worst-case scenario had come to pass. Twelve werewolves could tear through their group with ease, and if they had direwolves with them, the odds were even worse. For every werewolf, at least one wolf could be expected—if not two.

"Anyone skilled with a bow, get ready!" she called over her shoulder. "Shoot between the vines!"

"What are you doing, Faedi?" Lonan asked, knives raised.

"Trying the trick I used in the war," she told him as she raised her hand and swirled it over the ground.

Please grow.

Gradually, roots and vines rippled out from the earth before shooting up and around them, forming a dome to shield the camp's occupants. It wasn't as dense as she would have liked, but it was better than nothing. Every barrier helped.

As she worked, she caught the expressions of the forest-folk and freed slaves—some filled with fear, others with hope. The only one who stared in pure wonder was Emmaline. The child pushed through the group, weaving between taller figures until she stood before Faedi with a bright smile.

"Be careful, Miss Faedi."

"I will be," Faedi promised. "Now, go stay with the other children."

The howls escalated, more voices joining the cacophony. A sharp whistle split the air, followed by a rush of movement and Sophir's shouted warning.

The wolves were upon them.

Faedi spun around, her breath catching as she spotted glowing eyes in the darkness, surging toward them.

Ancients help us.

The night was filled with the sounds of clashing steel, desperate shouts, and the savage howls of were-folk. Faedi fought with everything she had, her body shifting into a half-wolf form to compensate for her injured arm, tearing into anyone who got too close.

The once-calm encampment had quickly transformed into a battlefield, full of chaos. Her earlier assumption about their numbers had been far too low. Each were-folk was armored and mounted on direwolves, accompanied by several others who bore no riders.

The clang of steel against steel rang through the night, each clash echoing like a thunderous bell. Desperate cries rose above the din, mingling with the feral howls of the direwolves prowling the fringes of the fight, their eyes glowing with fiery hunger.

Lonan was a phantom, barely visible as his form flickered in and out of the darkness. His knives flashed, slicing through armor and flesh. An attacker lunged at him, but he melted away into the shadows, reappearing behind the man with a swift, silent strike that left the were-folk crumpled on the ground.

Sophir tore through the enemy ranks, his scales shimmering like molten rock in the flickering firelight. Charging into the fray, he tackled four were-folk and whipped his tail at two others, sending them flying with bone-crushing force. With a roar, his claws ripped through armor as if it were paper.

Faedi's injured arm throbbed, but she shoved aside the pain, relying on her shifted form to keep herself and the group behind her alive. Muscles rippled beneath her fur as she dodged and weaved through the chaos, arrows whistling past her and into their attackers.

A were-folk lunged, sword raised high, but she rolled under the swing and extended her good arm, claws outstretched. Blood splattered across her face as she tore into his exposed thigh. He gasped, stumbling back, and she pounced with a snarl, aiming for his throat.

Hours seemed to pass as the battle raged on, but gradually, the howls faded. Snarls and barks turned to whimpers and whines, and terrified screams morphed into shouts of victory, even as the barrier of roots and vines was broken. Some of the less-injured attackers began to retreat into the darkness when their prey refused to yield.

Their pack arrived soon after, tearing into anyone they could grab, but Faedi ordered them to stay close. She didn't want them chasing anyone down—not when others could be waiting.

As the last of the attackers disappeared into the night, she stumbled back, her body returning to its normal state. She tipped her head back with a grin before releasing a howl, echoed by Lonan's and followed by a roar from Sophir.

Soon, the others joined in, celebrating with cries and shouts.

Faedi huffed, glancing back at the group. The immediate danger had passed, but the camp bore the scars of the attack. Livestock lay scattered, nearly half of them missing or dead, and many people were injured.

"Can the Watchers get here faster? Travel through the shadows?" She called to Lonan.

"I'll ask…and request more help," he replied with a nod.

"Butcher the dead animals now," she instructed the group. "Cook them. Start processing the hides. If they came for food, cooked meat won't appeal to them."

"Aye, you heard her," Jaref called, waving for everyone to get to work.

As the survivors tended to the wounded and salvaged what they could, Sophir pulled her aside and offered her water. She took a sip before he handed her a bundle of herbs. She smiled at him before quickly eating the wrapped mixture. The flavor was horrible, but it was the right blend.

"Why didn't you do that before?" He asked once she rinsed the bitterness from her mouth.

"Do what?" She looked up at him.

"When you fought the cultists in the forest and at your cottage, you didn't change forms," he said, tilting his head. "Why only now?"

"Because these were people like me," she replied, taking another sip of water. "The cultists didn't need another reason to kill me, and when I fought them, they didn't have silver weapons—but they might have had some hidden."

"Smart."

She smiled at him, realizing his comment was genuine rather than a jest. He was no stranger to hiding his true nature. Even after the fire, he had only removed his glamour when necessary, and she knew he would put it back on as soon as they left the encampment.

"Are you alright?" He asked as she had finished the water.

"I'll feel it in the morning," she laughed, despite her discomfort. "We should leave, too."

"You think they'll be safe without us?" Sophir frowned.

"Safer. They didn't take the livestock they killed. They weren't after food, and I don't think they were here for the Valorians or the farmers," she said, motioning toward the deceased, now covered by blankets. "They only killed those who got in the way and the animals that ran."

"What are you thinking?" he asked, shaking his head as Lonan approached. "They weren't cultists. Ilos' followers aren't welcoming to were-folk."

"They might not allow them in their ranks, but Torix said people do what they want with the right motivation. Fenkas did," she growled at the mention of her father and looked away.

"They'll be here by morning. More the day after that," Lonan announced. "Why are you mad?"

"I had a theory," she said, sitting on the ground and wiping her face with her hand.

"You think they were after us?"

She looked up at him and nodded silently. He muttered a curse and sat beside her, then laid back on the grass. Sophir soon followed, sitting on Lonan's other side as he watched the camp.

"We leave in the morning?" Lonan eventually asked.

"I think so," she replied, lying back as well. "I'm going to leave our pack with them… maybe Dusan too. They all work well together."

"We should tell Jaref tonight and leave before anyone wakes up. It's safer for them if they don't see our exact path," Sophir suggested.

Faedi sighed. He was right. If cultists demanded information from them, the survivors could tell them they had gone to Rowdon but not which path they had taken. There were spells that some blessed by divine magic could use to determine if someone's words were true. Maybe, since they were Valorian, they would be granted that mercy over torture.

"I'll go speak with Jaref now and take the first watch," Sophir said, standing and flexing his wings behind him.

"Tell him he can have our cart," she called after him before closing her eyes. "Should we leave the horses?"

"You can ask them to return here when the path gets too dangerous. The longer we have them, the faster we'll go."

Lonan slid an arm under her neck, cradling her as she rolled to face him. He was right; they needed whatever speed they could get. The sooner they reached the mountain, the more likely they were to get the help Torix hoped for—or King Haldin would kill them.

Maybe it would be less terrifying to be killed by family rather than by bastard god-worshiping murderers.

Before the first light of dawn graced the horizon, Faedi, along with Lonan and Sophir, was already on her feet. The camp lay eerily quiet, save for the soft rustling of wind through the new trees and the distant calls of early morning birds. Even their horses remained silent as they mounted.

"Watch over them," Faedi instructed Dusan and the wolves. "Don't let anything happen to them."

"Not the children, at least. They feed me," Dusan chirped before taking flight, circling the encampment.

Faedi carefully examined the sleeping bodies and the remnants of the previous night's chaos. The barrier—and they—had done their job. However, signs of the skirmish still littered the ground: broken arrows, discarded weapons, and patches of torn cloth. She glanced back at the camp, her heart heavy with concern for those they were leaving behind, but she knew they had no choice.

They would be safer without them there, especially once the Watchers arrived.

Lonan checked the makeshift saddlebags on the horses as Faedi combed her fingers through her horse's mane. His eyes scanned their surroundings while he worked, alert for any lingering threats or scouts. Meanwhile, Sophir approached and handed her one of the new cloaks Odessa had promised.

"Thank you," she said with a small smile, realizing that, for perhaps the only time, she was taller than him as he smiled up at her.

"You two should ride together," he suggested, nodding before mounting his horse.

Faedi took the lead, with Lonan's arms wrapped around her waist. Once they were safe, she urged her horse into a gallop, heading first toward the waystone and then south.

The horses seemed eager to run, relishing the chance to gallop freely after days of hauling a cart. Faedi smiled, understanding their joy. It felt wonderful to have the wind in her hair again—she agreed with the horses.

As they pressed on, the grasslands gradually brightened with the first hints of dawn, and the Rowdon Mountains loomed ahead. Their jagged peaks cast long shadows across the land as the sun continued to rise, and Faedi's heart pounded. Every stride the horses took brought them closer to the Dusk Elves— and to the grandfather who would either welcome her or kill her.

By mid-morning, they reached the ice plains of Rowdon. The rugged terrain offered a natural cover of mist and snow, but Faedi slowed the horses, unwilling to risk the ground beneath them. The last thing she wanted was for one of them to fall through the ice into a frozen lake or river.

"We should find places to rest well before sundown until we reach the Dusk Elves," Sophir suggested.

"Agreed," Faedi nodded, lifting a hand to shield her eyes from the light reflecting off the ice and snow.

"Any sign of Torix?" Lonan asked, scanning the landscape. "Everything looks the same to me."

"There are marks on some of these rocks—the snow doesn't stick to them," she pointed to one. "I just hope they're not too frequent for someone else to follow."

"Don't we want them to follow us?" Sophir asked just as the wind picked up around them.

"I do, but I don't want it to be easy for them. The longer they follow us, the safer everyone at the border is...and if they get lost out here, it's better for every- one," she replied, glancing back at him with a shrug.

Whether were-folk or not, wolves could survive in the cold longer than most—but even they had their limits. They hadn't eaten what they killed, which meant they would eventually need to hunt. If they ventured too far up the mountain, they might not return to the border. The Valorians and farmers would be safe.

Or at least, that was what Faedi hoped.

36

A Bitter Trail

Lonan

He spent most of the journey contemplating Sophir's retelling of the mysterious woman's words rather than focusing on the little girl they had left behind. She wanted to be found in stone, with frozen hearts and leaves. He wondered if ice, time, or something else had frozen the hearts. As he looked up at the jagged peaks of the mountains, blanketed in snow and ice, his thoughts drifted to a story his mother had told him as a child.

"Didn't the Gaelisks live in these mountains with dragons?" He asked, his voice barely rising above the wind that whipped around them.

"Centuries ago, yes," Sophir replied solemnly.

"We should return the horses; they aren't used to this climate or terrain. They know how to get back," Faedi murmured, speaking gently to the animals to calm them as she glanced between Sophir and Lonan. "We can continue on foot. Torix will be easier to follow here."

"I'll unload the supplies," Lonan sighed, gathering everything together. "What happened to the dragons and gargoyles?"

"There was a war, the same one that turned the north of Ashar into a wasteland. My grandfather's brother fought in it; he vanished with the Gaelisks. Before the war began, they made these mountains their home," Sophir explained as he helped Lonan with the supplies. "Dawn Elves and Deep Dwarves held the Gaelisks captive as slaves."

"For riches?" Faedi's eyes darkened, a low growl escaping her throat.

"Yes," Sophir nodded sadly. "There was an uprising led by the Shadow Elves when one of them went to the dragons, bringing tales and proof of the atrocities committed by the Dwarves and Elves. The dragons demanded freedom for the Gaelisks, and my ancestor was appointed as their guardian—someone to teach their young how to fly again and live outside of their slavery. Then, the mountain was attacked. No one saw the Gaelisks or my granduncle again."

"I'm sorry," Lonan murmured, lowering his head as he caught the twinge of pain in Sophir's voice.

"Who led the attack?" Faedi asked as she urged the horses off once they were free of their burdens.

"I assume it was either the Dwarves or the Elves, maybe both. The attack was swift; part of the mountains here was completely erased, leaving behind a crater… there was nothing left to determine who was responsible. Some say it might have been the Dusk Elves who resided here," Sophir said carefully. "Perhaps a disagreement between the freed Gaelisks and them. I don't know."

"Just another thing to ask my grandfather about, I suppose," Faedi muttered, facing the mountains and glaring up at the peaks.

"What's on your mind?" Lonan asked, genuinely curious.

"Just that I might be the heir of a horrible man," she said. "He damned the Umbrals, might have had something to do with the disappearance of the Gaelisks, and who knows what else."

"Historically, the Shadow Elves and Dusk Elves have been allies…" Lonan told her gently, wrapping an arm over her shoulders. "Maybe they killed whoever was responsible, and that's why there's no evidence."

"They weren't opposed to speaking when my family questioned them about the whereabouts of my granduncle," Sophir added, hoisting a large pack onto his back.

Lonan frowned when he noticed Faedi didn't seem entirely convinced. He couldn't blame her—not after what she had learned from her memories. Her father, the man she had loved and trusted to protect her, had been a traitor. He had ordered the cultists to kill her little brothers, to take her and Sylrie, and had likely made it out of the blaze alive. There was no logical reason for her to trust that her grandfather would be any different.

"Where is Torix's next mark?" Lonan asked, shifting the subject and motioning to the rocks around them.

"Over there," Faedi sighed, nodding before she started walking.

Lonan glanced at Sophir, who moved when Faedi did, and caught his eye. They shared a frown before turning their gazes back to her as she led the way. Lonan worried about what would happen if her grandfather wasn't honorable. The consequences for the Mire would be severe, but what concerned him more in that moment was what it would do to Faedi. She had already experienced the worst kind of betrayal, and if another person failed her, he feared it might break her.

The journey up the mountain was more challenging than Lonan had imagined. The wind was sharp, chilling him to his bones until they ached, and it was worse when they reached the snow. He had been wrong to think it might offer some reprieve from the jagged rocks; all it did was hide the ice below.

They had to travel slowly, carefully following in Faedi's footsteps. After several slips, Lonan realized it was only safe to step where she did. She seemed to be following an exact trail, and he figured Torix must have done something to the snow to make it safe for them, but nowhere else. He didn't want them to be followed. He was protecting the Dusk Elves.

"I can't tell if it's the clouds or if the sun is setting," Lonan shouted over the howling wind. "Do we make camp?"

He didn't want to admit it was because Faedi had begun to lean against rocks more frequently, taking heavy breaths as she cradled her arm. They all needed rest, but she required warmth the most. They had run out of her herbs two days prior, and he didn't want her to push herself into an injury.

"There's a cave ahead," Faedi pointed with her good arm. "We can rest there."

"Lead the way," Sophir called from behind them. He had remained in the back since they first found the ice, prepared to catch anyone who fell.

Lonan eyed the distance between their group and the cave; it wasn't far, but he didn't know if Torix's trail led there. If it didn't, it could take them a while to travel such a short distance. Like the Mire, the mountain air was thick, and he assumed some magic at play prevented trespassers. However, the similarity didn't make sense. There was no known heart tree in the mountains.

He sighed in relief when Faedi didn't slip on the way to the cave. Her movements were confident with each step, and he smiled momentarily before it fell bitterly. At least one man from her childhood had her safety in mind.

"Torix camped here," Faedi called over her shoulder as she wandered into the cave. "There was a fire."

"Should we make one?" Lonan asked, following behind and shaking the snow off his furs. "The wind and clouds are so wild, someone might not see smoke."

"We could use some of the furs to trap heat and leave a hole for smoke," Faedi nodded, walking through the small space of the cave. "He left wood."

"How do you know it's him?" Sophir asked from the mouth of the cave.

"I know his scent," she whispered, picking up a pouch left on the wood pile. "He left eventide seeds."

"Thank the gods," Lonan sighed in relief. "Work on your arm. We can make a fire and tea."

The fire didn't take long to warm the cave interior, with some of their furs hanging over the mouth to trap the heat. When the ones they wore were laid out beside the fire, Lonan realized that Sophir had brought extra from the cart. He smiled as he watched him sip steaming tea. For a city-folk, he was surprisingly competent.

Lonan sat beside Sophir in front of the fire, their backs to Faedi while she sat against the wall. He listened to her undress to expose her arm, whispering spells under the roar of the wind outside. She was trying to use the seeds on her arm to spur the growth of her vines.

She didn't want to face potential enemies without being able to draw Torix's bow.

Sophir offered Lonan a cup of tea. "Here."

"Thank you," Lonan nodded, accepting the drink and sighing after taking a sip. "This tastes better than it should."

"I think anything warm would taste good in this environment." Sophir chuckled beside him while examining the dried meats he had set out beside the fire. They were frozen solid by the time they stopped at the cave.

"Do you want tea?" Lonan glanced over his shoulder at Faedi. "It might—"

His words trailed off when he saw black vines slowly growing from her arm. Blood pooled and dripped from her scars with each new growth, and she trembled against the wall with shaky breaths. Her eyes were shut, her lip trapped under her teeth, and tears fell down her cheeks.

Yet, she didn't make a sound.

"Gods," Lonan gasped, scrambling over to her. "Dammit, Faedi."

"I'm fine," she whimpered, shaking her head.

Sophir kneeled on the other side of her. "Did this happen last time?"

"She was unconscious last time." Lonan shook his head. "It bled, but I didn't know it hurt like this."

"It's alright," Faedi promised, forcing a smile. "It isn't too bad."

"Here, drink," Sophir leaned closer, holding his cup of tea for her to sip.

Lonan grabbed the dried furs from near the fire to tuck around her for comfort while the vines grew slowly—achingly so. He tried not to watch them but couldn't look away as they crept over the scar to cover it. Sophir gently dabbed a cloth over the bloodied areas, holding a ball of crushed eventide seeds within the fabric in hopes of easing her pain.

Lonan didn't relax until blooms of eventides opened on the vines, releasing their silvery mist of pollen into the air—until Faedi sighed in relief and closed her eyes. Sophir began to pass out the thawed meat once she caught her breath, and they sat on either side of her while they ate their rations in silence.

Snowflakes, caught in the wind's fierce gusts, occasionally found their way through the gaps in the fur curtain covering the cave's mouth, only to melt instantly in the warmth radiating from the small campfire. The fire's soft, flickering glow danced across the stone walls, and Lonan knew it wouldn't last long. There weren't enough logs to last the night.

He tucked furs around himself and looked at Sophir and Faedi, who had done the same, shifting closer to Faedi. When the fire went out, they would have to rely on the trapped heat and what their bodies produced. It might not be comfortable, but Lonan wasn't concerned about their odds of survival.

Once the meal was done and the tea was gone, he brought his fur to his chin and closed his eyes. The sounds of the wind outside grew distant as he focused on the crackle of the fire and the gentle rhythm of Faedi and Sophir's breathing. The combination was soothing, acting as a lullaby, and his tense muscles relaxed as his breathing slowed.

37
The Weight of Ice

Sophir

His eyes shot open at the sound of metal striking rock, and he sat up, heart pounding. The cave's interior was pitch dark; no embers remained in the fire. Faedi shivered as the warmth they had trapped beneath the furs was disturbed. He strained his eyes against the darkness, searching for the source of the sound, but nothing seemed out of place. Yet deep down, he knew something was wrong.

"Wake up," he whispered, shaking Faedi and Lonan gently. "We need to leave."

"What's wrong?" Faedi mumbled, rubbing the sleep from her eyes.

"I don't know," he admitted, shaking his head. "It just doesn't feel right."

"Let's go then," Lonan agreed without hesitation, already rising to repack their supplies.

Within minutes, they were back out in the snow and wind. The scenery had not changed since they had slept—snow covered the rocks, swirling around their faces as Faedi led them once more along Torix's path. Just as before, Sophir walked behind her and Lonan in case anyone lost their footing. But his focus drifted away from them, his gaze sweeping over the rocks and peaks.

"It feels like we're being watched," he muttered, unease creeping into his voice.

"I wouldn't doubt they have a watch," Lonan replied, his tone serious.

"Or a hunt," Faedi added. "Torix is a born were, but he's a Dusk Elf. It may be common."

Sophir frowned as they continued. He doubted that Faedi or Lonan could pick up a scent with the wind's violence, but that also meant they wouldn't be tracked by theirs either. Wind was a natural feature of the mountains, yet he wondered if magic played a part in its relentless force.

He paused as ice crunched beneath his boot and looked down. They had followed Torix's tracks carefully the entire way, yet something felt off. He raised his gaze to Lonan and Faedi's backs as they walked ahead before tilting his head, studying the snow.

"What if this isn't Torix's trail, but the only trail?" He asked, watching as they turned to face him. "What if they know we're here?"

"Faedi?" Lonan looked back at her, and Sophir saw her eyes darken as she examined the path.

"It's magic," she confirmed with a nod—just as a howl pierced the roar of the wind. Her head snapped up. "That's not Torix. Follow me."

Without hesitation, she took off, running and leaping over rocks as she followed the magic. Lonan and Sophir weren't far behind, but it was difficult to keep pace with her. She was agile in ways Sophir was not, and Lonan could slip through shadows whenever he lost his footing. However, Sophir had one advantage that might help—if the winds allowed it.

Arrows began to rain down from the surrounding peaks.

"Watch out!" He dropped his pack before he leaped into the air, ripping his pendant free. It had been years since he had taken flight, always fearful of being spotted, but they had no choice if they wanted to escape their hidden attackers.

"Can you follow the magic if we're flying?" He called, straining to catch up despite the wind.

"What?" Faedi glanced over her shoulder, eyes widening. "Yes! Get Lonan first. They hate Umbrals!"

Sophir nodded and dove, reaching Lonan just in time to grab him before dodging another wave of arrows. He pulled him close and surged back into the sky, his back tensing against the strain. Below, Faedi continued her mad dash over the treacherous terrain, moving as though she had lived on the mountain her entire life.

"Archers to your left!" He warned.

Faedi rolled aside just as another volley of arrows struck the ground where she had been. With a swift motion, she outstretched her hands, summoning a curved wall of ice. The wind cut violently around it, knocking Sophir off course. He cursed, forced to redirect. As he turned, the arrows embedded in the ice wall exploded into hundreds of tiny shards, scattering in every direction.

"Go up! Follow me!" Faedi shouted while running, her form shifting.

Her fur seemed to merge into her body as she dropped to all fours, growing in size as black fur spread across her limbs. In the blink of an eye, a massive black direwolf darted through the snow, her bow and quiver still strapped to her back. Sophir offered a silent prayer of thanks that she wasn't white. He rose higher, dodging arrows along the way.

She darted around rocks and obstacles, unwavering in her path. Lonan watched the skies, calling out enemy fire before it reached them. With the wind growing fiercer, Sophir struggled to maintain control. Each gust threatened to rip Lonan from his grasp.

"I need to get lower." He warned, diving just as a particularly strong current nearly wrenched Lonan from his arms.

"Torix was supposed to tell the King we were coming. This shouldn't be happening!" Lonan held on tighter, his voice strained.

"Unless they killed him. I don't see any of his marks." Sophir growled. "Fuck!"

A massive bear emerged from behind a rock, slamming into Faedi and sending her skidding across the ice.

Without warning, Lonan vanished from Sophir's grasp and reappeared on the bear's back, dagger flashing. Sophir dove, catching sight of an elf charging at them, sword drawn. He swept low, grabbing the elf mid-charge and hurling them over the steep peak. But before he could turn back, something struck his neck.

His limbs went heavy. His wings limp.

The snow felt distant, numb, as he crashed into the ground. A sickening snap echoed through his body as his wing crumpled beneath him against a rock.

He knew he screamed, but no sound reached his ears.

Faedi and Lonan turned, eyes wide with alarm, but they were too far away. Shapes moved around them—elves clad in white and gray furs, some materializing out of thin air. They swarmed like ghosts, descending upon them.

Blood erupted from Lonan's mouth as an elf's kick sent him sprawling. Faedi's body shuddered as she reverted to her standard form, a silver blade buried deep in her shoulder—the arm with the eventides.

Sophir clawed weakly at the snow, trying to reach them. But he couldn't lift himself. He couldn't even feel his fingers in the bitter cold.

The world faded into silence. Darkness closed in.

Sophir's mind was groggy as he awoke, his body stiff and heavy. As consciousness seeped in, he realized he was gagged and restrained, his arms chained behind his back. His wings were pinned, and his shoulders ached awkwardly as he adjusted his position on his knees.

Where am I?

The air around him was thick and musty, suffused with the scent of mildew and decay. His head throbbed, and he wasn't sure if it was from whatever he had been poisoned with or the fall he had taken. What concerned him more was the unsettling thought that Faedi and Lonan might be in a similar situation.

"Is Sophir with you?" Lonan's voice was distorted.

Sophir blinked against the darkness, trying to make out his surroundings, but it was as if he had been plunged into absolute blackness. Panic began to rise within him as he felt the wall behind him—uneven stone slick with what he hoped was water.

"I don't see anyone with me," Faedi responded.

Dammit.

Blood coated his tongue as he tested the rough leather in his mouth. His lips felt chapped and raw. His legs were numb, as were his feet, and he had no way of knowing how much time had passed since the encounter on the mountain.

"Are you alright?" he asked, hoping they fared better than he did.

Minutes stretched into what felt like hours in the oppressive darkness. His mind raced with questions, his senses heightened in the absence of light. Fear mingled with frustration as he realized he had no means to escape—no tools, not even a glimmer of light to orient himself. There was no way for him to reach Faedi or Lonan.

"I'm fine. Lonan?" Faedi asked, though Sophir couldn't tell if she was lying.

Gradually, his eyes adjusted slightly to the darkness, and he began to discern vague outlines of the room—his cell. The ceiling was low, the walls rough, and the cold, damp floor pressed against him. There were no windows, and the door was spiked with a smoother material than the stone walls.

"I—"

Sophir's gaze snapped to the door when Lonan's voice cut off. No light broke through the cracks, and he didn't hear any footsteps. However, as he strained his ears, he caught the faint sound of muted voices—and laughter—before a muffled scream split the air.

What's happening?

He pulled against the chains as Faedi's panicked voice echoed in his mind, his arms burning with effort. Gradually, the room began to brighten with each tug. He glanced over his shoulder at the metal. Sigils he didn't recognize were etched into the chains, casting a golden light that intensified with every pull.

"Talk to us, Lonan."

Dust fell into his face as he yanked against the chains, ignoring it, just as he ignored the way his body protested each movement. He let out a low growl, biting into the leather gag, but another scream echoed through the darkness—Faedi's.

He roared into the gag, desperation clawing at him as he tried to break the chains from the stone.

"Please, talk to me."

Without warning, pain ripped through his body, stealing his breath as he collapsed to the floor. His muscles spasmed violently. He couldn't process the pain or how his body reacted—how it tried to flee and curl into a ball all at once. It was a sensation he had never experienced before—simultaneously burned, frozen, and electrocuted without a single physical sign of injury.

Another voice in his mind surprised him before he lost consciousness—a deep, gravelly voice, screaming his name—and calling for Faedi and Lonan.

38

King of Dusk

Faedi

A whip cracked, followed by a scream, then another crack, and another scream. Her body ached and burned with each fall of the whip—her eyes watered and a whine erupted from her throat.

Lonan.

Faedi slowly opened her eyes as her head pounded. The sensation was worse than after her first time getting drunk and smoking with The Watch. She tried to wipe her face, but pain jolted through her arm, and she quickly realized her hands were chained above her head.

Slowly, her vision cleared and adjusted to the dim light. Several torches lit the room, and the stench was horrid. Rows of cells lined the wall opposite her; in the corner, a shadowy figure lay slumped against the wall with their hands chained like hers, and in the center were four stone pillars spaced equally through the room. She was attached to one. Sophir was chained to the one on her right, his back to it, and his chest was bloody as a dark blue elf hit him with a whip. Lonan was chained to the pillar on her left, facing it while his back dripped black blood as he was whipped.

"The shadow's whore is awake," a Dusk Elf spat and wrapped a whip around his hand as he approached her with a smirk. "Why are you here?"

"We came to see the King. The Mire—" Faedi winced when Lonan screamed after another crack. "Stop it."

"Fuck the Mire. It will bleed until we are satisfied," he sneered. "So will you."

She watched him unroll the whip slowly before she looked up at her bound hands. There wasn't much she could do to defend herself without mobility, but there were some things she could still try. If her vines could grow in a room of stone, it wasn't something she had ever had to try before.

Please grow.

She closed her eyes as the elf drew back his arm in preparation to swing the whip and focused on her eventides. If she could recreate what she had done with the cultist before—less lethally—she might be able to stop the elves from attacking them. However, she wasn't sure they would move quickly enough. They had been slow to move before.

She cried out when the whip hit her chest and stomach but kept her eyes closed and remained focused on the flowers. Pain ripped through her again and again, but the next strike didn't come. Instead, she heard the elf curse and opened her eyes to see his whip stuck to her as vines grappled it.

"Stop!" Sophir shouted over the whips. "We have information about his daughter."

"She's dead, we know," the elf spat at Sophir angrily before he grabbed Faedi's face, and pain tore through her body as if her bones were breaking.

"She had children!" Faedi screamed as the pain continued. "Four. Three sons. A daughter. Two survived."

"Liar," his hot breath washed over her face, and the pain intensified.

Then, without any warning, it was gone.

Faedi collapsed when the pain stopped, her shoulders aching as if they would detach from the weight pulling on her arms. Weakly, she tried to right herself and scanned the room. The other two elves who were whipping Lonan and Sophir had stopped and were in the center of the room. On the ground was the elf who had beaten her, and on top of him was a sizable half-wolf creature with blood dripping from its mouth.

It snarled when the other two elves went for it and swiped wildly at them with its claws.

"That...is Faedi Yiva...daughter of Endi...and..." The words came slowly between heaved breaths, and Faedi's blood ran cold. "Torix Yiva...your heir... and I will kill...the next fuck...who touches my...daughter."

What?

"Release...her," the creature snarled again. "Now!"

Faedi stared at him with wide eyes as he stood and loomed over the elves. Slowly, his attention turned to her, and her heart caught in her throat when she locked eyes with him. There was something in his eyes behind the rage and sadness.

Every time she had run to greet him when he came to visit, he had given her the same look as a child.

The chains above her head rattled before her hands dropped to her sides. She blinked once, twice, and then he was in front of her. The beastly form was gone, and instead stood the man she knew him as. Her lip quivered once, and he immediately wrapped her in his arms.

"Release the others," he growled while petting her hair and rubbing her back. "Tell the King to prepare for guests."

"They need a healer first," she protested quickly.

"He needs to see what happened," Torix told her and pulled away. "He needs to order the healer for them. Politics are messy."

She turned her attention to Lonan and Sophir as they stood nearby. Both were bloody, but Sophir stood tall and held Lonan beside him gingerly. It made sense, in a horrible way, that Lonan would have been the worst treated of the three of them. However, her understanding of the situation didn't ease her anger.

The two guards, torturers, exchanged a look before they began to leave. However, when they walked too close to Lonan and Sophir, Faedi growled and dug her claws into the nearest one. She shoved him away, pointed to the wall on the other side of the pillars, and took a step toward the second elf.

"Do not walk near them." She demanded with a snarl. "Come within arm's reach of my bonded again, and you will not have heads."

She didn't hear their stammered attempts at a response over the shared warning growl between Torix and herself. They were quick to leave and remained against the wall until they reached the door before they left her alone with Torix, Lonan, and Sophir. Only when they were alone did she hold her stab wound and curse.

"Are you alright?" She rushed to Lonan and examined the multiple lashings on his back. Some were down to the bone.

"Penelope was worse when they were teething," he smiled at her. "Takes more to kill me."

"You need to learn how to shut up," Sophir grumbled before he frowned at Faedi. "He antagonized them."

"They called my mother a whore," Lonan explained quickly.

"She'll lovingly call you an idiot for getting a washboard's worth of scars over her honor." Faedi winced as she continued to examine the wounds. "You're sure I can't heal him? Not even a little?"

"Not if we want the correct show played," Torix sighed. "Your grandfather is honorable, but…two decades' worth of hatred and blame on the Umbrals will be hard to blame, even if you're alive and married to one."

"I can show the King what happened. I will show anyone who asks," Sophir told them, and Faedi looked up at him anxiously. "The blame is on that man, not you."

"What man?" Torix's voice turned rigid.

"Fenkas." Sophir turned his eyes from Faedi's to Torix's. "He told the cultists when to attack and told them to kill the younger boys."

Faedi straightened and hugged her arms to herself. She wanted to ask who Fenkas was and why he was there, but she couldn't form the words. The knowledge that he had led them there didn't make her guilt go away. She should have listened to Torix's rule. She wasn't supposed to trust any strangers in the forest, but she did, and people died.

"Was his body there?" Sophir asked suddenly, and Faedi followed his eyes to Torix. "We buried your wife and the boys."

"No," Torix shook his head. "He was the one I was hunting for. I thought he was a coward and fled…I did not think he would betray us. Neither did Haldin."

"Sylrie got out," Faedi whispered. "He went south."

Torix looked down at her with wide eyes. Hope. She knew that expression well and managed to smile up at him. Twenty-two years was a long time. He might have died in the forest, could have been captured, or he was out there somewhere. Alive and well.

"The King will see you."

One of the guards from before spoke from the doorway but didn't enter. Instead, he stood off to the side and waited with his eyes downcast. A mild tingle of satisfaction hit Faedi when she walked toward the door, and he stepped back against the hall's wall before bowing his head and beginning to walk.

"You should threaten to rip off body parts more often," Lonan chuckled before groaning. "It's very effective."

Torix offered Faedi his arm. "Let them walk behind us. When we enter, you two stand behind her; don't bow."

"He is a King—"

"Faedi is his heir, Lonan is a Prince, and you're an Itmis," Torix cut off Sophir. "You're bonded to her. Don't bow until you're introduced."

"I miss forest politics," Sophir rumbled, and Faedi bit back a laugh. "Pleasant mice were less complicated."

I miss them too.

After days of travel without a substantial break, Faedi's legs ached with each step as they were forced to climb. She guessed they were inside the mountain, but she hadn't realized they had gone so far underground. Still, she didn't complain. Out of everyone, she had the least amount of injuries, and she wouldn't whine when others were enduring worse.

As she walked up the steps, a distant sound occasionally thumped in between their echoed footsteps. She tilted her head, listening intently, and searched the stairwell. Nothing hung from the ceiling, only the occasional iron lantern casting light in carved-out boxes. The ancient stone under her feet seemed sturdy, yet the sound persisted every few moments.

Faedi glanced over her shoulder at Sophir and Lonan to see if they had heard it, but their focus was on the stairs. With the next thump, Faedi caught sight of Sophir's wing hitting the wall as it dragged awkwardly behind him.

She gritted her teeth and focused ahead of her, keeping her gaze on the guard's back. If they touched either of them again, arms and legs would surely go missing.

"I'll take them," Torix growled to the guard when they reached the top of the stairs, waving him off. After the guard left, Torix turned to them. "Catch your breath."

"We're putting on a show, right?" Lonan forced a smile. "Lead the way."

"Your legs are shaking." Torix rolled his eyes, sighing when Lonan didn't seem convinced. "Alright, it's your pride, not mine."

"He's too stubborn for pride," Faedi teased, following along beside Torix.

The halls were tall, carved into dark stone—smooth but lacking shine. Intricate carvings adorned the walls, depicting scenes of battles, The Ancients, and dragons in the sky with Gaelisks. Columns, shaped like ancient trees, lined the passageways. It was craftsmanship Faedi had never seen before.

The air was cool but far warmer than the harsh wind outside, carrying a faint, earthy scent tinged with smoke from the torches burning in iron sconces along the walls. Thick drapes of blues and greens hung open over stained-glass windows that revealed the snowstorm outside. Like the carvings, the windows depicted colorful creatures, and Faedi spotted flowers among them—eventides.

As they approached the throne room, the grandeur of the architecture intensified. The final stretch of the hall was flanked by statues of Gaelisks, each one carved with such detail that Faedi paused to inspect them. She turned quickly when she heard Sophir's wing hit something else and followed Torix.

The dark ironwood doors to the throne room towered from floor to ceiling. They were adorned with a mosaic of gems depicting a tree. The guards standing on either side bowed to them before slowly swinging the doors open, revealing the vast room beyond.

Faedi held her breath as they stepped over the threshold. Inside, the room was illuminated by grand iron chandeliers hanging from stalactites. The floor was polished stone, colored to depict a map of a land she had never seen on any map.

The throne sat atop a raised dais at the far end of the room, crafted from the same dark stone as the halls but encrusted with large blue jewels. Behind the throne hung an enormous tapestry depicting mountains surrounded by a lush, dark forest—a stark contrast to the blizzard outside. Yet, Faedi couldn't focus on the tapestry for long.

Not when the silver-crowned elf on the throne stood as Torix stopped them in the center of the room.

"You were banished, Torix Yiva," King Haldin announced, descending the stone steps from the dais. "You were cast out for failing your duties as a knight sworn to serve the crown and a sworn defender of my daughter—your wife. Why did you come back?"

"I received no word of my banishment," Torix stated plainly. His eyes burned with something Faedi couldn't recognize. "I've spent the last twenty and two years hunting for her murderers. I come today with her…our daughter, Fae-di Yiva, and her bonded partners, Prince Lonan Tagilson and Sophir Daygan."

Faedi glanced at Torix and bowed when he nudged her gently. She matched his movements as best as she could before straightening to stare up at King Haldin with wide eyes. His black hair was braided on either side, just as her mother had taught her to keep hers, decorated with silver rings and clasps.

His stern gaze bore into her, and she bit her inner lip, resisting the urge to fidget. The cultists had been less intimidating.

"What kind of animal is he?" Lonan asked her, and she released a shaky breath.

"A really big bear," she answered.

"He's a were-folk?" Sophir asked, his confusion almost making her smile.

"Faedi pictures new people as animals," Lonan quickly explained. *"She said you were like a swamp lizard."*

"I don't know if I should be offended by that or not."

"I said you were like a panther. He's being cheeky," Faedi sighed.

"Is this true?" King Haldin finally asked after an uncomfortable silence. "Do you have proof of these claims?"

"I was told I have a glamour on me and charms," Faedi told him, working to picture the King as a bear rather than an elf. "Until today…I thought I was the daughter of Endi and Fenkas Lirulin."

"Endi used a glamour on her and her brothers," Haldin turned his attention to Torix when he spoke. "Fenkas broke his oath."

"I can see it rippling over her." His gaze fell back on Faedi, and she quickly looked away.

"I had a picture of her—I guess with her glamoured, but…" Faedi trailed off when she realized what she was about to say. "It was…burned."

The last thing she had of her mother and brothers was gone. It was ashes, like them, and the bow Torix had given her when she was a child. They had all been burned to nothing, along with everything else she shared with Lonan.

Don't cry. Do not cry.

"Your Majesty, if I may?" Sophir spoke carefully. "I can show you Faedi's memories of the day your daughter died. I walked through them myself with her, and…Fenkas played a part in her death."

He placed his hand on Faedi's shoulder as he spoke, and she relaxed, if only a little while looking back at the King. His eyes moved from her to Sophir, then to Lonan, then Torix, before returning to her. His emotions were impossible to read, and Faedi's urge to hide only increased.

"Clear the room. Two guards remain," his voice boomed, and Faedi flinched despite her efforts not to. "If this is a trick—"

"I'm sure our deaths will be painful," Faedi interrupted bitterly before taking a breath and bowing her head. "Your Majesty."

"They will be," his jaw clenched, and his amber eyes glistened before he turned his attention to Sophir. "Show me."

"You will need to take a seat, Your Majesty."

39

Heir of the Tides

Faedi

*S*he paced the width of the throne room, her mind racing as King Haldin sat on the steps with Sophir behind him. Two guards flanked the King, their hands resting on their swords, while Torix sat beside Lonan. Each time she passed them, she clenched her fists, fighting the urge to heal their wounds. All of them, like Sophir, were bloodied and bruised, but the audience was gone.

Whatever political show Torix had intended to ease tensions against the Umbrals had been put on hold.

"Would it not mean the same thing if, when they came back, you were looking better?" She snapped, turning sharply to walk the other way. She stopped when she heard Torix chuckle. "What?"

"You're so much like her," he replied, shaking his head.

"Is that a bad thing? She told me it was cruel to make anyone or anything suffer," Faedi huffed, continuing her pacing even though her legs ached.

"Some suffering has a purpose, even when cruel," Torix said, his gaze piercing into her back.

"It's ridiculous, is what it is." She rolled her eyes. "Everyone in this room, save for the King and his guards, is bleeding. If they believe my memories and somehow accept me as an heir, my marriage to Lonan should be enough. Damn anyone who thinks otherwise."

Torix sighed. "And there's your grandfather."

Faedi glared at the guards as they turned their attention to her, letting them

256

know she would strike if they dared to harm Sophir again. She kept her pacing carefully positioned far enough away to resist the urge to heal them, but close enough to attack if necessary.

"I believe she gets that side from you," Lonan said, his laugh turning into a groan. "We'll be fine. Sophir's walk through your memory didn't take too long."

"It was at least two hours," she shot back, hands on her hips. "You all could get an infection."

"One that can still be healed," Lonan said with a smile, trying to lighten the mood. "Your abilities are better than most."

She crossed her arms over her chest, frowning at him. He raised his eyebrows at her, then winked, and she rolled her eyes with a huff. Even if he was right, she couldn't stand the thought of him, Sophir, and Torix walking around wounded. She would take any punishment over watching them suffer.

She smirked at Lonan. "So we at least agree I should do the healing over some stranger here?"

"Dammit, Faedi—" Lonan began, then laughed and shook his head. "I guess having the heir do the healing might send a message."

"You two are impossible," Torix grumbled, lowering his head.

"I know I won't sneak a knife in anyone's back," she countered with a shrug, though she winced at the thought. "You were banished, and they hate Umbrals... and I don't know what they think about Itmis."

Lonan and Faedi turned their attention to Torix, hoping he might have answers. Sophir had been beaten and attacked, but they knew little about any actual biases against his kin. She wouldn't trust anyone else to help him without keeping a close watch.

"There have not been any recent problems with them," Torix replied, glancing back at the guards. "Does the King hate dragon-kin as he does the Umbrals?"

The guards exchanged glances before shaking their heads.

"Was Fenkas a Krelin?" Faedi asked when the thought struck her.

"No," Torix sighed. "He was a were-folk like Endi and myself. My blood brother, he swore to protect her."

"She was one too?" Faedi couldn't remember seeing her shift.

"Yes, like her father," he said, rolling his neck and shoulders. "Unlike Dewgate and other places, were-folk are welcome in Dusk Elf society. A symbol of status sometimes."

Well, at least there's that.

Faedi scoffed and resumed her pacing. She knew that if she sat near them, she would be compelled to heal them, and all the pain they had endured in the name of political theatrics would have been for nothing. The blood on the floor was unacceptable, even if it felt like more than enough.

It took four more laps of the throne room before King Haldin and Sophir finally stirred.

She halted as the King stood, his gaze fixated on Sophir's back while Torix helped Lonan to his feet. Haldin said nothing, his eyes moving between their group before finally landing on her.

She didn't need to see his eyes to feel his anger.

Her breath hitched when he took a step closer, then another. She glanced at Lonan, Sophir, and Torix, their eyes fixed on Haldin, and bit her lip. None of this was their fault. Torix hadn't been there because he had trusted Fenkas to keep his oath. The Umbrals and Itmis were innocent, unaware of what had transpired. The only person in the room King Haldin could blame was her.

"If you require retribution for the loss of your daughter and to appease your people," she looked up at the King, her heart pounding, "punish me and leave them alone."

Sophir, Lonan, and Torix protested, trying to rush toward her, but the King's guards blocked their path. She knew they wouldn't hold them back for long. If Haldin wanted to unleash his fury on her, he would need to be swift.

"Stand down," he commanded, raising a hand to his guards, who stood ready with their weapons drawn.

He closed in on her, and she braced herself. If he was willing to condemn the Umbrals without sufficient proof of their supposed wrongdoings, she doubted he would hesitate to accept her offer. Not when he had witnessed everything firsthand.

There was a flicker in his eyes, a moment of hesitation before he raised his hand again, slowly. She forced herself not to break eye contact. If he intended to punish her, she wanted him to see the truth in her eyes.

As he brought his hand down toward her, she held her breath and bit her lip. His motion was fast enough to feel like an incoming strike, a slap, but then he slowed, halting just inches from her face.

Instead of a blow, he gently placed his hand on her injured shoulder, warmth spreading through her arm.

"You think I would punish you?" He asked, looming over her. "Blame you rather than Fenkas and Ilos' zealots?"

"Yes," she nodded, meeting his gaze. "You've blamed the Umbrals for years without speaking to them…and you saw what happened. I'm more to blame than they are."

Haldin lowered his head, eyes dark as he glanced back at the others. If Sophir had shown him the entire memory, he would know the truth: the Umbrals had arrived within minutes of the inferno starting, desperate to help. It wasn't their fault that everyone was already gone.

"I want healers tending to them immediately and chambers prepared," the King ordered swiftly before turning his attention back to her. "The Princess has returned…and we have matters to attend to."

The throne room bustled with life after King Haldin's announcement. Healers rushed in and out, servants scurried about measuring everyone for new clothes, and guards turned a massive wheel that raised the map of the continent from the floor. There was little time to take in everything; as soon as the healers finished, they ushered everyone away to rest and await their summons.

Faedi found herself alone in a lavish bedroom, its architecture mirroring the grandeur of the castle. The room was vast, with high ceilings adorned with intricately carved wooden beams. Large, arched windows framed with heavy drapes were pulled back to reveal the swirling snowstorm outside.

Her gaze drifted to the large four-poster bed positioned between the two windows. She studied its polished wood, which was covered in intricate carvings of creatures and floral patterns she couldn't identify. The bed was dressed in luxurious fabrics—a canopy of sheer silk, plush bedding, and decorative pillows of every texture imaginable. The headboard loomed tall and ornate, sparsely encrusted with jewels and markings that matched the posts.

Elegant nightstands flanked the bed, each holding iron candelabras that cast a warm glow across the room. The flames never melted the candles; no wax dripped down their sides, and the metal remained pristine.

Plush woven rugs covered the floor, with only a few bare patches in front of the fireplace, under the bed, and near the door beside the fireplace. She wondered if another rug lay hidden beneath the pile of pillows in the opposite corner by the bookshelf.

She turned sharply at a thump, half-expecting someone to check on her. The door remained closed, just as it had been since a servant had shown her to the room. Leaning her ear against it, she listened to the echo of footsteps in the hall.

They grew louder.

Staying near the door, she listened intently. She didn't know what to expect from the other Dusk Elves, especially with an Umbral in the room beside hers, an Itmis on the other side, and a banished man across the hall. Grudges died hard, and she wasn't ready to trust strangers to treat anyone kindly.

She stepped back as someone stopped outside her door and knocked. Other knocks echoed along the hall, and she bit her lip. Maybe King Haldin wanted to see them already.

"Yes?" She called when the knock went unanswered for too long.

The door opened to reveal a slender, dark blue-skinned Dusk Elf woman carrying a bundle in her arms. Faedi spotted silk, a basket, and caught the unexpected scent of lavender. The woman bowed and smiled, her wide, expectant eyes studying Faedi.

She seemed…nervous.

Shifting uncomfortably, Faedi bit her inner cheek. Prey animal or not, she didn't like being stared at, and she wasn't sure what was expected of her. She knew nothing of Dusk Elf customs.

"Did you…need something?" She tilted her head.

"Oh, I'm sorry, Your Highness." The woman straightened, presenting the basket. "I came to prepare your bath and brought clothes while the tailors finish your other garments."

"Were the others in the hall going to do that for Lonan, Sophir, and Torix?" Faedi cast a worried glance at the door.

"Yes, Your Highness," the woman nodded quickly. "His Majesty said he wanted everyone to rest and recover. After your journey and time in those horrid dungeons—I brought fresh herbs and oils for your bath."

Faedi caught the shudder that ran through the woman at the mention of the dungeon and sighed. A bath did sound like a good idea, but she couldn't shake her worry for the others. Focusing on the basket again, she crossed her arms over her chest.

"Are they being nice?" She asked Sophir and Lonan.

"Yes, they're encouraging a bath and rest," Sophir replied.

"They aren't even looking at me like they hated me a few hours ago. He's kind of nice, actually," Lonan added, and Faedi couldn't help but grin at his response. She understood his suspicion; after all, people could smile while they stabbed you in the back.

"Are we confined to these quarters?" She asked, turning her attention back to the servant.

"Oh no, Your Highness," the woman shook her head quickly. "You, your father, and your bonded are free to go wherever you wish. I believe His Majesty just wanted to ensure you were well rested."

"I suppose we shouldn't make him worry then," Faedi sighed, waving her hand vaguely toward the basket with a small smile. "A bath does sound nice."

"Wonderful!" The servant clapped happily, bouncing on her toes before hurrying to the door beside the fireplace.

Faedi followed her inside and raised her eyebrows at the sight of the massive tub, made from the same dark stone as the rest of the castle. The servant tugged a wooden chain, and hot water began pouring into it as she scattered oils and herbs across the surface. Once satisfied, she bustled about the room, setting out clothes, towels, sponges, and other items she might need.

Moving to the wall separating the room from the bedroom, the servant pulled a lever that opened the back of the fireplace. Heat immediately filled the room, and Faedi stared at the flames anxiously. Even in the cave, when she had craved warmth, she had never liked fire—especially after walking through her memories and the recent attack from the cultists. But she didn't have the heart to dampen the servant's merry mood. The woman appeared so proud of herself and excited to help.

"Would you like some privacy to get comfortable, Your Highness? I can come wash you when you're ready?" she asked, rolling her sleeves up her fore-arms.

"I…" Faedi glanced between the servant and the steaming tub, rubbing her shirt that covered the vines. She could be poisoned if she wasn't careful. "I should probably wash myself. After all the traveling, I'm filthy and honestly rather embarrassed. Thank you, though… um, what's your name?"

"Alaida, Your Highness," she replied quickly, bowing again with another smile. "I'll go check with the tailors while you take care of yourself. His Majesty plans to have a feast tomorrow before war talks."

"He does?" Faedi bit her lip, feeling a mix of excitement and anxiety.

"Oh yes," Alaida nodded eagerly. "He wants to celebrate you returning home and your marriage."

"I… everyone keeps saying I've returned, but… I lived in the forest my whole life." Faedi sat on the edge of the tub, shaking her head. "I don't remember this place."

"You don't… that must mean—I should check on the seamstress." Alaida dashed away before Faedi could respond, leaving her alone.

She is most certainly a rabbit.

Before Faedi could process Alaida's sudden departure, a soft knock echoed from the chamber door. She tensed, her fingers curling around the edge of the tub as she debated whether to answer. But before she could decide, the door creaked open.

King Haldin stood in the doorway.

Somehow, he seemed even broader—taller—than he had in the throne room. His presence filled the space in a way that had nothing to do with his stature. Even without his crown, his aura demanded obedience—but there was something in his eyes. Something raw—guarded, but aching.

"My child." His voice was deep but measured. Gentle, almost.

Faedi swallowed, standing awkwardly beside the bath, suddenly feeling as if she were caught in something far greater than herself.

Faedi inclined her head slightly. "Your Majesty," she said. "I—" She hesitated, uncertain of what to say.

Haldin's lips pressed into a thin line, and for a moment, he seemed as though he wanted to move toward her—like he needed some kind of contact. But he didn't. Instead, he took a slow breath, clasping his hands behind his back. "You do not need to bow to me, Faedi. I am your grandfather."

"I know," she admitted, gripping the fabric of her shirt. "But I don't…I don't remember." The words felt heavy; guilt curled in her stomach—though she didn't know why.

Something flickered across his face—pain that he quickly masked. "You've been gone a long time," he murmured. "Longer than you should have been."

She shifted on her feet. "How long was I supposed to be gone?"

Haldin's jaw tensed. For a moment, she thought he wouldn't answer. Then, with a sigh, he stepped further into the room.

"You were taken when you were still small," he said, his voice steady but thick with something restrained. "I had hoped…prayed that you would return quickly." His shoulders tensed, and she wondered if he had clenched his hands behind his back. "But years passed, and we heard nothing until I learned of the attack. I sent scouts—but all of you were gone."

She swallowed hard. "I don't remember anything before the forest."

He nodded, though his expression darkened slightly. "I know…it was to protect you." He hesitated, his gaze softening. "What your bonded showed me— it gives me as much hope as it does rage."

Faedi flinched, gripping her shirt tighter. "I hope to kill him if Sudek hasn't already taken him."

Haldin's expression didn't change, but something about him stilled, like he was holding his breath.

Faedi looked away, her heart hammering. "How much did you see?" She wasn't sure why, but she wanted him to comfort her. A hand on her shoulder, a hug…anything that might settle her nerves. "How much did Sophir show you?"

Silence stretched between them. Then, slowly, he exhaled. "I couldn't bring myself to watch more than Fenkas summoning the Orderlings. I knew what happened next."

She looked up at him, startled by the quiet intensity in his voice.

"But you are here now," he continued, his gaze searching hers. "You survived. You endured—as my heir should." He swallowed hard, his voice dipping lower as it quivered. "And you came home."

A lump rose in her throat, and she hated how much those words affected her. She didn't know if she was home or not. She wanted to believe it was, wanted to feel a pull of belonging—but she didn't. The mountain wasn't her home.

The Sauvern was.

Haldin must have seen something on her face, because his shoulders softened slightly. "You don't have to remember to be my granddaughter," he said gently. "That is not something time, nor distance, nor even memory can change."

She wasn't sure how to respond to that—though her eyes burned as tears welled in them.

After a pause, he took a step back, as if sensing he had said all he could. "I will have everything you need sent to your chambers and to your bonded," he said, his tone shifting back to something more composed. "Rest tonight. Tomorrow, we will talk more."

She nodded, though she wasn't sure she would be able to sleep.

Haldin hesitated once more at the door, his hand resting on the frame. Then, softer than before, he murmured, "It is good to see you, child."

Then he was gone, leaving her standing in the quiet with nothing but her own thoughts and the lingering ache his words left behind.

40

Hearts of Stone

Faedi

Alaida didn't return by the time Faedi's bath was finished, so she settled back in bed, staring at the intricate carvings on the ceiling. Various gems dotted the designs, catching each flicker of the fireplace. A small smile crept across her face as she realized they looked like stars.

Lonan and Sophir gradually fell silent in her mind after they all checked in with each other. No one had tried to kill them in their baths, and the food brought to their rooms wasn't poisoned. The only shared complaint was the separation between them, but they didn't want to offend the elves by slipping into a singular room.

Her attention shifted to the fireplace when one of the logs shifted, and she tugged her blankets higher. The thump echoed through the room, and her eyes narrowed; it didn't match the sound of the log.

"Do you hear thumping?" She asked Lonan and Sophir, frowning when silence was her only reply.

She huffed and rolled away from the fireplace, directing her gaze to the bookshelf. Sleep should have come easily after their travels and pain, but her eyes refused to grow heavy. Instead, her ears twitched with each sound, and her hair tickled her neck and face.

Thump.

"For the love of the Ancients," she groaned, rubbing her face before tugging a pillow over her head.

Thump.

"Just go to sleep," she mumbled against the pillow.

Thump.

She sat up and scanned the room with a frown. No one else mentioned the sound; no one even reacted to it. This meant she was either losing her mind or she was the only one who could hear it.

Insanity was likely.

Thump.

"Fuck," she whispered, sliding out of bed and pulling on the dark blue robe that had been left for her.

She frowned at her appearance. All she had was the silk nightgown and robe—hardly suitable attire for wandering around a castle in search of an insistent noise. Still, it was better than lying in bed, unable to sleep. A walk might exhaust her enough to find some slumber.

She approached the door and tested it. The knob turned freely, and the heavy wood door swung open quickly with a gentle pull. No guards were posted in the hall; the torches burned like before, but the air felt cooler.

Thump.

"Oh, hush," she scoffed, stepping into the hall and glancing both ways.

The throne room and the stairwell that led to the dungeon were to her left. To the right, she had no idea what lay beyond the rooms where she had seen Lonan, Sophir, and Torix go. The sound seemed to come from no particular direction; it echoed equally through the stone, and she frowned.

If she were an annoying thump, where would she be?

Her eyes narrowed as she tilted her head to listen to the air flow through the hall. There was a small gust with the next thump, and she looked to the right. It came from that direction.

Holding her robe a bit tighter, she began to wander down the hall.

As she walked, she sniffed the air with each new gust. Nothing smelled different; it was the same earthy scent she had gathered while climbing the stairs, with a faint hint of smoke and iron from the torches. However, when she reached a fork in the hall, she caught a new scent: evergreens.

She turned left after the next thump and continued. The occasional guards she passed in the halls said nothing; they only bowed and continued on their way. The servants were the same. None reacted to the sound, and she didn't ask them if they had heard anything. The last thing she wanted was to sound as insane as she felt.

Her legs burned as she continued, her bare feet numb on the cold floors. She stopped when she reached a dead end. An old tapestry covered the wall. Dark blue, almost black fabric was woven into the depiction of a tree, with eventide blooms adorning the sides of the design. A larger one was in the center, with silver threads woven into the fabric, peeking through like the bloom's pollen.

Thump.

The tapestry fluttered as a stronger gust blew from behind the wall, and she gently moved the fabric aside. Behind it, there was only stone, but the scent of evergreens grew stronger. She rested her palm against the wall and raised her eyebrows; the stone felt warm against her hand.

"She said to find her in the stone, with frozen hearts and leaves."

She recalled what Sophir had said about the woman—the voice that shouldn't have been there.

"How am I supposed to find someone if there's no door?" She huffed, rubbing her hand over the stone. Maybe there was a switch or hidden lever.

Thump.

The wall vibrated under her hand, and she pulled it away when something pricked her finger. Thin silver lines raced outward from the center, dust and dirt rippling off it. Then, without warning, the stone began to move.

She looked between the opening and the pinprick of blood on her middle finger. Of all the magic she had seen, this was one she had never encountered. Blood magic wasn't uncommon, but she had never heard of it being used that way. She also didn't use it herself.

"How does no one hear or smell this?" She whispered, staring down the pitch-black hallway. "Were-folk my ass."

Shaking her head, she stepped into the dark and held her hand out to ensure she didn't run into a wall. Her eyes should have adjusted to the darkness, but they didn't. As she cautiously shuffled over the stone floors, the air was heavy and thick, like mud.

She worried she might get lost in the vast darkness for a moment, but then a glint of something caught her eye in the distance. A pale light, silver like the threads on the tapestry, flickered with each thump. The sounds grew louder but not more frequent as she walked faster toward the light.

Gradually, the light began to spread like a soft cloud, stopping when it was within arm's reach. It smelled like eventides and evergreen, reminiscent of her home before her family was murdered.

Thump.

The stone trembled beneath her feet as she instinctively reached her hand into the small cloud. Its warmth was inviting, and she smiled as the scent intensified. Then it expanded, beginning to cover her arm. She wondered if she should be afraid and if the interaction might be dangerous, but she shoved the thought aside.

Despite any logic or reason, she knew she was safe.

An ashen blue-skinned woman beckoned a child with a wave of her hand as she crouched in the snow.

"Come look."

"Coming, Mama!" A small cloaked child rushed over but fell face-first into the snow. "I'm okay!"

Faedi tilted her head as she studied the vision. They were on the mountain, outside the castle, in what looked like a courtyard of sorts. The castle was nestled in the mountain behind them, but there was no blizzard. Everything was calm.

The woman picked up the child and hoisted her onto her hip. She wiped the snow from the child's face and slid her hood back, revealing a girl. Her skin was blue, her hair dark and wavy, framing her face, and bright gold eyes stared up at the woman happily. Her pointed ears had bits of black and white fur, and her tail wagged slightly under the cloak.

She was looking at herself.

"Do you see this flower?" the woman—her mother—asked as she knelt and pointed at an eventide. "They started blooming again after you were born."

"And Sylrie too," the girl giggled happily.

"Yes, and Sylrie too," Endi nodded, tapping the tip of the girl's nose. "They're here to welcome their friends."

"Flowers have friends?" Faedi tilted her head, waving at the flower. "Can I be their friend?"

"Yes, dear one, you are their friend. You and your brother will protect them."

The vision faded, and Faedi stumbled back as the cloud spread, illuminating the area. The darkness washed away, revealing a vast room as large as the throne room, if not bigger. Rows upon rows of stone figures covered the expanse, and on balconies up the walls, there were more figures—all of them facing behind her.

She looked over her shoulder to follow their stone gazes and shuddered as a chill ran down her spine. Two stone figures stood together: a woman collapsed in a winged man's arms, cradled against him. Her eyes were wide, but the carved expression on her face was peaceful. The man's expression, however, was stern. His dark eyes stared at Faedi, threatening—a silent warning to anyone who might approach.

Behind them stood a tree, covered in ice like everything else, but the black-vined eventides that adorned it were free of frost. They were as vibrant as the ones on her arm.

She took a careful step toward the tree, pausing when she didn't feel ice beneath her feet. Moss spread out under her, tickling between her toes, continuing with each step. Her eyes narrowed as she looked ahead before she jumped onto the ice. She should have slipped, but she didn't. More moss spread beneath her feet, and she bit her lip.

Lonan would never believe this.

Shaking her head, she resolved to walk around the frozen figures and approach the tree. If moss spread under her feet, she wanted to know what would happen if she touched it. Maybe it would unfreeze, or more eventides would grow.

The scent of evergreen grew stronger as she stood before the massive tree, studying its branches. It resembled the ancient heart trees in the Mire and forest, but it was different. The twins were ancient oaks, but the one in front of her looked like a willow and smelled like pine.

"What are you?" She asked, reaching forward to touch the tree. "I've never seen one like you before."

"Friend."

The tree's frozen leaves rustled as it responded, and she stepped back. Slowly, the ice began to crack and fall from its leaves and branches. Then, ice-covered stones began to crumble behind her as the thumps increased in speed and volume.

"You're a friend?" She asked the tree, feeling the hair on the back of her neck stand on end.

"Yes. We are friends. For a long time. This bark is new on you."

Growls rumbled behind her, and she turned. Dozens—no, hundreds—of figures stared back.

They were tall, nearly as tall as the Itmis around them, but where the Itmis bore scales, these beings seemed sculpted by the earth itself. Their pale gray skin shimmered like granite polished by centuries of wind, and crystals jutted from their shoulders, forearms, and brows in jagged, luminous growths—gemstones of sapphire, onyx, garnet, and quartz that pulsed faintly with inner light. When they moved, she could hear the faint grind of stone, like mountains shifting in their sleep.

Magic rolled from them in waves, thick and mineral—ancient, patient, and cold. The air smelled of rain on stone and deep caverns rich with ore. Some bore horned crowns of crystal, fractured and gleaming; others had translucent wings that refracted light like shards of glass. Each breath they took left faint trails of color hanging in the air, dust motes glittering like ground starlight.

She had seen sketches of them before—inked drawings in her mother's books. The same ones that had fueled the flames of her childhood home. Yet she had never imagined she would stand before one, living and breathing, the myths of her youth given form.

Gaelisks.

Their throats were striated with veins of black crystal that pulsed as though alive. Then the man holding the woman turned to face her, still cradling her in his arms. His hair was white as frost, his skin pale and faintly luminescent beneath the glow of the Gaelisks' gems. White wings folded behind him, their edges glinting with a faint blue sheen. The cold that radiated from him stung her lungs when she breathed.

He was a Verglass Itmis—a creature of winter skies, not stone. His ice-blue eyes met hers, glacial and deliberate, before he spoke.

"Heal her," he demanded, offering the woman, whose blood dripped down onto the moss.

"Oh Gods," Faedi gasped, rushing forward to cover the woman's bloodied abdomen with her hands. "How did this happen?"

"Magic," the man replied. "She did it to save them."

"She froze them?" Faedi asked, her voice trembling as she began to whisper spells.

"Yes."

She frowned while she worked the magic, praying to the Ancients that the woman's wounds would heal. The cut was jagged, as if done with a serrated blade or some other brutal weapon, and it continued to bleed as her skin slowly melded together. Movement caught Faedi's eye, and she glanced down at the man's tail as it twitched. Blood covered the tip of it, and she studied the sharp scales.

"Who is she?" She asked, glancing up at him when the bleeding finally began to slow. "One of them?"

"No," he shook his head. "A child who joined the fight."

Faedi's eyes narrowed. "The fight?"

"To save the Gaelisks from greed. She offered herself as a sacrifice, but…" He trailed off, observing the woman. "I don't want her to die."

"She won't," Faedi promised.

The wound took longer than she would have liked to heal, but eventually, the bleeding stopped, and the gash closed. She stepped back, lightheaded, releasing a shaky sigh as orange light crept into the room from where she had entered. The Gaelisks turned, baring their teeth as they hissed, and Faedi stumbled toward the light.

"It's alright," she slurred.

"We are among friends," the white-haired man announced as he followed behind her. "You look like you're going to faint."

"I'm fine." She shook her head, realizing too late that she shouldn't have when the room spun.

Maybe I'm not.

41
Ashes of the Past

Faedi

She stood in a vast, desolate landscape of ashes, the world around her shrouded in a cloudy haze. The sky was a shifting canvas of deep purples fading into indigo, streaked with veins of silver light that framed a black circle. Before her stood a figure cloaked in shadows that pulsed with a life of their own.

They were tall and imposing, their few exposed features marred by deep scars on their grayish skin. But it was their crimson eyes, burning beneath the shadowed veil, that held her attention. They watched her every move, their posture tense, as though reaching for something unseen beneath their cloak.

"Who are you?" Their voice rumbled like distant thunder, laced with an undercurrent of wariness.

"I don't give my name to strangers," Faedi replied, taking a cautious step back. "Is this a dream?"

"More like a nightmare," they growled, their gravelly voice tinged with a raw edge of fear.

She glanced down at herself. "So…we're asleep?"

Her eventides were gone, her arm worked despite the massive scarring, and her skin was more blue than gray. Her tail and claw-like nails remained, but the thin layer of fur that once covered them was gone. She was dressed in the same nightgown she had worn before passing out.

"We are," they confirmed, pulling her from her observations. There was something else in their voice—sorrow. It seemed they didn't want whatever they were dreaming about. Her eyes drifted from them back to the sky, to the eclipse. They were talking about Ilos' followers.

"You dream of wastelands?" She asked, looking back at them.

"Haven't been able to get it out of my head since they showed me," they growled, bitterness creeping into their tone.

"Who showed you?" She took a hesitant step toward them.

"A friend." They tensed but didn't back away.

She took another step, then another, disturbing the ashes beneath her feet. Their eyes widened with each step she took, and she worried they might retreat—or worse. But they remained frozen, caught between fear and something else she couldn't quite place.

"Who are you?" She asked as she approached. They felt painfully familiar yet foreign.

"Scarred," they murmured, their voice trembling. "Why are you here? No one is ever here."

"Your parents named you Scarred?" She stopped within arm's reach, staring up at them.

The shadows covered most of their face, casting eerie shapes over their scars, but their bright red eyes remained the same. Strands of black hair fell past their chin, and a thick tattoo streaked along their jaw and neck.

"No," they shook their head, motioning to their face. "Makes sense, though."

She tilted her head. "Kind of on the nose, isn't it?"

They looked her over and cracked a grin before sitting down in the ashes. As the shadows around them mixed with the disturbed dust, they braced their elbows on their bent knees. She mirrored their motions and sat as well. She could have wandered and searched for a way to wake up, but she felt no urge to run.

"Why are you here?" They asked after the dust settled.

"I don't know," she admitted, shaking her head. "I healed someone…and maybe she's a seer? We didn't really talk."

"Who was she?" They leaned closer, and she tensed.

"I don't know. She was frozen, and then she was bleeding." She bit her lip as their gaze darkened.

"Where?" Their eyes narrowed.

"In the stone with ice and leaves," she repeated what the woman had told Sophir.

"You woke up the Gaelisks."

Slowly, they lowered their hood without looking away from her. Their skin was grayish-blue, like fog, contrasting with their bright red eyes. The tips of their pointed ears poked out from their long black hair, moving slightly as they clenched their jaw. She could see it now—they were a dusk elf.

"Sylrie?" Her heart hammered in her chest.

Their eyes widened before they glanced around the area as if someone might overhear them, then returned their attention to her. As their brows creased, the tension in their jaw grew while they examined her. Their response to the name was all she needed to see.

It was him—he was alive.

Faedi awoke with a start, the soft linens and warmth of the bed a stark contrast to the dream she had just experienced. The silken sheets draped over her like a gentle caress, and as her eyes adjusted, she realized she was in a different room. Warm light from the fireplace bathed the space, but shadows stretched across her from the figures nearby.

As her senses gradually returned, she caught muffled voices from the opposite side of the room. The sounds were faint but distinct enough for her to recognize the familiar tone of her grandfather and an unfamiliar woman. Haldin was there.

She needed to tell him what she had seen.

Faedi attempted to sit up quickly, only to fall back against the pillows when the room spun around her. Her body felt drained, and despite the urgency of telling her grandfather that Sylrie was alive, exhaustion threatened to pull her back into sleep. She wanted to see if he was still there—to hug him, to talk to him, to find out where he was.

What if he doesn't know they're after us?

"—and it was Faedi who broke the spell?" Haldin's voice carried across the room, making her heart slow. "You're sure your magic didn't simply wear out?"

"That wasn't how the spell worked. The tree was always the one to decide, and it chose her." The woman's voice was calm and measured. "*She* was chosen by the hearts and The Ancients."

Faedi's heart fluttered at the mention of her name. She hadn't meant to affect the Gaelisks or the tree. She hadn't expected it to speak to her or to call her a friend. They had never even met.

"This bark is new on you."

She rubbed her head as she recalled the tree's words and the vision she had shared with her mother. They hadn't been glamoured—they were dusk elves on the mountain. Everyone said she had returned, but she hadn't believed it. Not until then.

"I told you centuries ago that when they were awoken, they would come here again. The eclipse will come, and they will want the children dead," the woman explained. Faedi couldn't tell if she was annoyed or merely weary—perhaps both.

"What is their obsession with us?" Faedi asked as she forced herself to sit up slowly. "What is so special about eclipse-born?"

Haldin turned to face her, as did the woman Faedi had healed alongside the dragon. However, only Haldin approached. The woman remained seated in her chair.

"There is a prophecy… It says children born during an eclipse are blessed by the gods to wield a portion of their power," the woman told her. "Not everyone is born with those abilities, mind you, but there are some among the masses who are."

"And supposedly I'm one of them?" Faedi remained unconvinced, but she caught the crease in Haldin's brow as he stood beside her.

"You are." The woman confirmed with a nod. "The heart tree would not have responded, and we would still be frozen if you weren't."

"Endi speculated you and Sylrie were blessed when you were born," Haldin admitted, lowering his head. "There was an attempt to steal both of you before your first name day."

"He's alive," Faedi whispered.

"What?" Haldin knelt beside the bed, reaching for her hand but hesitating before pulling away.

"I saw him…you did too. In my memory. But…after I healed her," she nodded toward the woman for emphasis, "I was with him. He was grown…scarred, but it was him. There were freed slaves from Valoria at the border who met him. He helped them."

"You're certain it was him?" Haldin asked. His eyes brightened, but his reluctance to believe rippled off of him.

"Twins of the eclipse are often connected." The woman interjected. "Some can speak to each other over great distances."

"We used to," Faedi nodded. "When we were children, but we couldn't after…"

She trailed off, trying to recall exactly what had happened. She remembered the markings on the doors, placed there after she was warned about the man in the light. But she couldn't pinpoint the moment their silent voices had disappeared. One day, they had simply been gone, and they had never spoken about it again.

"Did their mother use memory charms on them?" The woman asked.

"She did," Haldin confirmed. "She did it to almost everyone on the mountain. Endi swore there was more danger here than in the forest."

Maybe that was why Faedi hated lies. She had always known everything was one.

"I want them gone," she announced. "How do I get rid of them?"

"She didn't tell me. She may have told Torix," Haldin said, shaking his head before rising and heading for the door.

Faedi watched as he summoned someone from the hall, instructing them to bring her father. She wondered if Torix truly knew or if her mother had altered his memories as well. She wanted to believe he would have told her, but she wasn't sure.

Torix never spoke until he was ready—she knew that. But perhaps he hadn't spoken because he feared saying too much. Maybe he had kept his distance and measured his words carefully because he had promised her mother to keep it a secret.

Faedi understood that her mother had wanted to protect her children. But she also knew Endi was not daft. If she couldn't reverse the charms and spells, she would have put something in place. Someone—if not Torix—would know how to remove them.

Maybe Sophir knows how.

She glanced at the fire. If he could delve into her memories, there might be a way to go further back. He had already shown her how she had wielded magic beyond her skill and spoken in a language she didn't know. He might be able to uncover memories she had lost. However, she didn't want to wake him over a hunch.

Not after everything he had endured recently.

It felt like hours before Torix finally arrived, though Faedi knew it had only been minutes. His eyes were heavy with sleep, and he hadn't bothered to dress properly after being roused by the guard who escorted him. The moment his gaze landed on her, he rushed forward, sitting beside her without hesitation.

"What happened?" He demanded, his voice rough with sleep.

"How do we get rid of the memory charms?" Faedi countered.

"Endi didn't tell me," Torix admitted with a shake of his head. "It might be in her journals… but they're not in our room."

"Maybe they were hidden, and no one took them?" Faedi suggested, glancing between them before pushing herself up on shaky legs. "Like the door to the Gaelisks?"

"The what?" Torix stared at her, his arm wrapping around her waist to steady her.

"Only my line knew about the door," Haldin explained as he led the way out of the room. But he paused beside the woman. "Do you need anything?"

"No. We'll speak more later."

She bowed her head respectfully and offered Faedi a soft smile before being led away. Torix's grip on Faedi tightened as they walked, but neither he nor Haldin showed impatience when she had to stop and catch her breath. Faedi noticed the deepening frown on Torix's face as they continued down the stone corridors.

No words passed between them, and the air grew heavy with unspoken tension. It wasn't just her failure to mention Sylrie to Torix—there was something more. She caught the glance Haldin and Torix exchanged when her mother's journals were mentioned, and she noticed how they eyed each of the guards they passed.

They don't trust everyone on the mountain.

42
Broken Charms

Faedi

Long shadows stretched across the stone walls, cast by the torches that dotted the hall. Exhaustion from the night's events weighed heavily on Faedi, yet she neither complained nor asked to stop. She wanted the charms removed as quickly as possible.

Haldin led the way, his stride shorter and slower than it had been in the throne room. Torix remained beside her, his arm protectively wrapped around her waist until they arrived at the room where she had seen him led earlier. The heavy wooden door appeared no different from her own, but the scent that wafted from the room changed when Haldin opened it.

No one spoke as Torix shut the door behind him and guided Faedi to sit on the edge of the bed. She wanted to protest, to insist that she could help search without sitting down, but she was too tired to argue. Torix was also too stubborn to take no for an answer.

Perhaps she had inherited her stubbornness from him and not her mother.

"After you left, someone ransacked the room… I didn't notice anything missing, and no one found the Gaelisks—so I assume anything Endi might have hidden here is safe," Haldin said, remaining near the door.

Faedi stared at him. That didn't make sense. "You said she put charms on almost everyone on the mountain."

"She did. Only Torix, Fenkas, and myself were spared," Haldin confirmed with a nod before narrowing his eyes. "Why?"

"The servant in my room—she seemed like she knew something when I asked why you said I returned," Faedi said, shaking her head. "She ran off before I could ask her."

"Was it Alaida?" Torix asked, looking at Haldin after Faedi nodded. "She was one of Endi's maids."

"Do you think Endi trusted her enough not to charm her or gave her the key to remove the charm?" Haldin raised an eyebrow.

"Perhaps," Torix mused before turning his attention back to Faedi. "Should we summon her now or let you sleep first? You need to rest—you look worse than you did after your first solstice festival."

"Charms first, then sleep, then food… maybe food then sleep, or both," she trailed off, shaking her head as she looked around the room. "I can look while you get her, but tell her I'm sorry if she's asleep. Please?"

Haldin nodded before leaving to find someone to summon Alaida. Faedi sighed and pulled on whatever magic she could to examine the room. If they were lucky, whoever had raided the room earlier had not known the correct spells to reveal hidden magic. However, nothing in the room seemed unnatural.

The candlesticks were enchanted, like the ones in her room, as was the fireplace. Yet, there was another item on the writing desk in the corner that glowed. She tried to get off the bed, but Torix stopped her, raising an eyebrow in a silent command to point out whatever she had seen.

"On the desk," she nodded toward it and watched his face fall.

"I don't think that is the key," he told her as he approached the desk and picked up a framed picture.

He offered it to her after sitting beside her, his gaze fixed on the fire in the hearth. The enchantment was unlike any she had ever seen. The painting in the frame moved slowly, subtly. It depicted Torix and her mother in regal attire. Her mother wore a silver-trimmed veil, and they first looked at the artist who had painted the picture before turning to look at each other.

The love in their eyes was unmistakable—and Torix's smile was something she had never seen on him before. They looked so happy and in love, blissfully unaware of the horrors awaiting them before their children were grown.

"Was this your wedding?" she asked softly.

"It was," he nodded once without looking at her.

Faedi studied the moving picture, trying to ignore the ache in her heart. The tenderness between Torix and her mother was evident in every shift of their expressions, contrasting sharply with her memories of them. The realization that such joy had existed in their lives before the cultists shattered it made the weight of the room heavier.

"She told me she was pregnant with you and Sylrie right before this was painted," Torix whispered.

She looked up at him. "Really?"

He nodded again, his gaze still fixed on the flames.

"I saw Sylrie," she confessed, looking away when he turned to stare at her with wide eyes. "Even after I saw him get out of the house… I thought maybe he died from his injuries or worse, but…"

"But?" Torix slowly, carefully, placed his hand on her shoulder.

"We stopped to check on the farmers we helped leave Dewgate, and there were freed slaves from Valoria there. They told us a Dusk Elf, who called himself Scarred, helped them leave," she glanced at him briefly before staring at the wall. "Then, after I unfroze the Gaelisks… I passed out, and I thought it was just a strange dream, but I didn't have my glamour there, and he was there. He called himself Scarred, and I… I called him Sylrie—he looked shocked, scared, and before anything else could be said, I woke up."

Torix didn't speak after she finished, and his hand grew heavy on her shoulder. She didn't have the heart to look at him and wanted to flee when his hand began to tremble. However, she knew her feet wouldn't carry her far.

"It might have just been wishful thinking," she told him when the silence stretched too long.

"You two used to talk to each other," he said softly. "Before you could even speak to us, you were talking to each other. Maybe whatever you did with the Gaelisks… reconnected you with him."

She scoffed. "Or I'm gradually losing my mind."

"Have you tried to talk to him since you woke up?"

She looked up at him. The same hope she had seen in his eyes was there again, and her guilt grew. She shouldn't have mentioned the dream, even if it had seemed like a good idea. If she couldn't speak to him again—if Sylrie was dead, she would have hurt Torix again.

"No," she shook her head. "He was scared in the dream; I don't know if he would even respond to me."

"It doesn't hurt to try," he gave her shoulder a gentle squeeze.

Faedi looked up at him and sighed before nodding. He was right. The worst that could happen was that it wouldn't work, and nothing would change—unless it did, and Sylrie blamed her as much as she blamed herself.

What if he hates me?

She bit her lip and closed her eyes, taking a breath to steady herself. If he hated her, it was justified, and at least she would have closure knowing he was alive. He deserved to know who he was, who his family was, and unless he traveled to Rowdon to learn for himself, she was the only one who could tell him.

He deserved the truth—it was the least she could offer him after what had happened.

"*Sylrie?*" she called out in her mind, as she had with Lonan and Sophir, but there was silence. "*Syl, it's Faedi.*"

The silence that followed weighed on her like a heavy shroud. Then, faintly, there was something—a slight tremor of a response, a flicker of awareness.

"*Faedi?*" His voice entered her mind. "*That was you, right? In the dream?*"

"*It was.*" She looked at Torix with wide eyes and nodded when he raised his eyebrows. "*Where are you…is it safe to say?*"

Sylrie hesitated before responding. "*I think so? No one ever heard us before. I'm near Valoria. What about you?*"

Torix watched Faedi intently, hope burning brighter in his eyes. "What is he saying? Is he safe?"

"He's near Valoria," Faedi said with a nod, trying not to cry. Stating his location aloud made his existence feel more real. He was alive. "He wants to know where I am."

"Tell him," Torix urged with a gentle nod.

Faedi took a breath before continuing. *"Rowdon. Mama was a princess, King Haldin's daughter—Torix is our father. Fenkas was working with the cultists that attacked our home, and—"*

"I know."

Faedi froze. *"What do you mean, you know?"*

"Fenkas found me in the forest. He took me to Ashar—I got away, but... he told them there was a spell to block my memories, and they removed it. They tried to make me talk to you—they want you too."

A chill ran down Faedi's spine. *"I know. Someone said they want to sacrifice eclipse-born to Ilos."*

"They do," Sylrie confirmed. *"They think we have power from the gods, and sacrificing us to him will give him more power."*

Faedi clenched her hands into fists. *"Can you come here? I met the freed slaves you helped; they said you have a ship."*

"I will, once I finish business here. Let me know if there is a safe port in Rowdon. We never sail there, and I'll have more slaves with me."

"I'll ask Haldin," Faedi said, releasing a shaky sigh. *"Stay safe, please?"*

"I will—you too. I want you to tell me everything."

"Only if you tell me too."

"Deal."

Faedi trembled with excitement as Sylrie fell silent, her teary gaze lifting to meet Torix's. But her tears weren't from guilt; they were pure relief and joy. He said something—likely a question about Sylrie—but she couldn't hear him over the half-laughed sob that escaped her lips.

"He's alive," she managed to say as Torix wrapped his arms around her. "He's alive, and he's going to come here."

"Haldin can open the port, and you can tell him where to come," he said, gently running a hand over her hair.

"He said Fenkas took him to Ashar," she added, feeling Torix stiffen at the name. No words were needed; the low growl rumbling in his chest spoke volumes. If given the chance, he would tear Fenkas to shreds—and she would gladly help him.

Just then, the door opened, and Faedi buried her face deeper into Torix's shoulder. When she looked up, she saw Haldin entering with Alaida close behind him. Despite the late hour, Alaida's eyes sparkled with energy as she rushed forward at the king's silent gesture. Torix released Faedi but remained close as Alaida stood before them and bowed.

"His Majesty said I'm to remove the memory spells," she announced with a bright smile. "I'm sorry I didn't tell you earlier when you asked, but your mother specifically ordered me not to say anything unless asked by His Majesty or Lord Torix."

"It's fine. Thank you for honoring her wishes." Faedi nodded, wiping her eyes. "How does it work?"

"It's swift and mostly painless, I promise—but you may feel a bit dizzy and have a slight headache afterward. I've already asked one of the other servants to brew some tea for you. Although…" Alaida hesitated, eyeing her carefully. "You look dreadfully pale. It might be best if you sleep after, Your Highness."

"Alright," Faedi agreed, taking a shaky breath to steady herself. "What about the glamour?"

"That will be gone too, but I'm sure one of the enchanters could create one for you if you still want to appear…" Alaida gestured toward her with a subtle wince.

"That's a problem for later," Faedi said, shaking her head and sitting up straighter. "Let's do this."

"As you wish, Your Highness."

Alaida bowed her head, raising her hands and moving them gracefully as she whispered a spell. Faedi couldn't place the language and tilted her head, trying to decipher it, but her attention quickly shifted to the pressure building between her brows.

Suddenly, all she saw was white, and her body felt feather-light.

She had always heard that people saw their lives flash before their eyes before death, but she had never thought it was true. She had believed it impossible to witness everything from birth to death in mere seconds—until it happened to her. It was all there, overwhelming and consuming, and her head pounded as she struggled to process the images, sounds, smells, and sensations flooding her mind.

It was too much.

"N-hunt—need…Lonan—Soph—" She tried to speak, but a jumble of words spilled from her lips, mixing with her attempt to call out.

"She's going to faint," Torix's voice reached her, muffled and distorted despite his closeness.

He was right.

Scarred

Gulls called at the edge of the shore on Ceanea Isle. His bare feet sank into the cool, wet sand with each step. The gentle waves lapped at his toes, bringing with them the scent of salt and seaweed. Above him, the sky was a tapestry of deep blues and purples, stars twinkling like scattered diamonds over the water.

Since their arrival to drop off the freed Helgi, impatience had gnawed at him. He needed to clear his mind, to feel the wind on his face and the earth beneath his feet. But the endless expanse of the ocean never truly calmed him— not the way the forest in Yestrana did. That had always been a place he wanted to return to, yet he couldn't bring himself to face the ghosts of his past—knowing that everyone he loved was dead. Even so, they haunted him still.

He shook his head, pushing away the memory of his dream. A young Dusk Elf had looked so painfully familiar to his mother—the one who claimed to have woken the Gaelisks from their centuries-long slumber—the woman who had called him by his name.

"Sylrie?" Her face replayed in his mind, followed by the image of her tear-streaked face from the night he lost her.

"Fuck." He dragged his hand over his face and walked deeper into the chilled water, desperately trying to ground himself. "He died with everyone else."

"Who died?"

He turned to face K'than, the Dawn Elf who had refused to leave his side, and frowned. He shook his head, looking back at the sea as he sank into the water. The last thing he needed was to dig up the past; it wouldn't help anyone.

"Sylrie, it's Faedi." His eyes snapped open under the water, and his heart pounded in his chest.

Despite his fear, despite the logic that told him it might be some kind of trick, he spoke to her. Goosebumps prickled his skin as her voice filled his mind. She sounded older, but her tone was the same. He could almost feel her excitement mingling with his own.

She was alive in Rowdon and had woken up the Gaelisks.

"Go to the ones who are sleeping when it's time…you'll know when to go."

He broke the surface of the water and wiped his face. He didn't know what else could be if that wasn't a sign to go to Rowdon. If she was there, he needed to be there too. Even if it wasn't time, he couldn't resist the temptation of possibly seeing her again.

However, he hesitated, staring at the water with a frown.

"Faedi…I…I need to be sure it's you."

"How do you want me to prove it?" He could almost picture her wide eyes staring up at him—innocent and happy.

"Where did we hide at the equinox?"

"Trick question—we didn't hide; we explored and found a clearing. There was a woman there who gave us blackberry tarts, and then, when Mama found us, she was gone."

That was all he needed. They had never told anyone about the woman with the tarts—not even their mother. Without another thought, he turned to face K'than and began to make his way out of the water. There was a question in his eyes, but he didn't speak as Scarred approached. Instead, he took a hesitant step back.

"Dinner time," Scarred told him.

"Are you alright?" K'than's brows creased, and he stepped back.

"I'm fine," Scarred shook his head, starting back toward the village. *"How did you end up in Rowdon?"*

"I came here to ask for help for the Mire. There were cultists in the forest, and I think they're spreading a plague. We found a group close to the Mire, and they said the Dusk Elves might help. I followed Torix's trail and was told everything. They're trying to remove the glamour and memory spells on me now."

"Da's alive?"

"Yes, he's here with me now. He can't stop smiling—it's kind of weird. I've never seen him smile this much."

"Where did you go after the fire? I couldn't find you before Fenkas grabbed me."

"I…I don't know. For a while, everything was dark, and then I was with the voice in the light. I woke up close to Dietrich, and…I don't know what happened. I remember wandering around the forest trying to find Torix—then I was in the Mire."

His steps slowed as he walked down the narrow trail leading to their camp, ignoring the curious looks of the crew and villagers. He stared ahead, heading for the bonfire where he knew food awaited. It would be his last meal on the

Isle.

"So you stayed there? You've been in the Mire this whole time?"

"No, well…kind of. I joined The Watch and took a post near the edge, working a bit with the farmers in Dewgate. I didn't go into the city much—not after the last war. What about you? You said you were in Ashar. No one leaves there."

"I broke out and joined up with a group of mercs whose whole purpose is to free people from the flame. I've been with them for a while now—worked my way up, got a ship, a crew, and started taking my contracts."

He caught a glimpse of Danik near the fire and nodded to him before taking a seat nearby. He watched the crew interact with the Helgi villagers. K'than sat nearby, and he glanced at him when he felt his stare. For a moment, he wondered if he should tell him about the silent conversation that had just taken place, but he decided against it.

"How's Myst and Lonan? Are their parents alright?"

"Myst was attacked by cultists—they're blind, and Lonan…he's alright. I thought…the cultists attacked. We lived, but…"

He accepted a plate of cooked fish and vegetables, staring at the meal as he tried to piece together what Faedi had told him. Her words blended together in ways that made it hard to follow, but he understood enough.

Ilos' followers had tried to get her again.

"Are you alright?"

"The spells are…hurts."

"Faedi?" He lifted his head when she fell silent, glancing around. To the west. *"Faedi, what's happening?"*

He stared through the flames at the horizon. It would take days to sail around the Isle to avoid the jagged rocks surrounding it, or to go further out and around. Then, it would take even longer in unfamiliar waters. She hadn't mentioned if Haldin would open the port, either—he might have to port in Emsmeda or Dewgate and travel by foot. However, the warning he had received replayed in his mind: Dewgate was no longer safe for porting.

Rowdon or Emsmeda, unless he made his own.

"I have to go to Rowdon." He turned his gaze to Danik. "Faedi—she's alive. She's in Rowdon."

Danik's eyebrows shot up, and the group around the fire fell silent—even the Helgi turned their attention to him. They, like everyone else, knew that Rowdon's ports hadn't been open for centuries—not since the war to retake the Gaelisks.

"Are you sure? You haven't heard from her since…" He glanced at K'than, lowering his voice. "Are you sure it's not a trick from Ashar?"

"She was just talking to me. It's not Ashar," Scarred shook his head, trying to reassure himself.

"Have you asked her something only she would know? Nothing that bastard might have told them?" Danik narrowed his eyes at him.

"I did. It's her," he said, turning his gaze back to the fire. "But just in case…I told her I was near Valoria. I have to go to Rowdon. It's time."

"You heard 'em, ladies and gents," Danik called out. "Those of you who want to remain on the Isle, clear your things from the ship. Anyone who wants to move on to the next job gets on board. We're scrubbing off!"

"I don't know if you can hear me, but I'm coming. I promise."

Scarred stood at the edge of the ship, the wind whipping his hair into his face as he gripped the wheel beside Danik. He had expected Danik to try to convince him to wait until morning, but he hadn't. And none of the crew had stayed behind either. The camp had been broken down swiftly, and within an hour, everyone was on board.

He glanced over the side of the ship at the Helgi swimming alongside. Their dark scales gleamed in the starlight as they swam, jumped, and dove beneath the waves, moving like dolphins—except with poisonous weapons and barbs. They had promised to escort them into the frigid sea surrounding Rowdon, a way to repay them for saving their people. They would guide them through the treacherous waters. It felt like too much good luck after all the bad he had experienced.

Danik's voice broke through his thoughts. "You think there will be a welcome party for the Prince's return?"

"Prince?" Scarred turned to face K'than, who remained nearby, as he always did, and gave him a quick look-over. A pang of guilt hit him, but it was fleeting. His heritage hardly mattered. He wasn't going to Rowdon for power or status; his only intention was to be with his sister. If riches and glory came with that, he would do as he always had—the money would go to those who needed it.

"Yeah, Prince—I'm King Haldin's grandson," Scarred replied, his tone as gentle as possible. "I've been waiting a long time for this moment to go back."

"Why not go back before?" K'than asked, shaking his head. "When you escaped Ashar, you—"

"We were told the heir and Warden of the Tides could not return until he was called," Danik interjected, his eyes fixed on the sea ahead. "The flame has their prophecies; we have ours."

K'than lowered his head, hugging his arms to himself. "The priests said when the mountain opens, the second moon will come again, and darkness will cover this realm's plane—that the barriers between the others will be broken, and darkness will swallow everything. That's when they're going to kill everyone? The mass sacrifice to Ilos?"

"They want his flame to burn so brightly that it destroys everything that can cast a shadow," Danik replied, nodding. "They'll sacrifice all eclipse-born to him to increase his power to push back the darkness."

"But…you said where they kept you in Ashar was destroyed—do they even have the eclipse-born?" K'than asked, shaking his head, glancing between them curiously. "Do we even know how many there are?"

Scarred stared out at the sea, the sharp rocks jutting from the water. He'd never known how many eclipse-born there were in Ashar—only who he'd escaped with and the bodies he'd passed on the way. People were born and died every day; there was no way to estimate how many were born during eclipses.

"I know three are on this ship," he shrugged, glancing back at K'than. "I know my sister is one, two Umbrals in the Mire—that there's another we work with who is one… and that means there are at least seven where they don't want them to be. That's all that matters."

"If enough of us are too scattered around for them to sacrifice—Ilos doesn't win," Danik added, nodding.

K'than asked softly, "What if the darkness is just as bad?"

Scarred considered the question, his expression grim. There was a chance something horrible could happen if the followers of Ilos were right—that the people born during eclipses would unleash chaos and tear the world apart. But he doubted it. Unless some cosmic force drove him mad and overtook his better judgment, he wouldn't hurt people without good reason. Neither would Danik, nor Faedi.

The only group causing endless pain, tearing families apart, and killing thousands of innocents were the followers of Ilos. Whatever vision they had for the world, it was not one Scarred was willing to live in.

"I'm willing to bet on darkness," he said, his voice firm.

44
Stolen Moments

Sophir

Footsteps echoed softly across the room as Sophir stirred in the bed. His eyes opened slowly, taking in the familiar surroundings. The same servant who had attended him the day before was moving around the room, busy with clothes, armor, and breakfast, unaware that he had woken. She only stopped when another servant peered into the room, waving her over with urgency.

"They're awake," the one at the door whispered.

"Who?" the servant, whom Sophir assumed had been assigned to him, asked.

"*Them.*"

There was a brief pause, and Sophir watched as the servant at the door pointed at her throat. The other leaned forward after a moment, startled.

"How? When did that happen?"

"Late last night. His Highness found the Princess with them."

Faedi?

"Where is she now?" Sophir sat up and stared at the two servants. "Is she in her room?"

The servant in the doorway nodded hesitantly, and Sophir quickly slid out of bed. Without bothering to change from the silk sleeping pants he had been provided, he rushed past the two servants and down the hall toward Faedi's room. The door was slightly ajar when he arrived, and he felt a wave of relief when he saw her tail sticking out from beneath the blankets.

The servant in her room quickly turned toward him, holding a finger to her lips. Sophir tilted his head, regarding her. Despite her small size, barely more than half his height, she seemed unafraid to assert herself. He cracked a smile and nodded, leaning down to her level.

"What happened?" He whispered.

"Her Highness found the tree and awakened the Gaelisks," the servant explained quietly. "His Highness said she collapsed when they arrived, and the Itmis with them said she healed the Haxan who turned them to stone and ice."

"The Itmis?" Sophir raised an eyebrow.

"Yes, Lord Ighir and several dozen Verglas Itmis," she confirmed quickly. "His Highness is with Lord Ighir now. He went to them after removing Her Highness' charms and glamour. Everything is as it should be now."

Sophir straightened and glanced toward the door. Though he had been born long after Ighir had disappeared with the Gaelisks, the story intrigued him. Still, his concern for Faedi outweighed everything. The servant hadn't mentioned fire, but Sophir couldn't shake the memory of Faedi's state after her cottage had been attacked. She had been unconscious and in pain for far too long, her body not given adequate time to recover. He knew she had likely pushed herself too hard. The removal of charms wouldn't help—though it wouldn't strain her body, it could affect her already exhausted mind.

"Go see to your other duties. I'll take care of her," he nodded toward the door. "Have someone wake Lonan and send him in here."

The servant hesitated as if she might protest, but fled quickly when Sophir rolled his shoulders and unfurled his wings. Once she was gone, he crossed to the bed and gently brushed Faedi's hair away from her face. Her skin was no longer gray; it had a soft blue hue—like an evening sky just before sunset.

He traced her cheek with the back of his index finger, tilting his head to the side. It was soft, like before, but her velveteen fur was shorter. Her bonding tattoos, those from her union with Lonan, colored her skin beautifully. He smiled, relieved that they remained despite the glamour's removal.

When she rolled onto her back, he pulled his hand away and checked for injuries. Aside from the dark circles under her eyes, nothing appeared amiss. The flowers on her arm glittered faintly in the candlelight, her chest rising and falling with each breath. Her lips parted just enough for him to glimpse part of her elongated canines.

"I feel you staring," Faedi mumbled, her eyes opening to reveal their golden hue.

"I heard you woke up the Gaelisks," Sophir said, sitting on the edge of the bed with a smile. "How did you manage that?"

"I touched a tree," Faedi replied with a yawn, stretching her arms above her head. "Then I dreamed—remembered a lot."

"Oh?" Sophir tried not to notice how her nipples hardened beneath the thin fabric of her nightgown.

"I lived here before we moved to the forest," she explained, her cheeks darkening when her stomach growled.

"Hungry?" Sophir grinned, motioning for her to stay where she was. When she nodded, he picked up a tray of covered food the servant had left behind and carried it over to the bed. Steam rose when he removed the lid, and he sat beside her as she propped herself up on the pillows. He glanced from her to the tray of food before returning his grin and setting it in his lap.

"Are you planning on feeding me my breakfast?" Faedi raised a brow, a teasing smile forming on her lips.

"You are a Princess, aren't you?" Sophir teased, dipping a spoon into the breakfast stew.

"Only in name," she rolled her eyes. "I'm made for forests, not stone castles."

"I don't know, the attire suits you." He held the spoon out to her, smiling when she accepted the bite.

"This is hardly attire," Faedi gestured over her body with one hand for emphasis before stealing a piece of bread from the tray with the other.

"You're right," Sophir said, scooping another spoonful. "I do prefer you in less."

She narrowed her eyes at him, her cheeks flushing again as she ate the bite he offered. They continued for a while until Faedi leaned back and shook her head. Sophir glanced between her and the food. She had eaten a decent amount, but not the entire serving.

"Are you alright?" He set the bowl aside, leaning forward to brush the back of his hand against her forehead.

"I haven't hunted in a while," Faedi said, nodding toward the bowl. "You should eat too."

"Does the lack of a hunt prevent you from enjoying food?" Sophir asked as he pulled the bowl back into his lap.

"Yes. Cooked food starts to taste spoiled, bland, or like dirt… normally I travel with raw meat when I'm able, but…" She trailed off, looking around the room.

"I see," Sophir nodded. "What happens if you go too long without it?"

"I turn into a ravenous killing machine," Faedi teased, letting out a light laugh before shaking her head. "It's the same for anyone who doesn't get the nutrition they need. You get weak, sick, and then… pass out after healing someone."

Sophir frowned, recalling the last time she had likely eaten something that could satisfy her needs. Everything since her home had burned had been either smoked or dried.

"Why didn't you say anything?" he asked, staring at her.

"I was looking for animals the whole way," she shrugged. "I think, when everything happened last night, I asked someone to bring Lonan and me some fresh meat, but—have you spoken to Lonan this morning?"

"No, his door was closed. I was more worried about you," he admitted, glancing over his shoulder at the door. "I can find some for you two. There was sausage in the stew… they should have livestock somewhere around here."

"They keep animals in the valley behind the mountain; the storms are only on the outward-facing sides to keep people away," Faedi told him, pulling her knees to her chest and wrapping her arms around them. "Remembering is strange."

"Are they good memories?" Sophir asked, gently rubbing his thumb over her cheek.

"They are," she nodded, biting her lip. "Do you have to go?"

"Do you want me to stay?" he smiled when she nodded again. "Let me tell a servant to bring you and Lonan food, and then you'll have me here for as long as you want me."

"Alright."

Sophir leaned forward and kissed her forehead gently before standing from the bed. He opened the door and stopped the first person he saw—another servant and a guard he hadn't met before. He waved them closer.

"The Princess and Prince of the Mire require fresh meat delivered to their rooms. Sooner rather than later, if you can."

They bowed their heads and hurried off as Sophir stepped back into the room, shutting the door behind him. Without hesitation, he returned to the bed, smiling when Faedi opened the blankets for him. He laid down beside her, wrapping an arm around her as she covered them both, resting her head against his chest.

"Rest. They'll bring you better food soon," he promised, pressing another kiss to the top of her head.

She nodded quietly, and he closed his eyes as she traced circles over his chest. He wasn't sure which one of them drifted off first, but he knew that it was the first time in a long time that he slept without worry.

Sophir woke with a start to the sound of clattering dishes. His eyes snapped open, and he immediately noticed the absence of Faedi's warmth beside him. He sat up in bed, scanning the room, and froze when his gaze landed on her. She stood in the doorway, her robe loosely held together by one hand, the other gripping the belt, her wet hair glistening as it framed her flushed face. The faint scent of lavender and eventides filled the air—she had just bathed.

A relieved chuckle escaped him as he sank back into the pillows.

"Did you miss me?" Faedi asked, tying her robe tighter as she gave him a playful look.

"I heard the dishes, thought the servants had come back," he explained, watching her closely.

"They did come back," Faedi replied, stepping into the room. "Hours ago. I checked on Lonan while you were asleep, ate, and cleaned up."

She moved toward the bed, taking a brush from the mantle and running it through her hair. Sophir's eyes followed her movements, mesmerized by the way her hair swayed framing her delicate face.

"How is Lonan?" he asked softly, his concern evident in his voice.

"Exhausted," Faedi sighed, sitting on the edge of the bed. "He didn't sleep well last night. I made him go back to sleep."

"Made?" Sophir raised an eyebrow, amusement dancing in his gaze.

"I asked sweetly," Faedi said, scrunching her nose and narrowing her eyes at him. "And I petted his hair for a few minutes."

"I have a vivid imagination," Sophir chuckled, reaching out to take the brush from her.

"I know," she laughed, her voice light and teasing.

"Do you now?" Sophir's grin widened as he gently began brushing her hair, the soft strands slipping through his fingers.

"I saw you with Lonan," Faedi said with a knowing look, glancing over her shoulder at him with a playful wink. "You did partake in my heat."

Sophir leaned in, mimicking the playful scrunch of her face. "How much of that did you see?" he teased. "Did you like watching?"

Faedi gave him a shove, her laughter filling the room. "I saw enough, and it was insightful," she replied, her eyes sparkling.

"I haven't had a chance to talk to him about it," Sophir admitted, his tone softening as he brushed her hair. "I hope it wasn't... too much for him."

"He would have said something if he didn't like it," Faedi replied, leaning back against his chest. "Besides, I think it did both of you some good."

Sophir paused, his gaze softening as he looked down at her, noting the subtle crease of her brows, the way they pinched together when she was lost in thought, or when she was anxious.

"How so?" he asked, his voice low.

"You were both upset. Sometimes distractions can be a good thing," Faedi shrugged lightly, a hint of warmth in her voice.

Sophir's heart softened at her words. "True," he murmured, but there was a certain vulnerability in his tone as he continued. "I don't want anyone to think I'm using them for distractions. You both deserve more than that."

Faedi smiled up at him, her eyes warm and sincere. "I assure you, if either of us were uncomfortable, we'd let you know. Just as I'm sure you'd do the same."

Sophir leaned down, his breath catching as he whispered softly against her neck, "And what would you say if I told you you're looking particularly irresistible right now?"

Faedi tilted her head, giving him access to her neck as she sighed softly, a small smile tugging at her lips. "I'd say you should take your opportunity while you can. You don't find silk in the Sauvern."

Sophir's chest rumbled with a low laugh as his gaze flickered over her, taking in the way the silk gown clung to her curves. The way her breath hitched as he kissed the curve of her neck was enough to make his pulse quicken.

"You should take at least one of these dresses with you," he murmured, his lips brushing over her skin. "You would look absolutely ethereal in the morning fog."

"*Ancients*." Her gasp vibrated against his lips, her fingers threading into his hair as though urging him closer. "You'll need to take it off first," she whispered, her voice playful and sultry.

Sophir smiled as he slipped the strap of her gown off her shoulder, savoring the way her body responded to his touch. He kissed her neck once more, trailing his lips over her skin as she leaned back against him, her soft sighs warming him.

"Do you have plans before the feast?" He asked, his lips grazing her ear.

"No," she murmured, shivering slightly. "I like this plan."

"Good," he rumbled, his hands gently sliding the other strap down. The material loosened, falling just enough to reveal more of her soft skin.

"But this one…" his lips brushed against hers before he tugged the silk taut. "…this one won't make it."

Her gasp dissolved into his kiss, silk tearing between them, and nothing else in the world existed but the heat they shared.

45
Shared Desire

"For as big as he is, he's surprisingly gentle. This is different."

Faedi

The warmth of Sophir's hands radiated through her as he gently caressed her. He moved with a controlled grace, slower than before, careful not to rush. She bit her lip, wondering if the previous intensity was merely a product of the heat they had shared, or if this time, his desire for her was just as deep.

"Are you alright?" His voice was soft, a low murmur in her ear.

"I was worried you might not be," she admitted, glancing back at him. "You're… different."

Sophir's chest rumbled in response, a sound that soothed her, and he answered with quiet confidence. "Before, everything was so rushed, driven by your need. I didn't want you to be uncomfortable. This time, I want to take my time with you. To savor this."

Her cheeks warmed, but she only shook her head, words left unspoken.

"I meant what I said," he repeated, his tone low and sincere. "I want you."

Faedi let out a mewl as he kissed the curve of her neck, his touch gentle yet electrifying. His hand gently cupped her, pulling her closer, as his lips trailed over her skin. She could barely keep her eyes open as she absorbed the warmth of his presence, the way his touch sent ripples through her body.

"Keep your eyes open," he murmured against her skin, his voice firm yet tender. "And feel everything."

A slight shiver ran through her as his words broke through her haze, her heart racing. It was impossible to look away from him, and yet she felt a strange flutter in her chest, a desire to surrender fully to this moment.

Sophir's hands remained on her, guiding her with a tenderness that made her pulse quicken. There was a quiet intensity in the air, a stillness between them that made her feel both cherished and desired. As they moved together, she couldn't help but smile at the depth of connection that seemed to grow with every touch.

"You're so beautiful," Sophir whispered, his voice thick with emotion as he gazed at her, his eyes dark with longing. "I could never have enough of you."

Faedi's breath caught as she looked into his eyes. "We have things to do," she reminded him softly, though the words felt weak against the fire growing between them.

Sophir chuckled softly, brushing a strand of hair away from her face as he leaned in to kiss her again. "Later. There's time for all of that."

Warmth spread through her body, the slow caress of her own hand a delicate exploration of the sensations that had always stirred her when Sophir and Lonan had touched her. Her breath quickened as she let her fingers linger, brushing over the sensitive areas they knew so well, finding a quiet pleasure in the familiar motions.

Sophir's touch returned, his hands careful yet insistent as he continued to trace the curves of her body. His chest rumbled against her back, a low vibration that seemed to hum through her, heightening every shiver that ran down her spine. His lips, warm and eager, brushed along her neck, sending waves of heat through her, and she instinctively rocked her hips, chasing the sweet friction, all while trying to hold on to the moment, to keep her eyes open and focused on him.

The feeling was almost overwhelming. She let out a soft moan, her body trembling under his touch, but when she tried to pull away, his voice stopped her.

"Don't stop," he whispered, his words a low growl in her ear. "Go faster."

She gasped and turned her head to meet his gaze, her heart pounding as his tail wrapped around her arm, pulling her closer. He wasn't being forceful, but there was a possessive gentleness in his hold that made her shiver in delight. She could have resisted, could have moved away, but she didn't want to.

"Are you going to stop me?" She asked breathlessly, her voice trembling.

He chuckled softly in her ear, the sound rich with affection. "I will, if you close your eyes," he teased. "But look at you—so beautiful, so ready for me."

Her breath caught in her throat at the intensity of his words. She wanted to protest, to shy away, but the heat between them burned too brightly. She whimpered, her body writhing against him, and though she tried to close her legs, he was quicker, his hands moving to hold her open, gently but firmly.

"Sophir," she whispered, unsure if she was protesting or calling for him.

"Don't fight it," he murmured, his voice low and seductive. "Come for me."

That single command shattered her. She cried out, her body quivering, waves of pleasure washing over her in a rush. But before she had a chance to gather her thoughts, she was on her back, Sophir above her, his presence a powerful weight that made her heart race.

"Do you want to stop?" He asked, his voice thick with desire.

She shook her head, unable to find the words. Instead, she met his gaze, and in that moment, she surrendered to him completely.

He moved without hesitation, swift and sure, and the sensation of him entering her sent a fresh jolt of pleasure through her. She could hardly think, could hardly breathe, as she gave herself to him, her body reacting instinctively, desperately to his every move. There was nothing rushed about it—only a quiet, intense want, a need that matched hers.

Sophir's eyes locked with hers, burning with an intensity that left her breathless. He cupped her cheek with one hand, the other holding her waist, his gaze unwavering. He was so close, his body pressed against hers, and in that moment, it felt as though time had stopped. She couldn't look away from him, could only surrender to the emotions he stirred within her.

For a moment, it seemed like he had forgotten how to speak, lost in the intensity of their connection. But then, as his face softened in pleasure, he whispered something that made her heart skip.

"*Ma'lévin*," he said, his voice hushed.

My love.

The words broke her, sending her into a rush of sensations, her body arching as she cried out, her vision clouded by the intensity of her release. Sophir's grip tightened, and he roared above her, his release coming in waves, shaking him as he held her close. He kissed her again, tenderly this time, as they both tried to catch their breath.

Afterward, with their hearts still racing, she smiled as he brushed her hair out of her face, his touch tender and intimate. She didn't want to leave the warmth of their embrace, but there were things to be done—Haldin's celebration awaited, and there were matters to settle. But for a moment, she allowed herself to linger in his arms, content.

"It would be rude to skip a party in my honor, right?" she asked with a playful smile as she sat up, stretching.

Sophir smiled and kissed the side of her neck, his touch lingering. "I believe so, but… once the pleasantries are done, perhaps we could sneak away," he suggested. "Lonan could use more rest. I'm sure the two of us could help with that."

"I doubt he'll need much convincing," she said with a smile, leaning in to steal a kiss.

His eyes sparkled as he watched her stand. "Poor gown," he teased, his gaze appreciating her in the aftermath of their shared moment.

"Don't rip the next one off," she warned, her voice light as she began to search for fresh clothes.

"It was in the way," he said dismissively, his playful tone still heavy with desire.

"Don't you have a long-lost uncle to talk to?" She asked, glancing back at him over her shoulder.

"I do," he mused, but didn't move.

Faedi's brows creased as she studied him. His eyes were clouded, unreadable, and she wasn't sure if she should press him with questions. However, it didn't matter—not when he spoke first.

"Are you alright?"

She inched her head to the side and shrugged. "Why wouldn't I be?"

Sophir sighed and rubbed his chin. "Less than a fortnight ago, you were living peacefully. Now…you're home is gone, a man who raised you—"

"I don't need it repeated—I was there." She snapped and turned away from him.

Her heart pounded in her ears while she rummaged through the wardrobe. There wasn't time to sit and ponder on the past or how she felt about all of it. Not when there was *everything else*.

"Faedi…" Sophir's voice was careful. Too close to pity.

"I'm fine." Her back stiffened as her throat tightened. "I have to be fine—I don't want to talk about it."

Two thundering heartbeats passed before she heard him sigh.

"Would you prefer a distraction?"

Her stomach twisted. "Please?"

Sophir moved behind her, his hands trailing lightly up her thighs and over her sides, his touch both comforting and electric. One hand gently cupped her throat, and the other slid down her body, making her shiver as his presence pressed against her back.

"Sex shouldn't be a distraction," Faedi whispered, breathless as she leaned into him.

"It can be…if it's you," he murmured, his voice thick with longing. "You're irresistible."

She smiled, but it didn't reach her eyes. "We have important things to do."

Sophir's lips brushed against her ear, and his fingers brushed against her skin, sending a wave of warmth through her. "I'm taking care of one of those now," he said, his voice deep and teasing. "I called Lonan to check on him… and I owe him a promise."

"What promise?" she asked, her breath catching.

"I told him he could watch me take you—if that's alright with you," he said, the hint of mischief still evident in his tone.

By the time Lonan entered the room, Faedi was already on the bed, her body arching as Sophir moved behind her. Her breath hitched as she felt the rhythm of him, but it was the sudden sound of the door clicking shut that made her heart race in a different way.

Lonan stood frozen at the threshold, his eyes locking onto them, his lips parted in surprise. His disheveled hair fell into his face as he took in the scene. Without a word, he locked the door behind him.

The weight of his silence pressed against her chest—heavy, hungry, and feral.

Ancients, help me, don't just stand there.

Faedi's pulse quickened, not from embarrassment, but from the desire she saw reflected in Lonan's gaze. There was something more there now, an undeniable hunger, as if his very presence made her body respond all over again.

She felt Sophir's movements slow for just a moment, as though he too felt the shift in energy. Faedi couldn't pull her gaze from Lonan, who stood, transfixed, watching her with an intensity that left her breathless. Her pulse fluttered as she lost herself in him.

"Faedi," Lonan's voice was a low murmur, thick with desire. He spoke her name like a prayer, and her heart skipped in response.

A soft groan escaped her lips as Sophir's hand moved gently along her back, his touch warm and comforting, reminding her of the passion they shared. Still, it was the look in Lonan's eyes that made everything inside her stir, her body moving instinctively toward him.

Lonan took a step closer, his fingers brushing along her chin as he tilted her face upward to meet his gaze. She could see the raw longing in his eyes, the way his breath hitched when she looked at him. Her skin burned with anticipation as he leaned in just enough for her to feel his warmth.

"Do you want this?" Lonan asked softly, his voice thick with emotion.

She wanted to say something, but all that came was a soft, needy sigh as her body ached for more of him. Instead, she nodded, the words caught in her throat as she pressed closer to Sophir, her body calling for both of them, pulled by an invisible thread.

Sophir's hands slid around her hips, pulling her closer as he kissed the sensitive curve of her neck. Faedi's breath caught in her throat as she felt the weight of both of their gazes on her, the intensity of their presence overwhelming in the most beautiful way.

"Let me hear you," Sophir whispered against her skin, his voice a gentle command. "Let him hear you."

Faedi closed her eyes, her body swaying with the rhythm of their touch. Every movement, every glance, felt like it was drawing them all closer together, like an intricate dance they had always known, yet had never fully embraced. The connection between them was electric, filled with an energy that was almost tangible.

Lonan's hand moved to her cheek, his thumb brushing along the curve of her jaw as he bent down to kiss her gently. The kiss was soft, tender, and yet it spoke of a depth of feeling she hadn't realized had been waiting for them all along.

"Take your time," Lonan murmured, his lips lingering against hers. "We have all the time we need."

And in that moment, Faedi realized that this was no longer just about the heat of the moment. It was about connection, about love that was both wild and tender, a bond that wove them together in ways deeper than she could have imagined. She could feel their hearts, their souls, entwining, pulling her into something so much more than just passion.

When their lips parted, she found herself breathing heavily, her body still aching with desire. But it wasn't just desire for the physical—no, it was something more, something profound. The love between them, the need to be near each other, was something that could never be fully put into words.

In that quiet space, with the three of them close and breathing in the same air, Faedi realized just how deeply her soul had been touched by both of them. Her heart was full, her body sated, and yet she knew this was only the beginning of something far more beautiful than she could have ever dreamed.

Just when Faedi thought the moments could not become more overwhelming, Sophir pulled away, and a soft whine escaped her lips at the loss of his touch. Lonan, ever so patient, allowed her to turn and meet his gaze. Her eyes followed Sophir as he shifted further back on the bed, settling into a more relaxed position.

"What are you doing?" Faedi's voice was soft, laced with curiosity, though her face softened as she traced the lines of Sophir's body with her gaze, a quiet awe settling over her.

Sophir's smile was a slow, teasing curve of his lips. "Such a needy girl," he purred, his eyes gleaming with mischief. He curled his finger to beckon her closer. "Come here, let me savor you."

A shiver ran down her spine at the sound of his voice, the weight of his words sending a wave of desire through her. She could only whisper a prayer to the Ancients, feeling as though she were caught between two worlds.

Lonan, ever commanding, gave her a gentle but firm nudge. "Go to him," he said, his voice low and filled with authority. The sharp slap of his hand to her rear made her flinch, a mix of surprise and desire flickering within her. Despite the growing ache in her body, she crawled toward Sophir, the pull between them undeniable.

"Turn and face Lonan," Sophir directed softly, his hands steady on her hips. She obeyed without hesitation, feeling the weight of his hands guiding her, his touch so reassuring yet charged with something more. "Now sit, let go of your worries," he murmured, guiding her movements.

The intimacy of the moment left Faedi breathless. She lowered herself, bracing against his chest, her body instinctively moving with the rhythm of his touch. She couldn't take her eyes off Lonan, whose gaze was intense, filled with both tenderness and hunger.

"Lonan…" Faedi whispered, her voice barely audible as her body reacted, rolling with a need that was almost primal. His eyes locked onto hers, and she saw the raw yearning there, mirrored in the way he reached for her, his body aching to be closer.

Lonan's voice cut through the haze of sensations. "Return the favor," he whispered, his hands spreading Sophir's legs as he moved between them. Faedi's heart skipped a beat as she leaned down, drawn by the connection she felt so deeply. She pressed her lips to Sophir with a soft sigh, feeling the hum of approval echoing in the air.

The intimacy they shared felt both overwhelming and tender, each movement, each glance, a conversation of desire and trust. The connection between them was like a dance, each of them attuned to the other, the unspoken bond tightening as they moved together. Faedi was lost in the rhythm of it, the warmth of Sophir's touch, the electric charge in Lonan's gaze.

It was a beautiful kind of chaos, a melding of souls that left her breathless and trembling. In that moment, time slowed, every second becoming a memory she would cherish, a connection that was so much more than passion.

When they finally stopped, sweat-slick and breathless, Faedi felt the weight of their closeness, the bond between them pulsing with quiet intensity. Sophir, ever the protector, caught Lonan before he could fall, steadying him with a hand on his shoulder.

"Let's clean up," Sophir said gently, breaking the silence. He carefully lifted both of them as if they were weightless, carrying them toward the bath with a quiet strength.

"We may be late to the gathering," he mused with a smile, setting them down on the edge of the tub. "But the were-folk here will understand. We could use a wash."

Faedi laughed softly, the sound light and free, her body still humming with the aftershocks of their closeness. "You're probably right," she agreed, shaking her head in quiet amusement.

Even if their bond was no secret, she doubted anyone would want to witness the aftermath of such intimate moments—not Haldin, not Torix. No matter how much she had grown, there were parts of her that would always be their child, seen through their eyes. But for now, with Lonan and Sophir beside her, she had no need for anything else but the warmth of their touch.

46

A Toast to Reunions

Faedi

The grand hall of the Rowdon palace buzzed with festive energy as Faedi stood at the entrance of the throne room, flanked by Lonan and Sophir. Their arrival sparked a soft murmur of anticipation among the elegantly dressed guests. The vast chamber overflowed with Dusk Elves, Gaelisks, and opalescent-scaled Itmis, all gathered in celebration.

Long tables laden with an array of foods stretched across the room—platters of raw and roasted meats, delicate pastries, and exotic fruits glistening under the soft, golden light of the torches hanging from chandeliers that shimmered like clusters of stars. Crystal goblets filled with wine and golden flagons of mead were distributed among the guests. The laughter and clinking of glasses melded with the lilting tunes of the bards near the dais, creating a vibrant melody that filled the air.

As they walked through the doorway, Faedi felt the eyes of the attendees turn toward them. The murmurs died into a respectful hush. At the far end of the room, Haldin stood from his throne on the dais, dressed in regal attire. His robes, woven with silver and adorned with precious gemstones, shimmered in the firelight. Yet, he wore no crown, his attention fixed solely on them.

"Princess Faedi Yiva, Prince Lonan Tagilson, and High Knight Sophir Daygan," he announced, his broad smile warm as he refused to let anyone else speak for him.

A hush fell over the room as every head turned toward them, and Faedi felt the weight of their gazes as they bowed in unison. Shifting uncomfortably between Lonan and Sophir, she glanced down at her gown. It looked similar to the attire worn by the others, yet in this sea of people, she felt almost exposed. The cascade of twilight blue, silver, and purple flowed around her like liquid starlight, matching the finely tailored clothes Sophir and Lonan wore. Sophir, as ever, went without a shirt, his opalescent scales gleaming in the firelight. Lonan, too, was free of glamour, his pale skin replaced by swirling shadows that danced across him like mist.

As they made their way to the dais, the guests held their bows until they passed. Faedi's gaze lifted to Haldin as Torix moved to stand beside him. It wasn't until Haldin smiled at her with pride that her body relaxed.

"Tonight we celebrate not only the return of my granddaughter but also announce her union with the Umbrals and Itmis. We drink to the strength of the unity of our peoples," he proclaimed, raising a goblet in a joyful salute and beaming down at her.

Faedi glanced at the guests as they raised their drinks in a toast. The Gaelisks and Itmis present seemed more at ease than the Dusk Elves, and Faedi noticed there were far more of them than she'd seen in the chamber with the tree. The largest of the Itmis, whom she assumed was Sophir's uncle Ighir, stood on the other side of Haldin and gave a subtle bow of his head.

Turning her attention to the elves, Faedi fought the urge to flinch under their curious gazes. She looked like them and had been announced as their princess, yet they did not know her, and she could feel their scrutiny of her every move, their silent judgment. They were cautious, unsure of her place among them.

"Thank you, Grandfather," she said, bowing her head. As the party grew lively again after the toast, she sighed in relief. *"I think the memory spell was on more than just me and Sylrie—lots of the elves look confused."*

"What?" Sophir and Lonan's voices tickled her mind.

"It doesn't make sense," she murmured. *"I thought Aladia was the only one Mama told about the spell, but Sylrie's spell was removed."* She glanced between them and shook her head when they stared back at her in confusion. *"Right, I forgot to tell you. He's really alive—he's coming here soon."*

"I'm glad to know our beddings are good distractions," Sophir chuckled, and Faedi swatted his hand lightly.

"Speaking of Valoria, is now the time to ask him about the people on the border?" Lonan asked, raising an eyebrow as he glanced at her.

"Given the confusion of the people, it might be best to ask in private," Sophir advised as Haldin approached them.

"Grandpa and Torix wouldn't talk about anything in the halls," Faedi said, her voice a low murmur. *"I think they suspect people here on the mountain."*

"How are you feeling?" Haldin asked when he stood in front of them, Torix to his left and Ighir to his right.

"Well rested," Faedi smiled up at him.

"Much better. You have talented healers here." Lonan bowed his head with a light chuckle. "Your people still seem confused about Faedi being your heir."

"That will be settled soon enough," Haldin said, waving a dismissive hand. "For now, I wish to dance with my granddaughter."

"They shouldn't doubt your status too much; your family crest grows on you," Ighir stated, his voice calm before he turned his attention to Sophir. "We need to speak, nephew."

"Agreed," Sophir nodded, then smiled at Faedi before raising an eyebrow at Lonan. "Come with me?"

"Is it a private conversation?" Lonan shifted uncomfortably beside her.

"You're welcome to join," Ighir said with a nod. "Torix is as well. Old grievances seem to die hard here."

"That they do," Torix grumbled before waving for Lonan to follow them. "That's a problem for later, though. This party will go on all night."

Faedi smiled at Lonan and Sophir when they paused to kiss her cheeks—one on her left, the other on her right—before following Torix and Ighir. For a moment, she watched them go, making sure no one bothered them. Her smile grew when Sophir slid his hand over Lonan's lower back, pulling him against his side and curling his tail around him.

"May I have this dance?" Haldin asked softly, offering her his hand with a subtle bow of his head.

"I'll warn you," Faedi smiled as she accepted his hand. "I'm a horrible dancer."

"Maybe you just forgot."

Haldin led Faedi to the center of the room, where the dancers moved in sync with the gentle, rhythmic melody filling the chamber. As they took their place among them, the other dancers paused and gave them a wide berth. Faedi's heart hammered in her chest, and she bit her lip, glancing around nervously. The pressure of being announced as their princess felt like a weight on her shoulders, and she knew the eyes of the crowd were studying and judging her. But when Haldin placed a gentle hand on her waist, she focused on him, trying to shake off her anxiety.

"How is Scarred?" he asked, guiding her smoothly across the floor.

"He mentioned ports here?" Faedi replied, relieved when she didn't trip over her own feet.

"I will have them opened for him," Haldin promised, a twinkle in his eyes that made her feel a bit lighter.

"He freed Valorian slaves before—I think he's doing something similar now," she said softly, the music swirling around them. "They're with farmers who left Dewgate just north of the border...I was hoping—if...maybe—"

"What do you want to ask of me?" Haldin twirled her gently, his attention unwavering. "If it is in my power to provide, you have it."

"I want to bring them here or escort them to the Mire. Lonan summoned some Watchers with their bonded to help them, but they don't have the supplies or defenses to protect themselves." The urgency in her voice matched the tempo of their steps as they picked up speed. "They were attacked by a hunt when we were with them."

"Where did this happen?" Haldin lowered his head to meet her gaze.

"Near the border of Emsmeda and Rowdon," Faedi pointed to a spot on the giant map on the floor. "Right there."

"There are no hunts there," Haldin shook his head, furrowing his brows.

"There was, and it was a large one," Faedi insisted. "They had a healthy pack of direwolves with them too—enough for one mount and supply carrier each."

"Did you recognize any of them?"

"No, but we fought them off. I think they might have been after us though," Faedi said, turning her attention back to her feet, relieved that she hadn't stumbled. "They did not take the livestock they killed."

"Did they say anything?"

"No. Just screams and howls," she replied, shaking her head.

"It will be faster to bring them here. We have mounts that can make the journey within two days," Haldin nodded thoughtfully, tapping her chin to catch her attention. "We'll leave in the morning."

"We will?" Faedi's heart lifted at his nod.

"We do have a meeting to attend first," he added with a chuckle. "I suppose dancing was one of the things you could not remember. You dance as well as you did as a child."

"I stood on yours and Torix's feet to dance," Faedi scoffed, rolling her eyes at the memory.

"Yes, but you never crushed our feet like Sylrie."

His rich and warm laughter eased the tension in her shoulders. As she joined him in laughter, she looked around the room. Fewer eyes were on them now that the wine and mead flowed freely among the crowd.

"Scarred is taller than you," Faedi grinned up at Haldin.

Haldin tilted his head, his smile growing wider. "Is he?"

"Taller than Sophir, too," she said, glancing around until she spotted them with a group of Itmis near the wall. Her heart settled a bit, knowing they were still safe.

They continued to dance silently for a moment, their steps in perfect harmony with the music. For that short time, Faedi felt like a child again, at one of the solstice balls, happily dancing with her grandfather without a care in the world. Her brother was alive, Torix was nearby with his ever-watchful gaze, and Haldin's arms protected her from anything that might bring her harm.

Then the reality of her situation crashed over her like a wave, and her heart ached when she realized her mother was no longer beside Torix. Everything felt like a horrible mixture of different and similar all at once.

"What's on your mind?" Haldin asked softly, his steps slowing to a stop.

"The past," Faedi admitted, quickly wiping her eyes. "I'm sorry."

"Don't apologize," he shook his head, hooking his arm with hers to lead her away from the dance floor. "You should eat something. Aladia told me about the kitchen's…accident."

"What?" Faedi glanced up at him as they navigated through the crowd, which parted at their approach.

"You and Lonan were to be given appropriate nourishment the day you arrived," he explained, signaling for a servant to come forward once they reached the wall.

"You think it was on purpose?" Faedi frowned, watching the servant munch on a piece of barely cooked meat from the plate they brought.

"Aladia seems to think so," Haldin nodded, taking the plate once the servant bowed and offered it to him. "Mead, ale, or wine?"

"Anything," Faedi shrugged, smiling at the servant as they bowed again to retrieve drinks. "Is Aladia a…she doesn't smell?"

"It's a glamour. She is a bear, like your mother and myself. There are some trusted who hide themselves from the rest in the castle," he explained softly before snatching a piece of meat and eating it before Faedi could react. "She and your mother studied magic together."

Faedi nodded, taking a piece of elk that was fresh and nearly tender enough to melt in her mouth. She hadn't realized how starving she was until she swallowed and took a breath to steady herself. Were-folk might have been common on the mountain, but inhaling food like a ravenous animal was still rude.

"Is there anyone else who might have been able to remove the memory spells?" Faedi asked, grabbing another piece and quickly eating it.

"Why do you ask?" Haldin's eyes narrowed slightly.

"Scarred remembers." Faedi glanced up at him, raising her eyebrows. "This is probably a conversation for later?"

The servant approached again with two goblets, sipping from both before offering them with a bow. Haldin took the cups and held them closely while watching the servant. After what Faedi assumed was an appropriate time, they bowed and departed once he nodded in approval.

"Did he say how he remembers?" Haldin asked once they were alone again.

"The spells were removed in Ashar," Faedi answered softly after swallowing another bite. "Fenkas took him there."

"Can you ask him for more information?"

After Faedi had taken a sip, Haldin offered her one of the goblets. She hesitated, looking down at the dark liquid inside. The sweetness tickled her nose as she lifted it to her lips.

"*Sylrie?*" She called for him while she sipped slowly, recognizing the mead's flavor.

"*Is everything alright?*"

"*Yes, but Grandpa has questions. He wants to know what happened in Ashar and how the memory spells were broken.*"

"*I don't know who removed it, but they interrogated me after and wanted to know where you were. They thought we had an escape plan from the house.*"

"You were ten—how much does a child know?"

"They thought I knew a lot. Their questions didn't make sense though—they were asking about things that happened ages ago…before we were born."

"Like from Mama's history lessons?"

"Older than that. They kept asking about something called Dag'mör?"

A chill ran down Faedi's spine as she watched the mead swirl in the goblet, slowly darkening until the silver cup no longer reflected in it. The music and sounds of the crowd blurred and distorted around her.

"Dag'mör," Faedi replied, looking up at Haldin. His face was a blur, but he focused on her. *"They don't want us there—that's why they're there…and why they're using a plague."*

"They're doing what?"

"There's a plague in the forest. The only way to kill it is with fire. I used eventides to hopefully cleanse the soil, but—"

"Is it like Valoria?"

"Smells different, but yes."

"Fuck. Are the ports going to be open?"

"Grandpa said he'd open them. Are you coming?"

"If they don't want us there, that's where we should be. I'm leaving now. Let me know when you go to sleep…maybe we can talk again—I need a map."

"I will. I'll see you soon."

"Be careful. If Fenkas was a backstabber, there might be more in the mountain."

"You too."

47
The Antechamber

"There are too many eyes on Lonan. It seems they've accepted Faedi well enough, but no one looks pleased about her marriage to an Umbral."

Sophir

The crowd bustled as he weaved between guests with Lonan behind Ighir and Torix. His hand rested lightly on Lonan's lower back, hoping to offer him some reassurance as they navigated through a mass of people who had been ready to kill him not too long ago.

Finally, they reached a quieter area near one of the walls, where a group of Itmis and several Gaelisks waited. The sounds of the party were less overwhelming here, and the air felt less suffocating. Sophir moved until he and Lonan were directly at the wall, turning to face Ighir.

"Do you speak our tongue?" Sophir asked Lonan.

"No, Faedi is the linguist. Can you talk and translate if the conversation goes that way?"

"I will, don't worry." Sophir smiled at him before looking between Ighir and Torix. "You said we needed to speak?"

"You can walk in memories, yes?" Ighir raised his eyebrows.

"I can," Sophir nodded, glancing at a younger Gaelisk who approached. Unlike many others in the room, their horns hadn't been cut off, and their slate gray skin was free of onyx crystallized scars. They were one of the few who hadn't been rendered voiceless.

"Have you attempted to walk through the memories of ancestors yet?" Ighir's voice pulled Sophir's attention back to him, and he shook his head.

"No," he sighed, lowering his head. "There hasn't been an Astral who can do that in several centuries. My parents couldn't even do that."

"Do they still reside in the mountains?"

"They…" Sophir hesitated and glanced at Lonan before shaking his head. "They died some time ago. My family was cast out from the mountains."

"Should I ask why?" Ighir narrowed his eyes.

"It was before I was born, and they died not long after. The priests who raised us didn't know," Sophir shrugged dismissively, sighing when Lonan brushed the back of his hand against his.

"I'm sorry."

"I'm not," Sophir smiled down at him. "If we were cast out, it was because they did the right thing. Itmis laws are… outdated."

"And I thought Mire politics were difficult," Lonan remarked.

"I prefer Faedi's tree politics and mice," Sophir chuckled when Lonan did, shaking his head. "If there are ways to learn that aren't on the mountain, I'm happy to try and help. Is this for Gaelisks who were not… brutalized?"

"We younger ones still have our voices and wings," the Gaelisk responded softly. "But they are weak."

"We can teach them the old-fashioned way, but I'm not one to believe we have months to do so. Not with… current events," Ighir rumbled, placing his hand on the Gaelisk's shoulder.

"I may not be able to teach them through their ancestors, but I could teach them through you or the others," Sophir suggested, rubbing his chin in thought. "I haven't attempted to take multiple people into memory, but it could be possible. Although, it would be faster if my brothers and sister were here. At least then we could do five Gaelisks at a time."

"Is there a way to contact them?" Lonan looked between everyone. "Like my crystal to Watchers?"

"Doing so the easy way would alert many to our location, and not all Itmis are as friendly as us," Sophir told him, keeping his eyes on Ighir for his thoughts.

"We could ask Haldin for his thoughts and try the hard way."

"Do I want to know what the hard way is?" Torix shifted uncomfortably beside Ighir.

"The Helgi," Sophir rubbed his forehead with a groan. "It's been centuries since we called on that treaty, and it's my understanding that most do not leave their Isle. Not since the Valorian plague."

"They might answer to me, and Zarae mentioned knowing a Helgi before we were frozen," Ighir mused.

"Who?" Sophir asked, curious about the name he hadn't heard before.

"Zarae, the woman I was with, said she found you in one of our… friend's minds."

"Something tells me this is a conversation for later," Lonan said, raising his eyebrows as he looked between them.

"It is for closed doors," Torix announced just as a glass shattered nearby. "Now would be good. Should we get Haldin?"

"Yes," Ighir nodded, ushering everyone to a side door as he looked at the young Gaelisk. "Tell him it's time."

Sophir wanted to question him, but resisted as the noise of the crowd behind them grew. The sea of happy celebration turned to shock and confusion. Then, as the door shut behind them, Sophir glanced over his shoulder at the crowd. One elf, closest to the door, was pinned to the ground by a guard.

As they walked through the hall, Sophir observed the body language of everyone from their position at the rear, alongside Ighir. Torix appeared rushed but unaffected by the chaos they had just left behind, while Lonan kept glancing back at Sophir and the hall. The worry and confusion in his eyes were evident.

What's happening?

"What was that?" Lonan asked, looking between the two of them.

"Maybe they were testing to see who was surprised," Sophir suggested, silently nodding in agreement with Faedi's proposal.

Before they could delve deeper into their thoughts, Haldin rounded a corner with Faedi beside him. She hurried to join them, positioning herself between Lonan and Sophir.

"I think something was happening—or maybe I had a strange moment talking to Sylrie. Grandpa seemed to think it was all planned," she said, glancing back toward the chaos they had just escaped.

Sophir considered that they might have wanted to gauge their reactions to the memory spell or its removal, but there had been enough time for news of Faedi's return to circulate in the castle. Perhaps that was Haldin's intention.

"Aladia had to use magic to remove the spell. No one was casting in there," Faedi lowered her head. "Maybe the wine or mead?"

"It would be a clever way to spread a potion," Sophir commented.

"Would it affect the Gaelisks and Itmis who drank it? There were a lot of Verglas Itmis...I thought you said it was only your uncle who helped them?" Lonan pointed out, and he wasn't wrong.

"He might have had his people join, but my immediate family rarely spoke about him. It's...unlucky to talk about the dead, or the presumed dead, in his case," Sophir replied with a sigh, casting a glance at their uncle. There was so much they didn't know about him or his group still frozen in the mountain, and their time at the celebration hadn't been long enough or private enough to ask freely.

Sophir couldn't even comprehend their uncle's relationship with the woman he had been with. The thought faded before they could voice it as Haldin led them through another hidden door in the stone walls. A dimly lit corridor branched off from the main castle halls. The air was cooler, and the faded tapestries lining the walls hinted at a more ancient part of the castle.

As they ventured deeper, the corridor twisted and turned, each bend revealing a different scene from the castle's history, captured in old, dusty murals. Sophir could sense the tension in both Lonan and Faedi, their bodies stiffening as they moved, until Haldin finally stopped ahead of them.

He pressed his hand against a seemingly ordinary wall, and with a faint rumble, the stone shifted, revealing a concealed door. The room beyond was small and circular, with an arched ceiling covered in arcane symbols that pulsed with a subtle light.

"These are the same as the ones in the Mire," Faedi observed.

"This is the Antechamber," Haldin said, his voice low and serious. "It's a place of security—no magic can penetrate these walls. Here, we can speak freely."

As they entered the chamber, Haldin sealed them off from any potential eavesdroppers. Ornately carved tables and shelves lined the walls, filled with artifacts and scrolls. Between two shelves sat a bench, and on it was Zarae.

Sophir watched as she set aside a scroll, dusting it off before standing and bowing. There was no hint of the near-death experience she had faced the night before or of Faedi's healing.

"Were you frozen with the Gaelisks the entire time?" Sophir asked before anyone else could speak.

"I was," Zarae nodded, confusion flickering across her face. "Why?"

"How does Sylrie know about you, and how were you able to talk to Sophir in my memory?" Faedi asked, shifting to the side as all eyes turned to her. Sophir stepped closer to her. "I've never heard of a seer who can do that."

Zarae fell silent, looking at everyone in the room until her gaze landed on Ighir. Her expression changed when he rumbled low, prompting her to turn her eyes back to Faedi. Finally, she sighed and lowered her head.

"I've never spoken to your brother, but as for Sophir—I'm...bonded to Ragna, in a way—she and I were together in Ashar centuries ago. I promised her I would help her find her twin, and since that bond was made, I am connected to her—all of her," Zarae explained carefully. "While frozen, I spent my time in her memories, trying to find evidence of where her sister might be. They are wanted—both of them—by Ilos' zealots."

"Why? Are they eclipse-born too?" Lonan asked from the other side of Faedi.

"That, and more," Zarae replied, nodding. "They said she was god-touched."

"A what?" Sophir stepped closer, their curiosity piqued, but Faedi squeezed their hand to keep them grounded.

"God-touched, a true eclipse-born—just as her twin is. That is why they are hunting down eclipse-born and imprisoning them," Zarae explained, sitting back down on the bench. "They believe that if they sacrifice god-touched to Ilos at the eclipse, he will devour their power and grow stronger."

Sophir looked at Faedi and Lonan. They were targets because of when they were born, and The Order wanted to sacrifice them, murder them, to appease their god.

I'll slaughter anyone who tries to touch them.

Faedi narrowed her eyes at Zarae. "So...they think anyone born during the eclipses could be god-touched—so they're just going to sacrifice everyone they find?" When Zarae nodded in affirmation, Faedi looked away. "Great."

"And they want to destroy the Mire and heart trees because?" Lonan placed a reassuring hand on Faedi's shoulder as she hugged her arms to herself.

"I assume it's because heart trees connect the realms, and the Mire is home to one of the allied races," Zarae shrugged, shaking her head. "Ragna did not show me anything about their motives."

"You said she showed you everything," Sophir interjected, feeling a mix of frustration and urgency. Faedi gave their hand another squeeze.

"She does," Faedi confirmed. "Which means she does not know more of their motives. She only knows their movements now that she is free."

"She would only show what they wanted her to unless she was turned to their side," Sophir thought, unease crawling up their spine.

"You mentioned allied races. Do you mean the treaty between the Umbrals and Dusk Elves?" Faedi glanced at Haldin, who nodded silently.

"The alliance between the Umbrals and Dusk Elves is only a fraction of the bonds made." Zarae explained, "History was rewritten after the war, but bond oaths sworn to the gods are deeper than ink on parchment. So, Ilos' zealots seek to break those oaths."

Faedi began to pace the room, and Sophir followed her with their eyes. "That's why they killed my mother?"

"Yes," Zarae frowned. "If the bond between Umbrals and Dusk Elves is broken, they can keep you from returning to your home."

"What is so important about Dewgate?" Faedi asked, her confusion evident.

It didn't make sense for them to want them to stay where they were. The mountain was far more secure than the port city. If anything, they shouldn't want them remaining there, as they were much more challenging to kill on the mountain.

"It isn't just Dewgate," Zarae shook her head, standing to grab a torch. She walked to the center of the room to illuminate a design on the floor.

It resembled the map on the throne room's floor, but it was far older and more worn. Several lines were missing to separate the regions. Emsmeda, Lefral, Rowdon, and Detrich were completely absent, and almost the entire continent of Ystrana was marked as a forest.

Nearly all of it was the Mire.

"Mör's Mire," Faedi whispered.

"What?" Lonan's question echoed Sophir's own as they turned to Faedi.

"Ystrana used to be led by a council. It was housed in Dag'mör—Dewgate," Zarae explained softly. "Each region had its own elected leader, but those leaders were seated on the council to defend and protect Ystrana as a whole. However, three ages ago, after attempts to rebuild following the Great War, there was a shift in alliances. War broke out in Ystrana, and the countries separated."

Sophir watched her walk over the map, frowning at the unfamiliar history. None of the tales they had read spoke of this.

"Then, when the Dusk Elves heeded an oath-bound call to the Gaelisks and Shadow Elves," she continued, "Dewgate was abandoned. The Umbrals of the Mire swore to defend the land, and Gath'faunan, a dark fae, remained there to ensure that the city remained free until the Dusk Elves returned while the rest of their people were sealed away from this realm."

"How do you know all of this? If history was rewritten—" Sophir started, but Zarae interrupted them.

"I was awake three ages ago, and since then, I've had Ragna to fill in the blanks. She and I, like the other eclipse-born, are ageless."

"Who started the war in Ystrana?" Faedi asked, her gaze drifting to the edges of the map where other locations were depicted. They weren't on any maps Sophir had seen before.

"Who do you think?" Zarae looked up at them, her tone laced with frustration. "Ilos's devout and their allies. They infiltrated the regions and dismantled things from the inside, just as they did in Valoria—and I assume they are likely trying to do here and in Dewgate. They'll do anything to turn the prophecy in their favor."

Sophir remained focused on the map, the unfamiliar regions catching his attention. "Which prophecy?" He asked, his curiosity evident.

"The Seven Crowns," Zarae replied. "Each chosen by one of the Ancients to take their seat on the Ystranan council—the ones who will unite the realms, who will have the power to stop Ilos' purge of darkness—who will restore balance not just to this realm, but to all realms."

Lonan's voice cut through the tension, a mixture of curiosity and suspicion. "And you're one of the seven?"

"No," she sighed. "I was tasked with finding them and helping the gods awaken them once they are together."

"That's why you were imprisoned in Ashar?" Faedi asked, absentmindedly rubbing Sophir's knuckles with her thumb.

"Yes. They used me to track down each eclipse-born and kill them," Zarae explained, settling back onto the bench. "Then, I suppose after they realized the eclipses would continue to bless people born during them, they decided to imprison them and wait for the eclipse of both moons and the sun."

Sophir tilted his head, his curiosity mixing with concern. "They've never tried that before?"

Zarae shook her head. "There has not been a total eclipse like that for them to attempt yet."

Lonan walked over to Faedi and took her hand, his voice laced with concern. "How long has it been since the last total eclipse?"

"I'm not familiar with these regions. This map is..." Faedi trailed off, shaking her head.

"From before The Great War. I have not seen one in this lifetime—the last I saw was during The Great War, six ages ago." Zarae traced the parchment with her fingertips. "This is the first time in several centuries when all gods are alive and accounted for. The last of the eclipse-births happened while I was frozen."

Sophir's heart raced as he looked at Zarae. Her smile sent a chill down his spine.

"The next total eclipse will be sooner than later."

48

The Chosen Few

"There's no way that there's truth to the prophecies. Every region, every race, has its own version of it—but we're not really chosen by the gods. Faeturin wouldn't have let Faedi's family be murdered like that."

Lonan

He stared at Zarae, his heart pounding in his ears as he watched Haldin move around the room. He had no idea what Haldin was up to, nor did he care—not after the casual revelation Zarae had made. If Ilos' zealots had their way, they'd try to sacrifice them all soon.

"She's joking, right? Or maybe she's gone a bit mad after being frozen?" Lonan glanced at Faedi and Sophir, searching for a hint of agreement.

"Faedi did speak in the tongue of the Ancients when she was a child," Sophir shrugged, his nonchalance deepening Lonan's unease.

"I haven't done it since then—I wouldn't rely on that," Faedi subtly shook her head.

"Did your mother teach you how to speak it?" Lonan raised his eyebrows and turned away from Zarae when she smiled at him. As warm as her smile was, it chilled his blood.

"No—the language is dead. Even the priestesses at the temple in Dewgate don't speak it," she replied.

"And yet you did," Sophir nudged her, his gaze intense.

"You're oddly accepting of us possibly being chosen by the gods," Lonan squinted at him, trying to process the implications.

"I have my reservations," Sophir said, "but I saw what Faedi did as a child. She used magic that someone her age shouldn't have been able to use—it also wasn't the traditional magic of Guardians." He looked Lonan over. "And your mobility in the shadows isn't limited to the forest or the Mire. I was told Umbrals can only do that in their home territory."

Lonan stared at Sophir, momentarily confused. When had he used shadows outside of the Mire? Then it clicked—the fight in Emsmeda. Sophir was right; he shouldn't have been able to fight the way he had in the fields.

But that didn't make him god-touched. The map on the floor showed that all of it used to be the Mire.

He studied Faedi, sighing. If any of them was blessed by the gods, he believed it was her. After everything she had endured—her suffering—she remained kind and compassionate. She chose to help creatures and people alike, despite her distrust and fear of strangers.

It was the godliest behavior he could think of, and she was the only one who did it, even when it repeatedly hurt her.

"How long are you going to spend debating your divine gifts?" Zarae interrupted, looking between them. Then she clapped her hands suddenly. "Should I tell you the story of your patrons? It's one of my favorites."

"Our patrons?" Lonan squinted at her, curiosity piqued. Did she hear them?

"How they met in the crossroads," Zarae grinned at him, almost childlike.

"Zae, perhaps now isn't the time for stories?" Ighir sighed, moving to stand beside her, tousling her hair lightly.

"You're no fun," she huffed, a smile tugging at her lips. "Using the crystal to speak to the Mire will take at least an hour."

"Speaking of which," Haldin's voice called Lonan's attention. He turned to meet the King's gaze as he held out a crystal—similar to the one Lonan kept to communicate with the Watch. "Do you know if your parents still have their crystal?"

"I assume they do," Lonan nodded. "My parents were hopeful that you would see reason after meeting Faedi."

"Then we should be able to ascertain the status of the Mire and determine what we do from here," Haldin said, placing the crystal on a table etched with unfamiliar symbols.

"What do you mean?" Lonan tilted his head, watching the carvings on the table begin to glow and slowly travel toward the crystal.

"If the Mire is under direct threat, we will send our forces to defend them. However, if they have turned their attention to you three, it would be unwise to leave the mountain," Haldin explained.

"The Watch has not notified me of any large attacks or movements," Lonan told him, glancing at Faedi. Her brows were drawn together as she frowned.

"What if they go after both?" she asked softly.

"Then we will send reinforcements to the Mire, and I would advise the three of you to remain here," Torix interjected, and Lonan sighed in relief when Haldin nodded in agreement.

"This could take a while—if they are not near their crystal," Haldin warned.

A moment of silence stretched on as all eyes were on the crystal while they waited for a response. If Lonan hadn't had his crystal to communicate with fellow Watchers, he might have been concerned about the safety of his home. But he knew someone would have told him something—just as he would have been notified about the small settlement north of them.

"Can I tell the story now?" Zarae asked, laughing when Ighir groaned.

"Consider me intrigued," Faedi smiled, nudging Lonan.

"I am as well," Sophir agreed with a rumble before Lonan nodded.

"Have at it," he told her, unable to suppress his smile when she jumped excitedly.

"Find a seat, get comfortable," Zarae urged them. She rubbed her hands together and cleared her throat. "Papa always told it better, but I'll do my best. I just have to figure out where to start…"

Lonan traded a look with Faedi and Sophir, chuckling as he shook his head. Glancing at the numerous chairs and benches scattered about, he offered his hand to Faedi to lead her to a seat. Once she was comfortable, he sat beside her and waved Sophir over to join them.

"Maybe we should have brought snacks," Lonan grinned, laughing when Faedi stifled her laughter.

"I wish you would have. I'm starving—"

"Zae…" Ighir's exasperated sigh was betrayed by a grin that followed.

"Alright, alright, here we go…"

"In the crossroads where realms intersected—a place where gods coexisted in a delicate dance—light, shadow, and twilight mingled in a delicate balance. The goddess of the forest wove her essence into every leaf and stream, her presence a whisper of verdant magic. The god of shadows crafted the unseen depths of night, his influence a gentle caress in the dark. The god of the night sky painted the heavens with auras of protection, his gaze ever watchful.

"Though their realms were distinct, their paths often crossed in subtle ways. However, one twilight, when the boundary of day and night shimmered in hues of purple and gold, the goddess of the forest sought to make a new creation—a gift for the land she cherished.

"As she knelt in a meadow carpeted with luminescent flowers, a shadow fell across her path.

'Where have the trees gone?' the god of shadows asked as his form shifted with the darkness that grew over the land. 'I could walk freely here before; now I can only come with night.'

'Mortals took the trees to build their homes,' the goddess replied absently as she urged a seedling to sprout.

'Why did you let them?' he asked softly.

'The mortals are not made to withstand the elements and needed shelter,' she looked back at him, curiosity lighting her gaze. 'Do you not like the mortals?'

'I am not fond of the ones who fear the dark and try to destroy it.'

'This should help that,' she turned her attention back to the ground as vines sprouted from the earth. 'I will create new forests and drape them with these.

The magic surrounding the hearts of the forests will fertilize them.'

'Vines are much smaller than your trees,' he told her as he knelt beside her and studied the vine.

The goddess watched him silently and smiled when the vine turned black from his touch. Then, as buds for flowers began to form, they were black as well. It was an unexpected change, but not unwanted.

'It is not the vines mortals should be wary of, but the blooms,' she told him as flowers slowly began to open on the vines. 'Unless treated with care, these flowers can kill.'

'The mortals use fire,' he told her.

'And their poison is the strongest when put to flame,' she smiled again and plucked one of the flowers. At the base, it was as black as the vine but then turned to blue, and then to white at the tips of the petals. 'However, I do not know what to call them.'

'May I see?' another voice spoke from behind them.

They turned and watched the god of the night sky descend from his celestial heights to join them. When he beckoned the goddess for her new flower, she offered it and watched silvery pollen glitter from it as he inspected her creation— like stars being made before their eyes.

'Eventides,' he whispered before he offered it back to her.

'It hardly sounds threatening,' the god of shadows scoffed.

'Shadows aren't very threatening either,' she challenged with a coy smile. 'But mortals fear you all the same.'

'They fear all of us,' the night sky god mused. 'When they should fear the flames they wield so recklessly.'"

Eventides.

Lonan's skin prickled with gooseflesh as he turned his gaze to Faedi's arm, where the flowers glittered softly in the dim light. As far as he knew, they were the crown symbol of the Dusk Elves, created like everything else in this world. But to hear that their origin was tied to the meeting of gods made his heart race with anxiety.

Faedi's eyes never wavered from Zarae as she spoke, her words flowing beyond his comprehension. When Lonan lifted his gaze to her face, he froze. Her eyes were black.

"Faedi?" he asked softly, gingerly taking her hand.

"Hmm?" She blinked quickly, shaking her head. In an instant, her eyes were gold again, as if nothing had happened. "What?"

"Are you alright?" He squeezed her hand tighter. "Your eyes were… maybe I'm just seeing things."

"They were like they were when you were a child in the memory—when you spoke in the Ancients' tongue," Sophir confirmed softly, echoing his unease.

"Were they?" Faedi's brow furrowed as she rubbed her cheek. "Did I say anything?"

"They were, but you didn't say anything," Lonan assured her, shaking his head.

His attention shifted to the others, all focused on Faedi. Haldin and Torix looked concerned, while Ighir's expression was unreadable. Zarae, however, radiated pure excitement. If Ighir hadn't kept his hand on her shoulder, Lonan was sure she would have started bouncing around.

"I thought you only spoke it, but you... you've connected to one of them," Zarae said, her awe palpable as she stared at Faedi. She tugged on Ighir's arm. "See? I told you."

"Black eyes and the Ancients' tongue hardly means that she's been claimed," he warned with a gentle rumble.

"What do you mean?" Lonan's grip on Faedi's hand tightened.

"She's been claimed by one of the gods. She's a true eclipse-born."

Lonan looked back at Faedi, who seemed to stare at Zarae as if she had grown a second head. It was difficult enough to grasp the idea that they might be blessed by the gods, but to be claimed by one? If Zarae was right, it meant that Faedi would be a primary target for Ilos' zealots. As if her birth on an eclipse hadn't already made her a target.

"Sylrie," he whispered before looking back at Zarae. "If Faedi is a chosen... or if she is one of the seven, what are the odds they would have chosen Sylrie as well?"

"The man in the light spoke to him too," Faedi murmured, hugging her arms to herself.

"What man in the light?" Haldin shook himself from his silent stare.

"When they were little, they mentioned a man who came into their dreams and filled their vision with light—Endi put up more wards around the house after that."

"He did it again after the fire, to me at least... I didn't ask Sylrie if it happened to him. He said Fenkas took him to Ashar and he was tortured, though," Faedi continued, and Lonan wrapped his arm over her shoulders, pulling her closer. "I can ask him—the crystal changed colors."

He turned his attention back to the doorway as the room grew brighter. A familiar voice filled the air, and a smile stretched across his face when Myst's form took shape in the center of the room.

"Thank the Ancients they didn't kill you—Espen would have missed chewing on your boots." Their form was distinct enough for Lonan to see the smile on their face. "This is powerful magic. Can you see me the way I can see you? I need to find a crafter to make me something to wear all the time."

"We can see you," Lonan chuckled despite Zarae's earlier revelations. "How is the Mire?"

"Safe—full of refugees from Dewgate, but safe. I can't say the same for the city." Myst lowered their head. "The last group that came before we lost contact with Lady Callon said the plague was in the city. They torched the harbor when people tried to flee by ship."

"Is Elder Ravyn with you?" Sophir asked.

"No, but we know where he is. He and the other Guardians and Wardens are at the second twin. If they come here, they will be welcome like the rest, but they want to protect the surrounding forest and prevent the spread of the plague."

Faedi stiffened beside Lonan. "Are there more cultist groups in the forest?"

"None close to the Mire," Myst shook their head. "The bonded Guardians are using your eventides to deter them. They tried burning them—we found their corpses. The Nomads said they saw a hunt in the east… they shared a camp with some of Ilos' bastards."

"When did they see them?" Lonan's heart raced. There had been no cultists with the hunt that attacked them.

"A month—maybe longer. They said it was when they were on their way to us from their yearly trade in Dietrich."

"It would be foolish hope to assume they all died in the forest or got lost," Torix growled nearby. "If they aren't there, they have to be somewhere else. If they know they're here and the Gaelisks are awake—"

"We've received no reports from the pass," Haldin interrupted.

"Unless they're all in Dewgate," Faedi sighed, leaning forward to rest her elbows on her knees. "If they're spreading the plague, there's a chance they have immunity or a cure. They don't want us there—it would make sense to hold it… but they want to destroy the twins and the Mire."

"They want eclipse-born too. There's at least four here," Zarae chimed in.

"There's only one here in the Mire," Myst shrugged.

"And one on a ship coming here," Faedi added, shaking her head. "Where is Ragna? You said she was eclipse-born."

"She was in Dewgate for a while, but she left… I think the last time I saw her, she was in Dietrich. Things are kind of fuzzy now that I'm awake," Zarae frowned. "And I still don't know where her twin is."

"They could be regrouping somewhere—likely Valoria. The sea between us is calmer in the winter," Sophir suggested, crossing his arms over his chest. "Maybe they're waiting. Even vegetation in the Mire would be less dense in the winter, wouldn't it?"

"It is," Myst and Lonan replied in unison, while Faedi and Torix nodded in agreement.

"Light shines the brightest on fresh snow."

Lonan turned his attention to Zarae, who sat on her bench with her knees drawn to her chest, staring up at the ceiling. Following her gaze, he noticed the markings carved there. It was more of the language he couldn't read, the same as the one Faedi mentioned was in the Mire, alongside another map.

"Are you stating a fact or a prophecy?" He asked her.

"Both," she mused softly.

"How long can this connection hold? We need plans… and backup plans," Myst questioned.

"It will last as long as we need it," Haldin promised with a nod. "However, if the Mire and mountains are safe for now… I suggest we gather what information we can and speak again later. Faedi has requested we relocate a settlement on the border here—your Watchers and their bonded there are welcome to come as well."

"When will you be there?" There was a shift in Myst's tone and glanced at their projection suspiciously.

What are you planning?

"Tomorrow evening. We leave in the morning," the Dusk Elf King replied. "By the next day, everyone should be safe on the mountain."

"So we'll plan to speak in three days, then? That gives everyone time to gather information and relocate refugees."

"Three days," Haldin agreed with a nod.

As Myst vanished before his eyes, Lonan glanced at Faedi, who wore a similar expression of concern. Her eyes narrowed slightly before she stood, brushing dust off her dress with a huff. They both knew his sibling was up to something.

49

On Seafaring and Seduction

"On the last turn of the moon, I was worried about preparing for winter—now I'm worried about war and sacrifices. I wonder if chaos is on our side or not."

Faedi

While she examined the map Haldin had given her, she hummed an old tune—a lullaby her mother used to sing, before everyone went their separate ways for the night. Lonan and Sophir had only returned to their rooms long enough to gather clothes before they rejoined her. However, she had not moved from her place beside the hearth and still wore the luxurious gown from the party.

She couldn't put her faith in prophecies, but she could share the information they had been given. She could hope that she would see Sylrie again. Those were facts—prophecies were no better than rumors.

"Are you alright?" Sophir's voice came from a distance as she studied the shoreline and various marks in the ocean.

She wasn't sure if she needed to memorize everything on the map for him, especially since she knew nothing about sailing.

"Faedi?" Lonan placed a gentle hand on her shoulder. "Everything alright?"

"Yes," she nodded absentmindedly before pausing to look at them with a smile. "I just want to show him the right thing."

"Right. You can't take that with you in the dream," he sighed, glancing back at Sophir. "Any advice?"

"If he's a talented sailor, he should only need basic information—but since most people don't sail near Rowdon's coast…he might be unfamiliar with the territory," Sophir said, approaching to look over her shoulder at the map.

"So he could sink." Faedi frowned.

"It would help to know what territory he's familiar with," Sophir chose his words carefully, and Faedi smiled at him in silent thanks. He didn't want to add to her worries. "I know some who port in Dewgate for trade take a wide south-eastern path and go around the Ceanea Isle. They don't turn north until the last possible moment. Few brave the eastern route."

"What's the eastern route?" She stared up at him and shook her head. It made sense to go east to end up west; it was open ocean.

"Sailors call it an abyss." He pointed at the map where gray was smudged over the parchment. "Dense fog, sharp rocks, pirates, and only the gods know what else. Some say it's haunted by Lafral's fleets, who attempted to sail west and attack Ashar during The Great War—like their capital."

Faedi looked back at the map, biting her lip anxiously. The eastern route did not sound like a good path for Sylrie, even if he was a talented sailor. No one among the freed Valorians had said he was inept, but the idea of him sailing through there if it could be avoided unsettled her.

She shook her head. "If he's sailing west, which way should he take? He didn't say where in Valoria he is."

"Here," Sophir pointed beside the Ceanea Isle. "Through the Helgi Tides and between their Isle and the ice hills. It is dangerous—but less than the abyss."

"What are the ice hills?" Lonan asked as he poured drinks.

"Remnants of the Udror Mountains—where Ighir's people are from. They were the peacekeepers between the Itmis and Helgi, but I don't know if there is any bad blood with his disappearance."

"How fast would he be here if he took that way?" Faedi asked, not fully trusting the idea of him sailing through the ice hills, though it sounded safer.

"It would depend on where he is starting and his ship, but… around five days from this pass here," Sophir pointed between the islands. "Maybe less if conditions are good enough, but you could expect to add anywhere from three to twelve days."

"How long in the abyss if he's on Valoria's eastern shore?" Lonan offered them goblets of wine.

"If he knows how to navigate there…" Sophir paused to sip the wine as he thought. "Eight to fifteen total."

Faedi sighed and sipped the wine while staring at the map. No matter his path, Sylrie could wind up in trouble. She had to trust his judgment and hope he would remain safe. She also hoped no one would follow him.

If he was in Valoria, where Ilos' cultists walked freely, they could follow his trail to reach Rowdon and attack safely.

"I think I should remain behind while you get the people from the border," Sophir sighed and leaned against the mantle. "There are some Gaelisks who still have their wings, and they need to learn how to fly. Ighir asked for my help—I want to try and contact my brothers and sister to come help as well. Extra Itmis could be useful if the cultists mean to stage a large attack on this continent… as would Gaelisks in the air."

"Do you think Jaref will trust Haldin's word if none of us are there?" Lonan paced the room. "And that hunt might be watching them from a distance."

"Maybe… you think we should go with him?" Faedi asked as she set down the map and began to fumble with her dress.

"I think it's an idea worth considering," he sat on the foot of the bed with a sigh. "We don't know what the cultists are doing… and if there are people here who might be on their side, it's worth investigating. They might be more active while Haldin is away."

Sophir rumbled from beside the fire, and Faedi looked between them. If there were enough loyalists of Ilos on the mountain, Haldin's first absence in centuries would be the perfect time to stage a coup. However, they might not try, since they had the mass group of Itmis and Gaelisks.

It was impossible to know what might happen.

"I want to explore more in the antechamber and examine the mountain's defenses," Faedi admitted as she finally managed to slip out of the dress and paused to think. "But we need to make sure everyone is comfortable… and I don't like the idea of splitting up."

"I'd be happy to explore ideas—in bed," Lonan told her as he took her in, and her skin burned as Sophir stared at her as well.

She scoffed. "You two are impossible."

"We should make sure you're good and tired," Sophir chuckled and stepped closer to trace his fingertips up her side. "That way, you'll stay asleep to speak with your brother."

He isn't wrong.

"Unless you're already tired or not in the mood," he raised his eyebrows and lowered himself as if to kiss her. However, he paused with his lips just out of reach with a rumble.

Faedi looked up at him as she bit her lip and then glanced at Lonan. Neither one of them moved or said anything. Instead, they watched her and waited. Even Sophir's hand on her skin stopped short of her breast.

"What's wrong?" She asked them worriedly.

"He's waiting to see if you're in the mood," Lonan announced from his perch on the bed. "So am I."

"And if I'm not?" She asked, despite the warmth that spread through her.

"Then we'll go to bed and ensure you're not disturbed." Sophir pulled away and took a step back.

Faedi grabbed his hand without thinking to stop him from moving further away and shook her head. Sylrie had not told her when he would be asleep or announced he was going to bed. There was no reason for her to immediately go to sleep, and further study of the map would not do her any good. What mattered was that they wanted her, and she wanted them.

With the unknown movements of the cultists and their allies over them and Zarae's announcement in her mind, Faedi didn't know how much longer they could take time to be together. Whatever moments of peace they had left, she wanted to be spent with them in whatever way she could have them.

"I want to," she told them as she tugged Sophir's hand to lead him toward the bed. "There'll never be a moment when I don't."

"Agreed," Lonan stood and wrapped his hand behind her neck to pull her against him. He trapped her lips against his with a groan. Then he pulled away enough to beckon Sophir closer with his free hand.

Faedi smiled shyly when Sophir kissed Lonan and wrapped his large arms around them to keep them in place. She took the opportunity to kiss Lonan's exposed neck while he was occupied and laughed when he gave a shuddered gasp.

Lonan squeezed the back of her neck as Sophir's tail wrapped around her waist. Once Sophir was done with him, Lonan nipped her bottom lip before he went to his knees. Then, Sophir moved behind her and gently rubbed her sides while Lonan repeated the gesture on her legs between kisses.

Lonan and Sophir's slow worship of Faedi's body felt like sweet torture. She couldn't tell how much time had passed as they caressed, kissed, and nuzzled nearly every inch of her, but to her mild displeasure, they avoided her most intimate areas. She knew it wasn't without reason, but each time they seemed about to touch her exactly where she wanted, they pulled away.

It wasn't until she whimpered helplessly that they finally laid her on the bed and undressed. Yet, their slow torment continued. She stole kisses and touches when she could, clung to them when her body trembled with need, and nearly begged before they relented.

As before, when she had been in heat, Lonan laid back on the bed, and she lowered herself onto him with a satisfied moan before Sophir positioned himself behind her. Unlike their first time, Sophir used his tail on Lonan while they moved together, all the while continuing to kiss and caress each other whenever possible.

It continued until they were all spent and barely able to move. Faedi used the last of her strength to tuck herself against Sophir as he stretched his arm under her head as a pillow. Lonan curled behind her, his legs tangled with hers and Sophir's, holding her close. Then, Sophir tugged the blankets over them, kissed her forehead, and rolled to wrap his arm around both of them.

"What was your idea?" Sophir whispered.

"That Lonan and I leave with Grandpa, but we circle back," she replied, shaking her head. "I don't know if it's a good idea."

"It might give any loyalists here a false sense of security," Lonan mumbled, kissing her shoulder. "I don't like it though. Too many things could go wrong… he might have mounts capable of flying out here, but we're not experienced riders on flying mounts."

"I could ask Ighir to follow you," Sophir suggested. "Say he's testing the wind for the Gaelisks?"

"He should stay with you and them," Faedi shook her head quickly.

"Do you think the risk is that high?" Sophir pulled back to look down at her.

She shrugged.

"Maybe?" She pulled him closer with a sigh. "Between the cultists, Zarae's claims, and everything else? I feel like I knew more when I knew nothing."

"There might be more answers in the antechamber… and maybe Sylrie knows something too. We should wait to decide until you talk to him," Lonan said with a nod. "If we stay, Torix should stay too. Haldin has his trusted people, but of all of the Dusk Elves, we only have him."

"I agree," Sophir murmured softly. "Get some rest… we'll figure things out tomorrow. Nothing else can be done today."

They settled down soon after, and Faedi listened to their breathing even out and gradually slow. However, she couldn't bring herself to sleep. Not when anxiety gripped her throat.

She knew nothing about the origins of the gods beyond what the priestesses at the temple had said. During the Age of Creation, gods were created by the Ancients for specific purposes—then, on rare occasions, mortals ascended to godhood. But the gods hadn't touched the earth since The Great War.

If we really are chosen by the gods, will they intervene if Ilos' followers try to kill us?

The thought lingered in her mind, making it impossible for her to drift off to sleep.

50

Wine and Wrath

Faedi

As the darkness in Faedi's mind cleared, she didn't find herself back in the same ashen wasteland as before. Instead, she was in the hidden chamber where she had seen the frozen tree. But now, the stone floor was covered with lush moss, and the tree's branches were in bloom with vibrant red flowers. Petals danced slowly in the air, as if trapped in a gentle breeze.

Thump.

"What?" Faedi tensed as the sound shook her to her core. "I woke them up—"

"It's the tree—not the Gaelisks."

She turned when Sylrie spoke from behind her. He smiled at her and didn't hesitate to embrace her in a tight hug. She clung to his cloak, burying her face in his chest to breathe in his scent. Even if he might smell different when she truly reunited with him, she would take what she could get.

"It's a heart tree," he said into her hair.

"The twins in the forest don't do this," she said, shaking her head and holding him tighter.

"Maybe this one's twin is dead. I read somewhere that all hearts are connected, but there's a stronger connection between pairs," he explained while stroking her back. "Are you alright?"

"I am... there's just been a lot I've learned," she pulled away just enough to look up at him. "The eclipse-born... we might be godlings, and some of us were chosen by the Ancients for some prophecy. We don't know where Ilos' followers are, Lady Callon was imprisoned, half of the elves here look like they want to kill Lonan, there was an uproar at the party that I think Grandpa planned, the Gaelisks need Sophir to teach them how to fly, we need to help the settlement on the border, Myst is up to something, Zarae either makes perfect sense or none at all, and I don't know what route you're taking—you could wind up in an abyss with pirates, or killed by Helgi, followed by cultists, or—"

"Slow down," Sylrie chuckled as he sat on the ground, urging her to join him. "We'll start with the simple ones first… there's a Helgi on my crew, Danik. He's never failed to get me through the tides before. He's eclipse-born too. Now, I know Lonan, but who is Sophir and Zarae?"

"Sophir is an Astral Itmis—the High Knight of Dewgate and…" Faedi trailed off when she realized she hadn't told him anything about herself. "Lonan, Sophir, and I are bonded—more than just a Watcher and Guardian or Warden. We—I…"

"You're in love with them," he touched the ceremonial tattoo on her arm and smiled.

"I—" Faedi released a shaky sigh. "Lonan and I had our bonding ceremony before we left for Rowdon. Sophir was… a happy accident."

"And they love you?" His eyes lifted to hers, and she nodded silently.

"Good. I know I don't have a right to make threats since we've been separated for so long, but… I learned a few things in Ashar I wouldn't hesitate to do to them if they hurt you."

Faedi laughed despite the tears welling in her eyes and shook her head. Twenty-two years, and he was still the same. He was still her overprotective Warden.

"Is Zarae the one with the Gaelisks?" he asked softly, and she nodded again.

"Is she a seer?" he continued.

"I don't know, really. She's the one who said we were chosen by the gods and talked about the prophecy," Faedi explained, watching a red petal land in his hair. It matched his eyes.

"Alright," he sighed and scratched the scruff on his cheek. "I know cultists are gathering in the east. A lot of them are moving to the port cities on the western coast—we left before their ships could block ours."

"I thought you said you were leaving just a few hours ago." Faedi blinked up at him, shaking her head when he grinned.

"Didn't say where I was leaving from."

Her jaw went slack as her heart pounded in her chest. "Where are you?"

"With Danik at the helm, we'll be out of the Helgi Tides and in Rowdon's waters by morning." His eyes twinkled mischievously. "We'll port in Rowdon in two—three days if the wind is against us."

"I thought you… how?" Faedi exhaled, her disbelief evident.

"Funny how finding out your baby sister is really alive will make you finish a job faster," he chuckled and shook his head. "Technically, I was in Valoria… just already leaving. We were on the Isle, but… I was anxious to tell you where we really were."

"I don't blame you," Faedi shook her head quickly. "I asked Da if I could tell you where I was before. I only did it because he said it was safe."

"But now that we're on our way…" he looked away with a sigh.

Faedi smiled up at him before looking down at the floor and starting to draw in the dirt and moss. It was a crude recreation of Rowdon's southern shore, and she could only hope it was good enough for him. Trail maps were one thing, but she was no cartographer.

"Grandpa says the ports are here," she pointed where he instructed her to tell him. "He's leaving in the morning to get everyone from the settlement at the border. I'm worried though… that someone might take the opportunity to stage a coup while he's gone."

"Are you going with him?" he asked as he leaned over to examine the map.

"Lonan thinks we should stay behind with Sophir while he tries to teach the Gaelisks to fly," Faedi shook her head and glanced at the tree. "I suggested leaving with Grandpa but circling back."

"You said there was an uproar at the party?" He sat back and crossed his arms. His arms were larger than Sophir's.

"People started shouting, and guards were taking people prisoner before Grandpa took us to an antechamber to talk to Myst," Faedi told him with a nod. "I think they were removing the memory spell from everyone. He said that the only people who didn't have spells on them were him, Torix, Fenkas, and Aladia."

"Ladi… I remember her," he nodded and scratched his scruff again. "I think… you should stay, make a show of Grandpa leaving you in charge. Even if there's a group of loyalists on the mountain, you have an army loyal to you."

"To Grandpa," Faedi corrected him and narrowed her eyes when he shook his head.

"To you. He didn't wake up the Gaelisks—you did. They owe you their lives," Sylrie raised his eyebrows and smiled. "Stay together and if the worst happens, meet me at the port with them. Or have him train them at a nearby location, just in case."

"You have an army with you too?" Faedi raised an eyebrow.

"Danik can call on one. Ilos won't have the mountain, and I'll be damned if he has you," his growl vibrated in Faedi's chest. "Once I'm there, they're never separating us again."

Faedi stared up at him, her lip trembling slightly. "Promise?"

"I swear to the Oath Keeper," he took her hand and squeezed it. "And on The Ancients… but I'll be sure to give you some privacy to be with your bonded."

Faedi laughed as she pulled her hand away and shook her head. "Oh gods, you can still ruin a moment, can't you?"

"I expect the same treatment when I bed someone," he winked at her with a chuckle.

Faedi rolled her eyes as she stood. "I'm going to wake up now."

Sylrie mimicked her movements, shaking his shoulders while he laughed. Despite her feigned offense, she didn't deny him when he opened his arms for another hug. His laughter slowly faded as he embraced her until the only thing she could hear was the steady thump of the tree.

"Faedi?" His whisper was distant.

She shivered as her skin grew cold. "Hmm?"

"Keep Da with you. Don't trust any other wolves."

Faedi grumbled as light filtered through the windows, rolling over to hide her face against Sophir's chest. She wondered if she could drift back to sleep, but the faint knock at her door told her it wouldn't be possible. Aladia tiptoed inside, followed by a pair of servants carrying breakfast trays, hurrying about the room as they picked up their discarded clothes.

"I can get that," Faedi said, sitting up and clutching her blanket to her chest.

"I'm sure you could," Aladia smiled, shaking her head. "However, your grandfather wants to meet with you before he leaves. He called it a finale to last night's show."

"What happened last night?" Faedi glanced at Lonan and Sophir as they stirred.

"The memory spells your mother placed on everyone else were weaker and not tied to a glamour—he had them removed last night. He had his guards watching the crowd," Aladia explained as she passed the clothes to the servants after setting down the trays. "Go get Prince Lonan and Lord Sophir some clothes."

"I don't think I want a dress today," Faedi said, grabbing one of the furs to wrap around herself before climbing over Sophir to get out of bed.

As she uncovered the trays of food, she noticed a large plate with enough to feed all three of them—cooked eggs, sausage, cheese, fruit, and bread. She hesitated, remembering how Haldin had tested her food the night before.

"I test all of your food," Aladia informed her before approaching and taking a piece with a smile. "Don't worry; anything I bring you has been inspected closely. I made an oath to your mother to protect you—I swore it on the ancients and the Oath Keeper."

"Grandpa thinks there are loyalists here?" Faedi smiled at Aladia before eating the meat and pouring herself a glass of wine.

"He's had suspicions for years—but he played his part well."

"What was his part?" Lonan asked as he sat up.

"The distraught father overwhelmed by grief and hatred," Aladia said, bowing before she rummaged through the wardrobe. "He wasn't a threat to Ilos' followers if he appeared disinterested in the world's affairs."

"That's what everyone thinks about him," Sophir commented, his voice deeper with sleep as he sat beside Lonan.

"Only those closest to him know differently—and me. Everything started when the eventides bloomed here again," Aladia nodded, taking plates of food to the bed. "Plans, backup plans, and more plans for those. We knew we were on borrowed time."

Faedi picked out clothes from the wardrobe and sighed in relief when she saw they were more casual than the night before. As requested, Aladia had even picked out a pair of pants. They were lined with soft fur and trimmed with indigo and silver.

"I remember her showing one to me in the courtyard," Faedi said as she stepped behind the dressing screen in the corner, smiling when Sophir rumbled his displeasure. "She said they bloomed after Sylrie and I were born. She said we were going to protect them."

"She spoke to someone from Dewgate years ago, before you were born, who told her that their return would bring the Gaelisk's awakening and the return to our home...and the return of the gods."

She paused as she fastened the buttons on Faedi's shirt. Aladia had never mentioned prophecies before, but she had told Faedi that she was sworn to secrecy until asked. Faedi wondered if her request to remove her memory spells might earn her more information.

"Which gods?" Faedi called from behind the screen.

"I don't know. The woman she spoke to didn't tell her. She only said the gods would be accounted for—something about seven crowns."

"Did this woman have a name?" Sophir asked. "Or do you know what she looked like?"

"I don't know. She looked like one of us but didn't smell right—I can't recall her name… I'm sorry; her accent was thick—like a Faunan, but also...not."

Faedi stepped around from the screen as the servants returned to deposit Lonan and Sophir's clothes before hurrying off with deep bows. She smiled at them before her attention shifted back to Aladia and her bonded. While Lonan seemed interested in Aladia's retelling, Sophir's brows were tight.

Faedi tilted her head. "What is it?"

"Did she have horns?" Sophir asked, and Faedi watched his skin pale when Aladia nodded.

"What do you know?" Faedi asked quietly.

"Yes, which is strange. I've only seen Itmis and Vael with horns like that."

Faedi picked up her glass and sipped her wine. "Do you know them?"

"Maybe. There was one time—a few years ago, Lady Callon was upset about something and spoke with an accent. I don't think she's a Haxan, and Ravyn said something years ago...he was excited to give her a bottle of Vaelien wine."

"Plenty of people have accents," Lonan remarked.

"She has horns like that," Sophir murmured. "I felt them once when her glamour was weak, and there was a time her skin was darker—her eyes were different as well."

And now she's imprisoned.

There was something else. Faedi could tell by the way Sophir looked away and kept his brows pinched together. He was worried—and angry. The look in his eyes was similar to the one he had when Faedi burned the plagued person in the forest.

"We'll finish getting ready and meet with Grandpa. Where should we see him?" Faedi turned her attention to Aladia and managed a polite smile.

"In the throne room."

"Thank you—I'd like to speak with you later, once things are squared away?" Faedi glanced at Lonan and Sophir, who remained in bed, wondering if it was out of modesty or something else.

"Of course; I'm never far. I'll be just outside the throne room; all you need to do is call," Aladia bowed to them before hurrying out of the room.

Faedi waited several moments, allowing Lonan and Sophir to get out of bed and dress themselves. While she waited, she ate a bit more and washed the food down with wine when it sat like a rock in her gut. She didn't know why Sophir's anger bothered her the way it did, not when it was not directed at her, but she couldn't shake the expression from her mind.

"What is it?" she finally managed to ask once Sophir stepped beside her to pour his own wine.

"I consider Lady Callon a dear friend. Only she knew I was an Itmis," he rumbled softly, sighing when Faedi silently urged him to continue with a nod.

"The time I referenced, it was after the first time Lord Blavier demanded to watch us." Sophir downed his glass of wine with a grimace before continuing. "He had us bed one another for his entertainment—said we were too stressed with our duties, and...afterward, she ranted about how she 'had not whored herself out for the city just for him to tear it all apart.' I could tell by her behavior that it was not the first time he commanded that of her."

There was a long pause where the room fell silent. Faedi's heart pounded in her ears as she looked back at the food. Whatever appetite she had was gone.

"I hope the bastard is a walking corpse by the time we get there," Lonan growled as he tugged on his boots.

"I doubt that will be his fate," Sophir shook his head before doing the same.

"Evil people rarely get the endings they deserve." Faedi turned away from the bloody meat on the platter and stormed out of the room. "We shouldn't keep Grandpa waiting."

As she walked, her mind drifted to the anger she had seen in Sophir's eyes and how it mixed with shame and guilt. Her heart broke for him—and for Lady Callon. She knew the woman was good, a servant and protector of the people like Sophir. And she, along with Sophir, had been hurt by Lord Blavier for some twisted sexual entertainment.

"Can you teach me things from Ashar?" Faedi asked.

"What happened? Are you alright?"

"I'm fine—but there's a bastard in Dewgate."

"You don't like hurting people."

"I want him to hurt."

Two breaths of silence.

"I'll let you watch."

51

A Crown of Eventides

Faedi

*S*he'd barely calmed herself as they reached the throne room, her heart racing at the sight of Haldin standing at the center, dressed for travel and lightly armored. A wide smile broke across his face when he saw them, and Faedi hesitated long enough to bow, biting her lip as she approached him. Years had passed since she truly knew him, yet the urge to cling to him like a child was overwhelming. She longed to feel his hand tussle her hair again, to bask in that protective warmth she feared she might never feel again. It was the same longing she felt whenever she looked at Torix.

"Any news of our friends on the sea?" Haldin raised his eyebrows, and Faedi glanced anxiously at the guards and others in the room. But she relaxed as she breathed in their scents—everyone but Torix was a bear.

"They will arrive soon. We're to keep our eyes on the southeast—towards the Helgi Tides," Faedi replied, allowing a smile to bloom at the corners of her mouth. She watched as both Haldin and Torix grinned. "He mentioned possibly having freed slaves… and more eclipse-born."

"Are there any at the encampment?" Haldin asked as he passed a parchment to one of his guards. Faedi shook her head.

"We were told that they took newborn eclipse-born from the work camps in Valoria, and none of the farmers from Dewgate are there."

Haldin clenched his jaw and shared a brief, intense glance with Torix. The moment felt heavy, but he turned his focus back to Faedi, then to Sophir and Lonan behind her. Slowly, his expression softened, and he sighed.

"I prefer for the lot of you to stay here, but… there are concerns that they might panic when we arrive," he told them.

"You only want one of us to go—and you want me, specifically, to stay here?" Faedi frowned, her heart beginning to race again.

"I can go… Sophir needs to help the Gaelisks. It's only a couple of days."

"No." Faedi turned to look at Lonan, shaking her head subtly. It was easy to state the obvious, but she did not want them separated. Since they had bonded, they rarely spent more than a few hours apart.

"What if the people traveling with Grandpa try to kill you?" She raised her eyebrows at him. "You could tell the Watchers there that they're coming and then stay here."

"What if he needs help finding their exact location, or the Watchers there fear the worst and think he killed us?" He countered, placing a hand on her shoulder. "I'll go and be back in a few days. You'll hardly miss me."

"But what if I go instead, and you stay with Sophir?" She pressed, frowning deeper when Haldin quickly dismissed her idea.

"Given the oaths made, an heir must remain on the mountain."

Gods' forsaken oaths.

Faedi glanced at Sophir for some kind of support, but he merely shook his head with a sigh. He couldn't argue with the King—no one could, even if she wished she could.

"Three days?" She asked, looking up at Haldin with a glimmer of hope.

"We should reach there by nightfall," he replied with a nod. "As long as we can move them safely and quickly, everyone should be back by then."

"Your bonded will be by my side and under my personal protection until we return," Haldin promised gently as he stepped closer. "And you will take your seat on the throne and protect the mountain."

"Da stays?" Faedi glanced at Torix, her nerves calming when he nodded. She couldn't help but notice the smile tugging at his lips when he recognized what she called him.

She lowered her head and nodded, sighing. She needed to find out more about the oath that required an heir to remain, but she would have to ask later. Her mind felt fogged with worry about what might happen while Lonan and Haldin were gone. Something terrible could occur to them, or it could happen on the mountain.

"Alright," she finally said, looking back at Haldin and hugging her arms to her chest. "What should I do while you're gone?"

"Torix will walk you through preparations, and I want you to try and reach out to our other allies."

"We have allies?" Faedi raised an eyebrow, shaking her head slightly in disbelief.

"We do," Haldin smiled at her, tousling her hair with a chuckle. "We might have closed off the mountain for protection, but we kept some alliances beyond what the world believes. Zarae can assist you with that."

He tapped his nose, and Faedi nodded, understanding that he wanted her to return to the antechamber. She thought back to the crystal he had used and wondered who else he might have been in communication with. He had neglected relations with the Umbrals for so long that she had assumed he hadn't spoken to anyone from outside of Rowdon for just as long.

"Come with me," he motioned for them to follow, and Faedi grabbed Lonan's hand, unwilling to let him go until she absolutely had to.

Haldin led them through the castle toward the stables, with the guards and soldiers from the throne room trailing closely behind. Faedi paid them little mind, instead glancing around at the stone walls, memories of her childhood flooding her thoughts. She remembered how she used to race through the halls whenever Torix and her mother took her to see the animals. Sylrie had always been faster, but Torix had always let her mount the animals first.

A smile crept across her face at the memory as she followed Haldin's back. He had given her her first flying mount, a pegasus, before she had even learned to ride a wolf. Her mother had forbidden her to ride it until she could stay balanced on both a wolf and a horse, but Haldin had caught her many times in the stables, feeding the pegasus carrots and sugar.

The scent of fresh hay hit her as they crossed the dark wooden threshold of the stables. Whinnies and barks greeted them as they entered the massive royal stables, where stable hands bowed at their approach. This was the feeling she had been missing. It had only been days, maybe weeks, since she had been home with Lonan and all their creatures, but it felt like years.

"You're taking pegasi?" Faedi asked, noticing that none of the flying mounts were in their stalls. "Or something else?"

"Yes," Haldin glanced back at her with a smile. "I don't have as many as I would like. It could take a few trips to get everyone here, but we will ensure it's done as safely and quickly as possible."

"I assume children first?" Sophir chimed in from the other side of Lonan.

"Yes, and any sick or injured they might have," Haldin confirmed with a nod.

"Make sure Emmaline is alright," Faedi said to Lonan, smiling when he squeezed her hand.

"Of course," he nodded, glancing at Sophir. "She can't fly yet, can she?"

"No…" Sophir shook his head, clenching his jaw.

Faedi's brow creased as she studied his face. Her thoughts turned to the Gaelisks and their treatments. Only the young still had their wings, and a growl began to build in her throat. She stared up at Sophir, her worry deepening. "Does she have her wings?"

"Jaref said they're removed when they're infants in the camps."

Even if it had happened before Emmaline was old enough to remember, Faedi's blood boiled.

Lonan wrapped his arm around her shoulder, squeezing gently, and guided her to follow Haldin into an open clearing on the other side of the stables. Six men were already mounted on pegasi, surrounded by a mass of guards. Faedi stopped when Haldin turned to face them, her frown deepening as he gave her a sad smile.

"I know you don't like this idea, Faedi, and I know you don't care about fancy things, but I have something for you," Haldin said, reaching into his cloak and pulling out something wrapped in black silk. "If you're sitting on the throne in my stead, you should look the part of a true Guardian of the Tide."

Faedi took the bundle and stared at Haldin for a moment before unwrapping it slowly. Her hands trembled as she caught her first glimpse of metal, and she took a deep breath to steady herself as blue gems were revealed. She glanced back at Haldin, and he smiled, nodding for her to continue.

"I thought I'd never be able to put it on you."

Faedi released a shaky sigh as she fully uncovered the crown of thin platinum vines. Sapphires, diamonds, and other precious stones had been laid into the metal to craft flowers—eventides. Lonan squeezed her shoulder again, and she traced one of the flowers before managing a small smile at Haldin.

"I hope you hurry," Faedi said, offering the crown before whispering, "There's still a Warden to crown."

"That there is," he replied, smiling as he accepted the crown and placed it on her head.

The men on the pegasi bowed their heads, while the soldiers on the ground took a knee. Rustling behind her caught her attention, and she glanced over her shoulder to see the other guards and soldiers kneeling as well. Then Lonan's arm left her shoulder, and she turned to watch him and Sophir mimic the gesture, their gazes locked on her, filled with pride.

I believe both of you did plenty of worshiping last night, Faedi teased, grinning at them. Lonan's cheeks flushed, while Sophir bit his lips together, looking away with a chuckle. "I expect a kiss before you leave, my bonded."

"It would be my pleasure," Lonan winked at her before standing and wrapping his arms around her, capturing her lips with his.

Faedi clung to him for as long as she could, tangling her fingers in his hair. She breathed him in, taking everything she could before pulling away as tears stung the corners of her eyes. She blinked them away, forcing a smile.

"Ancients keep you," she whispered as he rubbed her cheeks with his thumbs.

"And you," he replied, kissing the tip of her nose. "I expect to see no less than twelve animals running amok in the castle when I get back."

Faedi laughed and shook her head as he turned to Sophir. She watched them kiss and share a similar embrace, but Sophir's brows creased as if he were in pain before he released him.

Without thinking, Faedi quickly hugged Haldin, not caring if it was somehow unfitting in front of an audience. She had never cared about appearances on the mountain as a child, and she certainly didn't plan to care as an adult. Royal protocol be damned; he was her grandfather first and King second.

Haldin chuckled, returning the embrace. His large arms almost wholly engulfed her, and she buried her face in his chest, sighing as he kissed the top of her head. Then he pulled away and smiled down at her.

"I expect you to provide Lonan updates while we are away," he glanced between them.

"Of course," Faedi replied, relaxing a little. She hoped the soul speech would lessen the sting of his absence.

"Don't give Aladia too much trouble with beasts in the castle—but it does need a bit of livening up," he added, a mischievous twinkle in his eyes. "There are young ones fresh from their mothers. Have the hands show them to you— we will need more mounts who are loyal."

Faedi nodded and stepped back. Haldin turned to Lonan and directed him to the pegasi. Sophir quickly wrapped his arm around her shoulder, holding her close as they mounted and took off into the snowstorm. They vanished from view sooner than she wanted, and she took a breath to calm herself.

Ancients, don't let that be the last time I see them.

"When he said mounts?" Sophir asked, pulling her from her thoughts as the area around the arena grew silent.

"Bears, wolves, elk, likely more pegasi. If it's the same as before, he might have some black griffins…there are Gaelisks without wings, who knows how many with Scarred, and whoever else Grandpa has for allies. We need trained mounts and armor to fit everyone," Faedi explained, turning to see Torix approach with a frown. He looked as displeased as she felt.

"And I thought the menagerie at the cottage was colorful," Sophir mused, bringing a smile to Faedi's face.

"Don't tell me there's already bad news," Faedi told Torix as he came closer.

"No, I just don't like seeing you upset," he shook his head, nodding toward the crowd. "They're waiting for your command."

"Grandpa didn't leave them with orders?" Faedi asked, scanning the crowd. He was right; all eyes were on her, and she resisted the urge to shy away from their gazes.

"He did—the orders are to follow yours."

Faedi looked back at Torix, frowning. Haldin had followed along with Sylrie's idea to make a show, even without her needing to mention it. This was grander than simply placing a crown on her head; he hadn't just left her to warm the throne—he had left her to command it.

This will either go well—or I will mess everything up.

52

The Burden of Oaths

Faedi

*M*aps and reports lay spread over the table at the foot of the dais in the throne room. They had more than enough stores to feed everyone—and another city's population—through the winter. Supplies of furs, metals, and magical ingredients were plentiful, but she couldn't shake the feeling of being overwhelmed. She didn't know where to begin, and everyone was looking to her for direction.

Keep it together.

"Get me a count of how many Itmis and Gaelisks there are," she instructed one of the bear soldiers. He bowed in response, and she watched him leave the room while others stood nearby, waiting for her next command. There was so much to consider, but she hesitated to speak freely. Even though Haldin had vetted some of the soldiers and guards, she couldn't be sure of anyone else's loyalty. She doubted anyone would admit to being a loyalist to Ilos' cultists if she were to ask.

"Rooms and supplies need to be prepared for those coming from the border," she nodded. "Some may be sick or injured. I want healers ready for them."

"Yes, Your Highness," a robed woman in the corner replied, bowing before ushering two other robed individuals out with her.

Faedi turned her mind to Sylrie. *"How many people do you have with you?"*

"I have a crew of twenty and a mass of roughly thirty Helgi escorting us. Danik can call for more if they're needed," Sylrie answered.

"You have Helgi with you?" Faedi asked, her curiosity piqued.

"Yes?"

"Give me a moment, please." She straightened and turned to Sophir and Ighir, who were waiting nearby. "You said you could get a message to your siblings

through the Helgi? One that won't draw attention?"

"Yes, their songs travel further and faster than ravens—and most can't understand it," Sophir replied, stepping closer to the table. "Why do you ask?"

"I have an idea," Faedi said, a grin spreading across her face. "What do you want them to sing?"

"Just that they need to come here." He narrowed his eyes. "Does your brother know a Helgi?"

"He says they're escorting his ship." Faedi's smile widened as she saw him chuckle and shake his head. "Can you give me updates on the Gaelisks?"

"Tell him my siblings were last on an island north of Dietrich—at the temple there," Sophir instructed.

Faedi nodded, watching him bow and turn to Ighir, signaling for him to lead the way. After they left, Torix stepped beside her.

"I don't like them leaving you alone," he murmured softly.

"We can make up for lost time," Faedi replied with a smile. "You can tell me if I say or do something wrong."

"You're doing well so far," Torix assured her, placing a hand on her shoulder. He leaned in to whisper in her ear. "Tell him the ports are open, and we want more fighters. I'll explain more tonight."

"Sophir has a message that he needs Helgi to send. He wants his siblings to come here; they're on Dietrich's northern island at the temple there. Torix says he wants more fighters and will tell me why later," Faedi relayed.

"I'll tell Danik to call for more Helgi and see what I can do about bringing in more mercs," Sylrie promised.

"If any of Ilos' zealots somehow make it up the mountain, they'll attack with fire. Any crops that are ready to harvest should be preserved," Faedi announced, glancing at Torix. "I also want increased patrols around the peaks and additional water prepared and stored."

Several more people bowed and left the room, and Faedi rubbed her face in an attempt to relieve her tension. She knew how defenses worked in the Mire, but she was too young to know anything about the mountain. It seemed impossible to erect an ironwood wall around it.

Unless we use ice.

"How many weavers are there who are adept with earth magic?" she asked, searching through the parchments on the table. "Do we have ironwood?"

"What are you thinking?" Torix asked as he joined her, looking at the maps.

"A wall—or a few," Faedi mumbled, just as a soldier stepped forward and bowed.

"Yes?"

"We have ironwood. Most of our weavers with that sort of magic man the crops and assist the healers with their herbs."

"Leave enough with the crops to supervise the harvest, but I want the rest to assist in crafting walls," Faedi instructed, grabbing a quill to sketch a map of the mountain. "The ironwood will support the wall and protect it from magical attacks. If they grow eventides on it, they should serve as a deterrent as well. I don't want too many entrances…"

"I'll have guards posted to protect them and the weavers while they work," the soldier assured her, bowing as he accepted the map from her.

"Walls should be started where civilians are most vulnerable, then move to protect food and supplies, and then the barracks. Everything else is secondary and well within the mountain," Faedi explained, raising her eyebrows when the soldier stared at her in surprise. "What?"

"You don't wish for the castle to be walled first?"

"No." She shook her head, gesturing to the paper. "I want civilians protected first, then what will keep us fed and warm. Those who protect us should be protected afterward. I also want evacuation routes planned for any civilians who don't live in the mountain. If the walls fall, they need to come here."

Torix hummed, and Faedi hoped it was approval as the soldier departed, shouting for his men to follow him. Once they were alone, save for a handful of guards, Faedi turned to face her father. He smiled at her, nodding in approval.

"Well done," he said. "That will win you some favor."

"I didn't do it for favor," Faedi replied, placing her hands on her hips with a huff. "I did it because the cultists will burn everything and everyone in their path. Anyone who can't defend themselves should have protection—a buffer to give them time to reach a location where there are people who can fight for them."

"I know that's why. I know you value life," Torix sighed, giving her a one-armed hug. "But the soldiers and civilians don't. No one here knows that you've witnessed what they're capable of before. That order to protect them first—that will win people over."

"Doesn't Grandpa protect civilians?" Faedi asked, studying the table.

"He does, but you're new. Even if memories were restored, it's hard for some not to hold a grudge. You've been gone for years. No one knows what kind of person you are."

Faedi glanced at the guards who remained and caught their approving looks before they quickly turned their eyes away. It felt strange to think about gaining favor this way, and she was uncertain how she felt about it. She didn't expect anyone to trust or adore her as their heir, but a desire to protect people seemed too simple to earn anyone's loyalty. Yet, she couldn't ignore the potential benefits.

Anyone loyal to Ilos might be swayed to join them, and if she was lucky, any sympathizers might rethink their allegiance to the cultists. They could report anyone who aimed to attack from within the mountain. Some conflict could be avoided.

Faedi sat at the long wooden table in the throne room, surrounded by reports, supply lists, and half-empty ink bottles. The golden flicker of the torches on the walls illuminated the parchment, but their light did little to lift the weight on her shoulders. Eyes were on her, as they had been all day, making it even harder to focus.

For hours, she scratched her quill across paper, calculating rations, checking supplies, and sorting through endless scrolls of numbers. She kept separate notes for Sylrie's crew, knowing it wasn't safe to share those details openly yet. Her braid had long since unraveled, and strands of dark hair kept falling into her face. She absently tucked them back as she shifted her attention to another column of figures.

"You should eat, Your Highness," Aladia said gently, placing a plate beside her.

Faedi sighed and leaned back in her chair, nodding at her. The sight of the food made her smile; it was all finger foods—no utensils required. The scent of meats and cheeses reached her, and her stomach growled, flushing her cheeks.

"I didn't realize how long I've been at this," she admitted, laughing softly at herself.

"From what I hear, everyone is impressed," Aladia replied with a grin.

"Da said something similar," Faedi said, picking up a piece of meat and glancing at her. "Sit with me, please. I've had people hovering over me all day."

"Of course, Highness," Aladia replied quickly, settling into the chair beside her. "Do you have battle experience?"

"I was taught in the Mire and helped defend Dewgate during the siege ten years ago," Faedi said, nodding as she accepted the wine Aladia poured. "Lonan and I both did."

"What's it like there?" Aladia leaned forward, resting her arms on the table, her wide smile encouraging Faedi to share.

"Loud and crowded," Faedi said, shaking her head. "I've never been one for crowds, but it's vibrant in its way, like here."

"You prefer the forest?"

"I do," Faedi admitted. "Dewgate felt suffocating, with the packed markets and noisy taverns. The only peace I found there was in the stables or the temple."

The city still left a bitter taste in Faedi's memories. After the war, Blavier had let too much slide—guards ignored violence and theft as long as it didn't impact the wealthier districts.

"So you don't plan to stay in the castle when we return?" Aladia's question caught Faedi off guard, and she shook her head.

"I don't know. Grandpa is King, and Lonan is heir to the Umbramire. I'm not sure where that leaves me," she admitted with a sigh.

"It puts you wherever you want," Aladia said with a wink. "But wherever you go, there will be more people than you're used to."

Faedi narrowed her eyes. "What do you mean?"

"Your grandfather will require guards for you," Aladia explained.

"Right… is that why they're over there watching me?" Faedi nodded toward the two guards stationed near the dais.

"Yes, Highness," Aladia confirmed, her soft laughter breaking the tension.

Faedi studied the guards as she took another bite of food. One was a bear—she could tell from his scent—but the other was harder to place. He smelled like a predator, though.

"Do you have names?" Faedi asked, raising her brows at them.

"Yes, Highness. I am Nare, and this is Bjorn," the one on the left replied with a bow.

"Bjorn," Faedi turned to the other man, studying him closely. A shimmer of glamour cloaked him. "Should I ask why you're glamoured to appear as a Dusk Elf?"

"You have the nose of a bear, Highness," he said with a smirk, bowing again. "I am here as my oath requires."

"An oath to whom?" Faedi asked, raising an eyebrow.

"To the Oath-keeper," he replied. "They want the mountain protected, and since you and your bonded are the first here—beyond Lady Zarae—that includes protecting you as well."

"So the Oath-keeper isn't aligned with Ilos?"

"No, Highness. They despise him and his allies, just as I do. Like many, we've endured their torture."

His voice carried a low growl as he spoke about the cultists, and it twisted something in Faedi's chest. She'd heard stories before, but hearing it firsthand made it feel heavier.

"And you're going to follow me everywhere?" Faedi asked, glancing at him and Aladia, who looked stunned.

"I have since you arrived," he replied, a crooked smile tilting his lips. "How do you think King Haldin and Torix found you so quickly when you woke the Gaelisks?"

Faedi narrowed her eyes, remembering that night. No one had been close enough for her to smell them—or so she'd thought.

"It's getting late, Highness," Aladia interrupted her thoughts. "You should head to the chamber."

Faedi nodded, standing and gathering the food and wine. "Right."

The sun had set, painting the sky with vibrant hues of orange and purple. Faedi knew it would be a long night, but she didn't mind the work. Anything was better than the gnawing anxiety as she waited for news from Lonan.

She didn't even know if their soul speech would reach this far, but she could only hope it worked as Sylrie's communication did.

53

Seven Hearts, Seven Realms

"They'll be lucky if any of them fly unaccompanied by the next moon—but if they learn to fly in these winds…they'll be able to fly anywhere."

Sophir

He sat on an icy hill overlooking the training fields, his wings unfurling behind him as he lazily caught the breeze. Below, the Gaelisks were working with the Dusk Elf soldiers, and he took a moment to rest his mind. It had been a long day of diving into multiple minds, preparing them for flight, and he felt utterly exhausted.

Beside him, Ighir stretched out in the snow, his arms tucked behind his head, a contented smile on his face. The wind tousled his white hair, almost perfectly blending with the snow. Sophir silently wondered if they would have enjoyed such moments together if Ighir hadn't been frozen in time.

"Do you think it's working?" Sophir asked, his sharp features softening as he stared up at the sky.

"I've prepared them mentally for flight and shown them how the wind turns, but we won't know until we get them in the air," Ighir replied. Sophir sighed and rubbed his face. "I just hope it's enough. My mind is… distracted with Lonan's absence."

Ighir chuckled beside him, but Sophir turned to him with a silent warning. Laughter was the last thing he wanted to hear while one of his bonded was so far away. Faedi was even too far for his liking, but flight and fight lessons couldn't happen in the throne room.

"Your bonded are capable people," Ighir said. "More than I thought originally."

"You have no idea," Sophir replied, smiling as he turned his attention back to the Gaelisks. "They've done nothing but surprise me since I met them."

Ighir fell silent for a moment, staring at the sky and the Itmis that circled above. A storm continued to rage around the mountains, but there was none where people trained and resided.

"What's your plan if this doesn't work?" He asked, sitting up to examine the field with Sophir.

"We teach them the slow way," Sophir shrugged.

"That could take months."

"We'll assign each an Itmis to assist them," Sophir said, nodding to himself. "The others can be trained on the pegasi Faedi ordered to be trained. If the message can reach my siblings fast enough, and the winds are favorable, they could be here before the week ends."

"You mentioned your sister has other talents?" Ighir offered him a skin of mead. "Do you think she may be able to reach their ancestors?"

"She might… and I would prefer them here anyway," Sophir replied. He didn't want them to be alone if there was a war. The priests at the temple could only help so much.

"You're worried the others could be eclipse-born?" Ighir quirked a brow.

"We are conscious the moment we are made—are we not?" Sophir mimicked his expression as he took a sip of the mead.

"We are, and the births of the Gaelisks were not tracked…there could be dozens of assumed god-touched here." Ighir rubbed his chin, looking thoughtful.

"I fear the gems they make are not the only reason why they were hunted," Sophir admitted. "Unless their greed truly runs that deep."

"Zarae hasn't mentioned anyone else being eclipse-born," Ighir shook his head before frowning. "However, her knowledge is fickle at best."

"Why is that? I've noticed she doesn't always seem present," Sophir remarked, shaking his head. Her behavior was unusual and troubling.

"I believe it's from her trauma," Ighir sighed. "She was a mess when I found her, and she barely made progress before we were frozen… Ilos is not kind."

Sophir frowned, offering him the mead again. "Do you know what happened to her?"

"Her bonded abandoned her…"

"He was eclipse-born?" Sophir's frown deepened as Ighir glared ahead.

"He is, and all fingers point to him siding with Ilos. I don't know what he was offered, but Zae was imprisoned, and I don't want to know what was done to her." His growl rumbled, shaking the air. "Whatever he was promised was not worth the damage done to that girl."

Sophir turned his attention back to the training field while Ighir took a drink from the skin. Ragna's face had remained unchanged during his communication with Zarae, but Ighir's added details shifted the context. Ragna was free; Zarae's focus wouldn't have been on protecting her.

Either it was on her bonded or on the other eclipse-born Ilos' followers had under lock and key.

"I could try to connect with their divine nature—unlock it," Sophir suggested after the silence grew too heavy.

"Have you tried that with your bonded?" Ighir's eyes were on him, and Sophir shook his head.

"No, but I think I saw Faedi connect when I was in her memories." He didn't look at his uncle.

"When she spoke in Ancient tongue and her eyes changed?"

"Yes… however, from what I witnessed in that memory, it seemed she was using shadows and not nature magic." Zarae had made it seem like Faedi was chosen by the god of the forest, but it didn't add up.

"The forest casts its own shadows. The earth is connected to everything—all realms," Ighir explained. "If she is chosen by the forest, she might be able to access multiple magics… the same could be true for you and Lonan."

"And that's why Ilos' zealots want eclipse-born sacrificed?" Sophir frowned at the thought.

"If there is some magic to give your lives and abilities to Ilos… he could kill another god or several."

Sophir nodded slowly, considering the implications.

"Why would he want to kill a god?" It didn't make sense to kill a god unless Ilos waited for another total eclipse, if that was a factor in a god's death.

"Greed, Power… Ilos was once a man." Ighir sighed and offered the skin back. "Beyond that, we need to determine who the crowns are. Zarae is rather confident that Faedi is one. I'm inclined to believe her, but that leaves six others."

"Do we know what separates the crowns from other true eclipse-born?" All of it still felt too far-fetched, but they had to gather as much information as possible. If they could locate potential crowns or god-touched, they could save them before the cultists got to them.

"I met one, and I could feel their untapped power—but as the crowns come together, the crowns will feel it themselves. Everyone will."

"But you do not feel that with Faedi?" Sophir asked softly. Faedi was powerful; he'd never deny that. But he didn't sense anything particularly abnormal when he was in her mind.

"There's something there, but… something is blocking her abilities." He shook his head. "Even when she healed Zarae—her magic was scattered."

Sophir frowned, resting his elbows on his knees as he thought back to the times he had witnessed her perform magic. There were some delays, or what might have been earth magic that he had seen Elders use. He assumed it was because she was younger than them.

Then, his mind drifted to the scars he had seen on her. The ones she confirmed were caused by torture—by the male voice in the light.

What if someone had tampered with her magic?

Sophir moved through the corridors of the palace, scanning every shadow and corner. Something felt off within the castle, but when nothing seemed amiss, he brushed it off as the absence of Lonan and Haldin. However, the unsettling feeling returned when he didn't see Faedi in the throne room.

As he approached her chambers, the dim light from the wall sconces cast a faint glow over the stone walls. The heavy wooden door to her room stood closed, but nearby, he spotted Aladia carrying a bundle of sheets in her arms. She didn't seem to notice him as he approached, but she turned to face him as he drew closer.

"She's in the chamber," Aladia told him before he could speak, her smile warm. "How are the Gaelisks?"

"They're well, thank you," he nodded, glancing around the hall as he realized he couldn't open the passages. "Could you take me to her?"

"Of course." Aladia smiled and shoved the laundry into a chute before waving for him to follow.

He followed silently as they wandered through the castle's less-traveled corridors. Instead of the clean stone walls and floors most people used, he noted a layer of dust on the sconces in the hall. Haldin likely only allowed a select number of people in this area, but Aladia moved through it expertly.

"Our reports say they are gathering in Valoria. Forces have moved there from Ashar," a voice echoed through the room as Aladia opened the door. Sophir stepped inside and examined the transcendent figure in the center of the room. Faedi stood with her back turned to the door while Zarae was seated on the same bench as the previous night. There was also a new presence—a male Dusk Elf who leaned against the wall near Zarae and nodded to Sophir as he approached Faedi's side.

"Any reports from the West?" Faedi asked before turning to look at him, her smile brightening his mood.

"None to give us any hope," the man replied, shaking his head.

"What do you mean?" Sophir asked, his concern growing before Faedi could speak.

"Detrich is in flames—many have evacuated to Emsmeda, but we fear whoever attacked Detrich will attack Emsmeda as well." Sophir's blood ran cold, and he took a breath to steady himself as the man continued. "Lefral is little more than a graveyard. It's my understanding that whatever sickness Dewgate's crops and livestock had came from there. There's also a group of Ilos' zealots hunting for something in the west while the rest aim to capture and destroy."

"What about the temple in Detrich?" Sophir asked, forcing himself to stay calm.

"Defaced like the one in Dewgate. They tortured and killed the priests."

Sophir glanced at Faedi, frowning when she squeezed his hand. She gave him a weak smile, but her worry was evident.

"I'm sure they got away."

They wouldn't know if the priests had escaped for several days, and that was if the Helgi could get the message that far. With Ilos' devotees about, they might not spread it that far.

"Do you know what they are looking for?" Faedi turned her attention back to the man.

"I believe it might be the sealed gates—the faunan and the Vael were sealed away after the Great War."

"If the gates are sealed, why would they want to find them?" The man beside Zarae straightened, crossing his arms over his chest.

"They want to destroy them—they believe that someone may be able to open them," Zarae commented idly.

Faedi glanced at her. "Who?"

"One of the crowns," she replied with a shrug.

"Do they know which one?" Sophir watched her return her attention to the scroll she held, sighing.

"If they do, they didn't let Ragna know." Zarae shook her head without looking up.

Sophir sighed and turned his gaze back to the transcendent man. Upon closer examination, he appeared to be some sort of elf, but Sophir couldn't make out the colors of his skin or hair. His style of dress suggested he hailed from the east—likely Ostria or Valoria.

"What if something else plays into the gates?" Faedi hummed, and Sophir watched her look between the maps on the floor and ceiling.

"Do you have a theory?" The man from the crystal asked.

"All of the heart trees are connected, right?" She stepped back and stared at the ceiling.

"They are," he replied, nodding.

"There's an Umbral song… about the hearts connecting the realms." She explained, and Sophir tilted his head. Lady Callon had said Umbral songs held hidden histories.

"It's possible—and could explain why they've destroyed heart trees in the east," the man beside Zarae nodded in agreement.

"The number of them may not be a coincidence either; there are seven hearts—seven crowns," Sophir added softly. "But are there seven realms?"

"The crossroads, mortal, Faunan, Udror mountains, Draetor… I don't know what the other two would be. There's a chance that history was erased before the Great War." Faedi pointed at the different regions on the maps. "There are two unnamed masses on these maps."

"The trees might know," Zarae suggested softly.

"Faedi said they don't know names for things." Sophir glanced at Faedi for confirmation.

"They don't, but if they tell me about a location, we might be able to find something out that way. I have questions for the tree anyway." She shrugged, turning to look at Zarae, who nodded.

"I'll stay here with the crystal to see if we can gather any more information."

"Ancients keep all of you. I will contact you when we leave," the man from the crystal said, bowing before he vanished.

Once the man from the crystal was gone, the other man beside Zarae approached them, scratching his chin. He regarded both of them with a nod before he moved to the door, checking the hall before motioning for them to exit. Faedi followed his instructions, and Sophir trailed behind, glancing over the man to take in his features as they walked.

Something about him felt familiar.

54

Memories of the Forest

"I hoped that more people would be against The Order—but I didn't think Grandpa would have a whole network of people plotting against them. How did he even get the contacts?"

Faedi

Sophir and Bjorn followed her through the winding corridors to the hidden chamber, her arms wrapped tightly around herself. Even though Sophir's presence provided her with some comfort, the worry about Lonan and Haldin gnawed at her mind. Night had fallen, and they should have received an update by now. Unless, of course, Lonan had reached the limit for soul speech.

"Who was that man?" Sophir asked softly, his voice breaking the silence. Faedi glanced around to ensure no one was nearby before answering.

"A contact in Ostria," she replied, her voice low. "He's part of a network trying to locate the freed people from Ashar and Valoria."

"He has an army?" Sophir raised an eyebrow, clearly intrigued.

"More or less," Faedi shrugged. "He says there's a group in Scyrei too."

"Dwarves?" Sophir asked, a teasing tone in his voice.

"Well, there are some dwarves, but mostly it's the people they have hiding there," Faedi winked at him, not wanting to mention any names. Even though her contacts were safe to speak of, she didn't think it wise to discuss those still in hiding.

As they continued down the corridors, the air shifted, carrying the scent of fresh earth. Sophir flexed his wings beside her, and Faedi smiled softly when he extended one around her, pulling her closer. *He must be as anxious as I am,* she thought.

"And the man following you?" Sophir asked quietly.

"One of my guards," Faedi replied with a smile, glancing back at Bjorn. "Grandpa had them swear to the Oath-keeper to protect me."

"Smart. He is glamoured," Sophir observed.

"I know," Faedi grinned, tapping her nose before turning a corner to the dead-end hallway.

The door opened with surprising ease, faster than it had when Faedi first found the Gaelisks. The air inside wasn't as frigid as it had been before, but it was cool enough for Faedi to see her breath. However, like in her dream with Sylrie, the ice had disappeared as the ancient tree came into view.

"What else do you know?" Sophir asked as the door clicked shut behind them.

"That he's only telling me so much. I think he doesn't trust speaking openly," Faedi smiled up at him, then turned her attention to Bjorn. "Isn't that right?"

"Yes, Your Highness," Bjorn nodded.

"Good thing he's locked in with us and the tree," Sophir rumbled, and Faedi grinned, shaking her head.

"You read my mind." She found a large patch of moss and sat near the tree, motioning for them to join her.

The air around them grew heavier as Faedi waited for Sophir and Bjorn to settle. The leaves of the ancient tree rustled, and Faedi glanced up at it with a soft smile. It was listening to them, waiting.

"Ask me whatever you want," Bjorn said, bowing his head before sitting down.

"Does my grandfather know what you look like?" Faedi tilted her head, studying him.

"No," Bjorn replied, shaking his head. "But he knows I have it." He rubbed his chin. "Zarae does, and you might."

"I might?" Faedi's curiosity piqued. She hoped his words were more ominous than intended.

"We've met in the past," Bjorn said cryptically.

"Any chance you could remove your glamour?" Sophir sat beside Faedi, positioning himself slightly ahead, as if prepared to protect her.

"I don't see the harm if it's only for a moment," Bjorn shrugged, then pulled a silver ring off his left middle finger.

The glamour covering him rippled and faded, revealing a man with long silver hair tied back in a braid. His right eye was red, his left was white, and a long scar trailed down over his left eye. Discolored burn scars marred his neck, contrasting against his tanned skin.

"You were the man with Ragna," Faedi stared at him with wide eyes.

"I am," Bjorn smiled and nodded.

"You're eclipse-born?" Sophir asked softly.

"I am," Bjorn nodded again.

"And chosen?" Faedi leaned forward, narrowing her eyes at him.

"I am that as well…" Bjorn mimicked her movements. "Although, I'm a bit more in tune with my divine patron."

"How so?" Sophir rumbled again.

"I was imprisoned for most of my life. For me, years of torture led to a greater connection to my patron."

"That's why you were with the cultists?" Faedi glanced between Bjorn and Sophir. "You and Ragna?"

Bjorn nodded with a sigh. "They believed we were broken enough to do their bidding."

Faedi recalled the chain glowing when Bjorn voiced his complaints about harming children, and the same had happened when he and Ragna helped her. They had waited until there were fewer cultists—only one to hold the chains. She rubbed her wrist anxiously, recalling the searing pain she had felt in the light.

"Thank you for helping that day," Faedi whispered softly.

"I wish we could have done more." Bjorn bowed his head, a sense of shame radiating off him like heat from a flame.

"When you say connection?" Sophir asked, his tone calmer now.

"I don't have any miraculous godlike powers or abilities. I can do some things, but it isn't consistent." Bjorn shook his head and chuckled. "I just—feel things. That, and I have an unnaturally long life."

"Like what happened when I was a child?" Faedi tilted her head, trying to understand.

"Similar to that, yes," he nodded. "There are some moments for us when we can channel our divine magic, but it makes us weaker for a time."

Sophir looked between them. "Like a limit to our mortal confines?"

"Either that, or something needs to happen to unlock our abilities," Bjorn shrugged. "Like the total eclipse or something else. I'm not sure how much we can rely on a prophecy that has been spread for years and translated into multiple languages."

"Is that why I can't get a scent from you—why you just smell like a predator?" Faedi studied him closely. Despite his scent, he was calm, and she hadn't seen a single threatening movement from him.

"No—my shape-changing ability is a gift. I assume it's from my patron," Bjorn nodded his head to the side before smiling. "They are the God of Vengeance."

Faedi's eyebrows shot up, and she glanced at Sophir. His reaction was unreadable, his brow furrowed as it always was when he was deep in thought, but he didn't comment. Instead, he looked at her when her gaze lingered and smiled.

"I can ask him more if you want to talk to the tree?" Sophir suggested softly.

"Alright," Faedi nodded and stood with a sigh before turning to approach the tree.

Its leaves rustled again as its branches swayed at her approach, and Faedi smiled. The tree's excitement was palpable, and goosebumps prickled her skin as soon as she touched the bark. She realized the conversation between Sophir and Bjorn had come to a halt, and she glanced back at them, her eyebrows raised.

"What is it?" She asked, noting their eyes were on her.

"I've never seen you talk to a tree before," Sophir shrugged.

"Nor have I. I was wondering if it would appear different from other Guardians," Bjorn admitted with a chuckle. "Should we ignore you?"

"Please? It's awkward having an audience," Faedi replied, returning to the tree with a sigh.

"I'll stop you if Lonan reaches out and you don't hear him."

Faedi nodded at Sophir's promise, taking a breath and closing her eyes. She didn't know if she would be too distracted to hear Lonan, but Sophir's announcement gave her some ease. It would be easier for her to focus on the tree's speech if she didn't have anything else to worry about. Trees in a forest were young, but heart trees were ancient, and their magic always left her with a headache.

The air around the tree grew thicker as Faedi brushed her fingers against the gnarled bark. Slowly, warmth began to pulse against her skin, and she laid her palm flat against the tree as she closed her eyes. Sylrie had been right—the thump pulsed from the tree.

"Maybe its twin is dead," she murmured to herself.

A wince crossed her face as a pressure built between her eyes, and a shiver ran through her. For a moment, there was silence—deep, all-encompassing stillness. Then, like a whisper in the wind, a voice seeped into her mind.

"My friend."

"Hello again," Faedi smiled at the branches, her skin tingling. "I have questions."

"It is late, and winter comes. You have come with questions?"

"I have," she nodded. "I know all hearts are connected, but I wanted to know if you were connected to other realms… other soil that isn't here."

"We are. Each realm has a heart, and every heart's twin is here."

"So the twins in the Mire are for this realm?" Faedi tilted her head to the side.

"No. They were the first you made."

Faedi stared up at the tree, her eyes widening. The tree didn't think she was god touched. It thought she was a god—the god of the forest.

Stay on track.

"What realm are you connected to—where is your twin?" she asked carefully, recalling Sylrie's thoughts. Its twin might be dead.

"It has been sealed away like the rest. They keep the shadows who were here before."

"The Shadow Elves?" Faedi searched the branches as they trembled.

"When others came for the stone ones—they used me to leave. Now the night, like you,

keeps their stone walls safe."

Faedi glanced back at Sophir and Bjorn while they spoke, but she couldn't hear what they said. Instead, all she could listen to was the tree and its steady, slow thump. A rustle in the branches pulled her attention back to the tree, and she frowned.

"Everyone thinks the realms are sealed away," she said softly.

"They are—you sealed them."

"Can I unseal them?" Faedi stepped closer to the tree.

"I do not know what this new bark on you can do."

Her frown deepened, and she shifted her stance. If Bjorn was right, she might not have the ability to unseal anything. Yet. There was a chance that she might have to wait for the next total eclipse unless there was another way. However, she wasn't confident that anyone in the other realms would be an ally. All she knew for sure was that Ilos' followers did not want the realms to be unsealed. He could still have followers there—working from inside to keep them shut.

"Should I try?" She asked, biting her lip as the tree seemed to shiver.

"The soil will crumble if you do not."

"How did I do it last time—in my old bark?" Faedi asked as her heart pounded in her chest.

If it thinks I'm a god, maybe I should talk like one.

"With ancient magic—desperation and rage. Your heart died."

Faedi stumbled back, clutching her chest as a searing heat flared through her body. The tree's words echoed in her mind as her pulse raced. However, beneath the rush of panic, there was an unsettling calm—as if the tree touched something inside of her. The world around her seemed to slow, and all she could hear was the tree's steady, rhythmic thrum—the pulse of the earth itself.

Her vision blurred for a moment, and shadows weaved in the haze. A figure stood in front of the tree as flames crept into her vision. Then, the figure came into view, and even though they appeared different, she knew it was the god of the forest.

She could feel them—she felt everything.

The pain that ached in her heart was too familiar—too powerful. Her heart was consumed by the weight of loss and fury. Ancient magic rippled around her, wild and untamed, and then black vines erupted from her as her heart shattered.

Faedi gasped and hit her knees as the images flooded her mind. The moss beneath the tree crept up her legs as the pulse of the magic continued to flow through her. It was the same in the memory.

"Faedi!" Sophir's voice cut through the haze as he appeared beside her, placing his hand on her shoulder to steady her.

"I...the forest sealed them," she stared up at him as Bjorn came to stand a few paces away. "Faeturin sealed the realms before."

"And?" Sophir frowned, his gaze flicking between Faedi and the tree.

"It says… their heart died—they were consumed," Faedi took a deep breath to steady herself before standing.

"We don't need you dying to fix what's broken," Sophir's eyes darkened. "The realms can stay closed off."

"The tree showed you what happened?" Bjorn stepped forward.

"I saw them—" Faedi closed her eyes and replayed the memory. "It said the soil will crumble if the realms aren't reconnected. The balance of everything will be thrown off… that's why Ilos' followers want to destroy the gates—the hearts—"

"We'll find a way that doesn't involve killing you," Sophir cut her off.

Faedi smiled up at him, but the uncertainty gnawed at her. The memory of her heart breaking, of the fire that once consumed her, lingered at the edges of her mind. She had been desperate then, driven by pain and rage.

But what hurt them before they died? Why were they so angry?

"I think there's another component," Faedi whispered while brushing her fingers against her chest where their heart broke.

"What do you mean?" Bjorn asked with furrowed brows.

"Just a thought—I don't know," Faedi shook her head and looked away from the tree. "Something happened to make them seal them… I didn't see it."

"Do you know if they were all sealed at once?" Sophir asked Bjorn.

"No," he shook his head. "If Zae knows, it's locked somewhere in her mind."

Faedi nodded, though her anxiety still gnawed at her. Either they would find a new way, or they would be forced to recreate what happened before. If everyone's claims were valid, the forest could choose someone else, but she didn't want to bet her life on it.

"Faedi, Sophir?"

55

Of Wanderers and Watchers

"They'll be fine. They are safe on the mountain and will protect each other. They're safe."

Lonan

The powerful wings of the pegasus beat rhythmically beneath him. Beside him, King Haldin flew close enough for them to shout a conversation over the wind. The sky had darkened as they slowly descended, scanning the area for the encampment.

In the distance, red and orange lights flickered. Lonan sighed in relief. It wasn't large enough to signal destruction; rather, it was the same communal fire he remembered from his visit with Faedi and Sophir. He smiled to himself, glancing over his shoulder toward the mountain.

"Faedi, Sophir? We made it to the encampment. Is everything alright?"

"The heart tree said they're the gates to the other realms," Faedi's voice echoed back, though it sounded distant.

"We found another eclipse-born as well," Sophir added.

"You're safe?" Lonan asked, hoping they were, but he didn't want to trust blindly. He didn't want to believe someone had started a revolt the moment Haldin had left.

"We're fine. What about you and Grandpa?" Faedi's voice was steady.

"We're fine. I'll let you know when we start sending people up," Lonan promised, smiling before signaling to Haldin. "That's the encampment over there."

"Just stay safe," Sophir's voice echoed in his mind as Haldin motioned with his arm, and his mount began to descend.

"It seems they haven't had much luck with structures," Haldin commented. Lonan frowned. He was right.

"It looks better than it did when we were here," Lonan replied, noticing a large longhouse near the fire. It appeared they had all decided to bunk together

350

for warmth.

As they descended with the others on their pegasi toward the encampment nestled against the miniature grove Faedi had grown for them, Lonan spotted smaller fires dotting the edges, casting flickering light over the few scattered tents. People milled about, but they gathered near the fire when they spotted their approach. Among them, he noticed several Umbrals taking point to surround the others.

The moment their pegasi's hooves touched the ground, the Umbrals approached with his pack as the others whispered among themselves. Lonan dismounted quickly, nodding to Haldin before closing the distance to the Watchers. However, he slowed when one of them caught his attention.

One wore a black blindfold and had a tiny bear cub beside them.

"What in the Ancients are you doing here?" Lonan rushed over to them. "You're supposed to be at home."

"And miss the real fight? I think not," Myst smiled and wrapped their arms around him in a hug. "I think it's a good idea if eclipse-born aren't in the Mire. It might give them more time to organize defenses."

"Is it that bad?" Lonan frowned at them, stepping back as Haldin approached.

"Not right now, but it could be later. If we can give them fewer reasons to send more people, I think it's worth exploring."

Lonan sighed and dragged his hand over his face, shaking his head slightly. It was sound logic, even if he didn't want to admit it. They would be safer on the mountain, where they could retreat into the stone walls rather than the forest, where cultists might hide. However, if there were allies of the cultists on the mountain, an attack could be launched as soon as they returned—or while they were gone.

Faedi and Sophir will tell me if anything happens.

"Are your parents aware of your plan?" Haldin asked, standing to the side and studying the group of Valorians and farmers. "Do they know the danger?"

"Our parents are aware, and I explained to these people what was happening. They've agreed to travel to the mountain," Myst nodded with a small smile.

"You're going with the first group, then," Lonan said. "I want a Watcher with each group."

They chuckled, shaking their head. "You got bossy, didn't you?"

"Did you expect me to be comfortable with you out in the open without—" Lonan cut himself off when Myst's smile fell, letting out a sigh. "Can you blame me for being worried?"

"No," they replied, shaking their head again. "But even if they want to take me wherever they took Vishal, it wouldn't do anyone any good. It's smarter to stay as a group… either we protect each other, or we're all taken together."

"No one will be taken anywhere if I have anything to say about it," Haldin growled. "As for the ones they have already taken, we'll plan something to do about it as soon as we know where they are."

"Vishal has not told me anything," Myst frowned, lowering their head as Lonan placed his hand on their shoulder. "Either he's been unconscious this entire time, dead, or… they've done something where he can't speak to me through our bond."

"Vishal is a stubborn ass; he's alive," Lonan reassured Myst, squeezing their shoulder. "We'll figure out a way to find him. Sophir might have some way to help."

They managed a smile at him, but Lonan could tell it was forced. It had been weeks since he was taken, and while Myst was known for their faith in many things, they still understood the odds. Even if the cultists did not aim to kill eclipse-born, people were flawed.

"We should tell them the plan and prepare the first group," Lonan announced, looking over the gathering crowd around them. However, he couldn't spot who he wanted to find.

"Where's Emmaline?"

As the people of the encampment bustled about, gathering their belongings, Lonan stood between Haldin and Myst. The icy wind tugged at his cloak, whipping around the encampment, and he frowned. Faedi's concerns had been valid; the air was already too cold. Even without the threat of Ilos' cultists, the encampment still wasn't developed enough to protect them from the harsh winter.

The mountain loomed behind them, its peak lost in the night, but its presence was ever-felt. Haldin's calm yet authoritative voice rose over the crowd as they urged the people to evacuate urgently. Myst, the other Watchers, and Lonan offered words of reassurance, though many didn't seem convinced. Jaref was quick to agree, urging everyone to gather only what supplies they could carry.

The Valorians and farmers moved with hurried and anxious energy, collecting what little they could—tattered blankets, meager supplies, and trinkets— while children clung to their sides. Lonan watched them carefully, noticing the fear in each Valorian's eyes. Unlike the farmers of Dewgate, they understood what Ilos' cultists were capable of.

Amid the chaos, a gentle tug at his cloak made him turn, and he immediately smiled when he saw Emmaline, with Dusan perched comfortably on her shoulder. She looked well, unharmed, but just as anxious as before. However, he couldn't tell if it was fear of her magic or the threat of the cultists that worried her more.

"You came back," she smiled up at him, and he knelt down to her level. "Where are Sophir and Faedi?"

"They're back on the mountain," he said, catching her eyes as they searched his face for answers. *Are they safe?*

"They're preparing things for when everyone arrives," he promised softly.

"They had to stay behind because there are people to help there too."

The little girl seemed to take some comfort in his words, though her brows remained furrowed, and her petite frame trembled slightly.

"Are you cold?" He frowned when she nodded. "Here—"

He removed his cloak and wrapped it around her. It almost swallowed her completely, but he didn't want her to get sick on the flight up the mountain or shiver so much that she fell. He glanced over his shoulder at Myst and nodded as a thought crossed his mind.

"See that person over there?" He pointed to Emmaline and waited for her to acknowledge them. "That's my older sibling. I want you to fly up to Faedi and Sophir with them. They'll keep you safe."

"I like their baby bear," she whispered softly.

"Espen? I'm sure they like you too," he chuckled as he stood and tapped Myst on the shoulder. "I want you and her on the same mount."

Myst regarded him, and he wasn't sure if they could see him or the child as Espen walked in a circle around them. They had mentioned before that the cub lent them sight, but he didn't know how often that happened.

"Of course," they nodded, then knelt to offer Emmaline their hand. "It's good to meet you. My name is Myst."

As they extended their hand, Emmaline took it with a shy smile, and Lonan watched the tension in her shoulders relax. Slowly, she reached forward and touched one of the necklaces that dangled from Myst's neck. Myst didn't stop her, only smiled and tilted their head to the side.

"You like that one?" They asked softly.

Emmaline nodded. "It's pretty."

"It's for protection," Myst told her before taking it off and carefully slipping it over Emmaline's head. "Sometimes, when I'm scared, it tells me what I should do."

"Really?" The child's eyes widened in surprise, and Lonan stared at his sibling with wide eyes.

The pendant was a relic, one left behind in the Mire by the fae when they were sealed into their home realm. For as long as he could remember, Myst always had it. They never took it off and protected it as fiercely as they did Espen.

"I want you to hold on to it for me," Myst said, nodding before they stood with a soft sigh. "The mounts are ready for the first group."

Lonan glanced at the soldier approaching Haldin before turning his attention back to Myst and Emmaline. Myst appeared calm as ever, nodding. However, he noticed the child tensing again, but Myst quickly placed their hand on her shoulder and smiled.

"Everything will be fine. I won't let you fall," they promised her.

"And I'll tell Sophir and Faedi that you're on your way. They'll be waiting for you," Lonan promised Emmaline before leading them to a pegasus.

Espen pranced around their feet as Myst, along with others from the encampment, were led to their mounts. Lonan glanced down at Emmaline once they stopped and watched her hide behind his leg with a sad smile.

"Just breathe and stay calm," he told her as Myst mounted the pegasus.

"Okay," her voice trembled as she nodded.

"The worst part is taking off," he assured her before gently lifting her and placing her into Myst's outstretched hands. Dusan hopped onto his shoulder with the transfer, and he eyed the falcon. *Not going with them?*

The falcon tilted his head to the side and blinked before ruffling his feathers. *I'll take that as a no.*

Lonan watched Myst tuck their cloak around the girl while he picked up Espen. He debated for a moment, unsure of where to put the cub, before carefully placing it into the pocket of one of the saddle bags. Thankfully, the cub didn't resist and only popped its head out from the leather pouch to look around.

"Ancients keep you. I'll see you soon," he smiled at them, raising his hand.

Emmaline smiled shyly at him as she held onto the saddle, and Myst held her closer with a nod. The pegasi, already restless, stamped their hooves and flapped their wings as the rest of the evacuees prepared to take off. They were off the ground as soon as the lead soldier shouted a command, and Lonan worked to keep his smile steady to reassure Emmaline.

He followed their ascent until they were just a speck in the sky, then lowered his head with a sigh. He wondered if he should have gone with them. Myst was strong and smart enough not to get into trouble, but they were an Umbral—and a blind one at that.

"Myst and Emmaline are with the first group. They just took off."

"I should have known they would be there," Faedi said as she shook her head.

"We'll keep them safe," Sophir promised.

Lonan turned to face Haldin, frowning as he rolled his shoulders. He wondered if it would be wise to stay at the encampment or move everyone over the border. Even if they didn't travel up the mountain, he wondered if people's fear of the Dusk Elves' wrath would deter others from following them. The cultists would still pursue them, but their allies, who didn't worship the same god, might hesitate enough to give them some peace of mind.

"If they're able to travel, we should move closer to or over the border," he suggested, glancing at the group that remained. "It will take at least two more trips if the pegasi can manage the weight."

"You sound like you've migrated before," Haldin chuckled with a nod. "It's a good plan. Let's round them up."

Lonan followed Haldin as he approached Jaref, hoping the old man wouldn't want his people to rest for the night. His gut told him that every moment they spent in the encampment increased their odds of an attack. The King of the Dusk Elves was out in the open and no longer silent on his mountain, an eclipse-born available to be taken, and several Umbrals to murder. If the cultists discovered them, they wouldn't hesitate to take their chance.

If they didn't know Myst was there, maybe there was still time before they came.

56

Bound by the Gods

"I can't shake the feeling that something bad is about to happen."

Faedi

Despite the delicious aroma, the food on the table in front of her held no appeal. The day had dragged on as they waited for the first arrivals from the encampment, and as night began to fall, there was nothing else to occupy her mind. Sophir had told her there was substantial progress with the Gaelisks, the port was prepared to receive ships, and there was no new information from Haldin's contacts.

She raised her eyes to Sophir, who stood on the balcony with his wings partially unfurled. His tail curled and uncurled around his feet as he clutched his goblet with pale knuckles. She could tell, without asking, that his mind was with hers.

All they knew for sure was that Lonan was safe with Haldin, they had begun moving the Valorians and farmers to the border, and Emmaline was with Myst on a pegasi. One that should have already arrived. They were missing, and there were few on the mountain they could trust to find them.

"Tell me about Ragna," Faedi said, turning her attention to Bjorn.

He glanced at her from his spot against the wall and frowned, but he didn't deny her. He kept his post nearby at all times, no more than ten paces away from her—unless she was in her room. She was sure he never wandered far from her door.

"I don't think it's a suitable conversation for dinner," he shook his head. "It'll ruin the meal you've barely touched."

"I'll take any conversation that keeps me from worrying over things outside my control," she countered, stabbing a carrot with her fork.

"I…" Bjorn hesitated for a moment, his eyes flicking to Sophir before he lowered his head with a sigh. "What do you want to know?"

Faedi grinned at him. "How did you meet?"

"She tried to kill me," he chuckled. "With good reason, of course—if you take into account the lies she was told. She thought I was my brother and that I was killing… me?"

Faedi sat back and shook her head. "So… she wasn't trying to kill you, she was trying to protect you?" Bjorn nodded, and Faedi glanced at Sophir. "And you'd never met?"

"Not officially, no." He cleared his throat, and Faedi turned her eyes back to him. "It's a long and complicated story. The most important thing to know is that she knows who her patron is, she's chosen by the Oath Keeper… which is fitting, I suppose—given my patron."

"Are your patrons friendly?" Faedi sipped her wine and raised her eyebrows.

"Mostly, unless angered," Bjorn explained, moving from the wall to sit at the table. "Oaths, Justice, Revenge, and Vengeance go hand in hand."

A smile crossed Faedi's face as she watched a blissful expression take over his. Even in his injured eye, which she doubted held any sight, there was a light to it. It was as if, despite being on the mountain, he was somewhere else. As if, maybe, he was with her.

Faedi knew it without him saying it. "You're in love with her?"

"Since the first time I laid eyes on her," he nodded slowly. "I think my patron knew that too—he was vocal about how I should stay with her."

"Our patrons give relationship advice?" Sophir spoke from his position on the balcony.

"Mine did," Bjorn chuckled. "Maybe it's because our patrons are connected too."

"Have you seen her since…" Faedi trailed off, glancing away. "Since the fire when I was little?"

"No," he sighed, and Faedi glanced back at him as he rested his forearms on the table. "But she talks to me."

Faedi tilted her head, grinning when he did. "Soul speech?"

"We're bonded, like you and yours." His lopsided smile grew. "She'll be here soon. She's probably got a ship right behind Scarred's."

"What about her sister?" Zarae had mentioned her previously, but Faedi hadn't thought to ask.

"No sign of her since Ragna and I were taken by cultists centuries ago… we told her to run and not get caught. Her visions are too useful to them."

"You sacrificed yourselves," Sophir stated as he approached the table and took a seat beside Faedi.

"We did. I swore to Ragna that I would do everything in my power to protect Tove, and I meant it," Bjorn nodded slowly, his smile turning bitter. "She's like Zae—too pure for this world."

Faedi frowned and slid her hand under the table to rest it on Sophir's thigh. She had more questions, but she wasn't sure if it was appropriate to ask when Bjorn appeared so bothered. He didn't need to tell her that there were other things on his mind—memories he didn't want to share.

Sophir squeezed her hand gently, and Faedi glanced up at him, biting her lip. He shared Bjorn's expression, and her brows creased as she wondered where his mind had gone. Given the situation, she assumed it was either eclipse-born or Lonan's absence.

"Do you know who our patrons are?" He asked Bjorn after the silence dragged on.

"If Zae's assumptions are correct…" Bjorn trailed off, rubbing his chin. "Your patron is the night sky—brother to Mumir. Faedi's is Faeturin, god of the forest, and Lonan's is the god of shadows—son of the Ancient dark."

"Do you know which gods Ilos specifically doesn't like or ones who were against him? If the cultists don't have them, we should find them first. Even if we don't have god-given abilities—we would be more effective together." Faedi leaned forward when Bjorn chuckled, shaking his head.

"Nothing," he said, pouring himself a cup of wine. "It's just nice to see someone agree to an alliance."

"I'm not a people person, but the enemy of my enemy is a friend. Just seems like a good idea," Faedi shrugged before taking a bite of her carrot.

"Right," he chuckled again, reaching for parchment. "I don't know how gods' opinions of Ilos might have changed over the centuries, but I can make a list… it will be a long one—there's a lot of gods, and I assume their chosen ones."

Faedi looked between Sophir and Bjorn while he scribbled on the paper. "What makes a god anyway?"

"Depends…" Bjorn mumbled. "There were the Ancients, then the ones they made specifically for the earth and their sentient creations—then others were born among them… and then some mortals or others rose to godhood."

Sophir leaned back in his chair with a sigh. "Like Mumir."

"Mumir was always a god—he was made by the Ancients and created drag-ons. It would be fitting if all of his kin's chosen were Itmis. Skies, sun, moons, stars…it's possible."

Faedi grabbed Sophir's arm when his startled inhale made his chair lean further back.

At least I'm not the only one still adjusting to all of this.

Bjorn wasn't wrong—the list was massive. By the time he finished, nearly the entire piece of parchment was covered in names written in his messy script. Some names were checked off, and their locations were known, like hers, but more were missing than found. She didn't get to dwell on it, though, because Bjorn cleared his throat, pulling her attention away.

He needs better handwriting.

She pointed at the scribble next to one of the names. "Is that a dash or a check?"

"Dash—she was vehemently against Ilos." He shook his head, sighing as a frown deepened his expression. "But I never found anyone she patronized."

"If their chosen are in a sealed realm, where Ilos' followers can't get to and sacrifice them…" Sophir trailed off, his voice rumbling with frustration.

She could tell he hated the thought as much as she did. Sealed didn't mean safe. Ilos could have followers anywhere. They couldn't assume anyone was safe, even if they were locked away.

"Is everyone with a dash unknown?" She asked quietly.

Bjorn nodded. "Yes…and they could be in sealed realms. I'm confident saying anyone with the Faunan is safe—their God King has always been an ally."

"What about people with the Vael?" Sophir tensed beside her.

"Anyone in Draetor could go either way. The Vael fell from Elyssarian ranks—they could be willing sacrifices or targets." Bjorn glanced over his shoulder, checking that they were alone.

She moved the food around on her plate, thinking back to the history lessons her mother had taught her. Long ago, there hadn't been different kinds of flameborn. The separation between them had only come after The Great War, but no one knew exactly why. The Elyssar had retreated into their temple cities, while the Vael seemed to vanish.

"Why did the Vael disappear?" she asked softly.

"They were punished for rebelling against Ilos and his allies," Bjorn shrugged. "Anyone who sided with our patrons was cast out. A realm was created for them so they could be safe and recover—but I doubt everyone there still thinks they picked the right side."

"So there could be a war in Draetor we don't even know about." She sighed. Maybe only the Faunan were the lucky ones.

Bjorn nodded, and she sighed as the rumble from Sophir grew louder. Torix had said the cultists had plenty of allies, and she doubted sealed realms could protect anyone from their flames. People would seize any opportunity to gain power, favor, or protection from Ilos' wrath.

She pushed her plate away, her appetite forgotten as a heavy weight settled in her gut. Despite all the power she held in communicating and organizing an army, it felt dwarfed by everything else. Refugees were missing, others were on a treacherous mountain path, and realms were sealed off with people who could be in danger.

And there she was, sitting in comfort, waiting.

"And the forest sealed the realms—leaving no way to help them," she whispered.

"Yes," Bjorn replied, nodding once. "What they helped you do as a child was only a fraction of what you'll be able to do later, but it was still part of it. For a moment, you weren't just a child—you spoke to us like our patrons do."

"Those were shadows," she started to protest, but he raised an eyebrow, cutting her off.

"What do you think trees make?"

"When I was with Torix, burying your mother and brothers, much of the ground that wasn't charred was covered in vines—eventides," Sophir said softly, squeezing her hand. "They weren't there in your memory."

He caught her gaze, and though his expression was stern, his eyes were soft. He believed she had grown them—that Bjorn was right.

If she had done it before, she could do it again.

57
Blood on the Snow

"I hope we're not moving them too late—we need to hurry."

Lonan

They left the encampment that night. Jaref had taken a vote among the refugees, and the first group flew off. Many were too wound up to sleep, and the rest looked to Haldin and Lonan for guidance. They were still on edge after the attack by the Hunt. Even though no more trouble had come after that, the fear of cultists and whatever else lurked in the night hung heavy in the air. The refugees trusted the Dusk Elf entourage and the Umbrals to protect them on the journey, so they voted to keep moving until they crossed the border—hoping that the invisible line might offer some safety.

They didn't stop until they were all well across the border. Only then did the group rest. The soldiers, Umbrals, Haldin, and Lonan took turns keeping watch, scanning the ice fields for any signs of movement. Thankfully, all was quiet. For now, they were safe, but Lonan couldn't relax. He wouldn't—not until he heard from Faedi or Sophir confirming that Emmaline and Myst had reached the mountains safely. Even then, he wouldn't feel much relief until he was there himself.

He needed to be with his bonded again.

When Haldin announced it was time to leave just after sunrise, Lonan was the first one up and ready to go. But he couldn't shake the anxiety that gnawed at him when Faedi told him that Myst and Emmaline hadn't arrived overnight. Haldin had tried to reassure him, saying they likely landed somewhere if the flying conditions hadn't been favorable.

Lonan hoped he was right.

As they made their way through the ice fields, the landscape was a stark contrast of white and blue. The early morning sun glinted off the frost-covered ground, and the cold cut through him like a blade. Haldin led the group with a determined pace, but the silence was unsettling. The crunch of snow underfoot felt deafening. The refugees huddled close, their faces tight with a mix of fear and determination. Their pack carried the weakest through the snow, though there were others who needed assistance as well.

The Umbrals took up that burden, along with their bonded, their shadows long against the snow, while the Dusk Elf soldiers led from the front.

Lonan stole glances at Haldin, watching as he scanned the horizon for threats. "How long before we should hear from the first group?" He asked.

"The storm on the mountain could delay them until this evening," Haldin replied, his voice cutting through the wind.

Hours passed with no sign of trouble, but the worry inside Lonan kept growing. Each time he thought of Emmaline and Myst, the urge to run ahead, to leave everyone behind, grew stronger. He knew it was foolish, but it did nothing to quiet the impulse.

As the sun climbed higher, the terrain began to change. Jagged ice formations loomed ahead, gleaming like teeth under a darkening sky. Snow clouds were rolling in. Haldin called for a break, giving the group time to rest and share rations. Lonan stood at the edge of the camp, unable to eat, his eyes fixed on the distant mountains.

"Lonan," Haldin's voice broke into his thoughts. "They'll be fine."

"Will they?" Lonan muttered, unable to hide the frustration in his voice. "What if—"

"Blind or not, Myst is a Watcher. And Emmaline survived the burning fields. They're survivors," Haldin said, but his face betrayed the worry he tried to hide.

Lonan turned away, shaking his head. He knew Haldin was trying to ease his mind, and part of him believed he was right. But it didn't change the fear in his heart. Myst was his sibling, and Emmaline was just a child. Even with Ytna's mercy, there was no guarantee they'd have Nori's luck.

As they resumed their march, the wind picked up, howling around them as Lonan tightened his cloak. He pressed on, his steps falling in line with Haldin's, though his thoughts were miles away. For all the strength and power he had from his status and training, at that moment, he felt weaker than a newborn.

If something happened to Myst or Emmaline, he'd never forgive himself. And if anything happened to Faedi and Sophir while he was away, he'd hate himself for an eternity.

The trail up the mountain was just as treacherous as before, if not worse. It wound higher and higher, more straightforward with Haldin leading the group, but still too narrow for more than two people to walk side by side. Snow and ice clung to the rocks, making every step uncertain. Exposed skin stung from the cold, cutting through even the thickest cloaks. Only a few days had passed since they'd been up there last, but winter had already arrived.

Lonan kept pace beside Haldin. He moved with grace despite the biting wind and treacherous footing, never faltering. Behind them, the refugees trudged on, exhaustion weighing down every step. It didn't take long for injuries to start—twisted ankles, broken bones, and one poor soul who fell from a ledge to their death. But there was no time to mourn. Haldin and Lonan urged them forward.

After Faedi's message that the others never arrived, they couldn't afford to waste time.

"We should stop soon," Haldin said, raising his voice over the howling wind. "The injured and weak won't make it much further without rest."

Lonan nodded, even though his instincts screamed against it. "The cave we rested in is hours away. Too many open spaces out here."

"We can't push them any harder. They're not built for this, Lonan."

"They—" A scream tore through the air from below, cutting him off. His muscles tensed, and his shadow flared to life, curling around him like smoke. Without a second thought, he bolted toward the sound, knives already in hand. The refugees were scrambling, eyes wide with terror as dark shapes moved in the storm behind them, too well camouflaged against the craggy rocks.

"Wolves," he muttered under his breath. Their scent had been masked by the storm.

Nearly half the group was separated, some stumbling up the path, others panicking and running back away from the beasts while his pack attacked anyone who got too close. Dark forms appeared on either side of the trail, more with every step he took. They were surrounded.

"Watchers to me!" He shouted, glancing at Haldin. "Get everyone you can out of here!"

He slipped into the shadows without a second thought, merging with the darkness as he darted forward. One of the wolves lunged at a refugee, knocking them to the ground, but his knives were faster. Black blood sprayed as he slashed its throat, the liquid hissing as it hit the frozen ground.

Howls echoed in the wind, spreading panic through the refugees as the Watchers and Lonan fought to hold the wolves back. Their blades cut through fur and flesh, but there were too many.

"They're on the pass!" Haldin's voice boomed over the chaos, and Lonan's blood went cold as flames erupted around them.

The fire surged, bright and fierce, creating a barrier between them and the wolves. Lonan glanced toward Haldin, who was charging into the blaze with his soldiers. The heat licked at his skin, cutting through the biting cold.

"Keep them back!" Haldin shouted again, slicing through the chaos with his blade. "We can't let them through."

His command pushed adrenaline through Lonan's veins. The flames lit up the terror on the refugees' faces, but they also illuminated the determination in the eyes of the Watchers. For a moment, the fire pushed back the shadows, and the wolves rushed at them. But Lonan didn't stop.

"Circle the injured!" He called to the nearest refugees, knives still poised. "Push them toward Haldin!"

He darted forward, driving his blade into the side of the nearest wolf. It howled, thrashing before collapsing in the snow. But as soon as one fell, two more took its place.

"To the ridge!" Haldin's voice rang out again, and flames shot up around them, igniting two of the refugees.

They fought forward, pushing against the relentless tide of wolves and fire. Each step felt like a battle as the icy ground threatened to send them sprawling. Lonan caught glimpses of injured refugees, some huddled together, others frozen in terror. Guilt gnawed at him, but he shoved it aside. Survival came first.

As they reached the ridge, Haldin unleashed a torrent of ice, creating a makeshift barrier between them and the flames. The wolves slammed into it, snarling and snapping, but the ice held for now. Lonan, along with the Watchers and soldiers, formed a defensive line, weapons gleaming in the firelight as they prepared for the next wave.

"We're under attack," Lonan called out to Faedi and Sophir, his breath ragged. *"At the ridge below the cave we stayed in. Wolves and cultists—they're hiding in the dark."*

"I'm coming," Sophir's voice came through the wind.

"He'll bring the Itmis," Faedi added, but Lonan frowned.

The Gaelisks would stay behind with her, protecting her if something went wrong on the mountain. But he didn't want Sophir to bring the Itmis, he didn't want him to leave her. Still, he couldn't argue. They needed the help.

The cultists were hiding in the dark. Either there weren't many of them, or they didn't want the mountain alerted to their presence. With their luck, it was probably the latter. They could be planning something worse—a larger attack, something more devastating.

"Make sure Faedi is safe before you leave," Lonan told Sophir. *"They're letting the wolves do the work. This feels more like a delay than a full assault."*

"Torix and the Gaelisks will stay with her," Sophir reassured him. *"Just hold on until we get there."*

Lonan nodded, though some of him still couldn't shake the worry. He looked up for Dusan and frowned. "Go to Faedi," he shouted into the darkness. "Find her."

But Dusan didn't fly south—he flew west.

58

Cold Awakening

Faedi

Golden flames split the heavens, searing through the clouds like the wrath of a thousand suns. The earth trembled beneath Faedi's feet, the very bones of the world splintering under the weight of their power. The gods were tearing the world apart. Every strike from their weapons sent shockwaves rippling through the land, shattering mountains and turning rivers into steam plumes. The cries of mortals and beasts echoed in her ears, and each of them rippled through her as if they were her own.

Because they were.

Her heart clenched, a deep, aching sorrow pulling at her chest as she fell to her knees beside two obsidian-armored men. The larger lay collapsed on the other, his wings ripped from his back and his helmet cleaved in two. She brushed tufts of messy black hair away from the smaller one's face, and a wail erupted from her throat as she looked into the lifeless violet eyes that stared up at her. They were gone, and she could not save them.

She could not save anyone—not from Ilos' flames.

Crashes of thunder from overhead pulled her attention, where the golden god of light and his army clashed with the gods in the sky. The mortals and beasts around her ran through the burned trees, hoping to reach the heart tree. To reach the portals to other realms.

They hoped for safety there, that Ilos' flames could not reach them, and that she would protect them as they fled. It was her job; they were hers to protect, yet she knelt hopeless as everything crumbled into ruin. If her allies, family, friends, and lovers continued falling, Ilos would follow them to continue his purge of darkness.

He can't hurt them if he can't get to them.

She stood and turned to face the twin heart trees, their upper branches intertwining in the smoke and flames while their bases were illuminated with shimmering magic. Beyond the gateway, there were realms untouched by the war raging above. But not for long.

"Hurry!" She called out, her voice carrying over the crackling flames and screams of the dying. "Get everyone through!"

She watched the mortals, their faces streaked with ash and tears, their bodies weary from running. They stumbled forward, their eyes wide with fear and confusion, but they clung to their last hope. Elves, dwarves, humans, faunan, and everything in between worked together to evacuate. All but the Umbrals ran for sanctuary.

The shadow race ran from the portals towards them, with their weapons and shields raised to defend the refugees. Like her, they would not flee; they refused to leave their home and abandon it to ashes. They would die to protect their home, and she would die with them.

The ground beneath her trembled harder, a fissure splitting the earth nearby. The enemy was too close. Their power burned brighter and hotter as they clashed. The golden flames crept closer, devouring everything in their path. She had little time.

One by one, the mortals fled into the light of the portals—mothers clutching their children, elders limping toward safety, soldiers with shattered armor and broken spirits. She watched them go, her hands trembling as she pressed them against one of the trees.

"We will protect them, friend."

"I know you will," she looked up at the branches and smiled sadly before she looked back at the portals.

A young man—one of the last—hesitated at the portal's edge and turned back to look at her. His eyes met hers, wide and filled with something that looked like fear, not for himself, but for her. She wanted to tell him to go, that it didn't matter what happened to her as long as they survived, but she could not. Not when a voice broke through the chaos.

"Faetorin!"

Her heart stopped as a young silver-haired woman tried to run through the crowd but was stopped by a large-framed fallen Elyssar. A Vaelor. She screamed, clawed his skin, and pulled against him, but he did not let her near the portal.

"Keep her safe," she told him. "Do whatever it takes."

"You have my word," he nodded while she continued to fight and flail in his arms.

"No! I can help!" The woman protested, "I can fight!"

Her tears shimmered on her cheeks as the ground buckled under Faedi. The flames roared as the trees groaned, its ancient bark burning as the golden flames consumed it. Ilos was too close, his rage pressed into the air around her.

"Stay alive," she whispered before she forced the portals closed with a scream.

The portal snapped shut, the light fading into nothing. Once strong and proud, the tree was burning, its roots turning to ash. The flames surged towards her, heat singeing her skin, but she stood tall, her eyes closed, her heart heavy.

She saved them. That was all that mattered.

The fire roared around her, and she knew she would not survive. But even as the flames closed in, the forest's spirit stirred around her one last time. A gentle breeze caressed her cheek, like a final goodbye from the land she loved and raised.

Please grow again, even in the ashes. Grow again.

Faedi blinked awake, the soft warmth of the blankets cocooning her in comfort. For a moment, she stayed still, using the sensation to ground herself as the remnants of the dream faded from her mind. Sophir was beside her, his breathing steady, and she smiled at the sight of his face, so peaceful in the starlight filtering through the window.

Before she could argue with herself further, the peace shattered when a chill pierced her thoughts as a voice broke through the fog of sleep.

"We're under attack."

Lonan's voice echoed in her head, sharp and full of urgency. She bolted upright, her heart racing as the heaviness of the blankets slid off her. She barely had time to register the shift before Sophir moved beside her, scrambling to dress.

"I'm coming," Sophir promised, his voice low as he pulled on his clothes.

Faedi was already on her feet, grabbing her clothing and shouting for their new ally. "Bjorn!"

The door opened immediately, and there he was—scarred, weary, still dressed in his armor. He hadn't slept, and the deep circles under his eyes told her as much. His hand rested on his sword, ready for whatever was coming.

"Sophir is leaving," Faedi said quickly, pulling on her tunic. "I want Ighir and the others to go with him. Lonan and Grandpa were attacked. Can you send guards for them?"

Bjorn nodded and disappeared down the hall without another word.

"You need protection too," he said, his voice tight as he laced his boots.

"I have the Gaelisks, Bjorn, Aladia, and maybe even some Dusk Elves who like me enough to keep me safe," Faedi replied, tossing his sword. "Grandpa and Lonan don't have that. They only have the Watchers and their bonded."

She hated that she was right. As powerful as the Watchers were, Haldin and Lonan couldn't trust all the soldiers around them, not with the cultists so deeply rooted in their lands.

"Ighir should stay here," he said, grabbing her shoulders before she could argue. "He'll want to protect Zarae. I don't think he wants her running into a fight. If they're willing, I'll take the other Itmis, but I want him here with you."

Faedi frowned, biting back a protest, but she knew there was no point. He wasn't going to budge. "Fine."

She walked beside him as they hurried through the corridors. The castle was eerily quiet, save for the faint clink of armor and the whispers of servants. The silence unsettled her. The pegasi hadn't returned yet; the guards she'd sent after them were missing, and now she had to watch Sophir leave.

Torix met them at the entrance to the throne room, his face lined with concern. He was in armor this time, a rare sight, and Aladia appeared behind him, her eyes filled with the same worry. They all knew what this attack meant—Haldin was in danger, and it wouldn't be long before she was, too.

"What are the odds this is a ploy?" Torix asked, his voice low.

"To leave the throne and Faedi unprotected?" Bjorn growled softly. "A damn good chance."

"She's safer here than they are," Aladia added, handing Sophir a cloak.

"I agree," Faedi said, trying to force a smile. "I want you both back safely."

"I'll fly him back myself," Sophir promised as he fastened the cloak. "By then, Emmaline and Myst will be here too. We'll only have to worry about…"

"Everything else," Faedi finished for him, her smile faltering as she hugged herself.

"Scarred might be here by then too," he said softly, nudging her as if trying to lift her spirits.

"Unless he's under attack as well," Faedi muttered, her thoughts already reaching out to Scarred. *"Are you alright? Lonan and Grandpa being attacked—they went for the refugees and—"*

"We're fine, but do not go after them."

"I'm not. Sophir is with the Itmis."

"Is Da still with you?"

"He is—but the first group never arrived, and he's the best tracker I know. Emmaline and Myst are—"

"Faedi—"

"I'm not leaving them out there to die or worse."

"Dammit Faedi."

"I'll be fine."

"You better be."

It was strange—her bond with him felt deep, deeper even than what she shared with Lonan or Sophir. She still didn't understand why they couldn't hear her when she spoke to Scarred, but she was thankful she had that connection. The cultists hadn't taken everything from her.

"It seems like every bit of good news we get leads to more bad," Ighir said as he approached, the other Itmis trailing behind him in flight armor.

"Can you stay with Faedi and Zarae?" Sophir asked his uncle.

"I planned on it," Ighir nodded. "I won't leave them or the Gaelisks. Just come back in one piece—I don't want to explain to your siblings that you got yourself killed."

Faedi watched as he chuckled, but her stomach churned. This was the part she hated most—the waiting, the helplessness. His smile softened when he turned to her, gently lifting her chin, his fingers warm against her skin. She bit her lip, the familiar nervous gesture she couldn't shake.

"You better come back—all of you," she whispered, her voice cracking as she met his eyes.

"We will," he promised, kissing her softly, and she closed her eyes, breathing him in, holding on to the moment. "We'll be back before you even miss us."

"I'll keep her busy with informants and defensive measures," Bjorn added with a grin, and Faedi bit back a groan.

"Sounds like you're trying to make me sleep until they get back," she muttered, glaring playfully before stealing another kiss. "I want updates—more than what Lonan's been giving us."

"I'll tell you everything," he said, his voice steady. "And you tell me everything Scarred tells you. If we need to fly to him after we get Haldin and Lonan back safe, we will."

"He said he's fine, and you're not going anywhere without me and Lonan after this," Faedi stubbornly told him.

"As you wish," Sophir bowed his head, then turned to the Itmis. "Follow me. Lonan said there are wolves and cultists. We go in fighting."

Faedi stood in the doorway, watching them go, the weight of everything pressing down on her. It was all too much. Haldin, Lonan, the cultists, everything. She clutched her arms around herself, praying to the gods that she wouldn't lose anyone else.

59
The Weight of Waiting

Faedi

Absolutely not."

Torix towered over Faedi, his growl low and threatening. He clearly did not like the idea of looking for the missing refugees, but Faedi wasn't going to let that stop her. They needed help, and Torix was the best.

"If people attack Lonan and Grandpa, they're at risk," she said, standing tall and staring up at him. "They need help."

"And you need protection," Torix snarled.

Faedi gestured around the throne room, at the group gathered in the space. "I have the Dusk Elves, an army of Gaelisk, Bjorn, Aladia, Ighir, and Zarae. I'll be fine."

Torix scoffed, rolling his eyes. Of course, stating the obvious wouldn't sway him, but she had to try that before resorting to more desperate measures. If he refused to leave, she would have to choose the next best option.

She glanced at Bjorn, who subtly nodded with a sigh. He already knew what she planned to do.

"If you don't go look for them, I will," she said firmly.

"The heir—"

"Will not sit on the throne while children and their bonded sibling are lost in the snow and ice," Faedi interrupted quickly, her voice sharp and full of defiance.

The air thickened between them, both of them growling at each other, their wills clashing. The others in the room stood silent, watching with bated breath, waiting for one to back down.

Torix's growl deepened, resonating through the room. His golden eyes narrowed, daring her to yield, but Faedi refused. She couldn't. Her heart raced as she stood her ground. Torix was used to giving orders, used to his pack obeying him.

But Faedi was not his pack—she led her own hunt.

"I'm not losing anyone else," she said, her voice quieter now but no less fierce. "I won't let them die out there without doing everything I can to help them."

Torix took a step closer, his presence looming over her. His form was almost suffocating, but there was warmth in it too. The room around them seemed to disappear, and for a moment, it was just them—locked in a battle of wills.

"They're not your responsibility, Faedi," Torix snapped, his voice low and harsh. "You have oaths to uphold, and the heir—my daughter—must stay safe."

"They are my responsibility," Faedi shot back, her voice unwavering. "Myst is my sibling by bond, the forest-folk are my family, the freed slaves were promised protection by the Guardian and the Warden of the Tides—if I abandon them, I don't deserve to sit on a throne."

Torix's nostrils flared, and Faedi could see the internal conflict behind his eyes. He was torn, she could tell, but so was she. She wanted to honor her grandfather's wishes, but she couldn't do that if it meant leaving innocent people to die or be captured.

"I won't stand aside and do nothing," she whispered, her voice cracking with emotion.

For a moment, his expression softened, but it was brief. Just as quickly, his features hardened again. He shook his head. "If you go, they'll follow. They'll abandon their posts here to protect you, and the mountain's defenses will fall apart."

Faedi clenched her fists at her sides, feeling her claws dig into her palms. "Then don't make me leave."

"Faedi—"

"We both know I can get past you if I want to," she interrupted with another growl, her resolve unshaken.

The tension crackled in the air, a palpable force between them. Bjorn's quiet presence behind her gave her the strength to stand taller. He was ready to step in if needed, but only with her consent.

Torix's jaw clenched, and his massive form loomed over her like a mountain, but something shifted in his eyes. Recognition, maybe understanding. He knew she wasn't bluffing.

"The last time I left you, everything burned," he whispered.

"I'm not a child anymore, Da," Faedi said softly. "And I'm not alone." She relaxed slightly. "You know it's the right thing to do."

Torix let out a low, frustrated growl and turned away, pacing momentarily before whipping back to face her.

"You'll stay here," he ordered, his voice stern. "You'll stay in this damn castle, and I'll go. I'll find them. But if anything happens to you while I'm gone—anything—I'll kill everyone here and never forgive you."

His words struck her deeply, but she nodded slowly, sighing in relief. "I promise," she said softly. "I'll be here when you get back."

Torix turned his attention to Bjorn. "Not so much as a skinned knee," he ordered, and Faedi couldn't help but smile.

Bjorn stepped forward, resting a hand gently on her shoulder. "I won't let her out of my sight," he said before whispering to Faedi, "You sure that was the right call?"

Faedi didn't answer immediately. She was sure, but it didn't make her feel better as she watched Torix leave the room. "It's the only call I could make."

She watched as a small group followed Torix in response to his howl, which pierced the air. The snow fell harder, the wind whipped through the castle's stone walls. Somewhere out there, Lonan, Grandpa, Sophir, Myst, Emmaline, and the others were fighting for their lives.

And all she could do was wait.

"You did what?"

"I had to. Someone we can trust needs to find Emmaline and Myst and the others. Da's the best person for the job."

"And that leaves you with one less person to protect you."

"Bjorn and everyone else are practically glued to me right now, and you're acting like I can't defend myself. I've done quite well in surviving and escaping danger thus far."

"If they're blocking the exits, how will you escape a stone fortress?"

"I'll figure something out. I'm good at that too."

"Dammit, Faedi."

"You seem to love saying that." Faedi sighed and rubbed between her brows.

Bjorn smiled at her as he placed plates of food down and sat beside her. "They aren't happy?"

"Not really, no," she shook her head and watched Aladia pour mead for them. "Would you be happy with your bonded doing something dangerous?"

He chuckled and sipped from his glass before patting the seat beside him for Aladia. "I wasn't at first—but I'm used to it now."

"How long until she's here?" Faedi raised her eyebrows.

"Not sure. I told her about the attack, and she just said she'd be here soon," he shrugged. "Either she's helping, coming here for backup, or she has other plans…we keep details limited—just in case."

Faedi stared at the food on the plates, frowning. She hated not having information. "Better than me. I feel like I'm going insane waiting for updates."

"Just because we do it doesn't mean I like it—sometimes you get used to unpleasant things."

That I understand.

She gently rubbed her arm and bit her lip. The pain was always there, even with the vines and flowers, but she had learned how to deal with the daily pain. It was like washing clothes in the cold river—eventually, the sting would numb.

"Well, hopefully, once we figure everything out and get everyone together, you won't have to be used to not talking to her anymore." She smiled at him before she began to eat. The food was flavorless, but she needed to stay strong. If everyone else was under attack, she knew there was a good chance she wouldn't be safe for long.

They won't waste a chance to get us while we're separated.

"Depends…we need to find her sister, and if she's not here…" Bjorn trailed off, frowning.

Faedi glanced at Aladia, who seemed uncomfortable in her seat beside Bjorn but didn't comment. "That was a big list," Faedi sighed. "Can the mountain hold defenses against the cultists and their allies?"

"It's stood for centuries, and all siege attempts for the past several ages have failed," Aladia nodded. "And if we truly have support from the Helgi, we'll have better defenses of our shores."

Faedi set her utensils down, narrowing her eyes as she took everything in. Beyond their primary goal of rescuing everyone Ilos' cultists wanted to sacrifice, they had no plan. Everything was purely defensive, and while she didn't want to draw any additional attention to themselves, she wondered if an offense might be a better defense.

"I think I dreamed of someone sealed in Draetor," Faedi whispered. "Of the portals to the other realms being closed."

Bjorn turned to face her slowly. She didn't need to look at him to know he was staring. "What happened in the dream?"

"People were dead," her voice trembled as she gripped the edge of the table. "The gods were fighting in the sky—someone was in one of the portals, a man was holding her back…I told him to protect her…then everything burned…I think I was seeing what Faetorin saw."

He was silent for longer than she was comfortable with before he sighed and offered her mead. He didn't speak until she took a sip. He wanted her to calm her nerves.

"The Great War, I remember pieces of it." His voice was softer than she'd ever heard it. "We were losing—too many of us died…gods and their chosen ones. Rhodri broke the earth into pieces after the realms were sealed. He said it was a plan he and Faetorin made…that if the forest died, he would do it to save whoever he could."

Faedi stared at the mead in her cup as it swirled around. Slowly, the dream, the memory, began to make more sense.

She sighed. "Faetorin was either going to die in the fight or die when he split the world."

"She was the earth," he nodded. "I assume he didn't want her to experience being quartered. They feel it—when what they are, what they're connected to is hurt or anything."

Faedi turned to look at him and narrowed her eyes. "Do we feel it too?"

He leaned closer to her; his one red eye shined brighter as he stared into her eyes. "I know you want to kill the man who posed as your father. That you want to burn him alive and make him hurt the way your mother and brothers did." Bjorn smiled when she leaned away, "I felt it as soon as you wanted it…several days ago, in Emsmeda."

Even if Faedi was willing to believe what everyone claimed about them being claimed by gods, she was still skeptical, but Bjorn chipped away at her doubts. It was easy to assume that she might want to hurt the person who got her family killed, but it was surprising he knew how and when she wanted it. Unless Sophir or Lonan told him, he wouldn't have known when she found out.

She raised an eyebrow at him. "Are you able to know if I get to do that?"

"No," he shook his head before smiling. "But if you were to…ask Vengeance for help, strength, or anything to help you get that goal, I would be bound to help however I could."

That sounded too good to be true. He had nothing to gain from helping her. "Just like that? No payment or anything? What if you meet him first and suddenly decide you like him?"

"He's an ally of Ilos," his jaw tensed with a growl. "The gods, even their chosen mortal tools, we can choose who we help. If someone were to pray to the forest and ask for help to…I don't know—keep them safe while they cut down all of the trees in the Mire, would Faetorin?"

What kind of question was that? "No."

"Then they would not have their help or yours," he smiled.

Aladia leaned back in her chair to look between them. "Seems kind of…ungodly to pick and choose who you help."

"Ilos has his underlings who do what our patrons won't," Bjorn pulled a coin from his pocket and held it up between his thumb and forefingers. "When he started the war, he had others backing him. Gods who turned against the Ancients, or mortals who rose to godhood through various means. For every one of us on our side—he has someone sworn to him to do the same service."

Faedi focused on the coin as he flipped it and watched it land in his open palm. "Can Zarae feel them?"

"No."

She reached to flip the coin over in his hand. "Can she feel Ilos?"

He nodded. "She can."

"Then what if the goal isn't to be sacrificed to Ilos?" Faedi took the coin from his hand and replaced it with one from her pocket. "What if the goal is to sacrifice us to his chosen people?"

Bjorn didn't move from the table, and his eyes stopped following her, as if his attention drifted elsewhere, while Aladia watched her. She seemed intrigued but didn't speak. Instead, her lips pressed into a frown.

Faedi tilted her head to the side. "Bjorn?"

He continued to stare off for several more moments before he blinked and looked back at her with a nod. "It's possible."

"Does that change any of the plans?" Aladia looked between them.

Faedi glanced at Bjorn while she bit her lip. The end result was the same if the goal was to perform a mass sacrifice—all of the eclipse-born needed to come together to defend themselves. If they were god-touched and had some untapped potential, they would be harder to fight if they were together.

"No," Bjorn and Faedi answered in unison.

Faedi turned her attention back to Aladia and nodded to herself. "We get everyone together that we can, and we fight. We survive."

60
Veil of Darkness

"We should have sent them to the Mire. A death in the Sauvern would have been kinder than this."

Lonan

There were more dead than living as Lonan fought through the fire.

Along with the Watchers and the remaining soldiers, he formed a defensive line. Their weapons gleamed in the firelight, casting long shadows across the ground that danced with their own life. His knives were ready, but time was running out. The flames were closing in, and there were too many of them—wolves, fire, and chaos pressing from all sides.

A howl rose above the noise, a signal, and the next wave hit hard. They came faster, stronger. Lonan slashed at a wolf that lunged at him, his blade cutting through thick fur and into flesh, but another was already at his back. He twisted, dodging the worst of the bite, but pain flared as its teeth grazed his arm.

"They're breaking through!" Someone shouted, but the roar of the flames swallowed the voice.

Lonan glanced at the ice barrier—it was already crumbling, the constant assault taking its toll. Haldin's magic flickered, his face pale with exhaustion. They wouldn't last much longer.

"Fall back!" Lonan called, his voice hoarse. "Push into the caves!"

Before they could even begin to retreat, the ice shattered. Wolves poured through, their eyes gleaming in the firelight.

They fought like hell. Lonan let his shadows free, moving through the chaos, knives flashing as he struck at the creatures, but it wasn't enough. One by one, their line broke. A Watcher fell beside him, his sword slipping from his hands as a wolf tore into his neck. Another soldier was knocked to the ground, screaming as flames engulfed him.

Lonan looked toward Haldin, but he was barely holding on, his strength fading as he fought to keep the fire at bay. Panic clawed at Lonan's chest. They were losing. They were going to die.

"We won't last much longer, Sophir," he called out through the bond as he slashed wildly at a wolf closing in.

"Hold on. We see you."

A gust of wind ripped through the battlefield, colder than anything Lonan had ever felt. Some of the fires died from the force of it. The wolves hesitated, their snarls turning to whimpers as shards of ice began to fall from the sky.

Dozens of Itmis landed among the chaos, weapons raised, their scales gleaming in the firelight. They fought with a symphony of roars that sent snow and ice cascading from the rocks. On the outskirts of the battle, a blast of ice shot out in all directions, halting the enemy's advance. In the center of it all, a black-scaled Itmis landed.

"There are fires all over the ridge," Sophir shouted over the battle. "Regroup, we need to move!"

Lonan didn't need to be told twice. He grabbed the nearest soldier by the arm and hauled him to his feet. Behind him, the wind howled, carrying with it the shouts of spells—cultists or some of their many allies.

"Are they near the castle?" Lonan asked as he rushed to Sophir's side. "Is Faedi safe?"

"The area was clear when we left, but I don't trust it for long. With everything we saw on the way down…" Sophir trailed off, shaking his head.

He didn't need to finish the sentence. His unspoken fear trickled through the bond. Whatever he had seen on the way down hadn't been meant for them— some of it had been meant for Faedi. If any attention remained on the Mire, it wasn't nearly as much as what was on the mountain. The cultists were making their move, and they weren't ready.

"We can't stay here," Lonan said. His mind flashed to Faedi; the thought of her alone in the stone fortress gnawed at him worse than his wounds.

Sophir stepped beside him and roared, his wings unfurling to block a blast of fire as it shot toward them. "We'll fly out. Hold on."

The remaining soldiers and refugees stumbled about, some barely able to walk, others dragging the wounded. Lonan scanned the ridge, searching for any clear path of escape, but there was only fire.

The Itmis held the wolves at bay, their roars mingling with the clash of metal and the screams of the dying as they worked to gather as many as they could. The only mercy left was ensuring they abandoned nothing but corpses. Lonan didn't want to leave anyone behind, but they couldn't afford to carry the dead— not unless they wanted to die with them.

Sophir slammed his tail into a charging wolf, sending it skidding across the icy ground before turning back to Lonan. "We're leaving. The others will see to everyone else. I'm not waiting."

He was right. It wasn't a fight they could win. Survival was their only option—getting the others to safety and returning to Faedi. If enemies waited on the ridges, the flight back wouldn't be easy. Sophir would have to fly wide to ensure their survival, even if it meant making Faedi wait longer.

"Get us back," Lonan said with a nod—then a sharp sting struck his side.

He spun and slashed blindly, but hit nothing. Then he looked down as wet heat spread across his leg. Blood soaked through his clothes, an arrow jutting from his ribs.

"Fuck."

Pain surged through him as the injury fully registered. His vision blurred, fire and blood blending into a feverish haze. He gasped for air, but every breath burned in his lungs.

"Have healers ready."

Sophir's voice boomed through the bond, but Lonan knew he wasn't speaking to him. He was speaking to the scream that echoed in his mind.

As darkness crept around Lonan, he remembered the first time he had been taken into the depths of the void. It had been vast, silent, and endless—a place that swallowed all light and sound. He had been young then, still learning to control his power, to bend the shadows to his will. He had thought he understood darkness, having wielded it and being part of it, but he had realized then that it was something different—something ancient, primordial, in the void.

"Do you feel it, Lonan?" A low rumble overpowered everything else. Sound seemed to coil and twist within the darkness, captured and held in place—just like him.

He nodded, though he wasn't entirely sure if he should answer. "I feel… stillness. Quiet."

The voice chuckled, a sound more like a vibration through his chest than anything audible. "You feel what you think darkness is, but that is not the truth of it. It is not the truth of you." A hand formed in front of his face and rippled. "Darkness is not the absence of light or sound. It is its own life force. Alive. It moves. It consumes. And it gives."

"What does darkness have to give?" Lonan asked as he searched for Sophir. He should have been with him, but he couldn't see him in the void.

"Life."

The darkness shifted and swirled, revealing a man of shadows. He was enormous, larger than any living creature Lonan had ever encountered. However, his size didn't intimidate him.

Lonan realized then that it had been his hand in front of his face. As he pulled back, the shadows around Lonan dissipated. Without thinking, he walked toward him, toward the power he commanded so effortlessly. The shadow chuckled again, and Lonan hesitated, realizing there should have been pain.

Did I die?

"Your body is safe, but your soul is restless." The massive shadow smiled, his pearly white teeth stark against the blackness surrounding him.

"Why is it restless?" Lonan asked, his eyes locked on the figure's hand, which continued to manipulate the wisps of shadow.

"It knows it must wake up," the figure said, his voice gentle. "As talented as you may be as the heir of the Mire, your power is nothing compared to what Ilos stole."

Lonan frowned, unsure of his meaning. "So I am god-touched, like everyone says?"

The shadowy figure before him chuckled again, his deep voice vibrating through the void like a distant thunderstorm.

"You are so much more," he said, his eyes fixing on Lonan with a nearly unbearable weight. "Not one of the seven, but no less powerful in your divine right. I had planned to make you my representative on the mortal plane, but you chose love instead of honoring your father."

Lonan narrowed his eyes. "Marrying Faedi was honoring my father."

The massive shadow pulsed, as if the very fabric of the void reacted to Lonan's words. His eyes gleamed—cold and distant, like stars swallowed by the dark—and a smile spread across his face, too sharp, too knowing.

"Tagil, King of the Umbrals, your father?" he mused. "This is what you believe? What you remember?"

Unease crept up Lonan's spine. He stepped back, but the shadows pulled him closer. It was as though the void wanted him to hear what the figure had to say. Clenching his fists, he felt the familiar hum of shadow magic swirl around his skin, ready to lash out if necessary.

"What do you mean? I don't remember anything," Lonan said, his voice steady despite his nerves.

The figure laughed as he moved closer, towering over him. "This mortal body may be the son of a mere Umbral king, Lonan. However, your first father is me. Darkness itself gave you life. I crafted you from the shadows themselves. You are my blood, my legacy."

Lonan's pulse quickened, but he kept his composure, glaring up at the figure despite the doubt creeping into his mind. The light hurt Faedi—why wouldn't the dark hurt him? "Then why come to me now? Why not before?"

"I come to you each time you are close to death," he said, his voice wavering. "I watch. I wait… and only when you are in danger do you open yourself to me."

Lonan shook his head, forcing down the anger bubbling up in him. "Sounds like you don't try hard enough."

The shadow narrowed his eyes. "Always the skeptic."

Lonan clenched his fists tighter. "It's kept me alive so far."

"No, not always," the figure agreed, his voice suddenly soft—almost tender. "But for you, it has been. Love will kill you, boy."

The words hit him like a cold gust of wind, cutting deep and sinking into places he didn't want to acknowledge. Images flashed through his mind while his heart clenched, and he fought to maintain composure. He watched them fall in dozens of ways, experienced the agonizing void left in their absence. All the while, the figure's words echoed in his mind.

"I won't abandon them," Lonan gasped, his voice raw.

The shadow watched him, his eyes gleaming with that knowing look that made Lonan wonder if he enjoyed every second of the torment. "You don't have to," he said. "But you can't isolate yourselves. You can't run and hide. You have to fight—if not for yourself, for them."

"Why?" Lonan asked despite his better judgment.

"Because Ilos has no replacements now that everyone is chosen... and when the second moon rises, he will only have one option," the figure explained before waving his hand in front of Lonan's face.

Screams ripped through his mind.

"He started the process with Faedi—years ago."

Pain tore through his body, and he dropped to his knees as the air was sucked from his lungs. Light filled his senses, and his skin blazed like fire. Every inch of him was ripped apart and sewn back together—over and over again—while the screams continued.

The voice in the light hurt us. Sylrie and me.

The pain was unbearable, unlike anything he had ever felt before. It wasn't just physical—it tore through his soul, as if the light were burning away everything he was. His breath came in ragged gasps as he clutched the darkness around him. Then... everything stopped.

"He will break them, Lonan, and you will only have yourself to blame if you don't protect them."

61

The Plagued

Faedi

The sharp, sudden pain lanced through her as if a blade had slipped between her ribs. She stumbled, clutching at her side. Lonan. It was him; she could feel it as surely as the blood pulsing in her veins. There was no mistaking that familiar weight, the dark pull of him, and then… something else, something sharp and wrong. It was the same as when she had been shot ten years prior.

She clamped her hands over her mouth to stifle a whimper, desperate to keep herself steady. Bjorn's hands gripped her shoulder, but she couldn't hear him over Sophir's voice in her mind, urging her to prepare healers. Her mind raced wildly, her skin prickling with dread.

"Where are you? How bad is it?" Her questions hammered through her mind, shouted through the bond, demanding answers.

Panic coiled in her chest. She wanted to scream, to tear through the palace walls and race to them, but she couldn't. The oath—the gods-cursed oath— bound her to remain in the castle while her grandfather was away—an heir of the Tides. The vines of those flowers twisted around her as tightly as any chains, pinning her there.

She sucked in a shaky breath, wrestling to control the fear that threatened to drown her. She couldn't go after him. She couldn't be there to pull him from danger or cradle his head in her lap while she healed him, and the helplessness clawed at her like a wild animal.

Ancients… please, let him be all right.

380

As the desperation simmered in her veins, she squeezed her eyes shut and tried to steady her breathing. The bond between them thrummed with distress—then went silent. She reached for it, grasping for it blindly in her mind while a sob shook her.

Bjorn's hands tightened on her shoulders, grounding her just enough to keep her knees from giving way. "Faedi," he whispered, his voice low. "What's going on? What happened?"

"Lonan's hurt," she gasped. "He's unconscious or…"

Bjorn moved to stand in front of her. "Sophir will bring him here. He'll have healers and you by his side soon."

That didn't ease the panic clawing at her heart. Sophir continued sending updates through the bond—fragments of thought, intentional speech—as he fled the battle. She wished she could see where they were, but all she could see was Bjorn's face. However, she could feel Sophir's worry; it rolled off him like a storm ready to break.

She swallowed hard, doing everything she could to focus on the world around her. Her fingers curled into fists, claws digging into her palms to keep her hands from trembling. She could only wait, helpless, until they returned.

"You're stronger than this," she told Lonan through the bond. *"You're coming back to me. You have to… you promised."*

Bjorn led her through the castle, shouting for healers to be gathered, and took her toward the stables. She didn't know if that was where Sophir would bring Lonan—he could land anywhere with him—but she didn't argue. She was too focused on trying to connect to Lonan to do anything else.

"We'll wait here for them," he announced, directing her to sit on a bench.

She nodded mutely, unable to speak as her throat tightened. Her skin was cold, tears welled in her eyes, and her heart pounded in her chest—she couldn't focus on anything else. The Ancients themselves could have appeared before her, and she wouldn't have moved.

As she sat on the bench, nearly paralyzed with dread, she forced herself to focus on each breath and heartbeat and clung to the thought of Lonan. Their bond remained silent, but the memory of his warmth and the depth of his presence faintly resonated within her.

Then, faintly, the bond trembled—a soft flicker of life, a fleeting connection. Lonan. She seized it, calling his name through the bond, pouring everything she had into that connection. He was alive, but his presence was faint and distant, slipping from her grasp as quickly as she sensed it.

Bjorn's steady voice murmured beside her, his hand resting on her shoulder as he continued barking orders. Gradually, his unwavering presence settled some of the chaos in her mind. If he could hold himself together while his bonded was in danger, she could do the same. She had to.

She looked up at him and gripped her knees for stability. "Can you feel it when she's hurt?"

He paused and turned his attention back to her. Then, after a long and silent stare, he nodded. "Every single time."

"Has she been hurt since you met me?" He never seemed as if anything was wrong while he was with her.

Bjorn stepped away from her with a sigh. "Yes."

She didn't press him for information, even if she wanted to know more. The times Lonan had been severely injured before—when the cultists attacked the cottage, when they were tortured—she had been too distracted by her own pain to recognize his. Or maybe she hadn't felt it because she was nearby. No one had ever really told her how deep the bond went.

She needed to know everything she could. It could help.

Cautiously, she spoke again and hoped Bjorn wouldn't be upset. "What else do you feel?"

His brows creased as he regarded her, his eyes searching her face, before he sat beside her and scratched his chin. "It depends… We learned how to silence the bond, for our sanity mostly…" He leaned back and stared at the ceiling. "Heightened emotions… pain, pleasure… I feel what she lets me. She's better at keeping herself quiet."

Her eyebrows raised. "But you're so serious all the time."

He laughed and shook his head. "Silencing the bond and putting on a brave face are two different things." Bjorn turned to straddle the bench and faced her. "I've had centuries to learn how to keep quiet."

"How do you keep yourself sane if you don't speak freely?"

Bjorn's gaze softened, and there was a hint of something wistful in his eyes, as though he remembered something long buried. He paused, his fingers tracing a small circle on the worn wood of the bench, and she could almost see the weight of his centuries pressing down on him.

"It isn't easy," he said quietly. "But bonds… they're complicated. They're a blessing and a curse. When you have someone, a part of you becomes them, and their burdens become yours. I keep myself sane because I don't want her to worry about me." He exhaled, his shoulders relaxing as he spoke.

Faedi mulled over his words, searching for anything to help her hold herself together. Anything that might make waiting easier. "But what if… what if I need him? If shutting him out feels… like I'm losing a part of myself?"

Bjorn's gaze held hers, and he spoke with a low, steady voice. "We don't get to choose how strong the bond feels, but you can learn how to manage it—without losing that connection you need. You have to anchor it in something stronger than the bond itself. For me, it's duty… my oath. The trust she has in me to honor it."

The word trust reverberated through her, softening the sharp edges of her worry. Trust—trust that Lonan would fight to return to her and do whatever it took. He had a strength, one as stubborn as hers, that had already seen him through so much.

Bjorn's words lingered between them, and she found herself nodding, the fear no longer as strong as it had been. "He's the most stubborn person I know," she murmured. "He won't let go."

A shadow crossed Bjorn's face as he glanced away, his mouth curving into a wry smile. "If he's anything like you, I'd wager he's already clawing his way back."

Before she could respond, hurried footsteps broke through the silence. They straightened, and she glanced behind Bjorn as he stood and turned. Aladia raced toward them, her cheeks flushed as she gasped for air.

"Refugees…" she slid to a stop and sucked in air. "In the courtyard."

Faedi and Bjorn sprinted through the castle behind Aladia as she led them through the winding hallways. Their footsteps echoed sharply against the cold stone, bouncing off the walls behind them. The air grew denser with each step, Faedi's pulse a thunderous beast as she steeled herself for whatever scene awaited their arrival.

They burst into the courtyard, and the sight that greeted them made her breath hitch. People—dozens of them, bloody, nearly frozen, and disheveled—huddled together near the entrance, their clothes torn and faces smeared with filth. Children clung to their parents, wide-eyed and silent, while others clutched meager belongings wrapped in worn cloth.

Bjorn tensed beside her as they took in the scene. He didn't need to say anything; her mind was beside his as she recognized the dress style among the refugees. They weren't Valorians or farmers—they were from Dewgate.

Faedi moved forward, lowering herself to the eye level of a young girl clutching a tattered doll. The child's wide, frightened eyes met hers, and she offered a soft smile, hoping to put her at ease.

"Hello," she said gently, keeping her voice low. "Are you hurt?"

The girl shook her head and clung to the doll as though it were her last thread of comfort. Someone in a black cloak stepped forward, their face bloody as they cradled a bundle in their arms. Faedi's blood chilled when she recognized them.

Myst.

"We found them on our way up," their voice was hoarse. The bundle in their arms shifted, and Faedi sighed in relief when she spotted red hair. "Dewgate is overrun with the plague. They fled—some of them are sick."

Bjorn was beside her instantly, scooping the child into his arms. "Bring the healers," he called over his shoulder. "Have one remain at the stables, just in case."

"Get them blankets and hot meals," Faedi instructed the nearby guards. "No one rests until everyone is taken care of."

Aladia nodded and quickly rushed to gather the servants, who sprang into action, leading some of the most haggard-looking people toward the throne room.

Faedi turned her attention back to Myst. "Tell me everything."

They nodded, the refugees' relief settling on her shoulders. Just as she straightened, a faint flicker in the bond sent a ghost of pain through her—a shadowed and distant sensation. Lonan. It was fleeting, slipping away as quickly as it had come, but it was enough to make her heart race.

"We were attacked on the way up," Myst's voice was muffled. Faedi nearly lost herself in the sensation of the bond but forced her focus back on them. "Espen helped us escape, but while we were trying to find a safe path here, we found them. There are groups all over the peaks. We didn't know who was friendly, so…we hid in the caves and only traveled at night."

A weary man with a gash along his arm approached, his voice low and grim. "A woman came to us in our dreams…she told us to flee—that there was a sickness in Dewgate. She told us the mountain was safe."

Faedi's brow creased. "Did she say anything else?" She wondered if it was the same woman who had come to her. "Did you see her?"

The man shook his head, his eyes haunted. "No, she…she was only a voice. She said to leave at once, that the sickness would take everyone. She said Lord Blavier would kill us all."

"What about Elder Ravyn?" He wouldn't have let them wander up the mountains without help.

The man lowered his head, and Faedi's heart stopped. "No one's seen him."

No—he was fine. He had to be somewhere else, making plans.

Bjorn's hand on her shoulder brought her back to the moment. His eyes were sharp as steel, but beneath that, she could see the worry etched into his face. "The healers will need to know if anyone has shown symptoms. We can't risk the sickness spreading through the castle…or beyond that."

Faedi nodded and turned to the refugees. "If anyone feels feverish, come forward now. We have ways to help you, but you must be honest." Her voice was gentle but firm. A few people stepped forward one by one. Myst moved with them, murmuring reassurances, their expression taut with exhaustion.

"You too?" Faedi asked.

"No," Myst shook their head. "But Emmaline took a fever this morning."

Bjorn's gaze flicked to Faedi. "We'll need to separate the sick from the rest. We can use the armory as a quarantine—it's isolated enough."

She met his eyes and nodded. "Good. Go to the throne room and help Aladia prepare cots. I'll take the others there…I've dealt with this before."

Bjorn paused, his eyes widening momentarily before he inclined his head and moved to direct the others.

Faedi turned to Myst, placing a hand on their arm. "I can take her," she offered gently. "You should rest."

They shook their head. "She's been by my side this whole time…either I'll start getting sick soon, or I'm immune. I can help."

They were right; Myst and Lonan had never left her side when he took her to the Mire with her fever. They had helped however their mother instructed them, and she knew Myst had a talent for magical healing.

They needed all the help they could get.

Faedi took a steadying breath, lifted her chin, and focused on the sick person who had stepped forward. "Follow me. We'll get you settled and fed while the healers work."

62

Blaze in the Night

"Don't die. You can't die. Faedi needs you—I need you."

Sophir

The wind tore through the night as Sophir surged higher, his wings beating fiercely as he held Lonan close to his chest. Lonan's body remained unnervingly still, his head lolling against Sophir's shoulder, and the only sound over the rush of wind was his shallow, uneven breaths. The wound in his side seeped through the layers of cloth Sophir had tied around it, staining his hands and chest with dark, sticky blood.

The wound was terrible, but he had no choice. He couldn't stop; he had to get Lonan to safety, to Faedi, before it was too late.

"Myst and Emmaline got here—they led refugees from Dewgate. They're saying Blavier spread the plague through the city," came the voice through the bond.

"Bastard," Sophir growled. *"Lonan's unconscious, but he's alive. We should be there soon. The Itmis scattered, and I lost track of them along the way."*

"I'm in the armory with the sick refugees…when you get here, go to the throne room. I don't want Lonan near any of this."

A flash of movement below caught Sophir's eye, and he instinctively tightened his grip on Lonan. Cultists—dozens of them—snaked their way up the trails beneath, hidden in the moonlit shadows and drifting clouds. They were armed, and the gleam of golden metal and the sharp movements of their bodies gave them away. He had already counted at least three groups making their way up the mountain, and with Lonan unconscious, he knew he couldn't risk being spotted.

Every instinct told him to stay in the shadows, but the higher he flew, the thinner the air became, making it harder to navigate the narrow ridges.

"Hold on," he whispered to Lonan. "We're almost there."

His back and wings ached, straining under the weight, but he pushed harder. His gaze remained fixed ahead, searching for the familiar, twisted rock formations that marked the final stretch of their journey. He expected to see the guards Faedi had posted to watch for assailants—unless they were already dead.

A memory flickered through his mind of Faedi's face just before he had left her, eyes wide and worried, her arms hugging herself for comfort. She had sent him for Lonan without hesitation, her own safety an afterthought. She had been terrified, even if she hadn't said it out loud. He had seen it in her eyes—just like in the cottage. She was always calm under pressure, but those two times, she had been so close to breaking.

Faedi was counting on him to bring Lonan back—for them to return to her.

Sophir tucked his wings closer to his sides, narrowing his path through the air to avoid the cultists below. The sharp tang of smoke from their torches reached his nose. They hadn't seen him yet; the absence of their eyes on him brought a strange relief to the pit of his stomach. However, he couldn't be sure how much longer that would last. They were getting closer to the last ridge, and he knew they wouldn't hesitate to cut down anything in their path.

"Ancients, let him hold on," he whispered. He couldn't see the full extent of Lonan's injury, but he knew Lonan was fading. His own strength waned with every beat of his wings, but he refused to stop. He wouldn't.

For Faedi, as much as for Lonan.

The rocky terrain of the mountain pass grew sharper, more treacherous. The cultists' voices echoed faintly below, but Sophir pushed higher, veering away from their line of sight. The frigid air stung his eyes and sent jolts of pain through his wings, but he didn't let up for a moment. His mind remained locked on Faedi, on the look of relief that would cross her face the moment she saw them again.

A sudden shift in the weight in his arms startled him. Lonan's head lolled to one side, his breathing ragged and uneven. Panic surged through Sophir, and a hot, unfamiliar sensation clawed at his chest. "Lonan," he shook him urgently. "Hold on. Stay with me."

Lonan didn't respond, but his chest rose faintly—just enough to give Sophir hope.

Ahead, light caught Sophir's attention, revealing the jagged rocks that marked the final pass to the castle. Relief washed over him, but it was short-lived; a figure stood silhouetted against the moonlit sky—gold glistening in the firelight. It wasn't one of Faedi's guards; it was a cultist scout stationed high on the ridge. Sophir froze midair, hovering just outside the torch's light, hoping the darkness would cloak them long enough for the scout to look away.

But he didn't. His gaze landed on them, and in an instant, he drew his weapon. The glint of steel caught the moonlight.

"Damn it," Sophir muttered, twisting sharply to the left, searching for anything to disappear behind. The cultist moved fast, raising an arrow and loosing it in one fluid motion. The arrow whistled through the air, missing them by inches, but the chill of its passing sent a shiver of unease through Sophir. He tightened his hold on Lonan, turning away from the ridge, hoping to gain enough distance to lose the scout.

The cultist shouted to his comrades below, his voice echoing through the mountain pass. Sophir cursed under his breath, knowing they had lost the advantage of surprise. He couldn't fight—not with Lonan in his arms. His only choice was to keep climbing, to reach the castle before the cultists overtook them.

The wind howled around them, carrying the cultists' voices, but Sophir ignored them, pushing himself harder than he ever had before. His wings screamed in protest, every muscle burning, but he forced himself to keep going.

"We're almost there, but cultists are close to the castle. I don't see the wall you ordered to be made either," he called to Faedi. *"I don't think there was enough time to prepare."*

"I'll send word for everyone to fall back to the castle; just get here safely."

Sophir couldn't evade them anymore.

Arrows whistled past his head, slicing through the darkness and scattering embers in their wake. The cultists were on him, their shouts echoing through the night, and the heat of their spells blazed against his wings as he struggled to keep altitude. Lonan's weight felt heavier with every wingbeat, and he clenched his teeth, driving himself forward through the wind and fiery assault.

The cultists moved in viscous waves, relentless as they clambered up the ridge, arrows and flames flying as they tried to strike from below. Sophir beat his wings harder, wincing as an arrow grazed the edge of his wing, splitting through the skin and leaving a trail of pain in its wake. The castle was close, but with every second, it seemed further away, obscured by the shadows of the cultists and the flashes of fire.

The moon glinted off a sea of golden armor beneath him, and he cursed under his breath. They knew he was coming—or at least suspected it. Lonan's ragged breaths came heavier against his chest, and he cursed again. Lonan was barely holding on. There was no time for delay.

With one final beat, Sophir angled himself upward, desperate to distance them from the cultists below. Cold and biting, the wind pressed in his ears, and he wrapped his arms tighter around Lonan. "Just a little longer," he whispered, half to him and half to himself. "Almost there."

Suddenly, a blaze of fire erupted from below, a cultist furling flames directly into his path. He twisted sharply, narrowly avoiding the searing heat, but the force of the turn sent him spiraling. His heart pounded a panicked rhythm that drowned out every other sound. He steadied himself, flaring his wings to slow their descent, but the cultists didn't relent. Another arrow shot past, so close that its razor-sharp tip grazed his cheek.

Blood trickled down his face, but he ignored it, focusing on the mountain that grew larger with every beat of his wings—on the stained glass illuminated by torches inside the castle. Ice walls had been raised on the outskirts of the ridges closest to the stronghold, and mounted guards patrolled them, but they were outnumbered.

"Ancients, we're so close," he whispered, pushing himself harder. His body screamed in protest, every beat of his wings raw agony, but he didn't let himself slow down. Their lives depended on it.

Below, another cultist raised his hand, gathering a ball of fire between his fingers. He was too close to avoid, and panic surged through Sophir as the man hurled the flames with a shout. He did what he could—he veered sharply and wrapped his body and wings around Lonan.

Pain exploded through him as the fire burned into his wings, the acrid scent of his own flesh filling his senses. He fought against it, but his wings were too damaged, his flight path too unsteady. The courtyard was still too far. If he didn't gain more height, he would crash into the ice wall, but he continued to spiral downward. His wings refused to cooperate, every attempt at movement sending fresh jolts of pain through him.

"Ancients help me," he groaned, forcing his wings to beat as hard as they could.

Another arrow sliced through the air, burying itself in his shoulder. The force nearly did him in, and he let out a strangled cry, his vision blurring with the pain. Lonan slipped in his arms, and he tightened his grip, desperate to keep him safe.

"No," he gasped, forcing himself to keep going. "Just a little further…"

With one final surge of strength, he angled himself toward the courtyard, preparing for a rough landing. He barely had control, his damaged wings throwing him off balance, and he braced himself for the impact, tightening his hold on Lonan as they rolled.

His back and wings crashed through the top of the ice wall, and the ground rushed up to meet them. He hit the courtyard hard, the force of the landing rattling through his bones. Pain exploded through his body as they tumbled across the snowy stone. He clutched Lonan to his chest, shielding him from the worst of the impact, but the landing left him breathless.

For a moment, he lay there, dazed and disoriented, the world spinning around him. Voices—shouts, hurried footsteps—surrounded him, but they were distant, muffled by the ringing in his ears. His vision swam, and he struggled to fill his lungs with air.

As the world blurred around him, a pair of bright blue eyes stared into his, and soft strands of red hair tickled his face. He couldn't hear her words or read her lips, but he recognized the expression.

Relief.

They had made it.

"Help him," he rasped, releasing his hold on Lonan.

She nodded, her gaze flickering elsewhere. His back arched as he cried out when she touched him.

"Ig!" Her voice finally reached him through the haze of pain. "Get them to the throne room!"

"Cultists—" he gasped, but she silenced him with a shake of her head.

"We know. They're surrounding us, but they're not getting close to the wall," she explained as she examined him. "They're waiting for something… we don't know what yet."

Pain throbbed through his body, but his mind raced with a different kind of agony. He had made it back with Lonan, but he didn't know about the others. He didn't know if Haldin was alive or dead. And the enemy was here.

It closed around them.

There were more cultists than in the cottage. And when they attacked, he didn't know if they would survive it this time.

63
Into the Depths

"How did these bastards slip by? They shouldn't be here—we should have had a warning."

Sylvie

Salt spray stung Scarred's eyes as he gripped the ship's rail, but he remained fixed on the dark silhouettes of the boats closing in through the storm. Their sails loomed like torn, red wings against the rolling sky, twisted symbols painted in gold streaks. He knew those symbols well—had seen them carved into flesh, marked on temple walls, and painted on the waters of once-thriving harbors. Cultists of Ilos. They were the kind who took pleasure in spilling innocent blood and reveling in the chaos that followed.

Rowdon wasn't far; they had been within a day's reach when the cultists' ship appeared on the horizon. Then, closing in, they tossed their grappling hooks over the rails, each hook biting into the wood and holding fast, pulling their ship to his like a noose tightening around a neck.

"Scarred!" Danik's voice cut through the storm, rough and battle-worn. Blood was smeared across his face, and he held a rapier in each hand, his eyes fierce. "There's another ship incoming!"

Scarred drew his sword and turned, finding his crew standing strong, weapons ready, eyes sharp with fear. Most of them had been with him for months, if not years, and they had always evaded trouble with the cultists. Beyond Danik and himself, they might not have been eclipse-born, but all of them knew the cruelty of Ilos' devout.

"Listen!" he shouted over the roar of the waves and the rising wind. "Don't let those bastards take anyone alive. We give them nothing!"

A murmur of assent rippled through the crew, hard and bitter, and flames erupted from the other ship onto his. The fire roared to life as the cultists hurled blazing pitch onto the deck, and heat surged around them, casting the ship into a hellish glow that swallowed every shadow in searing light. The fire ate across the timbers in jagged paths, licking up the mast, and the heat seared Scarred's skin even as the storm's cold rain tried to beat it back.

"Put it out! Sand buckets!" He roared, knowing every second lost would cost them dearly. But the cultists weren't waiting.

With a feral shout, a robed figure swung over from their ship, landing on the deck, blade drawn. Danik met him head-on, his twin rapiers flashing as they clashed with the cultist. Scarred turned, slashing his axe through the next cultist that scrambled up, his red-streaked robes and wild eyes marking him as a faithful zealot of Ilos. Blood sprayed as he fell back, but before Scarred could breathe, two more climbed over the rail, weapons ready.

The cultists fought like they had nothing to lose, each movement driven by that fanatical energy that made them nearly inhuman. They chanted Ilos' name with every attack, their voices rising in discordant harmony with the storm, and their ferocity threatened to overwhelm even Scarred's seasoned crew.

It nearly overpowered him.

The flames brought back his past, the one he had buried under years of torture and even more years of fighting to survive. His brothers' screams, those of his mother and Faedi, echoed in his mind as if he were there again. As if he were still a child, unable to save his family from death and pain.

Faedi made it—she's alive.

One of the cultists lunged at him with a hooked blade, nearly catching his throat, but he ducked low, slamming his shoulder into the attacker's stomach to knock him back. The cultist stumbled, slipping in the rain-soaked pitch, and Scarred took the opening to drive his axe through the man's chest. As he pulled his blade free, his eyes flicked to the rail where the enemy's grappling hooks held them fast.

"Cut the ropes!" He shouted. One of his men was already scrambling toward them, a knife clutched in his fist, but before he could reach it, a cultist barreled into him and dragged him down into a frenzy of thrashing limbs. Scarred reached them just in time, his axe cleaving into the attacker's skull, but the man's eyes were wide and terrified as he scrambled back to his feet, clutching a wound on his arm.

"Get below deck," Scarred ordered, but the man shook his head stubbornly.

"I can still fight, Scarred," he panted, his eyes flashing defiantly.

"Then get the ropes and stay out of sight!" Scarred snapped, pushing him toward the rail as he spun back to fend off another attacker. The cultist's sword swung toward his head, but he twisted, catching the blade against his own and driving it aside. The two of them circled each other, both drenched in rain and blood, and exhaustion began to seep into Scarred's bones.

K'than had warned him that sailing without rest would bite him, but he didn't regret it. Not when he was so close to seeing them again. He wouldn't let these bastards take him or kill him, not when he was so close to having his family again.

Behind him, the second cultist ship drew closer. They sent even more men across the gap between the vessels, their ropes and ladders swaying wildly in the storm.

"Danik, we can't hold both sides!" Scarred shouted over the clash of steel and thunder.

"Let them take the rails!" Danik called back, slashing through two of the cultists who came at him. "We can funnel them to the center—they can't take us all at once!"

He was right. They would let them flood the sides, then force them into a choke point at the center of the deck where they'd have no choice but to face them head-on. Scarred's crew rallied to the center, forming a tight line, shoulder-to-shoulder, weapons raised as the cultists surged toward them.

Some crew members and Helgi on board manipulated the water to clash with the flames the cultists shot at them. The enemy came with renewed fury, their faces twisted with zeal and rage, but the crew held their ground, striking down each attacker who dared approach. The deck was slick with blood and rain, and the air was thick with smoke and salt. The storm roared around them, lightning flashing across the sky, illuminating the faces of the cultists as they lunged forward.

Just as Scarred turned to check the ropes again, an explosion tore through the belly of the ship, blasting fire and splintered wood upward. The force hurled him off his feet, slamming him against the mast. White-hot pain shot through his side, and for a heartbeat, his mind couldn't process the chaos. His vision blurred as more eruptions followed, tearing the ship apart piece by piece as the cultists cheered with mad fervor.

A high-pitched whine rang in his ears, drowning out everything else, but through the haze of smoke and flame, he could still make out his crew shouting, some crawling desperately across the deck toward the rail, others staggering toward each other, eyes wide with terror. He pushed himself up, barely able to stand, and looked down to see blood seeping through a deep gash across his chest.

"Overboard!" He yelled, forcing the order out. "Everyone, get overboard!"

Then the deck gave way beneath him, and he plummeted, tumbling into the frigid, open sea as wood and flames crashed around him.

The cold was a shock that drove the pain from Scarred's mind in an instant. The sea surged around him, pulling him down as he kicked and struggled to find the surface. Dark shapes floated nearby, pieces of wreckage bobbing up and down. His arms flailed, and his lungs screamed as salt water forced its way down his throat, every instinct in him crying out for air.

His fingers caught a sliver of wood, and he gripped it hard, trying to keep himself afloat. The water around him was thick with oil and blood, slick and clinging. It coated his tongue and stung his eyes as he fought to stay above the waves. However, the relentless currents pulled him down, yanking at him like claws.

He was sinking.

He forced himself to think of Faedi. Of Da. Of Rowdon. He had made it this far; he would make it to shore. He tried to kick, but pain stabbed through his ribs, seizing his muscles, and the wreckage overhead closed out the last light from above. His grip slipped from the wood, and he sank deeper, dragged down by exhaustion and the weight of his injuries.

It was as if the sea reached to claim him, cold and crushing. His mind drifted back to the fire, the chanting cultists, and the twisted gold symbols. Faces from long ago, distorted by fear and grief, floated into his vision. Their eyes were ac-cusing, staring at him with a deep, unyielding gaze that was all too familiar.

He let go of the fight, just for a heartbeat—but that was all the sea needed.

64

Chaos in the Corridors

"I can heal them—I can help them. They'll be alright. Everything will be alright."

Faedi

Her hands worked through the motions almost instinctively as she tended to the ill and injured. The scent of herbs and salves clung to the air, mingling with the faint metallic smell of blood. The few refugees who stepped forward with more than minor injuries lay on cots in the makeshift ward they had set up. Some stared blankly at the ceiling; others were more concerned about their wounds than the threat of a possible plague.

She sat beside Emmaline on her cot, cleaning the child's cuts and wrapping them with as much care as possible. The rhythm was soothing, a balm to her frayed nerves.

"How do you feel?" She asked softly, watching as Emmaline stared at her hands while she worked.

The girl didn't look up, but her lip quivered. "My head hurts."

Myst stood from their perch beside the cot and smiled. "I'll get some tea."

Faedi managed a small smile as she tucked a blanket around the child. "You're safe here," she assured her, though the words felt hollow even as she said them. She wanted them to be true, wanted to offer everyone the safety they needed, but with the news that had filtered in—the cultists' movements, the unease in the castle, and Sylrie's sudden silence—it felt like a fragile promise. "Just rest. We'll have you feeling better in no time."

Emmaline nodded, her eyes softening as she leaned back, and Faedi took a moment to breathe, catching the low light flickering across the lines of exhaustion carved into the faces around her. The suffering, the terror—they were the same things she saw on the edge of her dreams, the things she tried to bury but always surfaced when she least wanted them to.

"Faedi."

She turned, blinking as Zarae appeared in the doorway. The woman stepped forward, her expression somber but steady as she took in the room. "Your bonded are back," she said.

"Where are they?" Faedi stood quickly, not caring about the stool she knocked to the floor. "Are they alright?"

There was a flicker in Zarae's eyes before she nodded. They were alive, but they were far from alright. "The throne room," she replied. "Go. I'll help in here."

Faedi hesitated, glancing at the refugees around her, but Zarae's gentle push gave her the nudge she needed. Turning, she barely managed to keep herself from breaking into a run as she left the room. Her footsteps echoed through the castle's stone halls, each step bringing her closer to the throne room.

The doors loomed ahead, and she hesitated for only a heartbeat before pushing them open. The light within was softer, casting long shadows across the floor, but as her gaze swept over the cots of refugees, her breath caught at the sight of Ighir perched on the edge of one.

Lonan and Sophir lay side by side, their faces worn and pale but whole. They were already wrapped in bandages, some deeply stained with blood, and neither of them stirred as she approached. Ighir stood as she drew closer and bowed his head.

"How bad are they?" She asked, looking between them.

His hand was heavy on her shoulder, but the weight grounded her. "The healers say they live, but they're saving their magic to ensure everyone gets the help they need," he explained softly. "We haven't seen any other Itmis, or Haldin."

The words sank in, heavy and cold, and a flicker of dread settled in her chest. If no one had seen the other Itmis or her grandfather, then there was a chance—no. She couldn't think that way. They were somewhere, likely flying in dozens of directions to evade the cultists, or they had taken cover to tend to their injured. And yet, even as she tried to reassure herself, the hollow edge of fear gnawed at her.

As she studied Ighir, she saw the same look in his eyes that she had seen in Zarae's. There was something else. "What aren't you telling me?"

He sighed and glanced over his shoulder. Faedi followed his gaze and spotted Bjorn near the balcony. His face was tight, his eyes hard.

"We received word of a fight at sea from the Helgi, who arrived at the port."

Faedi focused on Sophir and Lonan, tracing the lines of their faces, the dark smudges under their eyes, the faint rise and fall of their chests. They seemed fragile—a sharp contrast to the fierce power she had always associated with them. But they were alive. If they had made it, then Sylrie and her grandfather had too.

Ighir squeezed her shoulder, drawing her attention back to him. "They fought hard to make it back," he said softly. "And the Helgi are looking for survivors. If they find any of Ilos' followers in the water alive… what do you want done with them?"

Faedi swallowed hard, lowering her head to gather her thoughts. She wanted anyone who wished them harm dead, but she doubted that would help in the long run. They needed information—to understand the enemy's plans, their organization, and whether they had more allies nearby. Capture or kill might be their ultimate goal, but she needed to know how they intended to reach it.

"Tell them to capture any survivors if possible. We need to know their plans, their numbers, and whether they have more forces nearby. But if there's no choice—" she paused, weighing the words in her mouth, "then do what they must to protect themselves and us."

Ighir nodded. "I'll pass the orders along."

As he moved away to deliver the message, Faedi turned back to Lonan and Sophir, her heart tightening at their vulnerable states. Lonan's breath hitched, his brow twitching as if in pain, and she reached out instinctively, brushing her fingertips along his temple. His eyes opened—just a sliver—but recognition flashed in them.

"Faedi?" He rasped, his voice barely a whisper.

"I'm here," she said, soft and steady. "You're safe now. Just rest."

He nodded, his eyes drifting closed again as he slipped back into sleep. She stroked his hair back, then did the same for Sophir, wishing she could shield them both from every danger that threatened them.

Bjorn approached as she lingered beside them. His broad frame cast a long shadow across the room, but his face was lined with worry.

"Do you think bringing them here for information is wise?" He asked softly. "If there are loyalists among us…"

Faedi straightened, shaking her head. "I don't know. But we have to know what they're planning."

A muffled cry echoed from somewhere beyond the throne room doors, followed by the clatter of hurried footsteps. Her heart skipped a beat as she glanced at Bjorn, his expression mirroring the tense fear settling over her. She hoped it was nothing—maybe Torix had arrived with others, or someone had simply fallen ill—but the dread twisting in her stomach wouldn't ease.

Bjorn leaned closer, lowering his voice. "We need to do something with the ill and injured. We can't have them in the open—we can't protect them and ourselves if the worst happens."

A flicker of guilt passed through her. She had separated the groups to prevent the spread of the plague, but moving them now would take time, and she didn't know who among the castle's guards and servants could be trusted. Anyone left to defend those too weak to fight could slit their throats while they recovered.

Unless she left them with only people she knew she could trust. The antechamber was too small to hold everyone, but there was another place—one with only a single entrance, one hidden from most.

She took a steadying breath and nodded. "We seal them with the tree."

The corridors echoed with hurried footsteps as Faedi and Bjorn guided the last of the refugees toward the chamber with the tree. Sophir and Lonan had already been brought there by Ighir, though it pained her to leave them vulnerable. She knew Myst would look after them; she had refused to let them fight and wanted them to remain in the chamber to protect everyone and the tree.

Emmaline clung to Faedi as they walked, her hands tight and trembling around the bow. Her wide eyes remained dazed from fever, but beyond that, her fear was unmistakable. She knew something wasn't right, even with the gentle smiles Faedi attempted to reassure her.

"What's happening?" She whimpered, her voice barely carrying over the ambient noise of the corridor.

"We're putting you and the others somewhere safe," Faedi told her softly, hoping to calm her, even a little. "There's a heart tree there—it's been here for centuries, and it's my friend. It will protect you."

Emmaline's lips curved into a small smile, though it didn't reach her eyes. She was so young, yet already forced to understand far too much about fear and pain. Her eyes widened as they entered the chamber, her attention drawn to the massive tree at its center.

Aladia approached, her expression as grim as Bjorn's as she surveyed the people in the chamber. Her gaze settled on Emmaline, softening for a moment before flicking back to Faedi.

"I need you to watch over her. Protect her, no matter what," Faedi said, keeping her tone as steady as possible. "And swear to it…the way you swore to my mother that you would protect me."

Aladia's eyes widened before she reached out to take Emmaline's hand. "I swear it to the Oath-Keeper," she murmured, adjusting the child in her arms. "On my life, I will protect her."

Emmaline blinked up at Aladia, her tiny fingers curling into the fabric of her dress. She glanced between them, her lips quivering when her gaze landed on Faedi, but she didn't speak. Instead, her mouth set into a small pout.

"Stay with Aladia, alright?" Faedi leaned closer, pressing her forehead against Emmaline's. "You'll be safe."

The child nodded, her fingers brushing against Faedi's cheek before Aladia stepped back and bowed her head. Faedi watched them go, Emmaline peeking over Aladia's shoulder to stare at her one last time. She forced a reassuring smile before turning to Bjorn, who nodded and rested his hand on his sword.

Then, he smirked faintly. "Ragna will feel that."

Faedi squared her shoulders. "Good. She'll know something serious is happening then… I might have just voided the oath Aladia made to my mother."

Bjorn's smirk faded into something more thoughtful. "Some oaths are worth breaking."

They left the chamber together, Bjorn sealing the heavy doors behind them. Faedi cast one last look inside at the gathered group, biting her lip. Aladia and Myst would work together to protect everyone—and she could only hope it would be enough.

Her heart pounded once the doors were shut, the faint echoes of voices filtering through the stone walls. As long as she stayed away from the corridor, no one would have a reason to venture this far into the castle. No one would hear them.

Ancients, don't let anyone come down here.

Bjorn remained at her side as they moved through the corridors. The tension in the air was thick enough to cut with a knife, but the silence made her want to crawl out of her skin. The wind howling outside the castle had once brought her peace, much like the sounds of the forest around her cottage, but now, she couldn't shake the sinking fear that the mountain would face the same fate as her old home.

They had nearly reached the guards' quarters when the first crash echoed in the distance—a harsh, metallic clang, followed by a distant, muffled shout. Bjorn's gaze met hers, a grim understanding passing between them, and they drew their weapons as they picked up their pace. Whatever had started was already inside the castle.

Another shout rang out, closer this time, followed by the unmistakable clash of steel. As they rounded a corner, the sound intensified, flooding the halls with the chaos of battle. A handful of loyalists—faces covered, eyes alight with hatred—had already breached that section of the castle. They fought against the guards with fury, their blades flashing as they pushed forward, undeterred by the bodies of both their allies and foes strewn around them.

Bjorn and Faedi joined the fray without hesitation. Her bow was heavy in her grip, but the weight was familiar, grounding her. One of the attackers lunged toward them, but Bjorn was faster. He sliced upward with his blade, deflecting the strike, and Faedi drove an arrow into the attacker's eye with a snarl. He staggered back, his uninjured eye wide with shock as he collapsed. Faedi ripped the arrow free as blood spurted from the wound.

At least they weren't using fire—maybe the cultists hadn't arrived yet.

Their numbers were greater than she had anticipated. For every loyalist that fell, two more seemed to take their place. They weren't deterred by the winding corridors of the castle—they likely knew its layout better than she did. The realization struck hard: while she had spent decades in the forest, memorizing every tree and rock, they had spent that same time planning and preparing.

Once again, Ilos' zealots had the upper hand.

65

Light Upon the Mountain

Faedi

The silver flash of a blade struck close to Faedi's face, but she ducked just in time, the air parting with a rush of cold where it passed. Her vision swam as she twisted to strike back with her dagger. The harsh, searing light filled her eyes until she couldn't make out the surrounding shapes.

Then, like a snake slithering into her mind, he came to her.

"You think you're strong, Faedi?" It was a gentle hiss, soaked in mockery. *"But soon, you'll be nothing but an empty vessel."*

The words clawed through her as she shook her head, blinking against the light. Bjorn's hand landed on her shoulder. His voice echoed in her ear, asking if she was alright—but she couldn't respond.

"Do you feel it, child? That tiny, fragile thing you call strength breaking bit by bit. It's not enough. You're not enough."

She gritted her teeth, trying to force his words out of her head. Another enemy charged at her, and she lunged forward, her claws tearing into their side, but even as she fought, his voice lingered. Her breath hitched as a chill swept through her that no blade could have caused.

"Every soul you cherish is nothing more than kindling," he whispered in an icy breath against her mind. *"I will burn them all away, Faedi. And you? You will be left with nothing but ashes in your hands."*

She slashed out wildly, catching a flicker of fear in the eyes of the loyalists she attacked, and that fear sent him stumbling back. For a moment, she thought she'd beaten the voice, that he had left her alone. However, as she straightened to catch her breath, a burst of white light seared across her vision, blinding her again.

"What will you do when you can no longer remember them?" His voice cut through

the fog. *"Every precious memory you hold—I'll rid you of them. You'll have nothing left— just as you'll leave them with nothing."*

"No," she shook her head, trying to refocus on the figures moving around her. It was useless—the light twisted and changed, brightening until she feared it might burn her.

"Look at them," he sneered, his voice scraping through her mind like nails against stone. *"Fighting for you, dying for you…how many have you condemned already, Faedi? How many more will fall?"*

"Enough!" She snarled as her heart pounded in her chest. She slashed at the loyalists closest to her, using her momentum to shove them back as the pulse of light began to fade. However, the moment she steadied herself, the voice returned.

"You think this little stand means anything to me? That your little band of powerless god-touched will make a difference?" His laugh made her stomach churn. *"Your bonded couldn't even hold their own against mortals. What do you think you can do against the ascended?"*

She yelped when heat wrapped around her neck like a chain and flailed when arms grabbed her from behind. She was dragged, kicking and clawing, into a room, and darkness swallowed her. Then, something touched her face.

"Get away!" She slashed blindly with her claws before something grabbed her wrists.

"Faedi!" Bjorn's voice overtook the one in her head. "It's me, you're safe. He's taunting you—push him out."

She blinked, barely able to make out Bjorn's face through the blur of light and shadow clouding her vision. His strong hands gripped her wrists, anchoring her as she caught her breath, that voice still lurking at the edges of her mind. His touch helped, as did the wild bangs on the heavy door behind him, pulling her back.

The laughter faded slightly, and her body trembled. He nodded, his voice steady despite the chaos outside. "It's one of his tricks…don't let him in."

She pulled her arms free to hug herself and took a deep breath while she watched Bjorn press himself against the door to keep it shut. Guilt washed over her as she noted the strain on his face and heard the screams on the other side. She was supposed to be out there fighting with them.

Bjorn caught her eye and shook his head as if he knew where her thoughts had gone. "They'll survive a few moments without us. Breathe."

"He's in your head too?" Her head pounded.

He nodded with a growl. "Sometimes—and it's harder to ignore when no one else is in your head…bastard's more persistent when he's pissed off." His lips shifted into a bitter grin. "Just tells me we're doing something right if he's mad."

She wondered if that was true. "How do you do it?" She stood on shaky legs and stared down at him. "How do you keep fighting?"

"Put him in the dark," he replied and stood. "I think of things I know he hates, what I hope he fears. And I pray to the Ancients for strength."

She nodded, though her hands trembled, and sighed. If he hated the dark, all she had to do was think of Lonan. Of Sophir. There wasn't much darker than shadows and a moonless night sky.

"Go ahead, cling to them while you can. In the end, I will strip them from you one by one."

"I'm here." Bjorn offered her his hand, and she tentatively reached for it. "I won't let him break you. I swear it—to the Oath-Keeper and on my bond to her."

"You sure you should promise me that?" she frowned. She knew her fragility, even if she wanted to be strong.

He grinned at her. "I owe you, Faedi…far more than you know."

"Then let's make him hurt." She managed to smile as he led her out of the darkened room and into the chaotic battle that awaited them.

"Push them back!"

Faedi gritted her teeth, snarling as she slashed wildly at her attackers with her claws. Her bow had long since been abandoned when their numbers grew too fierce, and she fought with her teeth and claws in her partially shifted form. Bjorn followed suit, not long after her, just as the other were-folk in the castle— on both sides of the fight.

They were also equipped with silver weapons.

In any were-folk society, weapons of that nature were never mass-produced. They were locked away and reserved for only the most dire of circumstances. Faedi hadn't thought to order all of the silver weapons to be moved before the uprising, and her failure to do so stung almost as much as the cuts that littered her body.

Bjorn didn't leave her side while they fought, often putting himself between her and the others, but he never slowed. Ighir was easy to spot on the other side of the corridor, among the armored Gaelisks, beside Zarae who threw spells and swung a battle-hammer at anyone who got too close. Had it been under different circumstances, Faedi might have found the sight comical—her small, almost frail frame handling a weapon that seemed better suited for someone like Sophir to use—but there was no time for that.

The corridor was a frenzy of movement, a storm of claws, teeth, and flashing silver. The clash of metal against bone, the guttural growls, and the shouts mixed into a chaos that numbed Faedi's senses. Her muscles burned, and blood—a mix of her own and others'—painted her arms and chest as she clawed her way through the enemy line.

A flash of silver caught her eye as a loyalist lunged forward, blade aimed at her neck. She twisted just in time, the edge of the weapon grazing her shoulder. Pain flared hot, but she gritted her teeth and countered, her claws sinking deep into his side before she threw him to the ground, making sure he stayed down.

The silver weapons they wielded made every encounter dangerous; one wrong move, one misstep, and any of them could be fatally wounded. Sensing her brief pause, Bjorn took down another loyalist, his jaws snapping shut over the man's throat as he released a low, warning growl. The silver blade clattered from their hand as his form slumped, unmoving.

Despite their efforts, they kept coming, their numbers seemingly endless. Their frenzy and determination was unnatural, as though they were driven by something far more profound than loyalty. They fought as though they didn't fear death, as if something far worse awaited them should they fall back.

Through the fray, Faedi caught sight of Ighir and Zarae again. The Itmis was a whirlwind of movement, his blade flashing as he cut down anyone within reach. Zarae practically danced beside him, the weight of her hammer betraying her frame. Each swing sent a shock wave through the crowd of enemies, and when her spells erupted, they threw bodies back, creating precious breaks in the crowd for those of them who continued to fight.

"Push them back!" Faedi roared, her voice barely carrying over the chaos. "To the courtyard!"

Bjorn stepped closer to her. "What's the plan?"

She winced as she thought it over. It was dangerous and reckless, but the best she could come up with. "Split them up in the courtyard…form a line in the middle of a circle. That way, our backs are safe." She met his eyes and frowned. "It'll be ugly, though."

"Ugly's an understatement," he shook his head before he smiled. "But I'm in."

With Bjorn's agreement, Faedi silently prayed to the Ancients for support. She knew her plan was barely a plan—more of a desperate attempt to keep them from reaching the castle's lower levels—but it was all she had. It had to work.

The loyalists, as if they sensed the shift in strategy, fought harder to press them back. Their frenzied attacks grew bolder, more vicious. They moved in tight, coordinated clusters, their silver weapons gleaming as they cut through their defenses. A blade bit against Faedi's thigh, the searing pain only fueling her as she twisted, kicking out to knock the attacker off balance. Bjorn was on him in an instant, his fangs gleaming with blood as he took the man down.

"Move!" Faedi called out, her voice hoarse. The castle walls reverberated with the sounds of the fight as they pushed through, step by bloody step. Around her, she could see the toll it took on their side; their forces were tired and strained, but they didn't falter. Not once.

When they broke through the last hallway, the courtyard opened before them, a cold wind whipping through the air. Torches flared along the stone walls, and snow stung Faedi's eyes, but the air was clean. She took a deep breath and howled with as much volume as possible.

"Form the line!" Bjorn barked, gesturing for their fighters to split up. Half of them moved to form a semicircle near the rear, closing off access to the castle, while the rest of them held a line across the courtyard's center.

The loyalists spilled out after them, relentless, and charged into their formation. Faedi met the first head-on, ducking low and slashing up with her claws. Her hand jolted as her claws connected, blood splattering her face as they dropped to the ground.

Beside her, Bjorn was a blur, his movements more fierce than before. His face and body were stained with so much blood that Faedi couldn't tell who it belonged to. Further down the line, she caught glimpses of Ighir and Zarae and their unique forms of combat, which were chaotic but beautiful in their own way.

A shout went up from the other side of the courtyard. Faedi glanced over to see Itmis fly over the wall. It wasn't all of them, but it was enough to give her hope. They landed, their scales gleaming in the torchlight, and attacked without a moment to spare. Those they carried, some refugees and others soldiers, joined the fray as well.

The loyalists faltered for the first time, visibly shaken by the addition of the Verglas Itmis, who shot ice out into the crowd with ferocious roars. It was the opening they needed. Faedi shouted for their line to press forward, the order rippling through their fighters like a shock wave.

"Send them to the Ancients!"

With a roar, they surged forward, driving the loyalists back into their allies, who attacked them from behind. It was enough to send them stumbling and scrambling to regain themselves, but they didn't give them a chance. Faedi lashed out, clawing and biting, her hope growing with every moment—with every enemy that fell beneath them.

Ighir let out a mighty roar, a fierce sound that seemed to shake the ground beneath them. The loyalists hesitated, some casting glances back as though considering retreat. Those they looked to, the leaders of the insurrection, shouted orders, urging them to keep fighting—to kill them all.

Faedi hesitated when she recognized the fear in their eyes and took a deep breath. Every instinct screamed at her to push forward, to kill everyone who sought to kill them, but their fear gave her pause. If they slaughtered all of them, even the ones who wanted to flee, she would be no better than them.

"Surrender!" she shouted at them and grabbed Bjorn's shoulder to stop him. "Lay down your weapons, and you may live."

The ones closest to her hesitated, their grips loosening on their weapons. For a tense, charged moment, the courtyard stilled as some exchanged wary glances. One by one, weapons clattered to the ground, the sounds muted in the blanket of silence falling over the courtyard. Hope in their eyes flickered—rather than the hate that filled them before.

Not all of them surrendered, though. A hardened few clutched their weapons, their faces defiant. The leaders barked orders at them to stand their ground.

Their desperation cut through the air like a knife. However, without the strength of numbers and the threat of their allies looming on all sides, the will of most broke, leaving only a few to resist.

Bjorn growled, keeping a watchful eye on those who had surrendered. He nearly attacked the first, who dropped to their knees and bowed with their faces in the snow, but Faedi managed to hold him back. The others who tossed away their weapons mimicked the motion, and her back stiffened.

She turned her attention to the leaders and snarled. "Last chance." When they refused to disarm, she extended her hand, summoning what rested under the ice. "May the Ancients have mercy on you—because I won't."

66

The Tide's Vengeance

Faedi

The air was laced with the bitter tang of blood and ice. The bodies of the uprisers who refused to surrender were strewn across the courtyard, twisted into unnatural angles, each entwined in thick, eventide-covered vines. The vines glistened with frost, still pulsing faintly with the life ripped from the dead, the thorns sinking deep into flesh that had long since lost any hint of warmth. Faedi barely registered their faces anymore; she no longer saw wide eyes and gaping mouths. All she saw were enemies who had no place on the mountain.

Bjorn and Ighir flanked her, both tense, their eyes fixed on the figures gathered on the ridge beyond the wall. They were close enough for them to see, standing tall, robed in the heavy garb of the cultists, their symbols and insignia glinting dully against the cold, gray sky. Their figures were back-lit by the sullen sunset, shadows cast long and dark against the snow. Faedi's hands tightened at her sides; fists clenched so hard she could feel her claws digging into her palms.

That's a prime spot for archers—but they don't have bows.

One of the cultists stepped forward, his gaze fixed directly on her. The blood drained from her face, and her heartbeat slowed to a cold, hard thud as he lowered his hood, and recognition washed over her. Fenkas Lirulin. The man who had posed as her father, stolen her family's trust, killed her mother, and had her brothers burned—the man who tore her life apart.

"Oh, now this is rich," the voice purred. *"In all of your preparations—you forgot about him, didn't you? The one who betrayed you, the one who made you weak. You were so helpless back then. Do you think anything's changed?"*

Faedi clenched her jaw, forcing herself to stand tall and keep her expression unreadable. Fenkas took his time, his movements unhurried, as he looked down at them with a smile she could still remember. However, then, she knew it was sickly and false—twisted and demented.

"Little Faedi," he called out, his voice carrying across the frozen air, clear and mocking. "So nice to see you've survived all these years. A pity it had to be like this. We could have had a…different kind of reunion."

He paused, letting the words sink in, his eyes glittering with a cruel amusement that made Faedi's stomach twist.

Bjorn's hand brushed against her wrist, and a growl rumbled low behind her. She couldn't acknowledge them, not when Fenkas was watching. She couldn't let him see any hint of weakness, any sign of fear that clawed at her, that threatened to overtake her in a tidal wave.

"Whatever you're here for," Faedi said, forcing her voice to stay steady, "you're wasting your time. There's nothing for you here. Leave, or meet the same end as your sympathizers."

She gestured to the bodies, the vines still holding them in a grim embrace, their twisted limbs a testament to the force she could unleash.

Fenkas' smile only grew wider, more mocking. "Oh, I've come for something much bigger than you, child," he sneered. "I've come to claim the mountain in the king's name. And I offer you a choice. Surrender now, and we may spare the lives of the…less divinely touched. Resist…and they will all die here, just like the others who got in our way."

The growls and rumbles grew behind Faedi, but she didn't look back. Instead, she kept her eyes on Fenkas. She couldn't let him out of her sight.

"Surrender?" She spat, stepping forward, her eyes fixed on him with every ounce of hatred she could muster. "You think I would ever surrender to you? My parents might have trusted you—but I won't make their mistake. Not after you told them to burn them alive."

He chuckled, a dark and humorless sound. "Oh, sweet girl. You were always so stubborn. So foolish." His eyes narrowed, and for a brief moment, his mask slipped. His hatred and malice that lay beneath surfaced—the twisted soul that had taken so much from her. "But I suppose I shouldn't be surprised. After all, you were never very good at knowing when you were outmatched."

"Look at him," the voice whispered, dripping with disdain. *"Look at the one who took everything from you, standing there as if he owns you, as if he could crush you again with a single word. You know he's right, don't you? You're outmatched."*

Faedi pushed back the sudden surge of fury, focused on her breathing, the icy ground beneath her feet, the steady presence of her bonded and allies around her. She wouldn't let the taunts or Fenkas' threats break her. Not again.

"If you think I'm going to stand by and let you take this mountain, then you don't know me at all," she replied, each word slowly spoken to ensure it carried as far as it could. "I'll fight you and every one of Ilos' worshipers to the last breath. And I will make sure you pay for every life you've taken, every drop of blood you've spilled."

Fenkas' smile faded, replaced by something darker, something cruel. He reached into his cloak, and for a moment, dread welled up inside her, an instinctive sense of what was about to happen.

He pulled out something wrapped in cloth, stained in blood, and then, with a flourish, unwrapped it.

No.

Faedi staggered back, her heart hammering in her chest as she stared at the object in his hands. It was a head, its features frozen in death, its once-proud expression now twisted in a grimace.

Her grandfather's head.

Fenkas tossed the head down from the ridge, and it landed in the snow with a sickening thud, rolling to a stop at her feet. She could only stare, frozen in horror, as the truth sank in, cold and brutal.

A whimper slipped from her throat before she could stop it, a broken sound that held every ounce of pain and despair that she'd tried so hard to keep at bay. Her grandfather, the one she had been separated from for so long, the one she had forgotten for everyone's safety, her blood…was gone, taken by Fenkas, just like the rest of her family.

He watched her with a twisted smile, clearly savoring her reaction. Then he reached up to place her grandfather's crown on his head.

"I am the king now," he declared, his voice echoing through the air, cold and triumphant. "And I claim this mountain, this castle, and all who live within it, in the name of Ilos. Surrender now, Faedi. Swear your loyalty to me, and I may show mercy. Resist…and I will destroy everything you hold dear."

Something snapped inside her, a dark, raging fire that surged up from the depths of her soul, consuming everything in its path. The vines around the bodies in the courtyard tightened, twisting, pulsing with deadly energy that responded to her anger, her grief. She flexed her fingers, feeling the power rise within her, raw and unbridled.

"Mercy?" She hissed, her voice trembling with fury as the ground shook. "You spit false promises when we both know the only thing you're capable of is lies. This mountain isn't yours to claim—your blood is useless to the oath." She stepped forward over her grandfather's head as the hair on her neck stood on end.

"Your grandfather was more powerful than you, and he couldn't even win," it whispered. *"The oath is worthless—like you."*

She shoved the voice aside, focusing on Fenkas, on the cold, twisted face that haunted her past and threatened her future.

Fenkas only laughed, a cruel, mocking sound that sent a shiver down her spine. "Still clinging to little fantasies? The oath is void. The mountain is mine— the shadow elves will never return." His gaze shifted, sweeping over her allies as his smile grew darker. "I'll give you one last chance. Surrender, swear fealty to me, to follow Ilos' flame, and I might spare a few of you. Refuse…and you will all die."

Faedi didn't look at the others. She didn't need to. Every dusk elf knew of the oath, every Gaelisk was sworn to her, and the Itmis would follow Ighir. They had their loyalty. He had nothing.

"I hope you burn in his flames," she spat. "No one is surrendering to a coward like you."

He smiled again and raised his hand to signal his followers. The cultists with him began to descend the ridge while movement echoed from beyond the walls. However, he remained in place. He didn't move—he remained with that damned smile on his face.

She growled as wind whipped around them violently. "Bjorn?"

"Say it," Bjorn growled behind her. His voice low and dangerous.

"Vengeance…Belan guide me," she whispered, and the ice under her feet cracked, and her skin burned.

His breath tickled her ear as his growl synchronized with hers. "Take it, Faedi." Then he hoisted her in the air and tossed her onto his back. "Hold on."

What?

His bones cracked under her as fur burst from his exposed skin. Then, without warning, he surged forward. Metal groaned, a low, unnatural protest swallowed by the roar of his transformation. Massive claws split from his fingers as he scaled the ice wall like a spider, each movement sharp and jarring, until he launched himself toward the ridge.

"Fly!" He snarled, and she sprang off his back without thinking.

Movement in the corner of her eye caught her attention, and her heart stopped when she glanced to her right. Feathers of black, white, and brown, larger than her head, caught the wind and moved with each strain of her back.

Wings—I have wings.

When did that happen?

Every beat of her wings propelled her forward, faster, fiercer. Fenkas' mocking grin shrank as she closed in, and for the first time, his eyes betrayed him. There was a spark of fear as he waited in place. He finally understood; she wasn't going to hesitate. He was going to pay.

"You can't stop me, Faedi."

She let out a piercing screech as she dove, claws outstretched, her body slicing through the air like a blade. He raised a hand, a flicker of magic sparking at his fingertips, but she was faster. Her claws struck his arm, digging deep, and he staggered back, hissing in pain. The fierce and immediate satisfaction released everything she'd buried inside her.

One strike wasn't enough.

She veered up high enough to shift back to her dusk elf form, and in an instant of pain, she was hurtling down toward him again—this time, with her claws and rage. Her feet hit the ground, and she sprang forward, claws slashing at his chest. He stumbled, unprepared for the force, and his arrogance faltered, slipping into something darker.

"You'll regret this," he snarled. His voice was a low, venomous growl. "You always were a foolish girl."

"I'm not a child anymore," she spat back, stepping closer, refusing to let him catch his breath. "And you're going to regret betraying my family."

He laughed, a sound as cold as the mountain itself, and threw a punch. She dodged. The rush of air from his force grazed her cheek, and she returned a strike to his side. Her claws sank deep and grazed his ribs. He gasped, clutching his side, but his glare was filled with fury, his sharp teeth bared.

The ground trembled beneath them, a rumbling that seemed to mirror the storm inside her. She didn't let it deter her. Instead, she welcomed it and let it fuel the fire that had built in her core.

Fenkas' hand glowed with bright, twisted magic, and he launched a blast toward her. She managed to duck, the energy singing her shoulder as it passed. Pain flared, but she pushed it down like the rest of her pain, lunging forward and catching his wrist. With a twist, she forced his arm behind his back, pressing him down.

"You can't win," he growled, his voice muffled against the rocky ground. "You won't stand against his light."

"I already have," she said, leaning close to his ear, her voice laced with venom. "What do you think he'll do to you for failing him again?"

He sneered, managed to shift his weight, and threw her off balance. She stumbled back and rushed to steady herself, dodging another blast of magic as he scrambled to his feet. This time, he advanced with rage, his fists alight with the same bright, unholy glow. His power crackled in the air, heavy and suffocating, but she refused to yield.

He threw a flurry of punches, and she met each one, deflecting, blocking, some connecting, their strikes echoing against the ridge. Every blow sent jolts of pain through her body, but she matched his ferocity, unwilling to let him gain an inch.

The ridge beneath them shifted and groaned under their weight as if the mountain warned them of the danger, but she couldn't stop. She wouldn't until she saw him defeated. Until she ripped her grandfather's crown from his treacherous head.

Fenkas' face twisted in frustration as he took a step back, panting, his gaze shifting toward the group of cultists that were below them. They didn't interfere, they couldn't. Not when Bjorn was there—attacking them and keeping them from getting to her.

Fenkas roared, raising both hands, summoning fire that flared into a searing wave. Her instincts screamed at her to dodge, but she held her ground, her magic surging to the surface, twisting around her in coils of ice. Cold rushed down her arms as she extended them and met his flames with a blast of ice that collided midair. Steam erupted, and the ground quaked again, the vibrations intensifying as cracks split across the ridge.

The heat of his fire was overwhelming, even as she fought to hold it back with everything she had. Sweat beaded on her forehead, her arms trembled, but she pushed harder. She couldn't run, she couldn't give up, and she couldn't let him take anyone else away from her.

Then, swiftly, he switched tactics; the fire in his hands died as he rushed forward. She didn't have time to react before his fist collided with her jaw, sending her reeling. Stars danced before her eyes, and she stumbled, but she caught herself, a snarl escaping from her lips.

"That's all you have?" She taunted before she spat blood onto the snow. "Pathetic."

His eyes flashed with fury, and he lunged at her, but this time she was ready. She ducked, sweeping his legs out from under him, and he crashed into the ground. Before he could rise, she was on him, striking him with her claws again and again, each swipe and blow fueled by every ounce of fear, anger, and hatred she'd stored up over the years.

His face was a blooded mess, his breathing ragged, but he managed a twisted grin. "You think this ends here?" He gasped, his voice barely a whisper. "You'll burn, Faedi. Just like Endi. Just like Sylrie on his damned ship."

Sylrie? No… no, he's safe.

The words were a poison that sank into her chest, twisting, clawing, but she didn't let them stop her. She pressed him down, pinning him with the full weight of her rage.

But then he spoke words she didn't recognize, words laced with magic that filled the air with a sudden blazing heat. Instantly, flames erupted around them, a circle of fire that consumed everything in its path and vaporized the snow and ice. The heat was unbearable, searing through her skin, but she didn't release her grip.

If she was going down, he was coming with her.

The flames closed in, licking at her skin, burning through the edges of her vision as smoke filled her lungs. The ridge shook again, more violently than before; the earth shifted and crumbled, but she held on and refused to let him escape. He'd never escape anything again.

I'll take you to Sudek myself.

Heat seared her skin as if it were trying to peel her apart. Her hair crackled and burned, the scent of it sharp as fiery tendrils snatched at the long strands, curling them into ashes. The fire licked closer to her scalp, and agony flared, raw and vicious, but she clenched her teeth and smiled as flames began to engulf him as well.

Her eventides surged in response to the flames. The dark vines of enchanted growth wrapped tighter around her arm as if they were determined to keep her anchored, but the fire gnawed at them. The leaves were scorched and brittle. Her arm went limp as the growths were eaten away. Each lick of the flames sent a fresh wave of agony through her arm.

Then, like a shuddered sigh, one final time, a violent quake broke the ridge apart, and suddenly, they were falling, tumbling down the side of the mountain as the world turned to chaos. Snow and rock cascaded around them, a roaring avalanche drowning out everything else, and for a moment, there was nothing but the white fury of the mountain swallowing them whole.

67
Cracked Walls

Lonan

A dull ache in his side pulled him from the dark, a ghost of pain that pulsed in time with his heartbeat. It was the kind of ache that lingered after healing, a reminder that he had survived what had tried to kill him. The room was dimly lit, though a soft glow covered the ground and illuminated a trail toward a massive tree. He blinked, slowly piecing together where he was and how he had gotten there.

The scent of earth and vegetation filled the air, grounding him in a place that felt both familiar and foreign. Then, he saw Myst. They sat between him and Sophir, cross-legged on the floor, their hands resting on their knees. Thin, fresh bandages were wrapped around their arms.

His mind felt heavy, like wading through water, and he fought to push through the haze. It was almost surreal; he half expected to see the darkness around him. It was still there in his mind, but it didn't threaten to overtake him again. Instead, it was more of a comfort than anything else—a steady presence that grounded him.

He glanced at Sophir, who lay motionless beside him. Had it not been for the steady rise and fall of his chest, he might have worried he was dead. In the quiet, it was clear that Sophir was only beginning to recover. For a moment, Lonan just watched him, relieved that he was there, alive, despite the remnants of the battle they had fled from.

When Lonan shifted slightly, his joints protested. His ribs ached with every shallow breath he drew, and a flash of memory stirred—an arrow, the sharp scent of iron and sweat. The sound of something ripping. He forced it down, returning to the present. When he turned back to Myst, they hadn't moved or even blinked.

"Myst," he murmured, his voice rough. They didn't respond or seem to hear him at all. They were entirely focused on the tree, as though the ancient branches held something only they could see.

Lonan struggled to sit up, each movement an ache, but he managed. The air around the tree seemed different, even from the twins, charged with something he couldn't name. It was alive in a way most things weren't, the leaves whispering to each other in some language older than any of them.

Finally, he reached out and placed a hand gently on their shoulder. The contact seemed to bring them back, and they blinked, their gaze shifting from the tree to him as if seeing him for the first time.

"You're awake," they said softly, their voice laced with something Lonan couldn't quite place. Relief, maybe. Or was it sadness?

"I am," he replied, offering a small, tired smile. "Are you alright?"

They gave a slight nod but didn't smile back. "Tired."

"What happened?" Lonan asked, though he wasn't sure what else to say. The question seemed empty somehow, too simple to encompass everything between them.

"There's an attack. Faedi had everyone locked in here," they said, though their voice sounded distant, hollow. Their hand reached up, almost absently, brushing against one of the bandages wrapped around their arm. "You almost died."

Something about how they said it sent a pang through him, a feeling he couldn't shake. He wanted to reach for their hand, to offer some kind of comfort, but he hesitated.

A small sniffle caught his attention before he could find words to say to Myst. He turned his head, just in time to see Emmaline hesitating a few steps away, clutching the edges of the too-big cloak someone had wrapped around her. Her cheeks were flushed with fever, and her little hands trembled as she rubbed at her swollen eyes.

He barely had time to open his arms before she rushed forward, burying her face against his chest.

"I was scared," she mumbled, her voice muffled against his shirt.

He hesitated for only a second before wrapping his arms around her small frame, steadying her as she clung to him. "I know, little one," he murmured, smoothing a hand over her hair. "But you're safe."

Her tiny fingers curled into the bandages on his shoulders. "I thought you wouldn't wake up," she whispered. "Faedi left…and Sophir is still sleeping."

His chest tightened—his blood burned, and he rested his chin lightly against her head. "I'm here," he reassured her. "And nothing's going to happen to Faedi or Sophir."

She sniffled again, but nodded, and her grip loosened just enough for him to drag her into his lap. She was so small, so fragile—but Ancients, she had fought against so much already.

A quiet sigh escaped him as he held her close, the weight of her settling against him. He shifted his gaze to Sophir as her sniffles ceased. When he looked down at her, he realized she had drifted off to sleep. She needed to break the fever, but there was little he could do—but there were others with the tree who could help.

Even if he didn't want to let her go just yet—not after she had just gotten calmed down.

He looked back toward the tree. There was a presence there, a potent and steady energy that hummed beneath the surface. It was as if the tree was watching them, and Myst seemed almost…tethered to it. They never acted that way to the twins.

"Can you hear it?" Lonan ventured, trying to bridge the silence.

Myst shook their head. "It shudders every once in a while." They paused, their fingers still on the bandages. "I think it's reacting to the fight."

Lonan studied their face, catching the faint strain beneath their calm. They wanted to be out there fighting with everyone else. He couldn't blame them.

"How many Orderlings are out there?" he asked, careful to keep his voice steady though the question burned in his throat.

Their fingers curled around the edge of their bandages, twisting them as if grounding themselves to something tangible. "I don't know. The chaos inside got quiet, but they might just be outside now."

"Faedi? Where are you?" He held his breath, scared to make a sound while waiting for her reply.

The quiet in the chamber was fragile, a thin veil over the weight of things happening beyond the chamber. He turned his attention to Sophir's cot and reached to squeeze his hand.

Please answer me, Faedi.

Then, it hit him. Sharp, searing pain all over his body. The air left his lungs as he doubled over, and Sophir writhed on his cot. Myst stood in a panic, frantically checking over them, but Lonan couldn't hear anything, not over the sound of his racing heart.

Over the shrieking wind that ripped through the chamber as the tree shook. Its leaves scattered around the room, and he stared at it as he covered Emmaline the best he could. It was like the dungeon all over again. He couldn't see what hurt him—there was no injury.

Because it wasn't him who was hurt.

Faedi.

He whispered soft hushes to Emmaline when she stirred while he gasped for air. Sophir's eyes locked onto his as he did the same. They were unharmed, which meant she was the one in danger—and they were sealed in a chamber with an ancient tree.

"Take her," he told Myst as he offered Emmaline to them. "Myst—"

They cradled Emmaline close to them and nodded. "Go."

Despite the protests in his body, Lonan stood and rushed for the door. "Someone open this thing!" He slammed his fists on the stone. "I need to get to Faedi!"

The chamber shook, and dust and dirt fell from the ceiling as the ground rumbled under them. The others inside screamed, rushing for the door, and a chill shot down Lonan's spine when he heard children cry.

We are not dying in here.

He pounded on the door again. "Open the fucking door!" There was no response from outside, so he pressed his forehead against the stone. "I will tear this mountain down—"

"No need," someone called from the other side of the door. "There's a mechanism down here somewhere."

Lonan almost yelled at them to hurry up, he wanted to, but he didn't. Not when they might have been the only way to get them out. He didn't know if they'd help if he upset them.

Be nice. Be nice. Be—hurry up!

"Oh, there it is!" They shouted excitedly. It was Zarae. "Is it left or right…I can't…oh—" she was cut off as the door began to move.

Lonan didn't wait for it to finish opening and ran as soon as he could fit through the gap.

68

Shattered Ground

"She's alright…we'd know if she wasn't. She's not dead. Faedi is a survivor."

Sophir

Lonan and the sounds of battle led him as he hoped to find Faedi, but
nothing could have prepared him for what awaited them. Several ridges that once
stood above the courtyard had vanished entirely. The mountain was chaos.

He charged toward Ighir, Lonan at his side. "Where is Faedi?"

"She went down with the avalanche—they killed Haldin."

His grip on his sword tightened, the knuckles of his hand going white. He
wanted to leap after her, to tear through the ice and stone until he could pull
her back up. But before he could take a step, a shout pierced the air behind him,
pulling him back to the harsh reality unfolding around them.

"The wall is down!" Someone bellowed. Sophir turned just in time to see
a small group of cultists flooding through the breach in the wall. They came in
fast, cloaked in gold-trimmed robes and wielding silver weapons. He had been so
focused on Faedi that he had missed the damage the avalanche had caused to the
wall.

"Don't let them through!" Ighir shouted as he charged the group. Sophir
raised his blade and chased after him. There was no time to hesitate—Faedi had
fallen, but that didn't mean her home had to as well. Not when she could still be
alive.

The first cultist lunged at him, his blade aimed straight for Sophir's chest.
Sophir sidestepped, bringing his sword up to parry, then struck out with a quick
slash that found its mark. The cultist stumbled back, blood blooming across his

chest, but another was already there to take his place.

Sophir twisted, pivoting to avoid a blow from the side, but the second attacker was quicker. His weapon grazed Sophir's arm, leaving a searing line of pain. He gritted his teeth, bringing his blade around in a sweeping arc that sent the cultist spiraling to the ground. His arm burned, but Sophir forced himself to ignore it, to keep moving, to keep fighting.

The more he killed, the fewer would follow him when he went to look for Faedi.

"Stay together!" Ighir's voice boomed as Gaelisks and Itmis swarmed the cultists. His eyes were fierce, his focus unshakable, even in the chaos.

Another cultist lunged at Sophir, wild and desperate, his weapon swinging in a wide arc. Sophir caught his wrist, twisting until the cultist dropped his blade, then drove his elbow into the man's face. The cultist staggered back, and before he could right himself, Sophir swung his sword with every bit of rage he had, cleaving his head from his shoulders.

He glanced up, catching sight of Lonan at the far end of the wall. Lonan moved swiftly through the shadows, a terrifying force, slashing expertly through a knot of enemies. His movements were deadly, as if he were more shadow than man, gliding through the cultists with a lethal grace Sophir had never seen before. However, there was an edge of desperation in his strikes, the way his head kept turning toward the ridge, toward where Faedi had disappeared.

Flames came dangerously close to Sophir's face, snapping him back to the moment. He ducked, his heart pounding, and drove his blade through the chest of a nearby cultist. The ground beneath them trembled again, and Sophir glanced down at the blood-soaked ice.

The more prominent disturbances in the ice and snow had large roots slowly emerging through the holes. They weren't the thorny vines Faedi summoned— they were entirely different.

"Watch the ground!" Sophir shouted, warning their forces as more roots began shooting from the ground.

The ground trembled again as the roots continued pushing up, twisting and unfurling in black coils, snaking across the blood-stained snow. They seemed almost alive, like dark veins pulsing with an unnatural energy, reaching for the cultists' legs. Their enemies shrieked, yanking their feet free as they stumbled back, but the roots continued to advance, crawling, snaring the closest ones, and pinning them into place.

Then, from the castle, a new presence emerged. At first, it was only a shape moving through the shadows, then another, and another. Each figure was cloaked in dark armor that absorbed light rather than reflecting it. They moved in perfect, silent formation, each step measured, precise, and terrifying. They wielded curved blades, like crescent moons, forged from metal as dark as their armor. They appeared as shadows given form, and their skin, as dark as midnight, blended into the armor as though they were part of it.

A murmur ran through the dusk elves as they took notice, and shock and wary curiosity spread among them.

"The Helgi…" someone whispered, their voice filled with disbelief. "They came."

One of the cultists tried to flee, but before he could even turn, one of the newcomers closed the distance in a flash. With a single, fluid motion, they cut the cultist down, their blade barely making a sound as it sliced through flesh and bone. The others moved with similar precision, almost mechanical, their strikes deadly and efficient. Their skill was unmistakable, reminiscent of the Umbral's deadly finesse, but unlike them, they didn't disappear into the shadows. They hummed—strange tunes that built into shrieks.

Sophir turned as one of the Helgi, a tall figure with intricate designs carved into their armor, dispatched a cultist with ruthless efficiency. The figure's gaze landed on him, then Lonan. They inclined their head ever so slightly. They acknowledged them as allies—at least for now.

The cultists seemed to sense the power shift and tried to rally with shouted curses and raised weapons. But their desperation made them sloppy. They threw themselves at the Helgi, their blades slashing wildly, but the Helgi sidestepped with practiced ease, avoiding the attacks gracefully before striking back with lethal accuracy. It was like watching predators picking off prey—swift and precise.

By the time the fight was done, the courtyard was littered with bodies—both cultists and their own. The wall was reconstructed quickly, and the sounds of battle quieted. The distant rumble of the avalanche was the only thing left in the silence.

Lonan turned to Sophir. "We need to find her." His voice trembled. "We have to find Faedi."

One of the Helgi stepped forward, their armor decorated with numerous intricate carvings. Their gaze settled on Lonan and Sophir with strange intensity. "We were summoned to war—that was nothing." Her voice was soft, resonant, and song-like. "Where is the King?"

Lonan's jaw clenched, his posture stiffening. "That isn't all of them," he replied before bowing his head. "Haldin is dead…the heirs are missing."

The Helgi inclined their head, an unreadable expression flickering in her eyes. "Missing?" Sophir nodded mutely and looked back to where the ridge once stood. The Helgi followed his gaze before turning to face their forces. "Clear the field, help the injured, and form search parties."

With that, the Helgi broke into groups to follow the orders given. Ighir approached, his eyes fixated on the sirens before they turned their attention to him and Sophir. Their jaws were tight, like his, and he wondered if their hearts beat as furiously as his own.

Then, there was a moment of recognition on Ighir's face as he passed the woman who had spoken to them. He whipped around to grab her shoulder. The surrounding Helgi hissed, their sharp teeth bared, but Ighir wasn't dissuaded. Instead, he pulled her closer and lowered himself to look her in the eye.

"Vivi?" His whisper carried over the crowd.

She tilted her head, her eyes narrowing as she studied him before widening. "By the gods…" she breathed, wrapping her arms around his shoulders in a hug. "Ig, you bastard—you were dead."

He lifted her off the ground when he returned the embrace and spun around to face them again. "We need you out there with us, looking for them," he told her without looking away from Sophir. "You're still the best hunter in your clan, right?"

She hummed, and Ighir's expression changed. His smile fell, his brows creased, and the low rumble that came from him told Sophir whatever she said wasn't good news. He watched them communicate on a primal level—her hums and eerie sighs mixing with his growls and flicks of his tail.

Then silence stretched between them before she shook her head and turned to look at Sophir. "My hunters will kill what remains of Ilos' followers on the mountain—we will have the safety to look for your bonded," she spoke slowly, carefully, as if her common didn't come easily. "If you look for our brother too. He is…missing."

"They're all alive," Zarae's voice announced from behind Sophir. He turned to see her bloodied face. She blinked up at him and smiled. "None of them are dead. They're…not conscious…they aren't speaking…but they're breathing."

Lonan didn't wait for a breath before he turned on his heels and headed for the wall. "Then we have to find them before that changes." He stared up at it with a growl. "I'm not going to let that bastard take her from me."

His wings ached as they trudged through the debris, the snow broken and churned into an endless sea of ice and shattered rock where the avalanche had torn through the mountainside. The terrain was brutal, littered with broken branches, stones, and roots twisted like bones jutting from the earth. Every step was a struggle, but they couldn't stop.

"Anything?" Sophir called to Lonan, who was up ahead, his dark form barely distinguishable in the night. He shook his head without looking back. His movements were slow, his body tense as he scanned the ground with every step, his violet eyes narrowing at every dip and shift in the snow. He didn't need to say anything; his frustration and worry were clear in the rigid lines of his shoulders and the way his hand never left the hilt of his knife.

"Maybe there's too much snow to smell her," Sophir muttered, more to himself than anyone else, though both Lonan and Bjorn could hear. "She survived the forest for years as a child."

You better be alive, Faedi.

Above them, Ighir circled the sky, his white wings beating against the cold air as he scanned the mountainside. He remained silent in his search, but he was also alert for anyone who might try to follow, just like the small group of Helgi who traveled with them, spaced out to assist in the search.

The silence was crushing. Sophir hated it. Hated how every footstep felt like it echoed in the emptiness, how the world around them seemed too vast and hollow without Faedi's presence. She was somewhere, buried under all the ice and rock. She had to be.

Lonan stopped suddenly, crouching down beside a jagged outcrop of rock. His fingers brushed over something in the snow—a patch of red, stark and fresh against the white. Blood. Sophir's chest tightened as he moved closer, his breath catching as he studied it. It wasn't much, just a smear against the rock, but it was something.

Lonan's eyes narrowed as he studied the blood. "It's recent," he said, his voice low. "If it's Fenkas'…Faedi went down with him." He paused and looked around. "I haven't seen Bjorn."

He rose to his feet, scanning the snow for more clues, his gaze flickering across every break in the ice, every trace of movement in the wind. There was nothing, no other sign that she might have been that way, no trace of Fenkas or the cultists—only the blood.

"Do you think she could've gone further down?" Sophir asked, his voice tight. "It looks like the debris continues further down."

Lonan shook his head, glancing down the slope. "It's possible, but if she's buried…" He didn't finish the sentence and looked to their right. "I smell something."

He took off sprinting, and Sophir followed behind, over rocks and ice, until they spotted a cloak in the snow. It moved slightly, but the gold trim was impossible to miss. Orderling.

Lonan was on it before Sophir could blink, ripping it off the snow with a snarl. Even with the cold to preserve the body, the stench of death hit them. However, Lonan went to his knees and looked back at Sophir. "I found Bjorn!"

Sophir rushed over, sliding to his knees in the snow, and examined the man. He was sure Bjorn had seen better days, but he was alive. Barely. The right side of his face was burned, as well as his arms and chest, but he was breathing.

Lonan tapped the unburned side of his face. "Wake up, come on."

Bjorn groaned before his eyes snapped open, and he snarled at Lonan. Sophir pushed him back into the snow and rocks with a growl. "It's us," he warned him. "Where's Faedi?"

Bjorn resisted only momentarily before he blinked and looked between them. Confusion turned to shock, then to pain, and he wheezed when everything hit him. "I tried…" he shook his head while Sophir helped him sit up. "Fenkas— he set her on fire…tried to get her."

That explains why everything hurt the way it did.

Ighir landed beside them, and Sophir nodded him over. "Take him back to the castle."

"No." Bjorn protested and shoved Sophir's hands away. "I'm going to help find her." He said as he stumbled to his feet.

Sophir frowned at Lonan before watching Bjorn catch his breath. "You're injured."

"I owe her." He snarled as he started to limp through the snow. "So I'm going to help find her."

Lonan stood beside Sophir. "We need Ighir in the air anyway."

He'll be lucky if he doesn't die out here.

Despite Sophir's better judgment, they continued down the slope, moving as quickly as possible, their eyes scanning every inch of the terrain. The cold was brutal, but none of them slowed. None of them faltered.

Ighir circled above them again, flying lower this time. He must have seen something, a flash of hope that sent them moving faster, but there was nothing when they reached the spot. Only rocks and ice, snow piled high and untouched. He landed, his eyes scanning the area before looking at Sophir with a silent question.

"Nothing," Sophir muttered. It was impossible to ignore the weight of defeat that began to settle over him.

Lonan clenched his fists. "She's here," he said, his voice strained. "She has to be."

Bjorn looked between them, his brow creased and distorting the burns and scars on his face. "We—" he trailed off and turned his head. "Did you hear that?"

Sophir shook his head, as did Lonan. Ighir stepped closer to them and narrowed his eyes. They strained their ears to hear whatever Bjorn had, but none of them heard it. There was only the howling wind.

Lonan's shoulders slumped, his gaze fixed on the ground. For the first time, Sophir watched something break in him, a crack in the aura he wore like armor. His hand dropped from his blade, and for a moment, he just stood there, his head bowed, his entire form weighed down. Then, there was a break in the wind, and Sophir heard it.

An eerie screech.

"What is that?" Sophir looked between Lonan and Bjorn as Ighir took off into the sky to search for the source.

Bjorn shook his head, but his jaw wasn't as tense as before. "I don't know," he mumbled. "Sounds…maybe like a Helgi."

"Ighir's friend said their brother was missing," Lonan stepped closer to Bjorn. "Could it be him?"

A different shriek echoed before the wind picked up again. "That doesn't sound good…it sounds hurt." Sophir glanced over the snow as if some sign of Faedi might magically appear. "What do we do?"

Lonan sighed and closed his eyes as he tipped his head back. "If there's a chance that it's Sylrie," he spoke carefully, struggling through his words. "Faedi would be mad if we didn't go after him."

He was right—but mad might not describe how upset Faedi would be if they didn't help her brother. However, a slight change in the sky pulled Sophir's attention upward as Lonan opened his eyes to examine it. Vibrant blues, greens, and purples painted the sky, making the stars shimmer brighter.

Lonan covered his mouth to muffle a sob as tears rolled down his cheeks, and Sophir instinctively wrapped his arm over his shoulders. It was the one thing Faedi wanted to see when they were there—what she wanted for her name day—the Rowdon lights.

69

Song of Survival

"I refuse to die before I see Faedi and Da again."

Sylvie

His lungs burned as he gasped for air, and the cold pressed against him from all sides, harsh and biting. Blinking, he stared at the colors that painted the sky, their vivid hues pulling him from the haze of sleep. Slowly, he ran his fingers over his body, checking for injuries as memories of the fight on his ship rushed back—the way he had sunk into the waves.

He should have been dead.

Lying on his back, the ice seeped through his clothes, digging into his skin and aggravating the bruises and cuts he had gathered. The ache from them pulsed, and though his injuries had stopped bleeding, it was no comfort. His body protested as he forced himself to sit up.

Then he saw him.

Danik was sprawled in the snow a few feet away, face-down, his dark hair frozen to his skin. He was so still. A coil of dread wound tight in Scarred's chest as he crawled through the snow to him. Rolling Danik over, he brushed the frost from his skin—it was cold to the touch, but he was breathing. Barely.

"Hey," Scarred whispered, gently shaking him. When he didn't stir, Scarred pushed back his fear and slapped his cheek lightly. He feared he might hurt him, but he needed him to stay with him. "Come on, Danik, wake up."

A faint groan escaped Danik, and his eyes fluttered open, unfocused and dazed. A sliver of relief washed over Scarred, easing the pressure in his chest, but it was short-lived. Danik was too cold.

"There you are," Scarred sighed when Danik's gaze found his face. "Can you move?" Danik's brows pinched together momentarily, then he shook his head slightly.

"Hurts," he mumbled, his voice hoarse, barely a whisper. Scarred glanced down and noticed dark stains of blood on his clothes. The fabric was torn and stiff with frost, but there was no fresh blood. Not that it mattered—he couldn't afford to leave him exposed to the cold.

"It's alright, I'll find us something," Scarred murmured, more to reassure himself than Danik. He pulled Danik into his arms, bracing against the sharp jolt of pain in his ribs. It took his breath away when Danik let out a sudden, loud shriek. "Sorry," Scarred groaned, struggling to stand. He had lifted heavier things over the years, but Danik's weight threatened to drag him back into the snow.

The wind howled around them, its icy claws digging into his exposed skin as Scarred searched for any shelter. There was no sign of life, just endless snow and ice stretching in every direction, with frozen peaks in the distance.

"Where…where are we?" Danik's voice slurred, his head lolling against Scarred's shoulder.

"Rowdon, but I don't know where," Scarred admitted, tightening his grip on him. "But I'm going to find somewhere we can get warm. Just stay awake, alright?"

Danik nodded faintly, but Scarred could feel his strength waning. With every step, Danik's weight grew heavier, and his grip on Scarred's shirt slipped lower. Scarred's muscles screamed in protest, and his vision blurred from the effort. The cold bore into his bones, numbing his limbs, and all he wanted to do was sleep.

"Stay with me," Scarred whispered, as though the command would keep Danik alive.

Danik's head slumped against Scarred's shoulder, and Scarred teetered on the edge of collapse. His muscles trembled as he stumbled, hitting his knees. A sharp pain shot up his legs, and he couldn't hold back his startled shout. But it was drowned out by Danik's cry.

"I'm sorry, I'm sorry," Scarred whispered, cradling him closer as he struggled to stand. Then, he heard a faint hum, barely more than a whisper, coming from Danik. It was a strange melody, different from the sounds he had come to recognize, but it held a calming rhythm. The sound wove through the cold air and filled the space between them.

Danik's humming grew steadier, and as it did, an inexplicable warmth spread through Scarred, easing the tightness in his muscles. He stood more easily, his steps becoming more natural, and Danik's weight felt somehow lighter. It was a Helgi song, a soft tune that wrapped around Scarred like a protective cocoon, urging him forward.

Ahead, a dark spot broke the white horizon—a cave, its opening barely visible against the snow-covered landscape. Scarred's chest tightened with a spark of hope, and he stumbled toward it. They were so close.

"Hey," he muttered, feeling Danik's humming, then just a soft breath against his chest. "We're almost there."

Danik didn't respond, but his body shifted slightly against him. Scarred hoped it meant he heard him. With the last of his strength, he dragged them both into the cave and gently lowered Danik to the ground. The air inside was still frigid, but at least the wind was gone, and the walls shielded them from the worst of the cold.

Grimacing, Scarred searched the cave's interior. There was a crate in the back, and he rushed to rummage through it, breathing in the scent of dry wood and earth. It was a hunting cache.

"Thank Ytna," he whispered, pulling furs and kindling from the box.

His hands fumbled with the flint and tender, numb and clumsy, but a spark finally caught. A tiny flame flickered to life, dancing against the cave walls. Scarred slowly fed it small bits of kindling. Once he was sure it would live, he fed it larger fuel and then turned back to Danik.

Danik's face was still pale, his breathing shallow, and his injuries need-ed tending. Scarred knocked the crate over and dug through the contents for anything useful. He found a pack with bandages and medicine and returned to Danik.

His side was a mess of bruises and gashes, some of which had bled into the frost on his clothes. Scarred pulled furs closer before he began to gingerly peel Danik's clothes away. The medicine wasn't familiar—he was no healer.

"*Faedi…I need you,*" Scarred called out in his mind, holding his breath for a response, but it never came.

"Fuck," he muttered, shaking his head. Taking a steadying breath, he whispered, "You're going to be fine." He wasn't sure if he was convincing Danik or himself. His hands tightened the bandages, moving on their own as exhaustion threatened to pull him under. Danik's faint hum echoed in his mind, a lingering, dreamlike sound.

When he had done all he could, Scarred slumped back against the cave wall, too heavy to move. The fire crackled softly beside them, its warmth soothing the rest of the cold. He leaned back, watching the shadows play against the walls as his eyes grew heavy.

Before sleep claimed him, Scarred glanced at Danik one last time. His chest rose and fell, slow and steady. "You better wake up," Scarred muttered. "I didn't drag you through hell just for you to die on me."

Then, he surrendered to the exhaustion and drifted into a dreamless sleep.

Scarred woke with a start, every inch of him stiff and sore. An aching pain spread through his body where bruises and cuts still throbbed. Blinking, he noticed the dim light in the cave was fuzzy and blurred around him. It took a few breaths before he could remember where he was and the events that had led him there. As he shifted, he felt the weight of something warm pressed against his chest.

Looking down, he spotted Danik's hair poking out from beneath the furs that covered him. Slowly, he moved the furs to examine him. Danik's face was slack in sleep, his breathing even, and under him was Scarred's chest, wrapped in bandages. Danik must have taken care of him while he slept.

Scarred touched Danik's shoulder gently. "Danik," he murmured, not wanting to wake him abruptly. "Wake up."

Danik's eyes fluttered open, and a smile crossed his face when he looked up at Scarred. "You're alive."

"Could say the same to you," Scarred grinned at him, his voice rough like Danik's. "How are you feeling?"

"Cold, sore…but alive." Danik managed a weak chuckle. "You?"

"Never better." Scarred shifted, testing his injuries, and winced when a sharp pain shot through his side. "You did good with the bandages—I'm good as new."

Danik rolled his eyes, but his gaze softened as he traced one of the bandages on Scarred's arm. "You did most of the work getting us here."

They sat in silence for a while, both too exhausted and sore to leave the furs and disrupt whatever comfort they had. The contact between them was grounding, steadying, as if it reminded Scarred that he was alive. That he hadn't drowned in the sea.

He looked at Danik, noting the paleness of his skin around his scales and the shadows under his eyes. His glamour was missing. "Do I have you to thank for getting me out of the water?" Scarred asked softly. "I know I wouldn't have made it to the cave without your song."

Danik blinked, staring up at him. "I saw you go under—got you to the shore…but I don't know how we got here. I must have been out of it." He turned his attention to the fire and pulled the furs higher over them. "I don't feel the ocean."

"I couldn't hear it when I woke up before," Scarred replied, resting his hand on Danik's shoulder. "Whatever you did, I appreciate it. I owe you."

A faint color rose to Danik's cheeks, and he nodded, shifting closer as he wrapped his arm around Scarred. Scarred didn't protest; the cold was persistent enough to provide enough annoyance despite the fire, and he welcomed any comfort he could get.

He wasn't sure how long had passed or when he dozed off again, but he was startled when faint voices came from outside. With as much care as he could muster, he moved away from Danik and stood in front of him. His body ached and protested each movement, but he didn't care. He didn't know who was outside, and the fight on the ship was still too close in his mind.

Danik stood behind him and tried to move beside him, but Scarred stretched his arm out to keep him in place. "Maybe they won't notice us?"

Scarred shrugged and shook his head, then pointed to the fire as the voices grew louder. Were-folk were common among Dusk Elves, and they would have already smelled the smoke from the fire—or worse, their blood.

He reached for his axe and froze when he realized he didn't have it. The voices grew closer, and he strained to study the tones. They were urgent, but he couldn't determine much more than that before a shadow fell across the cave entrance. He held his breath, fighting back the growl that threatened to erupt from his chest.

Then, two other shadows appeared as the first entered the cave. He wasn't as tall as Scarred but was larger than average. His face was almost as scarred as Scarred's and burned. The other two followed, one with dark scales and horns with wings tucked behind him, and then the third figure—Scarred's heart skipped as he recognized his eyes first. Someone he would never forget: Lonan.

"By the Ancients…" Scarred breathed, lowering the arm he'd kept raised in front of Danik.

Lonan's gaze fell on him. A flicker of recognition crossed his face, his sharp and stern expression softening momentarily. He took a step forward, his gaze searching Scarred's as if he, too, was piecing together memories from long ago.

"Sylrie," Lonan's voice cracked, and he quickly looked away. Scarred didn't like that.

Scarred looked between the three of them. The Itmis was Sophir—he knew that already—but he wasn't sure about the third. But his name didn't matter. Not when anxiety twisted in his chest at Sophir's expression, which mirrored Lonan's.

Something was wrong.

"Where the fuck is my sister?"

III
Hiraeth

70

Whispers in the Flames

"I should have died with them in the raids."

Faedi

Light seared her eyes when there should have been darkness as she woke. There was nothing but the blinding glow and the lingering sting of fire, an echo of the agony still etched into her skin. It was as if the flames hadn't let go entirely, still clinging to her, searing deeper with every passing second. She tried to move, but could barely breathe.

She didn't have to hear him to know where she was.

"Hello again, Faedi." The light whispered, and she could hear his mocking smile. *"Look at you, burned and broken, not even a shadow of the warrior you thought you were."*

She refused to give him the satisfaction of a response or let him see how deeply his words clawed at her. Instead, she focused on what she saw before the light. Fenkas' face, scorched by the very flames he had summoned—her revenge for what he had done to her family.

"What was it all for, hmm?" He continued, his tone a twisted blend of pity and contempt. *"Running through the woods, thinking you could keep everyone safe. Your brothers. Your mother. Even now, you pretend you're strong enough to protect the mountain. Your bonded."* His laughter echoed, as chilling as it was familiar. *"But you failed, didn't you?"*

A flicker of anger rose, fighting through the haze of pain. Her skin throbbed, a blistering heat beneath the surface. She opened her mouth, but no words came out, her throat raw from the smoke and fire.

"You couldn't even protect yourself," he purred. *"All that strength you like to pretend you have, all of the Guardian magic you can summon—destroyed in a heartbeat. Because, in the end, Faedi, you're just like the rest. Ashes and bones."*

She squeezed her eyes shut, trying to block him out as Bjorn had said, but his voice slipped through every defense. Every fragile shield she attempted to raise.

"Remember them?" He asked, his tone turning almost gentle, deceptively soft. *"Torix and Sylrie, your only remaining family, sent on fool's errands because you asked them to. They're gone now, Faedi, or close enough. And who's to blame for that?"*

The heat of the fire crawled back into her awareness, a simmering burn that flared hotter with every word he spoke. Her arms were raw, her skin peeling back, exposing nerves to the open air. Her Eventides were gone; there was no trace of their black vines or vibrant petals.

She could almost feel his breath, cold and sharp, like a winter wind cutting through her. *"You're no god-touched, Faedi. You're nothing but a pawn. Do you think anyone followed you out of loyalty? No, they're waiting. Waiting for you to fall, for you to finally realize how weak and insignificant you are."*

With every word, her body burned hotter, a fierce, relentless pain she couldn't ignore, couldn't push away. It wasn't just her skin that felt like it was on fire—her very bones seemed to sear as if his words were scorching her from the inside out.

"Open your eyes, Faedi," he hissed. *"See what you've become. Broken, scarred, and useless. You're no heir, no queen, no protector. You're just another girl who thought she could save the world and lost everything."*

She gritted her teeth and squeezed her eyes shut. Did everything she could to prevent his words from entering her heart. She couldn't give him the satisfaction, but the burning persisted.

"You think this pain is bad?" He laughed softly. *"This is just the beginning. It only gets worse from here, little wolf."*

The words cut deeper than any wound, a twisted mockery of everything she'd fought for and lost. She knew he was feeding off her pain, her fear, twisting the knife deeper with each taunt. But a tiny, defiant ember burned beneath the agony, under the words that clawed at her spirit. Even if he was right—that she was broken, scarred, and failing—he was wrong about one thing.

She was the Heir of the Tides.

"That's it," he murmured, almost disappointed. *"Hold onto that tiny sliver of hope. It'll be sweeter for you to lose when I break you and make you mine."*

And just like that, his voice faded, leaving her alone in the blinding light, with nothing but the pain and the echo of his words, taunting, waiting for her to shatter.

How long have I been here?

Her time in the light before had been a blur, and she wondered if it had been Ilos' doing or if she had shielded herself from the memory. Before her family was murdered, the light had only appeared in her dreams and never lasted through a whole night—but after, it must have been days... maybe months. All she could remember was the aftermath—the pain.

He wouldn't kill her...he wanted to break her.

She strained to move, but like before, she was immobilized. Her wrists and ankles ached, as well as her neck and stomach, as if they were shackled. However, from her best recollection, she hadn't been captured. There should be no metal, but it bit into her skin and rubbed against the burned flesh that remained.

"Do you feel that, Faedi?" The voice slithered out of the brightness, smooth and amused. His tone was sickly sweet, making her skin crawl and her stomach turn. *"No shadows to protect you here. Just you and me."*

She swallowed hard, refusing to give him the satisfaction of a response—but it only seemed to amuse him further. His laughter echoed around her, bouncing off the invisible walls of light that surrounded her on every side.

"Come now," he cooed. *"Surely you didn't think it would be that easy to escape me? That I wouldn't come for what was mine?"*

The temperature seemed to rise, the light growing hotter, pressing against her skin until it felt like her flesh was sizzling. She bit down hard, fighting the scream that clawed up her throat. She wouldn't give him that, not yet.

This isn't real.

Then, a scream cut through the light—deep, feral, and unmistakable.

It was Sylrie.

"No!" She gasped, jerking against the bonds as she searched the light for him. The scream didn't stop; it echoed, twisting through the light, sinking into her bones, and with it came the sickening crack of her arm.

"You hear that?" He whispered, his voice dripping with delight. *"Your precious brother—the glorious protector who can't even protect himself. And it's because of you... he sailed into danger because you called him."*

She shook her head, squeezing her eyes shut against the light, but it continued to burn into her eyes. Sylrie's screams continued, raw and guttural, filled with pain that fueled her own. Bile rose in her throat as she failed to block out the relentless sound of his suffering.

"Stop it," she choked out, the words torn from her before she could stop them. "Leave him alone."

"Stop?" He mocked. *"Oh, no, this is only the beginning. We're just getting started."*

Then, the screams changed and shifted. Sophir's voice came, rough and strained, breaking as he cried out in agony. Her heart lurched, each scream driving into her like a blade. She didn't have to see him to picture what he looked like: bloodied and broken, his face twisted in pain, and she couldn't reach him.

"No!" She thrashed at the chains with everything she had, but it only brought fresh pain as the metal tore against her wrists. The light pressed harder, smothering her.

"*Look at you,*" Ilos purred, his voice smooth like silk. "*So full of fight… and yet, so powerless. They'll all suffer because of you. This is your doing.*"

Another scream pierced the air, and her heart stopped. It was Lonan, and he screamed her name in a horrid mixture of pain and fear. The light pulsated around her, pressing harder against her, and the heat intensified. Every tortured sound wormed its way into her soul, burrowing into places she hadn't even known could hurt.

It isn't real.

"*How are you so sure?*" He whispered. "*You can't save them from this.*"

The three screamed in unison, and a sob caught in her throat. She forced it down, gritting her teeth until her jaw ached.

It's not real—he does this when he's mad.

"*How do you know the mutt didn't tell you what I wanted him to?*" His breath singed her ear, and she tried to flinch away. "*It's rather convenient that there were people on the mountain who knew exactly what to say, don't you think?*"

The light pulsed again, and the screams grew louder, overlapping until they were a wall of sound that crashed over her. Other voices joined in, ones she couldn't immediately recognize, each of them screaming her name—distorting in pain.

"Are you mad?" She choked out. "That… so many people hate you? That we're going to find a way to kill you?"

Ilos' laughter filled the light. "*Oh, Faedi,*" he murmured. "*Divine blessings or not, how could someone as weak as you kill someone who's killed an Ancient?*"

She squinted at the light and snarled. "If an Ancient can die—so can you."

She wasn't sure if what she said upset him or if there was some kind of outside force, but the light fractured. Spots of darkness stretched around her and slowly clouded her vision. The voice disappeared after a thunderous shout, her body went cold, and she sighed in relief.

Maybe I'm dying.

A heavy, cold weight pressed down on her like a burial shroud, thick, smothering, until the weight of it sank into her bones. Cold flooded through her, numbing every thought and every memory until she wasn't sure if she was still alive or just a memory slipping through ice and silence. She tried to breathe, to blink, but her eyes were crusted shut, and the sharp bite of frost against her skin trapped her.

"*Faedi, where are you?*"

"*Answer us, please.*"

Then, something else—a pressure on her throat. It was subtle at first, almost part of the heavy cold, until it tightened, squeezing the last remnants of air from her lungs. Panic shot through her as she clawed blindly at the weight pressing her down, her hands slipping across rough fabric and skin. Light filled her vision, but beyond that, a shadow loomed over her.

The scent of charred flesh filled her nostrils as fingers dug into her neck, thumbs pressing into her windpipe, and she choked, her body thrashing against the weight. For a second, she thought it might be another torment of Ilos or a trick of her mind, but it felt too real, brutally so. The touch was fire against her frostbitten skin.

"Did you think it would be that easy?" A raspy voice hissed. "Did you think you could kill me and be done with it?"

She tried to scream, but the crushing grip on her throat swallowed the sound. Her hands scrabbled against him, trying to shove him off, but he held fast, his grip too strong. Still, she managed to open her eyes. Just in time to see a twisted gleam of satisfaction in Fenkas' eyes as the sky lit up in a beautiful array of colors behind him.

"Faedi, fight!" A voice whispered, faint and distant. It broke through the haze of pain, and her heart pounded in her chest.

She pulled every ounce of strength she had left and twisted, bringing her knee up as quickly as she could to collide with his side. He grunted, momentarily losing his grip, and she gasped in a sharp breath of icy air. She managed to roll away, pushing him off just enough to scramble away.

He didn't let her get far and lunged for her again. His fingers dug into her ankles, slicing her burned skin open, and she tried to kick free. "You can't escape me," he sneered. "I will deliver you to him."

More voices echoed in her head, tangled together in a desperate symphony. *"Don't give up."* Another voice urged, fierce and resolute. *"Keep fighting. We're coming for you."*

Her fingers brushed against a shard of ice, sharp and jagged, and without a second thought, she gripped it, slashing at him as he dragged himself up her legs. It cut across his face, drawing a fresh line of blood that splattered against the snow, and he howled. It took everything in her to back away and get to her feet as her right arm fell limp at her side.

He stumbled to his feet, his face twisted in pain and shock, but he charged her and tackled her back down into the snow. She gritted her teeth, pushing the ice into him. The resistance of his chest gave way as his blood coated her hand, hot and slick against the cold. Then, he was still, his weight pinning her to the ground as his wide eyes went glassy, staring at her with a final, hateful glare.

She could hardly process it. She was shaking and gasping, her vision blurring as she stared up at him—at the man who played with her and her brothers in the woods, the man who put flowers in her hair, the one who swore to protect her and her family.

"It wasn't real," a voice murmured, soft and soothing, but it was faint like a dream. A phantom whisper slipped through her mind. *"Go home, Faedi."*

She whimpered under his weight as the sky turned bright white. She couldn't escape. His blood continued to seep onto her as she thrashed under his weight, trying to get the heat of his body off her.

"*You're wasting time,*" Ilos sneered. "*Pathetic, really. Your kin needed you, and here you are, lost in your mind.*"

The light above her grew brighter, painfully bright, stabbing through the ice and snow, blinding her as she finally managed to roll Fenkas off her. She couldn't stay there. She had to move away from the crushing cold and relentless light, from him and every voice that echoed in her mind.

Faedi stumbled through the snow, her limbs numb, her skin raw and bleeding. The voices were still there, a tangled mess of whispers and shouts, filling her head until she could barely think.

"*Come back,*" she thought she heard Sylrie's distant and pleading voice. "*Faedi, please… I just got you again.*"

Her eyes burned, the light searing against her skin—or maybe the wind. She flinched, trying to shield herself and find shelter from it, but she couldn't see anything. She was exposed, vulnerable, as if all of her was laid bare under its glare, just like when she was little.

Then another voice broke through the others, one she couldn't place, soft and unfamiliar, yet somehow comforting. "*You're stronger than this, Faedi. Find your balance. Don't let him take you.*"

The words settled over her like a gentle spring breeze. She tripped and fell to her knees but forced herself to crawl through the snow. Her body screamed in protest, every inch of her numb and burning all at once. Then, warmth hit her.

She stumbled and fell against whatever she'd bumped into, her face pressing into coarse, dense fur that covered something solid and massive. Dazed and confused, she tried to lift her head, but her body refused to cooperate; her vision blurred in the light. Before she could grasp what she was leaning on, hands gently gripped her shoulders, steadying her.

The scent of pine and earth overtook the acrid smell of burnt flesh, almost comforting in its familiarity. Then, something slipped over her neck, settling against her collarbone, and the voices went silent. Warmth radiated from it, and the soft heat soaked into her skin as the light dissipated.

She tried to make out her rescuer's face, but the world was too blurred, her eyes too heavy to focus on any one thing. Then, darkness began to close in as she was lifted and held securely against fur and leather. Arms wrapped around her, and for the first time that day, she felt… safe.

Before everything faded, she last remembered a gentle, heavily accented whisper close to her ear. "Rest, he can't bother you now. You're safe."

71
Of Potions and Poison

Faedi

Warmth seeped into Faedi's skin, gentle and insistent, pulling her back from the cold that had wrapped around her bones. She lay still, savoring it, fearful that it would vanish if she dared to breathe and she would find herself buried under snow and ice—or drowning. Slowly, she let her eyes flutter open, squinting against the flickering light that danced beyond her vision.

The Rowdon lights stretched above her, their beautiful glow spreading across the sky in sweeping waves of violet, green, and blue. They twisted in and out of themselves as if painted by some unseen hand. It was a sight she had longed to see again, even when she hadn't remembered, but the sight was bittersweet. She wanted to see them with Lonan… with Sophir. She wanted Ravyn there too, but it had been so long since she had last seen him.

She let out a shaky breath, grounding herself, feeling the earth beneath her and the heat from nearby.

A low crackle of fire pulled her attention. Turning her head slowly, muscles stiff and aching, she watched the campfire blaze beside her. Its flames were steady, yet anxiety rippled through her despite the welcome warmth. The feeling grew when she spotted two figures seated by it—half-shadowed by the flickering fire. Two women she had never met before.

The first had short, unevenly cut hair, wisps falling across her forehead as she stared into the flames with an unreadable expression. She wore a cloak made of white fur, its thick folds draped around her shoulders, giving her a wild, almost regal look. But her eyes caught Faedi's attention—their bright red glint, like embers, unnatural and intense. They flickered with light, even more vivid and dangerous than the fire.

As Faedi took in her presence, the woman's scent drifted to her—sharp and earthy. Wolf.

The other woman was thinner and appeared more frail. Her large black eyes focused on the darkness beyond the fire. Her hair fell in soft waves, framing the sharp angles of her face, but it barely reflected any light from the fire. Like the first woman, she wore a cloak of fur—but black, and black spikes poked out from the fur.

The other woman's scent was stronger, but Faedi knew one thing about her the moment she took her next breath. She had poison on her.

As if sensing her gaze, the short-haired one turned, her eyes meeting Faedi's with a look that was equal parts curious and knowing. Her lips curled into a faint smile that held secrets Faedi wasn't sure she wanted to hear.

"You're awake," she said, her voice low and rich. "Good. I was beginning to think you wanted to stay with death."

Her words sank in slowly, and Faedi swallowed. Her throat was rough—raw. "How long was I out?" Her voice came out weaker than she expected. "Where am I?"

"Two days," the woman replied, her smile widening a fraction. "Somewhere safe."

A shiver ran through Faedi, though not from the cold. She pushed herself up slowly, acutely aware of the stiffness in her limbs, the lingering ache of frost-bite, deep bruises, and burns she hadn't yet dared to inspect. Her last memory came rushing back—the snow, the fight with Fenkas, his hands around her throat. The avalanche. Her grandfather.

A shudder ran through her, and she glanced around, half-expecting to see Fenkas' figure lurking in the shadows.

The woman's gaze never left her, eyes piercing almost through her. "You're not going to find him here," she announced as if reading Faedi's thoughts. "The snow took what you left of him."

Her words should have comforted Faedi, but they only reminded her of how close she had come to staying buried alongside him. "Who are you?"

Her smile fell, and her eyes returned to the fire. "Friends." She tilted her head slightly, the firelight catching the angles of her face. "Fellow future sacrific-es."

She extended a hand, offering a small flask, and Faedi accepted it cautiously. The cool metal pressed against her skin, and she winced. She sniffed the con-tents—sharp, bitter, alcoholic, and unmistakably medicinal. She hesitated, but the woman's eyes caught hers and held them—steady, unblinking, as if daring her to refuse.

"Drink," she said simply. "Unless you'd rather let the cold keep its hold on you. Or if you prefer a painful existence."

Without another word, Faedi took a small sip, the liquid burning down her throat before settling in her stomach like a hot rock. Warmth spread through her, easing some of the tension in her muscles. She returned the flask, and the woman capped it with approval.

Silence fell between them, broken only by the soft crackle of fire and the distant howl of wind through the trees. The Rowdon lights continued their dance above, casting strange shifting shadows across the snow. Faedi wanted to ask a thousand questions, to demand answers about who these women were, but something told her she should already know.

"Did you see Torix?" She asked finally, her voice barely above a whisper, hoping they would know who he was.

The red-eyed woman flicked her gaze between Faedi and the fire before nodding. "Yes, he is hunting for food." She pulled out a different flask and sipped from it. "I don't think he could stand watching you rest."

"He is a good father," the other woman chimed in from her place by the fire.

Faedi tried to keep her face blank, unsure if she could trust them. They planned to find eclipse-born and bring them together for safety, but not all eclipse-born would be on their side. Some could have sided with Ilos.

What if these two are loyal to him?

"How did you find me?" she asked, leaning forward despite her back's protest.

"Your scent is rather distinct," the red-eyed woman shrugged, her voice softer. "Even if they're not on you—it's rare to smell eventides in the snow."

Faedi looked between them, and her reply came before she could stop herself. "So are yours. Wolf and poison."

Sylrie had told her not to trust wolves.

"You drank my poison," the frail woman finally spoke, her voice soft, almost song-like. "It is like your flowers. Heal or kill."

The short-haired one raised the flask and tapped it with a clawed finger. She smiled at Faedi, one meant for comfort, and she relaxed slightly. Still, her mind spun with questions that barely distracted her from the pain lingering in her limbs.

"What are your names?" Faedi asked, needing something to call them. "Unless you're going for the cold and mysterious aura."

The short-haired one chuckled and glanced at the other with pure amusement. "I like her." The other smiled before her crimson eyes turned back to Faedi. "I'm Ragna—this is Lisea."

Faedi tilted her head, studying Ragna. She didn't look the same as in her memory, but it would be an odd coincidence for the name to be repeated. "Bjorn's Ragna?"

Ragna paused, blinked, then smiled softly and nodded. "Yes, I'm Bjorn's Ragna."

Faedi narrowed her eyes. "You look different."

"It's been just over twenty years now… and you're wearing something of mine."

Before she could respond, the scent of freshly killed game drifted toward them. Faedi knew it was him before she even saw him. Torix emerged from the tree line, his broad frame carrying an elk over his shoulders. His eyes immediately found hers, and for a moment, disbelief flickered across his face.

"Faedi?" His voice was hoarse, and his hands trembled as he dropped the elk. He crossed the distance in hurried steps, desperation in his movements.

Faedi struggled to sit up straighter, her back protesting, but she couldn't stop the small, tired smile that pulled at her lips. "Hi, Da," she said softly, her voice as tight as his. "I…"

She didn't know what to say.

"We'll go scout," Ragna's voice caught her attention, but she didn't look at her. She couldn't look away from Torix, even if she wanted to.

His eyes softened, a mix of relief and shock washing over his face as he knelt beside her. His hands reached out, almost as if he was afraid to touch her, but the fear in his eyes quickly faded as he cupped her face gently in his hands.

"You're awake," he whispered. His voice trembled, and her heart ached. She had hurt him… again.

"I'm sorry," she whispered back, the words spilling out before she could stop them. "I'm so sorry."

Torix shook his head, his brow furrowing as he pulled her into his chest. His arms were warm and solid around her, his heart pounding beneath her cheek. "You never need to apologize for being alive," he whispered into her hair. "Don't ever do that again, Faedi. I don't know what I would have done…"

She closed her eyes, burying her face against him as his words settled in her bones—comforting and painful at the same time.

"I'm sorry," she whispered again, though this time, he didn't reject her apology. Instead, his arms tightened around her as if to reassure her that he wasn't upset.

His fingers brushed through her hair, his grip gentle yet secure, like he was trying to ground her to him. "You're alive," he whispered. "That's all that matters right now."

The ache in her chest deepened, and she couldn't hold back the sadness welling inside her. Her throat tightened as the thoughts she had been avoiding came rushing back—Haldin's head tossed at her so casually. The sadistic grin on Fenkas' face. The screams of her little brothers. The charred bodies.

"Grandda—" she whimpered. The words she tried to say were bitter on her tongue, and she couldn't blink away her tears.

Torix didn't say anything at first; he only held her while she sobbed into his chest. It was only when she finally managed to calm herself that he pulled away to wipe her tears away with his thumbs. "I'm so sorry, Faedi," he said softly. "I should have come back… I shouldn't have left."

Her chest tightened at his words, her guilt growing, and she shook her head. He couldn't blame himself. She had convinced him to leave. And all the while, she had been glad that Haldin died—glad that it was him instead of her father.

She shouldn't be relieved.

"He died because I wanted to help the refugees—it's my fault—"

"He died honorably," Torix hushed her and wrapped his arms around her again. "Haldin upheld his oaths and died a true Warden of the Tide. What happened to him—what's happening now—it's not on you."

But it felt like it was. It felt like she had failed him.

"I just got him back." Her tears spilled over again. "I just got everything back, and Fenkas took it away again. The Order took it away again."

Torix nodded but remained silent. He didn't have to say anything, and she doubted there was anything he could say to ease the pain in her heart.

"I hate to interrupt," Ragna approached and stopped a few feet away, "but are you up for travel?" She offered Faedi the flask she drank from. "We shouldn't stay out here long. The avalanche took out a decent portion of their numbers, and the Helgi are on the warpath, but that doesn't mean they won't send people looking." A growl rumbled from her chest.

Faedi sipped from the flask and savored the sweet taste. "How far away are we?"

Ragna's eyes didn't leave the fire. "I don't know how fast the cultists will regroup."

A ghost of a frown appeared, and then she nodded subtly as her expression fell. "We're closer to the border than the castle. It'll be a rough hike." Then she chuckled as she looked up at the sky. The lights reflected in her red irises like fire in blood. "For mortals, anyway."

Lisea hummed. "And we are not mortal."

Mortal or not—the hike was slow.

The glamour only worked to keep Faedi's mind safe, but it didn't repair the damage done by the avalanche, and she didn't want to guess what state she had been in when Ragna and Lisea found her. What she recalled from her fight with Fenkas was a blur, and all she knew was pain. And, if she was honest with herself, not much had changed.

Through hours of travel, she had barely made a dent in healing her injuries. She was too weak, and neither Ragna nor Lisea were healers, but they were talented at using what they had—and battle dressings. Strips of fabric and fur covered her body to protect her wounds and stop the bleeding, and she had grown accustomed to Lisea's healing tonic. However, she wasn't brave enough to ask what was in it.

Like her, Lisea probably guarded her healing recipes closely, and Faedi didn't want to offend her.

She looked at the massive white wolf to her left, who trudged through the snow step-in-step with Torix. He insisted on carrying her whenever she couldn't hold herself upright for long and hadn't taken no for an answer. Not when she had no valid argument other than pride to deny him.

He hadn't carried her since she was a child.

"You think a lot."

Faedi glanced to her right at Lisea and stared. She wasn't wrong, but Faedi didn't know how to respond. Ragna and Lisea were new to her, and she didn't have Lonan to rely on for stability. Her solitude in the forest hadn't improved her interpersonal skills, and she had minimal trust in strangers.

She wasn't sure whether Lisea sensed her discomfort or if it was simply evident on her face, but the woman only smiled and looked back at the mountains.

"It's a good thing," she hummed. "Plans keep you alive."

Ragna rumbled a sound that mimicked approval, and Faedi cracked a smile. "So… you two are friends?" she asked carefully. They had seemed comfortable together at the fire. "Or new acquaintances?"

Lisea looked at Ragna, who only nodded their large head before she licked her lips. She was anxious. "Friends," she nodded. "Ragna has friends… they helped me and others. Now I… help her—with killing."

"With your poison?" Faedi asked without thinking, her cheeks warming when Lisea met her eyes.

"Yes," Lisea answered simply with another nod. "It helps us buy things we can't trade."

"I run a band of mercenaries—your brother works with me."

Faedi stared down at Ragna's head when she spoke, eyebrows raised. Sylrie had mentioned working with someone born during an eclipse, but he had given no names. He had told her what his job entailed, though. He said they helped and rescued people—he also said he had Helgi with him.

"Do you know my brother?" Faedi looked back at Lisea, hopeful she might have seen him since he had stopped responding to her. However, her hope vanished when Lisea shook her head.

"Danik—my brother does. He is…" she trailed off, pursing her lips with a hum. "First mate? They meet in Ashar and are friends for years. Always together. He sang to us—told us to fight for the mountain. Ragna says they are together— with your bonded."

Faedi caught herself smiling as Lisea spoke. Sylrie had a friend, someone he could trust, and he was alive. He was with Lonan and Sophir. He was safe—or as safe as he could be.

Her hand went to the pendant on her chest, and she tested the metal with her fingertips. She didn't want Ilos in her head again, but she didn't want anyone to worry needlessly about her, either. Even if Ragna told Bjorn she was safe and he relayed it to the others—she doubted they would feel much relief until they heard from her directly. She knew she wouldn't fully trust a third-party message.

She couldn't trust it.

72
A Faint Hope

Lonan

Four days in the snow, and we only found…them.

He stood against the wall, arms crossed over his chest, watching Myst heal the Helgi Sylrie had been with—Danik. Supposedly, he was the person the other Helgi wanted to find, but Lonan hadn't cared enough to ask any questions. Not when there were more important matters at hand.

Like his missing bonded.

For someone who was supposedly worried about his sister, Sylrie was surprisingly calm.

He hadn't moved from his place beside Danik, insisting the Helgi be healed first. It was either honorable or foolish, given how beaten up he was compared to the other man, but he also hadn't asked anyone about Faedi. He hadn't asked about his grandfather, his father, or anyone else. His attention was entirely on Danik—and Danik's was on Lonan.

If not for Sophir's nudge to his shoulder, Lonan might have stared a hole through Sylrie.

"What's wrong?" Sophir's voice tickled his senses, but Lonan didn't take his eyes off them. He did, however, blink—and caught Danik blinking too.

Lonan huffed and rolled his shoulders. *"He won't stop staring at me."*

"You did the same thing to me when I met you." Sophir's chuckle might have gotten a smile from him under different circumstances.

"That's because you were freaking Faedi out."

443

"Maybe you're freaking Sylrie out, and he knows." Sophir nudged him again, and Lonan rolled his eyes. No one could make Sylrie uncomfortable…except for Faedi, whenever she did something that could get herself hurt. *"You haven't stopped staring at Sylrie since we found them."*

"Of course I am. He's hurt, and he used to be the same size as Faedi. Now…he's taller than you."

"You're staring at him because he's tall?"

"I'm not going to sprout two heads, you know."

Sylrie's baritone voice pulled Lonan from his silent conversation with Sophir, and he straightened when he met his gaze. Sylrie almost looked amused, or he might have if he didn't look so utterly exhausted. He hadn't looked that way moments ago when his attention was on Danik.

Lonan shook his head and shrugged. "Sorry, it's just been a long time."

"Yeah." Sylrie's frown deepened before he looked between Lonan and Sophir. "So…you married my sister."

Lonan glanced up at Sophir before managing a small smile back at Sylrie. "Is that a surprise?"

"You're sizing him up, aren't you?" Sophir's voice rumbled in his mind, amused, and Lonan tried not to react.

"No…maybe?" He cast another quick look up at Sylrie. Thank the Ancients, Faedi was the one who talked with her hands. *"He's well within his rights to threaten me—and you. She's his sister."*

Sophir growled lowly, his tone dull but firm. *"He can threaten, but he's not touching you."*

Sylrie's chuckle pulled Lonan's attention back to him. He hoped Sylrie hadn't noticed how his cheeks warmed at Sophir's words. Maybe Danik had hummed something funny to him. He seemed to understand the sounds Danik made.

"I knew you two would get married—or it would have happened if…" Sylrie's smile faded as he trailed off, and Lonan winced.

"You didn't spend the last twenty-some years thinking she was dead?" Lonan asked, forcing the best smile he could muster. It wasn't Sylrie's fault for thinking she might have been dead. Lonan had thought the same thing for five excruciatingly long years.

Sylrie scoffed and lowered his head with a nod. "Yeah, that."

"Faedi told us you were in Ashar?" Sophir spoke up, his tail wrapping loosely around Lonan's legs.

Sylrie looked back up at them, and the subject of Ashar didn't seem as difficult for him as Faedi did. "For a few years, until we got busted out—been running with mercs since."

Lonan glanced at Danik and then to Myst, who straightened once they finished healing him. They turned to face Lonan, and he wondered if they could even see him. Espen was at their feet, but the cub's attention flicked between everything moving in the room. Guilt washed over Lonan when he realized he hadn't had much time to speak with them.

He was a terrible brother.

"So are there a lot of Helgi mercenaries, or…" Lonan trailed off, recalling how the Helgi fought—how they painted their skin black to match their armor. He'd never seen mercenaries that coordinated before, but then again, he hadn't encountered many mercenaries. No one like that ever ventured into the Mire and survived long.

The Helgi might survive there if they always fought like that.

Danik shook his head slowly. "Most of us prefer to stay with our own for protection—but a few of us joined up. We owe the band a debt…it's good luck to have a Helgi on a ship." He raised his eyebrows at Lonan and smiled. "Just like it's good luck to have an Umbral around in the forest, right?"

Lonan had to give it to him—he got a chuckle out of him there.

"Are you the one that asked them to come here?" Sophir asked softly, though his rumble echoed through the room.

Sylrie's grin at Danik was the only answer Lonan needed, but Danik's nod confirmed it. "We asked when the first ship closed in on us." He glanced at Sylrie before continuing, "We knew if there was one following us, more would come and attack."

"They're still a ways away," Myst commented as they tapped Sylrie's arm and pointed for him to sit down. "Your turn, big guy."

Sylrie didn't seem amused at being ordered around, but his expression softened when Myst muttered something about him being a 'stubborn ox.' With a sigh, he raised his hands and sat down with a wince. "Alright, you win." But once Myst moved closer, his eyes darkened. "You going to tell me what happened, or am I supposed to ignore that shit on your face? Where's your bonded Warden?"

Lonan flinched for Myst, but they didn't react. They might have blinked, but the wrap on their face hid it, and Espen only waddled around Sylrie's feet to chew on his boots. Sylrie would have been their Warden, just as Lonan would have been Faedi's—they had planned it as children. But then the fire happened.

"You're not shy about bringing up the heavy stuff, are you?" Myst scoffed and shook their head. Lonan knew they rolled their eyes. "We were attacked…by cultists, nonetheless. They burned my eyes, and Vishal…"

"No one's heard from him since the attack," Lonan finished when Myst trailed off, acting like the healing required more concentration.

Sylrie was silent, his brows knitted tight while he rubbed his chin. He was a far cry from the fun-loving child Lonan had known before. "Vishal…" he said the name slowly, as if trying to be sensitive or hoping to remember if they'd met before. "When was he born?"

"Two summers before me—on the solstice," Myst whispered. Their cheek glistened, and Lonan's heart clenched. It was the first time he had seen them show emotion over him.

Danik looked up at them and touched their shoulder with a low hum. "Then he's probably alive."

"Are you two really with Sylrie?"

Lonan's heart stopped when Faedi's voice reached him, and he whipped around to stare up at Sophir, who likely mirrored his look of shock—of hope. His jaw was slack, his eyes brighter than they'd been since the avalanche, and Lonan caught himself smiling. Like a fool.

"He's here, Myst is healing him. Where are you? We'll come to you." He fired off the message faster than he could process his thoughts, only slowing when Sylrie gasped. His sigh perfectly reflected Lonan's relief.

"Thank Ytna."

Lonan didn't realize Sophir had dragged him into another room until the scent of eventides filled his senses. One moment, they had been with the others; the next, they stood in her bedroom. Her scent still lingered in the air, the hearth remained unlit, and heavy curtains were drawn over the windows, shrouding the space in near-total darkness. Sophir stood in front of him while Faedi's voice echoed in their minds.

"They gave me a necklace. It keeps him out of my mind—but I can't talk to you either when I wear it."

Lonan exchanged a glance with Sophir, uncertain whether such magic was safe. When Sophir appeared unbothered, Lonan sighed. *"What happened to Fenkas?"*

"They said I killed him. I don't remember much of it, honestly."

"Have you always been able to grow wings?" Sophir mused, tilting his head as he traced Lonan's knuckles with his thumbs. The gesture soothed Lonan more than it should have.

"I'm a werewolf—but when Bjorn helped me... I don't know?"

Lonan chuckled at her confusion and shook his head. Of course, she wouldn't remember much—not with the murderous rage she had undoubtedly felt. All she had cared about was killing Fenkas. He didn't blame her. If he could fly, he would have brought Fenkas to her himself, just so she could have delivered the final blow.

At least then, they wouldn't have lost her in the avalanche.

A memory surfaced in his mind—the bird she had held when he found her, its feathers a different color, too large for such a small creature. Maybe— *"It could be one of those god-touched things,"* he suggested with a shrug. *"The unawakened abilities we keep hearing about? You've done things some Guardians can't before."*

"Maybe... but that doesn't matter. Are you two all right? Did the avalanche hurt anyone? Everyone was sealed with the tree and—"

"Everyone is fine. Helgi came after you fell and helped," Sophir cut in before she could worry herself into a spiral. *"Just focus on getting back to us in one piece. Please."*

Lonan smiled in relief when Faedi didn't continue her anxiety-driven tangent. However, the relief faded as he recalled something she had said. *"You said the necklace keeps him out of your mind…when did that start happening again?"*

Silence stretched for several breaths, and Lonan's heart pounded in his ears. Sophir's brows furrowed, his tail flicking anxiously behind him. She was either trying to remember or thinking of a way to word it without alarming them. He didn't like either option.

"Faedi?" Sophir prompted gently.

"I don't know…I don't know if it was him or maybe my self-doubt. He made me hear other people…what if he made me hear myself? He knew things…"

Lonan narrowed his eyes at Sophir and subtly shook his head. *"Does he actually know things, or does he just word them to make it sound like he does?"*

"I don't know."

"Ragna can talk to Bjorn, yes?" Sophir sighed, sliding his hands to Lonan's shoulders. Lonan knew what he would tell her, and he didn't like it, but he also knew it was what she needed.

"She can."

"Put it back on." They spoke in unison, locking eyes.

"Are you sure? He's not—"

"We're sure." Sophir shook his head with a low rumble. *"Better not to give him a chance. We'll be here, waiting for you to get back."*

"He's right," Lonan added gently.

"Alright… I'll see you soon."

Then, there was nothing. Only silence in the dark room. Instead of the hope he had felt minutes before, a pit of dread settled in Lonan's stomach. She was hiding something. He knew it. And he didn't like it—not when he knew the scars she carried, the evidence left behind from the last time she had been tormented in the light.

Lonan pulled away from Sophir and began pacing, fingers threading through his hair. "I swear, if she has a new mark from that fucking bastard…" He glanced at the hearth, shaking his head. "I'll make him fear the dark long before I kill him and make him see it forever."

Sophir wandered to the bed and sat on its edge with a sigh. "Can we kill a god?" He murmured, as if unsure whether he was asking Lonan or himself. "We've been lucky with our brushes against death, but… Bjorn had a list of gods—some are on Ilos' side."

Lonan turned to face him. "Who was on his side?"

Sophir licked his lips before leaning forward, resting his elbows on his knees. "I don't know… I was distracted." He shook his head. "There were a lot of names."

Lonan watched him, noting the way he avoided eye contact, his tail wrapped around himself. He looked like Faedi when she hugged herself for comfort. Something was wrong. Now, he understood why Faedi hated secrets so much.

"Tell me," Lonan demanded, stepping forward and cupping Sophir's cheek—a silent request for him to look at him. "What distracted you?"

Sophir slowly raised his head, meeting Lonan's gaze—searching, debating. "When Bjorn mentioned my rumored patron having siblings… it made me worry about my own." His voice wavered, almost timid. Lonan's breath caught. "Someone attacked the temple they were at in the north."

Lonan froze. He recalled Sophir mentioning someone—a sister—but he had never spoken much about the rest of his family. All he ever seemed to care about was what was immediately around them. "More zealots?"

Sophir's face darkened, and he turned away. "Yes. But we found out right before you were attacked," he admitted. "I was more concerned with getting you back alive… and then that bastard Fenkas—and Faedi."

He was right. There hadn't been much time to tell him. And even if there had been, Lonan wasn't sure any good would have come from it. Dozens of gods existed, and there was no clear way to know whether those they patronized would be allies or enemies.

Lonan sighed and sat beside him. "So what else did I miss?"

"Faedi wants to unseal the realms—the heart trees are portals." Sophir turned to face him but quickly lowered his head again. "I don't know if unsealing them is the best idea, but…"

"Once Faedi gets an idea, she doesn't let it go," Lonan finished with a sigh before scoffing. "The worst part is, she's usually right."

Sophir nodded. "I want to find a way to connect to my patron—I don't like not knowing these things."

"I don't like it either," Lonan admitted, rubbing his face. His mind wandered to the least helpful thought. "The only time I've felt anything different was when I was shot… but I don't think I want to repeat that."

Sophir's gaze dropped to Lonan's side. "I don't want to repeat that either."

73

A Fork in the Path

Faedi

We should reach the first pass by morning, but you should rest."

Faedi looked up at Ragna as she offered her fur cloak while she leaned against Torix. Neither Ragna nor Lisea made a fire, and she doubted they would. They were too close to the castle; if any cultists remained, a fire would be a beacon for their location. The pair looked like they could handle a fight, and she knew Torix could, but she could not. Her self-healing attempts had exhausted her, and her arm remained useless.

She might not be able to grow them again—the burns reached her bones.

"Any cultists?" Faedi asked before wrapping the fur around herself. She hadn't heard a howl from other hunts—but she didn't trust it. "Or anyone?"

Ragna shook her head. "No. Bjorn says the castle is quiet. Your brother was healed, and everyone is safe."

Faedi watched as Ragna twisted one of the rings on her finger, a simple silver band on her middle finger. She had seen her do it before, a nervous tick Ragna seemed to have whenever she wasn't in her wolf form. She hadn't mentioned its importance, and Faedi hadn't asked. Whatever it was, it was Ragna's secret that grounded her.

"What made the mountain fall?" Lisea's soft voice barely broke over the wind, drawing Faedi's attention. "The…av…avalanche?"

"I've been wondering that too," Torix grumbled, and Faedi winced.

He hadn't wanted her hurt, but she didn't know what she had done.

She hadn't given the cause much thought—or any. All she knew was that it had happened, and the aftermath followed. Lonan and Sophir hadn't mentioned anything about it either, and she doubted she should ask them. They had told her to keep the necklace on, and she knew they were right to worry. She wasn't in any state to fight someone out of her mind with how tired she was.

Then she remembered the roots she had pulled from under the ice. "I killed the uprisers with vines; maybe I disturbed it too much?"

Ragna raised a brow and looked between Lisea and Faedi. "How did you get plants to take root in the ice…and rock?" Her words slowed as she finished her question, kicking the snow for emphasis. "That's not…I've seen plenty of Guardians, but that's…impressive."

Faedi dismissed her with a shrug. "It isn't all rock and ice; there was soil there too. I could smell it."

"The mountain is solid."

Lisea's statement caught Faedi's attention, and she tilted her head to the side. Solid rock or not, the soil had been there. Wind could have easily moved it from the farms or other locations. However, when she considered what Lisea meant, her eyebrows pinched together. The people moved soil to create the farms and planted shallow-rooted crops in containers.

"Maybe…" Faedi bit her lip while piecing together her thoughts. "I might have used more magic than intended and disturbed the top. Everyone says the castle is fine, so…I don't know."

Ragna scratched her head, almost like a canine would, and shrugged. "Could be possible. Did you grow eventides?" She scented the air. "I can't smell any from there."

Slowly, Faedi shook her head. She couldn't remember what kind of plant it had been. "I just remember Fenkas' fire and…"

My grandfather's head.

Torix wrapped his arm over her shoulders and held her close. He didn't say anything or do anything else to call attention to her or himself, and she wondered if he knew where her mind had gone. He hadn't been there or seen what had happened, but she was sure he knew how horrible it had been.

"Might be worth investigating when we get back," Ragna nodded. "If it was strong enough to bring down part of the mountain, it could be risky to keep it there. The heart tree could be damaged."

The heart tree.

Faedi paused after Ragna spoke and bit her lip. Her concern had only been for the people she had sealed with the tree, not the tree itself. What would happen to the portal if the mountain caved in on it? What had happened to the other portals in the east when those trees had been destroyed?

"Bjorn told me about the people sealed in other realms…" She hugged the cloak closer around herself as the wind picked up. "Do you know how to unseal them?"

Ragna shook her head silently, and Faedi frowned. Even if she had known the chances of Ragna knowing were slim, she had hoped to get some kind of hint out of her. Beyond what she had seen in her dreams—she knew nothing about her supposed patron, but someone should know something.

She hugged her knees to her chest and rested her chin on them. "I need to figure out how to unseal them, right?" She glanced between Ragna and Lisea. "Or is it safer for everyone to stay locked away?"

"There was something that was said when I was in Ashar…" Ragna's voice barely carried over the wind as she spoke. "They insinuated that if they couldn't control the hearts—the portals…they would destroy them. The plague in Valoria wasn't set on the people but spread from the heart tree there. They used that after they destroyed the one in Ashar, and the aftermath was too severe."

"The earth was mad," Lisea shrugged with a hum. "They deserve it."

What if…

Faedi turned her attention to the ground and stared at the snow. The old magic she had sensed when she grew the throned vines was familiar, but she hadn't paid much mind to it. If a plant were to remain rooted in rocky territory, the roots would have to have a way to latch into the earth.

Every heart tree shared the same purpose, but there was always something different about them. Even the twins had differences.

She moved her feet deeper into the snow while considering the possibilities. "What if the heart tree caused the avalanche?"

Ragna approached her and kneeled before her, her red eyes ablaze as she watched her. Something must have clicked for her. "Ilos was fucking with you before…" she growled low before she smirked. "Tell me about the first time Ilos took you to the light. What were you doing before it happened?"

Faedi hadn't considered what she had been doing before she was taken to the light. It hadn't mattered to her before—not when the aftermath had ended with her in pain. All she knew was that it had started in her dreams, and then it had happened again after the fire and, of course, after the avalanche.

"I think the first time… was when Sylrie and I went to the twins…we were five."

Veth'iral, 2,679

Faedi and Sylrie were led into the forest by their parents, elder Guardians, and Wardens, their robes of deep greens rustling like leaves in the wind. The path was soft beneath Faedi's bare feet, the dirt cool and damp, and the air smelled of pine and moss. Sylrie's hand was tight in hers, his fingers sticky with the sap he had smeared on himself earlier when he had climbed the wrong tree and fallen. He always did that—climbed before anyone could tell him no.

But so did she—he was constantly climbing after her.

The impossibly tall twins stood ahead of them, their trunks separated by the invisible border between the forest and Mire. Their bark shimmered faintly, a soft silvery hue that glowed with an inner light. Faedi's breath caught in her throat. She had seen the trees before, but this time was different. Their auras caressed her like an unseen hand on her cheek.

"This is where your bond to the forest begins," one of the elders said, their voice deep and sturdy like an oak. Elder Peni. "Faedi, Sylrie, kneel before the trees."

Sylrie gave Faedi a sidelong glance, his amber eyes bright with excitement. For once, he didn't put himself in front of her to protect her; he only smiled. Together, they knelt, and the moment her knees touched the ground, a hum beneath the soil resonated through her—the twins' heartbeat.

"Place your hands on the tree," Peni instructed.

Faedi pressed her palm to the rough, warm bark, and Sylrie did the same. The forest seemed to exhale around them, and then it came: a voice.

"Your time will come."

The voice was neither male nor female, soft yet commanding, as if the earth itself spoke to them. Faedi glanced at Sylrie, and she knew he had heard it too. His hand found hers and squeezed.

Guardian. Warden. Those were the words the leaders spoke over them that day. Faedi knew what they meant—the magic and permissions they would be granted from the heart tree's blessing. Their weight settled on her shoulders, on her heart, but it wasn't unwanted. With the responsibility came peace.

That night, after they had celebrated and gone to bed, she dreamed of blinding, searing light that burned through the comforting darkness of sleep. It chased her, tearing at her with unseen hands and dragging her down into agony. There was laughter, sharp and cruel, and names whispered repeatedly.

"Ilos—Faetorin."

When she woke, she was screaming. Sylrie bolted upright beside her, sweat dripping from his brow, his face pale as ash. "It was just a dream," he whispered, but his voice trembled.

Faedi blinked the memory from her mind and stared up at Ragna, who continued to watch her. "We didn't sleep again that night." She looked away, frowning. "Eventually, we told our mother what happened, and she put markings on the doors. The dreams stopped after that... until the fire."

Ragna tilted her head to catch Faedi's eye again. "Did he call you Faetorin after the fire?"

"No." Faedi shook her head, recalling the second voice. "Someone did, though—I didn't recognize the voice. They said I was a child and argued with

Ilos. Then… I woke up in the forest. It was the first time I had marks left by the light, and it didn't bother me for years. What do you make of that?"

Ragna frowned and sat in the snow, lips pursed together. Something Faedi had said made her pause, but she wasn't sure what—unless it was all of it, which wouldn't have surprised her.

"Did you ever hear the second voice again?" Ragna finally asked.

Faedi scoffed, shaking her head. "No, but hearing them again would have been nice." Her attention drifted to her fur-covered body. "Might've hurt less—or not as long."

Lisea hummed softly, but Faedi didn't look at her. She didn't have to. The question hung in the air between them.

"Ilos is losing friends?"

Ragna shrugged. "Could be."

"Bastard shouldn't have any friends," Torix quipped, and Faedi smiled.

Ilos or his worshipers might have been losing allies, just as they faced the same risk. But Faedi wasn't sure she should put much faith in it. There hadn't been enough interaction to determine if the second voice had been an ally or not.

She tried to recall the voice, its words spoken in a different language she couldn't place. All she could remember was the break in the torment, the anger in the other voice. Then, after some time, it had told her to run.

At the very least, they had sympathized with her.

Sympathy might be enough—just like the people fleeing Ilos' cultists in Valoria. "So… what if he has people turning against him?" Faedi looked between them, raising her eyebrows. "Do we need to look for turncoats too? Or keep our focus on the eclipse-born?"

Lisea shook her head. "We make them come to us." She hummed again, and Ragna nodded, as if she understood. "We can't help if we're not safe."

"She's right," Ragna said, nodding again. "If people are leaving his flock or his higher ranks, we don't have the forces or time to look for them. We have to take care of ourselves before we can care for others."

Faedi bit her lip, considering the possibilities. The mountain was their strongest defense, but they couldn't stay there indefinitely. "What do we do about the mountain?" She focused on Ragna again. "It doesn't belong to the Dusk Elves, and if the portals to the realms are opened, we would have to leave."

"Dewgate," Ragna said with a grin. "That is your home—where you'll have to go. Our last reports say it's overrun with a plague, currently… but with enough work, it can return to its former glory."

Faedi instinctively turned west, toward Dewgate—toward the Mire. She frowned. The mountain had better defenses, but it wasn't where they belonged. Yet, she had never felt at home in the city. The forest was where she had always wanted to be. It was the only home she had ever known.

"And when do we go there?" As the wind picked up again, she asked, "We have too many sick and injured who won't survive the cold—too many of Ilos' devout waiting for the perfect opportunity to ambush us. They won't stop hunting us, and if the prophecies and rumors are true… it will get worse when the second moon comes."

Ragna rubbed her hands together and began pacing in the snow. She didn't seem surprised by Faedi's questions, but her face settled into an expression of concern. "Dewgate is without its lord," she said as she walked. "If we braved the trip, we could reclaim Dewgate now. There is Ancient magic there… and the Mire, where we have more allies. But we risk being attacked on the way there, or once we arrive. Or—we stay and wait for more of Ilos' cunts to attack us on the mountain."

Lisea hissed before shaking her head and standing as well. "We fight—either way." She shrugged, motioning around them. "But my kin fight better… not in ice and snow. Umbral fight better in forest. Wind isn't good for Itmis… the mountain could be our tomb."

"There's a heart tree here with people to free—maybe more allies," Faedi countered gently. "But I don't know how to open the portal… I don't even know if I can. And there are the oaths that keep the Dusk Elves there."

Ragna turned to face her. "Consider those oaths fulfilled—we need to talk to everyone."

But.

Faedi shook her head. Ragna was right. They couldn't decide without everyone else's thoughts, but they also couldn't waste time traveling back up the mountain for a traditional meeting. If they were going to move, they needed scouts ahead to ensure the path was safe.

She took a steadying breath, then closed her eyes and removed the pendant.

74

A Door Unopened

"We survived long enough to get here—but now what? Are we just waiting for The Order to come to us again? Can the mountain fend them off long enough? What happens after the eclipse?"

Sylrie

The scent of cedar and stone dust wrapped around him like an old memory he hadn't thought about in years, but recognized all the same. His head was heavy, his limbs weak, but he was alive—alive and warm, though an ache lingered in his shoulder.

Danik sat at the edge of the bed, his silhouette framed against the low light filtering in from the narrow window. His clothes were fresh and clean, and he looked far better than the last time Sylrie had seen him. Myst was still one hell of a healer.

"You're awake," Danik said softly, his voice steadier than Sylrie had expected.

"Barely," Sylrie croaked, his throat dry. He shifted to sit up, muscles aching. A hiss escaped before he could stop it, and Danik was by his side instantly, eyes focused on his chest and abdomen.

"Don't push it," Danik warned. "Your friend did good, but I doubt that's our last brush with death."

Sylrie let out a breath, nodding slightly, then took a better look at the room. It was smaller than he remembered, though that could have been the years stretching his memory. The carved stone walls were familiar, and the bed frame still bore scratches from the countless times he had kicked it out of frustration. The tapestry above the hearth had faded, but he could still make out the crest embroidered over it—an eventide.

"He kept it the same," Sylrie murmured.

Danik glanced back to follow his gaze, a faint smile tugging the corner of his lips. "Hard to imagine anyone changing anything. You're their prince."

Sylrie snorted. "I was, but now…I'm not."

"Your experiences don't change facts." Danik rested his hand on Sylrie's thigh. "You're their heir—just like your sister."

Sylrie looked back at him then, at the way his eyes softened, the lines of worry around his mouth still etched deep. "You think they're going to want someone like me? Having an eclipse-born as a ruler puts everyone at risk."

"Yes," Danik admitted. "Target of Ilos or not, he wants to rid the world of darkness—murder thousands of innocent people. I know for a fact that you would do any and everything you could to protect them." His gaze lingered on the room before meeting Sylrie's again. "And I'll be there to help you—like always."

The weight of his words settled over Sylrie, heavy but not unbearable. He hadn't thought about his inherited responsibilities in a long time, but there he was, in the room where it all started, with someone who had stood by him through more than he deserved.

He let out a long breath, fingers brushing the furs beneath him. "We'll see," he said quietly, not committing to anything yet but not pushing the thought away. "I shouldn't make any decisions until I talk to Faedi."

Danik chuckled. "Sounds smart." He glanced around the room again with a hum. Curious. "How does Dusk Elf rule work? Haldin was king, but…now there are two heirs."

Sylrie's eyes went back to the faded tapestry. "There's supposed to be a Guardian and Warden who work together to rule. After my grandmother died—"

"Sylrie?"

He sighed and lowered his head. *"I don't like you not talking to anyone. When will you be back?"*

"That's part of what I need to talk to you about. I have an idea, but you need to ask Sophir if possible. I think he might be able to help all of us talk."

Sylrie tilted his head and stood without questioning. Her ideas typically worked unless something had changed over the past two decades. He turned and looked back at Danik. "Faedi has an idea. We need to get the others."

Danik nodded wordlessly and stood to follow Sylrie from the room and to Faedi's. A guard stood outside—Bjorn, another eclipse-born—who inclined his head in a bow. His jaw was set as if he wanted to say something, but he only watched Sylrie with his crimson eye.

That's not a common trait.

Sylrie had thought the same when he met Ragna years before, but he hadn't thought to ask her who or what she truly was. All he needed to know was that she was an ally, an eclipse-born, and someone who hated Ilos' followers as much as he did. But as he looked at Bjorn, he couldn't help but wonder what was under his glamour.

"Faedi has an idea and wants everyone together," Sylrie told him, watching as Bjorn's unmarred eyebrow raised before he smiled and bowed his head again.

"I'll get them."

Sylrie watched him leave and scented the air. Predator, but more than just a wolf and not a Krelin. Bjorn smelled like Ragna—cold iron and ashes. *Tell me about Bjorn.*

"What about him?"

"Have you seen him without his glamour?"

"Only what he allowed me to see—but I think he's still hiding. Ragna is too."

"Why is he here?"

"Said he swore an oath to protect the heirs."

"Dusk Elf heirs or heirs of the ones here before us?"

Faedi fell silent, and Sylrie turned to face the door. The etchings in the stone, older than the tapestries that decorated the halls, were deep and worn in an old language. It was one he had never learned—his mother didn't speak it, and he had always assumed it was from the previous inhabitants of the mountain. Then, he thought back to Ashar when Ragna rescued him and the others.

"What were the guards shouting when we were rescued?" He asked Danik as he reached for the door handle.

Danik's eyes met his, and his brows creased. They never talked about Ashar; it hurt too much to bring up, but he didn't deny Sylrie. Instead, he sighed and shook his head. "Sounded like…Myrkiven? I never bothered to learn Asharian."

"Sounds close to Myrven in Elvish—common is 'shadow elf.'" Sylrie glanced at him. "Ragna said the heirs couldn't return until it was time…what if she wasn't talking about just me and Faedi?"

Danik scoffed and shook his head. "Rage doesn't scream princess."

"She's the product of the world that made her—just like us."

"I don't know if this is possible."

Sylrie leaned against the wall while Sophir addressed the room, looking around at everyone. Danik was on the other side of the hearth with his arms crossed. Lonan remained beside Sophir, Ighir towered nearby with a petite red-head beside him, Myst perched on the edge of the bed, and Bjorn leaned silently against the opposite wall.

Lonan was the first to speak. "You went into our minds before and interacted with us."

"Faedi and I have spoken this way before, too," Sylrie offered with a shrug. "Might be easier with an Astral's help."

Ighir nudged Zarae, who snapped to attention and raised her hand slightly. "I am also, mildly, connected to all eclipse-born—it is possible…maybe."

"What's the worst that could happen?" Myst asked with a shrug. "We die? At least then, we can't be sacrificed."

"There's a possibility that if we open this door—it'll be open for everyone," Sophir warned, shaking his head. "If we're already connected in some mystical way…we don't know where the other eclipse-born are or whose side they're on. Or their patrons, for that matter."

"Right—so we still die or become sacrifices," Sylrie mirrored Myst's shrug. "But…Faedi believes you can do it, and we need a plan."

Sophir muttered a curse and turned his attention to Lonan. It didn't take a mastermind to see they were murmuring, maybe even with Faedi too, and Sylrie cracked a smile when he lowered his head in defeat. He would do it—or try, at the very least.

"Everyone sit down," he pointed at the floor. His tail flicked behind him while he dragged his hand down his face. "You'll have to fight the urge to resist the intrusion in your mind."

Zarae skipped to the center of the room and sat down. "Use me as the conduit. I think it'll be easier that way."

Everyone else followed suit once Sophir nodded and sat in a circle around Zarae. Despite being the one to suggest Faedi's idea, Sylrie doubted it would work with everyone—more so without any of them sleeping. The few times it had worked before, Faedi and Sylrie had been asleep, and Sylrie doubted everyone would react well to the ashes he had seen Faedi in. He never liked the glimpses of Ilos' future for them.

Sophir kneeled behind Zarae and sighed before he wrapped his arms around her. Ighir tensed but didn't comment, and Sylrie closed his eyes when a tingling sensation tickled the back of his brain. Beside him, Danik hummed anxiously, but it soon faded into the sound of his heart beating.

Then there was nothing.

75

Ashes in the Crossroads

"If anything about this works—at least I'll be able to see them again. Once isn't enough, but maybe the sting of death won't be as bad."

Faedi

"I'll watch over you," Torix promised. Then, everything faded. In less than a heartbeat, she was no longer in the snow and ice.

The air no longer burned cold against her skin, and her lungs choked on the weight of ash that hung heavy like a shroud. The ground beneath her feet was barren, soft like silt but lifeless, stretching out in every direction as far as she could see. The sky above was a swirling mess of gray and black, a sunless void. Her heart pounded as she looked around for the others.

A ripple moved across the ground, a shimmering thread of silver light snaking through the dust. She stepped back, instinct urging her to keep her distance, but the tether curved toward her, thin and impossibly bright in the colorless world. Then, from the haze, another figure emerged.

Her voice cracked. "Ragna?"

The broad-shouldered woman straightened, shaking ash from her hair as she took in her surroundings. The woman before Faedi was unnaturally pale, unlike the scarred human she had grown accustomed to. Long, pointed ears stuck out from a mess of white hair, and her crimson eyes stared into Faedi's. "Looks like your idea worked."

She's a shadow elf.

Before Faedi could answer, another figure appeared—a tall, willowy presence with a cascade of silken hair, their black eyes sharp. Black scales shimmered on the edges of her face and neck, and no doubt under her clothes, as she glanced around. *Lisea.*

"This is…" Lisea's voice was low, uneasy. "What is this place?"

"It's what remains of the crossroads."

Faedi turned quickly to face the voice behind her and froze when she saw a woman she didn't recognize. Another shadow elf. Her white hair clung to her face, almost hiding her eyes that shimmered different colors, catching the ashes that drifted in the air.

"Tove!" Ragna ran past Faedi, almost knocking her over, and wrapped her arms around the other elf. "Ancients, how are you here? Are you safe? What—"

The woman laughed as she returned the embrace and held Ragna tightly. "He called everyone." She buried her face into Ragna's shoulder, and Faedi barely caught what she said next. "I'm safe. We'll be together soon."

In a blur, Bjorn was beside them. His massive frame wrapped around both of them as he laughed—cried. Like Ragna, his glamour was gone. He too, was a shadow elf, and Faedi took a step back from the scene when the realization hit her. Haldin knew what he was.

It was the only way he would have trusted an outsider to be so close and informed.

"Oathbound…" Faedi whispered as she looked over her shoulder for others.

One by one, they came. Sophir, his dragon-like form flickering as though caught between worlds, his wings folded tight against his back. Lonan stepped out of the haze with an effortless grace, his shadows dancing around him like a violent storm. Though confusion painted their faces, Sylrie arrived with another scaled man beside him.

Myst came next, their lithe form blending with the shadows and ashes, their eyes striking blue and sharp as their gaze darted about. Ighir appeared silently, his expression unreadable, though the tension in his posture spoke volumes. Zarae was the last to step forward, and Faedi caught glints that wrapped around her, silver tethers winding around her like anchors leading to each of them.

Lonan, Sophir, and Sylrie approached Faedi quickly, while the man who once stood beside her brother went to Lisea, and she embraced the trio as soon as they were close enough. She wanted to cry, and she nearly did, but the tethers moved again. Then, more figures began to emerge from the ashes.

The first one—a young woman, her face streaked with soot, her hands trembling as she stumbled back. Then another, a boy who couldn't have been more than six and ten, his eyes wide with fear. More followed, each connected by the same silver tether, their faces unfamiliar, their expressions ranging from confusion to outright terror.

Faedi turned to Zarae. "What's happening?"

Zarae inched her head to the side. "An unforeseen…happy accident?" Then she smiled. "This is…our family. Though I don't think it is everyone."

The crowd grew. Farmers, soldiers, scholars—men, women, children—all pulled into the ashes without explanation. Their murmurs rose, a cacophony of fear and uncertainty.

"Where are we?"

"What's happening?"

Faedi searched the crowd, not knowing where they were from—not knowing if they were allies of Ilos' devout. "Please, everyone, listen!" Her voice rang out, carried on the unnatural stillness of the air. "We're all here for a reason. Just… give me a moment to explain."

The crowd quieted, though unease rippled through them like a living creature. Faedi swallowed hard, looking to her bonded for strength. Sophir nodded slightly, his wings shifting as if preparing to shield her from any backlash, and Lonan rested his hand on her shoulder with a smile.

She took a breath and spoke again. "You've all heard the stories of eclipse-born, haven't you? Of those touched by celestial power, cursed—or blessed, depending on who you ask—with unspeakable abilities?"

The murmurs returned, some nodding, others frowning in confusion.

"That's what connects us," she continued. "We are eclipse-born. Whether you've known it all your life or never realized it until now, you carry that power. And because of that, we're targets." Her voice dropped lower. "Targets of Ilos' followers."

The name alone was enough to draw gasps from some. Others whispered questions to their neighbors, but the fear was palpable.

"Ilos seeks to kill us…maybe consume us," Faedi said, her gaze sweeping across the crowd. "To take the power we were given and use it to break the balance of the world. He means to sacrifice us on the next total eclipse."

"How do you know that?" A man called out. Faedi couldn't pick him out of the crowd.

"I've seen it," the woman with Ragna said. "I've seen the future he wants for the world…it's not unlike this one—what remains of his last attempt to steal power for himself."

Silence echoed through the crowd before shocked gasps erupted as Tove's eyes glowed and the ashes moved to take shape. They shifted and moved, making what looked like a temple of sorts. Then, a battle of translucent shadows made of black and gold played out around them. Faedi watched the people clash, run, and fall. Their forms were not of the ones that surrounded her but Elyssar—celestial beings at war.

It was the breaking of the crossroads—the beginning of The Great War.

Not long after it began, the shapes changed. The sky brightened before it started to dim and revealed an eclipse as flames ignited around them. Figures in robes surrounded them while the ashes took shape into large altars. People were laid out on them, chained and screaming, while the cultists closed in with weapons raised. Then, without warning, everything fell back into the vast nothingness around them.

"What he did here will be repeated over the realms—nowhere to hide, no one left alive…everything and everyone we love will be gone." Tove released a shaky breath. "No side will matter then."

"He thought by killing the gods in the crossroads he could take their power…and he did, for a while," Zarae explained as she walked to the group's center. "He didn't realize that they would continue to come back, though—that we're tied to the world they made."

Another voice rose from the crowd, a woman this time. "We're tied?"

"We are god-touched," another feminine voice rose in the crowd and crept closer. Her horns twisted around her head like a crown, and her golden eyes bore into Faedi's. "In a way, we are divine ourselves. We are the hands of the gods, trapped in our fates because of Ilos and made to suffer from his curse."

Sophir released a breath that warmed Faedi's ear. "Callon?"

"Hello again, old friend." She bowed her head before she righted herself and faced Ragna. "His forces are moving—the mountain will fall if you try to fight them there."

"This is insanity—we are not chosen by the gods, it's…blasphemy," another voice shouted, and Faedi searched for them in the crowd. Either they were in denial or one of Ilos' followers.

Sylrie stepped forward and raised his hand. "Who of you here are, or were imprisoned in Ashar? Who of you has been scarred by his golden flames?"

Faedi stared at him and raised her hand before looking at everyone else. The man with him raised his, as did Ragna, Bjorn, Tove, and Lady Callon. Slowly, others in the crowd began to lift their hands in the air—their fear enough to turn her stomach.

"Keep your hands raised if you are still imprisoned," Ragna stepped toward the crowd. Her anxiety was evident on her face, and she only relaxed when every hand fell. "Thank the Ancients," she whispered as she lowered her head.

"You got them all," Bjorn said before wrapping his arm around her shoulders and resting his chin on her head.

"For now, but being in one of his prisons is the least of our concerns." Lady Callon spoke again and looked between everyone.

Faedi raised her head. "Ilos wants a war and intends to create one. But we can stop him." She glanced over to the shadows near them. "We have to."

76

Silver Roots and Shattered Stones

Faedi

Ashes danced in the sky as they neared Dewgate's wall. The once-beautiful farmlands were barren, covered in a thin layer of snow, peppered with soot, and the air was acrid. Rot and poison. Torix was far ahead, scouting the perimeter, while Faedi walked beside Ragna and Lisea, wondering if Ravyn had seen the same in Valoria when he left.

The scent grew stronger as they passed the ruins of the farmers' homes and closed in on the towering stone walls. Never once had Faedi seen them damaged, but there they were—scarred and crumbling as if sagging under the weight of death. They couldn't protect the city from the threat that attacked from within.

There was no life there, not in the air or earth. Just remains of a place that had once been full of people. Of stories and beauty.

Faedi's heart tightened, and she searched for anything to give her hope. But there was nothing, only silence.

Ragna walked beside her, her heavy steps leaving deep prints in the ash that covered the ground. She was silent, her expression unreadable, but her unease radiated off her in waves. Faedi didn't take her for the kind to show fear, but Dewgate had an aura of death that even she couldn't shake.

Lisea stayed a little behind them, her eyes scanning the horizon. Her form seemed out of place against the devastation. She was the first to speak, her voice cutting through the thick quiet. "This place…someone burned it. The plague—" She paused, kneeling to examine the ground. "Someone was here before us."

Faedi kneeled beside her, swallowing the bile that rose in her throat. The remains Lisea spoke of were everywhere. Corpses lay fallen where they once stood, their limbs twisted like they had been caught in some final agonizing moment. Others were slumped against the crumbled walls or piled in what had once been the main square. The corpses of men, women, children—all of them plagued. What remained of their skin was stretched tight over their bones; black clumps of tissue remained that spoke of poison.

"This is recent," Faedi whispered. "They're still warm."

Lisea didn't reply immediately. She only stood, her brow furrowed in concentration as she surveyed the scene. The city pulled at Faedi's bones—the unease in the air, the weight of death that clung to everything. But under it all, the earth hummed with life. The soil remained untainted.

In the distance, the towering structure that had once been the temple of the Ancients loomed in ruin. All that remained was blackened and charred, crumbled like the wall.

"I hope this was the right choice," Ragna muttered, her voice low. "There's hardly any defenses left."

Faedi nodded, the realization creeping over her. Where the mountain might have been their crypt—Dewgate might serve them to Ilos on a golden platter. "The earth is healthy—the plague didn't spread to the soil."

Ragna clenched her jaw, then sighed as she lowered her head. "What magic this place has might've been the only thing to keep it safe. I just hope there's enough left for us."

"It's stronger this way," Faedi told her and began walking again, following the pull of the earth.

They wound their way through the ruined streets, the city's remains sprawled before them like a ghost of its former self. The once-bustling marketplace was a field of broken carts and empty stalls, littered with the occasional body, their faces frozen in expressions of terror. At the foot of the Lord's castle, the ground was scattered with debris—shattered stone, broken banners, the remnants of once-proud status that had been reduced to nothing more than rubble.

Faedi hoped Blavier suffered.

"Where is it leading you?" Ragna muttered, her voice barely over a whisper. "It's too quiet here."

Faedi couldn't argue with that. The silence was suffocating. The air was thick, and no sound came from the city. Not the chirp of a bird, not the rustle of leaves in the wind, not the distant sounds of the ocean. It was as though life had been utterly and wholly snuffed out.

"Underground, I think." Faedi finally managed to answer her. "I'm not sure."

"There are tunnels under the castle," Ragna announced, leading them through the gate.

Once they crossed the threshold, the charred wood and stone smell hit them fully. The walls were blackened, and the gates warped from the heat. But beyond them—past the desolate courtyard and the ruins—something glimmered faintly in the distance.

"That way," Faedi said, rushing past Ragna. "Something's over here."

They moved toward the light, careful to stay alert. Their steps were slow and cautious as they passed through the broken remains of the castle's grand entrance. The light seemed to glow brighter as they drew closer, an eerie glow coming from the heart of the ruins.

They reached the source of the glow in the castle's central chamber. A large, round stone was embedded in the floor, pulsing with a faint, silver light. It was the same shade as the tether that bound them all together when they had met in the ashes.

Lisea knelt, her fingers brushing against the stone. "What is this?" She whispered, almost to herself. "It is not...rock."

"I don't know," Faedi said softly and knelt beside her to examine it.

"It's a heart."

Faedi whipped around, expecting an attack, but she froze when she spotted someone stepping out from the shadows. Behind them, dozens of people cowered back. Then their scents hit Faedi, and she cracked a smile.

"Ravyn." Faedi stood and raced for him, throwing her good arm around his neck. "What happened?"

He held her close, cradling her head against his chest as she cried. Where were the other Guardians? What about the Wardens? She couldn't ask; she couldn't speak.

His arms were solid and strong around her, and Faedi pressed her face into his chest, soaking in his steady heartbeat against her. The scent of him—the earthy, familiar scent that had always been so comforting—was like a balm to her soul.

His hand moved gently through her hair, his touch tender, almost reverent. She wanted to stay there, to hold onto that moment where the world seemed to pause, where the chaos and danger melted away with the simple act of him being close again. She needed to savor it for as long as she could.

"I leave to find you help, and I find you looking like you crawled around in Draetor. What happened to you?" Dusan's voice reached her, but Faedi didn't pull away from Ravyn. She couldn't.

"Seeing everything...I thought the worst," Faedi whispered, her voice muffled by his shirt, though he seemed to hear her well enough. "Were you here?"

"No. I found people fleeing Dewgate; your pack was with them." His voice was soft as he explained his happenings. "I was told I needed to bring them back when the fire died—I was promised you were safe."

Who told him?

Faedi pulled away to look up at him and shook her head. It didn't make sense. He wasn't there when everyone spoke in the ashes.

He must have seen her confusion. "Lady Callon communicates through dreams," he told her before he pointed to the stone and led her toward it. "That's the remains of a heart tree…she said you could grow it.”

Faedi's fingertips tingled before another pull made her hunch over the stone. No—not stone. It was organic, but something else. She spotted rings over its surface just before her mind began to swim.

Thump.

“Faedi!”

Ragna and Lisea's shouts echoed and faded around her as Faedi stood in the darkness. The light was gone, but the sensation of life was stronger than ever, thumping into her like a heartbeat. With each pulse, silver trails spread outward from her, splintering off like roots reaching out into the unknown.

“When you open one, they'll all open again.”

She shook Tove's words from her mind. There was no heart tree in Dewgate, yet there she was. The sensation was the same. The pull of familiarity tugged at her, but it didn't speak to her as it had before.

Faedi touched the pendant around her neck and bit her lip, unsure if she should take the risk. Ilos might have known where they were going, but he didn't know when they would arrive. For all he knew, they were still on the mountain, but if she removed the necklace, he might find a way to discover they were already here.

Two and a half of them couldn't fight off a mass of his cultists—or whatever else he might have in store for them.

Thump.

Faedi watched as the silver trails scattered again, her thoughts drifting back to the map in the mountain castle. Each heart tree had been marked, but only one marked where the twins were. Then her mind wandered to when she had been named a Guardian by Elder Peni.

“Touch the tree.”

She had thought he was referencing the twin on their side of the forest, but what if… what if the base of the tree was buried underground? When Faethorin had sealed the portal, she had seen only one realm. There was a chance the twins were one heart tree.

Kneeling down again, Faedi ran her hand over the center of the stone. The silver light danced along its surface, and the thumps grew louder, gradually speeding up. They responded to her.

The pulse beneath her palm grew more assertive, and she flinched but didn't pull away. Instead, she pressed her hand flat against the surface, allowing the rhythm to seep into her.

Tove's words mingled with Elder Peni's command in her mind. The two phrases twisted together, like the twins' roots in the forest, while the pendant around her neck weighed her down. The comfort and safety it provided fell away, becoming a barrier. It had cut her off from Ilos, her bonded, and her brother. It had cut her off from the earth itself.

Thump.

The pulse beneath her feet grew more insistent, and the silver roots spread farther, reaching beyond the city. They wove through the corpses and rubble, extending farther still.

She unclasped the necklace.

The moment it left her skin, the air around her shifted. It wasn't an explosion but a ripple—a wave of energy that spread outward, shaking the walls and stirring the darkness around her. The silver threads flared brightly, briefly illuminating the chamber before dimming again.

The sensation hit her like a gale. Memories that weren't hers surged forward—roots twisting through the soil, towering trees rising above all else. Silver strands connected them through vast divides. And she walked through them.

They were memories, but not hers.

"Are you here to help me grow again, friend?"

Faedi looked down at her hand, staring at the apex of the roots, the mass of silver glowing beneath her skin. The tree was there, but it was broken—like her—damaged by Ilos' flames in The Great War. All those who fled to the forest, to the other twin for safety, had run because they had no choice.

She had healed herself before, after the cultists burned her with a taste of his power. Maybe she could do it again.

"Yes," she whispered.

The silver light beneath her hand pulsed, responding to her promise. Hesitant at first, flickering in and out, it seemed unsure whether to trust her. She pressed harder, her fingers sinking into the cool stone—the petrified stump—that hummed with memories of life and peace.

"Yes," she repeated, louder this time. "I'm here to help you grow again."

The roots shifted beneath her, trembling as the pulse quickened. The silver light spiraled outward, weaving under her. She closed her eyes, drew a deep breath, and let the ancient magic fill her lungs.

When the cultists burned her with their corrupted flames, she had pulled herself back from the brink. She took that pain, learned to live with it, and turned it into strength. Standing at the heart of the broken tree, she felt the same spark within her—a tiny ember waiting to catch.

She opened herself to it. "Please grow."

The light surged, and her breath caught as it flooded through her. It wasn't gentle. It was raw, wild, and untamed, coursing through her veins like a river breaking free of a dam. Her body ached as the energy poured into her, filling every corner of her being until she thought she might break.

But she didn't.

Instead, the ground beneath her shifted. The roots stretched and unfurled like a creature waking from a deep slumber. The silver glow brightened, illuminating the chamber in bursts of light that danced like glowbugs.

And then it began.

A small shoot broke through the cracked stone, glowing faintly in the darkness. It wasn't just any sapling—it shimmered with silver veins, its bark smooth and black as night. Leaves began to unfurl, not green, but a deep luminous indigo, edged in silver like frost on glass.

The tree grew fast, its trunk thickening, its branches reaching higher with every heartbeat. It was alive in a way that went beyond the physical. The air around it shimmered with an otherworldly energy.

It wasn't just growing—it was healing.

Eventides bloomed along its branches, their petals glowing like tiny stars. The blossoms were delicate but vibrant, their soft glow casting the ruined chamber in a serene, ethereal light. They weren't like the vines she had grown before. They were something… more.

An extension of herself—yet a being all its own.

Faedi stepped back when a light flashed in front of her. Her breath ragged, she stumbled back as the tree continued to grow. Its roots dug deep into the earth, sending energy ripples through the city. The beat echoed further, deeper beneath her.

"Faedi!"

Ragna's voice broke through the hum of power. Faedi turned just as Ragna knelt beside her, her face bathed in the soft light of the eventides. "Your arm… your… you." Ragna stumbled over her words, motioning to her. "What did you do?"

"What?" Faedi followed her gaze and looked down. Eventides were growing over her arm, but something resembling bark covered any bare space beneath them. "Oh… that's… new."

"New?" Lisea moved to stand in front of her, arms crossed over her chest. "Your calm is… spooky."

Faedi couldn't hold back the laugh that bubbled from her chest. "This is the least spooky thing that has happened to me." She tested her weight against the newly vined arm and pushed herself to stand. "I didn't know there was a heart here."

"It's still growing." Ragna began to ask while standing beside her. "Is it supposed to be shimmering like that? Or…"

Faedi leaned to look around Lisea, and her breath caught in her throat. It wasn't the shimmer of a glamour or the pollen from the eventides—it rippled deep in the tree's center. "Is that a portal?"

"I think it is." Ravyn put his hand on Faedi's shoulder. "Or at least the start of one."

Ytna's tits.

77
Return of the Tides

Lonan

Sual'viren, 2696

The first time Lonan saw Dewgate, he thought it was the most significant place in the world. Its walls stretched endlessly to either side, towering above the road and casting long shadows over the plains. The gates themselves were a marvel, carved with intricate designs that glimmered faintly in the sunlight—wards, he realized later, meant to protect the city from the very creatures his kind were rumored to be.

He shifted uncomfortably in his armor and examined his exposed skin for his glamour. To anyone else, he looked like a pale elf with black hair and violet eyes—almost elegant, in a way that made him itch. The glamour was flawless, as it needed to be, but he didn't like it. It wasn't him.

Beside him, Faedi walked with her usual shyness, her Mire bow strapped across her back and her lengthy, black hair pulled into a braid that swayed with each step. Her fresh Watch marks on the sides of her partially shaved head, which she defiantly refused to cover with her glamour, lifted his spirits slightly. However, the tension in her shoulders grounded him. She'd been as skeptical about the trip as he was, though she'd hidden it better.

"It's strange, isn't it?" she asked quietly, her voice barely audible over the murmur of the soldiers around them.

"What is?" he asked, glancing her way.

"They call to the Mire only when they need help—but put up wards to keep Umbrals away."

She wasn't wrong. The Lord of Dewgate, Blavier, had summoned them—calling on an oath ages older than the city's wall. The town was threatened, and its forces were spread too thin to defend it. So, they'd turned to the Mire. To the

Umbrals—and his people were oath-bound to protect it.

The irony wasn't lost on him. For centuries, his people had been treated as little more than fiends—dangerous, untrustworthy, best kept hidden away. Yet, when the city's survival was on the line, they'd reached out, desperate enough to call on the people they'd once spurned. He knew as well as anyone else that they would cast them away as soon as the battle was won.

"My father says it's an opportunity," he said, though the words tasted bitter. "A chance to show them we're more than what they think."

Faedi snorted softly. "Tagil is an optimist. If we save the city, you and I know they'll find another reason to hate us…just like the forest-folk."

He didn't argue. She was right.

The gates creaked open as they approached, revealing a city in chaos. Smoke curled up from several parts of the city, and the streets were filled with people— some injured, others preparing defenses. Soldiers moved in hurried groups, their armor clanking as they shouted orders and hauled supplies. It was overwhelming. The noise, the sheer number of people, and a pang of homesickness for the quiet shadows of the Mire hit him.

As they entered the city, a man in ornate armor approached them, flanked by two guards. He was Lord Blavier. He was older than expected, his face lined with worry and weariness, but his eyes were sharp as they swept over them.

"You must be the reinforcements," he said, his tone clipped but not unkind. His gaze lingered on Lonan momentarily, as if trying to place something, before he spoke again. "You have my gratitude. Dewgate will not forget this."

Lonan inclined his head but said nothing and kept his expression neutral.

The rest of the day was a blur of orders and preparation. Unsurprisingly, they were assigned to hold the line against any advancing forces outside the wall. The soldiers around them were polite but distant, their eyes wary when they thought they weren't looking.

That night, as the enemy forces approached, Lonan found himself wishing he could fight without his glamour—that he could be the thing people feared. The glamour protected him, but it was also a cage—locking away the genuine parts of him.

The first attack came just before dawn. The enemy surged forward in waves, their shouts echoing across the battlefield as they clashed against their defenses. Arrows flew, swords clashed, and the air was thick with blood and smoke.

He fought alongside Faedi, his knives a blur as he moved through the chaos. The glamour held, even as sweat poured down his back and his muscles burned from the effort, but it wasn't enough to keep the whispers at bay when the fight was done and they rested away from the fire.

"He's too fast," one soldier muttered as Lonan sat beside Faedi.

"Did you see his eyes?" another whispered. "They don't look right."

He wanted to vanish in the shadows and never look at the city again.

"Don't take it personally," Faedi said later as they patrolled the tree line. "They don't know you like I do."

He grinned at her. "Not everyone is lucky enough to be bonded to us."

"Like any city-folk could ever deserve to be bonded to you," she scoffed before she laughed. "No…that pleasure's all mine, Ni'Minn."

His heart pounded in his chest. That was it—that was the moment he fell in love with her.

The journey to Dewgate had been quieter than Lonan had expected, which only sharpened the edges of his nerves. Suspiciously quiet, to the point that every rustle of the wind through the grass had him scanning the horizon, searching for shadows that weren't his own. No cultists, no creatures, no traps. Just the steady rhythm of their footsteps and the occasional murmur of conversation from the mass that followed them. It felt wrong.

Sylrie walked ahead of him, his stride longer than even Sophir's, though Lonan could see the tension on his shoulders. Sophir stayed by his side, his wings tucked tightly to his back, his gaze sweeping over the landscape with the practiced caution of someone who'd seen one ambush too many. Danik brought up the rear with Bjorn, who had taken it upon himself to watch for anyone who might try to flank them. Myst stayed close behind, with Aladia and Emmaline in tow.

If it hadn't been for the small Itmis, Lonan doubted he would have smiled during the trip. The air was heavy, not with the oppressive weight of death that clung to the mountains, but with something… different. It was hard to name, but it prickled at the edges of his senses, setting him on edge.

"There's so many trees over there," Emmaline whispered in awe as they walked.

Lonan glanced back at her and grinned. "There's even more the further you go—in the forest and the Mire. Once this is over, we'll take you there… if you want. Some people think it's kind of scary."

"I want to!" Emmaline nodded eagerly before she announced, "I'm brave."

"I don't doubt that." He winked at her. "You're the bravest of us all."

Emmaline beamed at him, her little chest puffing up with pride at the compliment. She skipped a step closer, her small fingers curling around the edge of his sleeve as if she needed reassurance that he was still there.

"Are there big trees? The kind that touch the sky?" She asked, her voice full of wonder.

Lonan chuckled. "Some are so tall that if you climb them, you might just reach the stars."

Her eyes widened, glowing with excitement. "Really?"

"Really," he promised, nudging her playfully. "But you'd have to be careful. The trees in the Mire and Sauvern don't like just anyone climbing them. You have to ask nicely."

She gasped, gripping his sleeve tighter. "They talk?"

"In their own way," he said with a teasing smile. "Like how the wind whispers through the branches or the way the leaves rustle. You just have to listen closely."

Emmaline scrunched up her nose in thought before she whispered, "Do you think they'd like me?"

He pretended to consider it, tapping his chin dramatically. "Hmm… well, you are very brave. And kind. And you have the heart of an explorer. I think they'd like you a lot."

She grinned, practically vibrating with excitement, and squeezed his arm before letting go to spin in a circle. "Then I'll ask them to be my friends! I'll tell them stories, and maybe they'll tell me some too!"

Myst chuckled softly from behind them, while Sophir cast an amused glance in their direction. Lonan reached out to ruffle Emmaline's hair, laughing when she swatted his hand away with a playful glare.

"Alright, alright," he relented. "No messing up the hair of our bravest adventurer."

She nodded firmly. "Good. Because I want to look pretty when I meet my new tree friends."

"Of course," he agreed solemnly. "It's very important for tree diplomacy."

"And for mice," Sophir mused with a grin.

Emmaline giggled, the sound light and free as it cut through the tense air like the first rays of morning light. And for the first time in a while, Lonan allowed himself to breathe a little easier.

The closer they got to Dewgate, the more the land began to change. The scars of the plague were still visible—fields once fertile were barren patches of cracked earth, and the ruins of the farmers' villages stood as silent testaments to what had been lost. Yet, occasionally, life was fighting its way back.

Grass grew in patches under the thin blanket of snow, defiant tufts of green pushing up through the cold. Saplings dotted the horizon, their leaves a vibrant green that seemed almost too bright, too full of life. Birds flitted through the air, their songs breaking the quiet like hesitant whispers.

Then he saw it.

Beyond the crumbling wall of Dewgate, rising high into the sky, was a great tree. Its branches spread wide, their tips aglow with a silver light that pulsed faintly like a heartbeat. Eventides. The blossoms covered the tree, their pale glow unmistakable even at their distance.

He stopped in his tracks, the sight stealing the breath from his lungs.

"What in Mumir's breath?" Sophir muttered, coming to a halt beside him.

Sylrie turned, his gaze following theirs. His eyebrows raised, and his expression softened into something unreadable. "A heart tree?" He shook his head. "That's not…"

"It isn't possible," Bjorn said as he and Danik jogged to meet them. "What about the plague?"

"Eventides cleanse the earth," Lonan said, his voice unsteady. "Faedi used them before."

Danik crossed his arms, an unfamiliar hum coming from his chest. "New life doesn't grow this fast, even with magic. This…this is unnatural in every sense of the word."

Unnatural indeed.

"Not for the forest," Zarae said as she skipped to them, her battle hammer held behind her like a toy rather than a weapon. "Faedi did it."

"Why hasn't she said anything?" Lonan glanced at her as he stepped forward, unable to tear his eyes from the tree. The closer they got, the more he could feel it—a pull, a thrum of energy that resonated in his chest.

"Limited soul speech until we're all together and accounted for, remember?" Zarae smiled up at him. "Just in case everyone in our family isn't welcome at the table, y'know?"

Right, that.

He'd been so focused on the absence of cultists that he'd forgotten Zarae's warning to prevent Ilos from knowing too much. He'd complained about it at first, but only to Sophir because he was the only one he could talk to, and then Sophir had talked sense into him. Or kissed it.

He shook his head to dismiss the thought and kept walking while focusing on the tree. The energy it emitted wasn't hostile, but it wasn't comforting. It was old and ancient in a familiar and foreign way.

The city walls loomed before them, their stone weathered and cracked, barely standing. They likely would have fallen without the dense vines and roots that held them in place. Beyond them, the forest had reclaimed what the plague had tried to destroy. Plants of varied types climbed over the ruins, flowers bloomed in the crevices, and the air was thick with the scent of growth and renewal.

Yet, there was no one to greet them.

No soldiers. No citizens. No cultists.

Nothing but the whisper of the wind through the trees and the steady thrum of the great tree's presence.

"It's too quiet," Lonan said, his voice barely above a whisper.

Sophir nodded beside him, his jaw tight. "I don't like it."

Despite Zarae's caution, he wanted to reach out to Faedi. He wouldn't feel better until he knew she was safe, but she had the pendant to keep Ilos out of her head. If he reached out and she didn't respond, his anxiety would eat at him even if he had a logical explanation for her silence.

Sylrie scoffed and walked ahead of them. "Paranoid."

Excuse me?

Lonan stared at his back, temporarily frozen as he walked further away. It was as if he didn't have a care in the world that the sudden appearance of a tree wasn't a reason to pause and think. How would he know if it was safe or not? He hadn't been in Yestrana for decades.

"Faedi's going to kick your ass if you get hurt before she's officially reunited with you," Lonan called after him before he followed.

He glanced back at Lonan and rolled his eyes. "Who's the one that grows eventides faster than weeds?"

Good point.

"Has Faedi ever grown a tree of them before?" Sophir asked beside Lonan as they caught up with Sylrie. "I thought they only grew in vines."

Lonan paused to think while he walked. He hadn't seen her make a tree of eventides before, but there was the mishap with the blackberries one year. "No, but she has done things with other plants that weren't exactly natural." He grinned when Sylrie glanced back at him. "She might've covered the house in blackberries and accidentally made everything taste like them for an entire season."

"Fucking blackberries." Sylrie chuckled. "I thought she'd get sick of them after a while."

"Remind me to tell you about the jam explosion," Lonan said before the air shifted, and they all stood still just outside the gate. "You feel that?"

"Yeah." Sophir and Sylrie said in unison.

The air was lighter, far more fragrant and floral than even a tree of eventides would create, and the silvery specks in the air mixed with darker glimmers. There was other magic at work inside the walls.

"Are you waiting for an invitation?" A deep voice called from behind the wall, and they all looked to the gate.

Torix rounded the stone wall, an axe strapped across his back, and cracked a smile when Sylrie dashed toward him. Lonan looked away, or rather, he started searching for Faedi while the father and son had their moment.

Then, from behind him, Faedi stepped out with Ravyn beside her, and Lonan's heart stopped.

She was beautiful. Her blue fur glittered in the light and was streaked with white, just like eventides. Whatever burns she might have suffered from Fenkas were gone, and the vines on her arm were proudly displayed rather than covered.

At first, her smile was soft and timid, and without thinking, Lonan appeared in front of her and captured her mouth with his.

Her hands curled into the front of his cloak, gripping it as though he might disappear if she let go. She trembled against him, and he held her tighter to keep her secure. His heart pounded as he deepened the kiss, taking her in until they inevitably had to break apart for air.

He didn't let her get far, though, and smiled when she rested her forehead against his. "You're here."

"You knew we would be." He grinned before he kissed the tip of her nose. Then, he glanced at Sophir and chuckled when he noted how his hands were clenched at his sides. He wanted to embrace her as much as Lonan did.

Don't be a greedy bastard.

Lonan sighed and stepped back, allowing Sophir to move closer and hold her while he glanced around the crowd. Torix hadn't let Sylrie go yet, and Lonan couldn't help but sigh in relief. At least Faedi hadn't lost all of them in the attacks. He knew she would hurt and mourn for Haldin, but she had her father and brother still.

"Long time no see." Someone spoke from nearby, and Lonan turned to follow it.

He knew that voice.

Ravyn moved through the crowd, his smile a sight that made Lonan's heart stop. He didn't hesitate to wrap his arms around him, once he was close enough, and sighed in relief when Ravyn mimicked the gesture. "Ancients, I missed you."

"Hasn't been that long," Ravyn joked lightly, but his grip around Lonan tightened. He would have smiled, would have joked back, but he couldn't when he noticed how his hands trembled. "I missed you too," he whispered. "Truly."

Lonan didn't step back until Ravyn regained his composure and allowed himself to smile when Ravyn sighed with his own. He held his gaze, only for a little longer, until he caught a flash of red rush by him. Emmaline.

She ran straight for Faedi, and Lonan's smile grew when she had to peel herself away from Sylrie to catch the child who ran at her with outstretched arms. "Don't disappear again!" she demanded.

Faedi chuckled, holding the child close. "I won't," she promised. "No more avalanches."

A collective warmth settled over the group, despite the chill in the air, and Lonan savored it. After everything that had happened, such ease was precious, and he hoped it would last.

But he knew it wouldn't.

78

Echoes in the Void

Sophir

The streets of Dewgate were alive, though not as Sophir remembered them. The last time he had walked these roads, the city had been teetering on the edge of collapse—cultists in the alleys, illness spreading like wildfire. But now, as he walked, there was a quiet sense of renewal in the air. It thrummed around him, soft and persistent, like the promise of a song not yet sung.

He noticed Danik and Bjorn were no longer with them. He hadn't heard them leave, but he hadn't exactly been paying close attention. Bjorn was probably with Ragna or searching for her. Danik might've gone to the port—if more Helgi were coming, they'd likely arrive by sea.

Lonan walked beside Faedi on the opposite side, his gaze twitching with every step. "We need to contact my parents," he whispered. "They need to know it's safe here again."

Sophir's mind drifted back to the meeting in the ashes. He frowned. Other than Lonan and Myst, there had been no Umbrals. He came to a halt. "Myst's bonded wasn't there… was he?"

Lonan paused a few steps ahead, then turned, his unease shifting quickly into concern. "I haven't seen Myst since we were at the gate," he admitted, scanning the area. "Did you see them?"

Faedi shook her head. "I didn't see Myst at the gate." Her brow creased before she knelt beside Emmaline, smiling gently. "My friends made a safe place where everyone can gather while we work on fixing the rest of the city. I want you to go there with Aladia, alright?"

Emmaline pouted, glancing between them. "Are the friendly trees there?"

Faedi chuckled and pointed to the large tree of eventides. "That one is. And

476

my falcon friend is there too. Remember Dusan?" When Emmaline nodded, a soft smile formed on her lips. "He'll keep you safe. So will Aladia, right?"

Sophir followed Faedi's gaze to the dusk elf woman and relaxed when she nodded. Emmaline didn't protest further. She hugged each of them in turn before following Aladia toward the tree. Once she was gone, Sophir turned back to the matter that had them all on edge.

"Do we look for Myst?"

"I can soul-speak again—so no worries about anything bad happening," Faedi assured them with a smile. "I'll check the castle and temple. Meet back at the tree at sundown if we don't find anything."

Lonan stepped closer to her. "You're not going to run off and get hurt again, are you?"

She grinned and shook her head. "No, but Myst isn't here to make that promise—so let's find them."

Without waiting for a response, she dashed down the street.

Searching for Myst turned out to be far more frustrating than Sophir had expected. Dewgate was no small city, and much of it had become a chaotic maze of new growth and half-rebuilt districts. He and Lonan chose not to split up—covering more ground wasn't worth leaving Lonan alone while he was this on edge.

Hours passed as they navigated the city, asking after Myst with every person they met. No one had seen them.

"I'm starting to think they're not here," Sophir muttered, leaning against a broken column near the central square. The low sun caught the delicate vines weaving through the stone, even as the light faded. "If they were, someone would've noticed."

Lonan huffed, pacing in a tight circle, hands behind his head while shadows flickered at his feet. "They wouldn't leave without saying something," he insisted. "That's not them."

Sophir raised an eyebrow and pushed off the column. "Then where would they go in a city that used to ban your kind?"

Lonan's mouth twitched with frustration. "I don't know… but I know they're here. I can feel it."

Sophir tilted his head, a faint smirk curving his lips. "You feel it how?"

"I don't need to explain how my magic works to you."

"That's because you don't even know how it works."

Lonan narrowed his eyes, but a reluctant smile tugged at his mouth. "Touché." His mismatched gaze scanned the square again. "But something's off. Myst is stealthy—more than me. They could hide, but…" He trailed off, unsettled.

Sophir didn't know Myst well—not like Lonan or even Faedi and Sylrie. But seeing Lonan this unsteady was unsettling. He sighed and glanced toward the edge of the square, where a sewer grate sat ajar.

"Lonan." He nodded toward the opening. "Think Myst went underground?"

Lonan followed his gaze, expression darkening. "If they thought something important was down there? Absolutely."

Sophir sent a quick message to Faedi. *"Faedi, there are tunnels underground. We're checking there."*

"Keep me posted."

The tunnels beneath Dewgate were damp and deathly still, save for the occasional drip of water echoing somewhere ahead. The air was cool, earthy, tinged with filth—and something metallic that set Sophir's nerves on edge. They moved cautiously, steps quiet on the ancient stone.

"You'd think I would've memorized maps of this," Sophir muttered, lifting his torch. The flickering flame cast uneven shadows across the tunnel walls. "You think something down here could be important?"

"Sewers might connect to something," Lonan murmured. "The tree is big—its roots might have disturbed something down here."

Cracks in the walls grew more pronounced as they pressed on. "The dirt smells fresh now," Sophir observed.

Lonan didn't answer, distracted by the walls. He stopped abruptly, brushing his fingers over a barely visible carving—runic symbols, ancient and nearly worn away.

"What is it?" Sophir asked, stepping close.

"Old magic," Lonan whispered. "Same kind as the mountain. Same as the Mire."

Sophir frowned. The runes *were* familiar, though unreadable. There was a faint hum in the air—alive and buzzing beneath his skin.

A sudden gust of wind rushed through the tunnel. Sophir turned instinctively toward the dark. Then came the whisper—soft but urgent. Neither he nor Lonan spoke. They ran.

The passages narrowed, the air growing colder, until they emerged into a vast chamber. Sophir stopped dead.

The ceiling arched high above, every inch of the walls and floor covered in glowing runes—blue and silver light pulsing like breath. At the center stood Zarae.

She looked small beneath the towering ceiling, her hand drifting over the runes. When she turned, her expression was unreadable.

"Sophir," she said gently. "Lonan. I didn't expect to see you down here."

"Neither did we," Sophir said, raising his torch. "What is this place?"

"Have you seen Myst down here?" Lonan cut in. "Where is *here* anyway?"

Zarae's lips curved slightly as she turned back to the wall. "Myst hasn't been here—they went to the Mire, for reinforcements, I suppose." She explained. "This is beneath the temple. Another antechamber—like the one in the mountain. It's quiet here."

"Quiet?" Lonan echoed, stepping forward.

She looked back, her voice softer now. "Hearing everyone... it hurts sometimes. But not here—unless someone soul-speaks near me." She leaned against

the wall, arms crossing over her chest—not defiant, but protective. She was trying to shrink herself. "Ragna said it was dead here, but I think the tree brought
the magic back."

Lonan's shadows curled faintly around his feet. He stared at the runes.
"These symbols," he said. "They're the language of the Ancients, aren't they?"

Zarae nodded. "The oldest language. This was the convergence point before
the cataclysm."

"Convergence for what?" Sophir asked, a tight unease forming in his chest.
"What kind?"

She didn't answer at first. Then, kneeling, she brushed her fingers over a
spiral of runes. "Between mortal and celestial—where life began. And where Ilos
betrayed them."

She pointed to a nearby wall. Sophir followed her gaze to a patch of runes—
dim, broken. A hole the size of his head was smashed into the stone.

"What is this?" He asked, reaching out to touch the edge.

The moment his fingers grazed the stone, light exploded behind his eyes.

Pain slammed into him like a wave, blinding and scorching. His knees buckled, and he staggered back, clutching his head as something ancient and relentless clawed through his mind. Images and voices overwhelmed him—dozens
layered and crashing into each other.

"Mine."

"Sunamun!"

"Mother!"

"Murderer."

"Get away!"

He gasped, barely able to stay upright. Lonan's hands clamped down on his
shoulders, shadows curling around him like armor. Lonan's voice cut through the
din, sharp and commanding.

"Sophir! Breathe. Focus on me!"

Sophir latched onto his words like a lifeline, forcing himself to pull back
from the pain. The light dimmed slightly, the voices ebbing just enough for him
to hear the room again. Zarae's voice was sharp, laced with panic.

"Get him away from it! Now!"

Lonan's grip tightened, and he tried to drag Sophir back, his strength surprising given his lean frame—but not fast enough. The light surged again, and
Sophir's body jerked as his muscles spasmed.

Then, it was all gone without warning—followed by a scream nearly deafening him. He landed back on the floor, chest heaving as he drew in a ragged
breath. Lonan was over Zarae, who clutched her head, blood dripping onto the
stone.

"What…what was that?" Sophir managed to choke out.

"I don't want to find out," Lonan replied grimly.

Zarae's whisper made Sophir's blood go cold. "You heard her die," she said
softly. "Sunamun—the Ancient Light."

79

In the Moonlight

Faedi

The eventide tree stood tall and serene, its silvery leaves whispering in the breeze. Dusan perched among the branches, his wide eyes scanning the city with unwavering focus. He hadn't moved from that spot since the tree had grown.

He'd probably make a nest up there at some point.

Faedi rushed over to Torix and Sylrie, who stood beneath the tree, and took a moment to catch her breath. They turned to face her, their eyebrows raised, eyes wide—they knew something was wrong before she even spoke.

"Have you seen Myst?" she asked quickly, her voice edged with urgency. "They weren't at the gate."

Sylrie shook his head before glancing at Torix. "I haven't. Have you?"

"No—are you sure they weren't at the gate?"

Faedi shook her head, brushing a stray lock of hair from her face. "Can you help look? Sophir and Lonan are searching the tunnels."

Sylrie nodded and took off with a shout over his shoulder. "I'll check the docks and ask the Helgi to help search."

Faedi turned to Torix, hugging her arms to herself. "I'm going to check the castle and temple."

Torix surveyed the area with a low growl. "I'll check the barracks and call our hunts. They can search the perimeter."

"Thank you." She managed a small smile before sprinting toward the castle.

The castle and temple were empty. The destruction left in the wake of

480

Ilos' followers marred their once-grand facades. After that, she ran through the streets, hoping to catch Myst's scent. But the charred remains of buildings and the lingering stench of plagued corpses made it nearly impossible to track anything.

She didn't stop running until she reached what remained of Ravyn's stables. It was the only place she had ever felt safe in Dewgate. Even in the temple, she had always been anxious—always aware of eyes on her, of someone noticing Lonan's glamour. But Ravyn had opened his home to them and had never once made them feel unwelcome.

His mounts were gone, and she hoped he had gotten them out safely. The fenced corrals were broken, some pieces burnt to ash, the dark wood stained black from fire. But the structure itself seemed stable enough.

Maybe they're here because it's quiet.

Inside, the air was cooler, the light dimmer, but the scent of smoke lingered. Some of the furniture remained, but there wasn't even a mouse inside. The soot on the floor was undisturbed—Ravyn hadn't been home in some time.

"They're not in the castle, temple, or Ravyn's house."

"We'll meet you there."

The light in Ravyn's home shifted as moonlight filtered through the fractured windows, casting strange patterns on the wooden floor. Faedi sat near the hearth, knees drawn to her chest. How many nights had she sat there while Ravyn and Lonan sprawled on the floor, playing knife games without a care in the world?

Her fingers traced the faint grooves in the wood, worn smooth by time, as her thoughts drifted between past and present. The whispers of the eventide tree were distant now, replaced by the soft breeze that slipped through the broken glass.

Footsteps echoed outside. Faedi glanced up, her pulse quickening when the door creaked open and two familiar figures stepped inside. Sophir and Lonan. Their expressions unreadable until they moved into the moonlight.

Sophir was the first to smile, slow and warm, something in it tightening the ache in her chest. Lonan lingered a step behind, his gaze shadowed but full of quiet understanding. His presence was like a whisper against her senses—familiar, steady, safe.

"Good news," Sophir said, his voice low as he stepped closer. "Someone saw Myst go into the Sauvern."

Lonan nodded beside him. "Do you want to rest here or at the barracks?"

Relief washed over her, and she leaned her head against the wall as she sent a message to Syl. *"Myst went into the forest."*

Sophir shook his head with a small, amused sigh. "We need to work on their communication skills. Are you alright?"

"I'm with you two." Her lips curled faintly. "I'll be alright."

Lonan's shadows flickered at the edges of his form, his gaze searching hers. "We wandered the tunnels under the city," he murmured. "There's a lot of magic down there."

Faedi nodded. "Ragna mentioned runes. Did something happen?"

Sophir lowered himself beside her, his warmth grounding her against the cool wood beneath them. Lonan hesitated before kneeling at her other side, close enough that his presence surrounded her.

"I heard Ilos kill an Ancient," Lonan said, his voice soft. "Felt some of her pain." He reached out, brushing his fingers through Faedi's hair in an absent-minded gesture. "It hurt Zarae too, but we took her to Ighir."

So he wasn't lying…I wasn't either.

"Is she alright?" Heat spread over Faedi's face when he curled a strand of her hair around his finger and nodded.

"You could have said that before making me worry."

Sophir's hand found hers, fingers twining together. "Sorry," he murmured, his voice thick with something deeper. "You have no idea how much I've missed you."

Faedi's throat tightened. "I missed you too," she admitted, barely above a whisper. It took everything in her not to cry. "Both of you."

Lonan's shadows brushed against her skin like a cool breeze, his expression unguarded. "I thought I lost you." His voice was raw, heavy with emotions he rarely let surface. "Don't scare me like that again."

Faedi turned to face him, her heart aching at the vulnerability in his eyes. "Call it payback." She tried to smile, but a single tear betrayed her. "For getting shot."

His lips parted as if to argue, but instead, his hand rose to cup her cheek. His touch was reverent, and she leaned into him, closing her eyes. The weight of everything else faded in that moment.

Sophir's thumb brushed over the back of her hand, his presence steady, grounding. "How about no more payback?" He asked softly. "And no more getting separated."

The words settled over her, and she nodded against Lonan's palm. He leaned in first, his lips brushing against hers with aching gentleness. Faedi's breath hitched, and she clutched his shirt, pulling him closer. His shadows curled around them, their coolness a contrast to the warmth of his skin, sending a shiver down her spine.

When they parted, Sophir was there, his hand tilting her chin toward him. His kiss was different—firm, certain, a tether to something solid and unyielding. Faedi melted into him, her free hand finding his shoulder, her pulse a steady drum against her ribs.

When she finally pulled back, breathless and flushed, they looked at her, then at each other. A quiet understanding passed between them, a shared longing that needed no words.

Ancients, she had missed them.

Sophir exhaled, studying her before he glanced around the home. "Why did you come here?"

"This is the only place in the city where I feel safe," she admitted, a little sheepishly. "Ravyn's a good friend. I figured he wouldn't mind the visit."

Lonan leaned against the wall with a soft sigh, tucking his hands behind his head. "On the rare occasions we stayed here, Ravyn always offered his home—he didn't want us in an inn."

Sophir nodded with a quiet rumble. "Because of Blavier's laws."

"Technically." Lonan stretched his legs out, and Faedi instinctively leaned against him. "I wasn't supposed to be here anyway, so…are you going to arrest me?"

Faedi's scoff turned into a laugh when Sophir's gaze darkened slightly as he stared at Lonan. "You'd both enjoy that."

Sophir smirked, slow and knowing. "And you'd enjoy watching."

Lonan chuckled, wrapping his arm around Faedi's shoulders and pulling her closer. "I think we're bonded to someone with skewed morals."

Faedi felt the warmth of their bodies beside her, the familiar press of Sophir's tail flicking against her leg. Her heart pounded—not just from attraction but from the sheer relief of being with them again, of knowing they were safe, together.

She looked between them, her lips parting to say something, but words felt too small for the emotions tangled between them. Instead, she reached out, fingers tracing over Sophir's wrist, before shifting to look up at Lonan.

The silence between them was heavy with promise.

No more getting separated.

No more losing each other.

80

Defenses and Dancing

Faedi

The faintest edge of dawn painted the ceilings and walls of Ravyn's home in pale hues of blue and gold. Faedi stirred on the floor, the cool air brushing against her skin and sending a gentle shiver through her. Sophir's arm was draped over her waist, and Lonan's leg was hooked over hers on the other side. His soft breaths tickled her neck, but she didn't move.

The world was muted in that quiet, predawn moment—a pause before the city woke. But the faint echo of footsteps broke the serenity. She tensed instinctively, her ears catching the sound of people trading guard postings. Then came Dusan, perched outside the nearest window.

"There's movement in the forest."

Ancients, let that be good news and not bad.

"Lonan," she whispered, shifting slightly. "Sophir. We need to get up."

Lonan groaned, burying his face into the crook of her neck. "Too early."

She smiled, running a hand over his arm to nudge him. "We can't let everyone do the work for us. We need to help prepare."

Beside her, Sophir stirred. "She's right," he mumbled, his voice low and rough from sleep. "We don't need to be caught unprepared."

Lonan huffed a laugh but finally released her, sitting up and raking a hand through his tousled hair. His eye caught the faint glow of the runes as they began to face the rising sun. "We'd only continue the age-old tradition of rumors about Umbrals being self-serving and lazy," he said before he stretched and yawned. "But I doubt that would do anything for morale."

Once they were awake and ready, they made their way out onto the street. Dusan perched on Faedi's shoulder while they walked, preening her hair. It felt like ages since he had done that.

The air was cool and damp with morning dew; she could taste it before they crossed the threshold. A light fog rested over the streets while workers and guards bustled about, their voices a low murmur of plans and instructions.

However, the conversation's hum changed as they walked toward the tree. It was louder and tinged with urgency. A commotion rippled through the crowd gathered near the newly repaired fountain, and she caught pieces as they approached.

"Reinforcements—this morning."

"Guardians—Wardens in the forest."

Her heart quickened, and she exchanged a glance with Lonan and Sophir. They moved closer to the gathering; curiosity outweighed the weariness that clung to her limbs.

The crowd parted slightly as they approached, revealing Sylrie and Ragna. Neither one of them appeared ready to greet the day. They looked as exhausted as Faedi felt. While she knew nothing about what her brother might have done, she knew when she met Ragna's eyes.

She and Bjorn must have had a good reunion.

Ragna's gaze surveyed her before she smirked and bowed before approaching them. "Scouts spotted Guardians and Wardens coming this way."

Faedi's heart beat in her throat, and she straightened. "How many?" Her hope fell when Ragna shook her head. "That few?"

"Less than a dozen." She motioned for Faedi to follow her, and she did without hesitation. "I think some remained behind—cultists are all over the forest right now trying to spread the plague. The Umbrals know how to combat it, so I assume it's slow-moving, but… war doesn't care about life."

They followed Ragna through the thinning crowd, her pace steady but brisk. Faedi wanted to ask where Bjorn was. She didn't think she'd see Ragna without him nearby, but Sylrie caught her attention when he stepped behind her and gently grabbed her arm.

"I heard a hunt," he said softly, his tone a mix of hope and worry. She nodded and squeezed his hand.

They couldn't take a hunt for good news or a threat until it arrived.

As they neared the gate, the sounds of the city quieted, giving way to the low rustle of the forest beyond. Guards flanked the thick stone gates; their armor was still streaked with ashes and grime from cleanup efforts. They stood at attention, their hands resting on their weapons, but their gazes were fixed on the tree line in the distance.

The gates opened with a creak, revealing the misty path beyond. In the hazy light of dawn, movement stirred within the fog. A faint glimmer—a shimmer of silver and green—caught Faedi's eye. Then they appeared.

The Guardians moved silently, their steps as fluid as the wind rustling through the trees. Their forms seemed to merge with the forest, their armor a blend of organic and ethereal elements. The Wardens followed closely, their heavier footsteps marked by a soft clank of metal.

She couldn't help but draw in a sharp breath as the first Guardian stepped forward. His dark fur, red eyes, and black hair seemed to glow in the fog. Elder Peni. She raced towards him without a second thought, Lonan at her heels, and he caught her when she tackled him in an embrace.

"That surprised to see me?" He gasped but didn't let her go. "I thought you were going to stay in Rowdon."

"The cultists… we came back." She hugged him tighter and grinned over his shoulder at Lonan before her smile fell. "They're going to come for us."

Peni pulled back slightly, his piercing red eyes scanning hers with concern. "Then we'll fight them," he said firmly. "We're sworn to defend this city and the forest, and posh desert-folk won't change that."

Lonan clapped Peni on the shoulder, his smile softening the edges of his features. "You look good for someone fighting cultists and a plague," Lonan teased lightly, though his tone revealed his relief. "How is the Sauvern?"

Peni chuckled and shrugged. "And you look well for someone who can't seem to stay out of trouble," he shot back, but his expression turned serious as his gaze shifted to the crowd. "Ravyn sent word to send who we could. Everyone else is protecting the border."

"Glad to see you came, my friend." Ravyn approached through the crowd and smiled at Peni. "The plague is taken care of here, but the city needs new defenses."

"Yes." Peni stepped back from Faedi and scratched the fur on his chin. "The stronghold of eclipse-born does seem in need of repair."

Ragna stepped forward, her eyes on the others. "Were you followed?"

He shook his head. "No. We set traps behind us—even if they try to take the same path as us, they'll be delayed if they survive."

"Do I even want to know what you came up with?" Faedi narrowed her eyes at him but smiled when he winked at her.

"I've always liked this one," Dusan quipped, his eyes sparkling as he settled on Peni's large head. The man didn't budge, and Faedi sighed with a shake of her head.

She'd find out eventually.

The sun hung low in the sky, casting a warm, golden light across the city as the day's reinforcements and eclipse-born trickled in. By midday, the atmosphere shifted from quiet urgency to something more spirited. The tree—their heart— had become the central gathering point, its sprawling canopy offering shade and, some even claimed, promising hope.

Faedi stood beneath its boughs, watching as people gathered: those who traveled down the mountain, Guardians, Wardens, Helgi, and a small mix of others, their expressions ranging from anxious to joyful. The crowd grew steadily throughout the day, and with it, she realized a sense of familiarity—one of community.

At some point, someone decided they needed to celebrate. What spurred that urge, she didn't know. She did know that by late afternoon, tables had been set up near the tree, laden with food and drink from what supplies they had or grew. Music began to play—a lively, lifting tune from a group of Helgi who had brought their instruments—and people started to laugh and talk more freely.

She wandered through the gathering, weaving between groups of people. Sophir and Lonan stood near the crowd's edge, speaking with Ravyn. She caught snippets of their conversation—strategies, assignments, contingencies—but their tones were lighter than before. Sophir leaned casually against a stone bench beside Ravyn, his expression relaxed for once, while Lonan gestured animatedly, a grin tugging at his lips.

It was good to see them so at ease, even if only for a moment.

"Faedi!" A voice called, breaking her from her thoughts. She turned to see Sylrie waving her over. He stood near one of the long tables, his arm draped around Danik's shoulders. The latter looked slightly exasperated, but his smile was genuine. Ragna was there too, along with Bjorn, both halfway through a tankard of ale each.

She made her way over, her brother pulling her into a one-armed hug as she reached them. "About time," he said, grinning. "You've been absent all day."

"I was checking defenses," she replied, nudging him. "Someone has to be the responsible one."

Bjorn raised his tankard in a mock salute. "May the Ancients keep us."

Ragna rolled her eyes, but her smirk revealed her amusement. "May the Tides keep us." She winked at Faedi and smiled when Bjorn refilled her drink. "Might as well make the most of what time we have left."

As the sun dipped lower, the gathering grew livelier. Laughter echoed through the air, and even the most reserved began to mingle. Faedi included. It was a strange sight—ethereal warriors standing shoulder to shoulder with hardened soldiers, sharing stories and drinks as if they'd known each other for years.

She found herself at the tree's base, gazing up at its glowing branches. The eventide blossoms swayed gently in the breeze, their light casting a soft, soothing glow over the crowd. Children played around the base of it, Emmaline among them, and she couldn't help but smile.

"Beautiful," a voice said beside her.

She turned to see Ravyn, his ashen features softened by the tree's light. He held a cup in his hand, though he didn't seem interested in its contents.

"I was wondering," she said as she looked back at the tree, "if this tree could regrow… what about the ones destroyed in the east?"

Ravyn's eyes fell on her, but she didn't meet them. "The eventides clear plague from the soil—from the air. If you were successful in recreating this there… Valoria could stand a chance." He nodded, his eyes back on the tree.

"But Ilos' devout wouldn't let it stay. He has more followers in the east."

She nodded and glanced at him, studying his profile. There was a weariness in his expression that she recognized too well. "How are you holding up?" she asked softly.

He smiled, barely, though there was no light in his eyes. "Better than I have in the recent weeks, honestly." He glanced at her. "You know I asked Myst to take me with them when they left the Mire? Not because they're blind, but…"

Faedi raised her eyebrows when he trailed off and tilted her head slightly. "But what?"

He turned to face her, his head lowered. "The last time I left you, Lonan, and Sophir alone… two of you were hurt." His gaze lifted to hers. "I wanted to be sure you were alright."

She nodded, understanding the sentiment. "When Lonan and Sophir were… sometimes it's scarier knowing they're hurt and you can't do anything to help them."

He handed her his cup. "I know."

As Ravyn's gaze drifted back to the tree, she looked at the cup in her hands. They didn't need to discuss the pain and worry—not when everything around them was so lively. The last thing she wanted was to ruin the mood.

Before she could comment, a cheer erupted from the crowd, pulling their attention away from the tree. Behind them, a group gathered as dancing broke out among them. The music grew in volume, blending perfectly with the tree's heartbeat.

The cheer spread like wildfire, a ripple of joy sweeping through the crowd as the music took on a faster, more exuberant tempo. People began clapping to the rhythm, their hands rising in unison like waves cresting and falling. The dancers moved with wild abandon, their feet tapping and clothes swirling, creating a living, breathing tapestry of celebration.

Faedi glanced at Ravyn, who smiled. "Looks like they won't let the end of the world dampen their spirits."

"Maybe that's why they're dancing," she replied, the corners of her lips tugging into a smile. "Sometimes, joy is the best defiance."

As the crowd pulled closer to the makeshift dance floor, Sophir and Lonan emerged from the throng. Their grins matched and were infectious as they reached their hands toward her.

"You owe us a dance," Lonan said. "No escaping this one."

She laughed, shaking her head. "You know I can't dance."

"Never stopped you before." Ravyn nudged her. "We could show them how real Guardians dance."

Before she could agree or refuse, Lonan grabbed her hand and tugged her toward the dancers. She looked over her shoulder at Ravyn, who smirked as Sophir dragged him along. "Traitor," she mouthed, though she couldn't help but laugh.

The four of them spun in the circle, the energy of the music unrelenting as it guided her steps. It was fast and unpredictable, and she stumbled more than once, but the laughter that followed each misstep was genuine. The others around them cheered and clapped, their faces glowing with the tree's soft light and the flush of exertion.

The music slowed, its rhythm growing sultry, and without realizing it, they moved closer still. Ravyn's hand rested lightly on her back, guiding her into the sway of the dance. Sophir's fingers brushed hers as he stepped in, his black eyes watching her with quiet amusement. Lonan's arm draped casually over her shoulder, his shadows grounding her even as the world spun.

For a moment, the rest of the world—the worries, the battles, the looming uncertainty—fell away. All that remained was them, their joy, and the press of familiar bodies. Her heart raced, and heat crept up her neck.

"I… I need air," she stammered before ducking away and pushing through the crowd toward the temple.

81

*The Flame's
Call*

Sophir

The music thrummed in Sophir's veins as he watched Faedi vanish into the crowd. Her departure left a hollow ache in the circle they had formed. He glanced at Lonan and Ravyn, and without a word, they followed her through the dancers.

The laughter and movement around them faded into the background as the temple's towering silhouette came into view, its walls glowing faintly in the twilight.

"She was fine, wasn't she?" Sophir asked, his voice low but carrying enough weight to catch Lonan's attention.

"Until she wasn't." Lonan looked back at the crowd. "She doesn't like big groups—but they don't normally bother her when she's outside."

"Unless there's a big fire," Ravyn added.

Sophir studied his face, brows creased, then looked back toward the temple. He hadn't noticed anything was wrong until she ran. They had thought she would be fine because she usually handled large groups outside. But he should have known. She had always been anxious whenever people on the mountain surrounded them, and he had ignored it.

Dammit.

The temple loomed larger, its arched doors slightly ajar, spilling soft white light onto the path. Sophir caught sight of Faedi's silhouette further inside, near the collapsed altar on the dais at the back of the room. Her back was to them,

490

her head tilted toward the intricate carvings on the ceiling, and for a moment, he wasn't sure she had noticed their approach.

"Faedi," he called softly, stepping into the temple. His wings flexed instinctively, brushing the doorframe as he entered. Like the chamber below, the air inside was heavier, charged with Ancient magic.

She turned slowly, her expression tight—forced composure—though he caught a flicker of something in her eyes before she blinked it away. "You didn't have to follow me. I'm alright."

"Of course we did," Lonan said as he entered, his shadows flickering across the walls. He stopped a few paces behind Sophir. "We said no more getting separated, right?"

For a moment, she didn't answer; her attention remained on the gently glowing runes. Sophir might not have remembered how she was with crowds, but he knew she wouldn't speak until she was ready.

"It's nothing," she said finally, though her voice wavered as she turned to face them and held Sophir's gaze. "I just needed a minute to breathe."

"Lying about it isn't going to make you feel better," he countered as gently as he could manage. She flinched anyway, and her tail swished behind her anxiously.

Lonan must have grown just as impatient with worry. He didn't bother speaking; instead, he appeared beside her and took her chin, guiding her gaze to his. Silently, he leaned his forehead against hers and smiled softly. It was just like when they spoke outside their cottage when Sophir had first met them. Then, Faedi whispered something in Umbral.

"That's all?" Lonan whispered, and Sophir narrowed his eyes. Lonan must have had an inkling of what was bothering her.

Ravyn took a step forward. "Is everything alright?"

Lonan's soft chuckle pulled Sophir's attention back to Faedi, and he caught the deepened shade of her cheeks. She said nothing, but Lonan's concern melted into pure amusement.

Slowly, the tension in Sophir's shoulders eased, and he closed the distance between them. "I assume all is well?"

"Right as rain." Lonan smiled up at him, standing beside Faedi as he wrapped an arm around her waist. "She—"

"There are fires on the horizon."

An Itmis rushed into the temple, bowing his head. "It's an army."

The heavy beat of the soldiers' boots led them onward, the sound barely audible beneath the moaning wind. The pale morning light was overcast by the stretched shadows of the wall before them, its stone frame hulking against the horizon. Sophir kept his wings folded tightly against his back, the cold pricking along their sensitive edges. Ahead of him, Lonan moved like the specter he was—silent and composed, his eyes sharp as they scanned every shifting, crumbled ruin.

Faedi walked to his left, her footsteps almost weightless on the frosted ground. Her head was tilted slightly, as if listening to something beyond his perception. The tension in her shoulders mirrored his own. Even the wind felt wrong—too biting, too relentless—nothing like the gentle breeze at the party.

The Itmis soldier ahead kept glancing over his shoulder, perhaps checking that they were still there or, more likely, seeking reassurance. The reports were troubling: cultists gathering on the horizon, strange lights at night, whispers carried on the wind.

As they ascended the stone steps of the wall, Sophir's heart raced in his chest. He had surveyed the walls many times before—more than he could count—but the firelight in the distance was far from a welcome sight. There were hundreds more than the groups they had seen on the mountain.

"They knew we'd be here," Faedi whispered beside him.

He nodded subtly. "They know the Dusk Elves belong here and not the mountain."

Lonan stood beside him, his shadowy form merging with the dim light behind them. "They would have shown up wherever we went," he growled. "But it's hard to miss a new heart tree… I wonder if that's why Blavier had the rule about no Umbrals here. Ilos might've known you were bonded to me."

"He knew."

Sophir turned to look at Faedi; her eyes burned as she stared ahead. She hadn't told them everything Ilos had said and done to her, and he didn't think it was appropriate to ask. But there wasn't a single part of him that doubted her. If she said Ilos knew, then he did.

They watched in silence as the line of flickering lights grew. Sophir's pulse quickened. The cultists weren't hiding; they were setting up. He glanced down at the space between them. Even with the new growth, the ice and snow prevented much from flourishing, which would slow the enemy's advance. Yet, they waited.

Faedi shifted closer, her breath visible in the cold air. "Either they're afraid to move in the dark," she whispered, "or this is another waiting game."

"They do seem overly confident," Lonan replied. "They might be blind to the pain they cause, but they aren't idiots."

Minutes passed, each dragging slower than the last. The glints of light continued, accompanied by faint movements—figures shifting in the distance, too far to make out clearly.

Then it happened.

A low rumble, almost imperceptible at first, rolled across the land. Sophir turned, his eyes snapping toward the harbor.

Explosions erupted like fiery blossoms above the structures between them and the ocean, shattering the quiet. Smoke billowed as flames roared to life and licked the sky. Sails bucked violently, some torn apart by the force of the blasts, their splintered remains raining down like deadly hail.

"Dammit!" Sophir snarled, his wings flaring instinctively.

Lonan didn't flinch. His knives were in his hands, gleaming darkly. "They were a distraction—they knew we'd watch them and rally here," he said, his voice ice-cold. "They didn't want us to see their true numbers."

The cultists on the ridge moved then, their silhouettes emerging against the smoke-streaked sky. They carried banners scrawled with symbols Sophir didn't recognize, their weapons glinting in the dim light.

"We have to protect the wall," Faedi said, her voice steady despite the chaos swirling around them. "The Helgi will protect the shore."

Sophir nodded, stepping to her side. "Lonan?"

Lonan tilted his head slightly, his shadow form flickering as if he were ready to vanish. "We should meet them in the open. Delay them from reaching the wall for as long as we can."

Even if Sophir hated it, Lonan was right.

Lonan was already moving, his figure blending into the flickering shadows cast by the firelight. Sophir unfurled his wings fully, the cold biting against their sensitive membranes, and launched into the air with a single beat. Below him, Faedi followed Lonan down the steps from the wall, shouting for others to follow.

The cultists advanced steadily, their banners snapping in the wind. Their weapons gleamed, and though he couldn't hear them over the roar of the wind, he could feel the malice radiating from their ranks.

Sophir soared ahead, cutting through the smoke-tainted air to land with a heavy thud in their path. Dust and frost scattered beneath his feet as he stood tall, wings spread wide. Lonan emerged beside him like a wraith. Faedi came last, her hands glowing faintly with magic as she positioned herself behind them, a living barrier of roots and thorns already forming at her command.

"Turn back," Faedi said, her voice sharp and commanding.

The cultists didn't hesitate. Their formation shifted slightly, their ranks tightening as they prepared to engage. The lead figure—a man clad in gold armor—stepped forward. A wicked smile split his face.

"We are not here to bargain," he sneered, raising a gnarled staff. "Surrender all eclipse-born, or die with your illusions of safety."

"I prefer a third option," Lonan growled.

Before the cultist could respond, Lonan surged forward, a blur that collided with the man like a storm. The leader barely had time to raise his staff before Lonan's blades were slashing. The cultist stumbled back, blood streaking his armor.

The others charged.

Sophir launched into the fray, his wings propelling him forward with a powerful gust. His claws struck true, tearing through armor and flesh as he drove into their ranks. The cultists were trained well, their movements precise and coordinated, but they weren't prepared for the army they faced.

For the eclipse-born they sought had been trained by the horrors they created, with a will to survive far stronger than the commands of their god.

Around him, he caught glimpses of the others charging into the line— Ighir, Zarae, Bjorn, and Ragna fighting with a fire that only centuries of pent-up rage and fear could provide. The Dusk Elves, Itmis, and Gaelisks united to defend the city. Even the forest beyond them whipped violently as if it were fighting alongside them.

Faedi's magic surged behind him, and the earth came alive. Thick roots burst from the frost-covered ground, tangling the cultists' legs and dragging some down entirely. Others cried out as thorny vines lashed at their faces, tearing flesh and blinding them.

A blade swung toward him, and Sophir twisted, the metal glancing off his scaled forearm. He roared, the sound vibrating through his chest as he drove his claws into the attacker's neck. The cultist crumpled, and Sophir turned to face the next.

Lonan moved with lethal grace, his knives finding gaps in armor as if the cultists had been designed with him in mind. Each movement was calculated— he was a force of nature, untouchable and unyielding.

Faedi's voice rang out over the battlefield. "I have an idea."

82

Sentinels on the Shore

Sylrie

Smoke stung Sylrie's eyes as he crouched behind a shattered crate, his axe gripped tightly in one hand. The chaos of battle raged around him—shouts, explosions, the clash of steel against steel. Flames painted the harbor in hues of orange and red, casting eerie shadows that flickered along the cobblestones.

Danik knelt a few paces to his right, his sword dripping with blood as he wiped his face on his sleeve. His features were smudged with ash, but his eyes remained sharp. Lisea stood to his left, her curved blade drawn, gripped tight and ready. Sweat streaked her face, strands of hair sticking to her skin, but she seemed unfazed, her gaze locked on the cluster of cultists advancing through the wreckage.

"This is madness," Danik muttered, glancing at Sylrie.

"No arguments here," he replied, peering over the crate. The cultists pressed forward, their faces obscured by masked helmets bearing twisted symbols. One carried a crude metallic box with a sparkling fuse—like a cannon.

Ancients.

"That's a bomb," Sylrie warned.

Lisea's eyes widened before she broke one of the quills off her shoulder. She pulled a small wooden tube from her belt, inserted the quill, and raised it to her mouth. Sylrie realized what she was doing the moment she blew. The quill embedded itself in the eye hole of the cultist's helmet. He staggered back, dropping the bomb, which rolled into a puddle before the fuse sputtered out.

"Good shot," Danik said, already moving. He darted from cover, and Sylrie was right behind him.

They pushed forward, weapons raised. The harbor was in ruins. Flames consumed the wooden docks, and half-sunken ships groaned as they listed in the water. Smoke billowed, choking the air and reducing visibility to mere feet. But through the haze, more cultists emerged, pouring in like a relentless tide.

"More incoming," Sylrie warned.

"We need to push them back," Danik shouted, his voice barely carrying over the roar of the flames.

Sylrie nodded, stepping over the body of a fallen cultist. His boots slid on the blood-slick cobblestones, but he kept moving, his axe ready.

The cultists were relentless, their movements almost mechanical in their precision. They didn't flinch, didn't hesitate. They attacked individually, and he and Danik cut them down one by one. But for every one they killed, two more seemed to take their place.

A deafening explosion rocked the harbor, throwing Sylrie off balance. He stumbled, catching himself on the remnants of a shattered barrel. His ears rang, and for a moment, the world spun.

"Syl!" Lisea's voice cut through the haze, sharp and panicked.

Sylrie turned just in time to see a cultist charging at Lisea from behind. She was too focused on her next shot to notice.

"Lisea, down!" Sylrie bellowed, sprinting toward her.

Lisea dropped into a crouch just as Sylrie reached her, swinging his axe in a clean arc. The cultist collapsed, their momentum carrying them to the ground at her feet.

"Thank you," Lisea said breathlessly, looking up at him.

"Stay sharp," he replied, helping her to her feet.

Danik reappeared, his blade dripping with fresh blood. "They're using side alleys to flank us," he said grimly. "And there are others in armor—it's different."

His words sent a shiver down Sylrie's spine. He turned, scanning the battlefield. Through the smoke and firelight, figures emerged from the shadows— taller, broader, and moving with purpose. Their armor gleamed through the soot-streaked air, intricate sigils carved into the plates. These weren't the ragged, half-mad zealots they had been fighting. They were something else entirely.

"Ancients keep us," Lisea whispered.

"What kind of armor is that?" Sylrie narrowed his eyes. The metal plates were larger, covering their forms almost seamlessly, and the sigils glowed brighter than the flames around them.

"Whatever it is, I don't like it," Danik muttered, tightening his grip on his sword.

The armored figures continued forward, their steps heavy enough to make the ground tremble beneath them. They carried massive weapons—war hammers, halberds, even shields large enough to crush a man against a wall.

Plan. They needed a plan.

Sylrie's mind raced, the surrounding blaze a blur as he weighed their options. The ordinary cultists were bad enough, but if these new warriors reached the inner city, they wouldn't stop.

"We split them up," he said, forcing his voice to remain steady. "Danik, draw them toward the water. Lisea, keep to the shadows and pick off any stragglers. I'll—"

"Take the big ones head-on," Danik interrupted, already moving. "Don't get yourself killed."

Before he could argue, Danik darted into the fray, weaving between cultists with terrifying precision. His blade flashed as he cut down two of the robed zealots, drawing the attention of the armored sentinels. One of the massive figures turned, its halberd raised high, and lumbered after him.

Lisea shot Sylrie a look—half exasperated, half resigned—before melting into the smoke, her quills at the ready.

That left Sylrie.

The first Sentinel stepped into view, its war hammer held casually. It towered over the cultists, its armor gleaming faintly with an unnatural light. Twisted symbols glowed along its surface like embers.

This is going to hurt.

Sylrie squared his stance, gripping his axe tightly. The Sentinel advanced, its footsteps booming in the air, and then it charged.

The warhammer swung in a wide arc, and he barely managed to dodge. It slammed into the cobblestones with a deafening crash. Shards of stone flew, one slicing across his cheek, but he didn't slow. Moving inside its reach, he brought his axe down on its armored thigh.

The blade struck true, but instead of the satisfying crunch of metal giving way, a jarring clang vibrated up his arms. The Sentinel didn't even flinch.

Fuck.

It swung again, faster this time. Sylrie ducked, the hammer whistling over his head, and countered with an upward strike aimed at its helm. The axe bit into the edge of its helmet, knocking its head back slightly, but it wasn't enough.

The Sentinel roared—a low, guttural sound that reverberated in his bones. It reached out, one massive gauntlet closing around the shaft of his axe.

Double fuck.

With a wrenching twist, it tore the weapon from his hands and tossed it aside like a discarded toy. He stumbled back, drawing the dagger from his belt as it advanced.

The world narrowed, leaving only the Sentinel and himself. Every step it took was a countdown. He lunged, aiming for the joints in its armor, but it swatted him aside with a massive arm. Pain exploded in his ribs as he hit the ground, the air driven from his lungs.

Get up.

He forced himself to his feet, swaying slightly. The Sentinel was already coming at him again, its hammer raised for a killing blow.

Then, it staggered and dropped to its knees.

Through the flames, Sylrie spotted Lisea's silhouette before she disappeared into the smoke once more.

Without hesitation, Sylrie seized the opening, grabbed a discarded blade from a fallen cultist, and darted forward. With all the strength he could muster, he drove the weapon into the Sentinel's neck.

This time, the armor gave way.

The Sentinel let out a strangled roar, its massive form swaying before it collapsed with a resounding clang.

One down… how many more to go?

83

Hold the Line

Faedi

Frost crunched beneath Faedi's boots as she darted between the makeshift barricades, her breath fogging in the frigid air. The clash of steel and the cries of cultists filled the battlefield—a symphony of chaos and death. Her fingers curled tightly around her bow, the wood warm against her palms despite the cold. Ahead, Lonan and Sophir cut through the cultists with an efficiency that was both terrifying and awe-inspiring.

The cultists were relentless, throwing themselves against the defenses with a ferocity that bordered on madness. But they held the line.

"Faedi!" Sophir's voice rang out above the mayhem, his wings flaring as he leaped from a barricade and slammed into a pair of robed zealots. "We need more cover on the left; they're trying to flank."

She turned and scanned the battlefield. The left side was a tangle of shattered carts and hastily constructed barriers, where Dusk Elves, Itmis, and Gaelisk soldiers struggled to hold back a surge of cultists armed with crude explosives.

Raising a hand, she called on the earth beneath her feet, channeling its dormant energy. The ground rumbled a low growl that made her skin tingle before a thick wall of thorns erupted from the frozen soil. The barrier snaked forward, weaving between the defenders to cut off the advancing cultists.

The thorns shimmered faintly, their tips gleaming with venomous sap. Anyone foolish enough to try climbing would regret it. But there was no time to savor the creation. The cultists were regrouping.

Shouts rose above the chaos as they hauled forward another contraption—a ramshackle trebuchet, its wooden frame creaking under its payload.

"Lonan!" Faedi shouted, pointing to the siege engine.

He was already moving, his shadowy form melting into the fray. The cultists never saw him coming. One moment, they were loading the trebuchet; the next, they were clutching at their throats, blood spraying in dark arcs as Lonan's knives found their mark.

Faedi forced herself to focus, even as her chest tightened with the weight of battle. Every movement felt like a desperate gamble, every second a fragile thread keeping them from being overwhelmed.

Then, the forest stirred.

It was initially subtle, a faint rustling that carried on the biting wind. But it grew louder and deeper until it was unmistakable. The trees swayed violently, their branches twisting as if alive. Shadows spilled out from the tree line, but they were no mere tricks of the light.

They were Umbrals.

Dozens of them emerged, their forms shifting and insubstantial, their eyes glowing like blue and violet flames. They moved with an eerie grace, their limbs appearing elongated—as if they were one with their weapons—and sliced through the air as they fell upon the cultists.

Leading them was Myst, their presence unmistakable. Their form was fluid, a dark silhouette atop a darker mass. They moved like a storm given flesh, their knives tearing through the cultists with a ferocity that bordered on primal.

The cultists faltered, their formation breaking as panic set in. They turned to face the new threat, their weapons and magic swinging wildly at the Umbrals.

Lonan reappeared at Faedi's side, his knives dripping with blood. "So that's where they went," he said, his tone unreadable.

"I figured they had something like this planned." A small smile flickered across her lips as she fixed her gaze on Myst. "They're mad."

Sophir landed heavily beside them, his wings folding as he surveyed the chaos. "Good," he rumbled. "Anger might be what we need."

The battle finally began to shift. The Umbrals' arrival and the sheer shock they instilled were enough to give Faedi and her allies a fighting chance. For a moment, she thought they might just make it out alive—that they wouldn't die for the mere timing of their births.

Then, a metallic screech split the air, louder and deeper than anything she'd ever heard. It came from the cultists' ranks, and as the smoke cleared, her blood ran cold.

A massive group of figures strode forward. They were clad in dense armor that pulsed with unnatural light, their helms adorned with twisted, crown-like metal. Each carried weapons so large they dwarfed the average soldier.

"Ancients," she breathed.

The cultists rallied around the figures, their fear replaced with frenzy. A chill shot down Faedi's spine. Whatever upper hand they had was slipping away.

Sophir growled low in his throat, his wings flaring. "There are more like these at the docks."

"Sylrie says the armor is weakest at the neck," Faedi told them, her jaw tightening.

Lonan nodded, his shadows flickering as he prepared to strike.

Faedi tightened her grip on her bow, refusing to let the weight of the battle crush her. The energy in the air was different now—foul and unnatural. She hated it.

The figures moved toward them, the ground shuddering beneath their march. Behind them, the cultists surged forward, their chants rising above the din of war.

"Hold the line," Faedi commanded, as firm as she could manage despite the fear gnawing at her insides. "No matter what."

The others nodded, their expressions grim, as their forces braced for the onslaught.

The cultists' champions charged, weapons raised high, and Faedi's side met them head-on.

The clash was unlike anything she had ever experienced. Their strength was monstrous. Shattering. Sophir darted in and out, colliding with their enemies in a whirlwind of claws and steel. Lonan was a blur, his knives carving through the cultists that swarmed around them.

Faedi focused on their feet. Channeling the earth's energy again, she begged the vines to grow once more. By the grace of the Ancients, they did not need much coaxing.

Vines erupted from the ground, snaring their opponents' legs and slowing their advance. The armored figures roared in frustration, their weapons and magic cleaving into the bindings—just enough of a distraction for Sophir and Lonan to strike.

They pounced like predators onto prey, driving their weapons into the enemy's vulnerable spots. The Umbrals surged in, black fog rolling across the battlefield, and Faedi continued to plead with the earth.

Gods willing, the ground beneath them would no longer be barren.

84
On Winged Ancestors

"There's too many of them…why didn't they use all these forces when we were on the mountain? They could have overwhelmed us there—why wait until now?"

Sophir

The ground trembled beneath Sophir's boots as he planted them firmly into the churned earth, bracing for the armored brute's impact. His sword met the massive blade with a deafening clang, sparks flying in all directions. The strength behind the cultist's strike sent shockwaves up his arms, but Sophir stood his ground. His wings flared wide, catching the smoke-laden air, steadying him as he twisted and brought his axe down on the exposed back of the cultist.

The armor gave way with a metallic shriek, and the cultist fell, his blood pooling dark and steaming against the frozen soil. Sophir didn't pause to revel in the kill. Another cultist was already rushing toward him, weapon raised high.

Behind him, Faedi's voice rose in a frantic chant, her words pulling at the very fabric of the battlefield. Vines surged again, tangling the legs of the armored figures, buying them precious moments. Lonan's shadows darted in and out of the fog, his knives finding weak points in the cultists' armor with surgical precision. The Umbrals swirled around them like living shadows, their ferocity unmatched as they tore through the enemy ranks.

They could win this.

"Push forward!" Sophir roared, his voice carrying over the battle. "Don't let them regroup!"

The Dusk Elves and Gaelisk soldiers surged behind him, weapons raised as they threw themselves into the fray. For every cultist that fell, another took their place, but they matched their ferocity with their own.

Lonan was a blur to Sophir's right, his shadowy form darting in and out of reach. One moment, he was slitting the throat of a cultist; the next, he was driving his blade into the exposed neck of one of the armored figures. He moved like death itself, a predator who belonged in the chaos.

Faedi was holding her ground behind the line, her hands glowing with an unearthly light as she continued to channel the earth's energy. Vines and thorns erupted wherever she focused, creating barriers that slowed the cultists' advance. Despite her exhaustion, she didn't falter, her resolve as unyielding as the roots she summoned.

The battle blurred into a frenzy of motion and sound. Clashing steel. Roaring flames. Cries of the wounded. Pain. Sophir's sword swung again and again, each strike landing with brutal precision. His wings lashed out whenever he needed space, their strength knocking cultists off balance or breaking bones.

The cultists' numbers began to dwindle, their chanting faltering, and the flames lessened. The armored champions were either dead or tangled in the thorns, their holy flames unable to stop the masses from growing faster than they could be burned. A roar rose from their lines as the realization began to sink in: They were winning.

The Umbrals pushed forward, driving the cultists back toward the treeline. Then, the trees moved again, and screams erupted from those closest to the forest. Nearby, Ravyn shouted, celebrating as some of the smaller trees took life and began to attack.

Sophir caught Faedi's eye across the battlefield. She looked as drained as he felt, her face pale and streaked with blood and sweat, but hope flared in her eyes. She nodded at him, and he returned the gesture. They would survive.

Lonan appeared at his side, the shadows shrinking around him. "They're breaking," he beamed. "We press now, and they're finished."

"Then let's finish it," Sophir growled.

The push was brutal, but it worked. The cultists fell back in disarray, their chants dissolving into cries of fear and confusion. The last of their siege weapons burned, reduced to smoldering heaps of twisted wood and metal. Their leaders lay dead, their armored forms slumped in the dirt.

The battlefield quieted, save for the crackle of flames and the ragged breathing of survivors. Sophir's chest heaved as he stood among the wreckage, his sword dripping with blood. The wall of Dewgate loomed behind them, untouched and standing tall.

They had won.

Or so he thought.

The silence didn't last long. A distant sound cut through the stillness—a low, rumbling roar that sent ice into his chest. It wasn't a beast's roar or a man's cry. It was deeper, resonant, a sound that seemed to come from the sky.

"Mumir's breath," Sophir whispered, turning toward the horizon.

It can't be.

Beyond the smoke and the clouds, dark shapes moved against the sky. They grew larger with each breath—massive forms, winged. The roars came again, louder that time, carrying an unmistakable threat.

Dragons—dozens of them.

His blood turned to ice as the first of them came into focus, its scales glinting like molten metal in the light of the flames. Its jaws opened wide, revealing rows of razor-sharp teeth, and a torrent of fire erupted, carving a fiery path across the horizon.

And atop it sat a robed cultist.

Eena, help us.

The soldiers around them froze, their hard-won victory forgotten in an instant. Fear rippled through the ranks, spreading like wildfire as the mounted dragons drew closer. The ground trembled beneath their approach, each beat of their wings sending shockwaves through the air.

Ighir landed beside Sophir, his face mirroring his own. Dragons swore to never again interfere with wars among mortals, but there they were. Carrying their enemy. No better than standard mounts.

"I don't know if this is insulting…or if they deserve it," Ighir growled.

Sophir stared up at the dragons and scoffed. "I'd say both."

The first dragon roared again, its voice shaking the earth as it descended toward them. The soldiers began to scatter, their panic overtaking any sense of discipline. It was chaos all over again.

"Regroup!" Sophir shouted over his shoulder, turning to face their forces. "Form lines!"

Shouts echoed his as they tried to regroup, but it was useless. The dragons were too fast, too powerful. But Sophir knew it wouldn't be enough.

The battle they thought they'd won was far from over. It was just the beginning.

Ancients, let Faedi and Lonan survive this.

85

The Golden Herald

"When this is over…will this be over? Even if we beat them here and now—aren't they just going to come for us again? Are we going to spend the rest of our lives fighting?"

Lonan

The heat was unbearable, and the air was thick with fire and smoke, clawing at Lonan's lungs like a living thing. His vision blurred as he darted through the chaos, shadows dancing erratically around him. The dragons were everywhere—massive, nightmarish beasts that filled the sky with their presence.

The cultists rode them like harbingers of annihilation. Their robed forms were barely visible against the dragons' massive frames, but their commands were evident as they directed the beasts to attack. Fire rained from their maws, roaring infernos that devoured everything they touched.

Where was Faedi?

Lonan twisted, rolling to avoid a gout of flame that blasted the ground where he'd been standing moments before. The heat licked at his back, and he gritted his teeth as he came up in a crouch, knives glinting in his hands. His shadow form flickered around him, coiling and seething as if it shared his fury.

"Lonan!" Sophir's voice cut through the air as he rushed toward him, his wings churning the smoke. His hair was singed, his eyes blazing. "We might have a chance if we take down the riders."

Lonan didn't answer. There was no time for words, only action.

A dragon swept low, its massive claws raking the ground as it snatched up a group of soldiers. Their screams were cut short as the beast ascended, flinging their broken bodies into the flames. The rider on its back raised a staff, chanting a spell that sent bolts of light streaking toward their defenders.

Lonan surged forward, his shadows exploding outward as he launched himself at the dragon. The world blurred for an instant, and then he was there—on the beast's back, its scales slick and hot beneath his boots. The rider turned, their eyes widening in shock as Lonan drove his knives into their chest. They gurgled, blood spilling from their lips, and toppled from the saddle.

The dragon roared in fury, twisting violently in the air. Lonan barely managed to hang on, his free hand gripping the ridge of its spine as it bucked and writhed. His shadows surged again, anchoring him as he drove his second knife into the base of the dragon's neck.

However, instead of red blood—thick black ooze seeped out.

The beast shuddered, its wings faltering as it uttered a final, piercing cry. They plummeted, the ground rushing up to meet them. At the last moment, Lonan fell into the shadows and reappeared beside the dragon on the ground.

He took a ragged breath, watching the black blood pour onto the earth, melting the frost and seeping into the ground. It was the plague.

"Lonan, behind you!" Faedi's voice carried across the battlefield.

Lonan spun just in time to spot a cultist charging toward him, their staff raised high as flames shot out at him. Rather than run from it, he ran and slid on the ground toward them. His knives flashed white in his vision when they caught their thighs, and he twisted to dig them into their back. They crumpled with a scream, and Lonan didn't stop to watch them fall.

Another dragon soared overhead, its rider directing it toward the wall of Dewgate. It opened its jaws, unleashing a torrent of fire that engulfed a section of the defenses. Screams filled the air as their defenders scattered, their shields and barricades useless against the dragon's wrath.

The world was chaos—an endless fire, steel, and death storm. The dragons emboldened the cultists, their chants rising as they pressed the attack. There was no stopping them.

But Lonan refused to give up.

Sophir was a blur, his wings carrying him into the air as he grappled with another rider. His claws tore into the cultist's chest, ripping them from the saddle before turning on the dragon. The beast roared, snapping at him with its massive jaws, but Sophir was faster, darting out of reach and slashing at its wings.

Faedi stood at the edge of the battlefield with the other Guardians, their hands glowing with fierce light as they summoned more roots and thorns to slow the enemy's advance. Each took turns weaving spells and firing at anyone who got too close, but Lonan's worry was for her. Her face was pale, her movements slowing as exhaustion took its toll, but she continued.

Don't give up.

Myst charged ahead, a blur of shadows and fog as they carved through the cultists. Several Umbrals flanked them, their shadows twisting and writhing with Lonan's sibling as they tore into the enemy ranks.

They were holding the line—but barely.

Another dragon swooped low, its claws tearing through the defenders as its rider chanted a spell. Lonan's skin prickled with gooseflesh before he saw it—a bright ripple in the air. The spell erupted, sending a shockwave through their ranks that knocked him off his feet. He hit the ground hard, the impact driving the air from his lungs.

Before he could recover, the dragon turned its attention toward him, its massive head lowering as it prepared to strike. He forced himself to move, rolling to the side as its jaws snapped shut where he'd been a heartbeat before.

Lonan surged to his feet, his shadows coiling around him. The dragon lunged again, but this time he was ready. He jumped, driving his knives into the soft flesh beneath its jaw. The beast roared, thrashing violently as he clung to its neck, but Lonan dug his blades deeper.

The rider shouted something, their voice lost in the chaos, but Lonan was whipped around too violently to see them. Then, heat burned his skin as flames engulfed the dragon. He fell back, leaving his knives in the beast, and scrambled away as it crashed to the ground.

Around him, the battlefield was ablaze again. Even sections of the forest burned. The trees consumed. Charred skeletons of the home they had sworn to protect.

The forest burned, the flames spreading with every moment, its once-majestic canopy reduced to ash and embers. The air thickened with smoke, choking and suffocating. And still, the dragons circled overhead, their roars promising more destruction.

The cultists didn't care about the destruction; their focus was on entirely wiping them out. Lonan doubted they even cared about the sacrifices anymore. Not when he had already avoided too many death blows.

They were desperate—the battle wasn't going as they'd hoped.

But they weren't winning. Not really.

They were barely surviving.

The battle continued around Lonan like a tempest, each breath a struggle against the smoke and heat that choked the air. The dragons pressed their onslaught, their fire painting the battlefield in hellish hues. Their cultist riders chanted spells that filled the air with unnatural energy, their voices merging with the clash of steel and cries of the wounded.

Lonan slashed through another cultist who lunged at him, their blade missing by inches. But his strike was true. It carved through flesh and bone. The ground beneath him was slick with blood and mud, the frost long since melted, but he pressed on.

"There's more attacking the harbor!" Someone shouted from the left.

Sophir and Ighir darted overhead, clashing with another dragon mid-flight.

Their attacks focused on the beast's wings, sending it spiraling into the trees below. The following crash shook the earth, but there was no time to revel in victory. Another dragon replaced it, this one larger and more heavily armored, its rider adorned with ornate robes that glowed brightly.

Lonan forced his way toward Faedi, who gripped her knees as she caught her breath. Vines and other plant life continued to erupt from the ground, dragging cultists into the earth. Roots tore through the legs of the dragons, slowing their advance just enough for what remained of their forces to strike.

But Lonan could see the toll it was taking on her—on all of them. Their shoulders sagged, sweat dripped down their brows as they poured every ounce of energy into keeping their defenses alive.

"Faedi!" Lonan called, slashing through another cultist who charged him. "You need to fall back."

She shook her head, her gold eyes blazing as she straightened. "If we stop now, we'll all be ash!" Her voice trembled, but she didn't back down.

Before he could argue, the ground beneath them trembled violently, a deep, resonant quake that silenced the battlefield for a heartbeat. The dragons roared in unison, their cries echoing across the burning forest as if in response to some unspoken command.

Then came a scream that cut through the chaos like a knife.

Faedi.

Lonan's heart lurched as he turned toward her. She was stumbling, her hands glowing erratically as the vines and roots she'd summoned began to wither and recede. The earth seemed to shrink away from her, the once-dominant force retreating as if in fear.

And then it landed.

The dragon was massive, its gold scales gleaming with a sinister light as it descended from the sky. It landed in front of Faedi with an earth-shattering crash, its wings folding as it lowered its head to reveal the rider atop it. The cultist was draped in white and gold, their face obscured by a mask etched with jagged runes.

"No." Lonan gasped, breaking into a sprint as the world around him slowed.

Faedi's skin paled, almost white, as she stared up at the cultist who dismounted. Ravyn raced toward her from his spot on the line of Guard; his shout drowned out by the cultist's incantation. It filled the air with a sickening energy as the space before him shimmered gold.

"No!" Lonan roared, his shadows surging forward as he closed the distance between them.

The cultist raised their hands, light and gold coalescing into a writhing mass that shot toward Faedi. She screamed and reached out on either side of her, summoning another wall of vines and thorns—not to cover herself, but to protect the Guardians and soldiers behind her.

Lonan didn't think. He didn't hesitate.

In an instant, he was there, stepping in front of her and raising his shadows in a desperate attempt to shield her from the attack. The spell struck him square in the chest, and for a fleeting moment, he felt everything—the searing heat, the crushing force, the unbearable weight of the magic tearing through him.

Then...

86

Broken Bonds

Faedi

The world around Faedi froze, as if time had shattered in the wake of what she had witnessed. Her ears rang, drowning out the battle but not enough to silence the sound of her own scream.

He can't be gone.

Her knees weakened as the golden light faded, leaving behind nothing but ash. Her hands trembled violently as they reached out to the space where Lonan had been. The shadows that had surged fiercely around him moments before dissipated into the air, leaving her exposed and vulnerable.

"Lonan!" she choked, the name tearing from her throat. Her chest felt as if it had caved in, hollowed by a pain so deep it was all-consuming.

He was gone. Truly gone.

Her vision blurred with tears, the battlefield melting into a haze of fire and smoke. The vines she had summoned began to recede, wilting as if they, too, felt the loss. Her connection to the earth faltered. The vibrant energy that had surged through her moments ago was dull, lifeless.

"No…" the word was barely audible, a whisper against the roaring flames. "No, no, no!"

She couldn't see the battle anymore, the cultists or the dragons. All she could see was him stepping in front of her, his shadows surging like a shield—and then being obliterated instantly.

"Faedi, move!" Ravyn's voice cut through the fog in her mind.

She blinked, her gaze snapping upward. The cultist in gold stood where the dragon had landed, their hand still outstretched from casting the spell that had taken Lonan. Their mask gleamed in the firelight, its runes pulsating as though feeding off the destruction.

Sophir's roar split the air, a sound of pure, unbridled fury. He dove from the sky, his wings folded tight against his body as he plummeted toward the cultist.

She wanted to scream at him to stop, to flee, but the words caught in her throat. Her hands balled into fists, shaking with helpless rage.

Sophir hit the ground hard, his claws digging into the earth as he launched himself at the cultist. But they didn't flinch. They raised one hand, almost lazily, and when Sophir was close enough, they caught him by the throat.

"No!" she screamed, the sound tearing from her as she tried to stand, but her legs felt like lead. Ravyn grabbed her by the shoulders, holding her back as she struggled against him.

"Faedi, you can't—" he started, his voice straining as she fought to break free.

"Let me go!" she shrieked, twisting in his grip. "They'll kill him!"

Sophir writhed in the cultist's grasp, his wings beating furiously as he clawed at their arm. But they held him effortlessly, as though his strength meant nothing. The golden light around them intensified, bathing the battlefield in an eerie glow.

The cultist tilted their head, as though observing a curious insect. When they spoke, their voice was cold—emotionless.

"Oh? The brother…what a waste."

Before Faedi could even process the words, the light exploded.

The force of the blast knocked her backward, and she hit the ground. For a moment, she couldn't move, couldn't think. She couldn't breathe. When she finally managed to lift her head, her heart shattered all over again.

Sophir was gone.

No body, no blood—nothing but scorched earth where he once stood.

The scream that tore from her was primal. Raw. It came from somewhere deep inside, a place she hadn't known existed. Rage and grief coiled together, twisting into something monstrous.

"Faedi, we have to go!" Ravyn shouted, his voice desperate as he tried to pull her to her feet.

But she couldn't hear him. All she could hear was the cultist's voice, their words echoing in her mind. *What a waste.*

She stood, shoving Ravyn away with a strength she didn't know she possessed. Her vision narrowed, tunneling on the cultist who had taken everything from her.

They turned to face her, their mask tilting slightly as though they were amused.

"You…" she whispered, her voice trembling with a snarl. "You'll suffer for this."

The ground beneath her trembled as she called upon the earth again, but it felt distant and disconnected. The vines responded sluggishly, curling weakly around her feet. She screamed again, this time forcing her will into the earth— no longer pleading—demanding it to rise.

The ground cracked, fissures spreading outward as roots erupted in a frenzy. Driven by her rage, they surged toward the cultist, but they didn't reach. The dragon beside them unleashed a torrent of fire, scorching the roots before they could strike.

She stumbled, the backlash of energy hitting her like a physical blow.

The cultist raised their hand again, another spell forming in their palm. She watched it grow, the golden light spiraling into a concentrated sphere.

This time, there was no one to stand in front of her—except for Ravyn.

"Move, Faedi." He was at her side again, dragging her away as the spell hurtled toward them. It struck the ground where she had stood moments ago, the explosion sending both of them spiraling.

The cultist laughed—a hollow, chilling sound that pierced her heart. "Flee, little wolf," they taunted, their voice distorted by the mask. "Your forest is already ash."

She froze, her blood turning to ice.

Around her, the fires roared higher, their flames devouring the trees that had stood for centuries. The air was thick with smoke, and the suffocating haze darkened the sky above. Her forest, her home, was burning.

Again.

The cultist turned away, mounting their dragon once more. With a single command, the beast took to the sky, its wings stirring the flames below.

Faedi collapsed against Ravyn, the weight of everything crashing down on her. Lonan was gone. Sophir was gone. The forest would soon join them. Dewgate would as well.

"Not…" she whispered, sobbing as she clutched Ravyn's arm. "Not again."

She had failed.

Ravyn was shaking her, speaking urgently, but Faedi couldn't hear him. She couldn't hear anything over the deafening sound of her heartbeat—the sound of it breaking in her chest.

The fire raged around her, heat and ash burning her teary eyes. Her body trembled, rooted in place, unable to move or think. There was nothing but her heart and the cultist's taunting words echoing in her mind: *Your forest is already ash.*

"No," she whispered, her fingers clutching the ashen soil beneath her. It was scorched, lifeless, and hopeless.

Even in ashes, it will grow again.

The trembling in her hands spread through her limbs, becoming a deep vibration that mixed with her choked sobs. Grief and anger were no longer separate things—they had become one, a singular force demanding release. The air around her thickened, heavy with the scent of soil and rain, despite the smoke still choking the battlefield.

Something inside her broke open. Or perhaps it had always been there, waiting for a moment like this. A flood of energy surged through her—vast, ancient, and uncontainable. Her vision swam with green and silver, and she realized she was no longer kneeling on scorched earth but on a bed of vibrant moss.

The vines that had withered moments before stirred again, curling like awakening serpents. A low, thrumming sound filled her ears, rhythmic and primal, as though the earth's heartbeat had joined her own.

"Get up," a voice growled in her mind. *"You are not finished."*

She stood.

The cultist's dragon circled back, its rider calling out commands to the others still fighting. Flames spewed from the sky, but they no longer frightened her. They were merely another challenge to overcome, another reason to unleash the power building inside her.

The cultist turned their masked face toward her, tilting their head. "Still alive?" They sneered.

The ground beneath her feet shifted, and she wasn't sure if she moved or the earth carried her—maybe she was flying again. She didn't care. She launched herself forward faster than she thought possible, her hands outstretched. The cultist raised their arm to prepare another spell, but they faltered as the surrounding air darkened.

It wasn't just the shadows of the forest, but something deeper, something alive. Green tendrils laced with black streaks tore from the ground, chasing her as she climbed higher into the sky, borne upward by an unseen force.

The dragon under the cultist shuddered, its roar breaking into a wet, sickly gurgle. Its golden scales dulled, and its wings faltered mid-flap. A horrible crack echoed as it hit the earth, twitching once before going still.

The other dragons began to falter as well. Their roars turned to whines, their movements erratic as they crumpled to the ground one by one.

Faedi didn't care. She only had eyes for the cultist.

"You." Her voice snarled, unnaturally deep, layered with tones that didn't belong to her. Her hand reached for their throat as their dragon collapsed beneath them, and they stumbled to the ground. She landed before them, the impact sending shockwaves through the battlefield.

The cultist raised their hands, golden light flickering in their palms, but Faedi didn't wait. The vines that had once faltered surged forward, wrapping around their legs and arms, pulling them to their knees.

"You dare take from me?" she growled, the words foreign yet entirely hers. The vines tightened, drawing blood as they coiled. "You dare touch my forest? My people?"

Before she could finish, a roar sounded behind her—not from the dragons, but from an entirely different source. She turned just in time to see the gates of Dewgate burst open, dark figures pouring forth like a tide.

They moved with unnatural grace, their eyes glowing. They were almost like

Umbrals, though without shadows. Most had horns, varied wings, or both. Their faces were sharp, their expressions enraged, and they charged into the field to tear into the cultists with wild abandon.

Gathfauna—Dark Fae.

Faedi staggered, the surge of power within her faltering for a moment. They were sealed away. She didn't know how they got there. Unless...

The cultist in her grasp coughed weakly, drawing her attention back to them. Their mask had cracked, revealing a single eye filled with panic.

"You're tainted," they rasped, their voice trembling for the first time.

"No." Faedi smiled, tilting her head to the side. Mocking them. "I am the cure."

The vines surged again, snapping the cultist's body into the ground with a terrible noise that split the air. They cried out, and their spell flickered once before fading entirely. They were powerless, pinned beneath the weight of the earth itself.

But it wasn't enough.

All around her, the battlefield shifted. The flames that had threatened to consume everything flickered weakly before vanishing, not by water but by something far more profound. Green shoots burst from the scorched earth, growing at an impossible speed.

Eventides bloomed, their glowing petals chasing away the shadows and filling the air with a sweet, heady scent. They spread like wildfire, their light illuminating the battlefield in hues of silver and indigo.

Other flowers followed, their petals colored like flames. They covered the bodies of the fallen—cultists and allies alike—offering some final act of mercy.

The forest began to return, its heartbeat syncing with Faedi's. But the power coursing through her was too much. Her vision blurred, the world's edges dissolving into a swirl of colors and sounds.

The cultist beneath her cried out one last time before going silent, the vines dragging them into the earth. The Dark Fae cheered, their voices high and sharp, but their faces remained unreadable.

Faedi tried to take a step forward, but her legs gave out. The world tilted, and she fell to her knees, cushioned by the moss.

"Faedi." Ravyn's voice was distant, muffled.

She tried to respond, but her tongue was heavy, and her body unresponsive. But her magic continued to pour out. The ashes vanished, replaced by petals and leaves, the blood and mud covered by moss and soft grass. Saplings sprouted, growing quickly into large, ancient trees.

All around her, the forest bloomed—vibrant in color and energy. The vast expanse that was once between the forest and the city was already healed and full of life.

And Faedi was empty.

When darkness crept into her vision, she didn't resist. She willfully succumbed to it. Maybe, if she was lucky—she hoped—she would see them there.

87

Guardian of the Tides

Faedi

Her body ached as she woke—her muscles screamed with each breath, and her head throbbed in a dull, insistent rhythm. The rough, makeshift bedding beneath her scraped against her skin, the coarse fabric doing little to cushion her from the hard surface below.

The air was tinged with smoke and iron, though less heavy than it had been on the battlefield. She blinked, trying to clear the haze from her vision. Dim light filtered through cracks in what she realized were hastily assembled patches on wooden walls. The faint murmur of voices beyond them told her she wasn't alone, but it did nothing to soothe the rising panic in her chest.

Where am I?

A heavy hand came to rest on her shoulder, and she turned, her head spinning, her vision blurred. Slowly, Sylrie came into view, and her breath caught.

"You're safe," he said, but his eyes were haunted.

His features were pale and drawn beneath the blood-streaked bandages that crisscrossed his chest and arms. Bruises and minor scrapes littered his exposed skin, and he winced with each deep breath. His axe rested nearby, well within arm's reach.

The sight of him stirred a memory, a flash of chaos and fire. Her stomach twisted, nausea curling in her gut. She clenched her fists to anchor herself, and even that small motion sent a sharp pain stabbing through her.

Forcing herself upright despite her body's protests and Sylrie's attempts to lay her back, the room tilted for a moment before righting itself.

"What happened?" she rasped, her voice raw as if she'd been screaming. Because she had.

The memory of the battle surged again, but it was replaced by something darker—an unrelenting wave of grief.

Lonan. Sophir.

The images came rushing back, each clearer and more painful than the last. Lonan's shadow form dissipated under the blast of light. Sophir trying to escape the cultist's grasp only to be obliterated like Lonan.

They were gone.

She clutched her knees to her chest, her breaths coming fast and shallow. "No," she whispered, shaking her head as if she could will the truth away. "No, they wanted to capture us."

But the memories didn't stop.

Lonan standing between her and the cultist, his shadows extending to cover her—to protect her. The way he was overtaken by the light and then breaking apart until there was nothing left.

Sophir charging in, screaming in rage. Then nothing.

She had been powerless to stop it.

Tears came fast, hot and bitter, spilling down her cheeks. Her chest heaved with sobs, the sound of her grief muffled by Sylrie's chest as he wrapped his arms around her. She couldn't hear the words he said over the blood rushing in her head.

How had it come to this?

Everything they had known of the cultists, of their mission, said they'd be captured—they would be taken and sacrificed—that they would be bound to loyalists and the devout of Ilos.

But they killed them—they didn't care.

"Faedi," Sylrie murmured while he held her.

She shook her head. She didn't want words of comfort; she deserved none. They were gone because they were protecting her. If she had been stronger—if she had fled when they told her—if she hadn't wasted her energy earlier in the battle.

"You need to rest," he said, breaking through her thoughts.

"I can't," she choked out, shaking her head. "They're gone. I can't. They—"

His hold on her tightened, but he said nothing; he simply held her. His silence was unbearable, confirming what she already knew.

There was no fixing it—no getting them back.

"I should have done something," she whispered. "I should have—I don't know—stopped them, protected them." Her words broke into a sob, and she buried her face deeper in his chest.

"You were fighting for your life—for everyone's lives," he said gently.

"It wasn't enough," she snapped, her grief sharpening into anger.

He relaxed his hold, and he didn't speak for a moment. Then, softly, he whispered, "It never feels like enough. But blaming yourself won't bring them back."

She hated his words, even if she knew they were true.

"I..." A lump formed in her throat. "I didn't—didn't tell them I—"

"They knew," he pulled away and looked at her. His jaw clenched, and he looked like he might cry for a moment. But he didn't. He just watched her.

She sat back, staring at the cracked ceiling above her as fresh tears rolled down her cheeks. The world felt smaller, emptier, and unbearably cold. "I love them," she whispered. "I should have told them."

He lifted her hands, his eyes fixed on the bonding tattoos. Even in their absence, they remained and continued to shimmer like stars. "You told them," his eyes met hers. He was crying. "Trust me, Faedi, you told them."

She nodded, unable to speak. But even in the depths of her despair, a tiny spark began to flicker.

They're gone, but we aren't.

Lonan and Sophir fought for them and gave everything to ensure they'd survive. She couldn't let their sacrifice be in vain. She wouldn't let them waste their lives on her.

"Tell me what happened," she glanced at Sylrie. "There were…I saw Dark Fae."

He nodded silently, taking a break to steady himself. "Whatever you did out there… it opened the portal to their realm." There was something in his eyes she couldn't place. "They finished the army off. Their king… god, whatever he is… Zephyr, he's got his people working on the city."

She licked her chapped lips, processing what he said. She didn't know what she had done, but it didn't matter. All she knew was she was ready to take that bastard with her. Nothing, no one else mattered.

Ancients, she hadn't thought to ask about anyone else until her growl stuck in her throat. "What about Myst? The others?"

"Alive," he managed to smile at her, but it was hesitant. "Some are better off than others. Your falcon hasn't left the tree—attacks anyone who gets too close."

She sighed, closing her eyes to stop the tears from falling. "So we won."

"For now," he mumbled. It didn't feel like they did, but he wasn't wrong. Whatever victory they had was temporary.

She nodded slowly and wiped her tears with trembling hands. Her heart was still heavy but burned as she stared at her tattoos. They gave everything for her, for everyone, and she needed to do the same.

So, for them, she would rise—she would keep fighting.

The sun was high, casting a warm, silvery light over Dewgate. The air was fresh with timber and stone dust, the scents mingling with the faint sweetness of blossoms beginning to creep through the repaired streets. The city was alive with hammers striking steel and the murmur of voices—some hurried, some jubilant.

The battle wounds were healing. Almost all the scorched ruins were rebuilt, their once-charred skeletons replaced with sturdy stone and reinforced wood. Though quieter than it had once been, the harbor bristled with activity as new ships arrived, their sails painted with symbols from across the sea. Dewgate was whole again. Or as close to it as it would ever be.

Faedi stood on a raised platform in front of the heart tree, her hands folded tightly to keep from trembling, while Dusan sat on her shoulder. He hadn't left her side since she recovered. He didn't talk much but offered her silent support, much like Syl and Bjorn. If it hadn't been for them and Ragna, she would have lost herself in her depression.

Her breath caught in her chest as she scanned the crowd below—a sea of faces, all different yet united in their hope. Dwarves with their braided beards and tools strapped to their belts stood alongside towering Gaelisk warriors, their horns catching the light. Elves of varied backgrounds mingled freely. Humans were scattered throughout with the Itmis and Dark Fae. Their laughter rang out as they traded stories with their neighbors.

It was beautiful…and bittersweet.

She glanced at Sylrie beside her. His tall, muscular frame seemed almost untouched by the scars he bore beneath his finely woven tunic. He looked like he belonged there—powerful, resolute, every inch a leader. But his face, like hers, carried a shadow the moon couldn't chase away.

"Still standing?" he murmured, not looking at her.

"Trying," she replied, her voice softer than intended.

The platform creaked as the Dark Fae king, Zephyr, stepped forward, dressed in ceremonial robes trimmed in black and silver. They raised their hands to quiet the crowd, and slowly, the voices subsided—but Faedi's heart nearly drowned out his voice. She scanned the crowd and spotted Myst beside Tagil and Torix, and her heart clenched.

I'm sorry. I'm so sorry.

"People of Dewgate," Zephyr began, their voice strong and clear. "Today, we stand in a city reborn. What was broken has been mended. What was lost has been honored. And now, we look to the future."

A ripple of applause spread through the crowd, though it was muted as Faedi turned her eyes to the city square. To the statue erected there. One to honor the fallen, the stone covered with creeping vines of eventides and similar flowers she'd never seen before. Sylrie called them embertides. Rather than blue, their blooms were red—just like the embers Ilos' followers left in their wake.

The figures of Lonan and Sophir stared at her, and she couldn't stop a tear from falling.

"Centuries ago, this city was a bastion of hope, a symbol of resilience. And we will restore it to that former glory," Zephyr continued, their gaze sweeping over the gathering. "Today, we recognize the leaders who will guide us into this new era—those who have proven their strength, compassion, and unwavering dedication to this land and its people."

They turned toward them, their expression softening. "Faedi. Sylrie. Step forward."

Faedi swallowed hard, her pulse quickening as she stepped closer to the platform's edge. Sylrie moved with her, his hand briefly brushing against hers in silent reassurance.

Zephyr gestured to the towering walls of the city behind them. "Under their guidance, Dewgate has not only been rebuilt but fortified. New defenses stand as a testament to their vision and the unity of our people."

Faedi followed their gaze, letting her eyes linger on the walls. Steel ballistae gleamed in the moonlight, their mechanisms intricate and lethal. A new layer of enchantments hummed faintly in the air, their protective sigils glowing softly against the stone.

They were too familiar to the ones the cultists used for Faedi to look at for long.

"These defenses are not just tools of war," Zephyr said, their voice steady. "They symbolize what we can achieve when we stand together."

Another round of applause erupted, this one louder, more fervent. Faedi flinched.

Zephyr turned back to them, and their words settled heavily on Faedi's shoulders. "Faedi, you are the Guardian of the Tides—a protector of life and balance, a nurturer of the bonds that connect us all. Sylrie, you are the warden of the Tides—a warrior and a sentinel, a defender of this city and its people. Together, you will lead Dewgate into an era of peace and prosperity."

They extended their hands, one toward Faedi and one toward Sylrie, beckoning them to kneel. Faedi hesitated momentarily, her heart pounding, before lowering herself onto one knee. Sylrie did the same; his movements were slow, and he only kneeled when she was stable.

Zephyr placed a hand on each of their shoulders. "Do you swear to protect this city, its people, and the Tides that sustain this land?"

"I swear," Faedi said, her voice trembling.

"I swear," Sylrie echoed, his tone steady.

Zephyr stepped back and motioned with a wave of their hand. Ragna approached with a smile that didn't reach her eyes, carrying an ornately carved box. She nodded to Zephyr before she opened it, and Faedi's heart stopped.

Crowns.

Hers and her grandfather's.

I can't do this.

Faedi didn't want it. She didn't want to look at the beautiful metal twisted and woven like vines, but she couldn't move. She told herself she would fight for them, live for them. She couldn't run away—even if she wanted to.

The metal was heavy on her head before Zephyr finished placing it. "It suits you," he whispered. His smile betrayed the sorrow in his eyes. "You'll do Dewgate well. You'll do them proud."

Faedi's heart raced in her chest, drumming louder than the distinct thump of the heart tree. Then he was gone, and the crowd erupted into cheers. It was overwhelming, washing over her like a wave. She stood slowly, her legs unsteady beneath her. Sylrie rose beside her, his expression unreadable.

The ceremony continued around them—speeches, blessings, drinks poured, and gifts offered by their allies' representatives. Faedi accepted them all with a polite smile, her mind distant.

It wasn't until the sun dipped below the horizon that the celebration began in earnest. The square transformed into a festival, with shared music, dancing, and food. Laughter rang out, and the weight on Faedi's chest lifted momentarily.

But it didn't last.

She wandered to the square's edge, the noise fading into the background. Her gaze drifted to the horizon, where mountains loomed against the twilight sky.

"They would have loved this," she whispered.

"They would have," Dusan agreed. *"They would also love if you took care of yourself. You're not eating as you should."*

He was right. Faedi hadn't been able to stomach much since the attack—since they disappeared into ashes. No one told her to eat, but everyone who sat with her offered food and water. It was a silent request to eat something, but it was like charcoal in her mouth each time she tried.

The only one who didn't bring her food was Ravyn. He only ever brought himself and would sit with her for hours in silence. He was the only one she could break around, the only one who didn't have pity in his eyes.

Sylrie appeared at her side, his expression softening as he followed her gaze. "Everyone's pretty rowdy," he commented. It wasn't a complaint, more of a reason for his appearance—a lie covered with truth.

He didn't want her alone.

They stood silently for a long moment; the memories of Lonan and Sophir lingered in Faedi's mind. Their absence was a wound that would never fully heal. The pain of their loss was worse than her arm, worse than anything.

But as Faedi looked back at the city—the unity, the hope, the life that thrived despite the loss—she felt a flicker of something else. Not joy, not quite, but a sense of peace.

Like the peace she'd felt living in the cottage with Lonan.

It never dulled her pain, the constant loss she felt for her family, or stopped her fears. But it made all of it bearable.

Then, as the sky shifted colors with the moon's appearance, Faedi took a deep breath. The shadows of night took over the corners and crooks of the city. Stars shimmered in the sky, and she swallowed the lump in her throat.

The celebration carried on behind them, the laughter and music weaving through the night. Faedi thought it might have been a trick of the light—the stars reflecting in her tears—but when she blinked, it remained.

The second moon.

She glanced up at Sylrie, wondering if he saw it too. "We can do this, right?"

He nodded, his hand resting on her shoulder while he stared at the sky. His jaw was set tight. "We will."

They had to—for them.

The
End

Epilogue

The embers still burned in the heart of Dewgate, long after the fires of war had died. Ravyn saw them everywhere—in the glow of lanterns lining the rebuilt streets, in the reflection of the stars on the bay, and in the blue and red blooms of the eventides and embertides that clung to the city's stone walls. But mostly, he saw them in Faedi's eyes.

She had grown thinner since the battle. Grief had pressed down on her, carving sharp edges into her that hadn't been there before. She carried it like she carried everything else—silently, stubbornly, as if admitting to the weight would break her. But Ravyn saw it.

He didn't think she even noticed.

The city celebrated its rebirth, but Ravyn had never trusted celebrations. They were for the living, for those who could afford to let down their guard. He watched from the edges as the people of Dewgate danced and drank beneath the twin moons, laughter ringing through the air like wind chimes. It was a beautiful lie, this moment of peace.

Faedi stood apart from the crowd, her crown catching the light as she turned her face to the sky. Always looking for something just out of reach.

He made his way to her, the sounds of revelry dimming with each step. She didn't turn when he stopped beside her, but she knew he was there. She always did.

"They would have loved this," she murmured, echoing words they had said to each other more times than he could count. Sometimes he wondered if they would ever lose their meaning.

But they wouldn't… because they *would* have loved this. All of it.

He didn't answer right away. Instead, he reached into his coat and pulled out a small flask, offering it to her without a word. She took it without hesitation, lifted it to her lips, then grimaced.

"This is awful."

He huffed a quiet laugh. "It's strong."

She handed it back, her fingers brushing his for the briefest moment before pulling away. "Sylrie says we can do this."

"You can."

She exhaled, long and slow, then looked at him. "I don't feel like a Guardian."

"You are."

She fell silent again, watching the festival like she was trying to memorize it. Like she could hold on to it—something warm and real in the middle of everything else. Ravyn had seen that look before, in the eyes of warriors who had survived what should have killed them.

She was still standing. But she wasn't sure why.

"I'll never be him," she said finally. "I'll never be my grandfather."

"No," Ravyn said quietly. "You won't."

She flinched, but he didn't leave it there. "You're Faedi. And that's who they need."

She studied him, shadows flickering across her face. Searching, maybe, for something in his expression. For proof that he meant it. For permission to believe it herself. Whatever it was, she looked away first.

The second moon hung above them, casting silver light over the city, and Ravyn found himself looking at it too. He had never put much stock in omens, but it was hard not to wonder. Hard not to think about what it meant that it had returned now, after everything.

The people of Dewgate had their hope. Their symbols and their stories.

He had his.

Faedi exhaled again—steadier this time. When she spoke, her voice had settled. "Tomorrow, I want to visit the cottage… bring whatever home I can back."

"I'll come with you," he said.

She didn't thank him. She didn't have to. He would always be there.

The city burned with life around them, but for a moment, it was just the two of them beneath the second moon. Standing. Breathing. Moving forward.

For them.

For her.

And Ravyn planned to end anyone who got in her way.

Author's Note

First of all—thank you. Whether you devoured this book in one fevered sitting (I see you) or savored it piece by piece, I am beyond honored and grateful you chose to spend your time in this world with these characters.

Writing this story was a journey—one I didn't know if I could finish or not. But here we are!

Faedi (along with everyone else) is deeply special to me, and I hope she found a place in your hearts and minds, too. Their story was never going to be easy or tame: from Faedi's beginning as a PC in a D&D campaign and a character I cosplayed for fun during COVID-19, to her development as the Heir of Embers and Eventides—Faedi has always been a force of nature, a fierce lover and fighter despite her scars, and a believer in balance and justice. I wanted to capture that—the devotion, the pain, the fear, and love. And if you felt even a fraction of that while reading, then I did my job.

To my readers, new and those who watched this form from the beginning, you've made all of this possible. Every message, every review, every time you tell someone about my book—it means more than I can ever express. You are the Hunt, the flock, the fire that keeps this world alive.

And because I'm a walking spoiler—Faedi's story isn't done; the world is still growing. The hunt for the eclipse-born, The Seven, and the fight against The Order is far from over.

Remember, where there is light, a shadow will be cast. When the sun sets to reveal the night sky, stars will blaze. And even if the Earth casts a shadow on the moon, it continues to push and pull the tides.

Until next time,

M.W. Theodore

Acknowledgments

My deepest gratitude goes to my family for their amazing support throughout this journey. Thank you for enduring so many late nights and episodes of me walking around the house talking to myself and characters, for refilling my coffee cup, for handing me tissues, and for believing that I could do this.

Many, many, special thanks to Sam, Ryan, Alexandria, Mark, and Cealy for putting up with my constant badgering and messages filled with "does this look good?" for being patient when I forgot to send you updated files after my (many) late night editing sessions, and for listening to me rant about my "dumpster fire" in calls.

A big thank you to Anna for your amazing feedback and for the time and dedication it took to edit my brain baby.

 Appendix

Character Name Pronunciation Guide:
    Faedi — *FAY-dee*
    (Li-roo-lin/Yee-vah)
    Lonan – *LOH-nan*
    (Tah-gil-son)
    Sophir – *SOH-feer*
    (Day-gahn)

Side Characters
    Aladia – *Ah-LAH-dee-ah*
    Bjorn – *BYORN* (with a rolled "r")
    Blavier – *BLAYvee-er*
    Callon – *KAH-lon*
    Danik – *DAH-nik*
    Dusan – *DOO-sahn*
    Emmaline – *EH-mah-leen*
    Enoch – *EE-nuhk*
    Fenkas – *FEHN-kahs*
    Haldin – *HAHL-deen*
    Jaref – *JAH-ref*
    Lisea – *Lee-SEH-ah*
    Myst – *Mihst*
    Odessa – *Oh-DEH-sah*
    Peni – *PEH-nee*
    Ravyn – *RAH-vin*
    Rena – *REE-nuh*
    Tagil – *TAH-geel*
    Torix – *TOR-iks*
    (Yee-vah)
    Tove – *TOH-veh*
    Sylrie – *SIL-ree*
    (Li-roo-lin / Yee-vah)
    Zarae – *ZAH-ray*
    Ighir – *EE-gear*

Location Names – Pronunciation Guide
    Yestrana – *YES-trah-nah*
    Detrich – *DIE-trik*
    Dewgate – *DOO-gayt*

    Emsmeda – *EEM-smeh-dah*
    Lefral – *LEF-rahl*
    Rowdon – *ROH-duhn*
    Sauvern – *SAW-vern*
    Umbramire – *UHM-brah-mire*

Additional Locations & Names:
    Oprien – *OH-pree-en*
    Ashar – *AH-shahr*
    Ostria – *AH-stree-uh*
    Valoria – *vah-LOHR-ee-uh*

Isles & Unique Places:
    Ceanea Isle – *SEE-nay-uh Isle*
    Scyrei – *SKY-ray*
    Draetor – *DRAY-tor*
    Fauna Wylds – *FAW-nuh Wilds*
    Udror Mountains – *OO-dror MOUN-tinz*

Seas, Deeps, and Abysses:
    Wyrmshire Deep – *WERM-shyre Deep*
    Vanheim Sea – *VAHN-hyme Sea*
    Strafden Sea – *STRAHF-den Sea*
    Helgi Tides – *HEL-ghee Tides*
    Waywhich Abyss – *WAY-witch Abyss*

Terms
    Hrul'viras — *HROOL-veer-ahs*
(Umbral; Summer)
    Sual-viren – *SOO-ahl VEER-en*
(Umbral; Autumn)
    Súran – *SOO-rahn*
(Umbral; phrase meaning "my love")
    Sual-viren – *SOO-ahl VEER-en*
(Umbral; Autumn)
    Rakgrah – *RAHK-grah*
(Itmis; Itmis native tongue)
    Sual-viren – *SOO-ahl VEER-en*
(Umbral; Autumn)
    Súran – *SOO-rahn*
(Umbral; phrase meaning "my love")
    Tia'min – *TEE-uh-min*
(Itmis; "little wolf")
    Veth'iral – *VETH-ih-rahl*

(Umbral; Spring")

Vaelma – *VEHL-mah*

(Umbral; term of respect/endearment for elderly women. Translates to "Matron of Wisdom")

Races

Dwarves

Deep Dwarves – The Deep Dwarves, often referred to as the *Stromdár*, are a stout and resilient race that resides deep within the mountain ranges of the world. Known for their remarkable mining skills and mastery of stonework, the Deep Dwarves are a people who thrive in the dark, subterranean realms beneath the earth. They live in complex cities carved from the very stone they mine, and their culture revolves around their unshakable bond with the earth and the precious materials it offers.

Mountain Dwarves – The Mountain Dwarves, also known as the Halthroks, are a sturdy, proud, and industrious race that inhabits the mountainous regions above ground. Unlike their reclusive Deep Dwarf cousins, the Halthroks have adapted to life above the surface, building cities in the high mountain passes and plateaus, often near strategic trading routes. Their society is built upon trade, negotiation, and diplomacy, positioning them as the "middle men" between the more isolated Deep Dwarves and the other societies of the world.

Nomad Dwarves – The Nomad Dwarves, known as the Vorrnaks, are a hardy and resilient race that thrives in motion, living between the continents of Ystrana and Oprien. Unlike other dwarves who settle in mountains or underground fortresses, the Vorrnaks have developed a nomadic lifestyle, traveling between these two vast lands with the changing seasons. They are known for their prowess in trade, navigation, and diplomacy. While the Halthroks (Mountain Dwarves) control established trading routes, the Vorrnaks are the ones who connect these regions, creating a constant flow of goods and resources.

Elves

Cinder Elves – The Cinder Elves, natives to the harsh and unforgiving Valoria (the Burning Fields), are a striking and resilient race. Known for their ashen gray skin, white-to-light hair, and vibrant red, pink, or black eyes, the Cinder Elves have adapted to the extreme environment of their homeland. Valoria is a land of endless volcanic activity, scorching winds, and blazing heat, shaping the Cinder Elves into a people who thrive in such a brutal environment.

Dawn Elves – The Dawn Elves hail from the vast, sun-scorched desert region of Ashar, a land characterized by blazing sands, rolling dunes, and searing heat. With their striking golden features and ethereal beauty, the Dawn Elves are often revered as the "perfect" breed of elf, embodying grace, elegance, and strength. They are closely aligned with the Order of Ilos, the god of light, and are often seen as his chosen people—blessed with light and purity in both form and spirit.

Dusk Elves – The Dusk Elves are a mysterious and resilient race native to the city of Dewgate, a once-vibrant city now in ruins following the upheavals of the 10th and 11th Ages. As a result of political and religious conflicts, especially in the wake of the Age of Honor, the Dusk Elves relocated to Rowdon, a verdant yet protected region in the southeastern part of the continent of Ystrana. Though their connection to Dewgate still runs deep, their new home in Rowdon offers them both refuge and the ability to protect Shadow Elves and the Gaelisks— two races they have sworn to protect.

Shadow Elves – The Shadow Elves are an enigmatic and elusive race of Rowdon, before their dramatic disappearance during the 11th Age. With their pale skin, white hair, and their intrinsic connection to the shadow realm, the Shadow Elves have often been regarded with a mixture of awe and suspicion by other races. Their unique characteristics, such as their ability to become werecreatures, were gifted to them by the Dusk Elves as a means of survival and protection. The Shadow Elves have adapted to their new home in Rowdon, where they live in harmony with the land and the Gaelisks.

Umbral Elves – The glamoured disguise Umbrals are required to weare outside of the Umbramire.

Gath'faunan

The Gath'faunan are a shadowed lineage of the fae, bound to the twilight edges of the world where light and dark entwine. Often called dark fae by mortals, they are beings of mystery, power, and duality—feared not because they are inherently evil, but because they embody the raw, untamed aspects of magic that others dare not approach. Their magic is deeply tied to the night, shadows, dreams, and the unknown, drawing power from the liminal spaces where reality thins and the astral realms bleed through.

Helgi

The Helgi are a unique mermaid/siren species known for their ability to thrive in cold, deep ocean waters. They are a highly matriarchal society where both males and females can bear children. This extraordinary characteristic is rooted in their biology, influenced by a unique reproductive system that allows for a diverse and fluid approach to family structures. The Helgi are hunter-gatherers, relying on the ocean's resources to sustain their culture, and they are known for their deep connection to the waters they inhabit, which are often cold, murky, and difficult to navigate for many other sea-dwelling races.

Itmis

Astral Itmis – The Astral Itmis are the most powerful and revered members of the Itmis species, a celestial and dragon-like race that operates on a strict caste hierarchy. As the leaders and paragons of the Itmis, the Astral Itmis are the embodiment of cosmic energy, celestial power, and ancient wisdom. They are considered the founders of the Itmis race, believed to have been born from the stars themselves and to hold the key to many of the universe's most secret forces. Their power is unmatched, extending far beyond the material plane, and they are deeply connected to the cosmos, able to manipulate space, time, and the fabric of reality itself.

Crimson Itmis – The Crimson Itmis are a middle-tier caste within the Itmis hierarchy, known for their mastery over the element of fire. They are fierce, passionate, and relentless warriors who harness the destructive and purifying power of flames. Though they are not as esteemed as the Astral or Gold Itmis, the Crimson Itmis command great respect due to their role as the vanguard in battle and their ability to withstand the most brutal conflicts. With their fiery nature, they are often the first to engage in battle, acting as both shock troops and fearless leaders.

Verglas Itmis – The Verglass Itmis are a mystical and elusive race within the Itmis hierarchy, positioned as a mid-tier caste in the grand scale. Their elemental affinity is with ice and frost, a rare and beautiful magic that manifests in glimmering, crystalline structures and frosted spells. Known for their artistry and precision, the Verglass Itmis are often revered for their delicate yet powerful control over cold and frozen environments. Though not as physically imposing as the Tempest or Crimson Itmis, their abilities to create mirrors of ice, frost barriers, and illusions of snow are a testament to their creativity and strategic power.

Krelin

The Krelin are a humanoid race that combine elvish elegance with animal-like traits suited to life on land. They are known for their athletic builds, keen senses, and a deep connection to the earth beneath their feet. Their agile and strong physiques make them adept at both physical labor and combat. Though they share the ethereal beauty of their elvish kin, the Land Krelin also possess animalistic features that link them to the natural world, making them incredibly skilled hunters, trackers, and stewards of the earth.

Gaelisks

The Gaelisks are a stoic, ancient race resembling gargoyles in both appearance and nature. They have humanoid bodies with winged and tailed forms, their skin often a mix of stone, crystal, and marble-like texture. Their blood and tears, both infused with a crystalline essence, harden over time into crystals that are as much a part of their identity as their physical form. These crystalline structures are not only a mark of strength but also an emblem of their emotional depth and resilience.

Haxans

Haxans are humans who are born with an innate connection to magic. This magic is often the result of a mystical event, such as exposure to arcane forces during conception, the influence of powerful spiritual entities, or a divine blessing that imbues them with an unusual ability. The name "Haxan" derives from the ancient word for "touched by the unknown", and these individuals are often seen as living embodiments of mystical potential.

Humans

Humans are one of the most widespread and adaptable races in the world, known for their resilience, ambition, and diverse cultures. While they may not possess the innate magical abilities of many other races, their capacity for innovation, survival, and cooperation allows them to thrive in nearly any environment. Humans are typically characterized by their diversity in appearance, drive for progress, and their often complex societies.

Minotaurs

The Rhotar are a fierce and noble race of minotaurs who are deeply connected to the forests they inhabit. Towering in stature and known for their strength and cunning, the Rhotar have long been seen as guardians of the wilds. Their humanoid body is complemented by the powerful, bull-like features—horns, hooves, and the muscular build of a natural-born warrior. Though often misunderstood as brutish or simple-minded, the Rhotar possess a deeply rich culture centered around honor, respect for nature, and the pursuit of personal growth.

Umbrals

The Umbrals are a mystical and enigmatic race who dwell within the heart of the Umbramire, a dense, shadowy swamp that is as much a part of their essence as their ever-shifting forms. The Umbrals are deeply tied to the ethereal and dark energies of the swamp, which grant them both immense power and a unique nature. They are a gender-fluid, non-binary, and transgender people, capable of fluidly changing their physical forms and identities, embracing the freedom to choose how they present themselves. They are born from the mists and shadows of the Umbramire, and their existence is bound to this ever-changing, elusive place.

Werecreatures

Werecreatures are a fascinating and diverse race, capable of shifting between their humanoid form and that of an animal. They are divided into two categories: Born Werecreatures and Made Werecreatures. While both types share the ability to transform into animals, they differ significantly in terms of control over their primal instincts, temperament, and how they came into being.

Religions
The Order of Ilos

The Order of Ilos is a religion centered around the principles of light, hope, justice, and renewal. Followers venerate Ilos, the god of dawn, light, and renewal, and seek to bring light into the world, both literally and figuratively. Through worship, the faithful strive to illuminate the darkness with truth, love, and protection.

Varethism - Common Religion of Mortals

The faith of the mortals is a vast, interconnected system of worship honoring the Primordial Deities, their Creations, and the Lesser Gods who govern the aspects of life. The Mortal Religion is based on the Seven Realms and the deities who shaped them. It emphasizes balance, the cycle of life and death, and the mortal journey through the realms.

Wrydian

The Faith of the Itmisis a deeply spiritual and mystical religion practiced by the people who worship the ancient and divine forces that govern the world and the cosmos. The Itmis religion is rooted in the belief that everything in existence is connected through a web of cosmic forces, embodied in the gods, who shape both the physical and metaphysical aspects of life. This faith revolves around the balance of nature, the cycles of life, death, and rebirth, and the powerful influences of the celestial forces above and the primordial entities that define the world.

God Names & Domains
The Ancients

Halseia – *hall-SAY-uh*
Ancient God of Life
    Petha – *PEH-thuh*
Ancient God of Balance
    Rhodri – *ROD-ree*
Ancient God of Time
    Shivr – *SHIV-er*
Ancient God of History
    Sudek – *SOO-dek*
Ancient God of Death
    Sunamun – *SOO-nah-moon*
Ancient God of Light
    Xeler – *ZEEL-er*
Ancient God of Dark

Lesser Gods
    Aasis – *AH-sis*
Goddess of Luck
    Eena – *EE-nuh*
Goddess of Volcanic Coves
    Eryndar – *AIR-in-dar*
God of the Night Sky
    Faeturin – *FAY-too-rin*
Goddess of the Forest
    Ilos – *EE-lohs*
God of Light
    Mumir – *MOO-meer*
God of the Skies - Father of Dragons
    Syltorin – *SILL-tor-in*
God of The Hunt